# THE WAY THE
# CROW FLIES

Ann-Marie MacDonald

# THE WAY THE
# CROW FLIES

*A Novel*

HarperCollins*Publishers*

HarperCollins books may be purchased for educational, business, or sales promotional use. For information, please write: Special Markets Department, HarperCollins Publishers Inc., 10 East 53rd Street, New York, NY 10022.

A continuation of this copyright page appears on pages 715–19.

Originally published in Canada in 2003 by Alfred A. Knopf Canada, a division of Random House of Canada Limited.

FIRST EDITION

Illustrations by Wesley W. Bates

Library of Congress Cataloging-in-Publication Data is available upon request.

ISBN 0-06-057895-5

03 04 05 06 07 ❖/RRD 10 9 8 7 6 5 4 3 2 1

*For Mac and Lillian*
*So many "remember-whens"*

*We are doomed to choose, and every choice may entail an irreparable loss.*

*Isaiah Berlin*

*Part One*

## THIS LAND IS YOUR LAND

THE BIRDS SAW THE MURDER. Down below in the new grass, the tiny white bell-heads of the lily of the valley. It was a sunny day. Twig-crackling, early spring stirrings, spring soil smell. April. A stream through the nearby woods, so refreshing to the ear—it would be dry by the end of summer, but for now it rippled through the shade. High in the branches of an elm, that is where the birds were, perched among the many buds set to pleat like fresh hankies.

The murder happened near a place kids called Rock Bass. In a meadow at the edge of the woods. A tamped-down spot, as though someone had had a picnic there. The crows saw what happened. Other birds were in the high branches and they saw too, but crows are different. They are interested. Other birds saw a series of actions. The crows saw the murder. A light blue cotton dress. Perfectly still now.

From high in the tree, the crows eyed the charm bracelet glinting on her wrist. Best to wait. The silver beckoned, but best to wait.

# MANY-SPLENDOURED THINGS

THE SUN CAME OUT after the war and our world went Technicolor. Everyone had the same idea. Let's get married. Let's have kids. Let's be the ones who do it right.

It is possible, in 1962, for a drive to be the highlight of a family week. King of the road, behind the wheel on four steel-belted tires, the sky's the limit. Let's just drive, we'll find out where we're going when we get there. How many more miles, Dad?

Roads are endless vistas, city gives way to country barely mediated by suburbs. Suburbs are the best of both worlds, all you need is a car and the world is your oyster, your Edsel, your Chrysler, your Ford. Trust Texaco. Traffic is not what it will be, what's more, it's still pretty neat. There's a '53 Studebaker Coupe!—oh look, there's the new Thunderbird. . . .

"'This land is your land, this land is my land. . . . '" A moving automobile is second only to the shower when it comes to singing, the miles fly by, the landscape changes, they pass campers and trailers—look, another Volkswagen Beetle. It is difficult to believe that Hitler was behind something so friendly-looking and familiar as a VW bug. Dad reminds the kids that dictators often appreciate good music and are kind to animals. Hitler was a vegetarian and evil. Churchill was a drunk but good. "The world isn't black and white, kids."

In the back seat, Madeleine leans her head against the window frame, lulled by the vibrations. Her older brother is occupied with baseball cards, her parents are up front enjoying "the beautiful scenery." This is an ideal time to begin her movie. She hums "Moon River," and imagines that the audience can just see her profile, hair blowing back in the wind. They see what she sees out the window, the countryside, *off to see the world,* and they wonder where it is she is off to and what life will bring, *there's such a lot of world to see.* They wonder, who is this dark-haired girl with the pixie cut and the wistful expression? An orphan? An only child with a dead mother and a kind father? Being sent from her boarding school to spend the summer at the country house of mysterious relatives who live next to a mansion where lives a girl a little older than herself who rides horses and wears red dungarees? *We're after the same rainbow's end, just around the bend.* . . . And they are forced to run away together and solve a mystery, *my Huckleberry friend.* . . .

Through the car window, she pictures tall black letters superimposed on a background of speeding green—"Starring Madeleine McCarthy"—punctuated frame by frame by telephone poles, *Moon River, and me*. . . .

It is difficult to get past the opening credits so better simply to start a new movie. Pick a song to go with it. Madeleine sings, sotto voce, "*'Que será, será,* whatever will be will—'" darn, we're stopping.

"I scream, you scream, we all scream for ice cream," says her father, pulling over.

Utterly wrapped up in her movie, Madeleine has failed to notice the big strawberry ice cream cone tilting toward the highway, festive in its party hat. "Yay!" she exclaims. Her brother rolls his eyes at her.

Everything in Canada is so much bigger than it was in Germany, the cones, the cars, the "supermarkets." She wonders what their new house will be like. And her new room—will it be pretty? Will it be big? *Que será, será*. . . .

"Name your poison," says Dad at the ice cream counter, a white wooden shack. They sell fresh corn on the cob here too. The fields are full of it—the kind Europeans call Indian corn.

"Neapolitan, please," says Madeleine.

Her father runs a hand through his sandy crewcut and smiles through his sunglasses at the fat lady in the shade behind the counter. He and her brother have matching haircuts, although Mike's hair is even lighter. Wheat-coloured. It looks as though you could remove waxy buildup from your kitchen floor by turning him upside down and plugging him in, but his bristles are actually quite soft. He rarely allows Madeleine to touch them, however. He has strolled away now toward the highway, thumbs hooked in his belt loops—pretending he is out in the world on his own, Madeleine knows. He must be boiling in those dungarees but he won't admit it, and he won't wear shorts. Dad never wears shorts.

"Mike, where do you think you're going?" she calls.

He ignores her. He is going on twelve.

She runs a hand through her hair the way Dad does, loving its silky shortness. A pixie cut is a far cry from a crewcut, but it's also mercifully far from the waist-length braids she endured until this spring. She accidentally cut one off during crafts in school. Maman still loves her but will probably never forgive her.

Her mother waits in the Rambler. She wears the sunglasses she got on the French Riviera last summer. She looks like a movie star. Madeleine watches her adjust the rearview mirror and freshen her lipstick. Black hair, red lips, white sunglasses. Like Jackie Kennedy—"She copied me."

Mike calls her Maman, but for Madeleine she is "Maman" at home and "Mum" in public. "Mum" is more carefree than Maman—like penny loafers instead of Mary Janes. "Mum" goes better with "Dad." Things go better with Coke.

Her father waits with his hands in the pockets of his chinos, removes his sunglasses and squints up at the blue sky, whistling a tune through his teeth. "Smell the corn," he says. "That's the smell of pure sunshine." Madeleine puts her hands in the pockets of her short-shorts, squints up and inhales.

In the car, her mother blots her lips together, eyes on the mirror. Madeleine watches her retract the lipstick into its tube. Ladies have a lot of things which look like candy but are not.

Her mother has saved her braids. They are in a plastic bag in the silverware chest. Madeleine saw her toss the bag in there just before the movers came. Now her hair is somewhere on a moving van, rumbling toward them.

"Here you go, old buddy."

Her father hands her an ice cream cone. Mike rejoins them and takes his. He has chosen chocolate as usual. "'I'd rather fight, than switch.'"

Her father has rum 'n' raisin. Does something happen to your taste-buds when you grow up so that you like horrible flavours? Or is it par-ticular to parents who grew up during the Depression, when an apple was a treat?

"Want a taste, sweetie?"

"Thanks, Dad."

She always takes a lick of his ice cream and says, "That's really good." Bugs Bunny would say, *You lie like a rug, doc,* but in a way it isn't a lie because it really is good to get ice cream with your dad. And when each of you takes a taste of the other's, it's great. So Madeleine is not really lying. *Nyah, tell me anuddah one, doc.*

Maman never wants a cone of her own. She will share Dad's and take bites of Mike's and Madeleine's. That's another thing that happens when you grow up; at least, it happens to a great number of mothers: they no longer choose to have an ice cream cone of their own.

Back in the car, Madeleine considers offering a lick to Bugs Bunny but doesn't wish to tempt her brother's scorn. Bugs is not a doll. He is . . . Bugs. He has seen better days, the tip of his orange carrot is worn white, but his big wise-guy eyes are still bright blue and his long ears still hold whatever position you bend them into. At the moment, his ears are twisted together like a braid down his back. Bavarian Bugs.

Her father starts the engine and tilts his cone toward her mother, who bites it, careful of her lipstick. He backs the station wagon toward the highway and makes a face when he sees that his rearview mirror is out of whack. He gives Maman a look and she makes a kiss with her red lips. He grins and shakes his head. Madeleine looks away, hoping they won't get mushy.

She contemplates her ice cream cone. Neapolitan. Where to begin? She thinks of it as "cosmopolitan"—the word her father uses to describe their family. The best of all worlds.

Outside the car windows the corn catches the sun, leafy stalks gleam in three greens. Arching oaks and elms line the curving highway, the land rolls and burgeons in a way that makes you believe that, yes, the earth is a woman, and her favourite food is corn. Tall and flexed and straining, emerald citizens. Fronds spiralling, cupping upward, swaddling the tender ears, the gift-wrapped bounty. The edible sun. The McCarthys have come home. To Canada.

When you live in the air force, home is a variation on a theme. Home is Canada, from sea to sea. Home is also the particular town you came from before you got married and joined the forces. And home is whatever place you happen to be posted, whether it's Canada, the U.S., Germany, France. . . . Right now, home is this sky-blue 1962 Rambler station wagon.

Having adjusted his rearview mirror, Jack glances at his kids in the back seat. Peace reigns for now. Next to him, his wife opens her purse—he reaches forward and pushes in the automatic lighter on the dashboard. She glances at him, small smile as she takes the cigarette from her pack. He winks at her—*your wish is my command.* Home is this woman.

The Trans-Canada Highway has been finished: you can dip your rear wheels in the Atlantic and drive until you dip your front ones in the Pacific. The McCarthys are not going that far, although they did start this leg of their journey at the Atlantic. They have been driving for three days. Taking it easy, watching the scenery change, fir trees give way to the St. Lawrence Seaway, the narrow cultivated strips of old Québec all along the broad river, the blue shimmer of the worn Laurentian Mountains, the jet-smooth ride of the modern highway, *Bienvenue à Montréal, Welcome to Ottawa, to Kingston, to Toronto,* extending the summer holiday they spent with Mimi's family in New Brunswick—*Nouveau-Brunswick*—salt swimming among the sandbars of the Northumberland Strait, and at night the winking lights of the ferry to Prince Edward Island. They rose early to watch the priest bless the multicoloured fishing boats on opening day, *le premier jour de pêche.* Lobster feasts and noisy card games of Deux-Cents late into the night, neighbours arriving to squeeze in at the kitchen table, placing their bets with mounds of pennies and Rummoli chips, until the fiddles and accordion came out and Mimi's mother thumped out chords on the piano, her treble hand permanently bent into the shape of the hook she had used to make every quilt and rug in the house. *L'Acadie.*

Language was no barrier. Jack basked in the French, in the food, in the celestial confusion of a big family. Mimi's father had been lost years before, in a storm that capsized his lobster boat, and her brothers headed the family now. Big self-made men with a chain of seafood restaurants, who took to Jack from the start, when he and Mimi returned home after the war, engaged. Things happened fast back then, everyone understood, the brothers were barely out of uniform themselves. Jack was an *Anglais,* but he was theirs and her family embraced him with a fervour equal to that which fuelled their mistrust of the English in general. They accorded him the status of a prince and extended him the consideration usually reserved for ladies. The best of both worlds.

Jack eats his ice cream, one hand on the wheel, and makes a mental note to start jogging again once they get settled in. Over the past month his sisters-in-law, *les belles-soeurs,* have fed him like a prize calf. Flour, maple sugar, potato, pork and clams—the possible permutations are dizzying, delicious. And fattening. It seems there is nothing that cannot be transformed into *poutine.* What is *poutine?* It is what you make when you make *poutine.*

He has only had to loosen his belt by one notch, but Jack has a beautiful wife. One who still runs into the water like a girl, bikini-svelte despite two children, breaststroking through the waves, keeping her head up so as not to spoil her "do." Yes, he'll start running again once they get to their new home.

Behind him, his son's voice, disgusted. "Madeleine, it's melting right down your arm."

"No it's not."

"Maman," says Mike, leaning forward, "*Madeleine fait un mess!*"

"I am not making a mess!" Licking her wrist, salty skin and murky vanilla.

Mimi reaches back with a wet-nap. "*Tiens.*"

Madeleine takes it and wipes her hand. She tries to get Mike to hold her ice cream cone but he says, "No way, it's all gobbed." So Mimi holds it and, while Madeleine wipes her hands, she licks the ice cream drips. It is also a characteristic of mothers that they don't mind eating their child's soggy ice cream cone.

Madeleine returns the wet-nap in exchange for her ice cream but feels suddenly unwell. It's the wet-nap smell. Pre-moistened for your convenience. Disinfects too. The smell reminds Madeleine of throw-up. That's because, when you get carsick and throw up, your mother wipes your face with a wet-nap, so of course wet-naps come to stand for throw-up. They smell more like throw-up than throw-up. She passes the ice cream back to her mother.

"I'm full," she says.

Mike says, "She's gonna barf."

"I am not, Mike, don't say 'barf.'"

"You just said it. Barf."

"That's enough, Mike," says Jack, and Mike stops.

Mimi turns and looks back at Madeleine with the are-you-going-to-throw-up? expression. It makes her have to throw up. Her eyes water. She puts her face to the open window and drinks in the fresh air. Wills herself not to think of anything sickening. Like the time a girl threw up in kindergarten and it hit the floor with a *splash,* don't think about that. Mike has retreated as far as possible to his side of the seat. Madeleine turns carefully and focuses on the back of Dad's head. That's better.

As seen from the back seat of the car, it is as recognizable, as much "him," as his face. As unmistakable as your own car in a parking lot. His head, squarish, clean. It says what it means, you don't have to figure it out. His shoulders under his checked short-sleeved shirt. Elbow out the window, halo of light brown hairs combed by the wind, right hand on the wheel, glint of his university ring. Old Spice. Across the back of his neck, one faint line—a seam that stays paler than his sunburn. The back of Dad's head. It's the other side of his face—his other face. In fact, he has told you he has eyes back there. This is reassuring. It means he knows who starts most of the fights in the back seat.

"Mike, quit it!" cries Madeleine.

"I'm not doing anything."

"Mike, don't tease your sister."

"Dad, I'm not teasing her, she pinched me."

"Madeleine, don't torment your brother." Maman does not have eyes in the back of her head or she wouldn't say such a thing.

Mike crosses his eyes at her.

"Mike!" Her eight-year-old shriek like a handsaw. "Stop it!"

"*Tenez-vous tranquilles maintenant, hein?* Your father's driving," says Maman.

Madeleine has seen the muscles in her father's neck contract at her screech, and she softens. She doesn't want to make him have to pull over and face the back seat. That means a spoiled treat, and a good dose of shame for having ruined such a nice drive through such lovely scenery. His voice will be disappointed, his blue eyes bewildered. Especially his left one with the light scar that traverses his brow. The lid droops slightly, so that his left eye always looks a little sad.

"*Chantons, les enfants,*" says Maman. And they sing.

" 'Would you like to swing on a star, carry moonbeams home in a jar, and be better off than you are . . . ?' "

Billboards loom in farmers' fields, *Believe on the Lord Jesus Christ and Be Saved,* soldier rows of leafy beets that slow down or speed up depending on whether you focus on the dirt between the rows or on the blur of green, *Kodak, Dairy Queen, The Wages of Sin Is Death.* Barns, neat and scrubbed. The congenial whiff of cow-pies and wood fires reminds Madeleine of home—Germany, that is. She closes her eyes. She has just said goodbye to another house, on an air force base near the Black Forest. *Say goodbye to the house, kids.* And they pulled away for the last time.

Each house stands mute and innocent like a poor animal left behind. The windows wide-eyed, bereft of drapes, the front-door-mouth sad and sealed. Goodbye, dear house. Thank you for all the nice times. Thank you for all the remember-whens. The sad house left behind solidifies in memory to become a monument to a former time, a marker for the place you can never get back to. That's how it is in the air force.

This is Madeleine's third move, and Mike's fourth. He insists that she can't possibly remember her first move, from Alberta to Michigan, because she was only three going on four. Yet he claims to remember his first move, from Washington DC, to Alberta, despite the fact that he was barely three. Such are the injustices of living with an older brother.

"Dad," says Madeleine from the back seat, "I do so remember leaving the base in Alberta, don't I?"

"Sure you do. Remember the skating rink we made in the backyard?"

She looks pointedly at her brother. "Yup."

"There you go. But 'base' is actually an American term, old buddy. The correct term is 'station.' "

"Yeah," says Mike.

They left Europe in June and, for the better part of two months, Mike and Madeleine were indulged by their Acadian aunts and uncles in New

Brunswick, and ran wild with their cousins. Dozens of them: wild black-haired boys you are not supposed to have a crush on because you are related to them, sexy girls who shave their legs before they are twelve. They speak rapid French, just try to keep up, and if you've gone somewhere in a car with them, make sure you get in before it leaves again. Mike and Madeleine watched television for the first time in four years.

No one had a television set on the base in Germany. There were movies at the rec centre, reliably preceded by Looney Toons and Mickey Mouse. There were Friday night suppers with Maman, listening to Jack Benny on the radio before Dad got home from TGIF at the officers' mess. But TV opened up a brave new world of pageboys, chiffon scarves and madras shorts, of carefree teenagers and surfboards. The cousins were more Connie Francis than Sandra Dee, more Sal Mineo than Troy Donahue, but they had roller skates, cars and Dentyne. And big fridges. Welcome to North America.

Madeleine accepts the idea that she loves them all, *"parce que c'est la famille,"* says her mother. "Family" has almost as mythic a ring to it as "home." When they pulled away from Grandmaman's old pink bungalow, Dad said, "Let's head for home, what do you think, kids?"

Madeleine waved to Grandmaman, on the porch of the house that looked like a powdery peppermint. Big fat Grandmaman in her bungalow, brightly painted so Grandpapa could see it from his fishing boat out on the water. It was only the second time in Madeleine's life that she remembered visiting her grandmother, but her eyes filled with tears because "Grandmaman" is another word for "home."

"What do you say, Missus?" said Dad as they left behind the sea and dunes.

"Take me home, Jack," said Maman, and wiped her eyes behind her sunglasses.

For a split second Madeleine imagined they were driving back to Germany. To the green lawns and white buildings of the air force base and, in the nearby town, cobblestones, and sidewalk cafés; the tightly stitched countryside, no patch of land unspoken for, no inch uncherished, a different country every couple of hours on a Sunday drive. The German language she had taken to, the language of fairy tales—*Märchen*—in which she felt wrapped up and safe, like dressing up in her mother's mouton coat. The language that made people smile in surprise—women behind shop counters, who were delighted by her proficiency and teased her parents about their bad *Kanadische Deutsch* as they offered tastes of cheese and, always, *Schokolade für die Kinder.* The first German words she and Mike learned: *danke schön.*

If your father is in the air force, people ask you where you are from and it's difficult to answer. The answer becomes longer the older you get, because you move every few years. "Where are you from?" "I'm from the Royal Canadian Air Force." The RCAF. Like a country whose bits are scattered around the globe.

Each bit, each base, looks like every other, so there is a consistency to this nation. Like walking into any Catholic church and hearing the Latin Mass, you can go to a base—station, that is—anywhere in the world and understand it: the recreation centre, the churches, the post office, bank and fire hall, the parade square, the library, the airfield, the building where your father works. And the PX for groceries and everything else—"PX" is another American term they picked up in Europe.

If you live in what are called PMQs—Permanent Married Quarters— your house will be familiar too. There's a handful of designs, early suburban blueprints, mostly semi-detached, except for the tiny bungalows and the big house where the CO lives. Commanding officer. There is a flagpole on his lawn. By the time you're eight years old, you have probably seen the inside of each type of house in the PMQs. Sometimes in mirror image. And yet, somehow, each house becomes unique once a family moves in. Unique smells, instant accumulation of treasures, pictures and lived-in mess, all of it emerges from cardboard boxes that kids make into forts and play in for days before they collapse, and by the time they do collapse, the house looks as though the family has always lived there, because an air force wife can put together a home inside a week.

Each regulation lawn bristles with individuality—bikes, strewn toys, a different car in every driveway, each refrigerator opening onto a world of its own. Some people's fridges contain tins of Hershey's chocolate sauce. Others contain Hershey's tins that harbour lard and other horrible surprises; that is the McCarthys' fridge. Madeleine's mother wastes nothing, having grown up in the Depression. Although, considering that everyone else's mother grew up in the Depression too, perhaps it's an Acadian thing. Or merely Maritime—Canada's "have-not" provinces. So, despite the uniformity of design, no two houses in the PMQs are exactly alike until that in-between time when one family moves out and the next one moves in. In that space of time the house is no one's. It belongs to the taxpayers of Canada. During that no one's time, the house is scrubbed, disinfected, painted white, stripped of blinds, invaded by echoes. It stands suspended, like a deconsecrated church. Not evil, just blank. Neither dead nor living. It comes alive again when a new family pulls into the driveway and says hello to it.

Madeleine reaches into her new Mickey Mouse Club knapsack for her autograph book. Everyone in her grade three class back in Germany signed it. She opens it. . . .

*Yours until Niagara Falls,* wrote Sarah Dowd, the last letters tumbling down the page.

*Yours till the mountains peak to see the salad dressing, love your friend forever, Judy Kinch.*

*Roses are red, lilies are white, I love you dear Madeleine, morning, noon and night, your best friend, Laurie Ferry.*

The book is full. All have sworn to write. Madeleine and Laurie Ferry have sworn to meet on New Year's Day of the year 2000, in the playground of their PMQs in Germany.

The printed letters look lonely all of a sudden—gay pencil-crayon colours like party decorations after the party. She closes the book, puts it away and takes a deep breath of clover air. There's no reason to feel sad on such a beautiful day when you have your whole life ahead of you. That's what grown-ups say. She pictures her life rolled out ahead of her like a highway. How do you know when you're actually travelling along your life that was ahead of you but is now beneath your feet? How many more miles?

It's hard to move into a new house without thinking of the day when you will be leaving. *Say goodbye to the house, kids.* And you will all be that much older. Madeleine is eight going on nine now so she will be going on twelve next time. Almost a teenager. And her parents will be older too. She tries to remember that they are younger now, but she can't help looking at it in the opposite way: they are older than they were in the last house. And that means they will die sooner. Every house is a step closer to that terrible day. Which house will be the last? Maybe this one. The one we are on our way to say hello to.

The sun warms the lump in her throat and threatens to set tears overflowing her lids, so she closes her eyes and rests her temple against the window frame, soothed by the vibrations of the road. The wind in her hair is swift but gentle, the sun through her closed lids a kaleidoscope of reds and golds.

Outside, the afternoon intensifies. August is the true light of summer. Thick tenor saxophone light. Unlike the trumpets of spring, the strings of autumn. Visible grains of sunlight fall in slow motion, grazing skin— catch them like snowflakes on your tongue. The land is bursting, green and gold and bark. The stalks sway heavy with corn, slowing the breeze. The countryside reclines, abundant and proud like a mightily pregnant woman, lounging. "Pick your own," say handwritten signs. Pick me.

The Indians grew corn. This is the part of Ontario first taken from them by settlers. They fought here alongside the English, first against the French, then against the Americans in the War of 1812. Now there are reservations, their longhouses and villages survive as drawings in sixth-grade history books and life-size reproductions in tourist villages. Their tobacco is a big cash crop in these parts, but they don't grow it. The ground is still full of their belongings and many places have been named for their nations and in their languages, including Canada. Some say "Canada" means "village of small huts." Others say Portuguese fishermen named it Ca Nada: there, nothing.

*Welcome to Stratford, Welcome to New Hamburg.* . . . So many places in Canada where you feel as though the real place is in another country. If you come from London, Ontario, for instance, you might not say, "I come from London." You might have to qualify it with "Ontario." Having to explain this can sound apologetic even if you are perfectly happy to come from London. Ontario. New York was named after York in England, but no one ever thinks of York, England, when they think of New York. Mike would say, "That's 'cause the States has better everything."

*Welcome to Kitchener.* "Did you know Kitchener used to be called Berlin?" says her father, with a glance in the rearview mirror. "It was settled by German immigrants, but they changed the name during the First World War."

They stop for bratwurst and crusty white rolls, just like home. Germany, that is. Madeleine knows she must cease to think of Germany as home. This is home now—what she sees out the sunny car window. Impossibly long driveways that lead to gabled farmhouses with gingerbread trim. Immense fields, endless miles between towns, so much forest and scrub unspoken for, Crown lands, shaggy and free. Three days of driving through geological eras, mile after mile and still Canada. The vastness is what sets it apart from Germany. Part of what makes it Canada. "You could take the whole of Europe and lose it here in the middle of Ontario," says her father.

Madeleine leans her chin on the window frame. Picture the war in Europe, the planes and tanks and concentration camps, picture Anne Frank writing her diary, Hitler saluting the crowds. There is more than enough room for all of it to have happened in the province of Ontario.

"But it wouldn't happen here," says Madeleine.

"What wouldn't happen?" asks Dad.

"The war."

"Which war?" says Mike.

"The Second World War."

Mike points at her, then at his own head, and spirals his finger to indicate that she's crazy. Madeleine controls her anger. She wants to hear her father's answer. He says, "That particular kind of war could never happen here, sweetie, Canada is a free country."

"If it hadn't been for the war," says Maman, "Papa and I would never have met"—Madeleine squirms—"and you and Michel would never have come along. . . ." Her mother has a way of shifting a subject into a tilted version of itself. Stories of bombs and gas chambers do not go with the story of the air force dance in England where her parents met—The Story of Mimi and Jack. Maman sings, "'Underneath the lantern, by the barrack gate. . . .'" And that's it for any serious discussion of the war.

Madeleine's father is not an actual veteran, but he would have been had it not been for the airplane crash. Most of her friends' dads are veterans—pilots and aircrew. Her German babysitter's dad was a veteran too, of the Wehrmacht. He had one arm and their family went everywhere on a motorcycle with a sidecar. Some Canadian families made trips to see the concentration camps. Laurie Ferry saw piles of shoes at Auschwitz. But Madeleine's father says, "There's a difference between learning from history, and dwelling in the past." Her mother says, "Think nice thoughts."

Madeleine found an old *Life* magazine in the dentist's waiting room on the base. On the cover was a dark-haired girl not much older than herself. Anne Frank. She stole the magazine and pored over it guiltily for weeks, until it disappeared from her room. Maman had rolled it up, along with several other magazines, in order to line a pointed clown hat as part of Madeleine's Halloween costume.

"'My Lili of the lamplight, my own Lili Marlene,'" sings Mimi, one hand lightly stroking the back of her husband's head.

Jack relaxes behind the wheel. She sings the second verse in German. He is tempted to slow down, make the drive last, there is something so full about these suspended times. When it's just the two of them and their little family on the road between postings. No neighbours, no relatives, no outside world except the one whizzing past the windows. *Two drifters, off to see the world. . . .* Benevolent unknown world. Full tank of gas. A good time to take stock. You can see who you are. You can see what you have. You have everything.

He says to Mimi, "Sing it again, Missus."

Farms, wide and prosperous, red barn roofs painted with family names, Irish, English, German, Dutch. This is the southern Ontario heartland. "The Golden Horseshoe . . . ," says Jack to his family. Bounded by three Great Lakes: to the south, Lake Erie and Lake Ontario; to the west, Lake Huron. And although on a map its shape resembles more the skull of a steer, Jack is correct in adding, "It's also known as the Southern Ontario Triangle." The two descriptions conflate for Madeleine and she pictures a glittering golden triangle on a map, their blue station wagon seen from high above, crawling across it.

"Like the Bermuda Triangle?" she asks.

Her parents exchange a smile. "Nope," says her father.

Mike turns to her and mouths the word *stunned*.

Jack explains that in the Bermuda Triangle things are thought to disappear mysteriously, planes and boats vanishing without a trace. The Southern Ontario Triangle is just the opposite. It is packed with people—at least by comparison to the rest of Canada. There are factories and farms, the soil as rich as the cities; orchards of soft fruit down in the Niagara Peninsula and, spanning the whole, vast fields of corn, tobacco, beets, alfalfa; dairy cattle, horses, hogs and high finance. Windsor waves across the water to Detroit; General Motors, pension plans, let the good times roll off the assembly line. The U.S. is, in some places, a stone's throw away, its branch plants springing up to cluster on the Canadian side, reinforcing bonds across the world's longest undefended border. As President Kennedy said last year in Canada's Parliament, "Those whom nature hath so joined together, let no man put asunder." The best of both worlds.

"How many more miles, Dad?"

"A few. Just sit back and enjoy the scenery."

Cutting a swath through fields and woodlots are massive marching steel towers. Follow those mighty X-men and they will lead you to Niagara Falls—twelve million gallons per minute to fuel turbines that never stop, the engine of this province and the north-eastern United States. Pure power carried by those columns of upreaching steel, high voltage honour guard, girders of the golden triangle.

"Are we there yet?"

"Almost."

This part of the world was one terminus on the Underground Railroad, bordering as it does Michigan and New York state. There are still farms around here run by descendants of slaves who made that journey. People pass by and see a black woman driving a tractor and wonder where she's from. She's from here.

A certain amount of smuggling still goes on back and forth across the border—things and, sometimes, people.

Toronto is "the big smoke," and there are major tourist attractions like Niagara Falls, but at the heart of the Triangle sits the medium-size city of London. There are a lot of insurance companies there. Big American corporations have regional headquarters in London, and products destined for the entire North American market are tested first on the consumers in this area. The manufacturers must think there is something particularly normal about the Southern Ontario Triangle.

"Dad," Madeleine asks, "why don't they change Kitchener back to Berlin now that the war is over?"

"Both wars," he replies, "especially the last one, are still very much in living memory."

In living colour.

"Yeah, but Germany's not our enemy now," says Mike, "Russia is."

"Right you are, Mike," says Dad in his man-to-man voice, parade-square clipped, "though you don't really want to say Russia. Russians are people like anyone else, we're talking about the Soviets."

Soviets. The word sounds like a difficult unit of measurement: *If Joyce has three soviets and Johnny has twelve, how many soviets would they have if. . . .* Madeleine doesn't press the issue, but feels that Kitchener probably knows that Kitchener is not its real name. The name change makes it seem as though bright shiny Kitchener has an evil secret: "My name used to be Berlin. *Heil Hitler.*"

Dad clears his throat and continues, "There's an old saying: 'Those who do not remember history are doomed to repeat it.'"

Which is proof that, once your name is Berlin, you should keep it that way. But Madeleine says nothing. There is smart, and there is "being smart."

There is a wall down the middle of the real Berlin now. It's part of the Iron Curtain. Madeleine knows that it's not a real curtain, but the Wall is real. Twenty-nine miles of barbed wire and concrete. The grown-ups say "when the Wall went up" as though it sprang up by magic overnight. "History in the making," her father called it.

Before the Wall went up, the border ran down the middle of streets, through cemeteries and houses and apartment buildings and people's beds. You could go to sleep in the U.S.S.R., roll over and wake up in the free world. You could shave as a Communist and breakfast as a free man. Maybe they could build a miniature wall through the middle of

Kitchener if they changed its name back to Berlin. That's not funny. Communism is not funny.

"Dad, are they going to blow up the earth?" she asks.

He answers with a laugh, as though it were the first he'd ever heard of the idea. "Who?" he asks.

"Are they going to press the button?"

"What button?" says Dad. What snake under the bed?

Mike says, "It's not a button, it's a metal switch and it takes dual keys, one for each guy, and one guy turns his key, then the other guy—"

"And the chances of that happening," says Dad, in his my-last-word-on-the-subject voice, "are virtually nil."

"What's 'virtually'?" asks Madeleine.

"It means it might as well be zero."

*But it ain't zero, is it, doc?*

They drive in silence for a while.

"But what if they did press the button?" says Madeleine. "I mean, what if they did turn the keys? Would the earth blow up?"

"What are you worrying about that for?" He sounds a little offended. She feels somewhat ashamed, as though she has been rude. It's rude to worry about the earth blowing up when your dad is right there in the front seat driving. After you've had ice cream and everything.

"Would your skin melt?" She didn't mean to ask, it just slipped out. Picture your skin sliding off after it has melted. *Nyah, pass me a wet-nap, doc.*

"What makes you think that would happen?" He sounds incredulous, the way he does when she is afraid and he's comforting her—as if hers were the most groundless fear in the world. It is comforting. Except when it comes to melted skin.

"I saw a picture," she says.

"Where?"

"In a magazine. Their skin was melted."

"She's talking about the Japs," explains Mike.

His father corrects him. "Don't say Japs, Mike, say Japanese."

"Would it melt?" asks Madeleine.

"Can we talk about something nice, *au nom du Seigneur?*" says Mimi, coming to the end of her tether. "Think nice thoughts, Madeleine, think about what you're going to wear the first day of your new school."

*Melted skin.*

Maman lights a cigarette. They drive in silence. Refreshing Cameo Menthol.

After a while, Madeleine glances at Mike. He has fallen asleep. Maybe when he wakes up he'll play I Spy with her. If she doesn't act like a baby. Or a girl. They used to play together a lot, and shared baths when they were little. She recalls vivid fragments—boats bobbing, bubbles escaping from sinking ducks, "Mayday, come in, Coast Guard." She remembers sucking delicious soapy water from the face cloth until he grabbed it from her: "No, Madeleine, *c'est sale!*"

A bit of drool at the corner of his mouth makes him look younger, less remote. Madeleine's throat feels sore—she is tempted to poke him, make him mad at her, then she might stop feeling sad for no reason.

*Welcome to Lucan. . . .*

They are standing in an old country churchyard. Not old for Europe, old for Canada. Long grass obscures the gravestones, many of which have keeled over. One monument stands out. Four-sided and taller than the rest, still upright but chipped in places. Five names are chiselled on its sides, each name ending in "Donnelly." They were born on different dates, but they all died on the same day: FEB. 4, 1880. And after each name, etched in stone, is the word "Murdered."

The Donnellys were Irish. Jack tells the story of how they and their neighbours brought their feud with them from the old country to the new. "You have to ask yourself why," he says, "with all this space in Canada, they chose to live right next door all over again." There isn't much to the story. Most of it is written right there in the stone. *Murdered Murdered Murdered Murdered Murdered.*

Mimi calls from the car, "Madeleine, come, we're going, *reviens au car.*" But Madeleine lingers. "How did they murder them?" she asks her father.

"They came in the night and broke in."

"How?"

"With axes," says Mike.

"Come on, kids, let's go," says Jack, heading for the car.

"Did they get the people who did it?" she asks, transfixed before the stone.

No, they never did.

"Are they still out there?"

No, I told you, it all happened a long time ago.

"I don't know why you stopped here, Jack," says Mimi, leading her daughter away by the hand. "She's going to have *des cauchemars.*"

"No I won't," says Madeleine, stung by the implication that looking at an old gravestone might give her nightmares—she isn't a baby. "I'm just very interested in history."

Jack chuckles and Mimi says, "She's a McCarthy, that one." Madeleine wonders why anyone would want to be anything else.

Don't look for that monument nowadays. It was removed years ago, because too many tourists left with fragments of the stone. The McCarthys don't do that. They simply look and reflect, as is their custom. Rarely do they seek out "attractions"—mini-putt, go-carts—despite Mike's pleas and Madeleine's yearnings. Not only are those pursuits "tacky," but the best things in life are free. The wonders of nature, the architecture of Europe. Your imagination is the best entertainment of all, writing is the greatest technology known to man, and your teeth are more precious than pearls so look after them. "'Eat an apple every day, take a nap at three, take good care of yourself, you belong to me'— come on, *les enfants, chantez avec maman. . . .*" And Mike does.

Way up in the sky the moon is visible, a pale wafer. We intend to get there before the decade is out, President Kennedy has pledged it. Madeleine's father has predicted that when she and Mike are grown up, people will take a rocket to the moon as easily as flying to Europe. They were in Germany when Yuri Gagarin became the first man in space. Everyone was glued to the radio—the American Forces network with Walter Cronkite, "the voice of space." The Russians are beating us in space because Communists force their children to study nothing but arithmetic. Madeleine closes her eyes and sees the imprint of the moon against her lids. At least the Russians sent a man up there that time and not a dog, the way they did with Sputnik. That dog smothered.

"What was that dog's name?"

"What dog?" asks her father.

*Think nice thoughts.* "Nothing."

When John Glenn orbited the earth last February, the principal played the radio over the PA system and the whole school listened to the countdown. They cheered, and when Lieutenant Colonel Glenn returned safely to earth, the principal announced, "This is an historic day for freedom-loving peoples everywhere."

It is important to beat the Russians to the moon before they can send any more innocent dogs up there.

"How many more miles, Dad?" When Mike asks, it sounds like a question posed out of pure interest in maps and triangulated distances. When Madeleine asks, it sounds like whining. There is little she can do about this.

"Take a look at the map there, Mike," says her father in his man-to-man voice. It is a different voice from the one he uses with her. The man-to-man voice makes Mike seem important, which annoys

Madeleine, but there is also a note in it that makes her worry that Mike may be about to get in trouble for something even though he hasn't done anything.

"*Voici la mappe, Michel.*" Her mother turns and hands it to Mike.

"*Merci, maman.*" He shakes out the map importantly, peers at it, then: "I estimate arrival at 1700 hours."

"What time is that, Mike?" Madeleine asks.

"It's Zulu time."

"Mike, quit it."

"Five P.M. to civilians," he says.

"You're a civilian too," says Madeleine.

"Not for long."

"Yes, you're only eleven, you can't join till you're twenty-one."

"Dad, you can join the army at eighteen, can't you?"

"Technically, yes, Mike, but then who in his right mind would want to join the army?"

"I mean the air force."

"Well, during the war. . . ."

*During the war.* When her father starts this way, it's clear he's going to talk for a while, and probably tell them things he has told them before, but somehow that's the best kind of story. Madeleine leans back and gazes out the window, the better to picture it all.

But Mike interrupts, "Yeah, but what about now?"

"Well, now I think it's eighteen," says Dad, "but during the war . . ."

Mike listens, chin perched on the backrest of the front seat. Mimi strokes his cheek, his hair. Mike allows himself to be petted and Madeleine wonders how he has managed to fool their mother into thinking he is pettable. Like a fierce dog with bone-hard muscles that can only be patted by its owner, and its owner thinks it's fluffy.

" . . . you had fellas as young as sixteen training as pilots—they lied about their age, you had to be seventeen and a half. . . ." Her father was training at seventeen but he wasn't in the war. There was a crash. Madeleine closes her eyes and pictures his aircraft.

But Mike interrupts again. "Could I train at eighteen?"

"Tell you what, Mike, when we get to the station, I'll ask around. I know there's a civilian flying club and I don't see why we shouldn't get you up in a light aircraft before too long, eh?"

"Wow, Dad!" Mike punches his thighs. "Man oh man!"

Mimi reaches over and caresses the back of her husband's neck and he returns a casual glance that says, "No big deal," but really means "I love you."

Madeleine is embarrassed. It is as though she were suddenly looking through a door that someone ought to have closed. Mike seems not to notice that sort of thing.

"Dad," says Madeleine, "tell the story of the crash again."

"Yeah, Dad," says Mike.

"How about you settle back and enjoy the scenery, and when we get there I'll show you exactly where it happened."

Mimi sings, "*O Mein Papa.*"

Mike allows Madeleine to put her feet on his side of the seat. They sing for miles, until they forget where they are going, until they forget where they have been, and the drive becomes a dream, and that's what a drive could be back then.

*Welcome to Paris, Welcome to Brussels, Welcome to Dublin, New Hamburg, Damascus, Welcome to Neustadt and Stratford, and London. . . .* Welcome to Ontario.

So many unseen companions in this countryside, so many layers of lives. A collective memory has risen from the land and settled over the Triangle like a cumulus cloud. Memory breeds memory, draws it out of new arrivals, takes it in. The soil so rich, water so abundant, the bounty so green; it has absorbed us many times over, then breathed everything out again, so that the very air is made of memory. Memory falls in the rain. You drink memory. In winter you make snow angels out of memory.

Twenty-five miles north of London lies the Royal Canadian Air Force Station at Centralia. RCAF Centralia. Don't look for it now, it has lost its memory. A temporary place, for temporary people, it was constructed so that memory would not adhere, but slip away like an egg from a pan. Constructed to resist time.

The station is named for the nearby village of Centralia, but there the resemblance ends. The village is old and getting older. Gardens change in the village, shops go in and out of business, houses age, are altered, people are born, grow up and die there. But everything about an air force station is new. And it will stay that way for its entire operational life. Each house, each building will be freshly painted in the same colours they have always had, the cadets who jog across the parade square will always be young and about to get their wings. The families in the PMQs will always seem like the first families to move in, they will always have young children of about the same age. Only the trees will change, grow. Like reruns on television, an air force station never grows old. It remains in the present. Until the last flypast. Then it is demobilized, decommissioned, deconsecrated. It is sold off and all the aging, the buildup of time that was never apparent, will suddenly be upon it. It will fade like the face of an old child. Weeds, peeling paint, decaying big-eyed bungalows. . . .

But until that happens, the present tense will reign. And were a wanderer to return after being lost in time, she could walk straight up to her old house and recognize it. Open the door and expect to see Mum with a pan of cookies—"I've laid out your Brownie uniform on the bed, sweetheart, where have you been?"

No, this part of the world is not the Bermuda Triangle. But from time to time people do come here in order to disappear.

## WELCOME TO CENTRALIA

*I know it sounds a bit bizarre,*
*but in Camelot, that's how conditions are.*

Camelot, *Lerner and Loewe, 1960*

"WAKE UP, MADELEINE. We're here."

Royal Canadian Air Force Station Centralia. Six hundred and thirty-eight acres of government issue dropped into the middle of one continuous agricultural quilt. A good place to train pilots, farmland being ideal for emergency landings. Jack trained here during the war. "Welcome to the MON," his flight instructor had said: the Middle Of Nowhere.

He slows the car on the Huron County road. To their right, the station. To their left, the houses of the PMQs. "Let's take a tour, shall we?" he says and turns right.

Just outside the main gates, a World War Two Spitfire speeds on a steel pedestal, legendary little fighter, its propeller welded to a stop, clear canopy bolted over the single seat. *Per ardua ad astra,* says the plaque, motto of the RCAF: Through adversity to the stars.

"Dad, can you show us where it happened?" asks Madeleine.

"We'll get there, little buddy."

Jack would have flown a bomber had it not been for the crash. A big heavy Lancaster with four Merlin engines, the opposite of the nimble Spitfire. "That little airplane is one of the reasons why we're alive and free today," says Jack.

*Never in the field of human conflict was so much owed by so many to so few.* When Churchill said that, he was talking about the pilots who flew in the Battle of Britain. The Spitfire helped save Britain from Nazi invasion in 1940. When England stood alone, ninety-nine Canadian pilots stood with them, fending off the might of Goering's Luftwaffe while ordinary Britons watched from the ground.

The bolted and mounted Spitfire is another difference between Canada and Germany. Here the emblems of battle are proudly displayed, refurbished tanks and cannons, cenotaphs in town squares commemorating "our glorious dead" from the Boer War through to Korea. But in Germany there were no Messerschmitts shined up and on show. There were bullet-pocked buildings and heaps of debris, abundant ruins amid the "economic miracle"—the *Wirtschaftswunder.* It's a long word, like many German words, but Madeleine remembers it because it sounds like a magic spell. Her father explained what it meant and told them how the women of Germany rebuilt their cities brick by brick with their bare hands after each bombing raid, as undaunted as Londoners during the Blitz. Madeleine pictures them as though in a black-and-white newsreel, *die Trümmerfrauen*—"the Women of the Ruins." In headscarves, bent over foothills of rubble.

Jack pulls up to the guardhouse, chats and chuckles with the guard, who says, "Welcome to Centralia, sir," and salutes with casual courtesy—the type of salute that distinguishes air force from army. Jack touches two fingers to his forehead in response and pulls away. The Rambler drives slowly up Canada Avenue.

If her father had gotten to fly a bomber, he would have made more rubble in Germany. Unless they shot him down first. Hamburg, Dresden, Cologne. . . . Dad always shakes his head sadly at the mention of Dresden. When you hear the name Dresden, you picture beautiful china and wedding-cake buildings. They are gone now, bombs away. "Total war was Hitler's idea," says her father. Imagine going into someone's house and breaking all the plates. That'll teach you. All the women in the world couldn't put them back together again.

Madeleine watches the buildings go by, silent white siding with green trim, all neatly landscaped, labelled and laid out. The Protestant chapel, the Catholic chapel, the fire hall, the library. Shopping carts parked outside the PX, all quiet on this Sunday afternoon. Turning onto Saskatchewan Street now. . . .

They are driving very slowly. Like a military slow march, the muffled bootfalls a sign of respect or mourning. The McCarthys are carefully, reverently beginning to say hello to Centralia. Moving among a herd of unknown sleepy creatures, their future—don't make any sudden moves, don't anyone take a picture yet.

Up Nova Scotia Avenue, past administrative buildings where the dads work, past H-shaped barracks where the non-dads live. Heat shivering up from the parade square, chessboard black against the white buildings. The movie theatre—*Pillow Talk* is playing—the curling arena, the hockey arena—a flurry of activity behind the rec centre where kids are cannonballing into an outdoor pool. Madeleine watches it all inch by under the loving August sun. This is where whatever will be, will be.

As abrupt as a flock of gulls, a squad of young men jogs past, white sneakers in double-time, billowing singlets and blue shorts, sweat-stained cadets all sinews and Adam's apples. Some are African, others Asian, the rest Heinz 57 Caucasian. Mimi watches them pass, then raises her eyebrows ever so briefly at Jack, who mutters, "Avert your eyes, woman." She smiles. Jack underlines his mental note—he will definitely start running, once they've settled in.

He watches the young men jog away under the brutal accumulated heat of afternoon. He's been there. Here. Wore the coveted "white flash"—a triangle of cloth inserted in the front of the wedge cap to signify aircrew in training. One of the "Brylcreem boys," irresistible to the fair sex. He did his ground training, sweated over an instrument panel in a classroom, surrounded by a cyclorama of painted landscape and horizon, trying not to "crash" the Link trainer—an ingenious little flight simulator still in use—drawing the hood over its cockpit, flying blind, *trust your instruments.* They drilled it into you, *take off into the wind, even on the throttle, hands, feet and head.* . . . Speaking aloud the cockpit check, powering up for the first heart-pounding solo—God watches over your first solo, after that you're on your own. And later, at the officers' mess, legs still trembling, raising the glasses high, *Here's to being above it all.*

Jack trained here, but he would have gone operational in the skies over Germany—Mühlheim, Essen, Dortmund. Mission after mission to the "land of no future," as they called the Ruhr Valley, industrial heartland of the Third Reich, where an Allied bomber crew's life expectancy was even shorter than usual. But the war is history. Many of these cadets are training as NATO pilots. They will be assigned to squadrons around the world. They may never see combat, but they will take turns on Zulu standby, ready to scramble and be airborne within minutes of the alarm, armed with nuclear bombs and missiles, knowing that, if the balloon goes up, it could all be over one way or another in a matter of hours. Not just for a flight crew, or for hundreds, even thousands of civilians on the ground. But for all of us. It's a very different world now. Jack turns the wheel and the Rambler rolls into the shadow between two huge hangars.

Moments later they emerge onto a quiet expanse where concrete strips fan out to form a vast triangle within a triangle. The airfield. Perfectly still and baking.

Jack stops the car. Cuts the engine. Out on the runway, a shimmer of heat. "There's the old scene of the crime," he says. His tone is affectionate—a time-worn joke about a long-dead loved one. "Son of a gun," he says. Shakes his head. Mimi watches him. He turns to her and winks. Can't complain. He leans across and kisses her.

In the back seat the children look away, out at the airfield. Then Jack and Mimi are looking out too. It's as though the four of them were at a drive-in. Silent picture in broad daylight. The liquid air in this heat, a blurred screen.

Madeleine blinks. This is where Dad trained as a pilot. This is where he crashed. Surveying the smooth runways, she experiences one of those mental jolts that mark the passage between being little, and being a kid. Until now, she has pictured Centralia in the middle of the war—gritty landing strips swarming with cheerful men in fleece-lined leather bomber jackets, cracking jokes, sharing smokes, fearless and uncomplaining. Bombs exploding around the airfield, Dad dodging and dashing to his airplane. Although she knew very well that Centralia was in Canada, one aspect of being little was her ability to place it nonetheless at the centre of European hostilities.

When you are little, you can believe two things at once. Madeleine often had to remind herself that her father had not been killed in the crash—*how could he have been, when he is right here telling me the story of it?* Yet somehow she had come to think of it not only as The Story of the Crash, but also as The Story of When Dad Was Killed in the War. Now she realizes the absurdity of the images she harboured, and is chilled at how the latter title used to float through her mind with no sense of fear, no sense even of contradiction. All part of the semi-hallucinatory world she inhabited when she was little. Five minutes ago. She looks out at the airfield and feels as though she were waking from a dream. There are no bullet-riddled airplanes, no craters in the concrete, there are certainly no Lancaster bombers or even the bulky Anson trainers that her father flew. There are no weapons at all. The old Spitfire anchored back at the gates is the closest thing to a combat aircraft on the base. For there, ranged on the tarmac, are Centralia's main operational aircraft: Chipmunks.

Cheerful little yellow training machines. Cadets get their first taste of the wild blue in the cockpit of a de Havilland Chipmunk, then work their way up to sleek Sabres, Voodoos and CF-104 fighters, or hefty Hercules transports and Yukons. But not in Centralia. This is a Primary Flying School. And a Central Officers' School. With a Language School, an Engineering School and a Supply School, the whole place is one big school.

Centralia plays its role in the web of NATO defence but it is far from the Berlin Wall. Far from the Bay of Pigs, the Suez Canal, Cape Canaveral and the Russian Cosmodrome, far from it all. The Middle Of Nowhere. This is where Jack was awarded his medal: the Air Force Cross. *For valour, courage and devotion to duty whilst flying, though not in active operations against the enemy.*

The government built Centralia in 1942, part of Prime Minister Mackenzie King's vision of a vast network of aircrew training bases that prompted President Roosevelt to call Canada "the aerodrome of democracy."

Canada was one-third of the great North Atlantic Triangle, poised between Britain and the United States. This triangle worked in cunning ways. Under the Lend-Lease plan, many of the airplanes were built in the U.S.—"the arsenal of democracy"—but until the Americans entered the war the planes could not be flown into Canada without violating the United States Neutrality Act. So pilots would fly the new aircraft to Montana or North Dakota and land just shy of the border. Only feet away, a team of horses waited on the Canadian side. The airplane was hitched up and hauled into Canada, then flown to RCAF stations to supply the British Commonwealth Air Training Plan.

Recruits from all over the Commonwealth—Britain and every corner of its former empire—and many American flyboys, before they had their own war, came to Canada. Far from the front lines and out of range of German bombers, over a hundred thousand aircrew were trained—pilots, wireless operators, air gunners and navigators. They got their wings and fed the skies overseas, where they died in droves—most of them on night bombing missions, seven to a crew, in broad moonlight.

At that time Centralia was a Service Flying Training School, last stop before operational training in England, followed by the real thing. Jack was ready to go to England when he pinwheeled in his twin-engine Anson and exploded in the field south of the landing strip. Just short of the ditch. You can see the fringe of longer grass out beyond the taxiway. They pinned a gong on him for valour because he had done the right thing. It felt like reflex at the time but, as it turned out, Jack had made a courageous decision in the air, *though not in active operations against the enemy.*

Last April, when he got his posting notice, Jack laughed. Centralia. Son of a gun. Considered asking for an extension of his European tour of duty, but when he told Mimi, she said, "I want to go home, Jack." In all the years of their marriage they had spent only four in their own country. She said, "I want our next baby to be born in Canada." He smiled, needing no more persuasion than her desire for a third child. She loved Europe, but it was time. Time for the kids to know their country. Time, he knew, although she didn't say, to put some distance between them and the Cold War. When the Wall had gone up last summer, she had said, "We're too far from home."

This is the first time he has been back to Centralia. After the crash, he wore a bandage over his eyes for six weeks. His right eye is fine; he lost some peripheral in the left; he wears prescription sunglasses for driving and otherwise none at all except for reading. If he had been operational at that point, had he been injured by flak over Europe, they would have sent him back up once he recovered. No reason you can't drop your bomb load with an eye and a half. But he was CT'ed. Ceased Training. Like an obsolete aircraft, he was Struck Off Strength. He kept his wings but lost his aircrew category. His war was over. He was bitter at the time. He was young.

Mimi takes his hand.

Now he is back in Centralia. And Centralia is still a flying school, except these days the cadets come from NATO countries. And there are families. There are station wagons, barbecues and sprinklers. There is peace.

Most of his friends were killed.

He squeezes then releases his wife's hand, and starts the car. He rounds slowly back between the hangars. Time to show Mimi the social hub of RCAF Centralia. It's bound to be nice, they always are. High-polish wood and leather, sterling silver, white linen, and gardenias. The officers' mess. Worth squeezing yourself into a monkey suit, if you are an officer, and, more important, worth spending hours slipping into your best satin décolleté if you are an officer's wife. But formal events are far from the rule. Weekly dances require nothing more than a sports jacket and tie for the men, party dresses for the wives; bingos, raffles, barbecues and corn roasts are even more casual.

Mimi considers her husband's profile. She likes to tease him that he looks too young for her, although he is a year older. Something innocent about his blue eyes—it could be his lashes, golden brown and too long for a man. She wants to rest her head on his shoulder while he drives, the way she used to when they were courting. Feel his cheek light against her lips, his smooth shave, knowing he can feel her breath, wondering how long it will take him to pull over. . . . Jack looks unconcerned but she knows it means something to him, being back here. He teases her about being "dramatic" but she knows this is where he had his heart broken. Not by a woman, by an airplane.

She knows better than to talk about it, or to show him she knows by any sign other than being happy here. By plunging in and organizing their life, unpacking her formals along with the pots and pans, joining the Officers' Wives Club, sending his uniform to the cleaners. . . . Something she would never tell him: she is glad not to be married to a pilot. Salt of the earth, life of the party, some of their best friends, but . . . the worry for the wives when the men are flying. And the waiting after work when the men are together, drinking. High-strung esprit de corps, for all her husband's belief in how relaxed the air force is compared to the army. Mimi knows, but does not say, that men who are relaxed with other men are sometimes anything but once they get home. She is grateful to be a wife, not a cheerleader. She has the best of both worlds: a man in uniform whose first love is his family.

She looks away, not wanting him to feel watched. He is whistling through his teeth. He's going to be fine. *I have such a good man.* There is nothing more erotic than this knowledge, no Hollywood scene could rival this station wagon in the sunshine with this man and his children and the secret that only she knows: his face, hovering just above her own, deserted by his defences. At the mercy of his own strength, needing her to take it from him, keep it safe. Then give it back to him. She slips her hand onto his thigh.

Jack turns left on Alberta Street and follows the one curve on the base. A slow circular drive leads to a stone building couched in hedges and flower beds. Low-slung Frank Lloyd Wright, its granite facade a glamorous contrast to the architectural whiteout everywhere else.

"There you go, Missus," he says.

Flagstone steps lead to a pair of oak doors. Tilted wood-framed picture windows afford a glimpse of cocktail tables and chairs between burgundy-and-blue curtains—the air force tartan. The dance floor gleams. It is possible to fall in love with your wife all over again in the time it takes to escort her up to the open doors where the sounds of a swing orchestra greet you, along with the clink of glasses, the aroma of the buffet, the laughter of men and women. Enchanted evenings.

"*Bon,*" says Mimi. And they drive on.

Mike says, "Where's your building, Dad?"

"Oh we just passed it, buddy, it's back there on the right."

Receding through the rear window of the station wagon, a two-storey white building with a green shingled roof and concrete steps. Benign as a snowfort. That is where Jack will be running the Central Officers' School. That is where he will fly his desk.

Mimi takes a hanky from her husband's pocket and wipes the lipstick from his mouth, left over from their kiss at the airfield. Then she kisses him again and whispers in his ear, "*Je t'aime,* baby."

Life is beautiful. He lets the steering wheel unravel beneath his palm as he completes the leisurely turn back onto Canada Avenue. He is a lucky man. He wants what he has.

He knows that, had he gone operational in '43, he might well have been killed. The crash spared him. He has been given the gift that many of his friends sacrificed. He has children. It ends there, there is nothing better, not fast cars or caviar, not Playboy bunnies or money. Your children. And the woman who has your children. He says softly to Mimi as she squeezes his thigh, "Behave yourself, Missus." She glances down at his lap—"You behave, Mister"—and smiles. Pleased with herself.

As the Rambler passes the gates, the guard touches his cap and Jack lifts two fingers from the wheel.

They near the Spitfire again, and Madeleine feels the butterflies wake up in her stomach. We are finally going to our new house. Which one will it be? In Centralia there are 362 to choose from. In a variety of colours.

Opposite the Spitfire stands a wooden pole. It's not a telephone pole, Madeleine can see that. Way up at the top is a large birds' nest. And protruding from the mass of straw is a thrust of metal. Like a rusty mouth.

"It's an air-raid siren," says Mike.

It's unlike the ones she knew in Germany—freshly painted loudspeakers mounted on concrete posts. No birds allowed.

"It's left over from the war," says Dad.

"Did you ever hear it?"

"Nope."

She knows what an air-raid siren sounds like. There were drills on the base at 4 Wing. It's a terrifying sound that makes you have to go to the bathroom. "Does it still work?" she asks.

"Who knows?" says Dad, "but it sure would give the crows a fright if it did."

The Rambler crosses the Huron County road. No traffic on either side as far as the eye can see. MON. Madeleine turns and looks back up at the raggedy nest. Glimpse of a black wing, then a crow rises and flies away.

The Rambler enters the PMQs and Canada Avenue becomes Algonquin Drive. It leads through a little Levittown, planned suburb of semi-detached houses and bungalows in every colour of the rainbow. None of this was here in '43.

Each house is surrounded by a big lawn, a view of the cornfields never far away. Lawns can make slaves of their owners, but all anyone does in Centralia is water and cut, and the grass flourishes thick and green. Same with the maples that cast their twirling keys to earth, the blossom-raining elms, the shaggy bushes that erupt in snowstorms of confetti each spring, *Just married!* There are no fences. Crescents and bends form tulip-shapes, the whole place is hugging itself. Madeleine looks out the window at this bright new world.

Bikes and trikes and red wagons, sprinklers going, the distant roar of a lawnmower, the smell of freshly cut grass. Kids glance up, mildly curious, strange adults wave casually at the car, Jack and Mimi wave back.

"Who's that?" Madeleine asks.

"We don't know yet," says Dad.

"But we will soon," says Maman.

Or maybe they won't. The people who waved may be moving out just as the McCarthys move in. Or you may run into a family from two or three postings ago, and it's a great reunion but either way it's just as well to start off as old friends. That's how it is in the forces. You bond, you move on, there is no contradiction.

They drive past a park with swings, a slide, merry-go-round and teeter-totters. Paved footpaths run between the houses and open onto empty fields full of possibilities invisible to the adult eye. Among Centralia's PMQs there are sixty-four such empty acres—big grassy circles rimmed by the backs of houses. Someone's mother can always see you. No one worries about children in Centralia.

"Dad, why is it called Centralia?" asks Madeleine.

"Because it's at the centre of the world." Jack winks at his son in the rearview mirror.

"Every place is the centre of the world," says Mike, "'cause the world is round." And Centralia feels round, the looping streets, the neatly mown fields that fill the centres of these loops. Madeleine pictures a target. And in the crosshairs, Centralia. Bombs away. Rubble. Women in kerchiefs picking up the coloured pieces of the PMQs. Lego.

"Madeleine, stop daydreaming and look at your new neighbourhood," says her mother. "Where do you think your best friend lives?"

*Gee doc, maybe in that garbage can with Popeye the Sailor Man.* "I don't know, Maman." *I like to go swimmin with bare naked wimmin, I'm Popeye the Sailor Man!* Rude lyrics she learned from Mike. She pictures her Popeye ukulele. It's on the same moving van with her hair and the rest of their stuff—including, unfortunately, her accordion.

"Madeleine."

*"Oui, maman?"*

"I said, pick one and then later you'll see if you were right."

Madeleine rests her chin on the window frame and tries to guess where her best friend lives. The one she has not yet met. Does she live in the pink house, the green one . . . ? Suddenly she remembers that she already has a best friend, Laurie Ferry. But she can no longer quite picture her face.

"There's your new school, kids." Jack stops the car. Modern single-storey white stucco with big windows and a taller section at one end, the gym. J.A.D. McCurdy School, kindergarten through grade eight. Deserted, deep in its summer sleep. The flagpole stands empty. The swings hang motionless, the slide and teeter-totters static.

"Hop out and take a look," says Dad. Mike opens his door and Madeleine slides out after him.

Their parents watch from the car as they cross the playground without stopping to swing or slide, past the bike racks and up the broad front steps. In a week and a half they will line up here with other kids, some of whom they will know by then. Friends.

Brother and sister cup their hands around their eyes and peer through the glass of the big double doors. The first thing they see, once their eyes have adjusted to the gloom, is an arrangement of framed photos. Mike rhymes them off: "Sabre, CF-100, Lancaster. . . ."

Two larger photos preside over the rest. Queen Elizabeth II, "our gracious Queen," and her husband, Prince Philip. Their portraits greet you in the foyer of every Canadian school here and abroad. The Queen and Prince Philip, your old friends. Your godparents, in a way.

Hi, Your Majesty. Madeleine stares up at the Queen and thinks, this will be my last year in Brownies. This spring, I will fly up to Girl Guides. There is the congenial sense that the Queen has heard her and serenely agrees, "Why yes, Madeleine, it is high time you flew up to Guides."

"Thank you, Your Majesty."

"You're welcome."

Mike has strolled away and hoisted himself onto a window ledge to get a better look. She joins him and he hops down and gives her a boost. She gazes in. "I wonder which one is my classroom."

"This one is."

"It is not, Mike."

This classroom has the alphabet marching in block letters above the blackboard, and happy numbers skipping hand in hand. It is obviously the kindergarten classroom. The pile of pastel-coloured nap mats in the corner clinches it. Madeleine is going into grade four, you do not have naps on mats in grade four. Mike is going into grade seven.

"Due to my superior intelligence," he says suavely.

"Due to it's automatic when you're turning twelve," she says with withering sarcasm. Mike never withers.

"You have to pass first, stunned one."

"Like wow, man," she drawls, "you passed. How womantic, how positively gwoovy," snapping her fingers and swaggering like a beatnik, "Hey Daddyo."

Mike laughs. "Do Elvis."

She swivels her hips, wrinkling her brow over the microphone, dropping her voice, dribbling it like a basketball, "'We-hell it's won foh the money, two foh the show. . . . '"

"Do Barbie!" he yells, giggling furiously—it's so easy to make her go crazy. Madeleine goes up on tiptoes, sticks out her chest, points her hands, and totters about with a plastic face and mechanically blinking eyes. "Oh Ken, can you pick up my handkerchief for me, please?" she simpers. "I cannot bend my legs, I cannot bend my arms, eek! Oh Ken, save me. My hero!" Mike takes out an imaginary machine gun and Barbie dies in a hail of bullets.

Madeleine gets up. "Hey Mike, want me to do Sylvester? 'Thufferin' Thuckotash!' Want me to do Elmer Fudd? 'A hunting we wiw go, a hunting we wiw go—'"

But Mike takes off around the corner of the building. She follows. They run around the whole school three times, then they run to the teeter-totters and hang over the steel bar on their stomachs.

"Hop on," says Mike, and they teeter-totter violently while Madeleine hangs on for dear life, not complaining about the bumps, laughing every time she wants to cry, "Ow!"

He abandons the teeter-totter. Madeleine crashes onto her tailbone, laughs and follows, convinced her bum is flashing visible cartoon pain behind her. He has climbed halfway up the mesh of the baseball backstop by the time she reaches it. "Come on men, follow me," he cries, making explosion sounds, pulling a pin from a grenade with his teeth, "I need ammo!" and she tosses up a bandolier of bullets, "Thanks, corporal," he calls through the hell of battle—normally Madeleine is just a private, she swells with pride.

"Sarge!" she yells, "look out!"

Mike turns to see a Japanese soldier clambering up after him. Madeleine takes aim and snipes. "Got him!" she yells and, as the Nazi tumbles to his death, "*Auf Wiedersehen!*"

"He was a Jap," says Mike, "not a Kraut."

"Mike!" says Madeleine. "Don't say Jap and Kraut, we're not allowed."

Mike's head snaps to one side. "I'm hit!" His grip loosens and he half-tumbles down the mesh, bleeding, dying.

"Sarge! I'll save you!" She slides down the backstop, fingers and toes skimming the metal links, and releases her hold an impressive eight feet from the ground, tuck and roll. "It doesn't hurt," she announces before he can ask.

Their parents are still in the car, chatting. Mike and Madeleine are sweating. He pulls out an imaginary pack of smokes, and offers her one. Lucky Strikes. They lean against the backstop and puff, gazing across the road at a farmer's field and a stand of woods beyond. "First chance I get, I'm going to light out into those woods," says Mike.

"Can I come?" asks Madeleine, tentative—this could be pushing things too far.

"Sure, why not?" he says, and lets a squirt of clear spit escape his lips.

Times like this with Mike are precious. She does not want to move or say anything to wreck it. At times like this it is almost as if he has forgotten that she is a girl, and is treating her like a brother.

The sun tilts across their shoulders. Their shadows have grown up on the ground before them, long and lanky against the loose weave traced by the backstop.

"You ready to roll, kids?" Dad calls.

They walk back toward the car, comrades, no need to speak—as they say in the Marine Corps, *Deeds Not Words*. Their parents are smiling, amused at something. Madeleine reflects that sometimes your mother and father look pleased with you and you can't figure out why.

They pile into the back seat and it's funny how this is the first time since they arrived in Canada that Madeleine has not felt as though she were climbing into the new car in the new place. It's just the car. It's just Centralia, where we live, and that's our school, J.A.D. McCurdy.

"J.A.D. McCurdy made the first heavier-than-air powered flight in Canada, in 1919," says Dad.

*You 'spect me to remember dat, doc?*

A breeze lifts and the pulleys clank against the empty flagpole as the Rambler backs from the parking lot. On the first day of school the flag of our country will be raised. Not our flag, precisely, but the Red Ensign: the Canadian coat of arms, and in the upper left corner, the Union Jack. Canada does not have an official flag, we are not officially a country, we are just a dominion. What is a dominion? We're not sure. It's the name of a grocery store chain.

Madeleine is nervous now. Her hands are cold. The Rambler's creeping pace is taking them back through the PMQs, and closer to their house. Which will it be? Look for one with blank windows and an empty driveway. Algonquin Drive, Columbia Drive. . . .

At the corner of Columbia and St. Lawrence Avenue is a two-tone tan house with an orange VW van in the driveway. A plump girl with curly hair is Hula Hooping on the front lawn. As they turn right down St. Lawrence, Madeleine wonders, will I ever Hula Hoop with that girl? Will I get to drive in her van? Or is she moving away?

A purple house ahead on the left catches her eye because PMQ driveways are not usually full of old cars and washing-machine parts, or big German shepherd dogs that are not tied up. Who lives there? Scary people? That too would be unusual.

"That dog is loose," says Mike.

Mimi looks. "Tsk-tsk."

Her mother's *tsk-tsk* is the only time Madeleine is ever aware of her French accent. She puckers her lips and *tsk-tsk*s in a way English people think of as sexy. Madeleine twists her mouth to one side, à la Bugs Bunny, at the mere thought of the word. It makes her think of Bugs dressed up as a girl Tasmanian Devil, with a big bosom and red lipstick.

"What's so funny, squirt?" says Mike.

"Zat's for me to know and you to find out, *chérie,*" replies Maurice Chevalier, thanking heaven for "leetle girls."

The Rambler pulls into a driveway directly across from the purple house and stops. Dad says, "Say hello to the house, kids."

A two-storey white aluminum-sided semi-detached house on St. Lawrence Avenue. With a red roof.

Dad opens his door. "Let's inspect the premises, shall we?"

Madeleine is happy their house is white. Make of me what you will, it says, you need not behave in a yellow or green way in order to live in me. An asphalt path leads from the driveway to the front porch, which is located at the side of the house for privacy from your neighbours, who live on the other side. Jack gets out of the car, walks around and opens Mimi's door. She gets out and takes his arm.

Their parents always lead the way to the door of the new house. Mike follows, hands jammed in his pockets, observing the tradition but looking down. He is getting old enough to feel conspicuous—this walk up to their new house, an intimate act performed in public. Madeleine slides from the back seat and turns on the movie camera in her mind— I must remember this, the first walk up to our door.

They are coming to the end of their homeless sojourn. In these last few moments they are still vulnerable, soft-shelled. Roofless for another few seconds, open to the rain, to kindness, to cruelty. Jack climbs three concrete steps to the small porch, opens the screen door and reaches into his pocket for the key. Mike runs back to the car for something as Jack slides the key into the lock.

Then Jack does what he always does, over Mimi's squeals and protests. He scoops her up in his arms and carries her across the threshold. Madeleine covers her face and peeks through her fingers, mortified and delighted. Mike returns and tosses her mangy Bugs Bunny to her. "Come on, kiddo," he says. She hugs Bugs and follows her brother into the house.

To the left of the vestibule, stairs descend to the basement. Directly in front it's up three steps and a quick right to the kitchen—functional Formica, frost-free Frigidaire and Westinghouse oven, with just room to spare for a small table and four chairs. A window over the sink looks onto the front lawn. In Mimi's mind it is already curtained. To the left is the living room with fireplace and, immediately off it, the dining room. It never seems possible that the china cabinet and buffet will fit once the dining suite is in, but somehow they always do. A bay window in the living room overlooks the backyard and one of Centralia's big empty green fields ringed by the backs of houses.

Mimi squints, mentally arranging the furniture—couch under the window, framed oil painting of the Alps over the mantlepiece, reproduction of Dürer's Praying Hands on the kitchen wall. She leads the way up fourteen steps that turn on a modest landing, to three bedrooms and the bathroom. She makes the sign of the cross when she enters the master bedroom. Once the moving van has arrived, she will call up the Catholic padre and have him bless the house. Mimi is not as devout as her mother, but the master bedroom is where children are conceived.

Madeleine and Mike know better than to squabble over the choice of bedrooms. Maman is the commanding officer at home and she will assign quarters.

They troop back downstairs, footsteps clattering, voices hollow. Mimi turns to Jack, arms folded.

He says, "What do you think, Missus?"

She tilts her head. "*Ça va faire.*"

He smiles. Passed inspection.

The four of them stand in their new living room. The empty smell. Fresh paint and cleanser. The white echo of the place.

Tonight they will sleep in a motel. Tomorrow the moving van will come and, though they will eat in a restaurant again, they will sleep in their own house. On the third night, Mimi will make a fabulous supper in their own kitchen, and from then on the house will breathe with the smells of home. An invisible welcome will billow like sheets in a breeze when they walk in the door. *Hello.*

That night in the motel, tucked into a rollaway cot, Madeleine asks her mother to tell The Story of Mimi and Jack.

"*Oui, conte-nous ça, maman,*" says Mike, snug in the extra bed.

And Mimi tells the story. "'Once upon a time there was a little Acadian nurse called Mimi, and a handsome young air force officer named Jack....'"

If you move around all your life, you can't find where you come from on a map. All those places where you lived are just that: places. You don't come from any of them; you come from a series of events. And those are mapped in memory. Contingent, precarious events, without the counterpane of place to muffle the knowledge of how unlikely we are. Almost not born at every turn. Without a place, events slow-tumbling through time become your roots. Stories shading into one another. You come from a plane crash. From a war that brought your parents together.

Tell the story, gather the events, repeat them. Pattern is a matter of upkeep. Otherwise the weave relaxes back to threads picked up by birds to make their nests. Repeat, or the story will fall and all the king's horses and all the king's men.... Repeat, and cradle the pieces carefully, or events will scatter like marbles on a wooden floor.

# Here's to Being Above It All

*This organization operates in a complex system of values and relationships which may be conceptualized as a social system. The number of possible combinations of variables therein defies imagination. Possible combinations appear to be as limitless as the physical universe with its billions of galaxies.*

"Organization Theory; An Overview and an Appraisal,"
Journal of the Academy of Management, *April 1961*

JACK IS ALONE in his new office. He has just looked in on the commanding officer of the station and introduced himself, informally. He has not yet officially reported in or taken command of the Central Officers' School. That will come in a few days, once he has settled in with his family. Centralia is still on summer hours so things are pretty quiet, many personnel on leave. He has a little time before meeting some fellow officers for a casual lunch, so he has strolled over to take a look at his new digs.

He's in civvies. Mimi has already taken his uniform to the cleaners so it will be crisp for the handing-over ceremony toward the end of the week. This morning he wears tan trousers with a cream-coloured sports jacket she picked out for him in Paris. He pretends not to notice that it's raw silk, and he would never spend his money on himself this way, but he does submit from time to time to her sartorial interventions. She's the boss, after all.

He does what he always does when he moves into a new office: places a framed photo of his wife and children on the big government-issue oak desk. This office is much the same as the one he occupied at RCAF 4 Fighter Wing back in Baden-Baden, Germany. And the one before that in Alberta, and before that at the Pentagon, where he was an exchange officer in the Accounts Branch; a succession of smaller and smaller desks in shared offices all the way back to the supply section at the RAF station in Yorkshire during the war. This desk, these green metal filing cabinets, the shelves with *The Queen's Regulations and Orders* in three thick blue binders; the photo of Her Majesty, Queen Elizabeth II, the photo of the Governor General, a Department of National Defence map and four white walls—he could be anywhere. It even smells the same: floor wax and pencil shavings, the tang of shoe polish and wool uniforms. The view is similar too. Out his window, green hedges, white buildings, blue sky—no jet stream though. Just a single yellow Chipmunk banking into view.

The handing-over ceremony will occur in this office. It will be attended by the commanding officer—the CO—and the staff of the Central Officers' School. Jack and the officer he is replacing will shake hands, then co-sign a document in formal recognition of the change in command. Standard operating procedure—SOP—in the military: there must be no break in the continuity of command and control. Afterwards, a meet 'n' greet will be followed by lunch at the mess, during which a detailed schedule of one-on-one briefings between Jack and his senior staff will be drawn up. He will tour the facilities and meet the instructional and support staff, so that, by the end of the day, all concerned will have been made aware that Jack has taken up his position as officer in command of the Central Officers' School—OC of the COS. Another SOP: a leader must be seen and identified by his men, whether he is commanding a wing of jet fighters or a building full of desks.

Jack notices some paper stuck behind the radiator below the window ledge. He bends to retrieve it. *I'll be darned.* A copy of the *Schwarzwald Flieger—Black Forest Flyer.* The monthly magazine of RCAF 4 Wing, Germany. It's a small world. The issue is from February 1958, and on the cover, the newly elected Prince and Princess of the Fasching Karneval stand triumphant before the *Narrenzunft*—the Fools' Council. Fasching is the German lead-up to Lent—bigger and wilder than Mardi Gras. The photo was taken at the Kurhaus in Baden-Baden. He and Mimi were at a similar do one year later, two among dozens of personnel and wives who had turned out to mingle and celebrate with hundreds of Germans. He flips through. In among the birth announcements, squadron scuttlebutt, Little League news and ads, the schedule of events is printed—party after party, *Children's Fancy Dress Ball, Rose Monday Ball* . . . Canadians welcome. *Willkommen.* So many nice times. So many nice remember-whens. He tosses the magazine onto his desk. No doubt it belongs to the outgoing officer. He'll want to hang onto it for sentimental value.

When you get your transfer message telling you where you will be posted in a few short months, two factors determine whether your reaction is elation or disappointment or something in between. The first thing you look at is: who's in charge? Group Captain Harold Woodley is Centralia's current CO, a man whose reputation as a wartime pilot enhances his relaxed style of command, which is vintage air force and synonymous with firmness of intent. Jack was pleased. Veterans—especially pilots—tend to know that, although they are answerable to a big organization, that organization is made up of human beings, not just systems. The second factor is geographic, and this better be good or you'll have an unhappy wife on your hands—although Mimi could make a radar station on Baffin Island into a social mecca. The air force has an efficient informal communications network, otherwise known as the grapevine, and Jack knew Centralia's reputation as a great place for kids, with plenty to keep the wives busy. The city of London is just down the road, the small town of Exeter is even closer, not to mention countless villages, flea markets, auctions, and the great inland freshwater sea of Lake Huron for swimming, camping and picnicking. He knew that the officers' mess is well run and that the station as a whole has healthy links to the civilian community—curling leagues, charity events, all manner of sports and recreation. So, although nothing can compare to 4 Wing, Jack's reaction to his transfer message last spring—once he got over the irony—was pretty much on the elation side. But no matter where they sent him, he would have the sense of a fresh start; the optimism that imbues every change, coupled with his belief that no situation is beyond improving—after all, in the military, change is the only constant. He pulls out one of the heavy blue binders—*Administration*—and flips through.

His phone rings. Surprised, he reaches for it.

"Jack, it's Hal Woodley. My wife needs to know something ASAP."

"Fire away, sir."

"What's your wife's first name?"

"Mimi."

"Righto."

This job comes with a promotion. From squadron leader to wing commander—the equivalent of the rise from major to lieutenant colonel in the army. Wing Commander McCarthy is now in charge of upwards of a thousand students, department heads, course directors, instructors and admin personnel at the Central Officers' School. Aircrew selection and orientation, logistics and administration, construction and aeronautical engineering, military and executive development at several levels, leadership and management—it's all covered. There is even an exchange arrangement with the MBA program at the University of Western Ontario in London. There are Technical, Language, Finance, Management and Basic Officer Training sections, as well as an Office of Training Standards. Just about everything there is to know about the air force, apart from flying an airplane. Ground training.

He reshelves *Administration* between *Finance* and *Discipline*. He opens his desk drawers. Stray paper clips, elastic bands. A hefty stapler, tablets of lined yellow paper. A brass pencil sharpener in the shape of an airplane. He spins the tiny propeller.

Thanks to the air force, Jack got his MBA at one of the finest schools in the world—a single eye-straining year at the University of Michigan. He could earn better than double out in the civilian world—on civvie street. His job here is, in civilian terms, a management position comparable to a corporate executive vice-president in charge of operations. He will report directly to the CO, his time his own to organize as he sees fit. He is, for all intents and purposes, his own boss.

As such, Jack has devised a couple of rules for himself. Ask before telling. And listen more than you talk. His job is to know what everyone else's job is, to get everyone pointed in the right direction and then get out of the way. He's bound to encounter some resistance—resistance to change is only human—but if he listens, he'll find out what ain't broke and doesn't need fixing. And if he asks the right questions, his subordinates will tell him what he would otherwise have to tell them. Like many effective managers, he'll appear not to be working at all. Jack smiles to himself and reaches in his inside pocket for a folded personnel list. Rule number three: learn the names.

The next thing he'll do is seek out the station warrant officer—the equivalent of a factory superintendent, the fella who knows what makes the whole place tick, technically subordinate to Jack but in reality ranked just below God—and say hello. Jack consults his list: Warrant Officer Pinder. He refolds the list.

The third thing: Friday beer call at the officers' mess. All the news that's neither fit to print nor to speak aloud at a meeting will come out at these bull sessions. Jack only ever has one, maybe two beers, keeps his ear to the ground and enjoys himself thoroughly, standing around with the rest of the gentlemen and rogues, "telling lies."

Over the course of his first week he will study personnel files. He'll consult them the way a pilot consults a map before a mission. The paper acts as a guide but should never be confused with the real thing. Behind every name, rank and serial number is a human being. Barking orders may work in battle but gets you nowhere in peace-time.

And Jack is acutely aware that the Western world is in one of the longest stretches of peace and prosperity in its history. Not to mention anxiety. Everyday life resembles a hot-air balloon floating in a clear summer sky—it looks effortless from the ground, yet it's fed by fire, kept aloft by tension. Jack recalls his daughter's morbid reference to "melted skin." He and Mimi do their best to prevent their kids from dwelling on the threat, but in 4 Wing they, like the other air force families, stored a

week's supply of food and water in the basement locker of their PMQ;
there was an evacuation plan, and regular drills at the children's school.
Part of life. The Cold War has escalated, marshalling unprecedented
destructive force, most of which operates as an elaborate deterrent and
requires a large bureaucracy to administer it. This is a war that is not so
much waged as managed.

He pulls a frayed textbook from the shelf: *Principles of Management:
A Practical Approach.* We can do better than that. He has begun to
assemble his own management text, a compilation of the latest articles
coming out of the States, places like Harvard and Michigan. The world
is changing rapidly and the military, being among the largest corporations in the world, can either lead or lumber behind like a dinosaur.
Leaders today have to understand teamwork. That's the key to all the
latest advances in science and technology. We've virtually wiped out
serious infectious disease, we've got satellites orbiting the earth, you
can't open a newspaper without reading of another breakthrough. And
we do it without enslaving people—that's why thousands of East
Berliners voted with their feet before the Wall went up.

Jack is not alone in believing that the military chain of command is
not simply a series of orders and knee-jerk responses, but a model for
the flow of information and accountability. Air force types—especially
if they are veterans—tend to share this thinking. But it's important to
codify and teach it so that it's not dependent on unwritten traditions and
individual temperaments. He tosses the old textbook into the
wastebasket.

A cool head and a light hand are as important in an office as they are
in a cockpit. A man who can't keep his cool can't make a good decision.
So Jack's management style is relaxed, but when he makes a "suggestion" it is rarely mistaken for anything but an order.

This is something he learned from his flight instructor years ago,
right here in Centralia. Simon was famous for his suggestions. In the
air, from the instructor's seat beside Jack: "You may want to try
stalling the engine." And after seconds of deadly aerial silence, "Shall
we see if you can roll out of it?" The cool Queen's English, coming out
of a spin: "Good, now I wonder if you can land without bending the
kite out of shape?"

In April 1943, Jack and the rest of his class already had their wings
and were embarking on advanced training. They were cocky, eager to
go operational—to fly ops. Jack was not quite eighteen, none was over
twenty. Simon entered the classroom, his RAF cap pushed rakishly back
on his head, its sides permanently bent in the "fifty-mission crush"—the

long-term effect of wearing a radio headset in the cockpit, a badge of operational status. His tie loose, moustache pencil-thin, he sat on the desk, lit a cigarette and addressed them, wearing his upper-class accent like an old scarf.

"I know you sprogs think you know how to fly. You, and most of the great apes at the stick of any given aircraft, haven't a bloody clue how to fly, and it's not my job to teach you. It's my job to teach you sorry bastards how to stay in one piece long enough to bomb the *Scheisse* out of the Germans like gentlemen. Questions?"

"Squadron Leader Crawford, sir . . . ?" one skinny boy ventured.

"My name is Simon. Life is too short—especially yours, especially mine once I climb into the seat next to you—to waste time with a lot of syllables, so call me by my fucking name, there's a good lad."

They called him by his first name and revered him as an elder because, at twenty-three, Simon was an old man. A living exception to the rule "There are old pilots and there are bold pilots, but there are no old bold pilots." One of the few to fly both fighters and bombers. A decorated Battle of Britain ace who had requested reassignment from Spitfires to big lumbering Lancaster bombers "because being in a Lanc makes me feel more akin to a tin of Spam, and what's lovelier than Spam, really?" A different sort of risk, the opportunity to fly with a crew; Simon needed to keep himself interested. He came to them having survived a full tour of duty overseas: thirty bombing missions.

Simon was a great flight instructor because he never took control too soon. He waited to see if his pupil could handle it first, because once you went operational, nothing would happen according to Hoyle. Jack's hand shaking on the control column, head bursting on the verge of red-out after a steep dive at eight thousand feet, recovery at six hundred, his wheels touching down, one side then the other, then the other and the other again, then both—"Bit of a ropey landing, Jack."

Hauling himself over the side, legs almost buckling on the tarmac, Jack realized that Simon was still strapped in on the instructor's side. "You can go straight back up now, mate, or find yourself gun-shy next time round. Either way you're going to shake for two days."

Jack managed to reply, his voice trembling uncontrollably, "I'm easy."

Simon tossed his hat onto the grass next to the tarmac. "See if you can come level with this mark when we land."

He was assuming they would land, not crash. They went back up.

Later, in the mess, surrounded by buddies, Simon bought the beer: "Here's to being above it all."

At Jack's level, there was only an hour or so of required flying time with an instructor, after which you did your "circuits and bumps" on your own. But there were two or three pilots with whom Simon flew overtime. He said it was because they were bloody hopeless. Jack was among them. Top of their class.

Wearing night goggles, flying blind, able to see only his instrument panel, Simon drilling it into him, "Trust your instruments." Because when you can't see the horizon, your brain and body will tell you that right is left and up is down. You'll compensate for a felt left turn by banking right. You'll enter a terminal dive with no sense of velocity or direction, heedless of the approaching earth until your aircraft begins to come apart with the stress of speed.

Simon waited until the last second, then removed Jack's goggles so he could see he was in a sideslip, perfectly executed but for being a mere three hundred feet from the ground. "Power up, mate."

BAT. Blind approach training. Next time, Simon didn't remove Jack's goggles until they had landed smoothly. "Not bad for a Canadian."

Simon had a lot of attractive qualities but the one that inspired the most trust—and got you to do your first controlled stall at ten thousand feet—was his relaxation. It was also a quality that inspired fear, because you could never properly gauge the danger. Treetops piercing the fog. Unscheduled thunderheads. "Not sure I like the looks of that."

They flew for the fun of it. Got lost on purpose, followed the "iron compass" home, catching up with and overtaking freight trains below.

It's odd to think this of a man he has seen once in the past nineteen years, but if he were asked, Jack would answer that Simon Crawford is his best friend. Squadron Leader Crawford, DSO, DFC with Bar— *Distinguished Service Order, Distinguished Flying Cross, twice.* The ancient Chinese saying dictates that once you save a man's life, you are responsible for him. But the old sonofabitch needn't have taken it that far— Jack would have loved him anyway.

He leans back in his chair and clasps his hands behind his head. He has done well. Wing commander at thirty-six. He never would have believed it but he enjoys flying a desk. He likes the life, he likes the people. They know how to get things done without a lot of fuss. And if they survived as aircrew in the war, there's not much that can faze them. He isn't given to jingoistic declarations, but Jack loves the air force.

That's why it comes as a bit of a surprise to find himself staring out of his window at the unclouded sky, and imagining a different office in a different organization. An auto plant or hospital. An oil refinery in Saudi Arabia perhaps. Management skills travel well; he could work just about anywhere. Is it possible he's just the slightest bit bored? Or is it the sleepy effect of sun and cornfields, the hemispheric distance between him and the tension of the Eastern Sector, as they called the Soviet Union back in Germany? Does he miss the proximity of the Mk 6 Sabres back at 4 Wing? Life near the sharp end? The smell of jet fuel, the frequent reminder roaring overhead of why he is in his office doing what he's doing? "Anyone who wants a quiet life should not have been born in the twentieth century," said Leon Trotsky. Anyone who wants a quiet life should come to Centralia, thinks Jack, and smiles to himself.

It was good timing, running into Simon in Germany last summer. Because when Jack got his transfer message this April, he had Simon's number and was able to phone. "You'll never guess where they're sending me, Si. . . ." They both laughed when Jack said, "Centralia."

Simon called back a few days later. "Listen mate, I've got a favour to ask you. . . ."

Jack picks up his phone, then remembers that Simon asked him to use only pay phones. He puts it down again, gets up and leaves his office. He noticed a phone booth next to the PX, he'll call from there, then head to the mess for lunch.

The ennui that descended briefly in his office is dispelled by the fresh air as he emerges from the building and trots down the concrete steps. Simon described the favour as "glorified babysitting, really," and while it's true that what Jack has been asked to do is not exactly rocket science, it does promise to enliven this posting. He follows the sidewalk along a row of poplars, toward the parade square. Not a creature is stirring. Not even a Chipmunk.

Jack has heard that intelligence work can be numbingly dull, but he can't picture Simon bored. He does his best to suppress a tingle of anticipation. The favour will likely be just that. Dull. In any case, it'll be an excuse to hoist a few beers with Simon. Pry some Cold War stories out of him.

Jack tried once or twice after the war to track him down, but Simon had demobbed without a forwarding address. Then last summer, in a medieval town in northern Germany, he ran into him. Jack was with Madeleine, about to take her picture in front of the statue of the Pied Piper of Hamelin. The McCarthys were on holiday, making the most of their last summer in Europe, driving the Fairytale Route—the *Märchen Strasse*. They had visited the castle in the Reinhard Forest where the Brothers Grimm had stayed; they had toured Bremen, where the animal musicians fooled the robbers. Now they were in Hameln, the Hamelin of legend. Mimi had gone off with Mike for the afternoon.

Tomorrow they would trade and Mike would spend the morning with his father for a little one-on-one time.

Jack was focusing his Voigtlander slide camera on Madeleine, who smiled, squinting into the sun, the stone Piper towering behind her. Tourists milled about, passing in and out of frame behind the statue. Jack was ready to snap the picture when he saw a man pause to light a cigarette. *Son of a gun.*

"Simon!" he called, lowering the camera.

The man looked around and a smile broke over his face. "Jack?" he said, rounding the statue, coming toward him. "You still at large?"

Eighteen years can work a lot of changes in a man but Simon was unmistakeable. Not just his trim build but his voice, the way he carried himself—his whole manner seemed to say, *the most natural thing in the world, running into you, mate.* They smacked their palms together and shook hands, laughing. Reflex is a reliable indicator. Jack's reflex—and it seemed Simon's too—was pure delight; as though they were laughing at the punchline of a joke they'd left off telling in 1943.

"You sorry bastard," said Simon; then, glancing down, caught himself. "I beg your pardon, who is this young lady then?"

"This is our *Deutsches Mädchen,*" said Jack.

"Well how do you do, *Fräulein? Sprechen Sie Deutsch?*"

Madeleine replied, "*Ein Bisschen.*"

Simon laughed.

Jack said, "Madeleine, this is Squadron Leader Crawford."

"Jack, for Christ sake, I'm retired." Then, looking down at her, he said, "Madeleine, please call me Simon."

She hesitated, squinting up at him.

We should all age like Simon. Light blue eyes, shrewd behind the smile. The healthy smoker's skin, fine lines in a light leather tan that can look good on a man in 1961. Touch of steel through his honey-brown hair, combed quickly but neatly back. In his early forties and unlikely to change till he hits sixty-five. Camel cigarette cooking between his fingers.

He smiled down at Madeleine and said, "All right then, how about 'Uncle Simon'?"

"Uncle Simon," she said. And both men chuckled.

"What are your plans for the future, Madeleine?"

She replied without hesitation, "I'm going to be either a comedian or a spy."

Simon threw his head back and laughed. Jack beamed. "That's the stuff, old buddy."

Simon volunteered that he was a diplomat now.

"You're kidding," said Jack. "You're the most undiplomatic sonofabi—gun I know."

"That's First Secretary Crawford to you, mate."

"What the heck are you doing here?"

"As a matter of fact I'm on holiday. Meeting a friend."

Say no more. Jack was not about to pry.

Simon was actually based in Berlin now, having just been posted from the British Embassy in Moscow.

"What's Moscow like?"

"Cold."

He was on temporary duty at Military Headquarters in Berlin, working on Allied records indexes—a vast collection of German dossiers, both military and civilian.

Jack said, "How's your German?"

"Better than my Russian." Next year he would be in Washington. "I'm brushing up on my American."

Simon was the same. The self-mocking manner, affecting by turns Cockney and upper-class terms of endearment and scorn. He hadn't married. Jack showed him a picture of Mimi and he said, "What's a goddess like that doing with a poor slob like you?"

"Somebody up there likes me," said Jack.

"Well, we knew that."

The three of them went to a *Biergarten*. Madeleine had a sip from each man's glass, and made them laugh with her white foam moustache. The waitress brought stein after stein for *den Herren* and *pommes frites* and *limonade für das Mädchen*. It was a glorious afternoon.

The following April, Simon called and asked for the "favour." Jack listened carefully. He knew how to interpret the casual request. One of Simon's suggestions. Could almost feel him in the instructor's seat beside him. . . .

Jack steps from the sidewalk onto the blacktop of the parade square and the heat hits him. He heads diagonally toward the PX and the phone booth. He would not be surprised if Simon was MI6. British Secret Intelligence Service. MI6 agents don't advertise themselves; at one time not even their wives could know. Not a problem in Simon's case.

Jack feels for dimes in his pocket and experiences a twinge of excitement. A scientist is coming from the Soviet Union. A defector. The man needs a safe place to live for six months or so before moving on. "Make him feel at home," said Simon. "Poor bastard's bound to be a little on edge, a little culture-shocked. Cook him up some of that wonderful slop, what's that macaroni dish called?"

"Kraft Dinner."

"That's the one."

Another scientist has come over to our side; that's all Jack knows at this point. Simon was explicit in his way—"You might want to keep it to yourself"—the official term is need-to-know but Simon was never big on official terms. It might be fun to tell Mimi but she doesn't need to know, and in any case, Jack is not in the habit of bringing his work home. Hal Woodley doesn't need to know either. Simon pointed out that Jack will be acting as a private citizen, briefly playing host to the friend of a friend, strictly unofficial.

Back in 4 Wing, Jack and all other personnel had "war tasks" they would be called upon to perform in the event of an attack from the Eastern Sector. Jack's war task assignment was Intelligence. It required a top secret security clearance and involved debriefing pilots returning from exercise missions and reporting the results to the station commander and Air Division HQ. He is not unfamiliar with need-to-know. It occurs to him now to wonder whether Simon could have known that.

He reaches into his pocket and counts out the dimes. A Soviet scientist. Simon has referred to him only as "our friend from the East." Jack pictures a square-headed man with slicked black hair, thick black-rimmed glasses and a lab coat. What kind of science? Nuclear? "Rather an important chap," said Simon. *Our friend.* Why is Canada getting him?

Jack is about to open the folding glass door of the phone booth when someone says, "Wing Commander McCarthy?" He turns. A fat man sticks out his hand.

"I'm Vic Boucher, sir."

Jack shakes the hand. "Good to meet you, Vic."

Squadron Leader Vic Boucher. Built like a medicine ball, every bit as solid and almost as bald. "Welcome back to the land of round door-knobs, sir."

"And speed limits," adds Jack.

A friend of his back in 4 Wing is an old buddy of Vic Boucher's. They flew together in the war. Boucher was a tail gunner. Picture him now, squashed into the glass turret at the butt-end of a Lanc, and you want to grin. But he would have been trimmer then—the fear alone. A bomber crew's average life expectancy was six weeks; the tail gunner's, considerably shorter.

"I've been warned about you, Boucher."

"I'll bet you have," says Vic. "It's all lies. You coming to the mess, sir?" He straightens his tie. "Go ahead, make your call, I'll wait." His French accent sounds homey to Jack.

"Naw, *macht nichts,* let's walk." Jack pronounces it "mox nix," meaning "makes no difference" or, in air force parlance, "I'm easy." Like most veterans of German postings, he has mastered only a few choice survival phrases: *danke schön, einmal Bier bitte,* and *auf Wiedersehen.*

"Righto," says Vic.

"*Oui, d'accord,*" says Jack, and Vic laughs.

Jack likes the man immediately. One of his senior officers, in charge of training standards at the COS. And, most important, president of the mess committee. "I'm not going to let you rope me into any committees, Vic."

Vic laughs again. "We got an opening for treasurer."

"I'll keep you posted."

Jack invites him and his wife over for supper tomorrow night. Mimi will be happy to have someone to rattle away with in French. He walks with Vic, retracing his steps across the parade square. Simon will have to wait till after lunch. Pay phones may be secure but they are far from soundproof.

## The Mayflower

*Americans like what they have and want more of the same.*
"*How America Feels*" Gallup survey, Look, *January 5, 1960*

MADELEINE IS IN the driveway, leaning against the bumper of the Rambler, staring across the street at the messy purple house. Glinting at the foot of its front porch is something that was not there before. A wheelchair.

It is the only fully assembled rust-free object on the property, and it was suddenly there this morning when the McCarthys drove in from their motel. *Abracadabra!*

Madeleine is waiting for the moving van. She waited all morning and it looks as though she will have to wait all afternoon. She and Mike and Maman just ate lunch. Swanson TV dinners, minus the TV. Everything in its own little compartment like on an airplane. But lunch is over now, it's hot and there's nothing to do. Mike has gone off somewhere with another boy—no fair, he has a friend already. She looks down at her favourite plaid shorts with the fringed pocket, at her tanned legs, knees free of scabs because it has been so long since she had any fun. Her slip-on red runners bear the only signs of wear and tear. Her mother has tried to throw them out but they are just getting good, both big toes having worked their way through the canvas. The process can be hastened by dragging your toes as you coast downhill on your bike. *But my bike is on the moving van and the moving van will never get here.*

Madeleine's bike has fat tires—there is no such thing in Canada. Her bike looks like a little blue motorcycle, with an aerodynamic swell in the sloping crossbar that sports swift white letters, *Zippy Vélo*. It doesn't look like a girl's bike, nor does it look like the faux pas of a boy's bike, it's European. A Volks Bike.

The sun winks down on the road. Across the street and a few doors to the left, at the tan house on the corner, the mother of the Hula Hoop girl is unloading groceries from the orange VW van, but the girl is nowhere to be seen.

The neighbours who live in the other half of the McCarthys' white duplex are a dead loss. Maman calls them a "lovely young couple." They have a screeching infant at which they spend all their time gazing. The wife looks puffy and damp—Madeleine's mother has told her she is beautiful. Madeleine plans never to have babies, never to marry. She intends to live with her brother and never become doughy and moist.

The intimate weight of sun has muted the entire PMQs. As though everyone in the kingdom had fallen asleep. Madeleine feels the heat on her head like a hand. She stares across at the wheelchair. Light splinters from its steel frame.

At first sight it made her feel a bit queasy, the way things like that can. Crutches and leg braces. Strange twisty people in wheelchairs—you feel guilty and grateful not to be them or to be in an iron lung. *Say a little prayer for them,* says her mother, *and don't stare.* But Madeleine is staring now because the wheelchair is empty, there is no one around to get their feelings hurt.

"Where's Mike?" asked her father when he left this morning. Even then Madeleine was already wearying of her moving-van vigil.

"He made a friend and they took off."

"Why don't you go find some pals?"

"There isn't anyone."

He laughed his gentle incredulous laugh. "The PMQs are crawling with kids, old buddy."

Dad is so innocent. He thinks you can just go up to a group of kids and say, "Hey you guys, can I play too?" He talks of impromptu games of shinny back in the hometown streets, gangs of buddies roaming the New Brunswick woods, fishing, jigging from school, terrorizing the nuns, having a great time growing up together. Madeleine doesn't know a soul here, and how are you supposed to get to know anyone when school doesn't even start for a week? Mike always makes friends right off the bat. Boys don't care so much if you are new. Girls look at you like you're some kind of bug until they decide whether or not they want to play with your hair.

Madeleine despairs of the moving van and begins to leave the driveway. Taking baby steps, one foot in front of the other, heel to toe, because it will take longer to cross the street that way and the moving van will come sooner.

*Nancy Drew and the Case of the Mysterious Wheelchair.* Maybe they have a crippled mother. Imagine if your mother were crippled. "Come here, dear, so I can dress you." You would always have to obey her and answer nicely because how cruel to talk back to a crippled mother or to run away out of her reach. Imagine her making your sandwiches with her weak hands, wheeling over to the fridge for the mayonnaise. It makes Madeleine appreciate her own mother. It's good to appreciate your mother. She imagines her mother dead in order to appreciate her better: imagine if it were just me and Mike and Dad. Eating fried chicken every night and going to air shows. I'd wear Mike's hand-me-downs and people would think I was a boy. She reminds herself that the prerequisite for this all-boy Shangri-La is the death of her mother, and cuts the fantasy short. It's just not worth it if your mother has to die.

She breaks and runs in a heartburst of speed that takes her halfway down St. Lawrence Avenue in the direction of the school before she stops to catch her breath. On her left stands an empty green bungalow. She walks up to it and peeks in the living-room window.

Polished wood floors, fresh white walls. After the new people move in, she will remember spying on their empty house. She flops onto her back on the bungalow's overgrown front lawn and moves her arms and legs as though she were making a snow angel in the grass. Are there other worlds? Is it possible to sail to a place where there are towns under water, and talking animals? Sometimes Madeleine believes so fervently that she gets tears in her eyes. She stares up at the clouds. A mountain. A camel. Milton Berle—*Good evening, ladies and germs.* The mountain moves—a door opens up like a mouth. What was inside the

Pied Piper's mountain? Was it like Aladdin's cave, full of treasure? The mountain flattens and drifts apart to reveal the moon. It looks like a Communion host way up there, flavourless. Madeleine would rather go to sea than to the moon, would rather travel to the olden days than to the future. She would sneak up on Hitler at the Eagle's Nest and push him over an Alp like the wheelchair in *Heidi,* and she would warn Anne Frank not to stay in Holland. She plucks grass with both hands and sprinkles it over herself. If she stays here long enough she will be totally buried and no one will find her. Think how worried they all will be when she doesn't come home. Mike will be terribly sorry, and pray to God to bring his little sister back. Imagine the rejoicing when they find she isn't dead after all. And none of it will be her fault, because she just lay down in the grass quite innocently . . . and closed her eyes . . . *in the valley of the jolly, ho ho ho, green giant.*

On the back porch Mimi finishes a letter to her sister Yvonne, and starts one to Domithilde. Mimi holds nothing back from Yvonne, but Domithilde entered the convent years ago and can't be expected to appreciate the minutiae of family life. *Chère Domithilde, on est enfin arrivés à Centralia. . . .*

When she finishes the letter to Domithilde, she starts one to their German friends. *Liebe Hans und Brigitte, Finally we are here. Willkommen in Centralia!*

"Mrs. McCarthy?"

She looks up. A slim woman, a little older than herself, in spectator pumps and crisp belted dress, tastefully dyed strawberry blonde hair.

"I'm Vimy Woodley, welcome to Centralia."

Mimi gets up, reflexively touches her hair with one hand and extends the other. "Mrs. Woodley, it's so nice to meet you, please call me Mimi."

The CO's wife, and me in my ugly old shorts!

"Call me Vimy, dear." She's holding a plate covered in tinfoil. "Now it's not much, but you're to serve them warm."

Piggies in a blanket. *"Oh, mais c'est trop gentil."*

Vimy smiles and Mimi blushes at having addressed her in French.

"You're in good company, Mimi, you've got a French Canadian neighbour just up the street. Have you met the Bouchers?"

"Not yet."

"We'll have you over once you've settled in. Now a lot of people are away, and the Wives' Club won't be up to speed for a few weeks, but I'll pop a package in your mailbox to help you get your bearings. Just bits and pieces about the station and the area and the school and what-not."

"Thank you so much—Vimy?"

"That's right, dear."

"You're French?"

"I was named for an uncle who fought at Vimy Ridge. I'm just grateful they didn't call me Passchendaele."

"Or Big Bertha," quips Mimi and turns beet-red because nothing could be less apt, and it's too soon to joke so familiarly, but Vimy Woodley laughs.

"Vimy, will you come in for a cup of—for a glass of—?"

"Mimi, I wouldn't dream of it."

Both women know that the best Mimi is likely to do at the moment is a Thermos of Tang.

"Call if you need anything."

After lunch, Jack walks with Vic Boucher back across the parade square. A group of cadets emerges from the rec centre looking freshly scrubbed, gym bags over their shoulders. A number of cars are parked out front of the PX, women coming and going, some with strollers, others balancing groceries and toddlers, stopping to chat. Jack says, "Better double-check what the wife wanted me to pick up," as though using the pay phone were an afterthought.

But a cadet slips through the glass door and dumps a pocketful of change down the slot before Jack gets there. A Malaysian lad. Long-distance sweetheart—this could take a while.

"Come into the rec centre with me and use the one in the lounge, I've got the keys."

"Naw," says Jack. "I'll remember once I'm in there." And heads toward the PX.

"*À demain,*" says Vic.

Till tomorrow? Right, dinner. Jack must remember to tell Mimi the moment he gets home. *We're having guests tomorrow night.* He stands in the entrance and gazes into the grocery store. Strolls up one aisle, then down another. Buys a pack of gum.

When he comes back out of the store, Vic is gone. Tiny lies the size of splinters, they must be business as usual for Simon. SOP. Jack glances at the phone booth—still occupied. He heads home. There's no rush.

Madeleine runs as fast as she can up St. Lawrence Avenue, leaving a wake of green cuttings—it's here! Christopher Columbus's yellow ship rocks merrily across a painted sea on the side of the green Mayflower moving van. The rear door is already open, the ramp is down and a man in overalls is wheeling off her bike. She can feel already the spring of the saddle, pedals firm beneath her feet, trusty handlebar grips—oh my bike!

"Whose is this?" says the mover and winks, holding up the little blue bomber. He smells like tar; it's a friendly smell.

She rides over the grass, around the house and down the driveway, her legs working like pistons, before returning to the van, torn between the open road and the open truck where all their stuff is stacked in boxes and under blankets. She watches, seated on her bike, feet flat on the ground—she will have to ask her father to raise the seat, she has grown.

Mike is there with his new friend, Roy Noonan. Madeleine can tell they are making their voices sound deeper than they really are—shortening their sentences, forcing down their pitch. Roy has a black brush cut and braces and round pink cheeks. He is holding a balsawood airplane and Mike is holding the remote control. They have serious blank expressions on their faces. Madeleine knows better than to hope they might let her play with them. Who cares? The moving van is here!

Men carry down huge boxes and pieces of furniture—a quilted pad slips aside to reveal Maman's vanity table, that most intimate of altars momentarily on public view, like a lady passing a window in her lingerie. This is the first time the McCarthys have seen their own furniture since they moved from Alberta to Germany. It has been in storage. Here comes the couch where Madeleine curled up with her dad and read the paper before she could read, and that must be the glass top for the coffee table, marked *FRAGILE!* And what could be in the big box marked *RCA VICTOR THIS SIDE UP?* The television set! Cabinet of delights, last illuminated four years ago.

Things you forgot you owned are in those boxes. Our stuff. All the things we packed in Germany and all the things that slept in storage, reunited, first with one another, now with us. Toys and dolls that have made the incredible journey will emerge dapper and refreshed, "Of course we didn't smother." The cuckoo clock will awaken, mounted once more above the stove, a perpetual air of suspense hovering about its little door. Our own kitchen plates will smile up at us from the table, "We made it." Our cutlery, which will sleep in new but familiar berths in the kitchen drawer, and remember those little egg cups shaped like hens? We'll use those tomorrow morning. Here comes your own bed, borne shoulder-high in triumph down the ramp, and in that box are the precious photo albums that have evolved from black and white to colour—the next time we lift a cover, it will be to look on memories that are yet once more removed from the present. All these things have found their way to this specific spot on earth, 72 St. Lawrence Avenue, Centralia, Ontario, Canada. Our stuff.

As usual, kids gather tentatively around the van. A couple of kids who don't count because they're too young—their bikes still have training wheels. And the Hula Hoop girl.

"Hi."

"Hi."

They watch the van for a while. The Hula Hoop girl has curly copper hair, freckles and cat-eye glasses. She turns and asks, "What's your name?"

"Madeleine McCarthy. What's yours?"

"Auriel Boucher."

They watch the van some more.

"Where did you just move from?" asks Auriel.

"Germany."

"We lived there too."

"Neat. I was born in Edmonton."

"Neat, I was born in England."

"Neat."

It turns out that Auriel is hilarious, and she doesn't care if she's fat. Plump, that is. She's not really fat anyway, once you get to know her. And freckles are nice.

"I like your bike."

"Thanks," says Madeleine. "I like your top."

"Thanks," says Auriel. "It improves my bust." They burst out laughing.

You can't tell if Auriel actually has a bust behind her polka-dot poptop, but that's beside the point. Another girl joins them, Lisa Ridelle, in brand-new Keds.

"Hi Auriel."

"Hi Lisa."

"Hi," says Madeleine.

Wispy white-blonde pageboy, pale blue eyes, Lisa laughs at everything Auriel says. Soon she is laughing at everything Madeleine says.

"You laugh exactly like Muttly on *Penelope Pitstop*," says Madeleine, and Lisa laughs her rasping laugh.

"She's right, you do!" agrees Auriel, imitating her. Madeleine joins in and they all do the wheezy laugh like the cartoon dog. They have known one another for five minutes and already they have their own laugh.

"What grade are you going into?"

"Four."

"Me too."

"Me three!"

Lisa can turn her eyelids inside out, it's really creepy. "Do it again, Lisa." Auriel knows how to paralyze your hand. "Squeeze my thumb as hard as you can. Okay, now let go but don't straighten your fingers. . . ." Then she tickles your wrist lightly. "Okay, now try and open your fingers."

Madeleine can barely get them open. "Wow, I'm paralyzed."

"Do it to me now, Auriel."

"Want to set up a lemonade stand, you guys?" It's a hot day, they could make a fortune. But Lisa and Auriel are going to a baseball tournament overnight in the Bouchers' van. Auriel is catcher and Lisa plays shortstop. You can easily picture Auriel wearing the leather chest protector, the face cage and a backward cap—she would look exactly like a turtle. In a good way.

"Auriel, come get your tea, pet, Daddy's on his way." Auriel's mum is calling from the Bouchers' driveway. She stands next to the open VW van with an armload of baseball bats and shin pads. She has the same curly hair.

"Coming, Mums," calls Auriel.

Oh, to be like Auriel Boucher and Hayley Mills, and call one's mother "Mums." Mrs. Boucher is a war bride, you can tell from her English accent.

The moving van is almost empty. Madeleine watches her new friends run up the street to the Bouchers' house, just as her father rounds the corner. "Dad!" She hops on her bike and rides to him, pedalling furiously. "Dad, look!" He smiles and leans forward with his arms open as though to catch her, Zippy Vélo and all.

Everything is going to be fine, Centralia is going to be great.

"I'm glad to hear that, sweetie," says Dad as she leans her bike against the porch and follows him in. Boxes and furniture crowd the rooms, awkward herds as yet untethered to walls and corners. "Mimi, I'm home."

Already the echo in their voices has abated, absorbed by their things which have caught up to them, the rest of the family. Alive with all they have taken in over the years, these things will exhale memories of times gone by, filling the house with that untranslatable well-being the Germans call *Gemütlichkeit,* making it a place that is not a place at all: home.

For supper, the McCarthys have driven five miles north to the town of
Exeter for burgers and shakes. Exeter is neat and prosperous, but if you
hope to find an A&W you have to drive in the other direction, toward
London. There is a good family restaurant, however, and the four of
them slid into a booth.

The people in the restaurant knew right away that the McCarthys
were from the air force station. When it comes time for dessert, they
move from their booth to the counter, and Jack and Mimi chat with the
owners. They always make a point of meeting local people, whether
they are in Alberta or Alsace. People are people, let's make the most of
life. And they usually get a warm reception, even from those locals who
are suspicious of the stream of temporary neighbours who reliably
enrich the local community chest, but can otherwise unnerve the stable
population. It never takes Jack and Mimi long to belong. But it is not
meant to last and it usually doesn't, beyond a Christmas card or two
after the next posting.

"How's the pie?" Jack asks.

"Homemade," replies a woman of few words behind the counter.

"Say no more," says Jack, and orders a slice with cheese.

Madeleine watches the man at the grill flipping burgers. Is he the
woman's husband? He is thin and she is fat. *Jack Sprat.* . . .

"What'll it be, Madeleine?" her father asks.

She looks up into the pasty face of the woman. "Um. Do you have
Neapolitan please?"

"With a cherry on top?" asks the woman, without cracking a smile.

"*S'il vous plaît,*" says Madeleine without planning it.

The woman smiles and says, "Come-on-tally-voo?" then pinches
Madeleine's cheek, but not painfully. Ladies behind counters are similar
the world over. They like to give you things, they like to feel a hunk of
your face between thumb and forefinger.

Belonging and not belonging. Being on the outside and the inside at
the same time. For Madeleine it is as natural, as negligible, as breathing.
And the idea of growing up in the midst of your own past—among
people who have known you all your life and believe they know what
you are made of, what you are capable of—that is a suffocating thought.

"What about your IGA here?" asks Mimi. "They have a good
butcher?" A rich vein of conversation opens. Butchers from here to
London are discussed. This leads to children's shoes, the school board,
Prime Minister Diefenbaker, whether we're in for a cold winter, and the
space race.

"Well, Kennedy says he's going to do it and I wouldn't be surprised if he did," says Jack.

"What do we want to go to the moon for, anyhow?" asks the man at the grill.

Jack replies, "'Cause if we don't get there first, the Russkies will."

"Well, that's my point, eh?" says the man, wiping his hands on his white apron. "Gettin' crowded up there."

"Dad," says Mike. "Not we, the Americans."

"That's right, Mike, and don't you forget it."

"*Vive la différence,*" says Mimi.

The woman puts a parfait glass in front of Madeleine, Neapolitan topped with chocolate sauce, whipped cream and a cherry. "Wow, thanks," Madeleine says. The woman winks at her.

Madeleine picks up her spoon. Though she is at home everywhere and nowhere, there is the occasional sense of having misplaced something, someone. Sometimes, when the family sits down to dinner, she has the feeling that someone is missing. Who?

Jack asks where the best swimming and picnicking is to be found. Nearby on Lake Huron. He already knows this, but people like to be asked about where they live. And Mimi loves meeting people. They love her French accent and she loves that they can never guess where she is from. France? Québec? They pronounce it "Kweebec." No, and no. Where, then? Acadia. *L'Acadie.* Site of *le grand dérangement*—the great disruption of almost two hundred years ago that inspired Longfellow's romantic poem *Evangeline.* Mass expulsion of an entire nation from Canada's east coast, a human tide that flowed south, pooled in Louisiana to fertilize a Cajun culture, then trickled back up to thrive in pockets across the Canadian Maritimes, with roots that reach back to the seventeenth century. Mimi says, "That's why I'm so good at moving."

She laughs with the people behind the counter, and neglects to add that it was the *maudits Anglais* who kicked her people out in the first place. Americans tend to be more responsive than English Canadians to that part of the story, having seen fit to kick the damned English out themselves.

Jack enjoys teasing her when they're alone. "You're my prisoner," he'll say. "My rightful booty." If he really wants to get a rise out of her, he describes the French as a defeated people and says, "It's lucky for you the British were so superior or you and I would never have met." He knows he has won if he can get her to whack him. "That was always the trouble with the French. Too emotional." That's Mimi. Spitfire.

Jack and Mimi both come from New Brunswick's Atlantic coast. But they didn't meet there—she was French, he was English, why would they meet? He was working in a cardboard factory alongside three older men. At seventeen, he was the only one who still had all his fingers. When he realized he was also the only one who could read and write, he left. Lied about his age, joined the air force, crashed and remustered. When he and Mimi met in '44 at the dance in Yorkshire, where he was a supply officer and she was a nurse's aide at Number 6 Bomber Group, it seemed like a very small world indeed. Small world, big war. Lucky for them.

"This sure is a beautiful part of the country," says Jack to the man behind the counter.

"Oh, this is God's country," replies the man, topping up Jack's coffee.

It's simple, really: if you like people they will probably like you back. It helps that Jack and Mimi's children are polite and answer in full sentences. It helps that their daughter is pretty and their son is handsome.

"What are you going to be when you grow up, young fella?" asks a man in the booth behind them, a farmer in rubber boots and John Deere cap.

Mike answers, "I'm going to fly Sabres, sir."

"Well now," says the man, nodding.

"That's the stuff," says Jack.

It helps that Jack and his wife are attractive. Not just because Mimi is slim and stylish with her pumps and pencil skirt. Not because he is blue-eyed and relaxed—effortless gentleman, a natural polish that goes well with his mill-town respect for work and working people. They are attractive because they are in love.

It has worked. The dream. Post-war boom, the kids, the car, all the stuff that is supposed to make people happy. The stuff that has begun to weigh on some people—alcoholics in grey flannel suits, mad housewives—it has all made Jack and Mimi very happy. They couldn't care less about "stuff" and perhaps that is their secret. They are rich, they are fabulously wealthy. And they know it. They hold hands under the counter and chat with the locals.

Madeleine says, "I'm probably going to be in the secret service," and everyone laughs. She smiles politely. It feels good to make people laugh, even if you are not sure what's so funny.

Dessert is on the house. Welcome back to Canada.

They pull into their driveway as the sun begins to undo itself across the sky. Madeleine's interior movie music swells at the sight of its slow swoon over the PMQs; light spears the windshield, piercing her heart. Tonight they will sleep in their own beds in their own house for the first time since Germany.

In the basement, her father roots around in one of the boxes and Madeleine watches as he comes out with something more miraculous than a live rabbit. "The baseball gloves!" He tosses her one and they go out behind the house into the grassy circle. Mike is off with his new friend so she has Dad and the game of catch all to herself. The good smack in the palm, just this side of painful; the whizzing overarm return that he plucks easily from the air. The sun sinks between them so neither has it in their eyes, because when you play catch with your dad, everything is fair.

Oh no, here comes Mike with Roy Noonan. They have baseball mitts, they're going to wreck the game.

But they don't. The circle widens, the four of them toss the ball and an easy rhythm is established—thwack, pause, lift, whish, the ball cresting from glove to glove like a dolphin. Neither Mike nor Roy seems the slightest bit embarrassed to be playing with a kid sister, and the fact that Madeleine is a girl occasions no comment until, when the sun has faded to the point where they can no longer see the ball, and they follow Dad back to the house, she hears Roy Noonan say, "Your sister's pretty good for a girl."

And Mike's reply, "Yeah, I know."

What, about this day, has not been perfect?

When the kids have gone to bed, Mimi makes tea and Jack plugs in the hi-fi they bought in Germany. The station comes in crystal clear. "'Unforgettable . . . that's what you are.'" She sets the mugs down on the floor, he opens his arms and they dance under the sixty-watt bulb, swaying slowly in a clear patch among the boxes. "'Unforgettable, though near or far. . . .'" Her fingers curl through his, she brushes her face against his neck, his hand finds the small of her back, she is perfect.

"You want a baby from Centralia?" he says.

"I wouldn't mind a little Centralia baby."

"A little chipmunk?"

"I love you, Jack."

"Welcome home, Missus." He holds her closer. She kisses his neck lightly in the spot where the soft bristles of his hairline begin. "*Je t'aime, Mimi,*" he whispers in his shy French, bad English accent; she smiles into his shoulder. "'That's why, darling, it's incredible, that someone so unforgettable. . . .'"

He could take her upstairs now, but Nat King Cole is singing and, just as on their honeymoon in Montreal, there is the delicious confidence of putting off the moment. Life is long, I am going to make love to you for years and years. . . . "'thinks that I am unforgettable too. . . . '"

"Dad?" through the slats at the top of the stairs.

He looks up. "What are you doing awake, old buddy?"

"I can't sleep."

"Why not?"

"I've got butterflies," says Madeleine.

Mimi heads for the staircase. "You're cold in those baby-dolls."

"No I'm not!" Madeleine loves her baby-dolls. They are the closest thing to Steve McQueen sleepwear—boxer shorts and undershirt.

"Where's old Bugsy?" asks Jack.

Madeleine's heart leaps. "I don't know. I had him yesterday when we came into the house."

"Well where did you leave him?" Jack glances about.

"I don't know." Her eyes fill with tears.

Mimi mutters, "*Mon Dieu,* Jack, you could leave the well enough alone." But she joins the search while Madeleine sits, stricken, on the stairs.

Maman does not like Bugs. She thinks he's unsanitary. He has never been washed because there is a small record player or something in his stomach—when you pull his string he says several typical Bugs Bunny things. These days his voice sounds far away, his words obscured by static as though he were sending a radio message from outer space, *who toined out da lights?*

Jack is bent down looking under the couch when Mike's voice comes from the top of the stairs: "He's in my room where you left him."

"Michel," says Mimi, "what are you doing up?"

"I can't sleep with all the noise," he says, joining his sister on the landing in his cowboy pajamas.

Madeleine runs to her brother's room. Bugs is lying face down on the floor as though he's been shot. She turns him over and he looks as amused as ever, *Gee, doc, I didn't know you cared.* She picks him up and hugs him, wondering if Mike will be angry with her for snooping in his room. Bugs is the evidence.

But Mike isn't angry. He climbs back in bed, saying, "'Night, squirt."

Who is this nice Mike? Where's the one who used to get so mad at her? The brother who played with her and tortured her, the one she bit, leaving tooth-marks in his arm? Two tears run down her cheeks as her father picks her up and carries her to bed.

"What's wrong, old buddy?"

She doesn't know how to blame it on Mike because, after all, he has been perfectly nice. "I was just sad about Bugs. He's getting old."

Jack tucks the covers around her. "He looks pretty spry to me. He's got bags of mileage in him yet. Besides, Bugsy was never born, so you know what that means."

"What?"

"He's going to live forever." He sits on the side of her bed and says, "Now you snuggle down and go to sleep so you can wake up fresh as a daisy, 'cause I'll tell you what, tomorrow night we're going to have a barbecue and you can invite your new buddies."

"Okay, Dad."

"'Night-night, now."

"I made you some hot," says Mimi, handing him a fresh mug.

He sips and says, "Oh, I invited someone for supper tomorrow night."

"What?"

"Vic Boucher and—"

"Oh, Jack—"

"It doesn't have to be a big deal—"

"It's a big deal"—nodding, holding out her arms, surveying the chaos. Today she unpacked everyone's clothes, did the beds, unpacked the kitchen, washed every utensil, pot, plate and pan, but the rest of the house. . . . "You want me to entertain like this?"

"I'll throw something on the barbecue."

"What am I going to do to you?"—losing syntax when she's upset.

"I don't know, what *are* you going to do to me?" He winks.

"*Tu sais c'que je veux dire*, how can you invite people when"—throwing up her hands—"oh Jack . . . who are they?"

He follows her upstairs and her rant becomes a whisper, then disappears behind the bathroom door. He goes into their room and places his gift on her vanity table. A little something he has been carrying in his shaving kit since Europe.

She returns from the bathroom, unzipping her own dress, *you're cut off, monsieur,* but when she catches sight of the Chanel $N^o$ 5 spritz bottle she drops her arms and says, "Oh Jack."

"I'm still mad at you," she whispers when he turns out the light and joins her in bed.

He reaches for her, fills his hands with her breasts, miraculous, her skin warm as sand, inhales at her neck, he has shaved for her, she bites his shoulder. "Come on," she says. "That's right, baby," their first night in the new house, "that's right." It's so easy, like dancing with her, and when she lies beneath him and opens like a tulip Jack is glad to know she is stronger than he is, she must be to take him like that, to stay soft and welcoming the way she does, only her fingertips hard in his back, "Oh Jack. . . ." To stay soft the harder he gets, only her fingernails and her nipples, "That's right, that's right. . . ." Her mouth, her tongue, her half-closed eyes in the moonlight, face turned to one side, for no one else, for him, "Take what you want, baby, take it. *C'est pour toi.*"

Madeleine is wide awake in her new room. The sheets are nervous. They don't recognize these walls either. The pillow is stiff, no one can relax around here. The moon pours through the naked window that overlooks the grassy circle out back. She resists the urge to suck her thumb. She quit two years ago, bribed by Maman and Tante Yvonne with a brunette Barbie doll. Madeleine quit cold turkey, not because she wanted a Barbie but because she didn't, and it was so nice and so sad of Maman to think she was buying something special for her little girl. Madeleine pretended to be thrilled with the doll, who still lives in the pink satin-lined closet she came in. Sleeps there in her wedding dress, like a vampire. All Madeleine wants for Christmas is a set of six-guns and holsters. Girls never get anything good.

She has to pee. She gets up and creeps across to the bathroom with Bugs. Sits him down facing away from the toilet. Her pee sounds loud in the empty bathroom. She flushes the toilet—Niagara Falls—closes it, climbs onto the lid and looks out the window. Across the street, the porch light is on at the purple house. The wheelchair is gone, but beneath the light and its halo of mosquitoes sits a girl. Next to her lies the German shepherd dog, asleep. The girl should be asleep too, do her parents know she is not in bed? Is she allowed to be out in the middle of the night? And is she allowed to play with that knife? She has a stick and she's whittling it. Sharpening it.

THE NEXT MORNING, Madeleine saw the empty wheelchair again through the bathroom window. "Dad, whose wheelchair is that?"

He glanced out the window and said, "Beats me." And the two of them resumed shaving.

Her technique is identical to his, the only difference being that his razor makes a lovely sandpapery sound as it moves down his cheek while her razor, not containing a blade, is silent.

They wiped their faces with their towels and applied Old Spice.

At breakfast, Mimi told Jack that the kids were frightened of that big dog across the street—"No we're not," said Madeleine—"and all the junk in that driveway gets in my nerves." She wanted him to go over there and find out what was with that family.

"I'll bet they're perfectly nice," he said over his newspaper. "Just a bit eccentric."

"I had enough eccentric at home, *merci,* that's why I married you, Monsieur, to get away from eccentric." She caught the toast as it popped.

Now Madeleine crouches behind the confetti bushes at the foot of her front lawn as her father crosses the street. The wheelchair is gone again. Tools lie scattered in the driveway next to the old wreck that sits on blocks, hood up. She curls her hands into a spyglass and watches her father knock at the screen door. What if the door opens and a long green tentacle comes out and yanks him inside? What if the person who answers the door looks perfectly normal but is really from another planet and is merely disguised as a human being? What if Dad is merely disguised as Dad and my real dad is being held prisoner on another planet? What if everyone is an alien except me and they are all merely pretending to be normal?

The door opens. A man with a dark curly beard shakes hands with Dad. A man with a beard. In a frilly apron. Of all the strangest things you could possibly see on an air force base.

Her father disappears into the purple house and Madeleine comes out from behind the bushes. Should she go after him? Should she tell her mother? She returns to her lemonade stand at the foot of the drive-way. "Two cents," says the sign. In her empty pickle jar, nine pennies. Mike said, "Make mine a double, bartender." And Roy Noonan paid a nickel and let her keep the change. All the other kids are either too little to have money, or too old to take notice of her. After a while, two girls her own age stop and one says, "I hope you're washing those cups." Girly girls.

When Dad comes out he'll buy three and she'll have fifteen cents. Enough for a candy necklace, two Pixy Stix and two Kraft caramels, with plenty left over.

Jack's neighbour stands almost at attention, his posture an absurd contrast with his full-length frilly apron; its print faded and freshly grease-stained, it protects an immaculate long-sleeved white shirt and narrow black tie.

"Hi, I'm your neighbour, Jack McCarthy."

The man nods formally. "Froelich," he says, and sticks out his hand. It would not take a rocket scientist to figure out that Froelich is not military personnel. They shake hands. "Perhaps you wonder about the dog. He is harmless."

"That's nice," says Jack, "but I'm just here to say hello." Adding, with a grin, *"Wie geht's, Herr Froelich?"*

Froelich hesitates, then, "You take a coffee, yes?" He does not wait for a reply, but turns and heads for the kitchen at the rear of the small house. Jack waits in the vestibule. A carved wooden sign hangs by the door: *"Willkommen."* A record is playing in the living room; Jimmy Durante sounds crystal clear, Jack looks around the corner to see what kind of hi-fi it is—Telefunken, same as his own. *Eat an apple every day, take a nap at three. . . .* Jack whistles along under his breath and glances about. To his right, a heaped laundry basket on the stairs. In the living room, newspapers crest up against a worn armchair, toys litter the floor, which is covered by a dusty Persian rug smudged with dog hair. In the middle of it all, a playpen where two babies in diapers bounce rattles and a teething ring against the head of an older child who sits facing away from Jack. A girl, judging from the hair, not long but not short either—the extent of Jack's lexicon of feminine coiffure. A guitar leans in one corner, a coffee table is piled with magazines and books— one in particular catches his eye. He can smell something cooking—the simmer of an all-day soup at nine in the morning.

Froelich reappears with two mugs. "Cheers," he says.

*"Prost,"* replies Jack.

"Please to call me Henry."

Madeleine is relieved to see her father emerge from the purple house. Coffee cups in hand, he and the bearded man peer under the hood of the wheelless car and chat, while the man points at things in the engine.

Madeleine sees her father turn, still talking, and look at her. The bearded man turns too and they start toward her across the street. When they reach the lemonade stand, her father says, "This is our *Deutsches Mädchen.*"

Her parents call her this because she picked up so much of the language, courtesy of her babysitter, with whom she went everywhere—beautiful, bespectacled and bebraided Gabrielle, of the sidecar and the one-armed father.

Mr. Froelich looks down at Madeleine and says, "*Wirklich?*"

"*Ja,*" she answers, embarrassed.

"*Und hast du Centralia gern, Madeleine?*"

"Um, *Ich* . . . I like it okay," she says, seeing the German words tumble away like loose bricks as she reaches for them, turning to rubble in her memory.

"You come over to our house, Madeleine, we'll speak Deutsch, you and I."

He buys a glass of lemonade and drinks. "*Aber das schmeckt.*" His black moustache glistens, his lips are red and moist. He has a smile like Santa Claus. A thin Santa Claus, with a bald spot, a black beard and shiny dark eyes. And a bit of a stoop, as though he were leaning forward, the better to hear you. He is older than the normal dads.

"The Froelichs have a girl about your age," says her father.

Yeah, thinks Madeleine, and she has a knife. But she says politely, "Oh."

"*Ja,* we do"—Mr. Froelich nods to her—"perhaps a little older."

"Mr. Froelich teaches at your school."

"How do you feel about mathematics, Madeleine?" he asks, and smiles when she makes a face.

"Maybe Mr. Froelich can give you some tutoring." Jack turns to Froelich. "The Germans are way out in front when it comes to math, wouldn't you say, Henry?"

Jack buys a glass of lemonade, pronounces it "ambrosia" and returns with Henry Froelich across the street to the mismatched rust and rainbow collection of car parts, vaguely recognizable as some kind of Ford. Henry turns up the cuffs of his white sleeves, just once, then proceeds to tinker and chat. Jack smiles. Only a German would wear a white shirt and tie to work on an engine.

The Froelichs have lived in the PMQs for five years. Longer than any personnel. "What do you think of the mess, Henry? Worth the price of admission?"

"I have not seen it."

Jack is surprised. Teachers as well as VIPs from the civilian community all have the privilege of becoming associate members of the officers' mess, and most do.

"I haven't a tuxedo or a—how does one say, a 'dinner jacket'?"

"You don't need all that nonsense," says Jack. "Come as you are."

Froelich glances dubiously at his filthy apron, and the two men laugh.

"What part of Germany are you from originally, Henry?"

Froelich rummages in his tool box. "The north."

"Whereabouts?"

"Hamburg." He holds up a spark plug. "This type is Champion."

"Is that a fact?" Jack doesn't press him for details. Hamburg was carpet-bombed in the summer of '43. If Froelich was there, he's lucky to have survived. If he had family there, it's a subject best avoided. "I see you're reading *Silent Spring,*" recalling a book on the coffee table. "What's it like?"

"My wife is reading it, she has it from the book-every-month club."

"That's your wife's too, I take it." Jack indicates the apron.

Froelich smiles and wipes his hands on the faded swirl of roses. "Actually, not."

Jack thinks of the inside of the Froelichs' house—lived in, to say the least—and wonders what Mrs. Froelich is like. A thick woman with flaxen hair coming loose from a bun. Perhaps she works outside the home. Mimi is right, the Froelichs are eccentric.

He watches his neighbour bent over the engine, lips compressed in concentration. It is impossible to meet a man of his own age or older and not wonder what his war was like. And while it's true that you might not want to dig too deeply into a German's war record—not to mention those of their Eastern European allies—the majority of these fellows were just soldiers. Ordinary men like himself. In any case, Henry Froelich appears a bit old to have seen active duty.

"Look, we're having a couple of people over for a barbecue tonight. How about it, Henry?"

Froelich looks up. "We should be the ones to feed you, you only now have arrived."

It occurs to Jack that he may have just started World War Three with Mimi, but he presses on. "No big deal, come on over and take potluck." He sets his mug down on the roof of the old jalopy. "We'll see you tonight, eh, Henry?" Adding, as he heads back across the street, "And don't forget to bring your wife."

"Invite the whole street," says Mimi, a carpet tack between her lips. "I mean it Jack, *je m'en fous.*"

The kitchen curtains are already up, and the big oil painting of the Alps is hung over the fireplace—how did she manage that on her own? He watches her tap the nail into the kitchen wall with the hammer, then he hands her a wooden plate. "A little to the left," he says. "Good." In carved letters around its rim, *Gib uns heute unser tägliches Brot.* She has her Singer sewing machine set up in a corner of the living room, against the staircase wall, and, hanging in its usual place above, her mother's hooked rug of bright orange lobsters in the waves.

"Why are they cooked if they're still swimming in the ocean?" Jack always asks, and she always pinches his ear between her nails. She does so now—"Ow!"

"Dad," says Madeleine, banging through the screen door, "can you set up the TV?"

Mimi says, "No TV during the day."

"That shouldn't count in daylight saving time."

"She's going to be a lawyer, that one," says Mimi.

"I can at least set it up," says Jack.

"After you get the groceries." Mimi comes down the stepladder.

Madeleine slouches. In her hands, the pickle jar with all of eleven cents. "There's nothing to do."

"I'll give you something to do," says her mother. "You can dust the baseboards." Madeleine heads back out the door to play. Jack catches Mimi's eye. "Reverse psychology," she says.

"Advanced management." He closes in for a kiss but she fends him off and heads for the counter, where she rummages in her Yuban coffee can for a pen and writes out a grocery list. Mimi's kitchen—indeed her house—is a model of organization, with the exception of a six-inch square by the telephone: thatch of recycled envelopes, elastic bands, welter of pencil ends and—Jack swears—inkless pens, a tin pop-up address book inscribed according to her own arcane code. The phone rings, she picks it up. "Hello? . . . Yes . . . hello Mrs. Boucher . . . Betty. . . . Please call me Mimi. . . ." She laughs at something Betty says. "Yes, I know! . . . That's right. . . . Well I look forward to meeting you too." She laughs again. "That's right, sooner than we expected"—looking daggers at Jack— "They're all the same. . . . Now, you don't have to bring a thing, there's plenty of. . . . Around six and bring the kids. . . . All right, bye-bye." She hangs up and turns back to Jack with both hands on her hips. "Lucky for you, Monsieur. Betty Boucher is bringing potluck. She can't believe how Vic would tell you yes when he knows perfectly the house is still *toute bouleversée.*"

Jack takes the grocery list and gives her a kiss. The women have figured it out, they always do. He heads for the door, shoving the list into his pocket full of dimes. Which reminds him, he ought to call Simon.

From the big grassy circle behind the houses, Madeleine sees her father pulling away up the street in the car, and runs to see if she can tag along. But as she rounds the house, she sees the wheelchair across the street. Gleaming. Occupied.

She slows to a walk. Shoves her hands into her shallow shorts pockets, glancing casually from side to side, trying not to stare as she strolls down her driveway toward her bike lying at the side of the road. She sits cross-legged next to it, takes three marbles from her pocket and, as though it was her intention all along, begins to carve out a course in the cindery gravel. She steals a glance. It's a girl in the wheelchair.

She looks back down and flicks one smoky marble into another, sending it spiralling into a little hole. She glances up again. The girl is very thin. Her head lolls gently to one side, she has a lot of light brown wavy hair and her skin is very white. The hair is neatly brushed but appears to be too big for her head, which is too big for her body. Her freshly ironed blouse fits her like a loose wrapper. Her arms seem to be in constant slow motion—as though she were under water. A shawl covers her legs despite the warm weather, and Madeleine can see the tips of her narrow feet in white sandals, one crossed over the other. She is strapped in by a seat belt. Otherwise she would probably slide right out of her chair and onto the grass. It's impossible to tell how old she is. Madeleine looks back down at her marbles.

"Ayyyy. . . ."

She looks up at the sound, which is like a gentle groan. The wheelchair girl raises an arm—her wrist looks permanently bent, her hand clumsily closed. Is she waving? Is she looking at me?

"Ayyy!" An old-young quaver.

Madeleine lifts a hand. " . . . Hi."

Head rolling, the girl says, "Umeeah."

" . . . Pardon?"

The girl's head jerks back and, suddenly loose and loud: "Haahaaahhh!"

Madeleine is alarmed. Is the girl in pain? The corner of her mouth is pulled up. Is she laughing? At what? Well, she's retarded, maybe everything is funny to her. Madeleine gets up. Now the sound is like moaning, but it's only the dregs of the girl's laughter—a naked sound and infinitely gentle, it makes Madeleine feel afraid that someone may come along and do something terrible to the girl. It makes her want to go back inside her own house. But the wheelchair girl waves her closed hand again and repeats, "Umeah!" . . . *Come here!*

Madeleine picks up her bike and mounts it. She clothespinned a playing card to one of her spokes this morning—the joker—and it makes a putt-putt sound now as she coasts across the street. As she nears, she notices something unusual about the girl's chair—its wheels are attached by two heavy-duty coiled springs. Perhaps it's some kind of souped-up wheelchair. She realizes now that the girl wasn't waving; she's holding something. Offering it. Madeleine hopes it isn't a sweaty candy.

"What is it?" she asks in a kind tone of voice, leaning forward on her handlebars. The girl's eyes slide like marbles, then her chin drops to her chest and she appears to be looking for something in the grass, her head moving from side to side. As Madeleine draws closer up the driveway, she sees that the girl is actually looking at her out the corner of her eye. The way a bird might.

Madeleine hesitates, about to turn back—

"Wayyy!" The girl flails her hand. Clear drool flows from the corner of her mouth.

Madeleine comes closer. "Watcha got?"

The screen door of the purple house flies open and the German shepherd bounds out. Madeleine feels for her pedals but her feet get tangled up in her bike and she topples backward. The dog barks and lunges. Madeleine covers her face and feels the soft tongue on her elbows—the feel of pinkness—and an ache at the back of her skull where she has banged it on the driveway.

"You shouldn't never run away from a dog when it's chasing you," says a dead-level voice. "It just makes them chase you more."

Madeleine uncovers her face and looks up. The girl with the knife. Blue eyes. Husky eyes.

She sits up. The dog's tongue pulsates like a slice of wet ham between his fangs, and he stares off past her shoulder the way dogs do.

The girl says, "What do you want, kid?" She has the knife in one hand, a whittled stick in the other, its tip white and pointed.

Madeleine swallows. "What's your dog's name?" The girl squints and fires a neat round of spit from the side of her mouth. Madeleine wonders, does she cut her own hair with that knife? Shaggy rust to just below the ears.

"Eggs," groans the wheelchair girl, her head lurching forward with the effort of speech.

"What?"

"She told you," says the girl.

Madeleine rises cautiously to her feet and looks at the huge black and tan dog. Can his name possibly be Eggs? He turns and goes to the wheelchair girl, flops down and rests his chin on her twisty feet. He blinks but doesn't move when her hand drops down to pet him and her zigzagging fingers poke him in the eye.

"What are you doing here?" says the girl with the knife.

"She called me." It feels rude to call someone "she" when she's sitting right there, but Madeleine doesn't know the girl's name. Probably the girl doesn't know her own name.

The knife girl turns to the wheelchair one and says, "Was she bothering you?" Madeleine inches toward her bike. Me go home now.

"Noohhh," sighs the wheelchair girl, followed by the slight sobbing that is her chuckle. "I ju wah teweh my nay."

The girl turns to Madeleine and says, "She wants to tell you her name."

Madeleine stops and waits.

The wheelchair girl says, "Ahm Ewivabeh."

Madeleine doesn't know what to do. The tough girl shears a curl of bark from her stick. Around her neck is tied a leather shoelace that disappears beneath her grimy white T-shirt. At the corner of her mouth, Madeleine can see a paper-thin scar—it traces a line down toward her jaw, pale pink in the tanned face. She senses that this girl would fight like a dog. Sudden, savage.

Madeleine turns to the retarded girl and says, "Um. Hi."

"Well say her name, can't you?" says the knife girl.

Madeleine hesitates, then says, "Ewivabeh."

The wheelchair girl's head jerks back at an angle and her laughter shreds the air: "Ahhhhaaahaaaa!"

The knife girl stops whittling. "Is that supposed to be funny?"

"No," says Madeleine, honestly.

"'Cause if it is, you're dead."

"I know."

"Her name is Elizabeth."

"Oh," says Madeleine. "Hi, Elizabeth."

"Ayyy."

Madeleine looks at the tough girl. "What's your name?" she asks, surprised by her own nerve.

"Who wants to know?"

"Um"—she can feel a grin tiptoeing across her face, and tries to suppress it, along with Bugs Bunny, who threatens to take over—"Madeleine." *Charmed, I'm sure, doc.*

The girl spits again and says, "Colleen." Then she folds her knife, sticks it in the back pocket of her denim cut-offs and leaves, walking away barefoot up the street with her stick over her shoulder.

Madeleine picks up her bike. "'Bye Elizabeth."

"Wayyy!"

Madeleine waits with her hand outstretched while Elizabeth's closed fist wavers over it, then opens and drops something into her palm. Not a candy. Madeleine looks down at her hand. "Wow." A beautiful green boulder, swirled sea smoke. A glassie. The most valuable marble you could own. "Thanks Elizabeth."

Jack waits in the stifle of the phone booth beside the PX. He has fed the phone enough dimes to cover the call to Washington but he's concerned his time will run out before he gets to talk to—"Crawford here."

"Simon."

"Jack, how are you, mate?"

"Not so bad, yourself?"

"Can't complain. What's your number there, call you straight back."

Jack reads the number into the phone, then hangs up.

It was an obstacle course getting through to Simon—First Secretary Crawford. A series of English accents, from Eton to London's East End, told him he had reached the British Embassy in Washington. Bureaucracy, vast and self-perpetuating. Jack knows; he is part of it. Thank goodness there are people like Simon, who know how to cut through. The phone rings, Jack picks it up.

"Back in Centralia, eh? How's the old place look?"

Jack glances out—an airman carries groceries to his station wagon, where three kids bounce in the back seat and a beagle *haroos* in the back-back. "New," he says.

"Not a great deal to report, Jack. Our friend is still on hold. I'll let you know when he arrives."

"Do you have a ballpark?"

"Not really. I should think we'll move when the time is right."

Jack wonders how they'll get the man out. Through Berlin, perhaps. Will "our friend" be concealed in a car? Jack has heard about defectors being brought in that way—folded into the false trunk of a Trabant. "What about when he gets here? Do you want me to track down an apartment for him in London?"

"It's all taken care of."

"Good, that's good." Jack doesn't want to sound too eager. "Where do I pick him up when the time comes?"

"All you've got to do is look in on our friend once he arrives. See that he's comfortable, not too bored. Take him out for an airing once in a while. Usual care and feeding of your common garden variety defector."

"Does our friend have a name?"

"I'm sorry, of course. His name is Fried. Oskar Fried."

Jack pictures a thin man—spectacles and bow tie. "East German?"

"That's right. Though he's been stuck in the boonies for a few years."

"Where? Kazakhstan?"

"One of the 'stans,' no doubt. Come to think, you may as well take his London address. . . ."

Jack fishes in his pocket, finds a scrap of paper and writes down the address on the back of Mimi's grocery list. "So there's not a whole lot for me to do but sit tight."

"Welcome to 'the great game.'" It's the first reference Simon has made to the fact that he is an intelligence officer.

"First Secretary, eh? Isn't that Donald Maclean's old job?"

Simon laughs. "Technically yes, although I don't plan on a midnight flit to Russia any time soon."

They hang up with a promise to get together when Simon passes through with the defector.

*Oskar Fried.* Jack assumed the "Soviet scientist" would be Russian. The fact that he's German adds a congenial dimension to the already fascinating prospect of meeting the man—it'll be that much easier for Jack and Mimi to make him feel at home. Not to mention Henry Froelich right across the street—Jack meant to ask Simon whether he could invite Fried home for a meal. He looks at the address on the scrap of paper. A street near the university. If asked, Oskar Fried is here doing research at the University of Western Ontario. No one will ask. An academic with a German accent—hardly a rarity. And this part of the world is rich with German immigrant culture, pre-war and post. Simon has chosen a good place for Oskar Fried to recover quietly from whatever the ordeal of defection entails. It's simple, Jack reflects as he pockets the list: select a context in which people will answer their own questions. He opens the folding glass door of the booth and sets out for home across the parade square.

Oskar Fried is presumably a scientist of some importance. Why is Canada getting him? There's the National Research Council in Ottawa. There's the heavy water plant at Chalk River, which was cleansed of espionage back in '45—after the infestation by the Atomic Spy Ring that helped the Russians get the bomb. Fun 'n' games, thinks Jack, shaking his head at the memory of Igor Gouzenko talking to the press with a hood over his head after his defection. A real black eye for Canada. Chief among the names the Russian cipher clerk gave up was that of a Brit, Dr. Alan Nunn May—like Maclean, another Cambridge type—who had passed weapons-grade uranium to the Russians in the name of "world peace." Jack touches two fingers to his forehead in response to the smart salute of a cadet and steps from the black parade square to the cooler sidewalk, enjoying the stroll home. He sticks his hands in his pockets, absently rolling a bit of paper. He can almost hear Simon: "Take off those American gloves!"

Perhaps they were just overly privileged. Nunn May, and Guy Burgess and Maclean and their lot, wouldn't last a day on a Soviet collective farm. But that's history; Russia has the bomb and, God knows, so will China soon enough. What count now are nuclear missiles, ICBMs, and developing some sort of defence against them. Is that what Fried will be working on? Canada has a small number of nuclear weapons, but no warheads—at least, not that Prime Minister Diefenbaker will admit to. Jack stops in his tracks. The groceries! He makes an about-face and retraces his steps to the PX, digging in his pocket for the grocery list—it'll be great seeing Simon again, and finally introducing him to Mimi. She'll fix them a real Acadian feast. Then over to the mess, where the two of them will close the bar the way they used to—"Here's to being above it all." He regards the scrap of paper: *shredded wheat, milk, can peas. . . .* He peers at his wife's pencil scrawl. *Real jello*—no, that must be *red* Jell-O—*bag potatoes, hot dogs, doz. buns*—and here he's defeated—*mushmelbas?* What's a mushmelba? A type of mushroom? A cracker? Mimi ought to have been a doctor instead of a nurse, with her writing. He would phone home to ask, but he finds he's out of nickels and dimes. Oskar Fried. *Friede* means "peace."

He walks into the PX, takes a cart and, still staring at the encrypted list, wheels slowly up the aisle and straight into someone else's cart. "I'm sorry."

"That's okay," the woman says. "You're new."

"That's right. I'm Jack McCarthy."

"I think we're neighbours." She is perhaps three or four years older than he, pretty in a way. "I'm Karen Froelich." They shake hands.

"I just met your husband."

She smiles. Yes, she's pretty in spite of the lines around her eyes, her mouth—no lipstick. "I hope he offered you a cup of coffee."

"He offered me a beer," says Jack, "but we made do with coffee."

"Good." She brushes a strand of hair from her cheek, tucking it behind her ear. Her hair is not done but you wouldn't call her unkempt. She is simply not, as Mimi would say, "*bien tournée.*" Her gaze falls briefly as she says, "Drop by any time."

Shy, or perhaps vague. In any case, it isn't the usual air force wife invitation: *You and your wife must come over for dinner once you've settled in.* But he recalls that she isn't an air force wife.

"I'm afraid you'll be seeing us sooner than you think, Mrs. Froelich." And he repeats the invitation he extended to her husband earlier this morning. He is ready for a feminine objection echoing Mimi's and Betty Boucher's, but Karen Froelich just says, "Thanks," and begins a polite getaway down the aisle.

There is something girlish about her, although she must be forty. Worn white sneakers, stretch pants. And, it looks like, one of her husband's old dress shirts.

"What's, uh—" He feels suddenly awkward as she stops and turns; he is making too much conversation. "I saw you're reading *Silent Spring.*"

She nods.

"What's it like?"

"It's um. Disturbing." She nods again, as though to herself.

He nods too, waiting for more, but she just says, "Nice meeting you," and moves off.

Jack turns to stare at the shelves of cans in front of him, the way men do in grocery stores—*I could find Dresden at night from twelve thousand feet, but where are the canned peas?* He heads back up the aisle. "Mrs. Froelich," he calls, a little embarrassed. "Can you help me out here?"

"Call me Karen."

"Karen," he says, reddening for no reason, and handing her the grocery list, "I can't read my wife's writing."

She looks at it and reads aloud, "Four-seventy-two Morrow Street—"

Jack takes the list back and turns it over—*Simon, are you watching this? Christ.*

Karen looks at the scrap of paper, where he's pointing. "Marshmallows."

"Thank you!" says Jack. *I sound too relieved.* As they move off in separate directions, his heart is beating a little too quickly, out of proportion to the gaffe—the address was meaningless to her. No harm done. It's a healthy reminder to be careful, that's all. Not that it matters. Even the name Oskar Fried would be meaningless to her. It's largely meaningless to Jack. Some Soviet egghead in a bow tie.

He finds the fruits and vegetables mounded amid plastic grass, turns his gaze to the bananas, apples and pears, and shreds the address inside his trouser pocket. Potatoes . . . ah, there they are. Mimi didn't say how many. He puts two bags of them into his cart. Now, what else did she want? He reaches into his pocket for the grocery list and finds the shreds—that's it, shredded wheat. And what else? Hot dogs. And buns. For the kids. And marshmallows, of course. . . .

Madeleine is up in her room before lunch, surrounded by her worldly goods: books, toys and games, and her—she refuses to call them dolls—what's the word for dolls that aren't sissy? Bugs Bunny is in pride of place on the bed, his ears currently arranged in two chignons on either side of his head. At his right, she places a sock monkey named Joseph—she can't remember why he is called that, she only knows that when he was a sock he was pinned round her neck the time she had strep throat in Germany and she miraculously recovered. "*Guten Tag, Joseph,*" Madeleine says, and he smiles back with his button eyes.

Standing on a chair to reach her closet shelf, she stows the tattered game of Snakes and Ladders, then Monopoly—the British version, with pound notes and London street names—and the mystical game of Chinese checkers, with its precious store of coloured marbles, *Do not play with them outside.* She lines up her Narnia books on the shelf in the correct order. Given to her by a second cousin of her father's who is a Jesuit priest in Toronto. "Thank you Father What's-His-Name, these are the best books I've ever read."

She is perfectly happy thus employed, whiling away the time until Auriel and Lisa return from their baseball tournament, so she is surprised when her mother calls from downstairs, "Madeleine, there's a friend here to see you."

Surprise gives way to alarm as she tries to imagine who might be calling on her. Colleen? Elizabeth? Both? She slowly descends the stairs.

"Hi, I'm Marjorie Nolan," says the girl at the bottom of the three kitchen steps. "Welcome to Centralia, Madeleine."

"Marjorie's *maman* told her there was a little girl her age just up the street."

Madeleine looks at her mother. *I'm not a little girl.*

Her mother takes Madeleine's face between her hands and kisses the top of her head. "Go on out and play, *chérie,* it's a beautiful day," and pats her on the bottom. Marjorie Nolan smiles up at her, but Madeleine is doubtful. Marjorie has blonde ringlets and is wearing a dress in the summer holidays. Her hair and her short puffed sleeves give her a strange outdated look, like Pollyanna. Madeleine doesn't wish to be mean but she can tell right away that Marjorie is not her type.

"Would you like me to show you around, Madeleine?"

"Okay."

"Have fun, girls. Nice to meet you, Marjorie."

They walk, and Marjorie proceeds to give a guided tour of the PMQs. "Over there is the CO's house."

"Yeah, I know," says Madeleine. Everyone knows that the detached house with the biggest lawn—the one with the flagpole—is the commanding officer's.

Marjorie gestures. "And across the street, just behind the purple house, is the park with the swings and teeter-totters and things."

"I know, I went there already." She isn't trying to be rude, but it's hot and she would rather be reading or running through the sprinkler. It's too soon to leave Marjorie, however, so she says, "Want to run through the sprinkler?"

Marjorie giggles and looks down at her dress, "I don't think so, Madeleine." She sounds as though she's imitating a grown-up who is amused by something a kid has said.

"If you look to your right, across the highway and the railroad tracks," says Marjorie, "you'll see Pop's Candy Store. It's not part of the base. Teenagers hang out there. I don't advise it."

Madeleine gazes with longing at the bottle of Mountain Dew emblazoned across the screen door of Pop's. Then she looks back at the yellow ringlets bobbing on Marjorie's shoulders. At Marjorie's smile, pursed and waxy like a doll's. It comes unbidden to her mind: *Margarine.* "What do you want to do now?" she asks Margarine.

Margarine replies, "We're doing it, silly."

Madeleine resigns herself to walking one more loop of houses before making her escape.

"That's where Grace Novotny lives." Marjorie has stopped to stare at a pale pink duplex. They are in the far section of PMQs, on the opposite side of the school from Madeleine's house, an area laid out in mirror image to her own. This is where the non-commissioned ranks live, not that it matters. It's about skill, not rank. "We all depend on one another," says her father. "A pilot may outrank his ground crew, but his life is in their hands." This isn't the army, "where all you have to have is a pulse." So Madeleine is taken aback when Marjorie says, "Grace's dad's just a corporal." She has never heard anyone compare ranks before. The dads are always introduced as Mr. So-and-So, never by rank.

Marjorie says, "My dad's a squadron leader."

Madeleine doesn't reply, "Mine's a wing commander," because it would sound as though she were showing off. She can't help it if the only rank on the base higher than her father's is the CO's, and anyway, what's the big deal?

The pale pink house and lawn are the same as all the others, decently mown. A jumble of bikes and trikes leans against one wall, and in the driveway sits a big Mercury Meteor convertible with white leather seats and a pair of dice hanging from the rearview mirror.

"It belongs to one of Grace's sisters' boyfriends," says Marjorie. "She has four older sisters and they're all sluts." The word slits the air. Madeleine looks at Marjorie—perhaps she won't be so boring after all. She looks at the Mercury and pictures a greaser in a muscle shirt smirking behind the wheel, his arm draped around a chick, the speeding convertible piled high with girls in beehives and tight sweaters. *Sluts.*

"There are entirely too many children in that family, if you want my opinion," says Marjorie.

Madeleine's mother would say, "That's like saying there can be too much love. Each child—*chaque enfant*—is a gift from God." But Madeleine is secretly grateful that it is just she and Mike.

"Grace Novotny failed grade four last year, so she'll be in our class even though she's already ten, and if you want my advice, Madeleine, you'll steer clear of her. In fact"—and she chuckles—"that's an order."

That settles it, Marjorie is a stupid idiot. Her saying the word "slut" cannot make up for that.

"I'm not trying to be mean, but"—Marjorie cups her hand around her mouth and whispers into Madeleine's ear—"Grace smells." She giggles and looks expectantly at Madeleine. Madeleine obliges with a slight smile, then Marjorie squeals, "There she is! Run away!"

Marjorie runs off down the street, but Madeleine stays and looks at the pink house. Behind the screen door stands a girl. Her features are obscured by the mesh, but Madeleine can see a mass of curls, honey-coloured, down to her shoulders. She can't see anything weird about Grace, anything worth running away from—although she isn't near enough to smell. Even so, smell is nothing a bath won't fix. Unless your house smells, or you wet the bed. But the next moment, Madeleine does see something weird. It looks as though Grace is raising her hand to wave so Madeleine waves too. But Grace just puts her thumb in her mouth, and stands there sucking it. Perhaps Marjorie is right—best to avoid Grace Novotny. Don't make fun of her, the way Marjorie does, but don't befriend her either.

Marjorie is waiting at the bottom of the street, where a paved pathway leads between the houses to the rear of the school. "You'll be sorry," she chants.

"What for?"

"You shouldn't wave at her, Maddy, that's like petting a stray dog."

*Maddy?* "I don't care," says Madeleine.

They walk in silence, the asphalt changing to grass as they approach and then round the sleeping school.

"Are you mad at me?" asks Marjorie, folding her hands, bouncing them against the front of her dress.

"Why should I be mad?"

"Well, are you going to make friends with Grace?"

"No." Madeleine can hear her brother's voice in her own. A note of masculine impatience with stupid girls. She always defends girls when Mike criticizes them, but sometimes they can be really dumb.

"Will you be my best friend?"

Madeleine doesn't know how to answer. *Kinda soon to be poppin' the question, ain't it, doc?* She mumbles, "I don't know."

Then Marjorie tries to hold hands! Madeleine takes off, running to the swings, hops onto one like a cowboy onto a waiting horse and pumps till she is flying high.

Marjorie waits patiently below. "I suppose you've met the Froelichs," she calls in her grown-up sarcastic voice.

Madeleine watches as Marjorie fans her dress out like a ballerina and tiptoes in a circle. Madeleine stands up on the wooden swing and pumps harder.

"The Froelichs are trash, I'm sorry to say," says Marjorie. "Except for Ricky, he's a dreamboat!" She shrieks and runs to the teeter-totters.

Madeleine lets go at a great arcing height and sails through the air to a perfect landing. She joins Marjorie at the teeter-totters—at least they are doing something normal now. They rise and fall, politely avoiding giving each other the bumps.

"Whatever you do, Maddy, keep away from his sister, and I don't mean the retarded one, I mean the mean one, Colleen, she has a knife and she'll murdleize you with it."

Madeleine is starting to feel ill. According to Marjorie, the PMQs are full of reeking, retarded and dangerous kids, all of whom she may already have accidentally made friends with. Not to mention Marjorie herself. Madeleine experiences a pang of longing for Germany, for the base at 4 Wing, the clean fighter jets—young pilots who swung her up into the cockpit and saluted her father. The occasional B-52—part of United States Air Force Europe, USAFE—lumbering down the runway. There is a flight of B-52s in the air at all times, they are up there now, big blind dinosaurs, landing gear closing like pincers, hard segmented bellies full of bombs. Keeping us safe.

"And they have a vicious dog," says Marjorie, teeter-tottering sidesaddle.

"No he's not, he's friendly."

"He's a German shepherd, Maddy," says Marjorie sharply. "They can turn on you."

Madeleine closes her eyes and pictures the beautiful trees, rose bowers and fountains of the town near 4 Wing: Baden-Baden, in the heart of the Black Forest, the Schwarzwald. A spa town full of rich old ladies and their poodles—full of spies, said her dad, "reading newspapers with eye-holes cut out." The smell of pastry in the day and charcoal fires at night, the taste of mountain streams on a Sunday *Wanderung,* the language that smells like rich earth and old leather, *du bist wie eine Blume. . . .*

"Oh Maddy I feel sorry for you, you have to live right across the street from the Froelichs, I hope you're going to be all right."

"I have to go home," says Madeleine, dismounting, careful to hold the teeter-totter still for Marjorie.

"How come?"

"I have to have lunch."

"But my mum is making it for us," says Marjorie. "I already asked, and she's made cupcakes and everything."

"Oh." As soon as you feel sorry for someone, you are trapped. "Okay."

It's only one half-hour of her life, then she'll be home with Mike. He's making a model airplane with his normal friend, Roy Noonan. And Dad will be there. They'll play Chinese checkers and she will breathe the clean air of her own house. *What will I say the next time Marjorie comes to call on me?*

They walk across the baking green field and up St. Lawrence Avenue. Madeleine keeps her hand in her pocket in case Marjorie tries to hold it again. Marjorie lives in a yellow bungalow across the street from the little green one—it's still empty. She runs up her front steps and opens the screen door. Madeleine follows.

Inside the house, it is dark. Madeleine's eyes take a moment to adjust. It's stuffy. Cigarettes, but not the refreshing kind. Stale. Plastic covers on the living-room furniture, the curtains drawn. "Right this way," chirps Marjorie.

In the kitchen, the blinds are pulled down. "My mother gets headaches," Marjorie says, as though she's telling Madeleine that they have a maid and a grand piano.

Madeleine doesn't say anything. She sits at the brown Formica table and wonders if Marjorie has any brothers and sisters. There is nothing on the table. No dishes in the dish rack, no newspapers lying around, no junk. When Madeleine's house gets messy, her parents say, "Don't worry, it looks lived in." Marjorie's house does not look lived in.

Marjorie opens the fridge. "Hmmm, let's see." Madeleine sees past her into the brightly lit fridge, the stainless grille of shelves. Almost empty.

Marjorie makes them peanut butter sandwiches on white bread, cut into four with the crusts off. Garnished with pimento-stuffed olives from a jar. There are no cupcakes.

Marjorie pats her mouth with a cocktail napkin. "That was delicious if I do say so myself."

Madeleine flees without seeing Marjorie's room. "Thanks," she says. And runs all the way home.

"You forgot the milk." Mimi is unpacking the groceries onto the kitchen table.

"Can't make head or tail of your writing, Missus," he says, biting into an apple.

She pulls out the two bags of potatoes. "Jack McCarthy, how many potatoes do you think we can eat?"

He grins. "Make poutine or something."

"'Make poutine,' I'll make you!"

"Is that a promise?"

Mike bursts through the door and up the steps. "Can Roy stay for lunch?"

"*B'en sûr mon pitou.*"

Mimi is ladling out the last of the tomato soup, the pyramid of ham sandwiches on the table has dwindled, Roy is on his third and Mike is reaching for another, when Madeleine arrives.

"Where were you?" Mimi asks. "Where's your friend, does she want to stay for lunch?"

"Who?" asks Madeleine, then, "Oh, I went to her house for lunch."

"You ate already?"

"Yeah but I'm still starved." One last half a sandwich remains on the platter. Madeleine takes it and puts it on her plate, where it's joined by another half. She looks up at Roy Noonan, who grunts, "You can have it, I'm full."

"Thanks," she says, and catches sight of Maman winking at Dad. "What's so funny?"

Jack says, "Go ahead and eat up, sweetie, it'll put hair on your chest."

## How Sweet It Is

"The struggle in and for outer space will have tremendous significance in the armed conflict of the future."
　　*Soviet General Pokrovsky, two days before the launch of* Sputnik I, *1957*

"In the crucial areas of our Cold War world, first in space is first, period. Second in space is second in everything."
　　　　　　　　　　　　　*Lyndon B. Johnson to John F. Kennedy, 1961*

*Ladies, please believe me, this is a grand way to tenderize your meat. Get out your husband's hammer.*
　　　　　　　　　　　　　　　　Heloise's Kitchen Hints

ON THE MCCARTHYS' LAWN, the potluck is in full swing. Betty Boucher arrived with a platter of hamburger patties ready for the grill, a potato salad and a coconut cream pie, and her husband, Vic, followed with their barbecue, their kids and a clanking burlap bag. Jack already had hot dogs on the go over the coals, with a chicken on the rotisserie, Mimi brought out devilled eggs, a shredded carrot and raisin salad, a poutine rapé and a pineapple upside-down cake—not up to her usual, but this is day two, so *arrête!* Vimy and Hal Woodley came with a lasagna, a tossed salad and a bottle of German wine they'd saved from their last posting. Hal is a tall, fit man in his forties, with a salt-and-pepper moustache and close-cropped grey hair. "What a pleasure to meet you, Mimi." "Would you like a nice cold beer, Hal?" He is "Hal" to the ladies and "sir" to the men—unless he is in someone's backyard or on the golf course, but even then it's for him to say. The Woodleys' eldest daughter is away at university and their younger girl is "off with her friends." Auriel Boucher brought Lisa Ridelle, whose mother showed up to make sure it was okay and threw her arms around Mimi.

"Elaine!"

"Mimi!"

They haven't seen one another since Alberta.

"I didn't even recognize little Lisa!" cries Mimi. "You look grand, Elaine."

"I'm big as a house."

"What are you, six months?"

"Five!" Mimi insists that Elaine "go get Steve and join us, there's plenty." Elaine returns with her husband, a bottle of vodka, a plate of Hello Dolly squares and a snapshot of Lisa and Madeleine in the tub, age one. Madeleine and Lisa are amazed to discover that they have been friends for years. They giggle with mortified delight at the embarrassing photo, and Auriel examines it, flabbergasted. This was all clearly meant to be.

Steve and Jack slap one another on the back and Jack calls his son over. "Mike, this is the man who took your tonsils out in Cold Lake, say hello to Dr. Ridelle."

Henry Froelich has brought a bottle of homemade wine, and his daughter Elizabeth in her wheelchair. His wife has brought their twin baby boys, and a pot of chili con carne. Mimi takes in Mrs. Froelich at a glance—a man's old white shirt, faded black stirrup pants—smiles, receives the blackened pot from her and tells her the babies are beautiful—they are in rubber pants and undershirts. There are grass stains on the woman's sneakers. "Lovely to meet you, Mrs. Froelich."

"Please call me Karen."

Jack makes introductions all around. The Bouchers and the Ridelles shake hands with the Froelichs and agree that of course they know one another. The Woodleys appear to be more intimately acquainted. Hal asks Froelich if "their boy" is going to play varsity basketball this year, and Vimy asks Karen about her work downtown. A moment later—in the house, tipping an aluminum mould onto a plate while Jack opens more beers—Mimi says, "She's a funny one."

"Who?"

"Karen Froelich."

"Who? Oh, is she?"

"Well, you can see." She lifts the mould deftly from the jellied salad— peas and pineapple suspended in a jiggling, faceted green mound.

"She looks all right to me," says Jack.

"What do you mean by that?" She darts him a look, reaches for her cigarette, taps the ash.

"Well, not everyone's got your style, baby." He offers her a glass of beer. She shakes her head no, then takes it, sips and hands it back. Her red sleeveless blouse is turned up at the collar, her black capri pants reveal just the right amount of leg between hem and espadrille. The lipstick stain on her cigarette filter matches the kiss mark on his beer glass.

"Not to mention," says Mimi, "have you tried her chili?"

"No, but it sure smells good." He winks and she flushes. Like shooting fish in a barrel, getting her riled.

"Chili con carne, my foot. She forgets the carne"—butting out her cigarette, picking up her jellied salad. Jack grins and follows her back outside.

The grown-ups sit on lawn chairs, with plates on their laps and drinks at their feet. Lisa's mother, Elaine, laughs at everything Lisa's father says. Steve is the senior medical officer on base—"and resident golf pro," jokes Vic. The kids are at card tables placed end to end, Madeleine, Mike, Roy Noonan, Auriel Boucher, Auriel's younger sisters and Lisa Ridelle. The Froelich babies crawl around on the grass pursued by Auriel's two-year-old sister, Bea, in a bonnet and sunsuit. Karen Froelich feeds Elizabeth chili con carne—the sight of the food sliding in and out of Elizabeth's mouth makes Madeleine gag, so she tries not to watch, while trying not to seem to be trying not to watch.

Vic and Mimi argue in French; she swats him with an oven mitt and he cringes elaborately. "*Au secours!*"

"Vic, *parlez-vous le ding dong?*" calls Jack from the barbecue, presiding in his apron that says CHEF.

"I speak French, I don't know what your wife is speaking."

"*Ma grande foi D'jeu, c'est du chiac!*" Chiac, Acadian French, the "creative *langage local*," with as many variations as there are communities across the Maritimes.

"'*D'jeu'?! C'est quoi ça, 'D'jeu'?!*" Vic knows she means *Dieu*—God—but he imitates her in lilting feminine tones with an elaborate rolling of r's and she's laughing too hard to swat him again.

"Where did you find this one, Jack?" asks Vic, in his own Trois-Rivières twang. "She talks like a hillbilly."

"I picked her up in the Louisiana bayou."

Henry Froelich says, "Really?"

Mimi exclaims, "No!"

Jack says, "I found her in New Brunswick—"

Mimi nods and Jack continues, "on the Indian reservation—"

"Jack!"—using the oven mitt on him—"*allons donc!*"

Karen Froelich says, "Mimi, are you part native?"

Mimi's laugh decelerates to a polite smile. "No, I'm Acadian."

"That's why she speaks so uncivilized the French," says Vic in a parody of his own accent.

His wife, Betty, says, "You're one to talk, cheeky frog, murdering the language of Louis Quatorze"—she pronounces it "cat oars"—"with your heathen patois."

"Acadian," says Karen. "That's really interesting. There was actually quite a bit of intermarriage between the Acadians and the native Indians, wasn't there?" Her tone betrays no awareness of her faux pas.

There is a pause. Everyone is smiling. Jack knows that Mimi will assume the woman is catty, but he can't see anything but interest on Karen's face. She looks like a stranger in a strange land, here among the lawn chairs. Even her husband is recognizable in his way—a bearded, rumpled professor. But Karen is a woman with undone hair and no makeup, talking about the finer points of Canadian history. "That's how they got out of taking the oath of allegiance to England, right? Before the Expulsion."

Mimi smiles and shrugs.

Karen continues, "By claiming Indian blood."

Jack looks at Mimi. Will she roll with it? Tell the story of *le grand dérangement? That's why I'm so good at moving.*

Vimy Woodley comes to the rescue. "We know so little of our own history, really, don't we? I'm afraid I've never heard of the Expulsion."

Jack tells the story of the English forcing the Acadians from their homes two hundred years ago, and Mimi rallies: "That's why I'm so good at moving."

They all laugh, and Betty Boucher reaches for Mimi's hand. She says in her Manchester accent, thick as a good cardigan, "Well I'm English, love, and I'd like to say I'm sorry. There!"

At the kids' table, Mike stands up and whips his arm round and round like a propeller. When he stops, his hand has puffed and turned red with tiny burst capillaries.

"Wow," says Lisa, and turns her eyelids inside out.

"Neat."

Then they all follow Roy Noonan around the side of the house to watch what he can do with his braces and retainer. He leans forward with his hands on his knees and chews his tongue until a waterfall of clear saliva pours from his mouth.

"Kids," calls Maman, "come get your dessert."

Mike breaks into song: "Comet! It makes your bathroom clean"—to the tune of the Colonel Bogey March—"Comet! It tastes like Listerine"—leading them back the long way around the house—"Comet! It makes you vomit! So drink some Comet, and vomit today!"

Betty clears the table and asks Vimy if her daughter Marsha can babysit Saturday. Mimi scoops ice cream into cones for the kids and asks Steve his opinion on appendectomies.

"Well," he answers, "my motto is, if it ain't broke, don't fix it."

Mimi smiles up at him and says, "You sound just like my husband."

Hal is drafted by the kids to adjudicate the start of a pickup game of softball. Steve and Vic slip into the house for more beer, and Jack stands chatting with Henry Froelich. "What's your background, anyhow, Henry? Math? Science?"

A couple of beers in the Centralia summer evening and Hamburg 1943 is awfully far away—Jack can see nothing wrong in getting to know his neighbour. And Froelich doesn't appear to mind the question, seems relaxed despite his tie and long-sleeved shirt.

"My subject was engineering physics," he says, then raises his eyebrows as though gauging the degree of Jack's interest.

"Wow," says Jack. "What the heck is that?"

Froelich smiles and Jack tips the wine bottle over the man's glass. "Go ahead, Hank, I'm all ears."

"Well. . . ." Froelich crosses his arms and Jack can see him in a lecture hall—the axle grease under his nails could just as easily be chalk. "I studied, and then I taught, how things go."

"What things? Planes, trains, automobiles?"

"There are applications for all these, yes, and others. Propulsion, you see. But I was a very theoretical young man. I did not—um—dirty my hands, as they say."

"Not like now," says Jack, gesturing with his thumb at Froelich's motley-looking old jalopy across the street.

Froelich nods. "Yes, I grow pragmatic with age."

"I'm going to take a wild guess, Henry. You were a professor, am I right?"

"Yes I was."

"A doctor of . . . engineering physics."

"*Ja, genau.*"

"Well what the heck are you doing teaching the multiplication table out here in the middle of nowhere?"

Froelich laughs. Vic joins them. "What's so funny?"

Jack is about to dodge the question, not wishing to put Froelich on the spot if he'd rather not discuss his past, but Froelich answers, "Physics. My first love."

"No kidding, you a science buff, Henry?"

"He's a PhD," says Jack.

Steve joins them with a fresh beer.

"That's not too shabby," says Vic. "Nuclear?"

"Engineering."

Vic shakes his head. "If I had my life to live again, that's what I'd do, that's where the action is, eh? Avionics. Jet propulsion. Rockets."

It's on the tip of Jack's tongue to ask Vic if he didn't get enough of "things that go boom" during the war, blasting away in the back of a Lanc, but he remembers Froelich and says instead, "I'd be an astronaut."

"What do you want to do that for?" says Vic. "That's not flying, that's just sitting on a big bomb and praying." Froelich breaks a smile and nods. "'To the moon, Alice!'" cries Vic.

The others chuckle but Froelich looks a bit bewildered. Is it possible he has never seen *The Honeymooners?*

Steve muses, "The moon is an ideal setting for golf. Imagine how much longer it would take to play eighteen holes in zero gravity."

Jack knows Steve is two years younger than himself. But even without that information, he would know by Steve's particular brand of insouciance that he's not a veteran. Not that veterans can't be insouciant—Simon, case in point. But Simon's insouciance has an edge. Like Vic's bonhomie—he is still drinking in every moment, grateful to be alive. Like Hal Woodley, over in the field behind the house, pitching for the kids. This is what they fought for.

Jack says, "Well we better get there quick or you know what we'll find on the moon."

"What?" says Steve.

"Russians."

Vic and Steve laugh.

"Wernher von Braun said that and he oughta know."

"Who's he?" asks Steve.

Vic rolls his eyes, and Jack spells it out. "Von Braun is Mr. Ballistic Missile. Grand Pooh-bah of the American space program. NASA to you."

"Oh *that* von Braun," says Steve. "Had you going, didn't I?"

"Stee-rike!" cries one of the kids, and out in the field the teams trade places.

Steve says, "Why would anyone want to go the moon, anyhow? It's cold up there."

Like Moscow, thinks Jack, reminded of Simon's comment last summer. He takes another swig of beer. "Well what are we going to do, let the Russkies beat us at everything? At the rate they're going, they'll be there in '65."

Vic says, "The moon is, it's . . . the holy grail, it's the brass ring. . . ."

Froelich sighs. "Forget the moon just now, we are talking here about space, yes? A band of cold and dark one hundred miles above the surface of the earth, worthless—"

"Yeah," says Steve.

"—apart from that it is an extension of air space and this is where the next war will be decided." Jack pours Froelich more wine. "From up there"—Froelich points—"the Soviets can interfere with Western satellites, they can—how do you say—?"

"Neutralize," says Jack.

"*Ja,* neutralize missiles before they will leave the ground or the submarine. They also can launch a space station, they can arm it like a garrison and make extraordinary reconnaissance of earth. The moon is somewhat a minor scene, a. . . ."

"A sideshow."

"*Genau.*"

"USAF wants to make the moon itself into a permanent base."

"That's what the Russians are shooting for," adds Vic. "That's why they're ahead."

"But we're not in it for the same reasons," says Jack. "NASA is a civilian agency. Pure research."

"If pure research is the point," counters Steve, "why don't they just make a space station for experiments, why bother going to the moon?"

"Because the moon is something we all understand," says Jack. "Even a tribesman in darkest Africa can look up and marvel at what a feat that would be, and that's real power, when you capture the world's imagination. The U.S. needs to demonstrate its superiority to the world, and not just for show, for very practical reasons. You can't have the Third World looking to the Soviet Union for—"

"That's right." Vic gestures with his beer. "When you're sitting in a banana republic with a tinpot dictator—"

"And the Communists have got a man on the moon," says Jack, "and they're promising a chicken in every pot—"

"Sputnik was just the tip of the iceberg—"

"Look at *Vostok III* and *IV*—"

"What are their names? Nikolayev?"

"And Popovich," says Froelich.

Jack nods. "The 'heavenly twins.'"

The Russian cosmonauts have just completed a feat straight out of science fiction: a dual orbit of the earth in separate space capsules, passing within an incredible one hundred miles of one other for a total of 112 orbits, more than five times the distance to the moon. The Americans will be lucky to achieve a mere six orbits next month. The logical next Soviet step: a fantastic manoeuvre involving the mooring of two spaceships, and from there, complete control of space and target earth.

"And those are just the flights we know about," says Jack.

Hal Woodley joins them. They make room for him, imperceptibly straightening up.

"Think what else they got up their sleeve," says Vic.

"Nowadays," says Jack, "the real battles get fought in the press and in front of the TV cameras."

"So that's what happened to Nixon," says Woodley, and they all laugh.

Jack opens another beer, offers it to Hal. "Cheers, sir."

"*Prost.* Call me Hal, Jack." The others raise their glasses but, with the exception of Henry, avoid calling Hal Woodley anything at all, "sir" seeming overly formal for the setting, and "Hal" being inappropriate unless expressly invited.

"Think of the disappointment, eh?" says Jack with a grin. "You're a great Russian hero, a cosmonaut. You orbit the earth like a god, the whole world down below is your oyster, and where do they take you when you splash down? Back to some godforsaken desert in the middle of Kazakhstan!"

"I'd take six orbits over a hundred any day if it meant I could spend a week or two in Florida," says Steve. "The waitresses alone are bound to be easier on the eyes."

"Not to mention the food!" says Vic.

Froelich waits until they have stopped laughing. "By landing on the moon"—he speaks with the precision, the slight annoyance, of an expert—"the successful party demonstrates the ability to achieve instant liftoff which is necessary for the moon which is a moving target. When one is adding to this the superior Soviet guidance and control, there is the prospect also of ICBMs that launch to orbit where they cannot be shot down, then re-enter earth's atmosphere to strike a target—" As Jack listens he speculates; Froelich with his PhD could be teaching at a university, patches on his elbows. Maybe he's an eccentric, getting away from it all out here in the boondocks. Yet he clearly loves his subject.

Why would he want to get away from it? "Sputnik made the West very afraid," Froelich is saying. "But what is Sputnik?"

"Fellow Traveller, I think is the translation," says Jack.

Froelich ignores the comment and continues. "A small transmitter on the head of a rocket. And also the last resting place of a dog who did not ask to be a cosmonaut." The others chuckle, but Froelich does not smile. "Sputnik was not an intercontinental ballistic missile, it had to hit no target, just it had to . . . go up." And he points. "They did not have the ICBM, we have this—America has this—before Russia, but ordinary people in the West become afraid and this fear becomes useful to. . . ." He pauses, knits his brow, in search of the words. The other men wait respectfully for him to pick up the thread. Froelich is the picture of the absent-minded professor.

Hal Woodley supplies the missing phrase: "The powers that be."

"*Ja,* thank you," says Froelich. "By landing on the moon, the successful party demonstrates also the ability to rendezvous between two spacecrafts in orbit, and this is vital to making a military installation."

There is a moment of silence. He seems to have finished.

Jack says, "You're right, Henry, putting a man on the moon'll give us a nice warm fuzzy feeling, but the bottom line is security. The Yanks ought to pour their dollars into the air force space program."

"It's all politics," says Hal. "Look what happened with the Arrow."

A moment of silence for the Avro Arrow, the most advanced jet fighter in the world. Created by Canadians, test-flown by Canadian pilots, scrapped by Canadian politicians.

"And what did we buy instead?" says Steve with disgust. "Bomarcs."

"American hand-me-downs," snorts Vic.

"I don't know why McNamara is stalling," says Jack. "USAF's got all kinds of good stuff in the works like their, uh—they're working on those Midas satellites that tell you every time the enemy launches a missile, they've got a manned space glider in the works, what do they call it—?"

"The Dyno-Soar," says Vic.

"Yeah, *Time* had a whole spread. NASA's got Apollo but there's plenty of work to go around. Kennedy ought to throw USAF a bone."

Vic says, "Uncle Sam don't want to look like the Soviets, rattling the sabre in space."

Henry says, "You think space is not military now?"

"NASA is a civilian agency," argues Jack. "In fact, half the movers and shakers down in Houston are your countrymen, Henry."

"That's right," says Hal. "Look at von Braun and that other fellow—"

"Arthur Rudolph," says Jack. "Guy's a managerial genius."

Froelich shrugs. "They worked for Nazis."

"Really?" says Steve.

Jack winces. "Technically yes, but they were civilians. Scientists and dreamers."

Vic lifts his glass to Henry. "You got to hand it to the Germans, eh, when it comes to technology."

But Henry is still hunched, arms crossed, glass in hand. "Scientists and dreamers also caused the first atomic bomb to detonate at Los Alamos. They hold—held it together with masking tape. Very idealistic. It would stop Hitler. It kills instead millions of civilians."

There's a pause. Then Jack says, "It ended the war, though, didn't it?"

Hal says, "Although I wonder if you could've found a single general who'd've made that particular call."

Another pause. Vic sighs. "The Yanks always get stuck with the dirty work."

Jack nods. "Yup." Then smiles. "You know, Peter Sellers had the right idea. We ought to declare war on the Americans. They'll come in and hammer us, then give us a whole bunch of aid and we'll be better off than ever." Henry shrugs again, sips. Jack continues. "We're just lucky the nuclear types didn't get together with the rocket types over in Germany during the war—they'd've had nuclear missiles."

Vic says, "I wonder why they didn't."

Henry replies, "Because it is Jewish science."

The others look at him, but Henry does not continue.

"What's that?" asks Jack.

"Atomic science."

Hal asks, "What do you mean, 'Jewish'?"

"Einstein is a Jew," says Henry.

Jack flinches at the word—it sounds abrupt, rude: *Jew.* It sounds . . . anti-Semitic. Jack knows that isn't fair—just because Froelich is German doesn't make him an anti-Semite.

"Hitler rejects Jewish science"—Henry sounds more Teutonic than ever to Jack, clipped tones, confident to the point of arrogance—"also Hitler does not have the imagination to marry the rocket with the atomic warhead."

"Boy," says Steve. "So in a strange way . . . Hitler's anti-Semitism may have saved us from the big one."

Jack gives a low whistle. Henry says nothing.

Elaine calls, "What are you boys talking about?"

Jack smiles over at her. "Aw, fun 'n' games, Elaine, fun 'n' games."

"They're talking politics," says Mimi, carrying a TV table over with four plates of pineapple upside-down cake, "solving the world's problems." She sets the table down and winks at her husband.

Vic protests, "That's the third dessert tonight!"

"I don't know where you found the time, Mimi," calls Betty.

Jack notices Karen sitting a little apart, both babies asleep in her lap. Yet she doesn't look maternal so much as . . . what? He tries to put his finger on it. She looks as though she's on safari . . . like that woman who rescues animals . . . monkeys . . . lion cubs? What's the name of that book?

"Well stop being so boring," Elaine calls to the men from her chaise, "and come talk to us."

"Let them get it out of their system, love," says Betty, pouring tea, although Elaine is still working on a cocktail.

Froelich takes a bite of cake. "Thank you Mrs. McCarthy— *entschuldigen Sie mich, bitte*—Mimi. Delicious cake." He inclines his head in a formal Old World bow, and resumes energetically: "My point being, why go to the moon when we can so very well annihilate ourselves from here?"

The other men look at him. "I'm talking about avoiding annihilation," says Jack.

"Then why don't we get rid of the weapons?"

"Are you a ban-the-bomb type, Henry?"

"Sure, why not?"

"So am I," says Vic. "I'd like the Soviets to ban it first, though."

"The military are the biggest peaceniks of all," says Jack. "Unlike a lot of politicians, military types know what war is like."

Henry Froelich says, "And some civilians too. They know."

Hal looks Henry in the eye. "That's for sure, Henry. Lest we forget, eh?" He raises his glass.

"To friendship," Jack says.

"To friendship," the others join in.

Over by the barbecue, the kids are roasting marshmallows. Mike has made a torch of his, claiming to prefer it well done, *à point*. Madeleine approaches Elizabeth. "Would you like a roasted marshmallow?"

Elizabeth nods and sighs. Madeleine blows on the marshmallow, then holds the skewer out to her. Lisa and Auriel join her and watch as Elizabeth slowly savours the toasty white, her eyes half closed, a creamy moustache forming on her lip.

"Is it good?" Auriel asks.

"Yahhh." Elizabeth's head rests almost on one shoulder, then moves slowly in a half-circle and tilts back. Madeleine follows with the marshmallow. Elizabeth makes it look delicious.

Lisa says, "Know what, Elizabeth? If you take a marshmallow and squish it, it shrinks and you get ghost gum. Want to try it?"

"Yahhh."

Betty Boucher settles into a lawn chair and cuddles one of the Froelich babies. "With luck we'll get a family moving into that little green bungalow down the street, with a daughter over twelve."

"Wouldn't that be grand," says Elaine Ridelle. Most children in the PMQs are no older than Mike, hence babysitters are at a premium. Vimy's daughter Marsha is not able to babysit for the Bouchers Saturday night; the Woodleys are going away for the weekend.

Karen Froelich says, "Ricky can babysit." Perhaps she misinterprets the awkward silence that follows her offer as confusion because she adds, "My son."

Vimy turns to Mimi. "Ricky is a good friend of my daughter's, he's a lovely boy."

"He's a doll," adds Elaine.

Karen nods vaguely. The other women smile and change the subject.

Mimi has not yet met Ricky Froelich. She has no way of knowing what Betty and Elaine will tell her later: that Ricky is a good-looking youngster of fifteen, so responsible and well adjusted that many women in the PMQs wonder how he could possibly be a product of the Froelich household—not that the Froelichs aren't good people, they are just . . . far from average. But the fact that Ricky is a fine boy is not the point. The point is, boys do not babysit. What kind of mother would volunteer her son for a girl's job?

Vic crosses the lawn, heading for the street, and says over his shoulder to the women, "I'm not sure but I think he's just got the two dependents."

Betty asks, "Who?"

Vic stops and turns. "The American moving into the bungalow. They've just got the one child."

"Vic, you never tell me anything!"

"You never ask!"

"He's the new exchange officer," says Hal, joining the women. "A flying instructor."

"We'll have to have them over, Jack," says Mimi. "They'll be a long way from home."

"Aren't we all," adds Betty Boucher.

Vic was on his way home to fetch his accordion, but Mimi stops him: "Stay right where you are!" She turns to her daughter and orders, "*Madeleine, va chercher ton accordéon.*" Her daughter groans but Mimi overrides her. "*C'est pour monsieur Boucher, va vite, va vite.*"

Madeleine returns with her big red, white and black beast. Vic seats himself in a lawn chair, settles it onto his broad lap, undoes the snaps to let it inhale, then proceeds to bounce and hug the music out of it, elbows working the bellows, stocky fingers flying up and down the keys. Before long he has the children singing with him, then the women join in and so does Steve Ridelle. The young couple next door come out and join the crowd with their infant.

Madeleine sings *"Alouette"* with the others, and wonders where Colleen Froelich is. Did she do something bad and have to stay home? Is she spying on us right now?

Vic strikes up a jig, and Mimi sings, "'*Swing la bottine dans l'fond d'la bôite à bois.*'" Mike dashes behind the house and returns with the baseball bat. He holds it end to end and jumps over it back and forth in double time to the music, like a wild boy, throwing it up, catching it, step-dancing. Mimi whoops, everyone claps time. Madeleine is painfully proud. She watched her boy cousins and one of her big huge uncles do the same dance this summer while Tante Yvonne played accordion—except in Acadie they used an axe handle, not a bat.

Across the lawn, Jack and Henry join in the applause. Then Henry fills his pipe, tamps it down, tops it up, tamps it down. Jack takes out a pack of White Owl cigars and lights up. "You know, Henry, there is nothing I'd like better than to get rid of these things altogether. All the nukes. Hell of a thing to leave our kids. But we can't stick our heads in the sand. What about the missile gap?"

"If you believe in this gap." Froelich finally strikes a match, stroking the open bowl of his pipe with the flame, puffing it to life.

"Can we afford not to believe it?"

"Even their Secretary of Defense does not believe it."

"Yeah, McNamara backtracked pretty quick on that one, eh? Still, you never know what they've got in the pipeline." Jack spits out a speck of tobacco. "What's that you're smoking, Hank? Smells familiar." More acrid than Amphora, a Continental edge to it—dark, as opposed to milk, chocolate.

"Von Eicken. Deutsch tobacco."

"That explains it."

"Eisenhower warned his country it could be very dangerous to make a war economy during peacetime."

"Are we living in peacetime?" asks Jack, aiming a stream of smoke up into the deepening blue of twilight.

"Right here? Right now? Oh yes."

Jack nods a little, in time with the music—*If you're happy and you know it clap your hands, if you're happy and you know it clap your hands, if you're happy and you know it and you really want to show it. . . .*

"*Friede,*" says Froelich.

Jack looks at him sharply, then recalls. Of course. *Peace.* "You know, Henry, we can ban the bomb and do all that good stuff but we can't stop mankind exploring."

"You want very badly to go to the moon, my friend." The stem of Froelich's pipe is moist; his face has filled out with conversation, shadows turned to creases.

"Come on, Henry, you're a scientist—"

"I was."

"How can you not be excited about it? Pure research—"

"There is no such thing. Some questions receive funds, others do not. Who is rich enough to ask the questions?"

"Yeah but just imagine how it'll change our point of view if we do get there."

"The world will still be a dangerous place, perhaps more so if—"

"That's where you're wrong," says Jack, his cigar unfurling slowly. "Think how our petty wars are going to look from nearly three hundred thousand miles up. Think how we're going to feel flying through the dark. Can you imagine? Dead silence. And way down there behind us, there's the earth. A beautiful blue speck, lit up like a sapphire. We won't give a damn then who's a Russian or who's a Yank or whether you're red, white, black or green. We might finally figure out that we're all just people and we've all just got one shot at it, you know? This little life." He glances over at the others, gathered round the music. Mimi has her eyes closed, singing with Vic. "*Un Acadien errant*—a wandering Acadian—*banni de son pays*—banished from his country. . . ." The mournful minor key of folk songs the world over.

Henry Froelich says, "This is a beautiful idea."

Jack looks at him. The man looks sad all of a sudden, and Jack wonders what he has seen in his time. In his war. He is of an age to have seen a great deal. Past fifty, easily. Old enough to remember the first one—The Great War. Men who fought tend not to talk about it, but they readily acknowledge that they are veterans, even to a former enemy. Indeed, by now a fellow feeling exists among pilots who once strove to shoot each other out of the sky. But Jack cannot picture Froelich in uniform. He was more likely part of the war effort at an industrial level. Jack can easily see him on a factory floor: white shirt and clipboard, peering into the guts of a jet engine. Is he atoning for something? Maybe Centralia is a form of self-exile.

Froelich continues, his voice soft and dark like the black of his beard. "This rocket of yours, Jack, it can do all this perhaps. This is very noble. Very beautiful. Like a poem. But it does not come from a beautiful place, it comes from. . . ." He appears to have lost his train of thought. He glances about, takes a breath, raises his eyebrows briefly and recovers it. "You think it will take us up to heaven, *ja?* But it does not come from there." He taps his pipe. "Also it is very expensive. Unfortunately only war is rich enough to pay for such a beautiful poem."

Froelich pours himself more wine.

"Has it ever occurred to you, Jack, this? That Apollo is named for the sun? And yet the project is aimed at his sister, Artemis, the moon?"

Froelich looks at him, waiting for an answer.

"You got me there, Henry."

"Once upon a time there was a mountain cave. And inside the cave was a treasure." There is a glint in Froelich's eye. Jack waits. Is it possible his neighbour is a little drunk? "You see Jack, it is a fact that only the bowels of the earth can provide us with the means to propel ourselves toward the sun. Someone has to forge the arrows of Apollo. Even as someone had to build the pyramids. Slaves, yes? Which one of God's angels is rich enough, do you think, to pay for our dream to fly so high we may glimpse perhaps the face of God?"

Across the lawn, Vic and Mimi sing the second verse: "*Un Canadien errant*" . . . a wandering Canadian . . . if you see my country, my unhappy country, go and tell my friends that I remember them. . . .

"Tell me something, Henry. What are you doing here?"

"Oh well, after the war I met my wife in Germany, she volunteered at the U.N. camp where I—"

"No, I mean how come you're not teaching at a university somewhere?"

Jack fears he has been rude to his guest—he has known the man less than twenty-four hours and now he's grilling him. But Jack is used to getting to know people quickly. Because you do only get one life, and if someone can give you a tour of a road not taken, why would you not seize the chance? "I'm sorry, Henry, it's none of my business."

"No, it is a very good question, and I have a very good answer." Froelich smiles and the hard glint leaves his eye. He reminds Jack of pictures he has seen in *National Geographic* of emaciated holy men. Serene, starved. He answers: "I have everything I want right here."

Jack follows Froelich's gaze over to Karen, picking up the babies in the grass. To his daughter in her wheelchair.

"Cheers," says Jack.

"*Prost.*"

They drink.

The singsong has changed tempo again. Betty is warbling in a Cockney accent to her husband's accordion accompaniment, "'Will you love me when I'm mutton as you do now I am lamb?!'" Laughter, applause. And a lull—the children are gone. A few minutes ago, as though at some signal inaudible to the adult ear, they ran off, pelting down the street in the direction of the school. The lawn is suddenly peaceful and the women draw a collective sigh of relief. "Silence is golden," says Elaine. Betty's younger two are in the McCarthys' house, asleep on the couch.

Karen Froelich, having taken her babies home, has returned for Elizabeth. "Thanks, Mimi, it was a really nice get-together."

"Oh Karen, you're not leaving already."

"Yeah, come on over any time." She turns, saying to her husband, "Have fun, Hank."

Jack watches Froelich kiss his wife and say something in her ear as he lightly holds her hand. Again there is a certain quality in her expression, not precisely sad but as though she were smiling at something in the distance, or perhaps the past. She touches her husband's chest briefly. Jack watches her walk away, pushing the wheelchair over the grass. She is pretty when she smiles.

"Jack."

"What's that, Hank?"

"You make a nice party. Thank you."

Vic gets out from under the accordion, stretches his legs and reaches into his burlap sack.

"I'll put the kettle on," says Betty.

Elaine hands her cocktail glass to her husband. "Just a teeny one."

Vimy and Hal Woodley say their good nights—they're expecting a long distance call from their daughter at university, and in any case it wouldn't do for them to be the last to leave. With their departure a further slight relaxation sets in.

Vic upends his burlap bag onto the grass with a clatter. Jack asks Henry if Vic Boucher always travels with his own game of horseshoes, and Froelich replies, "I don't know. This is my first time to have a social occasion with him. And Dr. Ridelle too—Steve."

Froelich has lived in the PMQs longer than any of them, yet he has socialized so little. Perhaps this is the first time anyone has asked him about his real subject of "how things go." Jack senses that Froelich is a conversational treasure trove. You can almost feel the congenial heat of a fireplace when the man warms to his subject. And the sparks of impatience when he's going full tilt. Typical German, thinks Jack. Now that he knows how much Henry likes to talk, he will pick another argument at the first opportunity. He watches Vic drive the metal post into the lawn with his foot and reflects that it just goes to show you'll never find out anything if you don't ask—Vic comes up to them, gold and silver horseshoes in hand, "Gentlemen, *faites vos jeux*"—you could be living next door to an Einstein or a Picasso and never know it. It's important to know your neighbours. In the air force especially, because, in the absence of family and old friends, neighbours are what you have.

Froelich takes a horseshoe and raises it to eye level, taking aim. A burst of laughter from the women reaches them, the steel horseshoe glints in Henry's hand, sterling in the late summer sun like the wing of an aircraft, and Jack is suffused with happiness. Pure and untethered by any good reason, happiness born of this warm evening, the proximity of friends—brand-new yet so deeply familiar—the smell of grass and tobacco, the dying coals of the barbecue, the deep blue dome above, sunlight on silver in his neighbour's hand. He blinks into the big sun over the horizon because tears have come to his eyes and, to his mind, the words of a poem he learned years ago.

*Oh, I have slipped the surly bonds of earth*
*And danced the skies on laughter-silvered wings;*
*Sunward I've climbed and joined the tumbling mirth*
*Of sun-split clouds—done a hundred things*
*You have not dreamed of—wheeled and soared and swung*
*High in the sunlit silence. Hov'ring there*
*I've chased the shouting wind along and flung*
*My eager craft through footless halls of air.*
*Up, up the long delirious, burning blue*
*I've topped the wind-swept heights with easy grace,*
*Where never lark, or even eagle, flew;*
*And, while with silent, lifting mind I've trod*
*The high untrespassed sanctity of space,*
*Put out my hand and touched the face of God.*

The young air force pilot who wrote the poem also had an accident while training, and never got to go operational. He was killed. Jack watches the horseshoe leave his neighbour's hand.

QUICK, EVERYONE RUN to the schoolyard, there's a guy down there with a motor scooter and he's giving people rides!

This was the information picked up by kid radar that drew Madeleine and the others from the barbecue and the singsong, and sent them tearing down the street like wildlife from a burning forest. Before they could see it they heard the engine, revving like a souped-up lawnmower. They cut through between the houses at the bottom of the street and into the freshly mown field toward the school, where a crowd had gathered. There must have been at least fifty kids of all ages, on bikes, trikes, wagons and on foot—and beyond them, zipping past, his head and shoulders visible above the throng, a dark-haired boy. A teenager.

"Oh my God!" cried Auriel and crumpled.

Lisa likewise crumpled. "Ricky Froelich!" They burst into giggles, joined hands and ran toward the playground, turning to shriek, "Madeleine, hurry up!"

As Madeleine caught up, Auriel grabbed her hand, and the three of them ran in a line like cut-out dolls in time to see Ricky Froelich, on his red motor scooter, zoom off behind the school with a little kid on the back. Madeleine could also see that Mike had already barged to the front of the crowd with Roy Noonan. Music was coming from some-where—someone must have a transistor radio. Auriel seized Madeleine's arm. "There's Marsha Woodley."

"She babysits us," hissed Lisa urgently.

"Us too," Auriel hastily put in.

Marsha Woodley. Over by the swings, remote and serene, the CO's daughter. Flanked by two girlfriends. Twin-sets, penny loafers and ponytails. Marsha wears her cardigan draped around her shoulders, buttoned at the top, a pleated skirt and ankle socks. These girls don't attend J.A.D. McCurdy, they go on the bus to high school. High atop Mount Olympus. The transistor is in Marsha's hand—Dion's irre-sistibly swaggering voice—"'Well I'm the type o' guy who will never settle down. . . .'"

The motor scooter zooms back and deposits the little kid, and the crowd closes in. "Ricky! I'm next, take me, Ricky!"

He dismounts. A tall boy in faded jeans and a red cowboy shirt. Dreamboat. Colleen's brother—and Elizabeth's. Holy mackerel.

Auriel shoves Madeleine forward. "Ask him for a ride!"

"You ask him, you love him."

"I do not!" squeals Auriel and swats Madeleine.

Madeleine watches as Ricky lets Mike sit on the scooter by himself and twist the throttle. Auriel murmurs, "He doesn't even know I'm alive." Ricky trots alongside the scooter, holding Mike steady.

Lisa says, "Your brother's cute."

"Yuck!" cries Madeleine, shocked.

"Oh Mikey," swoons Auriel, and begins kissing her own arm.

Lisa succumbs to her raspy laugh and likewise smooches her arm: "Oh Ricky, oh Rock!"

Auriel erupts in giggles, barely able to speak. "Oh Cary Grant! Oh Gina Lollobrigida!" The two of them fall down.

Madeleine looks at her friends. They have lost their minds. Dion floats on the air, carefree and insinuating—as she watches Mike take off on his own around the schoolyard, his face red—he is trying not to smile. "They call me the wanderer, yeah I'm the wanderer, I roam around 'n' round, 'n' round, 'n' round. . . ."

Madeleine says, "Do you dare me to ask for a ride?"

Auriel and Lisa sober up immediately.

As Mike comes to a stop, Madeleine walks through the crowd and straight up to Ricky Froelich. "Can I have a try?"

"Not by herself," says Mike in his deepest voice, "she's too little."

"Mike, I am not!"

"She's my sister."

Ricky climbs back onto the scooter and turns to Madeleine. He has shiny black hair and dark brown eyes, his shirt is open at the collar. His Adam's apple moves as he says to her, "Hop on, pal."

Madeleine gets on the back and grasps the bar behind her. He twists the throttle and she feels herself jerked back as they accelerate across the pavement, then onto the field—it's exactly the way she imagines surfing must feel, the rubber wheels riding waves of grass, the soft seat vibrating beneath her. "Hang onto me," he calls over his shoulder, and speeds up. She slips her hands around his waist and threads her fingers across his stomach, warm and firm beneath his soft shirt. Her hands feel small. Panels of muscle stiffen as he leans into a turn, the feel of them reminds Madeleine of how boys look in their bathing suits—smooth chests, arc of ribcage just visible, and that line down the middle of their stomachs. . . .

"You okay back there?"

"Yeah," she calls.

She cannot stop smiling, her forehead against his billowing shirt, glad he cannot see her. Her hair lifts in the breeze, she leans her cheek against his shoulder blade and smells baby powder, Brylcreem; sees the sinews of his tanned forearm shift with each movement of his wrist, turning the throttle, squeezing the brake.

They speed from the grass onto asphalt and around the swings, while far away it seems the crowd of kids watches and the transistor plays. Is this what it's like to be in a movie? To feel so private, yet with a huge audience watching?

She leans with him as they round the school, hangs on a little tighter, feels the pearly snaps of his shirt beneath her fingers; there is no time, there is only now, the sound of a motor, the breeze on her arms, the warmth of the soaked-up sun radiating from his back, the ease of his voice singing along. They come out from around the school into the full tilt of the evening sun and the ride is done.

Madeleine climbs off, her legs trembling, a stranger to gravity. She doesn't think to thank him. She is deaf to the admiration of Auriel and Lisa. She rejoins the crowd and watches with her friends, but she feels like an emptied glass—that crestfallen feeling of walking out from a movie theatre in the middle of the day, out from the intimate matinée darkness and the smell of popcorn, which is the smell of heightened colour and sound and story, into the borderless bright of day. Bereft.

He gives a ride to every kid who wants one. Auriel, beaming and beet-red; Lisa, mute with pleasure. He even gives Marjorie Nolan a ride—she has no qualms about screaming and throwing her arms around him on the pretext of being afraid of falling off. And she hangs onto his hand after her ride is done, sticking to him, trying to drag him off his bike.

Through it all, Marsha Woodley watches, exchanging murmurs with her girlfriends, who squeal every time he buzzes the swings. Marsha doesn't squeal. She smiles and looks off to the side. Tucks a strand of hair behind her ear. Licks the corner of her mouth. Pale pink lipstick.

Finally, Ricky wheels the scooter up to Marsha. He dismounts and holds it steady for her as she gets on, and this time he gets on behind her so she won't have to straddle the seat in her skirt. He reaches his arms around her to grasp the handlebars, he tweaks the throttle, and they take off. Out of the schoolyard and up Algonquin Drive into the golden light of eight o'clock in summer.

Madeleine feels an ache. In a place she didn't know was part of her body. Starting around the wishbone in her chest and spreading out. A plunging sadness, to do with the scent of hay and motor oil, his billowing shirt and the sight of Marsha Woodley's skirt lapping at her knees. The crowd of kids disperses, and the three girls start for home across the green.

"I'm dying for a fag," says Auriel, and Lisa Ridelle pulls out a pack of Popeye candy cigarettes. The three of them light up and inhale gratefully.

"Sankyou, dahling."

"You're velcome, dahling."

"I'd vok a mile for a Camel."

They walk, the toes of their runners darkening with dew, sucking their candy tubes to a point. Walking parallel some distance away is Marjorie Nolan, shadowing them. Madeleine wonders why she doesn't just come over if she wants to walk with them. "Do you guys know that kid?" she asks.

Auriel looks across at Marjorie. "Not really, she just moved in." Which is surprising, considering that Marjorie was such a know-it-all today.

"Do you know her?" asks Lisa.

"Sorta."

"She looks weird."

"What's her name?" asks Auriel.

"Marjorie," says Madeleine, and then, "Margarine."

Auriel and Lisa laugh and Madeleine feels a twinge. She looks across at Marjorie, who is still not looking. *Fine, don't look, I was going to invite you to walk with us.*

"Margarine!" laughs Lisa, and Madeleine says, "Shhh."

"Yeah, Ridelle," says Auriel, "don't be so mean," then whispers, "Margarine," to fresh gales.

Madeleine laughs along politely. It's okay, Auriel and Lisa aren't the type to call Marjorie that to her face. Still, it's sad to have your name turned into margarine.

Mimi finishes washing the dishes. Jack dries. "That wasn't so bad," he says.

She doesn't look at him but smiles, dries her hands and reaches for a squirt of Jergens.

Mike comes in and opens the fridge. Mimi puts her hands on his head, kisses his crown and says, "*T'as faim? Assis-toi, là.*" He sits at the table and, as Mimi pulls leftovers from the fridge, takes a tiny green army tank from his pocket and proceeds to repair the treads.

"Mike," says Jack, and shakes his head. No toys at the table.

"But Dad, it's not supper or anything."

"It's still your mother's food."

Mike pockets the tank. Jack returns to his *Time* magazine. Mimi places a heaping plate in front of her son. "*Et voilà, mon p'tit capitaine.*"

"*Merci, maman.*"

She lights a cigarette, leans against the counter and watches her son eat. This will be his last year in children's sizes. He has his father's head, his father's way of eating steadily, neatly, the working of the jaw, the set of the shoulders and something about the eyes—though her son's are brown—the same long lashes, and that open quality, the focused unawareness that is masculine innocence. She can almost see the face of the man emerging from that of the boy. Her gaze is a thing of substance. Between a mother's eyes and her son's face, there is not air. There is something invisible and invincible. Even though—or because—he will go out into the world, she will never lose her passion to protect him. Girls are different. They know more. And they don't leave you.

From upstairs, Madeleine's voice, "I'm ready!"

Mimi moves toward the stairs but Jack gets up. "That's okay, I'll tuck her in."


"'And the children disappeared into the mountain, never to be seen again. All except for one child who was lame and could not keep up.'"

Jack closes the book. Madeleine gazes at the illustration—the yellow and red diamonds on the Piper's cloak, his pointed hat, his solemn beautiful face. He doesn't look cruel. He looks sad, as though at the prospect of performing a painful duty.

"What was inside the mountain?" She always asks this when he has finished, and he always considers for a moment, before replying, "Well no one can say for sure. But I think maybe it was like a . . . whole other world."

"Was there a sky?"

"I think there might have been, yeah. And lakes and trees."

"And they never grow up."

"You're probably right. They run around and play, happy as clams."

Meanwhile, in the outside world, their whole family gets old and dies, thinks Madeleine. She doesn't say this, however, because she does not wish to ruin the story for her father. It's the first time since Germany that she has asked him to read to her. She is getting a bit old for it, but it makes her new room feel cozier. And no one has to know.

"You almost ready to fall asleep?"

She hugs him around the neck. "Dad?"

"Yeah, old buddy?"

"Was Elizabeth born retarded?"

"She's not retarded, sweetie."

It's been bothering her. How can Ricky have a retarded sister as well as a delinquent one and yet be perfect?

"What's wrong with her?"

"She has cerebral palsy."

"What's that?"

"She can't control her muscles, but there's nothing wrong with her mind."

Madeleine blinks. Inside Elizabeth's head, she is perfectly normal. What must it be like to watch your hands try to pick something up? To hear your mouth slurring words when you know perfectly well how to say them? Like living in a very small room with a very big window.

"Can you catch it?" she asks.

"No, no, you're born with it."

"Oh."

"It doesn't mean you can't have a good life," he says. "She's a pretty happy gal, don't you think?"

" . . . Yeah."

Grown-ups are never frightened by things like that—horrible things that people are born with. Whereas, when you are going on nine, it's as though things from before you were born could still reach out and grab you by the ankle. You can feel the whoosh of how they just missed you.

"Have a good sleep, old buddy." He kisses her forehead.

"Kiss Bugs," she says, and he does.

She does not ask him if Mr. Froelich is a Nazi. It's a rude question to ask so late at night, after such a nice day. And she knows what he'll say: "No-o-o, what gave you that idea?" And she will have to answer, "Mike did," and Mike will get in trouble. Still, she would like to hear it from her own father that there is not a Nazi living across the street. "Hitler's still alive, you know," said Mike. And he told her how Goebbels killed his children with poisoned cocoa. *Goebbels*. It's what turkeys say. "Mr. Froelich could be a Nazi hiding out here," he said. "You can tell if he's SS, 'cause they have tattoos." But you can't see any tattoos on Mr. Froelich because of his long sleeves.

Dad switches off the light. "Sweet dreams."

"Dad, is Hitler dead?"

"Dead as a doornail."

She slides down under her blanket, savouring the smell of grass stains on her knees and elbows. A summer holiday night; she rode on a red motor scooter with a real live teenager, Hitler is dead, Elizabeth Froelich is not retarded, and school starts next week.

ONCE UPON A TIME, in a country that no longer exists, there was a mountain cave. And inside the cave was a treasure. Slaves worked to mount up more and more and more treasure. They worked day and night in the bowels of the earth, and fashioned the things of the earth into something celestial. They used the products of the earth: animals that had died billions of years ago were exhumed and refined; chemicals that had hidden in earth and air were caught, distilled and carefully recombined—these became its fuel. Minerals that had been harvested from the earth were purified by fire until they were strong and stainless, then forged into many shapes—this became its skin, its brain, its vital organs.

Everything has come from Mother Earth in this way. Cars, ploughs, televisions, clothes, electricity. Ourselves. Gathered, processed, moulded, ignited. If all this had happened in a flash, we would call it magic—lions freeing themselves from the clay, soldiers springing up from serpents' teeth, lightning snaking from the tip of a wand, language from our mouths.

But it did not happen in a flash. It happened over time. The age of the earth was necessary to create it all, and the minds and bodies of many people, and so it is called science. Humans can only work the magic in reverse. Returning it all to the earth and atmosphere in one great flash.

# STORYBOOK GARDENS

*Teacher: "It's harder teaching kids the alphabet these days."*
*Second Teacher: "That's right. They all think V comes after T."*
"Your Morning Smile," The Globe and Mail, *1962*

THE LITTLE ORANGE TENT in the Bouchers' backyard casts a magic glow in the afternoon. It's almost like being in a movie. The canvas smell, the close-up sound, full of promise, the frisson of truth-or-dare. Strewn with Archie Comics and Classics like *Water Babies,* and the jewel of Auriel's collection: the stack of *True Romance* comics which she inherited from her babysitter at their last posting, worn but intact, with their lavish drawings of blondes, brunettes and men with brutal jaws and sleek automobiles. The illustrated women cry gushy white tears. "It looks like Jergens," says Madeleine.

The opportunities for scorn are as endless and absorbing as the comics are seductive. The pup tent begins to feel like a den of iniquity. Madeleine is frozen, fascinated and appalled when Lisa closes her eyes, crosses her arms over her chest and says, "Oh Ricky, I'm dying, please kiss me." And Auriel does, right on the lips. Then Auriel dies, and Lisa is Ricky kissing her. Madeleine says, "Pretend I'm a spy and you're torturing me, okay? And I kill you and escape and Auriel is waiting with a stolen Nazi uniform. . . ." Mrs. Boucher always calls them after about half an hour. "Come and get some fresh air now, girls."

It is not wholesome to spend the entire afternoon in a pup tent.

These are the dying days of summer. This time next week, we'll be writing compositions entitled, "What I Did on My Summer Vacation." Our mosquito bites will still be itchy, still chalky pink with calamine lotion, but we'll be wearing shoes and socks, packaged into our new clothes, inserted at our desks in a row in a grade four classroom. Grade four. The bewildered days of kindergarten are so far behind. We are losing sight of the retreating shoreline of early childhood. It felt like the whole world; it was merely a speck. On the horizon is a land mass called adolescence. And between here and there, an archipelago of middle childhood. Swim from island to island, find the edible fruit, luxuriate in lagoons of imagination but don't get caught in a riptide close to shore, do not yield to a warm current; you'll be swept away with the sea turtles, who live so long and swim so far and don't know how to drown. When you are eight going on nine, you get stronger every day. You wake up more and more into the real world and yet it's as though,

around your head, there still float remnants of fairy tales, tattered articles of faith in talking animals and animated teacups. A rag-halo of
dreams.

Madeleine was kneeling next to her father on the couch, rubbing
his head while he read *Time* magazine. She asked, "Dad, what's a
dyke?"

"You know what that is, you saw them in Holland—"

"No," and she reads over his shoulder from the cinema listings.
"'When a rake and a dyke fall in love with the same girl, almost anything can happen—'"

"Oh, that's a—that's a—a type of garden tool."

Unconvinced but reluctant to hurt his feelings, she asked her mother
while she was helping to set the table.

"It's a woman who's sick in the head," answered Mimi flatly. "Where
did you hear that word?"

Madeleine replied, in the aggrieved tones of the wrongfully accused,
"I read it in *Time* magazine!"

"Lower your voice. Jack? What's she been reading?"

Jack said he figured it was about time to plug in the television set.
Madeleine cheered and ran outside to find her brother.

When Jack adjusted the rabbit ears, not one but three channels came
in clear as a bell, a fourth snowy but watchable. The Canadian
Broadcasting Corporation—CBC—and three from New York state:
NBC, ABC and the fuzzy one, CBS.

Maman's rule: "There's to be no eating dinner in front of the TV in
this house."

Dad's: "There's to be no TV while the sun's shining outside."

Then the whole family settled in to watch *Walt Disney's Wonderful
World of Color,* in black and white.

For Madeleine, it is exquisite agony to watch the child actors who
befriend the curious and resourceful young cougars and stray dogs. She
burns as boys in dungarees become trapped in abandoned mine shafts,
and girls nurse injured horses back to blue-ribbon health. How did
those kids get to be in those shows? How can I get there? They are
American, for one thing.

"When you're older you can move to Hollywood and become an
entertainer," says her father. But Madeleine doesn't want to wait. She
yearns for a career now. In show business. It keeps her awake at night.
Television fuels the flames. Bob Hope and Bing Crosby in their striped
jackets, straw hats and canes, cracking jokes and tap dancing. George
Jessel and his cigar. Baleful Rodney Dangerfield, sorrowful Red

Skelton; Don Rickles barking, Phyllis Diller carping, Anne Meara deadpanning, Joan Rivers rasping, Lucille Ball wailing. Madeleine doesn't get most of the jokes but she gets the big thing, which is: they are funny.

Afterwards, in bed with a book, the spell of television feels remote compared to the journey into the page. To be in a book. To slip into the crease where two pages meet, to live in the place where your eyes alight upon the words to ignite a world of smoke and peril, colour and serene delight. That is a journey no one can end with the change of a channel. Enduring magic. She opens *Peter Pan*.

The intoxication of television, the passion of new friendship, the yearning for Neverland and the smell of new clothes on the racks at Simpson's in downtown London, Ontario. All combine and accelerate to lift and spin her through the last weekend before school.

After back-to-school shopping in London, the McCarthys buy a picnic lunch at the big Covent Market building in the centre of town. *Wurst* and *Brötchen* from the Bavarian Delikatessen, where the ruddy-cheeked owners make a gratifying fuss over Madeleine and Mike. The smell of smoked meats and cheeses, fresh bread and mustard—it's the smell of a Sunday drive through the Black Forest, right here in southern Ontario.

"Small world," says Jack, when he finds out that the store owners knew the German bartender at the officers' mess in 4 Wing. Son of a gun.

They eat their picnic at Storybook Gardens. A park at the edge of town, on the Thames River, it resembles a miniature Disneyland. There is a wooden castle with drawbridge and a little choo-choo train that runs on a real track and carries passengers under twelve around the park. There are life-size figures from nursery rhymes—the butcher, the baker and the candlestick maker rock in their tub, Humpty Dumpty teeters on his wall, a dish runs away with a spoon. A big bad plaster wolf threatens three real live pigs who root about and live in miniature houses of brick, wood and straw, and a life-size witch smiles from the door of her candy-coated house. Unlike the Pied Piper, there is no room for hope that the witch may be good after all. Madeleine is disconcerted by the conspicuous absence of Hansel and Gretel. It implies that either the witch has succeeded in eating them, or they have yet to arrive; in which case, "Come here, little girl, you'll do very well." On the grounds there is also a greenhouse with tropical flowers, of interest only to adults.

When they return to the parking lot, a sticker has been applied to the rear bumper of the Rambler. Mimi finds it presumptuous—nothing like that would happen in Europe. Madeleine gazes at the sticker: bright yellow, it features the turreted outline of Storybook Castle and the path leading up to it, paved like Dorothy's yellow brick road.

On their way home, Jack takes the opportunity to happen onto Morrow Street.

"Why are we turning here?" asks Mimi.

"Just getting the lay of the land. You never know, we might want to retire here one day." He feels Mimi's hand stroke the back of his head, and he slows as they pass a yellow brick low-rise at the end of a leafy cul-de-sac. Number 472. Manicured lawn and hedge, kidney-shaped flower beds. Mums. A circular drive leads to the front doors, which are sheltered by a porte cochère.

"I don't know if I'm ready for that kind of excitement yet," says Mimi.

The place is like a mausoleum. Perfect. As the building recedes in the rearview mirror, Jack feels a butterfly stir in his stomach. He says, "Who wants ice cream?" A cheer goes up in the back seat.

"Jack," says Mimi, "we've had a lot of treats today already."

But it's too late. From the back seat, Madeleine chants, "I scream, you scream, we all scream for ice cream!" Mimi raises an eyebrow at her husband. Madeleine continues: "'Are you tired and listless? Take Dodd's Little Liver Pills for fast, effective relief.'"

Mimi and Jack exchange a look, suppressing a laugh. She says to her daughter in the mirror, "I hope you listen half so well in school this year."

## REMEMBER-WHENS

ON SUNDAY MORNING, Jack gets through the sermon at Mass by recalling Mimi in bed last night. Madeleine gets through by imagining how she would go about scaling the interior walls to the ceiling. Jack calculates in his mind how much he would need to put aside every week in order to buy his wife a mink coat. Every Christmas she warns him, as she prepares to unwrap her presents, "It better not be a you-know-what," and throws the box at him if he has spent too much on her. She always throws the box, and sometimes weeps if it is just *trop beau*. What better thanks could a man hope for? It's difficult, however, to squirrel away money when your wife is the comptroller of the family. Madeleine tugs the strangulating organza at her neck and imagines escaping on a motorcycle with Steve McQueen through a hail of bullets. ". . . Go in peace," says the priest.

"Come here, Mimi."

"Jack, what are you doing?"

"On your feet, woman."

"Oh Jack." And they dance. Three o'clock on Sunday afternoon. The priest has just left. He was here for brunch, and now Jack has put the soundtrack to *South Pacific* on the hi-fi.

"Let's get outta here," Madeleine says to Mike.

"Come here, you."

"Dad!" And she dances with her father.

"You dance divinely, Missy."

"Sissy," Mike rhymes from the couch, for which he gets a look from Jack. A complicit look that says, being a gentleman is part of being manly even though it might seem sissyish now.

Madeleine lowers her eyes, not to look at her feet but to hide her delight as she lifts one hand to her father's shoulder and places the other in his. When she was little she used to put her feet on his, but she is older now and her new patent-leather Mary Janes step in time with his Daks. She is still in her lacerating dress of pink spun glass, but has ceased complaining because Maman keeps telling her to offer up her suffering for the poor souls in purgatory. How many years off one's time in the purifying flames can be bought by eight-year-old girls in scratchy dresses? The saving grace of this getup is Madeleine's white Communion gloves: ribbed on the back like Bugs Bunny's. *Nyah, offer it up, doc.* That was flippant, sorry, dear God.

Jack says to her, "That's it, don't think about it, just relax and feel the music." They sweep together gracefully around the coffee table and he sings along softly with "Some Enchanted Evening". . . . Mimi joins in.

"Mike, dance with your mother," says Jack.

"*Voulez-vous danser, maman?*" And he offers her his hand.

"*Que t'es beau, Michel.*" Mimi resists kissing her son and they dance. She is teaching him to lead.

She puts on a big-band record she bought in nurses' training in Montreal. Chick Webb and his orchestra. Demon on the drums. "Time to cut the rug," she says, pushing back the coffee table.

They watch their parents jive, dangerously close to the crystal roosters from Spain, perilously grazing the oil painting of the Alps, rattling the end tables where the Hummels share pride of place with the Royal Doultons.

Mike and Madeleine take turns being whipped around like spaghetti at the end of their mother's arm—she looks fiercely serious one second and the next she is laughing like a teenager—at times like this, she seems more like a babysitter than their mother. "It's a wild party!" shouts Madeleine, and she and Mike dance in a frenzy, *wash-the-dishes-dry-the-dishes-turn-the-dishes-over!* Dad laughs until his face turns red and his gold tooth flashes. He snaps a picture. Maybe this Christmas we'll get a home movie camera.

After supper, a solemn rite. To do with love and loss. The loss of the past, and its transformation into precious memory. This alchemical feat always includes popcorn.

There is nothing so persuasive to deep recall as the hum of the slide projector in the dark. The audible fuzz that follows each colour slide as it sh-clinks into view. The longer ago the picture, the longer the moment of silence before Dad's cheerful voice in the dark: "That was a beautiful day, remember that day, Maman?"

A picnic among the pines of the Schwarzwald. Maman sitting on the plaid blanket, legs folded sideways, sunglasses and white kerchief. A tenderer-looking Mike, Madeleine with her long braids, squinting at the camera.

*Sh-clink.* It is not remembering so much as not forgetting. Madeleine contemplates the slides intently. Reverently. Each is an emblem of a vanished world. A doorway in a mountain, sealed forever.

*Sh-clink.* Monaco. The pink palace where Princess Grace lives. "That was the day I broke my heel and you got so mad at me," Mimi says to Jack. Certain things must be remembered after each slide. The pastry we had there, Madeleine got lost on the beach here—"I wasn't lost, I went for a walk."

"That was one of the nicest holidays ever, remember, kids?"

*Sh-clink.* Camping on the Riviera. Jack's crumpled straw hat and four-day growth of beard. "The best accommodation in Europe costs you either a thousand francs or five."

*Sh-clink.* "The fruitcake!" Grandmaman's fruitcake, which had been mailed from Canada the previous Christmas and took a whole year to arrive. Still moist and rummy. "A piece of that fruitcake every day, boy, I tell you you'd live forever," says Jack, as he always does.

"That was one of the nicest Christmases ever, remember Jack?" says Mimi.

"I remember."

*Sh-clink.* Alberta. "How'd that one slip in there?" says Jack. A tiny bundled Madeleine in a baby carriage perched atop a snowbank.

"I remember that," she says.

"You do not," says Mike.

"Do so!"

*Sh-clink.* Hameln. They have not looked at this slide before, so there are no comments that go with it yet. It is of Madeleine and Jack standing in front of the statue of the Pied Piper.

"There's Uncle Simon."

Jack says, "Where?"

Madeleine gets up and points at the screen, where a shadow spills across her father's trouser leg and the skirt of her dress—the silhouette of head and raised elbows. Simon, taking the picture.

This is one thing Madeleine has on Mike; she has met Simon. He taught their father to fly. He told her to call him "Uncle." He is a decorated veteran. He laughed at everything she said and asked her to come work for him. He did not look exactly like David Niven but that's who she has come to associate him with—the kind of dashing grown-up who might offer you a cocktail and think nothing of it. He said, "The best spy of the Second World War was a woman, did you know that?" And told her about a member of the French Resistance, Jeannie Rousseau—pronounced "Johnny." "Do you know what her code name was?"

"No."

"It was 'Madeleine.'"

She smiled shyly but she could feel her destiny stirring.

Johnny told the Allies about Hitler's secret weapon. "The V-2 rocket," said Uncle Simon. "That's why we were able to bomb their factory."

"Operation Hydra," said her father. "You were in on that show, weren't you, Si?"

Simon just smiled and said, "I and a few others." Then he looked back down at Madeleine. "We'd never have been able to do it without Johnny."

"Did you know her?" asked Madeleine.

"I'm afraid that's classified, old girl." And he laughed.

*Sh-clink.* Blank.

"Time for bed, kids."

"Aw Dad," says Mike, "can't we just have one more tray? Can we just see the hockey slides?"

The boring hockey slides from Cold Lake, Alberta. Backyard rinks and arenas and Mike and his friends with frozen snot, poised over their hockey sticks, no girls allowed. "Not the hockey, Mike!" Madeleine is suddenly savage.

"Temper down, now," says Dad gently.

"Yeth, the hockey," says Mike. "He shootth, he thcores! He-he-he-HA-ha!"

Mike can't even do Woody Woodpecker—"Shut up!" she screams.

"*Allons, les enfants, c'est assez!*"

"Come here, old buddy." And she goes to him. He picks her up. She hooks her pajama legs around his waist. She is too old to be carried upstairs to bed; she is so delighted and mortified that she mashes her face against his shoulder, but not before glimpsing Mike mouth the word "baby" at her, with his eyes crossed.

"Tell me a story, Dad," she says, using as mature a voice as possible.

"It's late, old buddy, you have to be fresh as a daisy tomorrow to start grade four."

Four. A benevolent number, brown and reasonable. Her school dress and ankle socks are laid out over a chair with her new shoes on the floor. It's as though she herself had sat down in the chair and disappeared, leaving only her clothes.

"Just one story, Dad, please." She still has her arms around his neck from when he leaned down to kiss her good night, he is her prisoner.

"Just one," he says.

"Tell me the story of the crash."

"Why do you want to hear that again, why don't we read. . . ." And he reaches for her *Treasury of Fairytales*.

"No Dad, the crash." This is not a once-upon-a-time type of evening.

"All right then. But after that, *schlafen.*"

There are some stories you can never hear enough. They are the same every time you hear them—but you are not. That's one reliable way of understanding time.

He sits on the edge of her bed. "It was right here in Centralia. . . ."

The story of the crash is already changing with you; it used to begin, *It was on a little training station called Centralia, way out in the back of beyond.*

"I was flying lead in formation. . . ." At the controls of his Anson trainer. Getting ready to join a bomber stream sixty miles long over the English Channel.

Madeleine rests her cheek on the pillow and gazes at his belt buckle, a fly perfectly preserved in amber. It's good to gaze at an object and listen to a story.

"I was coming in for a landing. . . ." In a month he'd be flying ops. At the controls of a Lancaster bomber—a real beauty of a beast. Suited up in full gear complete with Mae West—the buxom life-preserver for those fortunate enough to bail out over water.

"I was on final approach. . . ." Four other aircraft were set to land after him. Normally he would have a small crew in training on board but that day he was alone.

"I was flying the old twin-engine Anson. . . ." A very forgiving little aircraft, unless you're ground-looping on the tarmac—lovely in the sky, but a handful on the ground.

"The sky was clear as a bell. . . ." It's overcast but the ceiling is high, visibility good. Most pilots will fly their missions in clear moonlight over the Channel, slow and heavy with six tons of bombs to put on the target five hours away. They'll see their own shadows rippling across the grey sea below while watching for German fighters, Messerschmitts mainly, as the crust of Europe comes into view: patchwork fields and spires below like a diorama, visibility augmented by the criss-crossing cones of German searchlights, by the flames of each other's airplanes caught in the sticky web of light, the spritz and arc of anti-aircraft fire. And far below, their bombs tilting away, tumbling like dominoes toward earth, ending in soundless puffs of smoke. Some will make it back to Yorkshire—better to be hit on the way back, with less fuel and an empty bomb bay. If they're lucky enough to be hit but remain airworthy, they might be able to put out the flames by diving. If not, and they're lucky enough still to be alive, they and their crew might be able to squeeze past the equipment that crowds the narrow cabin and try to get out, climbing up the aircraft as it spins earthward. They rarely think about this. No one talks about it.

"I got clearance from the tower, so I banked left and started bringing her in for a landing. . . ." This time next month I'll be in England.

"Down below on the tarmac I saw another Anson rolling away from the flight line, and I took it for granted he was headed for the taxiway. . . ." The airstrips are black with recent rain but it isn't raining now, a bit slippery, no big deal. His worst fear has been that he will be sentenced to instructor school rather than posted overseas—the trick is to be good, but not too good. . . .

"At about a hundred and fifty feet I saw the Anson roll past the taxiway and turn onto the runway right smack dab where I was headed. . . ." Unconcerned as a bug on a leaf, the yellow aircraft below makes a slow right turn onto the runway and begins to pick up speed. "And I said to myself, what the heck is he doing?" *Something's fouled up.* "But there wasn't much time to think. . . ." Too late for Jack to go around again, and at one hundred feet a decision occurs in his central nervous system, causing his hand to pull up hard and lean right on the stick. "I figured I'd pour on the power, bank and get the nose up. . . ." His aircraft responds with sixty degrees to the left but no altitude; he is too low and slow for that at fifty feet. His port wing clips the edge of the landing strip, he cartwheels into the field, yellow plywood splintering off in all directions, *let her go,* he thinks, *less to catch fire,* he thinks, because at that point he has plenty of time to think, five spinning seconds. "But she spun in and there I was, tail over teakettle in the field."

What is left of his aircraft jams to a stop up on its nose in the dirt. At some point his head has snapped forward into the instrument panel— "I got a pretty good bump on the head"—the knob of the radio dial, most likely. It has all but taken out his eye. "But somebody up there likes me, I thought. . . ." Had he been operational at the time of the accident, he'd have kept his aircrew category—

Madeleine says, "But your eye was bleeding."

"Well I didn't know that then, I just figured I'd banged my head."

—twenty-twenty is nice but not essential, that's why you fly with a crew. All you really have to be able to see is your instrument panel, and Jack can see it fine, it's bent into itself below him. He is suspended over it by his seat belt, big drops of blood are splashing onto the shattered dial faces, the fuel gauge reads low and that's good news, where is the blood coming from? He touches his face. There's a storm raging behind his left eye—

"And Uncle Simon rescued you," says Madeleine.

"That's right."

A sound like a heavy zipper—Simon slices him out of his seat belt and hauls him out. Jack feels the earth travelling backwards beneath his butt—there are his boots bouncing along in front of him, how long have we been travelling like this?

"Simon saw the accident and he was the first one across the field."

Grass rippling past, a pair of elbows hooked under his armpits.

*There's been an accident,* Jack hears his own voice.

*Yes you foolish bastard, there's been a fucking accident.*

*Hi Si. Sorry, sir.*

He hears Simon laugh at the same moment as he glances up to see his yellow airplane—in a headstand twenty-five feet away, skeleton wings drooping—burst into flames like a flower unfolding, burning pollen on the air.

He wakes up in the infirmary. Why is the nurse smiling? Why does Simon offer him a shot of whiskey?

"You did the right thing, mate."

What is there to celebrate? His war is over. It ended thirty yards south of the runway at Number 9 Service Flying Training School, Centralia Aerodrome, April 7, 1943. SNAFU. *Situation Normal All Fouled Up.*

"And you got a medal," says Madeleine.

"That's right, I got my gong."

"But you couldn't fly any more."

"Nope, but it turned out for the best 'cause otherwise I never would have met Maman and you never would have been born, and what would I do without my *Deutsches Mädchen?*" Jack gets up from the bed and leans to tuck the blankets around her.

"Dad, tell the story of Jack and Mimi."

He laughs. "We said one story."

"But it is one story, it's part of the story."

"You're going to be a lawyer when you grow up." He switches off the light.

"Dad, what was the name of that place again?"

"What place?"

"Where Johnny said Hitler's secret weapon was?"

"Johnny . . . ? Oh, that was Peenemünde."

*Pain Amunda.* The name sounds like needles. "Did the Germans capture her?"

"I think so, yeah."

"Did they torture her?"

"No, no . . . she got away." He slips out the door.

"Dad?"

"Yeah?"

"What would've happened if you died in the crash?"

" . . . I didn't die."

"But what if?"

"Well. You wouldn't have been born."

"Where would I be?"

"I don't think you'd be anywhere."

What is worse? Being dead? Or not being born? How come we're afraid to die, but we're not afraid of before we were born? "Dad—?"

"Have a good sleep sweetie, think nice thoughts."

Jack closes her door halfway, to allow light from the hall to spill into her room. He goes to his bedroom and crosses to his dresser without switching on the light. That other Anson never should have been cleared for takeoff. The Air Force Cross was in recognition of his decision, in disregard of his own safety, to peel left into a certain crash, rather than risk trying to overtake the aircraft on the ground and land in front of it—a risk that, had it resulted in a collision with the fuelled-up airplane, would have killed its pilot, its instructor, its student navigator and its wireless operator. Along with Jack. *For valour, courage and devotion to duty whilst flying, though not in active operations against the enemy.* Jack reaches into his drawer and finds what he's looking for.

He crosses the hall to his son's room. On the wall, the Canadian Golden Hawks fly in formation, their gold and red Sabre jets in a starburst. Below the picture, the bed is neatly made, the boy is no slouch. He shakes his head at the new poster, however; where did he get that thing? *The United States Marine Corps Wants You.* Jack has a back-to-school gift for his son: a brand-new "RCAF 4 Fighter Wing" baseball cap from the boy's old team in Germany. He tosses it onto the bed and it bounces. Regulation corners. He smiles and heads downstairs.

His wife and son are sitting at the kitchen table playing gin rummy. Mimi gets up and puts the kettle on. "Jack, would you like a cup of tea?"

He finds his copy of *Time* among Mimi's women's magazines with their hairdos and recipes, and relaxes on the couch. In East Berlin a boy is shot attempting to escape over the "Wall of Shame" and takes an hour to die while people on the west side scream across at the guards to do something. He flips through—the sound of his wife and son chatting in the kitchen is all the more soothing because Jack doesn't understand French—President Kennedy in swim trunks, surrounded by women in bikinis. Infighting at NASA. Jackie Kennedy on waterskis. From the kitchen comes the whistle of the teakettle. Rockets and bikinis, what's the world coming to? Wernher von Braun demonstrates the Saturn booster engine for the President. U.S. military advisers are helping the South Vietnamese in "the most successful operation yet carried out against the Communist Viet Cong." Rocket-size crates on the Havana docks. . . .

Mimi places a cup and saucer on the side table next to him. He registers its arrival as though from a great distance—from the blackness of outer space, so that his failure to say thanks is not rudeness, merely a consequence of a law of physics. *Time*'s view is that Castro could have been easily "erased" if only Kennedy had properly backed the Bay of Pigs invasion last April, which it now terms "a synonym for fiasco."

Jack reaches for his cup. The pundits at *Time* think Kennedy is being soft on Communism, but what do they suggest? An unprovoked invasion? We might as well become Soviet citizens if we're going to adopt their tactics. He turns the page. "*OPINION Toward the Year 2000. The U.S. will defend Canada whether Canada likes it or not. . . .*"

"Jack?"

"What's that?" He looks up from his magazine as though surfacing from sleep.

Mimi is standing over him with the tea pot. She says, "I said, do you want some hot?"

"Oh. Oh, yeah. *Merci.*"

In Madeleine's room the ceramic face of a little Bavarian boy, surprised by a bumblebee on his nose, shields the night light. Tomorrow is the first day of school, the dawn of a bright new era. She closes her eyes. Colours flit rapidly behind her lids. She floats up, the bed listing like a sailboat. Was there really such a person as Peter Pan? If you believe hard enough, will you hear him crowing? Are there still talking ravens? *When I grow up I will have a dog. I will have a red sportscar.* The bed slips gently down the stream . . . *when I grow up. . . .*

THE CROWS WAITED until things had cooled down there. When the blue dress with the girl inside it had become just that, they dropped down—one, two, a third—to stand at a polite distance. And began to work the charms. Tug. Tugging at the bracelet. And one charm was free. The successful crow rose into the air with a flashing silver prize in its beak. Her name. Then the others flew away, and she was left alone.

# Back to School

*Write "all right." Both "all right" and "all wrong" are written as two separate words. Write "all right" and "all wrong" again.*

Macmillan Spelling Series, *1962*

MADELEINE DOES NOT NEED to be walked to school by her father, but it was their first-day-back tradition when she was little. St. Lawrence Avenue is full of kids in new clothes—cotton dresses and ankle socks for the girls, plaid shirts and high-top sneakers for the boys—all freshly ironed, barbered, braided and brushed. Some are being walked to school by their parents, but those kids are younger than Madeleine. She had intended to go with Auriel and Lisa, but at the last minute couldn't bear the thought of Dad watching his old buddy walk away without him.

Jack whistles through his teeth and glances about at the sunny pageant. Madeleine takes his hand to make up for the fact that she would rather not be seen walking hand-in-hand with him to grade four. He winks down at her. "Don't be nervous, old buddy." There is no harm in letting him think that's why she has taken his hand. She smiles for him.

They pass the empty green bungalow on their left. Whoever moves in there will be late for school. Mike is walking up ahead with Roy Noonan, wearing his new 4 Fighter Wing baseball cap over his fresh crewcut. He has a Spiderman comic book in his schoolbag—Madeleine saw him put it there but she didn't tell on him. Her dress has no pockets. It has a panel of crinkly fabric across the chest and a jazzy print of Africans playing bongos on the skirt—it's okay considering that it's a dress. She carries her white cardigan hooked by a finger over her shoulder—this is a less sissy way of carrying a cardigan, it's the way you would carry a bomber jacket if you had one. All she wanted was penny loafers; instead Maman bought the new Mary Janes. There is no way to pretend they are anything else.

She is hot on the outside and chilly on the inside. Butterflies. Her father says the best performers get them on opening night. This is opening day. Fresh scribblers. Fresh kids. Fresh teacher. Fresh self. She longs to let go of his hand and slant away like a kite. "Dad?"

"Yeah?"

"Um. Can you meet me after school and we can walk home together?"

"Don't you think you'll want to be with your buddies by then?"

"No."

"Well, we'll see. You decide at lunchtime, okay?"

She looks up at him, his eyes shaded by his hat brim. "Okay."

He is in his summer uniform. It looks just like his other one except, instead of blue, it's khaki. He wears his hat with the brim pulled a little lower than usual on sunny days to prevent his old eye injury from flaring into a headache. Madeleine loves his uniform—both the khaki and the dress blues—but her favourite part of it is his hat. The badge over the brim is beautiful: a red velvet crown edged in gold braid and beneath it, in brass, the albatross in flight, bold beak facing to its left. Some say it's actually an eagle, and there are still vigorous debates about this in the mess, but according to her father any right-thinking air force man knows it's an albatross. A bird of great good fortune. Unless you happen to kill one. Besides, an eagle is an American symbol.

Above his left breast pocket are sewn his wings. Even if an air force man is no longer a pilot, the wings remain part of his uniform. This spring, if Madeleine gets enough Brownie badges, she will fly up to Girl Guides. Then she too will have a pair of wings to pin proudly over her heart.

"Here we are," he says. The schoolyard. The sound of the crowd rises like a wheel of gulls over a turbulence of bobbing heads, eddies of stripes, polka dots and plaid, the occasional adult sticking up like a spar. Jack surveys the scene, his hand still around Madeleine's. He spots Mike in the crowd and touches the brim of his hat. Mike reciprocates with the bill of his baseball cap.

Madeleine says, "Well, I guess I better go," because it seems that otherwise Dad will wait for the bell.

"All right then." He leans down. "Do your best, sweetie. Do it your way."

She kisses his cheek, smooth Old Spice. "'Bye Dad."

He gives her the thumbs-up.

She enters the crowd, allowing it to close around her. She imagines that if she stood on tiptoe it would carry her along like driftwood. The shrieking is far away and in her ears all at once. She pauses at the swings to look back at her father. He is walking away up Algonquin Drive. She ought to have turned sooner and waved. You never know when will be the last time you see your dad. This could be it. The back of his head, his hat, smooth khaki uniform. *When Dad was alive.* She wants to run and take his hand again—

"Madeleine."

She turns. "Oh, hi Marjorie."

She bends to fiddle with her shoe strap in hopes that Marjorie will go away but Marjorie stays and says, "Oo-day oo-yay ant-way oo-tay o-gay oo-tay y-may ouse-hay or-fay unch-lay?"

"What?"

Marjorie giggles. "It's pig Latin, silly! Ig-pay atin-lay, illy-say!"

"Oh." Madeleine looks past Marjorie to see Colleen Froelich arrive in the schoolyard. Unhurried, face slightly averted. She wears a kilt and blouse that make her tan look darker, her legs harder and leaner. Like a kid someone found in a forest and put clothes onto. She has loafers. Good and scuffed. Madeleine wonders if she has brought her knife to school. Colleen's in grade six.

"Well oo-day oo-yay?"

"What?"

"Do you want to come to my house for lunch?!" Marjorie rolls her eyes with mock impatience. She is wearing a fluffy yellow dress.

"Hafta go home," mumbles Madeleine, scanning the playground, desperate now for a sight of Auriel and Lisa.

"What about tomorrow?"

"I don't know"—there they are, over by the teeter-totters—"I have to go." She retreats, adding as politely as possible, "'Bye." But before she can reach her friends, the bell goes.

She joins the stampede toward the steps. A row of teachers is suddenly there, a blur of instructions through a megaphone, something about grade ones on the right—the right of what? Who's on first? Kindergartners have already been shepherded through a separate door so they won't get trampled. "Quiet, boys and girls!"—school is officially starting. Madeleine lines up with the grade fives by mistake, vaguely aware that something is amiss, everyone at least an inch taller than she—"Psst!" She turns to see Auriel gesturing frantically for her to "get over here, you dork!" She steps out of the grade-five line and Auriel grabs her by the cardigan, yanking her to the safety of grade four.

"Gosh almighty, McCarthy!" whispers Auriel.

Lisa Ridelle is doubled over, laughing her silent ghosty laugh. The three of them giggle into their hands, a whistle sounds, squads of pupils begin filing up the front steps and in through the big double doors. Madeleine follows the caravan into the future. Who will my teacher be? Will she be pretty? Will she be nice? Will I understand fractions? *Que será, será.* . . .

"Good morning boys and girls, my name is Mr. March."

He is fat in a grey suit, but maybe that means he's nice. Fat people often are.

"Good morning Mr. March"—eternal grade-school singsong.

He has brown brogues. They are dusty. Perhaps he is too fat to bend over and polish them. That was cruel, sorry dear God.

The first thing Mr. March does is move the boys to the front. "I know what boys are," he says, revising his seating plan. He doesn't see the need to move the girls, or perhaps he doesn't know what they are. Madeleine is grateful because her desk is perfect: right across from Auriel, and one in front of Lisa.

A scraping of chairs; everyone rises to sing "God Save the Queen" and "The Maple Leaf Forever," and recite the Lord's Prayer. Then the rattle of chairs and outbreak of chit-chat as everyone sits down again. "Let's keep it down to a dull roar, shall we?" says Mr. March.

There is a bit of dandruff on the arm of his glasses, Madeleine sees it when he walks down the rows handing out the new scribblers for spelling. Pink. "Gordon Lawson," says Mr. March, consulting his seating plan. "Spell 'licorice.'"

"L I . . . C O. . . ." Gordon has wavy ginger hair freshly slicked, and the perfect number of freckles. "R . . . I . . . S—no, C, E."

"Very good, sir," says Mr. March. "The rest of you, look to Mr. Lawson. Emulate him."

Madeleine wishes Mr. March would ask her to spell something. A pink scribbler lands on her desk. *Hilroy* is emblazoned across the cover in bold cheerful script.

The first time you open a fresh scribbler. The clean smell. The paper sheen. Large scribblers, no longer little baby scribblers with wide lines. This is grade four. Copy the beautiful cursive letters that adorn the wall above the blackboard, each one repeated in upper and lower case like mother and child, doe and fawn. Study the map of the world that is pulled down over the blackboard. Canada and the British Commonwealth are pink. Ponder the cut-outs that decorate the walls between the big windows all along one side—hams and bottles of milk, fruit and poultry and other wholesome foods; bushels and pecks, gallons and yards; isosceles triangles cavort alongside wild animals and children from other lands in Eskimo parkas and Mexican sombreros. Up at the front, near the big oak desk, a felt-lined bulletin board on an easel. The only blank surface.

Madeleine arranges her new package of Laurentian pencil crayons next to her ruler and her new plaid pencil case. The air is bright with promise, the school pervaded by the aroma of fresh pencil shavings, orange peels and floor polish. No one has yet thrown up in the hallway, occasioning the spread of coloured sawdust; rain and snow have not yet soaked and musted the coats on the hooks at the back of the room—

those hooks are empty, it being still too warm for coats. It is difficult to believe, when you look out the row of big windows onto the playground and the bright PMQs beyond, that winter will really come. The seasons will change through that window, thinks Madeleine, I will turn nine through that window. . . .

"What is the capital of Borneo, little girl?" Mr. March asks.

Madeleine starts. Is he looking at her? "Pardon?"

He rolls his eyes. "'Beautiful dreamer,'" he sings.

The class laughs. He is handing out the scribblers for geography. Green.

"Hands?" says Mr. March. No one puts up a hand.

"How about you, . . ." consulting his seating plan, "Lisa Ridelle? What is the capital of Borneo?"

Lisa replies, "I don't know," barely audible from behind her curtain of white blonde.

Madeleine looks around. No one knows. Not even Marjorie Nolan.

"Well, you will by the time I'm finished with you, as will you all."

Directly in front of Madeleine is Grace Novotny. The part in her hair is crooked and her pigtails are fastened with plain elastics. It's true, Grace does smell—when Madeleine leans forward she gets a whiff. Perhaps she wets the bed. It's a sad smell. Madeleine leans back and resists the temptation to bury her nose in the crease of her new notebook. Let everything you do be perfectly neat this year, with no crossing-out or dog ears. Let everything be spelled correctly, and do not drop this scribbler in a puddle on the way home.

"When was the War of 1812?"

Madeleine looks up but she's safe. His head is turning like a periscope, looking for hands. A pause, then he says in a slightly weary way, "For your information, boys and girls, that was a joke." Polite laughter.

He passes out a thick red textbook. It's the grade-four reader, *Up and Away*. Madeleine opens it and is immediately engrossed in "Dale the Police Dog." He is a German shepherd who belongs to the Mounties. He guards their stuff and stops older girls from picking on younger ones. One day a little girl goes missing. "Dale's master let the dog sniff at the small sweater. Dale knew at once that he must go to look for someone who carried the same scent." Dale finds her asleep out in a field. Her parents have been worried sick. Dale looks like Eggs across the street. A blue textbook lands on Madeleine's desk with a thud and she closes the reader, aware of somehow cheating by reading ahead.

"I should make it clear right off the bat," says Mr. March, "that I'm not partial to shilly-shallying, dilly-dallying or chin-wagging."

Madeleine whispers to Auriel, "Except that his chin is wagging, or should I say 'chins'?"

"What did you say?"

Madeleine looks up, crimson.

He consults the seating plan. "Madeleine McCarthy. Well well, alliteration. Can you define alliteration for me?"

He must be looking at me, thinks Madeleine, because he said my name. But it's difficult to tell, because his glasses reflect the light and there is nothing in the set of his large face to indicate where he might be focusing.

Madeleine answers, "Um—"

"Word whiskers." He chants it in a fed-up way.

"It's when—"

"Full sentences please."

"A literation is when you throw garbage on the ground."

No one laughs, because no one, including Madeleine, knows what alliteration is. Mr. March says, "We have a wit amongst us."

Madeleine is mortified, but also relieved because Mr. March seems to have forgotten what he asked her in the first place. He continues handing out the blue textbooks—*Living with Arithmetic,* which makes it sound like a disease, which it is. Madeleine peeks inside. Sure enough, the enticing drawings, intriguing juxtapositions of rifles and cakes, cars and hats. "Into how many sets of 8 can you divide 120 children for square dancing?" What children? Where do they live? Are they orphans? "At the rifle range Bob scored 267 points. His father scored 423 points...." Who is Bob? Why is he allowed to have a gun? Insincere accounts of Mrs. Johnson baking pies, Mr. Green putting apples into boxes, hogs onto trucks, all a treacherous narrative veneer on the stark problems of how much, when, how long, and how many left over, the human characters mere evil imposters of numbers.

"What is the square root of forty-seven?" Mr. March asks, strolling up the aisle. Madeleine is alarmed—I didn't know we had to do square roots in grade four. He stops at the desk of a girl with long shiny black hair.

"I don't know," says the girl.

"You don't say," says Mr. March. His voice sounds as though he has let go of his muscles. Like something heavy sliding down a hill.

The girl he asked is crying! Quietly at her desk.

"There's no need for tears, little girl."

The bell rings. Recess.

"Side door, boys and girls," he says over the racket. The side door leads directly outside to the playground and they pour out into the sunshine, one jubilant scream of kids. The long wild fifteen minutes of freedom. The boys rush past the girls, taking over the baseball diamond, finding smooth spots on the asphalt for marbles, or simply chasing and pounding one another. Lisa, Madeleine and Auriel link arms and stride in step like robots across the playground, chanting, "We don't stop for anyone!" They walk right into the teeter-totter bar and collapse over it. They pretend they're swimming. They pretend they're flying.

The bell goes all too soon, and the grade fours file back in through the side door to find that the girl who cried is already there, cleaning the blackboard with a shammy. It's a treat to do that, Mr. March must have been trying to be nice, he's not an ogre. Her name is Diane Vogel. She's very pretty. Mr. March lets her write the title for the next lesson in chalk: *Botany.* Diane Vogel has beautiful printing.

Sitting back down in her row, Madeleine experiences that first reassuring proprietorial sense: my desk. My inkwell, which no one ever uses any more. Her father has told her it used to be filled with ink in the olden days, during the Depression. Boys would dunk girls' braids into it. She looks at Grace's higgledy-pigtails and wonders if any boy would be tempted to tease her like that. According to Maman, when boys do that it means they like you. *You got a funny way of showin' it, doc.*

Mr. March hands out crayons and construction paper and no one gets in trouble for the rest of the morning. They copy pictures of leaves and wildflowers such as Queen Anne's lace, "which grows in abundance in these parts," says Mr. March.

"Udderwise known as stinkweed," whispers Madeleine to Auriel, but it's okay, he doesn't look up from his desk. He's busy. While everyone draws quietly, he writes with a squeaky Magic Marker on sheets of yellow bristol board.

"How was your first morning of school, sweetie?" asks Jack, over tuna salad sandwiches, Campbell's cream of mushroom soup and, for dessert, *pète-de-nonne*—Acadian cookies. The name means nuns' farts; it's only rude if you say it in English.

"It was great."

"Good stuff."

No need for her father to walk her back to school, the mortality of the morning has fled. She runs to the end of the driveway in time to meet up with Auriel and Lisa. She turns and waves to him on the porch, then runs with her friends the whole way back to school, their cardigan sleeves tied around their necks for Bat capes.

Just before recess that afternoon, Mr. March says, "I need a volunteer." Hands shoot up. Mostly girls. Madeleine has not put up her hand and she feels a bit rude, so she half puts it up in order to be polite. Marjorie Nolan is jabbing the air with her hand, saying, "Oh!" with every jab. Mr. March consults his seating plan. "Marjorie Nolan. You will stay in at recess and do a job of work for me."

Marjorie looks about proudly as though she expects to see jealous faces. Madeleine is relieved not to have been picked to miss recess, and she is doubly relieved that Marjorie was, because she won't have to worry about hurting Marjorie's feelings by avoiding her. The bell goes.

"One at a time, boys and girls, in an orderly fashion."

After recess they return to see Marjorie installed at Mr. March's desk. She has a pair of scissors and is cutting out the last of numerous oval shapes from the sheets of yellow bristol board. Mr. March begins pinning them in a vertical row down the left-hand side of the felt bulletin board: each oval bears a name in black Magic Marker, one for every person in the class. There are multiple Cathys, Debbies, Dianes, Carols, Michaels, Johns, Bobbys, Davids and Stephens, so those names are followed by an initial. Across the top of the bulletin board, he pins more ovals: one for every subject. Reading, Writing, Arithmetic, Geography, History, Art.

Mr. March says, "Pay attention, class." He turns to the felt board and sticks something onto it. When he steps aside you can see what it is. Three felt cutouts: a hare, a dolphin and a tortoise. "It's up to you," he says.

Will you be a speeding hare? An adequate dolphin? Or a stupid tortoise? The tortoise is the only one smiling, which strikes Madeleine as odd unless you think of it as "Ignorance is bliss."

"Mrs. March made these cutouts and I have found them to be very effective," says Mr. March—as if he were talking about Ex-Lax, thinks Madeleine, and in order not to think of Mr. March on the toilet she pictures Mrs. March, a benevolent woman with a bun, hunched over a table with a pair of scissors, pining for children of her own. It doesn't occur to Madeleine to wonder why she assumes the Marches have no children.

She watches Mr. March's broad grey back as he amasses dolphins, tortoises and hares at the bottom of the bulletin board, peeling them from his soft colourful pile, pressing them to the felt board with finger and thumb. And there they cluster, waiting to embark on their various missions to hop, swim or crawl next to every name in every subject. Madeleine is confident of at least one hare, in reading.

"But fair warning, boys and girls," Mr. March says in his porridge voice. "Though you may fancy yourselves hares, remember the story of the tortoise and the hare. . . ." His glasses glint at no one in particular; he is looking at them and past them all at once, rather like those iguanas on *Wild Kingdom*.

"That hare was fast, but he had no powers of concentration . . ." —iguanas have somewhat porridgy skin, and they stare like Mr. March—"like Madeleine McCarthy."

Madeleine blinks. The class giggles. Everyone else has their spelling books open at page—what? When did that happen? She glances across at Auriel, who tilts her book helpfully—page ten. Madeleine opens her speller: *Unit 1: blame brakes flake grave slave shame mistake bare rare glare farewell average postage cabbage. . . .*

" . . . management, military, executive, finance as well as the admin course for junior officers. . . ."

Jack is in his office with his senior staff. The hooks on his halltree have sprouted air force hats; several more are ranked along the window ledge. One or two of his officers are likewise new to the station, so he has invited everyone for a general briefing. Vic Boucher has already gone over the series of special events—visits to and from Air Training Command Headquarters in Winnipeg, visits by school staff to the Staff School in Toronto, intramural curling and volleyball, etc. Now Squadron Leader Nolan is giving a rundown of incoming students. The man speaks into his clipboard; Jack leans forward, the better to concentrate—"Six hundred students in the COS, a hundred and forty flight cadets in the PFS, thirty-eight of them NATO"—but his gaze strays to the hats, then up to the window—"as well, we'll look to process something like seventeen hundred candidates through the OSU."

Jack pulls his focus from the blue sky, back to the briefing, as Nolan winds up. "Good stuff." He drums the eraser end of his pencil lightly on his desk and says, "Are any of you gentlemen familiar with what is known as the case-study method?"

One or two assents from the younger officers.

"Can someone give me the air force definition of leadership?"

A junior instructor, himself an MBA candidate, raises a hand. "Sir, I believe the standard definition goes as follows"—he looks a little lost in his uniform, is it possible that this young man has the slightest interest in aeroplanes? "'Leadership is the art of influencing others to achieve an aim.'"

He has answered by the book. A real ground-pounder. Name of Vogel. Ironic.

Jack nods. "Close enough," he says, "but what does it really mean, eh? 'Influence.' How? Who sets the 'aim'? How do you deal with resistance to change?"

A chief instructor, Squadron Leader Lawson, pipes up, "In the military I believe the accepted method is 'Change or else.'"

Laughter. Jack grins. "That's right, 'This won't hurt a bit, did it?'" More laughter. "In the military," he continues, "we have a chain of command, and in the heat of battle it's pretty cut and dried. But in peacetime—extended periods of peace like the one we're in—the tendency can be toward bureaucratic bloat, a loss of the sense of what it's all for. Although," he adds, "lest we forget, even in wartime there's always some general back in an office sticking pins in a map." Groans of assent, despite the fact that none except Vic—and Jack, in his way—are veterans. The eldest among the others is a hair too young to have served. Jack continues.

"I'm looking to take a bit of a more sociological approach. That's what's been going on for the past while at the good business schools, and it's been the trend in the real world for a few decades now. We're talking about something a little different from the traditional 'sir-yes-sir' approach. We want to dig a little deeper, get a little more complex, because the world is getting a helluva lot more complex."

"Better believe it," says Vic.

"Think of the military as a corporation," says Jack. "What business are we in? We're in the peace business. Who are our shareholders? The people of Canada. Our aim is to defend the country. In order to achieve that aim we must identify various objectives: to join with our allies in managing the threat of Soviet expansion; to monitor and respond to perilous situations within our own borders and around the world; to assess risk in the light of present-day weapons of mass destruction. What becomes key? Communication." He pauses and looks around. The men are relaxed on several chairs scavenged from neighbouring offices. Listening intently. "You may have a crack pilot, but if his ground crew used the wrong wing nut because the engineer submitted the right form to the wrong department whose initials changed last week and the orderly's bored with paperwork, you've got a potentially lethal domino effect."

"'And all for the want of a horseshoe nail,'" says Flight Lieutenant Vogel.

Jack pauses. Vogel looks down. Jack continues. "That's right. The question is, do our officers know how to manage people and the flow of information in order to lead effectively? It's our job to teach them."

He gets up and walks over to his bookshelf. "I've arranged for some of you fellas to sign on for the admin practices course up at Western, in London, and I've been pulling together stuff from some new books that are starting to float around out there." He pulls out a hefty wedge of bound mimeographed paper and drops it onto his desk. He flips through, creating a breeze. "These things aren't just bedtime stories, they walk you through every aspect of an actual business. General Electric, American Motors. . . . You can deduce the aims of an organization by analyzing its actions." He lets the pages fan shut again. "Human behaviour." He pats the book and gives the others a cagey look. "Think of Tom Sawyer as the original management whiz."

An officer near the back says, "How do you get someone else to paint the fence?"

"And give you the apple," adds another from the opposite end of the room. Laughter.

Jack says, "So far, military admin practices have erred on the side of action. We're looking to redress that. At the same time, you don't want the pendulum swinging so far that you get loads of analysis—every what-if in the book—and wind up crippling your ability to act. Not every leader can pull off both. A fella you'd fly to hell and back with might be hopeless on the ground." He wedges the book back onto the shelf, then turns, places both hands flat on the desk in front of him and looks them in the eye. "You've got to ask yourself, where do I fit into the picture? Am I looking at the whole picture, or just part of it? Which part can I influence?"

After a moment, one of his finance instructors says, "In other words, how big is my box?"

"Bang on," says Jack.

The door opens a crack and a young Flying Officer puts his head in. "Sir, it's a Captain Fleming on the phone for you, should I—?"

"Tell him I'll call back in a bit," says Jack.

"Yes sir," says the FO, withdrawing.

Vic Boucher says, "You moonlighting, sir?" The others chuckle. There are no captains in this room; there are flight lieutenants. In Canada, "captain" is an army rank.

Jack grins. "Some flatfoot up at National Defence HQ probably thinks he can up the army quota in the Flying School."

"'Army pilot?'" says one of the men. "Isn't that a contradiction in terms?"

Jack is going to enjoy this group. He glances at his agenda and asks Squadron Leader Baxter to brief them on some cadet personnel issues, then sits back. *Captain Fleming.* He keeps his eyes on the speaker, easily focusing on two things at once: "... with the Nigerian cadets, and while not all the Egyptians celebrate Christmas, we've made special provision for them to...."

Oskar Fried must be on his way. The blue sky through Jack's window, the row of hats, the smell of wood polish and pencil shavings peculiar to schools and government offices, all are warmed to mingling by the afternoon sun, and he basks in an unlooked-for sense of well-being. He is in no hurry to return Simon's phone call. If "Captain Fleming" calls, it means the matter is of ordinary importance. If "Major Newbolt" calls, it means drop what you're doing. Jack was amused when Simon picked the code names. While the Fleming reference is obvious if not ludicrous, he must remember to ask Simon where Newbolt comes from. He reaches for his pencil and resumes tapping as he listens—"... Ad Pracs, Accounting, Statistical Analysis...."

*Reading, Writing, Arithmetic, Geography, History, Art.* The felt animals have begun their migration across the bulletin board. Madeleine is unsurprised to see that she is indeed a hare in reading. She has, however, in spite of being an excellent speller, been designated a tortoise in writing. She is being penalized for penmanship. Apart from the fact that her writing still looks too much like printing, no matter how hard she tries, she always runs out of room at the end of each line and winds up with words scrunched in the verbal equivalent of a pileup on the highway.

It is five to three and Mr. March has chosen the best botanical drawings and prepared them with Scotch Tape: buttercups by Marjorie Nolan, tulips by Cathy Baxter and dandelions by Joyce Nutt. Madeleine drew excellent daisies with faces and long eyelashes—one is smoking a pipe, one is winking, a third has a moustache and glasses. Her disappointment at not being chosen is tempered by the realization that she is lucky to have earned a dolphin in Art for such unrealistic flowers, as it's apparent, now that she glances around, that the purpose was real-life. She casually folds her arms over her daisies.

Mr. March says, "Diane Vogel, proceed to the front of the class please." He lifts her up by the armpits and she sticks the three pictures over the window of the inside door—the one that opens onto the corridor. He sets her back down and says, "Thank you, little girl. You may return to your desk." Then he gestures to the door, like a lady on a Duncan Hines cake commercial: "Thus we turn our best face to the rest of the school."

Madeleine looks at the papered-over window. The art is facing out. At least we don't have to stare at Margarine Nolan's buttercups.

"You're getting company," says Simon.

"Oskar Fried is here."

"Not yet, this is something else, bit of a wrinkle."

Jack is in the phone booth next to the grocery store. He felt a little odd answering it; what if someone were to see him? No one did, but if someone had, how would he have justified answering a pay phone and proceeding to have a conversation? He was startled by the only answer that came to mind: adultery.

"They're sending a second man," says Simon. "Another officer will be joining the mission as your counterpart."

"My counterpart?"

"Your opposite number, as it were. A USAF type."

"Why are they involved?"

He realizes as soon as he asks that Simon is not about to answer, and indeed Simon replies, "Cooperation under the terms of NATO, dear boy, your tax dollars at work."

Jack recognizes annoyance beneath the casual tone, and senses that, if he asks now, Simon may actually tell him something. "Why do we need another man?"

"Because nature and the United States Air Force abhor a vacuum. They also abhor relying on anyone but themselves."

"Isn't this a joint effort?"

"Oh yes. As Abbott says to Costello, 'You follow in front.'"

"I didn't know MI6 worked so closely with the American military."

"Keep pumping me and I'll blow up."

Jack chuckles. "So what's our second man supposed to do?"

"For the most part, he's simply to be there on the ground, in case."

"In case what?"

Simon sighs. "They don't want to entrust Fried solely to a Canadian."

"We work with the Yanks all the time, what's the problem?"

"Well, Canada is leaky, for one thing."

Jack again sees Igor Gouzenko, hood over his head, naming names in Ottawa. But that was years ago. Along with the atomic spies at Chalk River. . . . "It is?"

"It's a bloody sieve."

"Look who's talking."

Simon groans. "Point taken, Messrs Burgess and Maclean have rather tarred our good English name of late. But I went to Oxford, mate, not Cambridge."

"So where do I meet up with this USAF type?"

"There's an exchange position at your station, yes?"

"That's right. It alternates between Americans and Brits"—Jack is a little taken aback. It hadn't occurred to him that the American would actually be posted to Centralia. Group Captain Woodley must be in the loop after all. "It's supposed to be a Yank this time but the fella's late."

"That's because they pulled the original man and posted another at the eleventh hour."

"An intelligence type?"

"No no, some fresh-faced kid. A little younger, a little quicker, perhaps, than the bloke they'd planned to put out to pasture up your way."

Jack is stung. "Si, it's still a training base, and a not too shabby one at that."

"No offence, mate, but we're talking bugsmashers and Chipmunks, are we not, and this pilot comes to you straight from USAFE."

*United States Air Force Europe.* "Wiesbaden?" Jack gets the picture. The American has just come off a tour of duty flying Sabres and F-104 Starfighters—widow-makers. "So what's the drill?"

"Well, it doesn't change much for you really, because the American chap hasn't been given the straight gen." *Gen*—general information. Intelligence.

"Why not?"

"I suggested to them that he didn't need to know yet and, in the end, they concurred."

Jack doesn't ask who "they" are. "They" are a committee; it will have sprouted from a branch of American military intelligence, it will have an acronym like countless other committees that proliferate and cross-pollinate in a big bureaucracy, and it might not officially exist. Somewhere there are human beings behind the letters, but they are as transitory as the initials themselves. If it's indeed possible to deduce the aims of an organization by analyzing its actions, Jack reflects, the aim of most bureaucracies is to confuse.

"So your American friend knows very little," says Simon. The chain of command will run from Simon, through Jack, to the American. "They suggest you brief him upon arrival."

"No problem," says Jack

"I suggest you may see fit to put that off until the last moment."

Jack smiles. "Whose suggestion would you suggest I follow?"

"No worries if you choose mine, I'll take any kicks that are coming." Simon goes on to explain that the American captain will arrive in Centralia knowing only that, during his year as an exchange officer, he will at some point be called upon to perform a special task.

"What task?"

"Well, naturally the Americans will have one of their own escort Fried south of the border when the time comes."

"So Fried is going to the States."

"And thanks to the Americans, you now know more than you need to." He sighs. "I don't know why I bother sometimes."

"No harm done, Si, who am I going to tell? I still haven't told anyone about the time you buzzed the nurses' residence in Toronto. So what's Fried going to be working on, jets? Missiles?"

"Rug-hooking, I think."

Jack laughs and opens the door of the booth with his foot to let some air in. The afternoon is heavy with sun. "So all this American fella knows is that at some point a Canadian officer will contact him and brief him."

"That's right."

"He doesn't know it's going to be me."

"No one knows it's you."

Jack removes his hat, wipes the band of perspiration from his forehead, and puts the hat right back on, because the sun pierces his eyes. "No one except Woodley," he says.

"Who?"

"The CO here."

Simon sounds relaxed as ever. "No, as I said, I've closed the loop on this one."

Jack pauses. It's one thing to feel he's acting as a private citizen helping Simon with a favour. But a foreign officer has been posted here for a purpose of which Jack's CO is unaware. Still, the man will function as a flight instructor; he'll step into a position that would be filled by an American in any case. His "special task" will take a day at most. And it's not as though he's coming from a hostile country. Simon is still speaking: " . . . only you and I know where Oskar Fried will be living. Only you and I know him by that name." Of course. Jack ought to have assumed it was an alias.

"One man to babysit, and one to stand by in the dark until it's time to escort Fried. Simon, that's a whole lot of hand-holding." He lowers his chin, getting the most out of his hat brim.

"It's overkill." This time Simon does not sound amused. "There's no need for this poor Yank to move to Canada, uproot his family for a year, just so he's in position for a task that would otherwise cost him a day. I don't like it."

Jack hears Simon in the instructor's seat beside him, *not sure I like the looks of that.* Never anything so adamant as *I don't like it.* He feels momentarily disoriented, as at the sudden cessation of an engine, and regains his bearings with a pragmatic observation: "It's a waste of the taxpayers' money, that's for sure."

"Whenever you increase the points of entry in a mission, you lose control. That's when you get gremlins." Simon's voice is clipped, precise as chalk on a blackboard. "This Yank's no doubt a good man, but the Americans, in their customary zeal, have increased the target area. The chances of a fuck-up will now likewise increase. It's sloppy and bloated and it annoys the hell out of me."

Jack waits for more, but Simon is silent. "We could use you here at the management school, Si."

Simon laughs and sounds like himself again: "Word of advice, Jack. Number one: If there's ever another conventional war, join the intelligence service. You'll be relatively safe, and you'll know more or less what's actually going on. Number two: Observe carefully what the Americans are doing. Then do the opposite."

Jack laughs. "When's this fella getting here, anyhow?"

"Any day now. Name's McCarroll."

"Sorry, I meant Fried."

"Oh. Shouldn't be long."

"Why here, Simon?"

"You're an inquisitive bastard."

"I'm interested, I can't help it." He leans against the glass, glancing over at the PX. "Listen, you know what I'm looking at right now?"

"Enlighten me."

"Chicken legs thirty nine cents a pound, homo milk is on special, and there's a Red Rocket by the door, drop a nickel in the slot and you can go to the moon. There's a four-year-old astronaut in it right now."

"Going stir-crazy?"

"Naw, it's a great place, just not exactly where the action is. What's out your window? The Pentagon? The White House?"

"The domino theory in action: I tell you one thing you don't need to know and you go at it with a crowbar. I'm not telling you a bloody other thing, sunshine."

"Come on, Si, toss me a bone, you old sonofagun."

Simon sighs. Jack waits.

"Well, the first factor in selecting this location is you, of course."

Jack savours it silently.

Simon continues: "Then, as you may be aware, there is your country's reputation as a way station for weary travellers."

"You mean refugees?"

"In a manner of speaking. Canada is an easy route to the U.S. In this case, that's working in our favour."

"But why park him here, why not ship him stateside straight away?"

"Canada is also both far enough removed from and closely enough allied to Britain and the U.S. to provide haven."

"Because Fried is working on something the Soviets and the Americans both want," Jack hazards. "Which means they'll look for him in the States first. But by the time he gets there, he'll have a new identity—he'll be Joe-Blow Canadian crossing into the U.S." Jack is of course aware that Britain, Canada and the U.S. share intelligence—cooperation among these countries is often smoother than cooperation within them, due to inter-service rivalries. But he has never seen it up close—a case study. "What do we all get out of it?"

"Goodbye Jack."

"Hang on."

"Christ, what now?"

"Who the heck is Major Newbolt?"

Simon laughs. "You're going to have to do your homework, lad."

"Let me know when I can buy you that drink."

As he turns to leave the booth, Jack sees that a small lineup has formed. Cadets standing at a respectful distance, waiting for the phone. They salute; Jack touches the brim of his hat and heads across the parade square for home. *Something the Soviets and the Americans both want.* . . . He doesn't have to look up in the sky, he knows it's there—even when you can't see it.

"I believe that this nation should commit itself to achieving the goal, before this decade is out, of landing a man on the moon, and returning him safely to earth." Kennedy said that last year, but the Soviets have kept right on eclipsing American efforts, making heroes of Russian cosmonauts smiling out from the pages of *Life*. Luniks, Vostoks, manned rockets bearing the red star, hurtling skyward, gaping fire, two launch pads for manned flight at Baikonur in Kazakhstan compared with the lone Pad 14 at Cape Canaveral. The first U.S. attempt to match Sputnik blew up on the launch pad—the British press dubbed it a "Flopnik!" Oskar Fried is a scientist from the winning side, and the United States Air Force has gone to great lengths to import him. When Jack recalls recent articles and editorials about American military determination to compete with NASA, the connections seem suddenly crystal clear. He quickens his pace, his leg muscles feel taut and tireless, he could easily run home.

The Soviets are not like us; while we're "mooning" about space exploration, they are turning their best military brains to the problem of space flight, pouring unlimited state funds into it, unconstrained by a congress or parliament. That's why President Kennedy has approved billions for NASA. That's why the U.S. Air Force is clamouring for a piece of the pie, convinced it ought not to be left entirely to the civilian agency. Jack glances up; there it is, mild disc. To fly there. To stand in the darkness of space and view our earth, milky blue, fragile jewel. There is not a human being on the planet who could remain unmoved by the enormity of such a feat. That's why, apart from immense strategic advantage, there is such prestige attached to it. Hearts and minds and muscle. Jack feels certain now it's why USAF is determined to acquire its own Wernher von Braun, in the person of Oskar Fried. He watches a fuel truck lumber past him up Canada Avenue toward the hangars, and behind it, Vimy Woodley at the wheel of a big Oldsmobile with a carload of Girl Guides. He returns her wave. One of those young gals is bound to be her daughter. When he gets home he'll tell Mimi to line her up to babysit Friday night. It's high time he took his wife into London for a fancy dinner, just the two of them. He glances at his watch. Five-twenty; Mimi will expect him by now. He quickens his pace, feeling springs in his heels, wings on his feet. When Jack was a boy he idolized Flash Gordon. It was science fiction then. Now it's just a matter of time.

He recalls Henry Froelich the other night, questioning von Braun's civilian status. Yes, von Braun worked for the Germans during the war, but he was a scientist, and why shouldn't the Americans turn his skills to their advantage now? Not all men of science are paragons of virtue—Josef Mengele wasn't the first to prove that. But von Braun worked on weapons, not human beings. In this he was no different—certainly no worse—than the scientists on our side who developed the first atomic

bomb. Froelich was right, they did hold it together with masking tape
for that first test blast down in Los Alamos; men and women in khaki
shorts, eggheads, civilians—Jack has seen the photos. Von Braun is of
that ilk. The Einstein of rocketry. He masterminded Hitler's "secret
weapon," the V-2 rocket, granddaddy of the Saturn and every ICBM on
the planet. And he did it at Peenemünde. The research and development facility that Simon helped to bomb in '43. Jack shakes his head—
talk about a small world.

He strides past the Spitfire, eager now to see his wife. She will hand
him a martini *avec un twiste*. They have been separated for the space of
an afternoon, yet he feels as though he's on his way home from the airport—*can't wait to see you baby, look what I bought you when I was in.* . . .
And as he crosses the Huron County road that separates the station
from the PMQs, a perfectly reasonable explanation occurs to him for a
person arranging to receive a call at a pay phone—apart from adultery,
that is. He might have had a sudden impulse while passing the phone
booth. Might have stepped inside and phoned a store—Simpson's, say,
in London—to inquire about a brand of perfume as a gift for his wife.
The salesperson might have had to go to another floor, then call him
right back from a different phone. . . .

He enters the PMQs, alive with children and tricycles. The smells
of many suppers perk his appetite and add to the edge in his stomach.
He looks up at the sound of his name and returns Betty Boucher's
greeting.

"How are you, Betty?"

"I hope they're treating you all right, Jack."

"Can't complain."

"Dad! Catch!" His son tosses the football on the run as another boy
tackles him, bringing them both down. Jack catches the ball, trots
twenty-five feet, turns and bombs it back across three lawns. The
boys dive.

"Mimi, I'm home."

She smiles at him as he appears in the kitchen doorway and tosses his
hat onto the halltree. She doesn't ask him why he's late, that's not her
style. She's in stockings and pumps, never slippers after five, the strings
of her white apron go round her waist twice, she hands him a martini,
butts out her cigarette and kisses him.

"Something sure smells good," he says.

*"Fricot au poulet."*

Mimi has supper on the stove, every hair in place, and she's put away
under the sink the old maternity dress and rubber gloves that she wore

to scrub the floor. Clark Kent changes in a phone booth. Superwomen are more discreet.

He slips his arms around her waist. "Where's Madeleine?"

"Out playing."

"What are you doing between now and supper?"

She whispers her answer in his ear.

"What would your *maman* say?" He lets his hands slide down over her bottom, and pulls her to him.

She rests her elbows on his shoulders and looks up at him. "Why do you think my *maman* had thirteen kids?"

He laughs. "You got eleven to go, Missus, what kind of Catholic girl are you?"

She bites his neck. "A smart one."

He follows her up the stairs. He picks up her apron on the way, then her blouse, then a shoe. He waits to catch the other one and it crosses his mind—something Simon said that Jack didn't dwell on at the time: *No one knows it's you.* Can that be literally true? Is it possible no one in Ottawa—at External Affairs or in the Prime Minister's Office—knows of Jack's involvement? They would have to know about the American captain, even if Woodley doesn't. Still, integration of the two militaries is nothing new, USAF could send whomever they want to up here without saying why. But Ottawa would have to know about the plan to shelter a high-level defector. How else would Simon acquire the authority to operate here? Not to mention a Canadian passport for Oskar Fried.

"Catch," she says, her other shoe poised in her hand.

And he does.

## MUSCLES

WHY IS THERE ALWAYS one kid in the class who smells? Whom everyone shuns? Kids who have failed a grade inhabit a different world. As though exiled in a desert, even if they are right beside you, they are far away, breathing the bewildered air of a waterless planet. By Friday of the first week it's established. At recess, Marjorie runs up to Madeleine, touches her and says, "Grace germs, needle!" then gleefully inoculates herself.

Madeleine ignores it, even though she can see other kids poised to run, waiting for her to pass on the germs to one of them, then hastily give herself a needle. She does not. She goes round the corner of the school, touches the stucco wall to get rid of the germs, then quietly inoculates herself, murmuring, "Needle."

Grace doesn't seem to notice that no one likes her. She grins to herself and sucks her thumb, then rubs her lips to wet them. She picks her nose and eats it, there is no other way to put it. If you had just arrived from Mars, you might think Grace was pretty. Enormous blue eyes like a doll's, and naturally wavy hair which is sandy streaked with blonde; imagine it clean. Her lips a perfect Cupid's bow; picture them not chapped. Then imagine Grace actually looking at you. Without her eyes swerving and her hands twisting her grimy cuffs.

It was mean of Marjorie to start the needle craze, but it was clear before then that Grace was destined to be the class reject. On Tuesday afternoon she ate Elmer's Glue paste from the pink blotting paper you get for art. And on Wednesday she picked her nose and wiped it on her desk in front of everyone. Mr. March made her stay after three for "remedial hygiene." Madeleine glances up at the felt bulletin board. No wonder Grace has nothing but smiling tortoises next to her name in every subject.

"Turn to page sixteen in your *Girl Next Door* reader," says Mr. March, and they all get out their books. "Madeleine McCarthy, read from where we left off." While many kids dread reading aloud, Madeleine loves it, so she is glad to hear her name. She opens the book and reads flawlessly, "'Muscles and Ice Cream'. . . ." The story is about Susan, a girl in a wheelchair, who goes to the hospital so she will be able to walk again. " . . . one of the nurses showed us the exercises. She kept saying, 'Try hard, Susan, and soon you will have big, strong muscles, but now you get some ice cream.'" Madeleine pictures Elizabeth standing up, muscles bulging like Hercules, shattering her wheelchair. She reads on, "'If you want big, strong muscles, I'll show you how to get them,' Bill said. . . ." Bill is one of those imaginary older boys who are nice to girls. Everyone knows boys are not like that. Ricky Froelich is, but he's different. "'Bill showed Nancy a good way to build strong muscles.'"

"Thank you, Miss McCarthy," says Mr. March, and continues up the row with his pointer—when he taps a desk, that person has to start reading. Everyone prays he will not tap Grace's desk, because Grace has to sound everything out. He taps Lisa's desk.

Lisa reads, barely above a whisper. Mr. March keeps saying, "Speak up, little girl," but Lisa gets softer and softer, her face redder and redder, until finally she stops and stares at her desk. Madeleine is worried Lisa may have to stay after school for "remedial reading." Or worse, be demoted from dolphin to tortoise.

Mr. March taps Grace's desk. An audible groan from the class. Grace hunches over her book and reads, "Wha-at gamms . . . games do you often p-l-ay that gy . . . gi-ve you-r mus . . . moose . . . musk. . . ."

"Class, what's the word?" intones Mr. March.

And the class chants in unison, "Muscles."

Please don't make Grace sound out the word "exercise."

"Gordon Lawson, continue reading please."

Thank goodness. Gordon is an all-round hare.

During recess, Madeleine and Auriel console Lisa, who is still trembling, so when they return to the classroom Madeleine is shocked to see that she herself has been demoted from hare to tortoise. In Reading. *What's up, doc?*

Mr. March must have noticed her dismay because after everyone has sat down he says, "It's for your own good, little girl. Reading aloud is one thing. Comprehension is quite another. That takes concentration."

*Concentration.* Madeleine feels slightly ill. A tortoise. No fair. How can she get back up to hares? After school she will tell her dad. He'll know what to do.

Don't dwell on it right now. It's Friday afternoon and the beautiful kindergarten teacher has come into the classroom.

"Hello grade fours, my name is Miss Lang."

"Hello, Miss Lang," says everyone.

She is here to announce the beginning of Brownies. The boys refrain from sniggering, she is that pretty. "How many Sixers do we have in the class?"

Several girls raise their hands, among them Cathy Baxter—no surprise, she having emerged as the boss of the girly-girls—and Marjorie Nolan, who has neither emerged nor settled yet in any group. Madeleine is not a Sixer, she is not even a Seconder, she prefers to be a lone wolf in Brownies and not have to inspect anyone's nails or keep track of dimes—the nifty notebook with pencil attached notwithstanding. Maybe this year they will get to go on a camping trip. She looks at Miss Lang in her A-line dress and pictures her sitting cross-legged roasting a wiener over a campfire.

"Oh my," says Miss Lang at the show of hands, "it looks as though we have quite a few chiefs and not enough Indians."

The class laughs sincerely. She has a beautiful figure. But more than that, Miss Lang has charm. What incredible luck that she, and not just someone's boring old mother, is Brown Owl—"bird of great good fortune." Like the albatross.

"How many of you expect to fly up this spring?" she asks. All the girls raise their hand, even Grace. She ought to have flown up to Guides by now, or at least walked up. But then she ought to be in grade five too. There are no Brownie badges for cutting the cuffs off your own cardigan with a pair of school scissors.

"Good," says Miss Lang, in her voice that reminds Madeleine of a jazz record they have at home: *Vibes on Velvet.* The cover is "adult": a lot of half-naked chorus girls in a burlesque pose. *Burlesque.* It sounds like barbequed shrimp, and it means sexy but not really dirty. The album cover is, however, way dirtier than the Sears catalogue, even though the amount of bare skin is about the same. Perhaps that's because the ladies on the album cover know they are being sexy, whereas the Sears underwear ladies look as though they think they are fully clothed—hmm, think I'll just hang out the wash in my living bra.

"Madeleine McCarthy?"

Everyone is looking at her, especially beautiful Miss Lang. Madeleine reddens and says, "Pleasant. I mean present."

The class bursts out laughing. Up at his desk, Mr. March rolls his eyes. *Oh no, I'm going to get it. Again.*

Miss Lang smiles. "I'll take that as a yes."

*Yes to what? Oh no.*

But Miss Lang isn't angry. She has a way of making any girl she talks to seem pretty. When she says, "We'll have you flying up this spring, Grace, I know it," in that moment even Grace Novotny seems clean.

At five to three Mr. March stands up and announces, "The following little girls will remain after three . . . ," and he consults his seating plan. "Grace Novotny . . ." No one is surprised. Grace is a tortoise only because there is no worm category. Madeleine wonders why Mr. March has to look at his seating plan in order to remember her name when this is her second year in his class. " . . . and Madeleine McCarthy." His glasses are still trained on his clipboard.

Madeleine is immediately hot. Her legs, her face—*what have I done? I daydreamed about Miss Lang. I pictured her in a bra. But I read perfectly—Susan and her stupid muscles. It's bad enough to be demoted to tortoise. But to be kept after three. . . .*

The bell goes. The rest of the class rattle to their feet; already the smell of failure is clouding around Madeleine's desk as she remains seated. She has been paired with Grace Novotny. *Madeleine germs, needle!* Auriel catches her eye as she leaves and Madeleine grins and draws a cut-throat finger across her neck.

"And don't forget show-and-tell on Monday, boys and girls." Mr. March sounds disappointed in them already.

Lisa and Auriel are sitting waiting for Madeleine at the end of the school field, and making dandelion bracelets.

"What happened?" asks Auriel.

Lisa is chewing the end of a weed, she offers one to Madeleine. Everything's going to be fine. Madeleine bites into the tender white shoot where the sweetness is.

"I got a detention," she says, cool like Kirk Douglas. "First of all he says, 'Come here little girl'"—making a triple chin, bugging out her eyes, doing a fat English accent—even though Mr. March doesn't have an accent. Lisa writhes silently on the grass, Auriel hangs on every word.

"What'd he make you do?"

"Exercises," says Madeleine and rolls her eyes.

"Exercises?!"

"'To improve your powahs of concentration, little geuhl,'" she drawls.

"What a creep!" cries Auriel.

"'What maroon!'" says Bugsy, then Woody Woodpecker takes over. "He-he-HA-ha—!"

"Holy cow, Madeleine, you sound just like him!"

"—he-he-he-he-he-he!"

Auriel and Lisa join in. Although few people can really do Woody Woodpecker, everyone enjoys trying. "He-he-HA-ha!"

They start rolling across the field—we could just roll all the way home instead of walking, want to? Then they stop, sprawled on their backs, and let the sky go topsy-turvy overhead.

"He should have his head examined," says Auriel, getting up and starting to twirl.

"He should have his head shrunk," says Lisa, following.

"He should have his stomach shrunk," says Madeleine, and they are all twirling—now run! Run dizzy all the way home, as the pavement lurches and spins between your footfalls.

When they get to the corner, they agree to meet back here in play clothes in five minutes. "Synchronize your watches, ladies," says Auriel. And they do, although none of them wears a watch.

"What took you so long?" says Maman.

"Lisa and Auriel and me were playing," Madeleine answers, running up the stairs into the kitchen—ginger cookies, oh boy!

"Madeleine, look at me."

Madeleine crosses her eyes and stares at her mother.

Mimi laughs in spite of herself. "You're not to play, you're to come straight home and change, then you can play."

"*Oui, maman, comme tu veux, maman,*" says Madeleine, swiping a cookie.

Mimi raises an eyebrow and takes a puff of her Cameo—this one has settled in nicely at school. No worries there. She bends and gives her daughter a kiss on the forehead. "That's for speaking French."

Madeleine groans but she is pleased. She feels free, it's Friday, tonight we'll play hide 'n' seek in the twilight, then we'll watch *The Flintstones,* and tomorrow we go camping at the Pinery on Lake Huron. She feels suddenly ten feet tall and invincible. She flies out the front door, sails off the porch, zooms zigzaggy up the street, her arms outstretched like a Spitfire—I could run and run and never get tired. Spin the earth beneath my feet like a giant marble.

Here is what happened after the bell.

It was very quiet. Mr. March sat down and scraped his chair in until his stomach met the edge of his big oak desk. Grace giggled.

"Stand up, little girl."

His glasses glinted in the afternoon sun. Madeleine couldn't tell if he was talking to her but, since Grace made no move to stand, Madeleine did.

Then Mr. March said, "You need to improve your powers of concentration."

"Sorry, Mr. March."

"Don't be sorry, little girl, we're going to see what can be done about you."

"Okay."

"Come here."

He doesn't sound angry. Maybe this isn't a detention. Maybe it's extra help. Madeleine walks down the aisle toward his desk. Grace giggles behind her. Madeleine stops in front of his desk.

"Do you know the capital of Borneo, little girl?"

"No, Mr. March."

"Come closer."

She comes around to the side of his desk, which is like a big enclosed cube on three sides—you could easily hide a cake underneath it. He takes his hanky from his breast pocket.

"Can you touch your toes, little girl?"

"Yes."

"Well?"

Madeleine touches her toes.

"That will help send blood to your brain," says Mr. March.

She straightens up again.

"Can you do backbends, little girl?"

Madeleine does a backbend, ending up in an arch with her hands on the floor behind her head, her hair hanging like grass—she can easily walk around like this but she refrains, afraid of showing off by accident. Plus, even though she knows her dress is not immodestly pulled up, she feels a bit funny doing a backbend with a dress on in the classroom after three—her light blue pleated pinafore. She can hear him rustling but she can't see anything except the upside-down door with the art papered over the window.

When she straightens up, Mr. March says, "You need to do more exercises, little girl. Show me your muscle."

She resists the urge to turn and look behind her, because even though the glare is gone from his glasses, it really does seem as though Mr. March is looking past her at someone else. Someone called "little girl." He reaches out and takes her by the upper arm. She tries to make a muscle but it's difficult when your arm is being squeezed.

"Say 'muscle,'" he says.

He doesn't even want me to spell it, *this is so easy, doc.* Madeleine says, "Muscle."

She watches his profile and waits as he squeezes her arm. She says, quietly, "Ow."

"I'm not hurting you."

He lets go and says, "Rub your arm. That will make it feel better." So she does. "Rub it," he whispers, looking straight ahead, sitting forward in his chair, belly jammed right up against his desk. He is breathing through his mouth. Maybe he has asthma.

Suddenly he sighs and turns to her and says, "I don't see why I should tell your parents about your problem just yet, little girl. Do you?"

"Um. No sir."

"Well we'll see. Run along now."

Madeleine goes back to her desk to get her homework and Grace gets up and rummages for her homework too—Grace's notebooks are already dog-eared.

"Not you, little girl."

And Grace sits back down.

Mr. March says, "You may stay and clean the blackboards."

Madeleine leaves the classroom and walks by herself down the deserted afternoon hall, wondering how she can improve her powers of concentration. The word itself has a headachey sound. Why is it called a Concentration Camp? Where is Borneo?

She arrives in the foyer and looks up at the Queen. All this looked so strange and new that day long ago when she and Mike peered in. She didn't know then that she would be the kid who acts up in class and gets a detention. She looks up at the Queen and says, "I won't from now on, Scout's honour," although she is a Brownie. "Scout's honour" is more potent than "Too-wit, too-woo," it's what Mike says when he's making a solemn vow.

When she walks out onto the big front steps and sees that Auriel and Lisa have waited for her in the field, she runs to them, allowing the breeze to take away the after-three feeling.

At supper, Madeleine doesn't have a very good appetite, despite the delicious Friday night fish and chips.

Mimi says, "*Viens,* let me feel your forehead." But she doesn't have a temperature.

Mike says with his mouth full, "Can I have your french fries?"

"Mike," says Jack.

"What?" Bewildered, aggrieved.

Mimi looks at her daughter. "What is it, *ma p'tite? Regarde-moi.*"

Madeleine blushes under Maman's gaze. She feels guilty even though she has done nothing wrong. But everyone is acting as though there were in fact something wrong. Is there? Mimi strokes her hair and says, "Hm? *Dis à maman.*"

Jack shakes his head discreetly across the table at Mimi. Madeleine is turned away from him and doesn't see. She opens her mouth to confess to her mother about being kept for exercises after three, but Mimi says, "What is it, Jack?"

Jack rolls his eyes and smiles. "'Why did you kick me under the table?'"

"Sorry," says Mimi.

Madeleine and Mike are both bewildered now, but that's nothing new in the land of grown-ups.

Jack removes Madeleine's plate, handing it to her mother, and says, "What do you say, old buddy, have you got room for dessert?"

Madeleine nods yes and feels her face cool, back to normal.

After supper, Jack invites his daughter to read the funnies with him on the couch. She snuggles in and he explains the joke in *Blondie,* then casually inquires, "How was school today, sweetie?"

"Fine."

"Just fine?"

"It was okay."

"What's on your mind, little buddy?"

"I got put in tortoises for Reading," she mumbles.

Jack doesn't laugh, he knows it's serious stuff. Once he has got her to explain the rating system, he asks, "Why'd he do that?" Madeleine feels her indignation afresh, remembering now how she had planned to tell Dad all along, before the exercises made her feel grateful to Mr. March for promising not to tell.

"He made me stay after three"—it feels good to own up to it.

"What for?"

" . . . Exercises."

"What kind of exercises?"

Madeleine doesn't say "backbends." Now that she is here sitting on the couch with Dad, she feels it was a bit bad of her to do backbends in a dress in front of Mr. March when they weren't even in the gym.

"For my concentration," she says.

"But you're a great reader."

"I know."

He considers a moment. "Maybe you weren't paying attention. Tell me about Mr. March." And he puts down the newspaper.

"Well. He talks really slowly. He has glasses. He doesn't like us."

Jack smiles. "I have a feeling I know what's going on."

"What?"

Dad knows about the backbends. But he doesn't sound mad. He sounds as if he is going to say, *Mr. March made you do backbends so the blood would flow to your head. That's perfectly normal,* and Madeleine is relieved, she has not been bad after all.

"You're bored," says Dad.

"Oh."

"Einstein failed the third grade, because he was bored. Churchill failed Latin. President Kennedy can speed-read a book in twenty minutes but he did very poorly as a kid in school."

*I'm bored. That's all it is.*

"Now, I'm not saying it's good to be bored. It's a problem. You've got to make a challenge for yourself to keep things interesting."

"Okay."

"What's your aim here?"

"Um. To get back to hares."

"What's your first step going to be?"

"Um. Don't daydream."

"Well yeah," says Jack, nodding, taking it under advisement. "But how are you going to manage that when he's so darn boring?"

Madeleine thinks, then says, "I could have a nail in my pocket and squeeze it really hard."

Jack laughs less than he wants to, then nods. "Yeah, that might work in the short term, but what about the long term, once you get used to the pain?" She doesn't have an answer.

He folds his arms. "Well . . ."—looks at her speculatively—"there's something else you can do, but it's not going to be easy."

"What?"—eager for the challenge.

He narrows his eyes at her. "Let Mr. March think you're interested. When he's talking, look straight at him"—he points at her—"not out the window, never take your eyes off him as long as his lips are moving. That'll be the best exercise in concentration of all. There are very few good teachers in the world, they're a gift."

"Like Uncle Simon."

Jack chuckles and rubs her head. "That's right, old buddy. But meantime you've got sorry old Mr. March. I've met him."

"You have?"

"Sure, when Maman and I registered you at the school, so I know what you're talking about. He's no genius. But let me tell you, you're lucky you have him for a teacher."

"I am?"

"Yes, because there are lots of Mr. Marches in the world and very few Uncle Simons. You have to be able to learn from the Mr. Marches and that's up to you. 'Cause at the end of the day, Mr. March isn't going to be around to take the blame. Do you understand what I mean?"

"Yup."

"Press on," he says, as adamantly as if he were addressing a young pilot. "There's an old saying for when the battle is raging and you've been hit."

Madeleine waits for it.

Dad regards her steadily, his right eye dead serious, his left eye no less so, if a little sad—it can't help it. "You put your head down, and you bleed a while. Then you get back up and keep on fighting."

Madeleine will look Mr. March in the eye and never miss a word. He will put felt hares next to her name. He will be amazed. And there will be nothing he can do about it, she will be so concentrated.

Jack smiles at the expression on her face. Spitfire.

He returns to his *Globe and Mail* and reads the joke on the front page: *Your Morning Smile: The man still wears the pants in the typical family. If you don't believe it, look under his apron.* He'll have to show that one to Henry Froelich. He skims. *200 MiGs in Cuba.* Turns the page: *The Cold War Comes to Latin America.* . . . Fun 'n' games.

In bed, Mimi puts down her *Chatelaine* magazine and asks, "Did you find out what was wrong?"

"Wrong with what?"

"Madeleine."

"Oh, yeah," says Jack, "she had a little problem daydreaming. Got nailed for it by the teacher, Mr. Marks."

"Mr. March," says Mimi. "Is it serious?"

"Naw," he says, "she's got it under control."

Mimi lays her cheek on his shoulder, strokes his chest; he covers her hand with his and squeezes. Continues reading his book, *Men and Decisions.*

She says, "She seemed so upset."

Eyes still on the page, "Oh I don't know, I think maybe. . . ."

"What?"

"Well maybe she was more upset by the cross-examination," he says, as though idly speculating.

Mimi lifts her head a little. "Did I cross-examine her?"

"A bit." His tone says, *No big deal.* He is not looking to criticize her.

She pauses, then nestles in, runs two fingers across his nipple, says, "You're such a nice papa."

He smiles. "Yeah?"

She raises herself on one elbow; he closes his book and reaches for the lamp switch. "Come here, Missus."

The sand dunes of Pinery Provincial Park are the perfect setting for Desert Rat warfare. Mike plays with her all weekend. They battle and escape and die elaborately, tumbling down the dunes—impossible to hurt yourself no matter how high you jump from, sand in your hair, a sandcastle that takes all day, sand in your sandwiches. Into the clean water of Lake Huron, riding the breakers all that windy Saturday, and that night, tucked into her sleeping bag next to her brother, Madeleine closes her eyes and sees the water cresting endlessly to shore on the movie screen inside her lids. Just smell the canvas of the good old tent, the friendly musk of the air mattress and, when the campground is quiet and you hear the sizzle of the last campfire of the last camping trip of the season being doused, listen to what was behind the silence all along: the waves in your ears, soundtrack to the surf behind your eyes.

On Sunday evening when they return, there is a moving van in the driveway of the little green bungalow.

## THE QUIET AMERICANS

*The nature of this national identity is a question Canadians agonize over. . . .*
*When asked, they can describe it only in negative terms. They may not know*
*what it is, but they are sure of what it is not. It is not American.*

Look, *April 9, 1963*

"CLASS, SAY HELLO to Claire."

"Hello, Claire."

Funny how a new kid makes you feel as though the rest of you have been together for ages. Suddenly you are a group and there is an air pocket around the newcomer. She does not belong. Even Grace belongs, in her way.

Claire McCarroll arrived just after the nine o'clock bell, with her father. Holding his hand. Mr. McCarroll resembled all the other dads in Centralia, but if you looked closely at the badge on his air force hat you would see an eagle with outspread wings, thirteen stars encircling its head, one claw clutching an olive branch, the other several arrows. Above his left breast pocket were his wings, outstretched on either side of the shield of the United States of America, topped by a star. His uniform was a deeper blue than those of the Canadian dads, and when he moved, the weave imparted a grey sheen. The effect was pleasingly foreign and familiar all at once.

Claire was dressed in baby blue, from barrettes to ankle socks. She carried a Frankie and Annette lunchbox suspended from her wrist like a purse. No one ever stays at school for lunch so Madeleine wondered what she had in there. Auriel passed a note to Madeleine that read, "Is she your long-lost sister?" They did look something alike. Dark brown pixie cuts, heart-shaped faces and small noses. Except Madeleine was taller and the new girl had blue eyes, shyly downcast. No one had yet heard her speak. She reminded Madeleine of a porcelain figurine—something lovely for your mantelpiece.

Mr. March shook hands with her father, then escorted Claire to her seat—he can be nice sometimes. The American dad hesitated in the doorway and waved to Claire. She waved back and blushed. Madeleine understood that. Finally her embarrassing dad left and everyone stared at Claire as she sat and folded her hands on her desk. And everyone—at least all the girls—noticed her beautiful silver charm bracelet.

Mimi, Betty Boucher, Elaine Ridelle and Vimy Woodley are in mid-protest on Sharon McCarroll's front step.

"We wouldn't dream of it," says Vimy.

Sharon has invited them in but the ladies have only dropped by to welcome her, deliver an information kit and a plate of squares, and extend the formal invitation for the young woman to join the Officers' Wives Club. Sharon was immediately endearing because she instantly asked them in, allowing them to decline vigorously. She's a pretty little thing. Mimi is reminded of an actress . . . which one?

From the front porch it's plain to see that the McCarrolls' house contains the usual forest of cardboard boxes and errant furniture, but Sharon is neatly turned out in pumps and a bright little short-sleeved dress, a *Willkommen* plate already graces the wall of the tiny front hall, alongside a commemorative plaque of her husband's squadron at Wiesbaden, and the smell of baking is coming from her kitchen. Impressive, but not surprising in an American service wife. Their ability to march in and out on a dime and a blaze of home-baked, fully accessorized glory is legendary.

What is surprising—and the women will discuss this later—is that Sharon McCarroll is not what you would expect of a fighter pilot's wife. Especially an American one. She is shy. Soft-spoken. She makes Mimi, and perhaps the other women too, feel . . . American.

"We're just the welcome wagon." Elaine Ridelle is in pedal pushers and tennis shoes, still managing to look girlish six months into her pregnancy.

"We aren't here to see you put the kettle on, love," says Betty. Betty unfailingly wears a dress—in this instance a crisp shirtwaist. Not due to any Old World view of proper female attire, but because she knows how to bring out the best in her figure, which is pleasingly plump. "Put a pair of trousers on me and I'd look like a beached whale," she has said. Which is an exaggeration, but Mimi respects a woman who knows her own good and not-so-good points. Mimi herself is in a pair of lemon-yellow cigarette pants and a sleeveless white knit turtleneck.

"You've got your hands full enough already," she says, handing her new neighbour a foil-covered Corningware dish, and before Sharon can object, "It's only a *fricot au*—a lamb stew."

Sharon is so young. Betty and Mimi are moved to take her under their wing, and Elaine says, "Do you and your husband golf, Sharon?"

At which Sharon smiles, looks down and half-shakes her head, no, and Vimy says, "Give the poor girl a chance to catch her breath, Elaine."

"That's okay," says Sharon, a gentle Southern sigh in her words. Lee Remick, that's who she reminds Mimi of.

Vimy says, "Here's your survival kit, my dear, my number's at the top and my house is over there." She points up the street to the detached white house with the flagpole on its lawn. She hands the young woman a binder and adds, "My daughter Marsha babysits, and that's probably enough out of us for the moment."

Mimi observes Vimy closely. Her manners, her ability to put others at ease; that is the definition of breeding, and a must in a CO's wife. Mimi learned a lot from her mother and her twelve siblings back in Bouctouche, New Brunswick, but she didn't learn what women like Vimy can teach her. Jack will one day be in Hal's position, and Mimi knows she will have to entertain "wheels," as Jack calls them, in her own home. She will be promoted too. The men all have to take exams and pass courses in order to qualify for advancement; the wives have to train on the job. Mimi notes how Vimy smiles graciously, and doesn't shake Sharon's whole hand, but instead lightly presses her fingers.

Of course, they all end up trooping into the little green bungalow, because Sharon insists—not in hearty tones, or with brash protestations of Southern hospitality, but by blushing and retreating to her kitchen, where she puts the percolator on and takes a pan of hermits from the oven.

"This is Bugs Bunny. He's a rabbit."

Laughter. Madeleine pauses. Silence, all eyes upon her. Mr. March has ordered her to go first. She has looked him in the eye and proceeded to the front of the class. Clean slate. Concentrate.

"I like Bugs because he speaks his mind," she says loud and clear.

Laughter. She didn't mean it to be funny. She's merely telling the truth. Show-and-tell. *Just the facts, ma'am.*

"His favourite food is carrots and his favourite expression is, 'Nyah, what's up, doc?'"

Laughter. She can feel her face reddening. She consults her recipe cards, where she wrote her presentation in point form with the help of her father.

"He is wily. He lives by his own rules and he always gets away from Elmer Fudd. Once he dressed up as a girl and sang, 'The Rabbit in Red.'"

Giggles.

She departs from her notes and sings tentatively, in Bugsy's voice, "'Oh da wabbit in wed . . . '"—a little soft-shoe—"'yah-dah dah-dah-dah dah-dah de wabbit in wed.' And he put on false eyelashes and even, you know"—she spreads her fingers and makes a circular gesture over her chest; the class screams with laughter. She raises one eyebrow, twists her mouth like Bugs and improvises—"Falsies, I pwesume." Rapidly now, can't put a foot wrong, "Like the time he pretended to be a girl Tasmanian Devil with lovely big red lips?"—one hand behind her head, the other on her hip—"'Well hello there, big boy,' meanwhile he's got a bear trap in his mouth for teeth, chomp!—'Yowww! Yipe-yipe-yipe!'"

It is out of hand. Mr. March quells the merriment. "Enough mirth. You may sit down now, Miss McCarthy."

Madeleine instantly sobers up, gropes for her recipe cards where they have fallen under Mr. March's desk and returns to her seat. It's just as well that she has been cut short. It means that she didn't have to pass Bugsy around the class—standard operating procedure for show-and-tell. She doesn't like the idea of everyone handling him—although Bugs probably wouldn't mind. Nothing sticks to Bugs.

Grace Novotny has brought in a rag doll named Emily. It's home-made. "My sister made it for me." One of the sluts, thinks Madeleine involuntarily, then feels terribly sorry for Grace having a kind slut for a sister. Grace can't pronounce the letter "r." She says *sistew*.

Grace whispers something into the side of Emily's soft dirty head, then Emily gets passed around. Some kids are openly mean, handling the doll with their fingertips, holding their noses. Grace doesn't seem to register any of it. Madeleine holds Emily in both hands, not by her fingertips. Emily is grimy, but a lot of dolls are if they are loved. What if there is pee on Emily? There probably is if Grace sleeps with her. She is missing a felt eyebrow, her mouth is stitched in red wool. The effect is not of lips but of lips stitched shut with red wool. She wears a bikini, yellow polka dots like the song.

When Emily has been passed back to Grace, she tucks her in her arm and, without warning, starts singing, "Itsy Bitsy Teenie Weenie Yellow Polka-dot Bikini."

There's a difference between kids thinking you are funny, and kids laughing at you. The class is laughing as much as they did for Madeleine but it's different, and Mr. March is not stopping them. Madeleine doesn't find it funny but she tries to laugh in the way of "you're funny" as opposed to "you're retarded," in order to make the laughter okay, but it doesn't work. She gives up and waits for Grace to finish. Luckily Grace doesn't know all the words—she repeats the first line a few times, then sits back down.

Mr. March reads the name of the next person on the list, "Gordon Lawson." Gordon, with his clean freckles and tucked-in shirt, shows and tells about fishing flies. It's a relief even if it is terribly boring.

Jack takes a walk over to the Flying School. He plans to inquire about lessons for his son at the civilian flying club but he has an errand to do first. He heads down a corridor identical to the one in his own building, with its battleship-grey linoleum, until he gets to a door with "USAF Exchange Officer" painted in block letters on the frosted window. Through the half-open door he sees the USAF hat hanging on the hall-tree in the corner. He taps his knuckles against the glass. He expects to hear the usual hearty "It's open," and is prepared to extend his hand with a joke—something about IFF: identification friend or foe. Prepared for a super-friendly hotshot American pilot. But there is no sound. Instead, the door opens all the way and a young man stands before him. He salutes with the velocity of a karate chop and says, unsmiling, "Hello, sir." He looks just about old enough to be a Boy Scout. Jack says, "Wing Commander McCarthy," and shakes McCarroll's hand. "Welcome to Centralia, captain."

"Thank you, sir."

"This is a robin's egg." Claire's palms are cupped around a pale blue shell. It was in her Frankie and Annette lunchbox, nested in tissue paper. "It fell and I found it."

Does she have an accent? It's hard to tell, she speaks so softly.

"Speak up, little girl," says Mr. March.

"I found it," says Claire, and yes, you can hear a little sway to her words.

Claire goes to offer the blue egg to Philip Pinder in the front row, but Mr. March stops her. The egg is too delicate to be passed around the class. "Especially to the likes of Mr. Pinder." The class laughs in agreement. Even Philip Pinder laughs. Madeleine is relieved that Claire will be spared the agony of a broken robin's egg. Mr. March is kind at heart.

Everyone wishes Claire would talk more, in her American accent, but all she says in conclusion is "I collect them sometimes." *Sometahms.* That does it. At recess the girly-girls want to be her friend and several boys show off in her vicinity. Philip Pinder sings at the top of his lungs, "'Roger Ramjet he's our man, the hero of our nation, the only thing that's wrong with him is mental retardation!'"

Cathy Baxter puts one hand on her hip and says fed-uppedly, "Philip," and he squeals away like a racing car. Cathy Baxter is the boss of the girly-girls and their skipping ropes, and Joyce Nutt, who is the prettiest, is her second-in-command. They all surround Claire to marvel at her bracelet. Claire doesn't brag or say a thing, just holds out her wrist obligingly as Cathy goes through the charms one by one—

"Marjorie, don't butt in."

"Sorry, Cathy."

Thus, while Madeleine can see the physical resemblance, she knows— heading for the swings, climbing on and glimpsing the shiny pixie cut in the centre of the small crowd below—that she and Claire McCarroll are nothing alike.

"The following little girls will remain after the bell"—and he consults his seating plan even though he knows everyone's name by now— "Grace Novotny. . . ."

Well that's not surprising, Grace didn't "tell," she sang, and not terribly well.

"Joyce Nutt. . . ."

Joyce Nutt? What did she do? She is one of the skipping-rope girls and they never get in trouble—

"Diane Vogel. . . ."

Diane is also a skipping-rope girl, but not a bossy one. It seems she too requires improved concentration because, as Madeleine has just noticed, Diane has suddenly become a tortoise in spelling.

"And Madeleine McCarthy."

After all her efforts at concentration, she is required to remain after three. Due to mirth. Her stomach goes cold. She showed off and now she's in trouble. And yet she wasn't trying to show off. How do you tell the difference?

She and the others wait at the back of the empty classroom, ranged along the wall with the coat hooks, while Diane Vogel does her backbend up at the front. Mr. March spots her by holding her steady between his knees so that she won't fall and hurt herself.

"Can you spell Mississippi, little girl?"

"Thank you, sir," says Blair McCarroll as Jack slides a glass of beer to him along the bar at the mess.

McCarroll is, as Simon predicted, fresh-faced. His jaw has a freshly chiselled look, his profile clean and buffed. The hardness of youth is apparent behind the pleats and creases of his uniform, and in his neck rising from his starched collar, which has yet to wilt against any excess of flesh. The wings over his left breast pocket attest, along with a row of stripes, to his service as a fighter pilot. But in his manner there is none of the swagger of his trade. He has not seen fit to rumple his lapel, push back his hat, loosen his tie or look Jack in the eye with the force of a punch. A flush stains his cheeks at the slightest provocation.

"So what are you doing up our way, McCarroll?" asks Jack. "Going to learn to fly?"

The men laugh—two or three flying instructors here to welcome McCarroll, along with several non-aircrew officers from the school.

McCarroll glances down at the high gloss of the bar, then up again. "Well your pilots are some of the best in the world," he says in his mild drawl. "I consider it an honour to help out with the training."

A few men exchange looks, nod. Okay.

"You seem like a reasonable man, McCarroll," says Jack with a grin.

"Please call me Blair if you like, sir." He glances at the others. "And you all."

Vic Boucher orders a plate of fried scallops. "Who's going to join me?"

Ted Lawson says to Jack, "How about it, sir? *Einmal Bier?*"

A fresh round is bought, they move to a table, work is discussed along with plans for the next formal event—a dinner and dance in honour of the Air Vice Marshal from Air Training Command Headquarters, who is flying in from Winnipeg for Battle of Britain day. Jack groans inwardly at the thought of squeezing into his formal mess kit—his monkey suit. McCarroll will have no such problem; lean and anything but mean, he reminds Jack of a young seminarian. The kid is probably steady as a rock in the cockpit, perfect reflexes uncorrupted by bravado—the machines these lads fly nowadays are hair-trigger. Nothing like the old beasts Jack piloted.

Hal Woodley joins them, removing his hat, loosening his tie; the other officers straighten up and make room, greeting him, "Sir." A waiter brings him a clean ashtray and a Scotch.

Jack leans back again in his bucket chair amid the kibitzing. He watches McCarroll listening politely. It's an odd feeling, knowing something about another man that he is unaware of himself. Especially when it affects that man's family, thinks Jack. There's no harm in it, of course—both he and McCarroll have a special, if simple, job to do. But McCarroll doesn't know it, and won't need to know it until Simon gives Jack the word. McCarroll and his wife will eat, sleep, perhaps conceive a child here on this station. Their daughter will go to this school instead of another, and McCarroll doesn't know why. Yet. It doesn't sit perfectly well with Jack, this secret knowledge. Something about it—an inappropriate intimacy. The odour of some-one else's tousled sheets.

"What's the word, Jack?" asks Woodley.

"Well, things are ticking over pretty good. I got Warrant Officer Pinder on side, I figure my job's halfway done."

Woodley chuckles. "Don't get him too far on side, he'll fill your ice-box with deer meat and it's all you'll eat for a month."

The topic turns to fishing. Jack weighs in on New Brunswick salmon and Hal Woodley tells a story about an Indian guide up in northern British Columbia. *It's not right.* Jack shifts in his chair. Woodley should not be in the dark about why McCarroll is here. Like everyone else at this cocktail table, McCarroll is under Woodley's command, and any orders he follows while stationed here should come through Woodley. Jack is sitting next to an American officer who is not strictly subject to the chain of command. *This is wrong.*

" . . . and he said, 'Aw, you should've been here yesterday, Mr. Woodley, they was bitin' then.'" Laughter erupts. Even McCarroll has relaxed enough to join in. Jack feels a smile stretched across his face. My problem, he thinks, is that it never seemed as though I was going behind Woodley's back until McCarroll showed up and put this whole thing in uniform. It was supposed to be "unofficial." He sips, mildly relieved to have at least analyzed his discomfort. No, none of this is by the book, and Jack is unaccustomed to that. But the fact remains, we're all on the same side. This favour will be over and done with soon enough, and no one need ever be the wiser.

He bends to rise from his chair and experiences an uncomfortable sensation around his throat. As though he were carrying a little excess weight and, in the act of bending, the displacement of extra flesh had exerted a slight pressure on his neck. He lifts his glass of Scotch for a toast. "Here's to being above it all."

He feels the Scotch open his throat, says, "Cheers," by way of leave-taking and heads for the doors.

Knowing more about other people's lives than they do themselves—Jack reflects that, after all, it's nothing new for him. In Germany, at 4 Wing, he often had advance notice of exercises and drills, even postings. He knew whose leave would be cancelled, whose wife would be disappointed, who would get his preferred posting and who would be going to a radar base in the Arctic. It was part of his job to know and, sometimes, to decide. It never gave him a moment's pause. How different is this, really? He reaches the doors and glances back at the lounge full of officers. In a far corner is Nolan, alone at a table—not unusual in and of itself, there's no law that says a man always has to be "all in together, fellas." What is unusual is that Nolan is eating supper here again. At first Jack assumed Nolan's wife was away, but he was told earlier this week, by Vic Boucher, that Mrs. Nolan is some kind of invalid. Jack pushes through the big oak doors and fills his lungs with fresh air. He exhales the cigar and cigarette atmosphere, the aroma of liquor and beer and uniforms. He enjoys the company of his fellow officers, he enjoys his work, but all that is only a means to an end. Real life is what his wife is cooking up for him at home, this very moment.

When Madeleine emerges from the side door, she sees that Lisa and Auriel have not waited but are halfway across the field, walking slowly so she can catch up with them. She has already started running across the playground when Marjorie calls from the swings, "Hi Madeleine."

Madeleine doesn't stop. "Hi."

"Wait up."

"I can't." But she slows down, not wanting to catch up to Auriel and Lisa with Marjorie in tow.

"How come you had to stay after three?" Marjorie is breathless with the effort to keep up.

"'Cuz," says Madeleine.

"'Cause why?"

"To do exercises."

"Do you get to be a monitor?"

"No. I don't know."

"Can I play with you and Auriel and Lisa?"

Madeleine shrugs. "It's a free country."

Marjorie looks down.

Madeleine says, "Here," and hands her a chocolate rosebud.

Marjorie gazes at it and with an intake of breath says, "Oh Maddy, where did you get it?"

Madeleine mutters, "Mr. March."

Marjorie pops the rosebud in her mouth and, before she can say thank you, Madeleine takes off like the Road Runner, leaving Marjorie in a cloud of cartoon dust.

She catches up with Auriel and Lisa. "What happened?" Auriel asks.

Madeleine looks at them solemnly. Tucks in her chin, unhooks her eyeballs from their moorings and says, "'Mm-bedea-bedea, that's all folks!'" As they zigzag toward home, she steals a glance over her shoulder at Marjorie trailing behind them. Madeleine didn't want the rosebud anyway.

"How was school, old buddy?"

They are on the couch, reading the paper before supper; Madeleine is snuggled under his arm.

"It was fine. There's a new kid."

"I figured as much."

"She's American."

"Mm-hm." They read "The Wizard of Id." Then he asks, "What's the situation report?" Jack has decided not to bring up the subject at the dinner table, he knows she feels private about it.

"I got put back up to Dolphins," she says.

"There you go, this time next week you'll be a rabbit again."

"Hare."

"Did you do like we said?"

"Yes."

"Did you look him in the eye and not miss a trick?"

"Yes."

"Good stuff."

Madeleine waits for him to ask if she had to stay after three again, but he doesn't. And why would he? The whole point was getting out of tortoises, and she has done that. Why would he suspect she might have been kept after three again? And anyhow, it was her own fault. She stepped on another land mine, she has to learn where they are. A bad teacher is a gift. Do you really want to tell Dad how you disrupted the class due to mirth? After we talked about winning the war of concentration? You know what you must do. You have your mission. Operation Concentration.

"Dad?"

"Yeah?"

" . . . Are backbends good for you?"

"I suppose so, yeah."

Jack turns a page of his newspaper. *KHRUSHCHEV SAYS WEAPONS IN CUBA SOLELY FOR DEFENCE. . . .*

"Do they improve your concentration?"

"What's that, old buddy?"

"Backbends."

"Oh, I don't know, how would they do that?"

"By making the blood flow to your head."

"Yeah I suppose they would. Why, have you been doing backbends?"

"Yes."

"When?"

"After school." She adds, "On my way home." That's not really a lie. Mr. March's desk is on her way home, she has to pass it in order to get to the door.

"Don't work too hard, sweetie." He puts down the paper because she looks so serious all of a sudden. "Listen now"—he pulls her onto his knee—"maybe it's time to throttle back, what do you think?" He tells her to forget all about tortoises and hares for a while, because "half the battle goes on back here," and he taps the back of his head, "while you're out playing or in bed asleep dreaming. You've got to be careful not to burn the candle at both ends."

Dad doesn't know what backbends are. She tries not to think about them while he hugs her. They don't belong here on his lap. Mr. March's knees in a vise grip on her hips, "spotting" her.

"Dad, can I watch TV now?"

"Why don't you go out and play, there won't be many sunny days left."

"*To Tell the Truth* is on."

"It'll be on next week too, don't you think, eh?"

"Yeah." She returns his smile and gets down off the couch. Her legs feel heavy.

When she imagines telling him about the backbends, she thinks of herself doing one right in front of him, and that makes her feel sorry for him because he would be so bewildered. But Dad wasn't wrong. She got out of tortoises.

Jack returns to his paper. Bleeding hearts in Britain are demonstrating, *Ban the Bomb!* Self-described Communists. That sort of leaning was understandable in the thirties but is unforgivable now. Have these people never heard of Stalin? He turns the page. Sees his daughter still standing in the middle of the room, looking a little lost. Maybe she's had a falling-out with her friends. "Did you say there was a new girl in your class?"

Madeleine nods.

"Why don't you go call on her. Make her feel at home."

"Okay."

Her legs are so heavy and the sun is so bright, it feels like miles down to the little green bungalow. She squints, feeling almost sick.

"Hello Madeleine, honey," says Sharon McCarroll. She has the same sweet Virginia voice as Claire.

Claire McCarroll has a bedroom full of unbroken toys. Shelves of dolls, and games with no pieces missing. That's because she is that rare and blessed creature, an only child. She doesn't so much play with Madeleine as watch Madeleine play. She is like someone in a foreign country who knows a few polite phrases: "You can play with it." Claire is not used to defending her stuff. She even lets Madeleine hold the bird's nest on her dresser. It has the blue egg in it.

"Wow," says Madeleine, "you have an Easy-Bake Oven."

"You can play with it."

"'It's Kenner! It's fun!'" and Madeleine squawks like the cartoon bird, "Grawk!" Claire giggles and it sounds like water bubbling up. It is so sudden and happy that it makes Madeleine laugh.

"Pull my string," says Madeleine. And Claire pulls the imaginary string. Bugs Bunny says, "Nyah, what's up doc?" Claire laughs again. "Pull it again." Claire does.

It's too nice out to play inside so Mrs. McCarroll lets them take Claire's Easy-Bake Oven outside. They sit on the grass, peering through the oven door, waiting for the light bulb to cook the tiny angel food cake. Madeleine is in play clothes but Claire is still in her dress.

There is not a great deal to talk about.

The cake is ready. Claire opens the oven. "You can cut it," she says, blushing.

Madeleine divides the cake scrupulously and they take as long as they can to eat it off tea-party plates. Then they do somersaults to aid digestion. Madeleine sees Claire's underpants even though she isn't trying to look. She imagines Claire doing a backbend at Mr. March's desk, then closes her eyes to get rid of the picture. She squeezes them shut only to see Claire's underpants, their pattern bright and clear on the insides of her eyelids. A storm of yellow butterflies.

That week at school, Claire is much sought after. But it wanes. She is so genuinely what she seems—quiet, shy—that there is no point continuing to make a fuss or fight over her. She never picks a best friend, which is what everyone is waiting for her to do. Offerings are made: "Claire, do you want one of my Smarties?"

"Yes please, would you like a cookie?"

Regardless of who makes the offer, Claire accepts it and offers something back. She doesn't understand that you shouldn't enter into any exchange with Grace Novotny, that it taints you. Claire just doesn't get it, even after a whole week. She doesn't join any huddles, she swings on the swing alone, not high. She may go down the slide, braking carefully with her hands on the way. And she rides to and from school on her bike every day, even though the PMQs are too close for anyone to have to ride.

Her bike has fat tires like Madeleine's, and underneath its custom paint job perhaps it is also a Zippy Vélo. But Claire's father painted it pink and white, a decorative diamond pattern like the Pied Piper's cloak gracing the fenders and chain guard. It has a pink seat, pink bell, pink plastic wicker basket and—pièce de résistance—two glistening pink plastic streamers.

Claire is definitely not a reject, and since everyone kind of likes her and nobody dislikes her, no one notices that she has no friends.

## Policies of Containment

*As a parent you undoubtedly want to protect your youngsters from missteps and mishaps in the sexual sphere. You undoubtedly want to assure your children of sound sexual information and of freedom from marriage-impairing inhibitions.*

Chatelaine, *August 1962*

Going to school in the morning is often very different from coming home in the afternoon. Wednesdays are best because she never has to stay after three. No one does. Mr. March conducts the school band, and Wednesday afternoons they practise from three to four-thirty. Lisa and Auriel are in the band, playing triangle and recorder respectively, but Madeleine has managed to avoid it by promising her mother to practise her accordion faithfully. She has started lessons with Mr. Boucher.

Every morning she leaves her house in time to join up with Lisa and Auriel and they sing all the way to school. *American Bandstand* rate-a-record. Madeleine throws wide her arms and belts plaintively, "'Whe-e-e-ere the Boys Are . . . !'" Auriel is not shy either, she will twist right there on the side of the road, and sometimes it feels too early in the day to be laughing that hard. They have named themselves The Songelles. Spinning their hands, snapping their fingers, locomotioning all the way down the street.

If they leave for school early enough, they can double back to the corner of Algonquin Drive and the Huron County road, where the teenagers wait for the bus to high school, and catch a glimpse of Ricky Froelich and Marsha Woodley holding hands. He carries her books.

The bell rings and every morning, amid the scraping of chairs, the after-three exercises seem very far away, banished by the comfortable daily routine that begins with singing "God Save the Queen"—if you watch carefully, you will see that Claire McCarroll sings different words to it, but not loudly. American words. What's more, there is now a gerbil living in a cage at the back of the classroom, imparting a friendly rodent smell of wood shavings. His name is Sputnik.

"Turn to page twenty-five in your Macmillan speller. . . ."

At recess there is the minor annoyance of avoiding Marjorie Nolan, who has yet to settle with any one girl or group. "Want to come to my house for lunch, Madeleine?" Why can't she find her own friends?

There are many girls like Marjorie: girls with pursed lips and opinions on other girls, and clothes that are clean at the end of the day, let her find them. Why is she not in Cathy Baxter's group? They skip double-dutch and have no shortage of lesser girls willing to be ever-enders—Marjorie could start out as one of those, then move up through the ranks. The bossy girls. They always have an important secret that's "for me to know and you to find out." They throw underhand in baseball and have their art put up on the wall on Fridays. They are perfect for Marjorie. But although Marjorie is an excellent skipper, makes perfect paper fortune-tellers and gets hares in almost every subject, when she agrees with them or says, "I love your sweater, Cathy," they merely pause and Cathy rolls her eyes; then they all go on with what they were talking about before they were so rudely interrupted by no one. Madeleine has begun to feel a creeping responsibility. Am I going to have to be her friend because no one else will?

"Turn to page twelve in your *Canadian Treasury of Song* books." Mr. March sounds a note on his pitch pipe, raises a thick finger, brings it down, and the class sings: "'Land of the silver birch, home of the beaver, where still the mighty moose wanders at will. . . . '"

As the day progresses, Madeleine watches the felt animals on the bulletin board carefully.

"The following little girls will remain after three. . . ."

Once or twice a week. Sometimes all of them, sometimes just some of them. What did those other girls do wrong today? Beautiful sad Diane Vogel, intelligent Joyce Nutt, and Grace Novotny. Not even Grace is capable of being a total reject all the time, yet she is always required to remain.

They line up at the back of the room where the coat hooks are. When it is Madeleine's turn, she walks down the aisle and he looks at her in that unseeing way that makes her think, maybe I am just a pigment of his imagination. Auriel and Lisa don't ask her about it any more, no one does. They are simply the little girls who are required to remain. The exercise group. No one in the class wonders what the exercise group is any more, it just is.

It's easy to get home by twelve past three because Mr. March never keeps them more than ten minutes, so no one gets in trouble for being kept after three; because no one is late enough for their parents to notice.

"If you don't tell them, I won't," says Mr. March. "Of course, that all depends on how well you do after three."

That's nice of him. Bad enough to get in trouble with your teacher, but who wants to get in more trouble with your parents?

A few weeks into school and it feels like months, the unstructured days of summer having given way to lessons and sports and Brownies. Madeleine and her friends are taking ballet, tap, jazz and highland dancing over at the rec centre, from a tall bony lady called Miss Jolly who looks exactly like a licorice Twizzler in her leotard. Miss Jolly laughs her toothy laugh at Madeleine's most gracefully intended efforts. "You're remarkably supple, Madeleine, but I'm not sure dance is your forte." When she gets them to do the twist, Madeleine feigns a stomach ache. The thought of writhing sexily around with all the other little girls gives her a queasy after-three feeling.

The grown-up social whirl is likewise in full swing. There are cocktail parties on Friday nights and a do at the mess every Saturday. Madeleine's parents have started curling Saturday mornings, and during the week the ladies get together for coffee parties and bridge parties.

The latter are the best because they happen on school nights, and involve a cornucopia of snacks and baked goods that translate into treats the following day.

One Thursday evening in late September, Mimi hosts four tables of four players each and permits Madeleine to stay up and say hello to the ladies. Madeleine looks longingly at the crystal bowls of bridge mix on every card table, at the tiered plates of gooey Nanaimo bars and butter-tarts. An orange sunset chiffon cake sits proudly on a pedestal dish, and there are hot and cold hors d'oeuvres—wiener bites, Swedish meatballs, pickled things on toothpicks. The living room is bright with laughter, conversational clusters throwing off sparks like the combination of cashmere and freshly washed hair; on the buffet, the silver service glitters along with tiny glasses of crème de menthe; lipstick adorns the rims of teacups, patent-leather purses are parked on the floor like miniature cars; it all mingles with the scent of perfume and cigarette smoke, to heady effect.

Madeleine is in her polo pajamas and quilted robe. "Hello Madeleine, sweetheart, how is school treating you?" Kind, elegant Mrs. Woodley. "It's very good, thank you." Mrs. McCarroll is over by the fireplace listening to Mrs. Lawson, who is patting her hand—Gordon's mother is almost as inviting as Mrs. Boucher, a comfortable-looking woman. Mrs. Noonan is nice but a bit cross-eyed. Madeleine hears Mrs. Ridelle's voice in the kitchen, "Come on, Betty, live a little!" She is shaking an aluminum Thermos. Johnny Mathis sings on the hi-fi about wanting to have children. Madeleine is mesmerized by the scene. If she stands perfectly still and unfocuses her eyes and ears, she can see and hear everything at once:

". . . cheap at half the price—"

". . . get out, really?!"

". . . knows how to put on the dog—"

". . . posted to Brussels—"

". . . hasn't joined."

"Who hasn't?"

"Sylvia Nolan, she still hasn't joined the Wives' Club."

". . . case of nerves—"

*Sylvia Nolan.* Marjorie's mother, the one with headaches. Madeleine's eyes dart about—is Mrs. Nolan here? Is she going to tell about the exercise group? Of course not. *She still hasn't joined the Wives' Club.* And what exactly is there to tell, anyhow? Suddenly Mrs. Baxter is there, beaming down at her—a big-boned woman with big-boned blonde hair and bold red lips. "You must be friends with my Cathy."

Madeleine half smiles, at a loss how to reply. Mrs. Nutt, a slim woman at Mrs. Baxter's side, says quietly, "You're in Joyce's class, how do you like grade four, dear?" "Fine, thank you." Mrs. Nutt takes her place at a card table and says something to Mrs. Vogel, who looks like Judy Garland—beautiful and on the verge of crying from happiness. Have Joyce Nutt and Diane Vogel told their mothers about the exercise group? Are Mrs. Nutt and Mrs. Vogel talking about it right now? Are they going to tell Madeleine's mother?

"Madeleine."

"*Oui, maman.*"

It's bedtime. Mimi wraps a chocolate ladyfinger in a cocktail napkin and gives it to Madeleine, saying, "Now straight to bed, or the *bonhomme sept heures* will come and get you."

Her mother has been to the beauty parlour today. Her hair is perfectly and simply formed, like her green and black sleeveless dress. Madeleine walks slowly upstairs, and watches Maman thread her way through the room and take the needle off the record. She turns, claps her hands twice and announces, "*Allons, les femmes,* let's get down to business." Everyone laughs and obeys. Madeleine lingers, her eyes on Mrs. Vogel and Mrs. Nutt, willing them to move to separate tables. They do. She is relieved that Mrs. Nolan is not here, but wonders at the absence of Mrs. Novotny. Then she recalls Marjorie's words, "Her father's just a corporal." Mrs. Novotny isn't an officer's wife, so there would appear to be no danger that Maman will hear about the exercises from her.

"*Madeleine, vite, vite. Bonne nuit, ma p'tite.*"

"Do you know the capital of Borneo, little girl?"

Madeleine only tells her father the good stuff. She doesn't mope in front of him any more. She doesn't want him to think their plan isn't working. It's working. She is only ever a tortoise for a couple of days, then gets promoted back to dolphins. But never to hares. It would be sad for him to think he hadn't fixed the problem. He has fixed it. And when she is with him, the after-three exercises become a very small and separate thing.

She helps him mow the lawn, with her hands next to his on the bar, and they discuss things over the roar of the motor. She tells him about the kids in her class—the bossy girls and the Philip Pinder boys and the rest except, of course, the exercise group—and he teaches her new words, "peer pressure" and "group dynamics." He helps her write a speech on the topic of humour, laughter as the great "panacea." She is mercilessly mocked in school for her use of such a big word, and responds by using it as frequently as possible, regardless of context. She and her father speculate as to why God allows war and cancer and the suffering of innocent dogs, they discuss what she will do when she grows up, going over the pros and cons of various professions—conducting what he calls a cost-benefit analysis. He asks where she wants to be in five years, they assess short-term versus long-term goals and how they can all lead to Ed Sullivan. One Saturday they pack a lunch and hike for miles on dirt roads far from the base, just the two of them with a Thermos of Nestlé's Quik and a supply of peanut-butter sandwiches. Times like this become memories almost instantly, part of a gilded past that somehow coexists with the present. Remember-whens to look back on even as they are happening, bittersweet and aglow with sunshine fading to sepia—the late September dust suspended in the wake of a single passing car, leafy smell in the air, blue sky reflected in his sunglasses.

She keeps meaning to ask him what the capital of Borneo is, but she always forgets.

"The following little girls will remain after the bell. Diane Vogel, Grace Novotny, Joyce Nutt, Madeleine McCarthy and Marjorie Nolan."

Marjorie looks around proudly and her dimples appear. When her eyes meet Madeleine's she looks away haughtily. Only Margarine Nolan could possibly be proud of being chosen for the exercise group. Madeleine feels her face grow hot at the realization that Marjorie has no idea what the exercise group really is. What if she tells on us? *Tells what?*

They line up along the coat hooks. Madeleine leans back until she feels the hook grind against her spine, then slip sideways to find a spot between her ribs. Like a chicken carcass.

You stand against the coat hooks until he calls you. Or until he tells you to sit back down at your desk and write a spot quiz. Then he lines up the rosebuds on his desk and you all go up and take one, and leave. "Side door, little girls."

Diane Vogel is up there behind the big oak desk with him. Madeleine watches and waits. I wonder what kind of exercises he makes the other girls do? Do they do the same ones I do? Do they think they're in the smart group, or the stupid group? Or the bad group? Which group am I in?

Grace Novotny does backbends behind his desk while he spots her, holding her steady between his knees so she won't fall. He doesn't want any foolish accidents.

Joyce Nutt does backbends too, but beside his desk, never behind it. And he doesn't spot her. Doesn't he care if she falls?

Madeleine glances down the line. There are five of us now in the exercise group. Almost enough for a six in a Brownie pack. And we are all Brownies, although we will certainly get our wings and fly up to Guides this spring. Except for Grace—she may have to walk up.

No one talks, not even Marjorie. Her lips are compressed as though to prevent herself from talking. She has figured out that this is a rule, and once Marjorie knows something is a rule, she goes around like a monitor.

Everyone waits while Grace does her exercises. All you hear is the sound of the gerbil burrowing in his cage and the sound of Mr. March breathing—it's hard work for him.

Three minutes past three. The cutout turkeys are up on the wall in anticipation of Thanksgiving. Smiling and dressed like the people who are going to eat them. Happy pilgrims on their way to get their heads chopped off. There are also horns of plenty with squashes and corn tumbling out.

Grace Novotny walks back up to the coat hooks.

"Come here, little girl," says Mr. March. No one knows who he is talking to until he says, "The one in the white blouse," and Madeleine proceeds to the front of the class.

"Do you know the capital of Borneo, little girl?"

"No, Mr. March."

"What were the names of Columbus's ships?"

"The *Niña,* the *Pinta* and the *Santa María.*"

"Correct. Let's see if you can get two out of three. What is the word for a female peacock?"

"I don't know, Mr. March."

"The answer is peahen. Say peahen."

"Peahen."

"Say peacock."

"Peacock."

"Pea."

"Pea."

"Cock."

"Cock."

"Come closer. Closer. That's it. I want to see if you're getting any stronger. I want you to keep up with your exercises, otherwise I won't be able to give you a passing grade in health, stand still."

We don't even have health as a subject; he is crazy.

"Let me feel your muscles, little girl. Oh that's a big one. I'm not hurting you."

His cheeks jiggle and he stares at her but it's as if he were looking at nobody at all. Where is Madeleine? The man is touching her freshly ironed blouse; it has a brooch of the Acadian flag, white red and blue, Maman pinned it there this morning, poor Maman.

"Let me feel your chest muscles. They're growing aren't they, do you rub them every day? And your tummy muscles, and your—oh you're sweating aren't you?" Mr. March touches her underpants. It feels good.

"Do you know what will happen if your parents find out what a bad child you've been?"

Her head is terribly hot. She shakes her head, no.

"They'll send you away." *Into the forest.* She feels her heart beat against her ribcage, sees it huge and red pulsing against the bars of bone.

"Here, little girl, feel my muscle—that's it—squeeze it, it's strong." It is rubber, there is a smell. Blank it out or you'll throw up.

"Are you strong? Let me feel how strong you are. How hard can you squeeze?" It is loose skin on the outside and hard on the inside, it is raw.

"Rub it."

He puts his hand around Madeleine's and it must hurt him to rub it like that, the skin pulls away from the top of it like on a turkey neck, the hole is where he pees.

Then he pushes her away, and maybe he will call the next little girl up to his desk and maybe he won't.

Madeleine walks back to the coat hooks. It takes a long time and yet her feet have not stopped walking from Mr. March's desk, so probably it has taken the normal amount of time. She presses her spine against the hook, and the next thing she notices is that Marjorie Nolan is up behind his desk, but she doesn't remember Marjorie being called or leaving the coat hooks; Marjorie is just there at his desk all of a sudden. Her legs feel heavy, tired, as if she had been standing for a long time. But it's only seven minutes past three.

Marjorie has her hands out and Mr. March is filling them with candy—that's not how we usually do things in the exercise group.

"I'm the candy monitor," says Marjorie, suddenly back at the coat hooks. She struts along the line, and when she gets to Madeleine she says, "You only get it if you're good and not stupid, so forget it, Madeleine."

Madeleine wants to say, "I don't give a care," but her lips are dry.

Marjorie licks a red Smartie, applies it as lipstick, then pops it into her mouth and crunches it. "You'll be sorry, Madeleine."

Out the side door with the others. Once again Madeleine is thankful for the side door, because imagine meeting the principal, Mr. Lemmon, or Mr. Froelich, and having them wonder what it is you have been doing in the classroom after three—behind the door with the turkeys taped over the window.

They disperse. Silent as usual, except for Marjorie, who tries to chit-chat as though she were a member of a keen new club. Madeleine avoids her.

"Hi," says Claire McCarroll. She's riding her bike around the school-yard, her pink streamers glittering in the breeze.

Madeleine's head feels swampy, her underpants feel dank, she pictures their yellow butterfly pattern but remembers that those are Claire's, not hers, hers have a ladybug pattern, Maman bought them at Woolworth's, no one ever imagined that a teacher would touch them, that's what happened today. Also, usually you just feel his thing poking through his trousers when you do your backbends, which are otherwise just normal backbends and the poking could be an accident or a pocket knife. Now you can never say to anyone, "Oh we just do backbends." You can't say anything.

"Where did you get these bruises?" asks Mimi, examining Madeleine's upper arm.

"Just hacking around," says Madeleine. "Auriel and I were giving Indian sunburns." Which is not a lie, they have done so on occasion.

Mimi narrows her eyes. "*Vraiment?*"

Madeleine blushes. Does Maman notice that the bruise is the shape of a grown-up's hand? But Mimi says, "Are you sure you haven't been playing with that one across the street?"

"Who?"

"Colleen."

"No."

"Well just remember, Colleen Froelich is too old for you."

Mimi turns back to the stove in time to save the Hollandaise sauce.

"How was school today?" asks Jack over supper.

"It was good."

"What did you do?"

"Turkeys." Madeleine reaches for her glass of milk and knocks it over. "Woops!" Mimi catches the glass before it tumbles to the floor, and Jack shoots his chair back to spare his trousers.

"Butterfingers," says Mike.

"Michael, help your mother," says Jack.

Tears spring to Madeleine's eyes. "Sorry."

"Don't cry over spilt milk, sweetie."

Mimi takes a tea towel, goes down on one knee and dabs at Madeleine's blouse. Her daughter bursts into tears. Mimi puts her arms around her and pats her back, and Madeleine covers her eyes and wails. "*Madeleine, qu'est-ce qu'il y a?*" Mimi takes her gently by the shoulders and looks at her. "*Eh? Dis à maman.*" But her little girl turns away and goes to her father. He has his arms open. She climbs onto his lap and begins immediately to calm down. Jack winks over Madeleine's head at Mimi. Mimi smiles for him, and turns back to the sink.

Mike rolls his eyes as he wipes up the milk. Madeleine's humiliation is compounded by the knowledge that her brother is right; she's crying for no reason, proving what a girl she is.

"What's wrong, sweetie-pie?" asks Dad.

She answers, "I don't want you to die," triggering fresh sobs.

Jack chuckles and ruffles her hair. "I'm not gonna die!" He makes her box him to show what a tough old rooster he is. "Tough old roosters don't die in a hurry, that's it, hit me right here."

After supper he plays with them—her favourite game from when she and Mike were little. Dad is the spider. His spider fingers curl slowly in the air, the suspense builds, you wait for him to strike, wanting to run away, wanting to wait till the last second, "Gotcha!" Then he tickles you until your stomach aches from laughing, and the only way to make him stop is for whoever is free at the moment to give him a kiss.

"Mike, Mike! Kiss Dad!"

But Mike won't, he's too old to give Dad a kiss.

"No fair!" she cries, "I kissed him for you!"

"So?" says Mike from the couch, "*C'est la guerre,*" and he flips through *The Economist.*

The spider has her by the ankles, she's trying to get out of the quicksand, clawing the rug, "*Maman! Donne un bec à papa! Vite!*"

A moment's respite. Then, oh no! The spider is tickling again—it's great, it makes you crazy—

"Mike!" Now the spider has her by the arms—"Maman!" Laughing—Now he pulls her into jail—"Somebody!" Now he clamps her between his knees in a vise grip. Madeleine stops laughing. She keeps the smile on her face but her stomach has dropped. Dad is tickling and she writhes and laughs, acting normal, but she is feeling hot and not very well, she cannot move. His knees are pinned on either side of her hips.

"The woolly spider's got you now," he growls, as usual.

*Let me go.*

"Maman!" she calls, laughing like a girl who is playing with her dad.

Those are Dad's trousers right in front of her. What if she bumps into him? The hot smell is around her, the living room is getting dark. He leans forward and gives her a whisker rub.

"What's all the commotion?" Maman appears in the doorway, her yellow rubber gloves dripping.

"Kiss Dad," Madeleine says, quiet now, making a smile.

Maman kisses him and the spider lets go. Madeleine smiles at him in appreciation of her favourite game. He laughs, pats her on the head and picks up his newspaper again. Madeleine heads for the front door.

"Madeleine, *attends une minute,*" says Maman, looking down from the top of the three steps.

"What, Mum?"

Mimi walks down the steps and says gently, "You're too big to play like that with your father."

Madeleine runs across the street and cuts through the Froelichs' yard to the park beyond, with the swings and the merry-go-round. She sits against a big tree. An oak. It hears her. She is too big. Maman knows there was something bad about that game. If you play with your dad and he bumps against you and you feel his thing, it's because you are too big to be playing with your father.

But Madeleine didn't bump against him. It's up to her, however, to make sure it never happens, because it would not be his fault. She would have only herself to blame. Her mother knows what Madeleine knows. Games where you are trapped between his knees are not good. Her father is too innocent to know it's a bad game. Dad doesn't know what could happen. He doesn't know what you know. He would be helpless while you bumped against his trousers, he would be bewildered with a thing in his pants. Madeleine presses her back against the good bark and cries with her forehead on her knees. The tree hears her. *Poor Dad. Poor Dad.*

"Jack," says Mimi in bed that night.

"Yeah?"

"Madeleine's too old for those games."

"What games?" he asks, scanning his *Time. The U.S. policy of merely trying to isolate—or contain—Cuba has had dismal results. . . .*

"Tickling games, I saw the look on her face."

He lowers his magazine. "You mean the old woolly spider?"

"Yes. She's too old, she was embarrassed."

"Was she?"

"Oh yes, I think she only plays to please you."

Jack blinks. "Really?"

She smiles at him. "I hate to break the news, Papa," she says, "but your little girl is growing up."

"You think I embarrassed her?"

"A little bit, yes."

He takes it in. "But it's okay to play with her otherwise," he says.

She smiles. "You don't have to lose your old buddy. But you want to leave some room for your young lady."

She gives him a kiss and reaches for her *Chatelaine*. She flips through
. . . *the average salary paid to women is only half that paid to men—*

"She's just like her maman," says Jack.

Mimi laughs. "Don't I know that."

"She's a spitfire." He gives her a kiss, then, "I didn't mean to embarrass her."

"I know."

They read.

His: *Since last October, the U.S. has boosted its force of military advisers to more than 10,000 and is now spending $1,000,000 daily to beat the Viet Cong. . . .*

Hers: *Thanksgiving recipes your family will love.*

Once upon a time, in a republic that no longer exists, there was a handsome and brilliant young man called Wernher von Braun. He came from an aristocratic Prussian family, and he shared the passion of his generation. Rockets. They were, as yet, merely a dream; humanity's chance to rise far above the violence of earthly existence, to where our petty differences would shrink in the immensity of space. A dream of peace in our time. Wernher studied physics and joined a club of amateur enthusiasts who built small rockets of their own, launching them on weekends.

He caught the notice of an army officer who shared his dream and belonged to an organization with pockets deep enough to fund it. In 1936, Germany was recovering, freeing itself from the yoke of poverty. There were finally people in power—vulgar people perhaps—who nonetheless knew how to get things done. It was a wonderful time to be young.

Wernher was twenty-five years old when he was put in charge of the army's secret project to build the biggest, most powerful rockets the world had ever known. But first they needed to find a safe place to forge their dream. Wernher's mother said to him over Christmas dinner, "Why don't you take a look at Peenemünde? Your grandfather used to go duck hunting up there." Wernher fell in love at first sight with Peenemünde's wilderness, alive with deer and birds, its lost sandy beaches and Baltic sea breezes. The first trees fell before the bulldozers on April 1. Scaffolding and test stands were raised, rail tracks were laid, barracks were built and a neo-classical campus sprang up to accommodate designers, physicists, engineers, aerodynamicists, technicians, administrators and all the gifted young people who would make the dream a reality.

The slaves came later.

# OKTOBERFEST

*At the altar the future splinters gloriously into a spectrum of split-level houses filled with appliances, rosy-cheeked children and boyishly handsome husbands. At a time in history when a girl, according to the latest predictions, can live to be a hundred years old, she really only has plans for the first forty years of her life. . . . We're trapping them in a marriage marathon.*

Chatelaine, *July 1962*

BY THE FIRST WEEK of October the leaves were not yet in their glory, but they were on their way. Scarlets and fiery yellows made their appearance, acorn squash scored green and ochre, fancy orange turbans and gnarled gourds mounded up in bushel baskets out front of the IGA and on stands at the foot of farm driveways. Turnips and the last of the corn on the cob, potatoes, beets, carrots and radishes, the local bounty flush from the earth. In the small town of Exeter, the bakery smelled even more divine with the change of temperature, not yet crisp but cool enough in the mornings to contrast deliciously with warm gusts of cinnamon buns and pumpkin pies. The fall fair opened up behind the old train station and Jack took the kids; they made the rounds of the midway—bumper cars, games, and a decent roller coaster designed to make you want to hold onto your cotton candy, especially if you'd already eaten it. In the PMQs women were washing windows, signing their kids up for figure skating and hockey, and reminding their husbands to put up the storm windows one of these weekends, while the men started thinking about putting the snow tires on the car.

If you had shown a much younger Mimi McCarthy, Marguerite Leblanc, as she was then, photos of her life now—dancing beneath a crystal chandelier at the officers' mess with a handsome man in uniform, keeping house with all the modern conveniences, her children both with their own rooms European travel, her name on a joint account—she would have thought it was a fairy tale. Not that she hadn't set her sights on it to begin with. Marguerite became Mimi long before she met Jack. When she was about Madeleine's age, in fact. Mimi reaches for the Palmolive and runs the tap over the breakfast dishes.

She was the only girl in her family to leave her hometown, to pursue post-secondary education, the only one to go overseas. The war helped a lot of young people to break free, but Mimi's get-up-and-go did the rest. She loves her sisters, she even loves most of her sisters-in-law, she is glad they're happy, but she would not trade places with them for anything. She has kept her figure, she is still in love with her husband and, at thirty-six, she yearns for another child.

The desire is romantic, almost erotic—caught up in how she feels about her husband, still her date, still fun, but completely her own. She imagines how much easier it would be with the next baby, knowing all she knows now. She enjoyed the first two, of course, but she was so far from home. Washington, then Alberta. No one told her what it would be like. There was no one to take the baby for a moment; no one to see what needed to be done and simply do it, on days when the house resembled an asylum—nothing but crying and spilling and spitting up, until she too sat and cried. No one just to be there. Only your own mother and sisters can do that, and they were half a continent away. In the air force, wives go to great lengths to help one another, with no expectation of it being reciprocated in this posting, knowing that someone will help them when they need it down the line. But friends can only do so much.

Not every woman is cut out for this life. A few buckle—divorce is rare, the strain shows in other ways. Mimi has seen it: the too-cheerful voice on the phone in mid-afternoon; the first drink of the day as a reward for housework, the second as an accompaniment to *As the World Turns;* the nap before her husband gets home; until one day she sleeps through, and he finds himself opening a can for himself and the kids and making her coffee before the guests arrive—"She's just a little under the weather." And to be fair, not all husbands are equal. It takes two to make an unhappy marriage. Mimi is lucky.

She looks out her kitchen window while she scrubs the frying pan; the rubber gloves spare her hands. A bird flutters past, a sparrow with grass in its beak. Across the street, the Froelich boy lifts his sister into the old station wagon, then puts her wheelchair in the back, the way he does every morning. He kisses his mother goodbye and sets off running through the park behind his house, to catch the school bus. Mimi's own children have already left for school and, although high-school classes start later, he will just make it. Karen Froelich bundles the two babies into a basinette in the back seat, then pulls out of the driveway.

She must have a job of some kind. It would explain the state of the Froelich household—Mimi caught a glimpse when she returned Karen's chili non-carne pot. Karen probably takes the children to a babysitter, then goes to work. The Froelichs don't appear to have two incomes; still. . . . Mimi returns the steel wool to the side of the sink, reminding herself to pick up some little tray or holder for it next time she's in town.

The babies are foster children, that much is known. Betty, Elaine and Vimy were all in Centralia when the infants arrived on the scene. Where do they come from? An unwed mother? People are paid to foster children, aren't they? In which case, why does Karen Froelich work? The Froelichs don't attend church. Either church. Are they atheists? She must remember to ask Vimy Woodley.

She scoops soggy bread and bits of shell from the drain and pushes back a strand of hair with her wrist. Mimi stopped working when she got married, and what woman would choose to work once she had a child? At first she wondered how Karen Froelich managed, what with the babies and a handicapped child, but now she suspects that the woman simply doesn't manage. Has chosen not to. Poor Henry.

One morning, Mimi saw their girl Colleen heading up the street in the opposite direction from the school. Mimi lifted the phone receiver with her soapy glove, only to recall that the child's mother was not at home. She dialled the school instead and asked for Mr. Froelich, embarrassed but feeling responsible even if the mother did not. Henry answered that Colleen was home from school today, not feeling well. When she delicately informed him that his daughter had left the PMQs along with her dog, Henry had said not to worry, the fresh air would do her good. Well, *chacun à son goût*. But it's not surprising that the child goes around like a ragamuffin. Mimi sweeps the floor.

What is surprising is that Ricky Froelich is so well turned out. Vimy has joked that she and Hal can't find a thing wrong with him, although she was a little concerned when he and Marsha started going steady. He comes from a "different" sort of family, said Elaine Ridelle over a hand of bridge, to which Vimy replied, "Don't we all." But in any case, the Woodleys will be posted this spring and that will be that. Another advantage of living on the move.

Mimi puts the broom away and turns to the calendar on the fridge, where each square is packed with her tiny writing—the Oktoberfest dance at the mess, the church bazaar, hockey and figure skating, volunteering at the hospital in Exeter, Vimy's cocktail party in honour of the visiting air vice marshal, dentist appointments, Brownies, Scouts, Jack's trip to Winnipeg, Jack's trip to Toronto, the first curling bonspiel, hair appointment. . . . She circles Thanksgiving and jots down "Bouchers," because Betty has confirmed that they'll be coming. She hesitates, and adds "McCarrolls?" then picks up the phone to call her young next-door neighbour, Dot Bryson. The girlish voice answers and Mimi hears the baby screeching in the background. She tells the young woman to bring the child and come keep her company: "You'll be doing me a favour." Mimi smiles into the phone—she can almost hear tears of relief in the voice at the other end.

She puts the kettle on, then bends to the cupboard under the sink where she keeps her hideous hausfrau clothes and begins to pull out Mason jars and line them up on the counter. She will can for five days. Chow-chow, red chili, corn relish, dills, bread-and-butter pickles and Jack's favourite, mustard pickles. Next week is *confitures*.

Thanksgiving falls on October 8 this year, and there will be a turkey draw at the mess as usual, with so many birds on hand that everyone is bound to go home with a Butterball. The social highlight of October, however, is Oktoberfest. The strong local German immigrant flavour, combined with the fact that so many personnel and their wives are veterans of German postings, means that Centralia's is bound to be something special. The officers' mess has been gearing up for weeks. Jack has tried to persuade Henry Froelich to bring his wife and join the party.

"*Ach,* I don't have—"

"You don't need a tuxedo," said Jack, adding with a wink, "Besides, it's Oktoberfest, you can wear lederhosen."

Henry Froelich smiled and shook his head. "I think no."

"I'm sorry, I forgot," said Jack. "You're from northern Germany, you wouldn't be caught dead in lederhosen."

They were having an after-supper glass of Froelich's homemade wine in the McCarthys' driveway. Henry had Jack's lawnmower in pieces.

"What's your better half got to say about it?"

"My . . . ?"

"Your wife, Karen. Does she like to dance?"

"She prefers the less formal occasion."

Jack nodded. "Like this," breathing in the early autumn evening.

"Just so," said Henry, and bent to his work, wiping grass and grease from the blade. Jack watched him for a while, his immaculate cuffs turned up once at the wrists, fingers stained with grease, shirt and tie protected by the old apron.

"Tell me, Henry, are you ever going to drive that thing or are you planning to donate it to the Smithsonian?" Jack nodded across the street to the Froelich driveway, where a litter of auto parts was growing around the hybrid chassis now recognizable as a '36 Ford Coupe; its doors and fenders, its broad running boards and low-slung front end, all scavenged from different wrecks and welded together. In the midst of it all was Henry's son, bent over the engine. "Like father like son, eh?"

Froelich smiled, obviously pleased. "It's for my boy, when he is sixteen. That is when I go completely grey, when he will be driving."

"Hank, I'm getting worried; that car is like the loaves and fishes, every time I look there's more of it. I just hope you don't get as interested in my lawnmower as you are in that car, or I'll be up to my knees in grass next summer."

"Don't worry, Jack, your Lawn-Boy is very much less interesting than the Froelich-wagen. You maybe like to know that when finished, this car will contain parts from many other makes of automobiles, as well as a secret ingredient from a washing machine to improve fuel efficiency."

"Wow, really?"

"*Nein.*"

Jack laughed.

"I will work on your car next," said Henry.

"*Nein,* yourself!"

Jack sipped the wine and blinked at the taste—terrible stuff.

Henry asked, "How do you like the wine? We pick ourselves the chokecherries at the Pinery."

"Chokecherry, eh?" Jack nodded. "Not too shabby."

"'Shabby'?"

"That's the highest compliment you can get from an air force type. It means just great."

"Good, good, I bring you a bottle, I have plenty."

Jack said casually, "Henry, why don't you let me treat you to the Oktoberfest dance. You and Karen come as our guests. . . ."

Froelich slipped the blade onto its axle, reached for his wrench, tightened the bolt but didn't reply. Jack feared he might have made a faux pas, implying a money problem, which had not been his intention. "You'd be doing us a favour. It's just what the party needs, an honest-to-goodness German, and you wouldn't believe the food. How long since you had a good bratwurst, eh?" Again he sensed that he'd said the wrong thing. Perhaps Henry thought he was criticizing Karen's cooking.

Henry tossed the wrench aside and fished in his toolbox for a screwdriver. "You are very generous, Jack, and I would like on another occasion to accept your gift, but I am not German." He snapped the lid on over the engine.

Jack flushed. What had he missed?

Henry twirled the wing nuts into place. "I am Canadian," he said, and smiled. He pulled the cord and the motor roared to life.

On the Friday before Thanksgiving, Jack came home from beer call at the mess with an immense frozen turkey. "Mimi, I'm home!"

"Oh Jack," she cried, "you won!"

"Yup," he said, thunking the thing down on the kitchen table.

The young woman from next door rose with her baby. "Hi Jack. Mimi, I better run."

Jack said, "How are you . . . ," and hesitated.

"Dot, you must stay," Mimi put in, tactfully supplying the girl's name.

"How are you settling in, Dot, okay?" Yes, her husband was in the accounts office, name of Bryson.

"Just great, Jack, thank you," she said, blushing, then left, in keeping with domestic etiquette. Mimi saw her to the door, then returned to kiss her husband—he was so proud of that turkey, shrugging, saying, "It's over to you now Missus, I only dragged it home."

She poured him a beer and teased him about forgetting the neighbour's name, gratified that a pretty young thing like that should get barely a glance from him. He took a second glass from the shelf and poured half his beer into it for her. "I already had two at the mess. You don't want to bring out the beast in me, do you?" He winked.

"*Ça dépend.*" She clinked glasses with him.

There are men who, if they make it home for Friday night supper at all, are too "happy" or too belligerent to sit at the table and eat with their children. Snoring in their uniforms on the couch or glazed in front of the television set. Perfectly nice men, and thank goodness Mimi isn't married to one of them. Her older sister, Yvonne, is, though; married to one of those men whom other men find harmless.

Madeleine watched her mother slide the huge turkey into the oven at noon, and when Maman said, as she always did, "*Bon.* There goes Monsieur Turkey," Madeleine could not help but see the pallid flesh in a whole different way. Like someone's bare backside—ashamed and curled to hide their face. And when Maman had taken the loose skin around the neck and tucked it under the body, Madeleine felt somehow that the turkey was embarrassed to be dead and naked. "I'll call you when the neck is ready," said Maman.

The McCarrolls were coming to Thanksgiving dinner. American Thanksgiving was not until November and, as Mimi told Sharon over the phone, "We can't let you be the only ones in the PMQs without a turkey dinner next week." The Bouchers were supposed to join them, and the women had pooled their card tables for the occasion, but at the last minute Betty phoned to say they were in strict quarantine. "Steve Ridelle's threatened to paint an X on our front door if we don't sit tight all weekend." Their youngest, Bea, had come down with mumps.

Twenty-four pounds of turkey and only four adults and three children. "What a feast!" said Jack.

Madeleine passed around a plate of Ritz crackers with smoked oysters, and celery sticks with Cheez Whiz. Jack lit the first fire of the season in the fireplace and poured a rye and soda for Blair. Mike joined them in the living room with a ginger ale while the women saw to the kitchen. Jack was grateful for his son's presence, because McCarroll had not become more loquacious with the passing weeks—like pulling teeth, getting the fellow to talk. Mike kept up a steady stream of questions about flying, and it occurred to Jack that McCarroll appeared more at home chatting with the boy than he ever did at the mess with his fellow officers. Pity he didn't have a son.

"What's in store for you next, Blair? I take it you're only here for the year."

"Ohio, sir."

"Call me Jack." Blair nodded and flushed. "Wright-Patterson air base?"

"That's right, sir."

"They got some pretty good R&D going down there, eh?"

"That's what I'll be doing. Human factors testing."

"What the heck is that?"

Blair became almost animated. "I'll be testing high altitude full and partial pressure suits. Space suits."

"Wow!" said Mike.

"'Course I'm aiming for Edwards, then . . . who knows, maybe Houston."

Jack raised his eyebrows appreciatively and nodded—McCarroll is gunning for astronaut training.

Mike said, "I'm going to start flying lessons in the spring." He looked at his father.

"That's right, Mike, I'll wander over and check out the civilian flying school next week."

In the kitchen, Mimi made gravy and Sharon heated up the pan of candied yams she had brought.

"That smells so good, Sharon, I'll have to get the recipe from you."

"Okay," said Sharon. The entire conversation had been like that:

Mimi's gambits followed by Sharon's shy non-starters. It wasn't so noticeable around a bridge table, but it was a tad difficult one on one. Mimi's impulse was always to hug Sharon, but you could only hug someone so many times without getting to know them. Mimi had prepared for the Thanksgiving meal well ahead, so that, other than gravy, there was little to do, but she set Sharon to work carving radishes into rosettes in order to make the silence less obvious. "Why don't you put on a record, Jack?" Charles Aznavour would be a great help.

Claire had brought a box of animal crackers as a hostess gift for Madeleine—it came with a string attached so that you could pretend it was a purse or a briefcase.

"Wow, Claire, thanks." Upstairs in her room, Madeleine showed Claire her books and toys and the beautiful green glassie Elizabeth had given her, as well as a plastic bag containing bread mould that she was incubating under her bed. At their age there was no social embarrassment over silence; Madeleine pulled out *Green Eggs and Ham* and read aloud, although she had it mostly memorized. They sat on the floor against the bed and Claire leaned against her—which felt perfectly normal somehow—and listened, and laughed.

"Madeleine! Claire! *Venez,* come get a treat," called her mother.

In the kitchen, Mimi lifted the neck and giblets from the sauce, put them on a plate and offered them to Mike and the two little girls. Madeleine's parents always say these are the best parts of the bird, perhaps because you get to eat them straight out of the pan when you're starving and tantalized by the roasting smells. Or perhaps it's because during the Depression you were lucky to have anything at all—gizzards for supper, fried bread and molasses for dessert. Still, Madeleine has always savoured these bits, so when Maman offered her a morsel on a fork she took it willingly. But she declined a second one; she had become suddenly aware of chewing someone's stomach. And when Mike offered to share the neck, she said, "No thanks." She folded her hands and watched while Claire McCarroll daintily picked the meat off it and ate.

They sat down at the table and Jack poured from a bottle of good *Qualitätswein* that Blair had brought. "That *schmecks,* eh?" said Jack.

Oddly enough, Madeleine found she wasn't hungry. Her parents had mercy on her and, apart from some minor encouragement, she wasn't forced to empty her plate. She ate a slice of Mrs. McCarroll's excellent pumpkin pie in order to be polite, and a piece of Maman's wonderful chocolate pound cake in order not to hurt her feelings, and when the guests left, went to bed with a stomach ache.

Maman said, "Well that's what happens when you only want dessert." But she gave Madeleine a glass of ginger ale and stroked her forehead until she fell asleep.

In bed finally, Jack and Mimi laughed. "Not exactly the life of the party, eh?" Lovely people, the McCarrolls, but *mon Dieu,* sometimes silence wasn't golden. "Do you think they talk when they're at home?" Well it was a good reminder: next time they had the McCarrolls, they'd make sure to invite not just one other couple but two—in case of mumps.

They stretched out gratefully and reached for magazine and book.

Hers: *How to Tell Your Child about Sex*

His: *Decision in the Case of Dr. J. R. Oppenheimer*

On the Tuesday after the long weekend, Madeleine walks down the empty school hallway with her cut-out turkey. Thanksgiving is over and the next special art they do will be for Halloween. The turkeys and the horns of plenty have come down, including those over the window of the hallway door, but Mr. March has replaced them with a patriotic collage of red maple leaves in Saran Wrap.

It's ten past three. Mr. March said as usual, "Side door, little girl," but Madeleine said without turning back, "I have to go to the bathroom," and exited by the hallway door. He didn't say anything. He didn't even call her back to complete her sentence: I have to go to the bathroom, *Mr. March.* She didn't have to go to the bathroom, she simply wished to avoid Marjorie handing out the candy. So she automatically lied.

She is on her way to the foyer when she passes the grade eight classroom on her right and sees Mr. Froelich cleaning his blackboard. There are fractions and x's and numbers with minuses next to them, a clash of jagged chalk smearing now into white dust, disappearing like a headache under Mr. Froelich's smooth brushstrokes. She watches, soothed, unaware that her feet have stopped until she hears, "Why are you still here, Madeleine?"

His sleeves are rolled up to his elbows. His arms are skinny white under his black hairs.

"You want to help me clean the board?" he asks. "Or maybe you better hurry home, eh? Your mutti will worry."

But Madeleine comes in and stands beside him, watching his arm move in a broad arc across the board.

"What's that?" she asks, aware that it is rude to ask about marks on a person's body. It's bad manners. But she has automatically asked

Mr. Froelich about the mark on his arm without thinking, because often after the exercise group she has a feeling of just waking up, as though she has sweated out a flu in the night and may still be dreaming. And when you are dreaming, you say whatever comes into your head.

Mr. Froelich doesn't seem offended. He glances down at his arm where the blue marks are. He says, "Oh. That's my old phone number," and begins to roll down his sleeve, but Madeleine reaches out and puts her hand on his arm. This also is a strange thing to do, and she is watching herself do it—you shouldn't just go around touching people, especially grown-ups, that too is rude. But her hand rests lightly on his forearm; she is looking at the small blue numbers there.

"Does it rub off?" she asks.

"No."

"'Cause it's a tattoo."

He nods.

She asks, "Were you in the SS?" It feels like a normal question.

He shakes his head. "No."

She looks up at him. "Were there some good Nazis?"

"Not that I know of. But people are people."

"I know."

He waits. Looking at her, but not staring. They stay like that for a bit. He is like talcum powder, like a nice priest. The smell of chalk is gentle.

"Are you feeling all right?" he asks. *"Was ist los, Mädele?"*

*"Nichts."*

He puts his hand out and touches her forehead. His fingers are dry and cool. She begins to wake up. *"Du bist warm,"* he says.

A man's voice behind her says, "Everything okay?"

Madeleine looks up, her hand still on Mr. Froelich's arm. The principal, Mr. Lemmon, is standing in the doorway. He always has a five o'clock shadow and looks worried.

Mr. Froelich feels her cheek and says to Mr. Lemmon, "I wonder if she's a little feverish."

"Are you okay, Madeleine?" asks Mr. Lemmon.

Madeleine nods.

"Shall we walk home?" Mr. Froelich asks her.

"No thanks," she says. "I'm going to run all the way."

He smiles and says, "All right then, you run."

She walks out of the room, past Mr. Lemmon. The hallway looks brighter now—she can see more of it. Perhaps someone has opened a window somewhere, it feels cooler. There is no running in the halls, and she knows Mr. Lemmon is watching, so she restrains herself until she reaches the corner, then she turns and bolts through the foyer. Past the Queen, past Prince Philip and all their fighter planes, she doesn't slow her pace before the glass doors but runs at them, the heels of her palms thrust forward to bash down the metal bar that opens the latch. She accelerates off the steps, stretching her legs as far as possible—*Elastoman!* She runs, arms outflung, paper turkey fluttering from her fingers.

Halfway across the field, she sees someone emerging from the dry corn on the other side of Algonquin Drive. Colleen Froelich. She has something in her hands, a rope; green and yellow, too short for a skipping rope. And Colleen Froelich doesn't skip. Madeleine calls to her but Colleen ignores her and keeps walking. Madeleine follows and calls again, "Hey, Colleen, watcha got?" Colleen doesn't answer.

She tries again. "How's Eggs?" Colleen gives no sign she has heard.

"Hey kid!" yells Madeleine, her throat seared by anger, "I asked you something!" Colleen's back is impervious. Madeleine runs to catch up. "I said, how's Eggs!" she screams. Dizzy with the force of it.

Colleen stops and turns around suddenly, so that Madeleine almost bumps into her and the thing she is holding. A snake. Madeleine's anger deserts her. She doesn't like snakes.

"What the hell're you talking about?" says Colleen.

Madeleine takes a step back and says in a small voice, "Your dog. Eggs."

Colleen narrows her icy blue eyes. The enormity of having messed with her dawns on Madeleine. The snake drips from Colleen's fingers, she winds it around her wrist and says, "His name is Rex, you *re*tard."

Madeleine is shocked. Colleen has used the word that people use on her own sister. Madeleine starts to say something nice about the snake, hoping to make everything all right, but Colleen turns her back and starts walking away again.

Madeleine's anger roars back, she scoops grit from the side of the road and hurls it like shrapnel. "Everyone hates you, kid!"

That night she asks her father, "Dad, in the olden days, did people write their phone number on their arms?"

"In the olden days they didn't have phones." Jack gets up and puts away the *Treasury of Fairytales*. "Whom do you know with their phone number on their arm?"

"Mr. Froelich."

"Mr. Froelich?"

"Yeah." She hesitates. She doesn't want to make her father think Mr. Froelich was a Nazi, but she needs a definite answer. "He has a tattoo."

"A tattoo?" Jack sits back down. "What does it look like?"

"It's blue. It's here." She points to her forearm.

Jack takes a breath. Holy Dinah. But he smiles at his daughter and says, "That makes sense. You've heard of the absent-minded professor?"

"Yeah."

"Well that describes Mr. Froelich to a T." He kisses her forehead. "'Night-night, sweetie."

"Does it mean he was a Nazi?"

"No." He has spoken too sharply, he softens his tone. "No, no, sweetie, nothing like that, don't ever think that."

He turns off her light and slips out. She hugs Bugs, relieved. As she closes her eyes it strikes her as odd that, within the course of only minutes, she should have had such a gentle time with Mr. Froelich, and such an opposite time with Colleen. How can Colleen and Ricky come from the same family? The only one in her family Colleen seems related to is Rex.

Mimi gets up from the kitchen table and pours Jack a cup of tea. She has been writing out cheques, paying bills.

Jack says, "Son of a gun."

"What?"

"I think Henry Froelich is Jewish." He pronounces it *Jeweesh* with his vestigial east coast accent.

"Oh Jack, everyone knows that."

"Who's everyone?"

"I don't know. Vimy told me. I asked if they ever went to church and she told me Henry is Jewish. I don't know what *her* excuse is."

"Whose?"

"His wife's."

"No one tells me anything."

"Well what difference does it make?"

"Nothing, except. . . ." Mimi returns to her paperwork. She sets the baby bonus aside—Michel has grown out of his new sneakers already. Jack continues. "Henry was in a concentration camp."

Mimi makes the sign of the cross.

Jack sighs and shakes his head. "Holy Dinah."

"I'm glad we never went there. . . ." She doesn't even want to say the word. *Auschwitz*. "*Pauvre* Henry." There are tears in her eyes.

Jack reaches across and takes her hand. "Why are you crying, Missus? The war's over, Henry's fine, happy as a clam."

Mimi shouldn't be shocked by the information, she knew it was a possibility as soon as she learned Henry was Jewish, so she is surprised at her inability to get the words out. Maybe she's getting her period—in itself a disappointing event—maybe that's why she is overreacting. What she can't manage to say without crying: Henry may be fine but his family is not. His first family. Not only parents and relations, but children—she is suddenly certain. She blows her nose, she's fine. She resumes working on the bills.

Jack finds himself replaying conversations with Henry Froelich. *Einstein is a Jew.* It had sounded anti-Semitic from Froelich's lips last summer. Of course there is nothing wrong with the word "Jew"—especially if you are one—but there is something about the single syllable, it sounds less polite than "Jewish." Perhaps the noun sounds anti-Semitic because Jack has rarely heard it pronounced by people other than anti-Semites. Vivid in his memory are radio broadcasts of Hitler railing against *"die Juden!"* And in newsreels after the war, when the horrors began to come out, a narrator's voice describing in solemn tones "the persecution of the Jew . . ."—even then it bore a stigma, the shame of death. And Jack has known few Jews—Jewish people. There was one family in his hometown in New Brunswick, the Schwartzes—they played rugger like anybody else, fished, never had a Christmas tree, no one gave it a second thought. Jack has come across the odd Jewish fellow in the air force, but they are Canadian. You don't expect to run into too many German Jews. Not any more. His cheeks burn a little at the thought of how often he has jokingly accused Henry of being "typically German." Not to mention that crack about lederhosen. Christ. Well, the tattoo explains why Froelich is content to be here, teaching grade school.

"Doris Day is Jewish," says Mimi.

"Really?"

"Mm-hm."

# DOMESTIC SCIENCE

*If you are a highly excitable mother with certain needs, you may find it impossible to get along with a daughter of similar temperament and needs.*

Chatelaine, *July 1962*

MADELEINE SPENDS THE NEXT week and a half looking over her shoulder, scared Colleen Froelich is lying in wait, ready to pound her. But nothing happens. And while she is relieved, she is also oddly disappointed.

Life goes on as usual, and on Saturday October 20, Mimi asks Madeleine to help her get ready for the Oktoberfest dance.

Madeleine kneels against the side of the tub while her mother, wearing a sparkly shower cap, takes a bubble bath. She gets Madeleine to scrub her back with a loofah—"that keeps a lady's skin nice and soft"—and shows her how to push her cuticles back in order to avoid hangnails.

Madeleine holds the towel, then waits while Maman powder-puffs her underarms after shaving with her electric Lady Sunbeam. "You can start shaving when you're twelve, Madeleine." Madeleine doesn't point out that she has already been shaving with Dad for years. She follows her mother into the bedroom and watches her put on itchy-looking underpants and matching lace bra, leaning forward into it, expertly reaching behind to fasten it. Then her garter belt, then her stockings— "always roll them first, like this, then point your toes"—resting one foot on her hope chest, *"comme ça,"* stroking her leg to draw the stocking up to her thigh, "so you don't get runs," and fastening it to the garter belt with the rubber snaps.

"Help me with my girdle, Madeleine." It doesn't matter if you are slim, "a lady is not fully dressed without a girdle." There are a million hooks and eyes. Finally, she slides her silk slip over her head, and sits down on the cushioned stool at her vanity table—*"Donne-moi le hairspray, s'il te plaît, ma p'tite."*

At this point, Mike joins them and sits on the end of their parents' bed with a Hardy Boys book. This is one activity he has not abandoned: he still comes in to watch Maman get ready to go out for the evening and chat with her in the mirror. Madeleine can't figure out why he doesn't consider it to be sissy.

They speak French together, easily, rapidly. Madeleine tries to make out the gist of what they are saying. Maman calls him her *"p'tit gentilhomme,"* and when he is with her he acts like a little gentleman, too.

He tells her of his latest victories: first in the hundred-yard dash, picked to play centre on his hockey team, the highest mark in science. He is going to be in the NHL. Then he is going to be a doctor. Who flies Sabres. "*Tu peux faire n'importe quoi, Michel.*"

Madeleine looks at her brother and it seems that, when Maman says it, it's true: he can be whatever he wants to be.

She enters her parents' open closet, walking between her father's suits and shirts as though through a curtain, breathing in—wool, shoe leather, faint cigar smell and fresh cotton. Her mother's voice reaches her as though from a great distance. "*Madeleine, où vas-tu?*"

She comes out and returns to her mother's side in front of the big round mirror, and watches as she tilts her head back, lowers her lids and applies black eyeliner with a tiny brush, "only in the evening, Madeleine," then forward to apply mascara, "but *fais attention, pas trop.*" She puts on her lipstick, "always stay inside the lip line." Madeleine nods to her mother in the mirror, contemplating the possibilities of the red lipstick on her own cheeks and nose. Bozo.

Maman places a tissue between her lips and presses, then, "*Aimes-tu cette couleur, Michel?*"

Mike looks up from *The Mystery at Devil's Paw* and replies that it's a very nice colour indeed. Madeleine looks at the discarded tissue, a blown kiss, and pictures Marilyn Monroe with her carsick eyes. Dead now and in her grave.

"Do me up, Madeleine."

Madeleine zips her up and breathes in her perfume—"My Sin" by Lanvin. Mingled with VO-5 hairspray. Mysterious and alluring.

"*Comment vous me trouvez, les enfants?*" Maman is wearing a dirndl. Low-cut laced-up embroidered bodice with a full red and white skirt. It cost a fortune in Garmisch.

"*Très chic,*" says Mike.

"*Sehr schön,*" says Madeleine, and Mimi hugs her.

Downstairs Jack says, "Frau McCarthy, you're a knockout." He is in Harris tweed, plaid tie, brogues and a green Tyrolean hat with a feather. Mike finds a flash cube and snaps their picture before they leave for the mess.

Marsha Woodley babysits them as usual and, as usual, Mike behaves as though she were there to babysit Madeleine only. He tightens the cord on his plaid housecoat and strokes his chin while inquiring what channel Marsha would like to watch.

Marsha is so nice, Madeleine feels she can't shun the offer to "play Barbies." "I used to be crazy about dolls too when I was your age,

Madeleine." Marsha has brought Barbie's convertible, which mitigates things somewhat, but she insists that Ken drive. Madeleine is relieved when Mike offers to show Marsha his airplane models.

"Sure, Mikey," she says.

His manly frown doesn't flicker. "After you."

He has lost his mind.

A knock at the door. Madeleine runs to answer it. There on the other side of the screen, standing in the dusk, is Ricky Froelich.

"Hi pal," he says. He is leaning, one arm against the wall.

She turns and hollers, "Marsha! It's Ricky!" Then to him, "Come on in."

"Naw, that's okay."

Marsha comes up behind Madeleine and says, "Hi."

"Hi. Aren't you going to invite me in?"

Marsha rolls her eyes, and says with an interrogative inflection, "Of course not."

Madeleine is tingling. Please, Marsha, please say yes.

"Ricky," says Marsha, in a tone both teasing and warning, "I'm babysitting."

He grins. "I can read bedtime stories."

Mike arrives at the top of the kitchen steps. "Hi Rick," he says in his deepest voice.

"Hi Mike, how's she going?"

"Good. Wanna watch a movie?"

"Sure, but that's *verboten,* eh?"

"How come?"

"Boss won't let me."

"Aw come on, Marsha," says Mike.

"Yeah," says Madeleine.

Marsha turns to them. "Okay you guys, skedaddle."

They do. And watch from the window on the upstairs landing as Marsha steps out onto the porch with Ricky. They can't make out all of what is being said, but they watch intently the subtle dance unfolding below. Marsha, arms crossed over her chest, looking down, hovering just within the arc of Ricky's arm, raised and leaning against the door now. His head is bent close to her ear. She shakes her head, they hear her giggle. The next moment Ricky glances to either side, then kisses her. Her head tilts back and he leans into her. Then he leaves, jogging back across the street to his own house. Marsha rests her back against the door, hugging herself, biting her lower lip.

"Marsha, the movie's starting," calls Madeleine.

They watch *Thomasina*. Madeleine tries hard not to cry and feels better when Marsha does. Mike does not once make fun of the movie, and when it's over he says, "Not too shabby." Madeleine wants to scream at him.

Later, from the bathroom window, Madeleine sees Ricky Froelich sitting in the light of his front porch, strumming his guitar. She opens the window and strains to hear the soft chords and his easy voice singing a lonesome Hank Williams tune. She kneels on the toilet lid, folds her arms on the windowsill, rests her chin and stays for a long time, listening. He sings song after song, some in a strange-sounding French. Sad ones, so as not to wake the neighbours.

Shortly after midnight, Mimi slips into her daughter's room. Madeleine is sound asleep hugging that filthy old Bugs Bunny. Mimi places a little cocktail umbrella, striped like a rainbow, into Bugsy's plastic-gloved hand.

The next morning, Madeleine runs into the kitchen with her prize. "Maman, look what Dad brought me!"

Mimi picks up the whistling kettle, about to say, "Maman brought you that." But she catches herself. "You have the nicest papa in the world." She pours the tea.

Madeleine twirls the tiny umbrella, "'Singin' in the rain—'"

"Help me set the table for after church, *ma p'tite*."

Madeleine groans. "How come Mike never has to help?"

Mimi says sharply, "Don't 'how come' me, Madeleine, just get the move on."

Aunt Jemima smiles jovially from the box of pancake mix. Why can't she be my real mother?

After Mass, Jack relaxes with the paper until Mimi calls him for brunch. "Boy, something sure smells good," he says, turning to call, "Mike, come and get it!" Mike comes in with the sports section, and he and his father sit behind headlines while Madeleine and Mimi put plates of bacon and eggs and pancakes in front of them. *Soviet Forward Base in Cuba. Hockey Record: Sunday—Toronto at Boston, Montreal at New York.*

Madeleine slouches in her chair. Why is her mother suddenly turning her into a slave? A scullery maid, as in fairy tales of wicked stepmothers. She picks up her fork, noticing that Maman has taken the broken egg as usual.

Mimi says brightly, "All right, that's enough news at the table." Both Mike and Jack blink and look up innocently, then obediently fold their papers, put them aside and start eating. Mimi winks at Madeleine, who stretches the ends of her mouth sideways in a technical smile meant to fool no one.

Mimi sips her coffee and resists the urge to light a cigarette. She takes a forkful of egg, a bite of toast, reminding herself that it's important to eat with her family even though her appetite is often suppressed by cooking, leaving her hungry and prone to snack between meals. That's how women gain weight. Although she wonders if her slimness has something to do with her inability to get pregnant. Maybe if she were more like her own mother, or her sister Yvonne. . . . But there is nothing to say that she won't get pregnant. She simply hasn't yet. She smiles at her daughter. There are times when Mimi too would love to sit back on the couch with a magazine and have someone cook her a meal. Iron her blouse. Occasionally it does feel like drudgery. That's normal. It's important, however, not to communicate those feelings to your daughter—that's a recipe for future unhappiness. It's important to foster pride in what is, after all, the most important job in the world. There is just one problem: she's too much like me.

## DUCK AND COVER

*Can we really reduce nuclear war to a nuisance level and believe that a few feet of concrete and an assortment of tinned goods will be sufficient to preserve our own special little world while fifty-megaton bombs with a destruction radius of twenty miles are being dropped about the country?*

Chatelaine, *February 1962*

"'THERE WAS A TURTLE and his name was Bert
and Bert the turtle was very alert
When danger threatened him he didn't get hurt
he knew just what to do!
He'd duck! And cover.
Duck! And cover. . . . '"

The chorus of voices sounds like the Walt Disney Singers on a story record. Bert is a cartoon turtle, and after he retracts into his shell several times, the cartoon part ends and real kids appear in freshly ironed clothes, running from a playground to a doorway where they duck and take cover. Then a serious man's voice says, "Don't look at the flash." The kids cover their eyes.

Mr. March is showing this film because the free world is in grave peril.

At seven o'clock last night, Madeleine watched her father's profile when President Kennedy came on the television. "Good evening, my fellow citizens. . . ."

He's handsome, thought Madeleine. Our prime minister, Diefenbaker, is not—his hair looks like a plastic bathing cap.

" . . . This government, as promised, has maintained the closest sur-veillance of the Soviet military buildup on the island of Cuba. . . ."

It was Monday night and she was disappointed, because Lucille Ball was supposed to be on but the announcer had said, "Tonight's program has been pre-empted in order that we may bring you a message of extreme urgency from the President of the United States." Her father's mouth had become a line, his whole profile had become a line. The fam-ily was on the couch, watching.

Cuba is where Ricky Ricardo is from. Lucille Ball is actually "a great beauty," Dad has said, but you can't tell because she is so funny. Would you rather be beautiful or funny?

" . . . Within the past week unmistakable evidence has established the fact that a series of offensive missile sites is now in preparation on that imprisoned island. . . ."

"What's the matter?" asked Madeleine. Had they built another Wall?

"Shhh," said Mike.

President Kennedy continued in his clear Boston accent. "The pur-poses of these bases can be none other than to provide a nuclear strike capability against the western hemisphere, ranging as far north as Hudson Bay, Canada—"

"Time for bed," said Maman.

"It's only seven o'clock!"

"*Allons!*" She took Madeleine by the hand. Mike got to stay up.

Madeleine waited until Maman's footsteps retreated down the stairs, then she crept out of bed and to the landing, where the television sounded even louder than in the living room. President Kennedy was still speaking. " . . . the Soviet government stated on September 11 that, and I quote, 'The armaments and military equipment sent to Cuba are designed exclusively for defensive purposes. . . .'" She inched toward the edge of the landing and crept down one stair. Now she was able to observe her family through the railings and imagine what it would be like if she were not alive.

" . . . That statement was false."

The President's voice continued, a hollow backdrop to her reverie—what if she was actually invisible? What if she was dead now and didn't know it?

" . . . Nuclear weapons are so destructive and ballistic missiles are so swift. . . ."

What if she was a ghost?

"Our own strategic missiles have never been transferred to the territory of any other nation under a cloak of secrecy and deception. . . ."

What if she spoke and they didn't hear her? Then she would know she was dead.

" . . . and our history, unlike that of the Soviets since the end of World War Two, demonstrates that we have no desire to dominate or conquer any other nation or impose our system upon its people. . . ."

She opened her mouth but refrained from making a sound, suddenly reluctant to find out.

" . . . In that sense, missiles in Cuba add to an already clear and present danger. . . ."

She was unable to move. Growing cold, lips parted, unable to make a sound.

" . . . the costs of worldwide nuclear war in which even the fruits of victory would be ashes in our mouth. . . ."

She was turning into a statue. If someone in her family did not look up at her soon, it would be too late. They would try to revive her and her arm would break off.

Her mother looked up. "Madeleine." *I'm alive.* "What are you doing up?"

Madeleine was surprised not to be scolded. Instead, Maman tucked her in and sang softly, "*Un Acadien Errant.*" Madeleine knew she was supposed to feel better and fall asleep. Feel better about what? She closed her eyes.

An hour later she snuck into Mike's room.

"Mike, what's the big hairy deal?"

"The Russians have got nukes in Cuba and they're aimed at us."

"Oh. So?"

"So. It means World War Three."

"Oh. Is Dad going to have to fight?"

"We'll prob'ly just all get incinerated unless we have a bomb shelter."

"Do we have one?"

"Nope, but I'm going to build one."

"Can I help?"

"It's not a game, Madeleine."

"I know that."

At breakfast the radio was on as usual, men's voices, dark and shiny like black suits. " . . . who is going to blink first? Castro has said that any attempt to—" Maman switched it off.

"Dad, is there going to be a war?"

"Who told you that?"

"Mike."

He got a look from Dad. "I doubt that very much."

Silence.

Mimi poured more coffee. Jack turned a page of his *Globe and Mail.* Madeleine saw the headline, *U.S. NAVY WILL BLOCK ARMS FLOW TO CUBA.*

"Kennedy's no fool," said her father.

"He's a good man," said her mother, and Madeleine was surprised to see her make the sign of the cross and turn away with her lips moving—praying. President Kennedy is Catholic, of course he's good.

Mike asked, "Are we going to go on alert?"

Dad said from behind the paper, "Why would we do that, Mike?"

"The Americans've gone to defcon 3."

"What's that?" asked Madeleine.

"It's routine," replied her father.

Maman buttered toast. Sliced it.

Mike said, "Is there still going to be a game tonight in Exeter?"

"Of course, Mike, why wouldn't there be?" Dad sounded annoyed, but maybe it was just his man-to-man voice.

After a moment, Mike said, "Dad, when can I go up in a Chipmunk?"

Dad sounded distracted, as though he had never heard of a Chipmunk. "What?"

Mike slouched. "Nothing."

Madeleine contemplated her father's newspaper, imagining eyeholes cut out in President Kennedy's face for spying. Her eyes wandered down the column . . . *proclaimed a quarantine.* That is when someone in a house is sick and you put a mark on their door so no one can go in or out. There was a quarantine in Cuba. She recalled a fascinating picture she had pored over in Mike's grade six history book of the Black Death. Shrivelled people in cloaks, with no teeth; the blue-bonnet plague. "Is the plague in Cuba?"

Her father lowered the paper. "What? No . . . well, that's one way of putting it." Her mother glanced at him and he added, "Naw, the U.S. is just makin' sure Cuba doesn't get any more weapons, that's all." Then cleared his throat.

Madeleine ate her Cheerios. Her crunching sounded very loud. The newspaper stayed perfectly still. Mike sprinkled sugar on his Sugar Crisps.

After a while Dad said, "We were more worried when the Wall went up."

Maman lit a cigarette and said, "That's for sure." And everything felt normal again.

Mr. March puts away the projection screen and pulls down the map of the world. "Here is Cuba"—he uses his pointer—"and here is Centralia." He taps again. "Anyone who thinks the Russian missiles could not reach Centralia is sorely mistaken."

They are doing a special grade four air-raid drill: when Mr. March smacks his desk with the pointer, they all duck under their desks and cover their heads with their hands, like Bert the turtle in his shell.

"Good," he says, adding, "This is one exercise where I expect you all to be tortoises."

Obliging laughter.

Jack walks to work. It looks like a normal day. Children on their way to school, fresh laundry on the lines. When he kissed Mimi goodbye she asked him if he was worried and he said, "Naw, not really. It's a whole lot of sabre-rattling." She smiled and asked what he wanted for supper tonight, and he left feeling better for having reassured her. Able to concentrate on what lies ahead. He is eager to get to work. To do something. That's the best remedy.

And there will be plenty to do. Centralia is a primary flying school where cadets earn their wings. A place where officers are trained to improve their leadership and management skills. Hardly a tactical centre. But it is a military base. U.S. and Canadian aircraft could be dispersed here to get them away from target areas. He fully expects to be advised by the commandant of an increase in the military alert status—virtually routine and in accordance with the NORAD agreement. Merely one stage in a series of flexible conditions geared toward an orderly transition from peace to war. He takes a deep breath. Merely good management.

As he leaves the PMQ patch and crosses the Huron County road toward the Spitfire, he is as close to marching as he ever gets, speaking his thoughts in his mind to the rhythm of his footfalls—*logistical support, air transport, aid the civilian population in the event of an attack, in the event of an attack, in the event of an attack*—He touches the brim of his hat in response to the guard on duty, who has delivered an uncharacteristically stiff salute.

In the space of a day, the world has changed. The ordinary has begun to look precious. It's a familiar feeling. He felt it in Europe last summer when the Wall went up. And yet, for all the imagined horror, nuclear and conventional, there was the sense that Europe had been through many wars. This is different. This is home. A foreign attack on North American soil. . . . Nothing would ever be the same. He glances up at the old air-raid siren. Naive relic. Not much use except to the crows who have built their nest there. Our early warning will come from the DEW line high in the north. We'll have fifteen to eighteen minutes to hide. Where?

On the far side of the parade square, a group of officers including Vic Boucher and Steve Ridelle is gathering. Everyone is in early. Jack quickens his pace.

The First World War was supposed to be "the war to end all war." The Third World War will end everything. The most likely scenario is the destruction of key cities on both sides, the U.S.S.R. taking the brunt in the short term, the long term being universal disease, starvation, death. The planet will no longer be able to support life as we know it. And so far this is the only planet we know. . . . Tears spring to his eyes, surprising him, at the thought that it may end for man before he can reach the stars. He blinks, embarrassed in spite of himself, unaware that his mind is doing what minds do best—keeping the worst thoughts at bay, replacing them with manageable ones: the search for other worlds cut short, versus the annihilation of your children.

He joins his colleagues. "Well, like the Chinaman says, eh? 'May you live in interesting times.'" They laugh.

Warrant Officer Pinder is there. He looks coiled, his brush cut bristling, busted boxer's nose ready for a fight, which for him means a clean sweep of every nut, bolt, blanket and engine on the station. "Morning, sir," he says to Jack and salutes. Group Captain Woodley joins them. They all salute. Woodley informs them that there has been no change in the alert status of the Canadian military. There's a pause, then Jack says, "Unbelievable."

"The scuttlebutt is," says Woodley, "start preparing, but do so 'discreetly.' The Prime Minister doesn't want to alarm the public."

Vic Boucher says, "That's like serving the soup while the house is on fire so's not to alarm the guests."

They stand there at a loss, perhaps a dozen of them. In uniform, *ready aye ready*. With nothing to do. Stranded. As though they had just missed a bus.

Mimi gets up. She has been praying in her kitchen. Our Lord doesn't mind where you pray, He doesn't require a hat or a missal, He sees past rubber gloves and surely He wants His creation to survive. She is in her dreadful hausfrau clothes. She will clean from top to bottom today, then she will cook one of Jack's favourites: a *bouillie* of spare ribs, potatoes, cabbage, turnip, carrots and string beans. Today is not a day to drop in on a neighbour for coffee. She does not wish to become caught up in fear and speculation. That doesn't help the men do their jobs, it just gives them one more thing to worry about. This morning she kissed her husband goodbye as usual, and when he told her not to worry, she smiled and told him to come home hungry. He was relieved. That is her job.

At noon, Jack heads for the mess. As of tomorrow morning, the Americans will enforce a strict blockade or "quarantine" on all offensive military equipment under shipment to Cuba, unless Khrushchev agrees to dismantle the missiles there. Britain has issued a statement in support of the quarantine, and so has the rest of the free world—with the exception of Canada. By noon, Prime Minister Diefenbaker has done nothing but call for "calm and the banishment of those things which sometimes separate us"—meaning Canada and the U.S.—while at the same time proposing that the U.N. go to Cuba and "verify" the presence of offensive weapons. He is implying that Kennedy is lying. Either that or Dief is terminally indecisive.

"We're on the brink of war and our prime minister wants to strike another committee," says Steve Ridelle.

"There's nothing worse than a hands-on manager," says Vic.

"Especially when he's sitting on them," says Jack, and they all laugh.

A bunch of them are brown-bagging it but have gathered at the mess to talk, because there is not much more for them to do in the face of the crisis. Weapons of sudden mass destruction are aimed at the western hemisphere, Soviet ships are steaming toward Havana, as they unwrap the wax paper from their sandwiches. American troops are conducting the biggest peacetime manoeuvre ever in West Berlin, as Russian armoured columns advance.

"What've you got, Steve?"

"Looks like some kind of fancy bologna."

"Those are pimentos."

"What can I say? Guess I ain't got no class."

Jack says, "Dief is playing politics with national security 'cause he doesn't want to be seen to be dancing to the American tune."

"I don't get it," says Jack's neighbour, Bryson. "We're all sitting under the same flight path. Part of the same target area."

Jack knows the young officer is thinking of his new baby at home—all the men at this table are fathers. He reaches for his coffee and sees Nolan entering the mess. He lifts a hand, intending to invite him over, but Nolan appears not to notice. He finds a table at the far end and sits with a book.

"Who does he think is going to protect us if we're too gutless to do it ourselves?" says Lawson. "Britain?"

"Fat chance," says Vic.

"Never mind that we saved their bacon in two world wars," says Ted Lawson.

"Dief would rather stand up and sing 'God Save the Queen' while the whole map turns red," says Baxter.

Vic leans forward, his French accent coiling tighter as he speaks. "If we don't be—if we are not prepared to participate in the defence of our own borders, we might as well be the fifty-first state."

"The Americans will defend us whether we like it or not," says Woodley.

"So much for sovereignty," says Jack. "Use it or lose it."

They eat. The bartender sends over a plate of pickled eggs, on the house.

"What about the Bomarcs?" asks Vogel. "They must be armed by now."

No one answers at first. It's a naive statement. Diefenbaker has refused either to arm the American missiles or to say straight out that they are not armed.

"Don't hold your breath," says Vic.

"Dief wants to make hay out of both sides of the nuclear debate," says Steve.

"He's trying to fight his way to the middle," says Jack.

"No such thing when it comes to nukes," says Vic. "That's like saying you're a little bit pregnant." Steve and the others laugh. Jack merely smiles, and Hal Woodley's calm expression doesn't change; he lights a cigarette and tosses the pack onto the table. Jack reflects that even if it turns out Canada has lost her nuclear virginity, Canadians will be left to wonder just who has the authority to fire the outmoded missiles. Do we or don't we? Only our Prime Minister knows for sure.

As though Hal Woodley has read his thoughts, he says, "That type of secrecy is very dangerous in a democracy."

"It's called lying," says Jack.

They eat in silence. There is probably not one among them who wouldn't like a beer right about now, but no one is going to order one unless Woodley does. Woodley accepts a top-up of his coffee from the waiter. After a moment he says evenly, "The security of the U.S. is the security of Canada, and vice versa. That's not just the NORAD agreement, it's the Basic Security Plan. Dief has to honour it."

Jack feels like apologizing to Blair McCarroll for Canada's poor showing. The young man is quiet, as usual. Jack watches him staring down at the lunch his wife has packed for him—ham and cheese on a kaiser, homemade pecan tart. If Jack feels useless, think how McCarroll must feel. He should be in the cockpit of a tactical interceptor, patrolling the Florida coast. Jack is tempted to reach for a cigarette. He quit years ago, when his daughter was born. He shakes his head. "What's Dief waiting for?"

Vic says, "We need a Mackenzie King, we need a St. Laurent."

"We need a Frenchman," jokes Steve.

"Anyone but this prairie haystick," says Vic.

"Hayseed." Jack winks.

"I don't mind where he's from," says Vic. "Saskatchewan's full of good people—"

"Better believe it," says Hal Woodley.

"What I mind," says Vic, "is this guy—"

"Dief the Chief," puts in Steve.

"He doesn't know what he doesn't know," says Vic. "And he doesn't want to know."

"He's asleep at the switch," says Jack. And there is nothing to add.

"'It's a world of laughter a world of tears, it's a world of hopes and a world of fears. . . . '" Mr. March has declared that there is no finer patriotic gesture than to sing in the face of peril. Twenty-nine grade four voices, raised in unison: "' . . . It's a small world, after all! It's a small world after all, it's a small world after all, it's a small world after all, it's a small, small world. . . . '"

Elaine Ridelle has phoned Mimi twice, then popped over. She's terrified. She asks where Mimi hides the sherry. Mimi pours her a drink and calls Betty Boucher. She speaks discreetly, almost in code, but Betty knows right away what's up—Elaine has already popped in on her and found the Pimm's.

Mimi puts the stopper back in the decanter and changes out of her hausfrau clothes as Betty arrives with her four-year-old and a bushel of apples to peel; between the two of them they will have Elaine more or less shipshape by five. She is seven months pregnant and afraid the world will end before she gives birth. Betty tells her she ought to be more worried about giving birth to a lush, and puts the kettle on. They do not discuss the crisis, beyond Betty's comment that she isn't about to have her day ruined by "that Russian pipsqueak."

They are joined by Dot from next door with her baby, and, almost as an afterthought, Mimi calls Sharon McCarroll. Elaine may be the squeaky wheel, but Sharon is farther from home than any of them—except of course Betty, but Betty lived through the Blitz. Sharon is crying as she speaks, but far from hysterical. She forms her sentences as diffidently as ever. "I'm just worried about my family, Mimi—you know, my folks in Virginia."

Mimi takes the phone receiver into the dining room and lowers her voice while Betty distracts Elaine in the kitchen. "Of course you are, but you know it's going to be fine."

"At least my folks don't have to worry so much about us, being up here and all," says Sharon, brightening.

"That's right."

"I'm praying, Mimi."

"We all are, dear, and we're praying for your president."

She hears a small sob at the other end of the line. "Thank you."

"Listen, *ma p'tite,* it's going to blow over, meantime we have to just worry it out, and I hate to do that alone."

"Oh Mimi, would you like me to come over?"

"That would make me feel a whole lot better."

The four of them play a round of bridge and exchange trade secrets, among them the exact nature of their housework clothes—ugly old maternity tops, diaper bandanas and ragbag slippers, the shock their husbands would get if they ever caught them like that. All except Sharon, who, when pressed, admits to changing into slacks and an old V-neck sweater. Silence, then the others laugh till they weep, while Sharon smiles, a little puzzled, and Mimi gets up and hugs her.

On the way back to work, Jack finds that Blair McCarroll is walking with him. He says to Jack with no preamble, "In a way I'm glad I'm up here, on account of my family's here too. Safer for them." Jack nods. McCarroll continues, "But I feel like a damn fool." Jack nods again. "Not doing what I'm trained to do," says McCarroll in his farm-boy drawl.

Jack wishes he could tell Blair why he is up here; that it's not entirely pointless. Instead, he claps a hand on the younger man's shoulder. "We're a hundred percent behind you, McCarroll. And you're right about your family. Just as well, eh? Safer here in the middle of nowhere."

Blair returns the stoic smile.

"The following little girls will remain after the bell. . . ."

Perhaps Mr. March places a higher value on their survival. He has kept them behind to practise duck and cover under his big oak desk, "which is bound to provide more shelter in the event of an air raid."

Marjorie squeals and skips to the front. Grace grins, looks back at the other girls ranged against the coat hooks and follows Marjorie. He makes them both duck and cover under his desk at the same time. Then they emerge and it's Madeleine's turn.

Back in his office, Jack stares at the phone. He wonders if he ought to go out to the booth at the edge of the parade square and call Simon. If the Soviets pull another Berlin Blockade in response to this crisis, it's game over for anyone trying to defect to the West. So much for our hopes of depriving the Soviets of the scientific expertise of people like "our friend," Oskar Fried.

That's what the new warfare boils down to. Technology. Brains. We've grown soft in the West, we read manuals on how to raise our children, we offer basket-weaving courses at universities and spend untold hours in front of the boob tube. Meanwhile, in the U.S.S.R., a generation of engineers is coming of age. Khrushchev is right. They are perfectly capable of burying us.

He pulls a paper-clipped wedge from a mimeographed stack and inserts it into a large binder; articles and essays he has culled from various American management publications—might as well keep busy.

A heading catches his eye, *Scientific and Professional Employees*. He reads: *Scientific and professional employees have less orientation toward their employer and more toward their work and their profession—that* makes sense. Pure science is a higher calling. *They are more matter-of-fact and less talkative, participative and social.* That certainly doesn't describe Henry Froelich—he is shy, but once you've coaxed him out of his shell. . . . Will Oskar Fried be the same? That is, if he makes it out of the Soviet bloc? *The true scientist intends to work at his specialty regardless, and the fact that a specific employer has hired him is somewhat incidental.* Jack pauses. That's why scientists such as Wernher von Braun remain above the fray—although Henry would counter that such a thing is impossible. But rockets are rockets. And now they are ICBMs that we pray we will never use, and Saturn engines that will power us to the moon. And von Braun has switched employers, he works for us now—the Americans, that is. *Aware of his ability and contribution, the scientific employee has high status drives, leading to some discontent and frustration.* Jack lifts his gaze to the window and begins to construct a mental composite—a profile—of Oskar Fried.

Perhaps he is defecting not just for ideological reasons but because he's had it with the bloated Soviet system, which tends to reward corrupt apparatchiks, fugitive Cambridge spies and the odd cosmonaut—not to mention the periodic purges, which are not necessarily a thing of the past. Could it be that Fried is tired of a drab life labouring in obscurity and fear? That he craves the kind of prestige and rewards the West has to offer? The good life? Who could blame him? He is coming alone. Perhaps he is unmarried, or a widower. Perhaps he has nothing to live for back in the U.S.S.R.

Jack's gaze has come to rest on the photo of Mimi and the kids. If a man came into his home and threatened his family, Jack would kill him. Simple. He turns a paper clip between thumb and forefinger. But there is nothing simple about this situation. The men on the other side of the world don't need to leave their homes in order to destroy his. Mountains used to afford nations a defence. Bodies of water, deserts and, until recently, sheer distance. That was why thousands of Allied aircrew were able to train in safety, at this very station among others, before heading overseas to defeat Fascism. But nowadays there is no such thing as "out of range." Global village. And all it takes is one idiot. . . .

Meanwhile, Canada's defences have not been activated. Jack's hands are tied. He can't so much as order a blanket broken out of mothballs, should it become necessary to provide relief for the civilian population. His own government has decided that Jack's children don't need to be defended. He hasn't felt this angry, this useless, in years. Not since 1943, in Centralia.

The phone rings. He grabs it. "McCarthy here." Her voice at the other end is relaxed. An ordinary day.

"Fire away," he says, his disappointment only fleeting. The heat in his face, the pulse at his neck recede as though the sound of his wife's voice were a cool cloth to his head. "Milk? . . . yup . . . butter. . . ." He drops the paper clip and reaches for a pencil.

Madeleine walks out the side door of the school. She has her art with her, a construction-paper bear. His head is square—she was unable to draw and cut out a circle, no matter how she tried.

The afternoon is grey and gauzy, no sun except for a dirty yellow stain against one end of the sky—the only indication that there is still such a thing as east or west, or that it makes any difference.

It burns probably because of the chalk on his finger, but that is just a sting and it will stop soon, for even though it's her first experience of being stabbed, she sees no reason why it should sting forever, nothing does.

The other girls disperse, unwrapping their candy. Madeleine doesn't take the candy any more. The others put out their hands and for once in her life Marjorie Nolan has the power to say, "You can have this one."

Madeleine did not know you could be stabbed so hard and not die or go to the hospital, she did not know anything could get up there—that must be where the pee comes out, and she can already tell that pee will make it sting more, although maybe it will also disinfect since that is what stinging often does.

Right now she is more worried that her head may not return to normal size. The moment she left the school, it began to swell and expand until it became huge, like the grey cloud that has become the sky this afternoon. If she closes her eyes she can feel herself growing impossibly tall and weightless, her head ballooning up up and away, her feet far below and tiny on the ground in their scuffed Mary Janes.

Walk fast and make a breeze to cool the sting, there is moistness in the air, that will help, it will also dry the underpants, which are damp and wadded like a bandage.

She doesn't continue through the baseball field toward home. Instead she crosses the parking lot and turns up Algonquin Drive, the PMQs on her left, the farmer's field on her right.

The good thing about stabbing is that she is now certain she's no longer afraid of needles. Once you have been stabbed, a needle is nothing. And that's what you get for secretly hoping he would touch your underpants.

She veers onto the road and walks down the middle. She'll hear if a car comes along. She could walk into that low field between the furrows, follow the sugar-beet road. The farmer might come out with his shot-gun. She could pretend to be a scarecrow or simply walk into the bullets, she would like to feel them bouncing off her. That farmer doesn't own the world, no one does, *blow it up, earthling.*

She could keep walking in a straight line until she finally gets home for supper, years from now. Why does anyone stay anywhere? Why don't people just roll like marbles over the tilting earth? How does any-one know there is such a thing as themself? She starts to zigzag down the road, weaving between the broken yellow lines. Perhaps this is why mothers say not to stray on your way home. Because they know you might keep going. She turns onto the Huron County road.

The white buildings of the base spread out to her right, opposite are the PMQs, their colours muted, no expressions on their faces, and up ahead the Spitfire, indifferent. Madeleine sees everything all at once with-out looking at anything. All appears grim and indistinct, stripped of one layer of light, stripped of distance and difference beneath the uniform grey that has lowered the sky—the ceiling, as pilots call it. High above that blur, the day is eternally blue and sunny—this grey, these clouds change the whole world for us down here and yet they are no more than a curtain or a piece of stage scenery. Her father is over there somewhere to her right, and to her left is her mother. They are specks, words.

Mr. March's expression does not change, his glasses glint as usual. You would never know by looking at his face that he has his hand up a little girl's dress. Madeleine doesn't think of it as "my dress." It's as though she's seeing the plaid pleats from the level of her hem—there are her bare legs, and a man's grey sleeve up between them as if she were a puppet. It stings. She melts away from the pain like a Popsicle from a Popsicle stick. Do not speak, your voice is far away in another country. Do not move, your arms and legs are not attached to the pain, there is nothing for them to do but wait.

Her feet will not stop walking—past the turnoff to the PMQs now—like Karen in *The Red Shoes,* she will have to find a kindly woodcutter to chop them off. She begins to run heavily, pounding her heels because this is the way to feel that your feet will not be chopped off. The air is like layers of damp tissue paper clinging one after another to her face. As she runs, she opens and closes her fists, twisting her wrists, because this is the way to feel that your hands will not be chopped off, or just come off by themselves and float away like pieces of Pinocchio. *Stand still, little girl.*

The ragged *caw* of a crow, a sound like something scrawled in black ink on the air. She looks up on the run. One is returning to its home atop the pine pole where the air-raid siren protrudes from beneath the mass of twigs and hay, the rusting mouth open as though in mid-cry, or like a fountain run dry. She runs past the Spitfire on its pedestal, aimed upward, its gun barrels filled in and painted over. It won the Battle of Britain. How come someone didn't kill Hitler? Why didn't someone just walk up to him with a gun? Anne Frank would have lived. If only she could go back in time and kill Hitler. If only a car would come along right now with a strange man in a peaked cap who says, "Get in the car, little girl," she would kill him, smash the door on his head. Here comes a car, let it be a kidnapper, *I will bash his head in with a rock.*

But the car passes. She picks up a rock and hurls it after, then turns and runs again, past the airfield on her right, dragging the toes of her Mary Janes, wrecking them, this is the way to pound someone when there is no one to pound. *Put your hands around my neck, little girl. Now squeeze. That's it. Harder.* Standing beside his desk. Feeling the muscles packaged in the fat, and that strange floating thing in the front of his soupy neck like turkey bones. His eyes bug out, why doesn't he clean his glasses? Perhaps because he is using his hanky on his thing. It sticks up under the white fabric like the chalice in church. Madeleine didn't ask to think that, it just came into her head, and God controls everything, "So don't blame me!" she yells, jutting her chin forward, marching now. But there is no one to hear her, the base is far behind, and the roofs of the PMQs are sinking behind the gentle rise and fall of autumn fields.

Her head is back to normal size, of a piece with her body again, and the air no longer seems so flat and far away. The grass looks real now, the pebbles at the side of the road look real and so is the feel of her paper bear crumpled in her hand. The Huron County road has become a corridor of birches and maples, farms opening on either side like the pages of a book. The light has changed, no longer flint but liquid. Cool grey has gathered, multiplying shades of hay, bales of shredded wheat dotting the fields, old gold of dry stalks, the abrupt river-green of a pumpkin field—miraculous splashes of orange, gifts the size of beachballs under each broad leaf. The fading grass of the roadside leans thick and chewy, dirty hair brushed against fenceposts. A turnip lies where it bounced from the back of a truck, milky purple like the inside of a seashell. She thinks, if I never went home again, I wouldn't starve.

She smells rain and slows her pace. The velvet scent of hay, a cud-mown field to one side; a big brown head heaves round and looks at her across the fence, its moist mother-eye. Somewhere a red-winged blackbird, its dark sweet song close up in the misted air, like a bird in a movie. Telephone wires criss-cross overhead, trapeze artists swinging voices from pole to pole, balancing nests and conversations. She stops and faces the field to her right. Beyond the ditch running with weeds is the corn. Papery yellow, standing at attention like veterans, decorated and depleted, still marching in columns, ribbons furling from empty stalks.

The first big drops fall. Massive and far apart they come, exploding dust at her feet. She tilts her head back, catching drops that taste both soft and metallic, they tap her face like fingertips, impossible to tell where the next drop will fall, as rapid as thoughts. She looks ahead again, feels her bangs flattening against her forehead, water streaming down her nose to her lips. If she never went home again, she wouldn't go thirsty.

Up ahead, a willow tree sweeps the ground where the Huron County road intersects with a nameless dirt road. The tree stands at a slight sway, as though in sidelong greeting, underwater green and fading with the season, trembly with the rain that, at Madeleine's approach, sounds lighter against its many small leaves, the song of a long-haired soprano. She sees it shimmer in the rain, a tree made entirely of wands. Perhaps this is where she will spend the night, a broad and level limb for her bed. She parts the green curtain and beads of water melt along her arm and down the back of her neck as she enters the cool dry arch, and at once the sound changes. It's like being in a tent in the rain. She smells, before she sees, that she is not alone. Wet animal. Familiar.

Rex is lying at the base of the tree, his fur steaming, droplets of light around his neck, the tips of his ears. An old clothespin bag sits on the ground next to him. "Hi Rex." He must be lost. His tail pats the ground at her approach, but she stops because she has seen something out the corner of her eye. Holey white running shoes, light brown legs. Colleen, sitting on a branch. She has a long stick stripped of leaves, it bends from her hand supple as a whip.

She slides off and drops to the ground. Madeleine takes a step back. Colleen reaches down to the clothespin bag and, without taking her eyes off Madeleine, brings out a canvas pencil case, unzips it, dips in and comes out with a tuft of tobacco and a rectangle of white paper. Madeleine watches her roll, lick and seal the paper, then put it between her lips. Colleen takes a book of matches and lights up. *Success without College* promises the cover. She inhales, squinting through the smoke, and leans against the tree, cigarette between thumb and forefinger. Her dirty white T-shirt glows clean in the green shadows. The leather string around her neck disappears beneath her shirt to form a tiny bump in the centre of her chest.

Madeleine asks, "Can I see your knife?"

Colleen reaches into the pocket of her cut-offs.

Its handle is carved in yellowed bone. "From a bear," Colleen says, unfolding the blade, polished and ultra-thin with use and care. She holds the knife flat across her palm. Madeleine reaches for it. "Don't touch it," says Colleen, not closing her palm.

"Why not?"

"'Cause it's not a toy." Colleen talks with her face slightly averted, pale eyes narrowed. Madeleine sees the fine white scar at the corner of her mouth, faint frown.

"I'm not ascared of you," says Madeleine.

"I don't give a shit."

"I know," says Madeleine, shocked yet curiously at ease.

"Know-it-all, eh?"

"Come here and say that," speaking before thinking.

"I am here, stupid." The corner of Colleen's mouth rises, sarcastic amusement in her eyes.

"So you is," says Madeleine, her mouth to one side like Bugs Bunny. She reaches out and takes the knife. Colleen makes no move to stop her. "On guard!" declares Madeleine, and slashes the air like Zorro. Colleen just watches. Madeleine holds up her soggy bear with his smearing smile and impales him—"Take that!" She taps her chin with the point of the blade and invites Colleen to "come on, hit me right here." She starts laughing helplessly, arms limp and noodly—"Goodbye cwuel wowld!"—staggering, knife flailing, cross-eyed, pretending to stab herself. Rex stands and barks.

Colleen takes a drag, then flicks her cigarette aside and holds out her hand for the knife. Madeleine returns it, weak with laughter. Colleen folds it and shakes her head. "You're a maniac, McCarthy."

Madeleine replies in a bright voice, as though reading aloud, "*Oui, je suis folle, je suis une maniaque,*" starting to do a mechanical twist.

Colleen says, "*C'est ça quoi ja di, ya crazy batar.*" Which is how Madeleine finds out that Colleen speaks a kind of French.

"It ain't French, it's Michif," says Colleen.

*Michif.* Sounds like "mischief."

Colleen hooks the clothespin bag over the end of her stick and walks out from under the tree, back into the rain. Rex follows.

"Colleen, wait up."

Madeleine catches up and they walk in silence. She takes off her shoes and socks. The rain hits the ground in a perpetual mist, it falls so hard. It's easy to run in a hard rain, puddles become trampolines, it's like running on a path in the woods, impossible to get tired. Mirage-barns waver across the fields, thunder shakes the trees at the foot of a mile-long farm driveways. Paws and bare feet and soaked running shoes. She smells wet dog. There is no smell in the world more comforting except perhaps a campfire. Although a campfire is melancholy too, because you sit around it with your family in the big dark, knowing that your love and who you are stretch only a little way into it.

"Where're we going?" asks Madeleine.

"Rock Bass."

It isn't a whip, it's a fishing rod.

There is still a bit of summer left down there. The greens are vivid with a sheen like old leather. Blades of grass still tall but easily bent and broken now, they will not spring back if you step on them. Leaves are still fleshy at the stems, fused to their twigs but only weeks away from that moment when they may all blow off at once. When is that moment? Some years the breezes come gradually, taking a few leaves at a time, while other autumns are still and calm, trees fully clothed and many-coloured until November, when with one huff and puff the woods stand suddenly naked.

"Are we there yet?" asks Madeleine. They have stopped at the crest of a ravine. Below is a stream which, come spring, will be more than a creek and less than a river. On the opposite bank, a maple tree grows. The rain has slowed and the drops say *hush hush hush* against the red and amber leaves. It's an afternoon sound.

It is amazing to think that, while we are at school or asleep or watching TV, the woods are here. Breathing, changing, their stately grace made up of countless frantic lives lived high and low, each rustle and cry part of that sweeping rhythm. Breathe in, it's summer. Breathe out, it's fall. Stand still, it's winter. Open your eyes, springtime.

The maple tree is so quiet, yet it is passionately changing. Part of it is dying. The pretty part. Its sadness will soon be exposed, its true age and wisdom, casting up its gnarly prayers. That is the beautiful part.

"This is Rock Bass," says Colleen, and skids straight down the ravine to the stream below. Rex follows. So does Madeleine. There are stepping stones but they wade across.

There's a flat rock under the maple and, nearby, the remains of a campfire. Colleen takes an Eight O'clock Coffee can from her clothes-pin bag, removes a wax-paper lid and lifts out a fat worm. She hooks it onto the end of her line, it curls in spasm, she casts into the stream, then stands on the flat stone and waits.

Madeleine squats on the ground and waits too, hugging her knees. She reaches for a charred stick and writes her name on the stone. Her name looks like her face and she wishes it looked fiercer. The vowels look as though they could be stolen and carried away wide-eyed, and there are too many syllables—each one a weak point of connection, separable like a joint. She wishes she had one syllable, compact, inviolable. Like Mike.

She says to Colleen's back, "How come you didn't pound me that day?" Colleen keeps her eyes on the stream. "You're not worth it."

Madeleine rubs the palms of her hands with soot from the stick. "Why not?"

"'Cause I'm not going back, that's why." Colleen flicks her line back over her shoulder and recasts.

"Back where?"

"None of your goddamn business." She sounds calm. Content.

Madeleine wipes her hands together as though the soot were soap, then smells them. They smell like a campfire now. Clean. "Why would your parents send you back?"

"Not my parents." Colleen glances down at her and Madeleine is reminded that she is afraid of this girl.

She revises her question. "Why would you get sent back?"

"For violence."

*Violence.* The word looks like a slash of red and black. Madeleine can see the muscles in Colleen's calves, dusty and lean—still brown, although summer is long gone. They contract as she shifts forward. She's got a bite. She pulls in a small fish. It whips about, grey and yellow at the end of her line, staring. She unhooks it and tosses it back. "You ever hear of Children's Aid?"

"No."

"You're lucky."

The sun comes out from under the grey coverlet of this rainy afternoon just in time to begin its descent into evening. Madeleine has no idea what time it is. The airfield comes into view on their left and she feels as though she is waking from a dream. That's when she realizes that she has lost her shoes.

"Where were you going, anyhow?" asks Colleen.

"Nowhere."

"If you say so."

Madeleine says, "I was running away."

"I done that."

"Yeah?"

"Lotsa times."

"Where'd you go?"

"Once to Calgary," says Colleen. "We stoled a horse. Me and my brother."

"Ricky?"

"Who else?"

"You ran away all the way to Calgary from Centralia on a horse?"

"Not from here. From a place in Alberta."

"What place?"

"None of your goddamn business."

They walk. "I was born in Alberta," says Madeleine. Colleen is silent. Madeleine asks, "Where were you born?"

She doesn't expect an answer so she is surprised when, after a moment, Colleen says, "In a car."

"On the way to the hospital?"

"No. It was around the border somewhere. Either in Montana or Alberta."

Madeleine pictures Mr. Froelich pulling over to the side of a lost highway, trying to boil water over a campfire while Mrs. Froelich has a baby in the back seat. She puts her hand out and feels Rex's wet nose nudge her. "What's Children's Aid?"

Colleen spits neatly from the side of her mouth. "They come and put you in a training school if they think you're bad enough."

"Oh. What's a training school?"

Colleen shrugs. "It's a jail for kids."

Up ahead, the PMQs look as tame as animals in a corral. The Spitfire looks friendly once more and the white buildings of the base as cordial as a collection of barbershops. But a feeling is growing in the pit of Madeleine's stomach. Apprehension. "Are you going to get in trouble?"

"What for?" says Colleen.

Madeleine doesn't have in mind the smoking or the swearing, because presumably Colleen does neither in front of her parents. But skipping school can't be concealed. How else could Colleen have already been hanging out at the willow tree with her play clothes on? "You played hooky."

"So? It's my life."

Madeleine glances at her profile—serious mouth, narrowed blue eye trained on the horizon—and wonders if this means she and Colleen Froelich are friends now.

"Boy, are you ever gonna get it!"

It's Mike, standing on his pedals, pumping furiously toward her up Columbia Drive. "Maman is going to kill you!"—slamming on his brakes, coming to a showy side-stop. "Where the Sam heck have you been?"

"Have a hairy fit, why don't you?"

Mike shakes his head, looks at the state of her. "*Va-t'en dans la maison, toi.*"

Roy Noonan and Philip Pinder's tough older brother, Arnold, ride up from opposite directions. "I got her," Mike tells them.

"Where'd you find her, Mike?" asks Arnold, as though she were a lost cat.

"I wasn't lost!" yells Madeleine.

"Oh yeah?" says Mike. "Where were you, then, making mudpies with the girls?" The boys stare at her. Roy offers to ride her home double—her house is only a stone's throw away, is he off his rocker?

Mike says, "Thanks, you guys, I'll take it from here."

"Welcome," they grunt, and ride off.

Madeleine turns to gauge Colleen's scorn at her humiliation, but Colleen is gone.

"Is Dad home yet?" Madeleine asks, as she trails after him up the driveway toward her execution.

"You better hope not," says her brother, leaning his bike against the house, taking her elbow as though she were his prisoner. She yanks free and pulls open the screen door.

Her mother comes out of the kitchen and stands at the top of the three inside steps; she is on the phone. "Never mind, Sharon, here she is." She hangs up. "*Dieu merci.*" Her eyes are red. She reaches down for Madeleine.

At the touch, her relief turns to anger, she hauls Madeleine up the steps and spanks her bottom through the living room, toward the stairs. As they pass the kitchen, Madeleine sees Mike at the fridge calmly pouring himself a glass of milk. "She was with Colleen Froelich," he says. "*Elle a perdu ses souliers, maman.*"

The French comes so fast that Madeleine can't understand a word, although it's not difficult to imagine what her mother is saying—she has called half the PMQs, she just got off the phone with Mrs. McCarroll, where are your shoes?! And in English: "You're not to play with the Froelich girl, do you hear me?"

She shoves her through the door of her bedroom and slams it shut. "*Bouges pas! Attends ton père!*"

Madeleine sits on the edge of her bed. The early evening light warms the flowered spread and her frilly pillowcase. Her giant pixie dolls with their cracked faces stare merrily—Christmas gifts from Tante Yvonne. She shoves them to the floor and reaches for Bugs, pats him and rearranges his ears, folding them back so he can relax. "That's a good Bugsy." She looks down at her muddy bare feet, her streaked dress, blackened hands. Discovers speckles of mud on her face. Waits in the unnatural bright silence of her closed bedroom. She lies down. Her feet are cold although it's warm out. Bugs nestles against her shoulder.

She hears the front door open downstairs. Her father's muffled voice, cheerful as usual after work. A hush. His measured tread on the stairs. Getting closer. Her stomach goes cold. *Wait till your father gets home.* His cold blue disappointment, his sad left eye; his white temper that she has only ever seen directed at other drivers and at printed instructions for the lawnmower. And sometimes at Mike. Her doorknob turns slowly and he peeks his head in. He is still wearing his uniform hat. He gives her a quizzical look. "What are you doing having a nap before supper, sweetie, are you sick?"

"No."

He doesn't know. Maman didn't tell him.

"Well come on down and help me read the funnies. Maman's made a delicious supper."

It's a miracle.

Throughout the meal, not a word of Madeleine's transgression. The radio is already off when she comes down to the kitchen. Her father usually listens to the headlines before saying grace. Instead, Maman puts on Maurice Chevalier, then replaces him with Charles Trenet when Dad mutters something about "that collaborator." She eats everything on her plate without complaint, including the mashed potatoes with turnip mixed in—why does Maman have to ruin perfectly good potatoes?

After supper Mimi takes Mike to a basketball game in Exeter. Ricky Froelich is playing for the South Huron Braves. Jack was going to take him but he is staying home with Madeleine instead. Maman kisses her goodbye and whispers, "You're so lucky to have such a nice papa."

Her father doesn't watch the news, instead he and Madeleine play a game of checkers at the kitchen table. After a while he says, "Maman tells me you were late getting home from school."

So he knows. But he's not mad.

"Yeah," says Madeleine, keeping her eyes on the checkerboard.

"Where'd you go?" Dad is likewise contemplating a move.

"For a walk."

"Oh? Whereabouts?"

"Rock Bass."

"Where's that?"

"It's a ravine. You go down a dirt road."

"I see." He jumps her, and she jumps two of his. "By yourself?"

"Well I met Colleen."

"The Froelich girl?"

"Yeah. She was fishing."

"Did she catch anything?"

"A bass."

"A bass, wow."

"She let it go, though. She has a knife."

"Really?"

"But she doesn't play with it, it's a tool, not a toy."

"She's right about that."

They play. She wins.

"What happened at school today, old buddy?"

"Um . . . we had a film."

"What about?"

" . . . Duck and cover."

"Duck and cover?"

"In case of an atomic bomb."

"I see." He folds up the checkerboard. "And did Mr. March get you ducking under the desks?"

"Mm-hm."

"Is that why you ran away?"

Madeleine opens her lips. No sound comes out so she nods.

"I might have to have a word with Mr. March."

"No," she says.

"Why not?"

*Do you know what will happen if your parents find out what a bad child you've been?* "He's nice," says Madeleine. She tries not to breathe out. She sits very still—don't let the smell go into the air.

"Maybe so," says her father. "But he's out of line."

Madeleine waits. Does he know? Can he smell it? *They will send me away.*

"Listen to me now, sweetheart." *The Children's Aid will come and take me to jail.* "He's exaggerating the danger. President Kennedy has to show the Soviets who's boss, that's all." President Kennedy. Does he know Mr. March? *There is a nukular missile aimed at Centralia. I'll give you something to cry about, little girl.* "The world is waiting to see who's going to blink first. And you can bet it'll be the Soviets 'cause they know we mean business this time."

Madeleine blinks.

He says, "You can't appease a tyrant." Pease porridge hot, pease porridge cold. "You've got to stand up to him. That's what we learned in the war, never mind ducking and covering." He sounds disgusted. Cowards duck and cover. Collaborators.

"Like Maurice Chevalier?" she asks.

"What's that?"

"Nothing."

He closes the paper and gets up, gesturing for her to follow. Am I in trouble now? No, Mr. March is. No, the Soviets are.

He spreads a map of the world on the dining-room table. He points out the places in Europe where she has been. Copenhagen, Munich, Paris, Rome, the French Riviera. . . ."Tell Mr. March about that the next time he asks you for capital cities."

He asks where she'd most like to go in the whole wide world. She can't decide, so he traces a finger up the Amazon and describes the animals and natives she could see. "You could go with a guide on a bamboo raft." Then he does the same with the Nile, lined with pyramids. "You could ride a camel across the desert." And right here in pink, our own vast country. "Take a canoe up the Yukon River, live on salmon and pan for gold." She can go anywhere.

"You can grow up to be anything you want, the sky's the limit. You can be an astronaut, an ambassador—"

"Can I be in movies?"

"You can do anything you set your mind to."

"Can I go on Ed Sullivan?"

"I want you to promise me something," he says, looking her in the eye.

"Okay."

"I know you love to go out in the woods and roam with your buddies, I used to do the same thing. But when I was a kid there weren't so many cars and we knew everyone for miles around. We're new here in Centralia"—we're always new—"and Maman gets worried when she doesn't know where you are. Tell you what, promise me you'll check in after school, change into your dungarees and tell Maman where you're going, then you can wander up to Rock Bass to your heart's content, so long as you're back for supper."

"Okay."

"That's the stuff."

"Dad?"

"Yeah?"

"I was running away."

He laughs. Madeleine didn't know it was funny. She smiles, everything must be okay. She follows him into the kitchen.

"I'll tell you a secret," he says, opening the freezer, taking out the ice cream. "I ran away lotsa times when I was a little fella. I'd fill my pockets with cookies, and Joey Boyle and I would light out over the school fence."

"How come?"

He looks surprised at the question. "For fun." He jams a scoop of vanilla ice cream onto a cone. "You're like me," he says, handing it to her. "Adventurous."

Madeleine eats the ice cream, and smiles like a girl eating ice cream. He does not know about after-three. If he did, we wouldn't have looked at the map and he would not be talking about when I grow up. Dad has welcomed her into the sunny tribe of scamps in knickerbockers from the olden days: the days of the world's best candy, when each house was different and one was haunted and there was a Main Street with a drugstore soda fountain. And he has laid the world at her feet for when she grows up. The dark of after-three must never be allowed to touch the sunshine world of when Dad was little. Luckily, she is the only link. And she can keep them separate. Like a secret agent fending off both sides of a shrinking room.

"Dad?"

"Yeah, old buddy?" Everything is okay.

"Can I see your medal?"

She follows him upstairs. He reaches into his top drawer, behind his clean hankies. He places a small wooden box in her hands and opens it. Against a bed of blue velvet, suspended from a red and white ribbon, gleams the silver cross: two thunderbolts conjoined with wings, overlaid with propeller blades. In the centre, Hermes, the god with winged heels. *For valour, courage and devotion to duty whilst flying. . . .*

"Uncle Simon gave you that," she says.

"Well, Uncle Simon didn't give it to me. But he helped."

"'Cause he taught you to fly."

"That's right."

"And he rescued you." She strokes the medal. She is going to cry. Why? After everything has turned out to be okay after all, don't cry,

Madeleine, Dad didn't die in the crash. She bites the inside of her cheek and stares at the medal. Dad will not die for a long long time.

"Dad?"

"Yeah?"

"Where's Borneo?"

"Let's go down and find it on the map."

Borneo isn't even a country. It's an island in the Indian archipelago. There is no capital city.

Dad tucks her in and says, "I've got something I want to give you." A tattered book missing its back cover. On the front, a picture of a boy in old-fashioned britches, holding a can of whitewash, a half-painted fence behind him. *The Adventures of Tom Sawyer.* "It's old. But I bet it still works."

Madeleine opens it. Inside on the flyleaf is a bookplate: *This Book Belongs To* and, in a primary scrawl, *John McCarthy.* "It was mine when I was a boy. Now it's yours."

"Wow. Thanks Dad." She holds it carefully. She can smell its old-book smell, mushroomy. "Are you going to read it out loud?" She wants to read it on her own but she doesn't want to hurt his feelings if he has his heart set on reading it to her.

"Nope." He gets up from the side of her bed. "I think that's the kind of book best read on your own time, to yourself. And when you finish that you can read *Huckleberry Finn.*"

"Dad?"

"Yeah?"

"Maman said I'm not allowed to play with Colleen Froelich."

He hesitates. Then, "Maman was pretty worried when you didn't come home."

"I know."

"She probably figures Colleen's not such a great influence."

"She's not an influence," says Madeleine, as sincerely and respectfully as she can.

He smiles. "She knows how to fish, eh?"

"Yeah."

"Well she can't be all bad, then, can she? You leave it with me, okay?"

She bites her lip, this time to suppress her joy. "Okay." He kisses her forehead and leaves her tucked in and reading.

He walks downstairs. Imagine, scaring a class full of eight- and nine-year-olds like that, what kind of a teacher—? Duck and cover, my eye, if this thing blows it's sayonara, buddy, you can kiss your arse goodbye, never mind all the backyard bomb shelters the Yanks are selling to each other to go with their swimming pools. If Kennedy had had the guts to call off that half-baked invasion at Bay of Pigs a year and a half ago, the world might not be in this mess—he finds a beer in the fridge—or if he'd had the guts to all-out invade.

He goes to the living room. Bay of Pigs was a textbook example of a failure of decision-making. Not the making of a bad decision, but the failure to make a clear one. All Kennedy accomplished was to inflame the situation—like poking at a hornets' nest. Still, he's doing the right thing now. Seeking the best advice—unlike our prime minister, who's allergic to advice. Jack bends and flicks on the TV, then sits on the couch and waits for it to warm up. Kennedy isn't backing down, but neither is he firing the first shot. "Speak softly and carry a big stick." A war of nerves. It takes guts. And Kennedy has a few, if his own war record is any indication. More than just a pretty face from a rich family. Good old Irish bootlegger stock, and that's what Jack and anyone with any sense is really pinning his hopes on—bare knuckles crossed with a Harvard education. He would love to be a fly on the wall in the White House Cabinet Room, where the Executive Committee is meeting round the clock. The Excomm. History in the making.

The CBC comes on, and Pierre Salinger tells a Canadian reporter that Secretary of State McNamara and his team are living on sandwiches and coffee as they make and revise plans for every contingency. Across the United States, housewives are stocking up on canned goods as talking heads explain how to survive a nuclear attack, without explaining why anyone would want to. Meanwhile, in Canada, heads are firmly lodged in the sand. No new developments. He switches to CBS and watches while Walter Cronkite explains "the way it is." If there has to be a nuclear war, just as well to hear it from him.

There is a limit, however, to the amount of news that can be broadcast, even in the midst of an international crisis. Jack changes the channel and feels his shoulders begin to relax in spite of himself as he watches Wayne and Shuster.

Up in her room, Madeleine is engrossed. *Shortly Tom came upon the juvenile pariah of the town, Huckleberry Finn. . . .* She knows she will have to turn off the light when Maman gets home. *Huckleberry was cordially hated and dreaded by all the mothers of the town. . . .* This is the first grown-up book that she has ever read silently to herself, unmediated by her own voice and her father's. Reading has just become even more intoxicating. *Huckleberry came and went at his own free will. He slept on door-steps in fine weather, and in empty hogsheads in wet—* what's a hogshead? A hog's head?—*he did not have to go to school or to church, or call any being master, or obey anybody; he could go fishing or swimming when and where he chose, and stay as long as it suited him; nobody forbade him to fight; he could sit up as late as he pleased; he was always the first boy that went barefoot in the spring and the last to resume leather in the fall; he never had to wash, nor put on clean clothes; he could swear wonderfully. . . .*

If you believe hard enough, is it possible to enter the world of a book? If you pray to God for a miracle, can He transport you to St. Petersburg, Florida, long ago? Set you down by the Mississippi in a pair of tattered overalls, as a boy? Madeleine squeezes her eyes shut and prays. *Please, dear God, turn me into a boy.* God can do anything. Except change Himself into a rock with no powers, then change Himself back again, because then He would never have been a real rock. Don't think about that—like infinity, it is a mystery and it will make you dizzy. Have faith. Keep reading, and when you wake up in the morning, perhaps the miracle will have occurred. . . .

By the time Mimi gets home with Mike, Jack has found another news special, another pundit, " . . . but do we have a viable emergency measures plan? My guess is. . . ." He switches off the TV, she kisses him and asks, "How's Madeleine?"

"Oh, she's fine. But I tell you, I'm going to have a word with that teacher, what's-his-name."

"Mr. March. Why, did something happen at school?"

"Fella needs a good thump on the nose."

She pauses, halfway out of her coat. "Why, what did he do?"

"He's scaring the life out of the kids with this nonsense over Cuba, that's why she ran off after school."

"Oh." She slips her coat off. "Well I don't like her playing with the Froelich girl."

"The Froelich kid is harmless, it's the wife you don't like," and he winks.

"Dad?"

"Yeah Mike?"

"Are we on alert yet?"

"Nope. How was the game?"

"Great. Rick scored two baskets."

"Good stuff."

Mike heads for the kitchen to get the leftover *bouillie* from the fridge.

"Jack, make sure you don't, you know. . . ."

"Don't what?"

"Well I want you to be careful, don't embarrass Madeleine when you talk to her teacher."

"Why would I do that?"

"'Cause you'll get mad, you know how mad you get."

He laughs. "I won't get mad."

"Maybe I should go instead."

"Naw, don't worry, I'll play it cool. Drop by the classroom tomorrow, right at three, once the kids have gone. Tap on his door."

She kisses him again.

Sometime after midnight, Madeleine creeps from her bedroom to the top of the stairs.

"What're you doing?" It's Mike in his cowboy pajamas, on his way to the bathroom.

"Nothing," she whispers, her arms full of sheets.

"You wet the bed."

"I did not." She starts to cry.

"Don't blubber," he whispers. "Get changed."

He goes into her room, turns over the mattress, then takes the sheets downstairs, puts them in the washer and turns it on.

Their parents wake up and Mike tells them that she was sick.

"Not feeling well, old buddy?" Dad asks, picking her up. Madeleine rests her head on his shoulder and slips her thumb in her mouth for just an instant. Maman isn't fooled. Nothing is said, but a plastic sheet appears on Madeleine's bed. She can tell because of the crinkle.

# I Cannot Tell a Lie

"I just don't see any other solution except direct military intervention right now."

*General Curtis LeMay to President Kennedy, October 19, 1962*

*Best advice: keep your cheeks up. Do this by starting to smile ever so slightly. This gives the muscles of the face a lift, uptilts the corners of the mouth and relaxes the forehead muscles.*

*Chatelaine, 1962*

At breakfast, Jack looks up from his paper. "They're going to test all the sirens in southern Ontario today." He asks Madeleine, "You remember hearing the sirens once or twice in 4 Wing, when I'd have to go off on a drill?"

Madeleine remembers—that is, her insides do. Her knees do.

"Well it's the same thing," says her father. "Nothing to worry about."

After breakfast, Mimi says, "Madeleine, come here, what's this?" She is standing in the bathroom with the laundry hamper open. Madeleine's underpants are in her hand. There is a brownish stain.

"Um. I don't know."

"Did you have an accident?"

Madeleine turns red. "No!" Mimi sniffs the underpants. Madeleine turns away; Maman is horrible.

"It's blood," says Mimi.

Madeleine can't swallow. She just looks at her mother.

"Are you bleeding now? Let me see"—reaching under Madeleine's school dress, pulling down her underpants—

"Maman!"

"Don't 'maman' me, *je suis ta mère.*" She examines Madeleine's underpants—spotless—then pulls them back up. "What have you been doing?"

"Nothing." Madeleine can feel her cheeks on fire.

"Sit down, Madeleine."

She sits on the toilet lid.

Mimi says, "Look at me."

Madeleine does.

"What happened to you, *chérie?*"

Madeleine swallows. "I fell." She sees the air begin to float sideways, as though it were slightly liquid.

"What were you doing?"

Madeleine blinks to make the air stand still. It works. Maman is still looking at her.

"It's okay, Maman's not going to be angry."

Madeleine says, "On a bike."

Mimi sighs and says, "Madeleine, did you take your brother's bike again without asking?" Madeleine nods yes—I'm not lying, I have taken his bike a couple of times without asking. "And you hurt yourself on the crossbar."

Madeleine nods again. It's true, that actually happened once and it really hurt. "It really hurt," she says.

"I can see that," says her mother, stroking her cheek. "Oh Madeleine, when I was your age my papa wouldn't let me have a bike."

"Why not?"

"Because of this." She holds up the underpants. "*Écoute bien.* I've said I don't want you riding boys' bikes, not your brother's, not anyone's, do you understand why now? Next time you find blood on your panties, *ma p'tite,* you have to tell Maman." She tosses the underpants back in the hamper. "Because that's part of growing up."

She kneels in front of Madeleine and strokes her pixie cut. "A few years from now you'll bleed a little bit once every month, and that's how God prepares your body so that one day you can get married and have babies."

"Oh."

"But you're a long time from that, don't look so worried."

"I don't want to get married."

Maman winks and sings, "Someday, My Prince Will Come."

She leaves the bathroom. Madeleine stays to pee. It takes a while because it stings.

Mimi hands Jack his hat as he heads out the front door and says, "I love you."

"I love you too, Missus."

"When are you back today?"

"Why, are you entertaining the milkman?"

"I can do better than that."

He grins. "That's what I'm worried about."

They made love last night. It's a likely time of the month. Whether it was reckless or hopeful to risk conceiving a child at a time like this makes no difference to how she feels at the thought. So happy.

Jack kisses his wife—not the usual peck goodbye, almost a going-off-to-war smooch—right on the front step. She laughs and pushes him away. "I'll be home early," he says. "I'm dropping by Madeleine's classroom."

"At ten o'clock this morning, the quarantine began," says Mr. March. "I don't have to tell you what that means."

The class is silent. Someone is in big trouble.

Mr. March says, "If one single solitary Soviet ship crosses the quarantine line, it will be sunk." He taps his pointer across his palm. "How many of you have bomb shelters at home?"

No hands go up.

"Well what are your parents waiting for? Nuclear winter?"

Obliging laughter.

He whacks the pointer across his desk and everyone dives.

"Ricky Froelich babysat me last night," says Marjorie at recess.

"Tell us another one, Nolan," says Auriel. Lisa and Madeleine have been carefully threading Auriel's oxfords with red licorice shoelaces.

"He did so," says Marjorie, widening her blue eyes. "Honest Injun."

She has joined Majorettes. She has brought her baton in for show-and-tell and is twirling it in an arc over her head. Showing off.

"That was so funny I forgot to laugh," says Lisa.

"For your information," says Madeleine, "Ricky had a basketball game last night." The baton falls to the asphalt and bounces on its rubber tip. Madeleine looks up and sees Grace Novotny hovering behind Marjorie.

"Hi Grace." She feels a bit mean, aware that she has greeted Grace only in order to enjoy Marjorie's annoyance when she sees that she's being followed by the class reject. But Grace says "Hi" back and Marjorie doesn't seem the least bit surprised.

"You're just jealous," she says.

"Jealous of what, pray tell?" Madeleine's voice drips with scorn.

"Of me 'cause I'm Ricky's girlfriend."

The three of them laugh sarcastically, "Hardy-har-har."

"And!" shouts Marjorie. "I happen to be the boss of the exercise group!"

"Shut up," says Madeleine, getting up and walking away casually, willing her friends to follow her. They do.

"And you're not," Marjorie chants. "You-ou're no-ot—"

Madeleine stops and faces her. "What's so big about the exercise group?" It's a dangerous question. Marjorie puts on a simpy smile, tilts her head and swivels in place.

"You know what, Marjorie?" says Auriel. "If you had a brain you'd be dangerous." Auriel always knows what to say. "Come on you guys, let's go to the teeter-totters."

When the bell goes, Madeleine catches sight of Colleen, but they don't greet each other. Colleen is in grade six, after all. But more than that; it's impossible to imagine playing with Colleen at recess. She is an after-school friend. And after-school is as far from the grade four class at J.A.D. McCurdy as the Mississippi is from Centralia.

Jack leaves his office at a quarter to three. He will just make it in time. He quickens his pace to avoid a knot of fellow officers strolling across the parade square; he knows what they're talking about and he's sick of talk. The mood around the station started out energetic this morning, almost upbeat—typical air force, chipper in the face of danger. But a general frustration set in when the advancing afternoon brought nothing new from Ottawa. Dief has yet to endorse Kennedy's "atomic diplomacy" or place the military on alert. He's stalling. Waiting to see what the Brits will do. Jack shakes his head: are we a country or a colony?

Although the other NATO allies including the British have all made statements supporting the Americans, neither Britain nor Europe have obliged Kennedy by elevating their state of military alert, but that's not unreasonable—any sudden move in Europe could light the spark in Berlin. But Canada isn't Europe. Twenty-five Communist-bloc ships and several submarines are now on course for Cuba. If they breach the quarantine, the Americans are ready to fire the first shot. This is no time for Canada to play wait-and-see.

"*Bonjour* Jack."

Jack waves but doesn't pause. The U.S. military has gone to defcon 2: Strategic Air Command is patrolling the skies, more than forty ships and twenty thousand men are in position to enforce the quarantine. The American CINCNORAD—Commander-in-Chief of NORAD—has requested that Canada increase the alert status of its Voodoo fighters, allow USAF to disperse aircraft to Canadian bases and permit U.S. air-craft in Canada to load nuclear weapons. None of this is a secret; it's all there in black and white, delivered to your front porch with the milk. But the Canadian armed forces are obliged to prepare for war under a cloak of secrecy, while trying to decode coy signals from elected leaders who want us to be kind of ready, but not to appear at all ready. Jack clenches and unclenches his fist.

Dief is courting disaster. Apart from the fact that we all stand to be killed, his mixed messages have put the government in danger of abdicating civil control over the armed forces, at the very least creating a gulf between the military and the civilian population. This is supposed to be a democracy. If the prime minister wants us on alert, why doesn't he say so? And do it publicly? *The Globe and Mail* summed it up this morning: *Any attempt to sit on the fence in this period of crisis, to remain uncommitted, would be interpreted around the world as a rebuke to the United States and as aid and comfort for her enemies. Such a course is unthinkable.* Unfortunately, it's the course we are on.

Jack checks his watch as he passes the PX and the phone. He is angry, but feeling less useless than he did this morning. He has a job to do.

"The following little girls will remain after three. . . ."

Madeleine stands against the coat hook, waiting. If it bleeds again, what will she tell Maman?

Jack enters the Mobile Equipment building and walks across the concrete floor past a tractor mower, a bus and several forklifts, to a rank of black staff cars, and signs one out.

He pulls out into the full force of the afternoon sun. He touches his breast pocket but he has left his sunglasses at home—he had no way of knowing he'd be driving today. No point going home to get them, that would entail telling some silly fib to Mimi. Besides, the windows of the Ford are tinted and Jack does have his hat. He lowers the brim over his eyes, he'll be fine.

He points the car south on the Huron County road. It's a nice day for a drive. If anyone asks—which nobody will—he has zipped down to London to meet with a guest lecturer for the COS.

Simon called this afternoon. Oskar Fried is here.

"Proceed to the front of the class, little girl. Yes, you. The one with the pixie cut."

The Spitfire is still visible in Jack's rearview mirror when he returns his eyes to the road and recognizes the Froelich boy running on the shoulder, coming toward him. He is pushing his sister in her wheelchair with its homemade shock absorbers—sharp little rig—the big German shepherd trotting alongside, the little convoy kicking up a halo of dust. Jack smiles and touches two fingers to the brim of his hat as he passes. Rick waves.

He watches them retreat in his mirror and it occurs to him that the Froelich boy is missing school this afternoon—unless this outing counts as part of his athletic training—because it has barely gone three o'clock. He adjusts his mirror and gets the feeling he's forgetting something. What?

Madeleine has left by the side door and is halfway across the field, running all the way home, when the siren sounds. Her legs seem to decelerate and—even though she can still feel the wind in her hair, still see her Mary Janes carrying her as fast as they can—everything goes slow-motion. The siren has changed the air, made it thick, her legs are heavy, thighs like wet cement; the sound rises, rises, wailing; she squints against it as against a blare of light, she cannot look up, the siren is obliterating the sky, painting it metal, it is thickening the liquid in her body and liquefying what was solid. She is cold, cold, there is terrible sorrow in the sound, it is the real sound of what it was like to be Anne Frank, and nothing can save you now, even the birds can't be saved, even the grass. . . . And then it stops. It's a normal sunny day again.

Jack reaches for the car radio and turns it on, twisting the dial across the band, looking for news of the crisis. . . . *represents a major shift in the balance of power. . . .* His excitement at meeting Oskar Fried has been put into perspective. It's no longer an adventure, something to spice up the sleepy prime of Jack McCarthy's life. No longer theoretical, as Henry Froelich might say. Oskar Fried has come to join our side in the war we call peace. When "Major Newbolt" called this afternoon, Jack went straight to the phone booth and returned the call. "Our friend has arrived," said Simon. Jack was surprised. Fried already in London? Just twenty-five miles down the road? Simon had to have worked pretty quickly—Berlin must be locked down tight by now. Still, Jack had expected, if not advance notice, then Simon himself. Had looked forward to introducing him to Mimi, showing off his family, then sinking a few over at the mess. But Simon has already been and gone. Nothing personal, mate.

   . . . *on September 11 when Gromyko denied that the weapons were offensive in nature. . . .* Jack turns up the volume.

Madeleine runs the rest of the way home, then all the way upstairs, and checks her underpants. It's okay. She knew it would be. He didn't do any poking today. Just strangling. Of himself.

Simon said, "You might want to look in on him tonight."

Jack knows it was no mere suggestion. In any case, he has no intention of waiting until this evening. Not only is he eager to meet the man—to shake his hand in this week of weeks—but he's also not in a position to disappear for an unexplained evening visit to London. He would have to offer an explanation, and that would mean lying to his wife. Lies are like clutter on a radar screen: they obscure your target.

*. . . and the first direct confrontation between the two superpowers. . . .*

Jack asked Simon about procedure. "Can I have him to the house for Sunday brunch? What's the drill on introducing him to my family, making him feel at home?"

"Your call, mate. I suggest you meet him first."

"Who should I say he is?"

"Tell the truth as far as possible. His name is Oskar Fried and he's a German scientist."

"At the university?"

"That's right. On sabbatical. Keep it simple."

"How did I meet him?"

"You met him in Germany, through your German friends—you did have German friends?"

"Of course." But Jack and Mimi had the same friends. If the scientist were someone closely enough acquainted with Jack to look him up on arrival in Canada, Mimi would have at least heard of him. Simon makes it sound simple, but Simon isn't married. "Here's what you need to know," he said, and gave Jack instructions as to how to pick up the money he would wire. No more than six hundred dollars a month. It sounds like plenty to Jack, and will seem like a fortune to someone who has spent the last seventeen years behind the Iron Curtain. It must be difficult even to get a decent meal there. In that respect it's not unlike living in England, thinks Jack, and smiles, reminding himself to say that to Simon next time they're talking.

*. . . risk war unless Khrushchev agrees to dismantle all offensive weapons. . . .*

Madeleine pulls her jumper off over her head, undoes her strangulating school blouse, pausing only to smell her hands—they smell fine—and hollers from the top of the stairs, "Can I go fishing?!"

Colleen has not invited her but she doesn't want to be with Auriel and Lisa yet, so—

"Madeleine, don't yell!"

If she were allowed to watch TV right after school, all her problems would be solved, but she is not. She could be watching *The Mickey Mouse Club*, or *Razzle Dazzle*, with Howard the Turtle and beautiful Michele Finney, and the after-three feeling would ebb away. "Can I?!" She hurtles down the stairs, jumps the last five steps, whips perilously around the banister—

"*Doucement, Madeleine!*"

She stands stiffly in front of her mother, feeling like a collection of hard sticks in her play clothes, this is what a wooden puppet must feel like—

"Permission to go fishin,' ma'am." She salutes, banging her head, crossing one eye.

Mimi laughs; Madeleine takes it as a yes and turns to flee.

"*Attends, Madeleine!* Where do you fish?"

She stops and turns. "Rock Bass."

"*C'est où*, Rock Bass?"

"It's down a dirt road, you can almost see the airfield, it's close." She doesn't mention burnt-out campfires, she doesn't mention Colleen Froelich.

"Who are you going with?"

"Um. Can I call on Colleen?"

"You know what I said about Colleen Froelich."

Madeleine suppresses a groan, because she senses that her mother may be about to relent on the Colleen issue.

"All right. But I want you home in one hour."

"Yabba-dabba-doo!" She races from the kitchen.

"And no TV over there," calls her mother behind her.

Madeleine jumps down the three steps to the front door—she would like to burst right through the screen, the way the Cartwrights burst through the Shell sign at the beginning of *Bonanza*. She runs like a hard puppet across the street, but slows and turns back into a real live girl when she sees Ricky Froelich. He's drinking from the hose. He is in red jeans and a sweaty white singlet. The water runs down the front of his shirt, pasting it to his chest; his Adam's apple bobs as he swallows, his collarbones rising and falling with his breath.

"Hi pal." He holds out the hose and she sips, ice-cold; then he offers it to Rex, who bites the water, pink gums and white fangs. The best drink in the world.

"Hi Elizabeth," says Madeleine.

"Ay Ademin."

She walks up to the Froelichs' front door and knocks on the glass panel above the screen.

"Go on in," says Ricky. But Madeleine doesn't. It's as though there were an invisible force field around other people's front doors, you can't just walk up and open them. Just as you can't open someone else's fridge.

Mrs. Froelich appears. "Hi Madeleine, come on in."

Madeleine doesn't have time to say, "Can Colleen come out and play?" She follows Mrs. Froelich in and back to the kitchen. There are dirty dishes on the counter. Breakfast things still on the table.

She says, "Mrs. Froelich?"

"Call me Karen, kiddo."

Madeleine opens her mouth to say it but cannot. Now she can't call Mrs. Froelich anything. She watches silently as Colleen's mother feeds the baby boys, each in a battered high chair. There is a splotch of crusty baby gunk on her vest. It's a long plaid wool vest, loose and groovy. Madeleine slowly, deferentially sits down on one of the chairs, a tear in its vinyl pad, and wonders what will happen next. Mrs. Froelich has long straight hair parted in the middle with silver streaks. Her face looks different from the other mothers. You can't picture her sitting at a vanity table. No offence, but Mrs. Froelich looks like a young witch—a good one.

Colleen walks through the kitchen, mutters "Hi," then goes out the back door. Madeleine is unsure whether to follow so she stays put. Ricky comes in with Elizabeth and starts talking on the phone. He makes a peanut-butter bender and eats it in one bite. He makes another and hands it to Madeleine. He is talking to Marsha Woodley.

Even when he's all sweaty, Ricky Froelich looks freshly showered. He shaves too, she can see a patch of stubble at his chin and along his jaw, his cheeks are stained red with air and exercise. His legs are long and lean, one foot crossed over the other. His hands do everything casually and perfectly, such as make a sandwich and hold it for Elizabeth to bite. Even if his house smells like old stew and Elizabeth is drooling peanut butter, Ricky Froelich is clean. Like a teenager on TV, he seems carefree. He seems . . . American.

Mr. Froelich comes in, smoking a pipe and carrying a German newspaper.

"*Madeleine, wie geht's, hast du Hunger?*"

"No, I just had a peanut-butter sandwich, *danke.*"

"Good, fine *und* dandy, *komm mit mir, wir haben viel Lego in den* living room." His dark eyes twinkle, his red lips moist around his pipestem, like Santa.

She follows him into the living room and sees a mountain of Lego piled next to the playpen. And sitting on the floor next to it is Claire McCarroll. It's like discovering an elf under a mushroom cap, Claire in the Froelichs' living room. With her bracelet full of lucky charms. She is building a house out of Lego.

Madeleine sits next to her and starts hunting for wheels to make a car to go with the house. Mr. Froelich puts on a record. A woman with a deep voice sings a tune that Madeleine recognizes, but with French words, *Qui peut dire, où vont les fleurs. . . . ?* Madeleine hums along.

Mr. Froelich says from his armchair, "You like Dietrich?"

Madeleine nods politely, yes. Who is Deetrick?

There is the soft sound of Lego clicking together and the occasional rustle of Mr. Froelich's newspaper. Madeleine sings along softly in English, ". . . *gone to soldiers, every one. When will they ever learn? When will they e-e-e-ver learn? . . .*"

Maman needn't have worried. The Froelichs don't even have a TV.

Jack follows the curve of the cul-de-sac that is Morrow Street and parks at the foot of the manicured lawn of the yellow brick low-rise. . . . *in other developments, U.N. Secretary General U Thant sent identical letters to Mr. Khrushchev and President Kennedy—* He switches off the radio.

He gets out and walks up to the front doors beneath the porte cochère. He enters the empty vestibule and sees a house phone. Through a glass wall to his right is a small lobby, likewise deserted. Couch, leather armchair, coffee table with three or four magazines fanned out. A potted benjamina gathers dust in one corner.

He scans the framed directory on the wall and finds what he's looking for: *O. F. apt. #321.* As he dials the number he glances at the wall of small metal mailboxes: the discreet typed initials reappear there, *O.F. Our Friend.* Of course! Jack shakes his head. Simon.

The line rings a third time. There is a brief pause followed by a reedy voice. "*Ja?*"

"Hello, Herr Fried? This is Wing Commander McCarthy, sir. I'm here to welcome you."

There is no reply. Instead, Jack is startled by a loud buzzer. He hangs up in time to grab the handle of the glass door. Two steps lead up to the elevator. He takes them in one stride.

After a sluggish liftoff, the elevator stops at the second floor and an elderly lady gets on. Jack nods but she seems not to register his presence.

When the doors close and the elevator rises, however, she looks up at him. "Down," she says accusingly.

He exits at the third floor. The smell of lavender follows him out and down the hall, where it's joined by the fug of a thick gravy. Someone's dinner will be ready long before five.

It crosses his mind that you would never in a million years walk into this apartment building, along this corridor with its carpet-muffle of orange and red paisley, through the duvet of dinner smells and geriatric perfume, and expect to find a high-level Soviet defector. Simon has selected everything for invisibility.

The door marked 321 is at the end of the hall. A corner unit. Jack removes his hat, stands in front of the peephole and knocks. He has butterflies in his stomach. Simon has been characteristically low-key about the whole thing, but the facts speak for themselves. Jack is about to meet—has been entrusted with the well-being of—a man whose life and work and presence here derive from the crucible of international relations which at this very moment are affecting the lives of everyone on earth. He takes a deep breath. Considers knocking again.

Finally, a fumbling behind the door. Slide of a deadbolt, the knob turns, the door opens a few inches. Above the safety chain, a stripe of white face, scant grey hair. Spectacles.

"Herr Fried?" he says. "I'm Jack McCarthy, sir. *Willkommen in Kanada.*"

The door closes. The slide of the safety chain and it opens again, a little wider. Jack extends his hand. "It's an honour to meet you, sir."

Oskar Fried takes his hand briefly. The man feels frail.

Jack looks into the light grey eyes. Fried's face, delicately lined parchment, pale. He is somewhere between fifty and seventy-five. "May I come in, sir?" he asks, because Oskar Fried has made no move. He appears shell-shocked. He must have been through one hell of a trip.

Fried turns and retreats slowly, almost at a shuffle. Jack follows him into the apartment. The smell of tobacco. Familiar. The lights are off, the curtains drawn, as though he were in hiding—which he is, though presumably the Soviets haven't the first clue where to look for him. Jack glances around. The dull greens and browns of a furnished apartment; the tobacco masks a generic air freshener designed to mask a generic loneliness—the smell of the solitary male. Wall-to-wall indoor-outdoor, respectable lampshade yellowed with years of nicotine, a cheap print of Niagara Falls over the perfectly decent couch. Jack will have to get the man out to the PMQs for a visit to a real home as soon as possible.

"How are you settling in, sir?" he asks. *"Uh, brauchst du, uh, brauchsten Sie etwa?"*

Fried doesn't smile at the attempted German, but says by way of reply, "Do you bring money?" His voice is thin, his accent more raw than Henry Froelich's. Uneroded.

Jack smiles. "I've got it right here, sir."

He takes a small brown envelope from his inside breast pocket and hands it to Oskar Fried.

Fried takes it. "I thank you," he says, with an Old World inclination of the head that puts Jack in mind of Froelich again.

"You're most welcome, sir."

Oskar Fried is a spare man—as though he had been drawn with a pencil. His glasses are wire-rimmed, not the robust black frames Jack had pictured. He was right about the bow tie, otherwise there is no trace of the meaty Brylcreemed physicist he had envisioned. Fried's white dress shirt is buttoned up but still loose at the neck, revealing the narrow cords and loosening flesh of undernourished and advancing years. Jack recognizes the permanently starved look of some Europeans—no amount of good food can possibly make up for the war. Henry Froelich has that look, although, even with his stoop and lean cheeks, Henry's face is warm and mobile. Oskar Fried looks to be etched in sandstone. Seventeen years behind the Iron Curtain will do that. His suit jacket and trousers are of indestructible brown wool manufactured sometime in the last fifty years. But even in a lab coat, he would look like . . . a clerk. Jack feels disappointed, then immediately guilty. The man is exhausted. Traumatized. Stranger in a strange land.

Jack walks over to the window—"May I?"—and opens the curtains, squinting at the flash of daylight.

Fried jumps to his feet. *"Nein, bitte."*

Jack draws them closed once more and turns to see Fried holding an ice bucket. He blinks to readjust his eyes and sees that the bucket contains bits of bark and stone. Growing up from its midst, supported by a coat hanger, is a flower. Purple, almost black.

"Orchid," says Fried.

Jack smiles and nods.

*"Dunkel,"* says Fried. "Not light."

"It grows in the dark," says Jack.

Fried nods, almost smiles.

Jack feels a rush of pity for the man. Is it possible to be farther from home than he is now? And has the U.S.S.R. ever really felt like his home? He may very well have found himself in the wrong part of his homeland at the end of the war, trapped in what was suddenly East Germany. Forced to make the best of it. And now, a chance at freedom. He has been brave enough to grasp it, this wisp of a man. And perhaps generous enough too. "Herr Fried, I want you to know that we appreciate what you're doing."

Fried listens closely, nodding.

Jack continues, slowly and clearly, "I want to thank you for coming."

"You are welcome," says Fried.

Poor bugger holed up here, taking the thanks of the free world from some RCAF type he doesn't know from Adam. Answering to a name not his own. "Look, sir, when you're settled in, you call me at work, okay?" Jack takes the money envelope from Fried and writes down his office number and below it his home number. "This number here," says Jack, pointing to it, "is my home. But only for emergency, *verstehen Sie?*"

"*Ja.* Emergency."

Once Jack has arranged to bring Fried out to Centralia—for brunch this Sunday, perhaps—there will be no reason for him not to use the home number. But until Jack has been able to introduce Mimi to the "visiting professor," and to think of a plausible friend-of-a-friend scenario, it is best that Fried call him only at work.

"Would you like to come for a quick spin around the city?"

"Spin?"

Jack moves his hands as though on a steering wheel. "In *ein Auto*. A drive?"

"Yes, I drive."

"No, would you like to come for a drive with me? Now?"

Fried shakes his head.

"Well when you change your mind, sir, this is a beautiful part of the country—*sehr schön*." He points to the sad painting on the wall. "Niagara Falls. Magnificent. And if you like flowers"—Fried nods— "there's a greenhouse at Storybook Gardens, wouldn't be surprised if they had orchids."

Jack rubs his hands together and looks around—hi-fi, good, no TV, however, although there is a set of rabbit ears on the windowsill. Too bad, it would help Herr Fried's English. "Have you got enough food, sir?"

Jack steps into the small galley kitchen and opens the fridge. Fried follows and stands at his shoulder.

It's well stocked—Simon has seen to that—but it's bound to get lonely, eating alone night after night.

He longs to ask Fried what he will be working on; to hear his opinion on the current crisis in Cuba, get him to talk about the space program. But that subject is off limits for now, Simon has made that clear, and anyhow the poor chap is already spooked. Culture-shocked.

"Sir, would you care to join my family this Sunday for—?"

Fried is already shaking his head, but Jack continues, "My wife's a great cook and she speaks pretty good German, *besser denn mein,* eh? In fact we've got a German neighbour, a science type like yourself—"

Fried says, still shaking his head, "I do not do this—"

"It's entirely up to you, sir, I just want you to know you're welcome and it's fine with Mr. Crawford—Simon."

"*Ja,* Si-mon," says Fried, as though it were two words.

"Now, you know what to say if anyone asks why you're here?" Jack puts his hat back on and adjusts it.

"Guest professor of Western University, London."

"That's right."

Jack takes a last look around. There is nothing more for him to do. The fridge is stocked, there is toilet paper in the bathroom, and on the small dining table is a map of London. Simon has seen to everything. Except for a TV. As an afterthought, Jack goes to the map and circles Storybook Gardens.

"Orchids," he says, eliciting a faint smile from Fried. "*Auf Wiedersehen* for now, sir."

"Goodbye," says Fried.

The door closes behind him and Jack hears the slide and schunk of locks, followed by silence. He can feel Fried looking at him through the peephole, waiting for him to leave. He turns back the way he came, down the silent swirl of red and orange, and dismisses a mild sense of anticlimax. Well, what did he expect? A glass of schnapps and a chinwag about the space race? Give Fried a week or so, Jack thinks, and he'll be thirsting for company. Jack will have him out to the house for supper, relaxed and nursing his pipe—that's what the tobacco smell was, he realizes now, Fried and Froelich smoke the same brand. The two of them might very well hit it off—both Germans, both men of science displaced by war. Jack reaches the elevator and pauses at the recollection that Henry is Jewish. Well, what difference should that make to Oskar Fried? Jack has committed that error once already: assuming that Henry was an anti-Semite because he was German. He presses the button and waits. Fried is a scientist. He of all people is likely to be above that sort of thing—what does it matter if you're black, green or blue when you're splitting the atom? Maybe Jack can pour a few good Löwenbräus and get them talking politics—if not science. Introduce his kids to Fried, knowing that one day he can tell them they met a real live defector. A Soviet scientist, straight out of the history books.

The elevator opens and he steps in. As the doors close, he hears a small dog yapping from somewhere in the building; otherwise he encounters no one on his way back to the car.

Madeleine has built a tank and a station wagon. Claire has finished her house and built a church which they have agreed is also the school and the A&P. They are arranging farm animals around their new subdivision when the phone rings in the kitchen.

"Hello? . . . Hi Sharon . . . ," says Mrs. Froelich. "Yeah, she is." She laughs. "Well I wouldn't mind if she did . . . no big deal . . . sure, I'll send her home. . . ."

Madeleine watches out the Froelichs' living-room window as Claire walks away down the driveway. Marsha Woodley is there at the foot of it, talking to Ricky. Claire reaches out and takes Ricky's hand. Marsha takes Claire's other hand and the three of them walk down St. Lawrence Avenue like that, toward the McCarrolls' house, just as though Ricky and Marsha were her parents and Claire was their little girl.

Jack drops off the staff car and returns to his office to find a message telling him to call the CO. He asks his admin clerk, "When did this come in?" Has he been missed? His clerk answers, "An hour ago, sir." Jack dials the CO's extension—what will he say if Woodley asks where he has been? Jack doesn't relish the thought of lying to his commanding officer.

He needn't have worried. Woodley was calling to advise him that the Prime Minister has finally ordered an increase in the alert status. The Canadian armed forces are at "military vigilance"—a level just short of the U.S. defcon 2. But Diefenbaker still has not made a statement in support of the U.S. And the alert is to be implemented secretly. "You've got to be kidding," says Jack.

Our Voodoo interceptors "may or may not" now be armed with Genie nuclear missiles which we "may or may not" have in our possession.

"Fun 'n' games, eh?" says Hal.

"Bunch of Mickey Mouse politicians."

"Let's keep our eye on the ball, shall we? Old Dief needs all the help he can get."

Jack gets the message. There has been enough bellyaching about government in the past couple of days; the people of Canada elected Diefenbaker for better or worse, and that's who the military is working for. The new state of alert will have little effect on the operations of RCAF Centralia. They are in for more high-tension thumb-twiddling; all the more reason to cool it with the complaints.

"Righto," says Jack.

"'*Wiedersehen.*"

Jack crosses the Huron County road and enters the PMQ patch. He feels tired for some reason. Kids are out playing. In the Boucher driveway, a team's worth of hockey equipment is laid out to air, and up ahead, in Jack's own driveway, the Rambler is parked awry, which is how he can tell Mimi's been out shopping. Everything looks normal. But that's just a veneer. Normal has begun to mean that we could all be annihilated in a matter of hours. He takes a big breath of autumn air. *You never had it so good.* Who said that? How can something be so true and so false at the same time?

He sees his daughter come out of the Froelich house with the German shepherd dog. Jack would rather she didn't get so close to that animal—they can turn on you. But she's fearless, clutching its fur, her eyes squeezed shut as the dog "guides" her across the street. And he remembers what it was he was going to do today. Drop in on Mr. Marks.

He watches her arrive at the front step and open her eyes. The dog lopes home; she turns and sees Jack and runs to him. He opens his arms, catches her and swings her around—"Dad, give me an aeroplane!"

He takes her by an ankle and a wrist and spins. She's fine. She has forgotten all about "duck and cover." He won't alarm her by bringing up the subject again, with its attendant spectre of annihilation.

"Eat up, Mike," says Jack. But the boy picks at his dinner. One-word answers to all Jack's questions. "How was school?"

" . . . Okay."

"Sit up straight, mister, and eat what your mother cooked for you."

He feels a degree of annoyance that he knows is out of proportion to the situation. He would like to blame it on the current world crisis but he knows it predates that. The boy is becoming sullen. Mimi says he has entered the "awkward age." Jack replied, "In my day, we couldn't

afford an 'awkward age,' we were too busy putting food on the table."
And she came back with that French astringency: "You want him to
have the things you never had, well this is one." He was stung, but
glad that his wife is able to best him so reliably in these matters. It
gives him permission to be "a nice Papa." Because lately he has had the
sense that he is flying blind when it comes to the boy. His own father
never would have stood for these truculent one-syllable retorts. But
then Jack wouldn't wish his own father on anyone.

Mimi says, *"Qu'est-ce que tu as, Michel?"*

The boy looks up at his father. "Dad, are we on alert?"

Jack stabs his mashed potatoes with his fork. "There's nothing for
you to worry about, Mike. The only ones who should be worried are
those poor old crows, they must've got an awful fright when the siren
went off today." And he winks at Madeleine.

"What if there's a war, are we just gonna sit there?" asks Mike.

Madeleine expects him to be told that there isn't going to be a war,
how many times do I have to—? But her father eats steadily, chewing, chewing his potatoes, his lips getting thinner. Is someone in
trouble?

"What does history tell you, Mike?"

"What do you mean?"

"'Waddyamean?'"—imitating his son's surly tone. "I mean, what
did we do when war broke out in 1914?"

"We fought."

"That's right. And in 1939?"

"Yeah, but—"

"We were first in with the British both times and we fought and we
died and we won."

"Yeah, but the Americans—"

"The Americans were late into both wars."

"Yeah but this time the Americans—"

"The Americans are what stand between us and Communism."

Mimi murmurs, "Jack."

"We can't even defend ourselves. Arnold's dad says—"

"I'm not interested in what Arnold's dad—"

"We're too chicken to even go on alert!"

Jack mashes homemade chow-chow into his potatoes and doesn't
reply. Mimi says, "Madeleine, have you decided what you want to be for
Halloween?"

Madeleine is surprised at the question. It has never occurred to her
to abandon the sacred clown costume she has worn for the past two

years. Halloween costumes are not to be traded in lightly, they are . . . like
vestments. "A clown," she answers.

"*Encore? Mais il est trop petit maintenant pour toi.*"

"Can't you make it bigger?"

Mimi shrugs. "Sure, but I thought maybe we could make you a new
one. You could be a ballerina or a—"

"I want to be a clown again."

"We're cowards, that's all," says Mike.

"I've got news for you, Mike. . . ." Her father puts down his fork.
Madeleine holds her breath—is Mike going to get it? But Dad sounds
calm. "We are on alert."

"Jack—"

"It's true," he says to Mimi. "You won't see it in the papers but he's
got a right to know. We all do. As Canadians."

Madeleine's face is hot. She waits. Dad says each word slowly. "An
elevation in the alert status of the armed forces is a routine precaution"—as if he were explaining something that would be perfectly
obvious to anyone but a silly ass. "It's called crisis management and it's
only common sense. It sends a message to the Russians: 'Listen, fellas'"—
he points his fork at Mike—"'we mean business, so hands off our buddies
'cause if you mess with them, you're messin' with us.'" He jabs his
potatoes several times in quick succession. "This whole thing'll blow
over. Castro is a puppet and it's only a matter of time before his own
people see that." Castro is a puppet. Madeleine tries not to laugh.
"What bothers me," Dad is saying, "is we've got these jokers up on
Parliament Hill who are indulging in the lowest form of Canadian
nationalism." He pauses. Madeleine bites away the grin on the inside of
her cheek. "Anti-Americanism."

The word hangs in the air, until finally Mimi says, "Can we have
dessert now, *ma grande foi D'jeu?*"

Jack laughs. "You should be running the Excomm, Missus."

After supper, Jack sends his daughter down to the basement to play with
her brother so that she won't hear his optimistic dinner-table dismissal of
the crisis contradicted on the six o'clock news. He watches U Thant
deliver his calm and desperate plea in the U.N. and wonders if he went too
far over supper—will Madeleine have nightmares again? He listens for
sounds of a squabble from the basement, but the kids are quiet down there.
They're getting all kinds of alarmist misinformation out there, at school
and in the playground. They ought to hear some actual facts at home—
not gloom and doom, but enough reality to inspire confidence in him.

Aerial photographs appear on the screen, taken by U-2 spy planes: launching pads, somewhere in the hills of Cuba. He switches off the TV and tells Mimi he is stepping outside to stretch his legs.

Over at the Froelichs,' a living-room lamp stands in the driveway, lampshade and all. It casts a rosy glow on the exposed engine of the automotive heap. Froelich is in his apron and white shirt-sleeves, bent under the hood with his son. They work to the accompaniment of a tinny transistor radio. Jack saunters across.

"Hank, how're you making out there?"

"Not too shabby, Jack."

Ricky looks up and greets him, and Jack says, "I've seen you out there running with your sister, Rick, how far do you go normally?"

"Till one of us gets tired, I guess. Seven or eight miles."

"Good stuff."

Froelich fills his pipe with his grease-stained fingers, Jack takes out a Tiparillo.

"Forget the car, Henry, why don't you build a great big bomb out here instead, and aim it straight at Ottawa?"

Froelich puffs his pipe to life. "You are angry, Jack."

Jack is surprised. "Naw, I'm not angry, I'm just frustrated with how our fearless leader is handling things. Or not handling them as the case may be." He puffs. "Yeah, you're right, I'm angry."

The boy disappears under the car and Jack lowers his voice. "How do you figure the chances we'll all be blown sky-high this time next week?"

He is surprised at his own question—at how he has phrased it. He wouldn't express himself this way at work. Like his fellow officers, he is not given to alarmist language—they are not Americans. Not yet, anyway. But he has blurted the question to Froelich, perhaps because he senses that Froelich is not easily alarmed.

Henry says, "Will you pass me the wrench? The middle one, *ja. Danke,*" and bends to the engine. "Jack. My first opinion is, this crisis is predictable."

Jack nods. "Bay of Pigs."

"Also the Americans still have their base in Cuba."

"At Guantánamo, yeah."

"And also America has already many missiles on the Soviet doorstep."

"Turkey. But those're obsolete. And the Yanks didn't put them there in secret."

"I don't know how comfortable this is to people in the target."

"True. But I trust the Americans not to use them."

"The Americans have used them already."

"Right." Jack pulls on his cigar. "But that was to end a war, not to start one. I don't trust the Soviets as far as I can spit."

"I do not trust either," says Froelich, and Jack finds it difficult to tell, knowing the syntactical idiosyncrasies of Froelich's English, whether he means *I don't trust the Soviets either,* or *I don't trust either of them.* Such are the hazards of translation. Imagine trying to analyze the latest missive from Khrushchev. We'll all go up in a mushroom cloud because of a preposition. But Froelich is saying, "I think they play a dangerous game, the Americans and the Russians, and they play this together."

"Can I use the torch, Pop?" asks Rick.

"What do you mean, Hank?"

Froelich turns to his son. "Yes, no, find your safety glasses, then yes"—then turns back to Jack. "I agree with Eisenhower."

"You liked Ike?"

"He warned of too much military industries. We force the Russians to keep up. People grow rich from these industries and they become to have political influence."

"It's called the arms race," says Jack.

"I think it is what the British call, 'silly bugger.'" He wipes carbon buildup from the old distributor cap.

Jack laughs. "So you don't think the world is going to end tomorrow?"

"The world has ended many times, my friend."

Jack thinks of the numbers on Froelich's arm, concealed by the white shirt. He would like to find a way to apologize for . . . having been a jackass. But referring to a subject that Froelich has not seen fit to broach might only distress the man . . . and compound Jack's faux pas.

Henry says, "Pass me the Robertson's red." Jack hands him the screwdriver. Overhead the stars are crisp and bright. Jack looks up at the moon, cold and calm. Look long enough and you may see a satellite. The Froelich boy's transistor radio catches invisible signals from the air, as though netting schools of fish, and translates them into a male voice singing in a falsetto about the girl he loves—in Mecca.

"The United States also acts in secret, for example U-2," says Froelich.

"How else are we supposed to know the Russians are arming Cuba to the teeth?"

"What about Gary Powers when he has invaded Soviet air last May?"

"We used to do that all the time in Germany," says Jack and grins. Froelich glances up. Jack explains, "Our fellas'd climb into their Sabres and scream across into the Eastern Sector to test the Soviet response time. The Russkies'd send up their MiGs and chase us back home. They did the same thing to us."

"If this was so harmless," says Froelich, "why did Eisenhower say it was a weather plane for NASA?" He relights his pipe.

The aroma reminds Jack of home. Germany. He and Mimi and their little family—something complete about their lives over there. The sense that every day the world got a bit better. Cities healed, one brick, one spire at a time, flowers bloomed in window boxes. Perhaps it's just nostalgia . . . for the smiles that greeted them when people found out they were Canadian. A new alliance forged from the intimacy of enmity. The past and the present had made a pact and the result was the future. Perhaps they were simply happy there. He is taken aback at that thought, because it would imply that he is something other than happy now. But, the current crisis notwithstanding, he is happy, surely. He is not aware of being unhappy. He taps the ash from his cigar and watches it float to the ground.

"Bottom line is, Henry, Castro is a puppet and Kennedy is an elected leader."

"It's a pity Americans are not so fond of democracy outside their own borders." Sparks fly from the back of the car, where Ricky is welding.

"That's not true, Henry, what about the Marshall Plan, look at"—Jack almost says Germany, but catches himself—"Western Europe, look at Japan."

"Look at Latin America, look at Indochina—"

"Uncle Sam can't solve the problems of the whole world—"

"Part of the world just asks him to stay away—"

"Would you rather live in the Soviet Union, Henry?"

"To question U.S. is not to love U.S.S.R., a socialist is not a Communist."

"Are you a socialist?"

"We are both."

"Both socialist *and* Commu—?"

"*Nein!* You and I both are socialist."

"How do you figure that, Hank?"

"You get sick, you go to hospital, doctors fix you, you don't go broke."

"Medicare—"

"Is socialist."

Jack laughs. "You're right, some of our best policies are—"

"Soviet Union is not even Communist, is totalitarian." Froelich looks at his wrench as though he were angry at it—"Ricky, where have you put the pliers?!"

The sparks die, Ricky's face pops up and he pushes the welding goggles back on his forehead. "They're right there, Pops, hangin' off your belt."

"Oh. *Danke*."

Jack sees Rick duck down again and the shower of sparks resumes. With luck, that boy will never have to fight a war. "Stalin killed more people than Hitler," he says, and regrets it immediately—but why should he pussyfoot around Henry Froelich? The man is not asking to be patronized—he keeps that tattoo covered for a reason.

"So?" says Henry. "One, one hundred, six million, this is supposed to make someone feel better? They are all butchers."

"I'm just agreeing with you, Henry, that's why you don't see Americans jumping over the Wall to get into East Berlin, that's why the brain drain is all one way."

"Brain drain?"

Jack pauses. This is a conversation he would be having whether or not he had ever heard of Oskar Fried. It's fine. "It's just a way of saying that, given a choice, many Soviet scientists would jump at the chance to come here and work."

"Ah"—Froelich nods—"you speak of defectors."

"I guess so." Jack inhales the smoke along with the sharp air as Froelich straightens, intent upon the engine, scratches his neck, leaving a streak of grease above his white collar, and says, "Can you ever trust a traitor?"

Jack is taken aback. He answers, almost peevishly, "They're not necessarily traitors. Some are idealists."

"That's what those Englishmen called themselves. The ones who defected. . . ."

Just then the screen door opens and, beyond the pool of light around the car, Jack sees a girl walking toward them in the dark.

"Ricky. . . ."

It's Karen Froelich.

"Yeah Mum?"

"Lizzie's asking for you, hon."

The kid wipes his hands on a rag and heads into the house.

"How are you doing, Karen?"

"Oh I'm fine, Jack, how are you, are you worried?"

"What, me? Naw. What do you make of all this nonsense?"

She does not demur or "leave that to you men," she says, "I think it's bullshit."

He hesitates, then asks, "How do you mean?"

She folds her arms across her chest—her sloppy man's vest is the last article of clothing that would suggest female characteristics, and perhaps that's why it's impossible not to notice her breasts suddenly take shape with her gesture.

"'Cause between the two of them they can already destroy the planet a couple of times over." Her tone is offhand, in contrast with her words. "They don't need Cuba as an excuse." She pronounces it "Cooba."

Jack says, "Is that what you think they want to do?"

"No, I think they want to, you know, scare us. Distract us so we won't notice . . . all the other stuff, you know?"

He nods. But he doesn't know. He glances at Froelich, who watches his wife. He is in love with her. It must take a lot of love to run that household, those kids.

"Cuba's just caught in the middle," she says. "Under Batista, they were just America's whore. Fidel's the best thing that ever happened to that country."

Jack can't decide what is more startling: her use of the word "whore" or her use of the word "Fidel." Not to mention "bullshit."

"I like the Kennedys at home"—her voice deceptively young in the darkness—"they're really getting it together with civil rights down there. But the right-wing press has been baying for Castro's blood for months, so. . . . Are you guys hungry?"

Jack shakes his head. "No, I'm uh—thanks Karen." They watch her go back in the house.

Jack shifts his eyes from the screen door, and spits out a speck of tobacco. "We can only hope Khrushchev dismantles those weapons. It's like General MacArthur said, eh? Never fight a war you don't intend to win."

"Ach, win schmin, it's all good for business, no?"

"It's about more than that, Hank, and you know it."

"What is it about, my friend?"

"It's about democracy. It's about the fact that you and I come from worlds apart and wind up standing here in your driveway, disagreeing about something that in some countries would get us flung in jail for even talking about. And that includes Cuba."

Froelich draws on his pipe and releases the leathery aroma in a white stream. Jack sends a chain of smoke rings up to drift and distend in the October sky. The two of them look up at the spangled dome. It really is a remarkably clear night. A beautiful night on earth.

Froelich says, "You want *ein Bier,* Jack?"

"*Ja, danke.*"

"What the heck is this?"

Jack is in his basement, surveying a ramshackle of cardboard boxes that he had neatly collapsed and stacked after the move in August. They now form tunnels under blankets reinforced with every book from the bookshelves, as well as the bookshelves themselves. Heavy hardcover volumes secure the blanketed extremities—Winston Churchill's memoirs, all six volumes, *The Rise and Fall of the Third Reich,* along with several years of carefully preserved *National Geographic* magazines, the *Encyclopaedia Britannica,* the Huron County phone book and God knows what else. Sleeping bags that had been laboriously rolled and stored for the winter now curtain an entrance arch fashioned from one end of the old metal baby crib. Jack reaches out and rescues part of today's newspaper from the literary thatch-work as Mike's head appears between the sleeping bags. His daughter emerges. "Hi Dad, want to come in?"

"Watcha got in there?" asks Jack.

"Rations," she says, "and water."

"What are you up to, Mike?"

Mike switches off the flashlight and crawls out. "Makin' a shelter."

"A bomb shelter," says his daughter, delighted. It's a game to her, and that's as it should be.

"Up to bed now, sweetie."

"We haven't finished, Dad—"

"Up you go."

As she disappears up the steps, Jack says to his son, "Are you trying to give your sister nightmares again?"

"No." The boy turns red.

"What did I tell you at supper?"

"We're on alert."

"Well that's not make-believe, it's real. I told you that 'cause I figured you were mature enough to understand."

"I'm mature," he mumbles.

"Well then, what kind of game are you playing here, Mike?"

"It's not a game, it's how you do it, I saw it on TV."

"You saw it on TV. Do you believe everything you see on TV?"

"No."

Jack turns to go back upstairs. "Take all this nonsense apart now and put everything back the way you found it."

"Dad—"

"On the double."

"But—"

Jack stops and turns, pointing a finger. "You heard me, mister, I want this thing gone. Dismantled."

He climbs into bed next to Mimi and tells her about Mike's "bomb shelter." Now that he's describing it aloud, it's actually kind of funny. She kisses him and says, "He's like his father."

The boy is just trying to do his bit. It's hard sometimes to remember that he's just a child. "Remind me tomorrow," he says, "I want to take Mike over to the arena after school, pass the puck around."

Mimi strokes his chest and rests her head against his shoulder. As he reaches to turn out the bedside light, she says, "Did you talk to Mr. March?"

"Mr.—? No, I . . . got a little busy toward the end of the day, but she seems fine now, don't you think?"

"I think so, yeah."

The next words come easily. "I had to go into London. Meet with a guest lecturer for the officers' school. Ran a bit late."

"Mmm," she says.

He closes his eyes.

"Jack. Are you sure it's okay for Madeleine to play with the Froelich girl?"

"Colleen? Sure, why not?"

"I hope so, because I let her go over there today."

That's right, he was going to have a word with Mimi about that. Just as well she has come to it on her own. "Good," he says.

He listens until he hears her breathing change, then carefully turns onto his side. The first lie. But how is it different from the others he has told her in the past few days? "It's just sabre-rattling. Nothing to worry about." They are not really lies. They are another way of saying, "I'll look after you." Another way of saying, "I love you."

In the privacy of the darkness, the fleecy comfort of his sleeping family, Jack reflects on Oskar Fried alone in his furnished apartment. That is how we will win this war—how we will ensure that there is a world for our children to inherit. By getting as many Oskar Frieds as possible to come over to our side. And in a small but direct way, Jack is helping. He closes his eyes again and revises his expectations of Oskar Fried. Let the man cloister himself in his apartment if that's what he wants. He isn't here to make Jack McCarthy's life more interesting. He is here to help win this cold war that is set to boil over.

But Jack's eyes will not stay closed. His lids have that spring-loaded feeling. He gets up, goes quietly into the hallway and looks in on his daughter. She is asleep. Damp child's brow, wrinkle of flannel PJs and grimy old Bugsy. My child is safe.

## BIG WARS AND LITTLE WARS

*A Russian quite recently said*
*'In color TV we're ahead.*
*Your pictures confuse,*
*With all sorts of hues,*
*But ours are the best—they're all red.*
TV Guide, *fall 1962*

IT'S RAINING MILDLY after school the next day. Madeleine has just come from playing naked Barbie dolls with Lisa Ridelle. Auriel was at the dentist. It was entirely different being two rather than three. They sat, somewhat at a loss, on Lisa's bedroom floor, looking through her mum's movie magazines. Then, to Madeleine's dismay, Lisa brought out her Barbie and Ken—she hadn't even known Lisa possessed them—and undressed the dolls until they were both bare naked. She stuck a straight pin between Ken's legs for his "thing" and made him lie down on top of Barbie. Madeleine said, "I just remembered, I have to go." She felt an overpowering dread backing up from her stomach, like a sewer, as Lisa began to speculate with carefree horror on "the facts of life." Madeleine hoped she'd left in time, before the smell came out of her and filled the Ridelles' house.

Now she is safely outside, with the soft aroma of rain and worms. It's raining just enough for the worms to be out basking. She and Colleen are crouched, collecting them from the side of the road in front of Madeleine's house. A pair of yellow boots appears. Marjorie. "You know what, Colleen?"

"What?" Colleen barely glances up.

"Madeleine isn't really your friend. She's just using you."

"Go away, Margarine." Madeleine doesn't bother to look up from under the hood of her red raincoat. She is not collecting worms so much as training them. Right now she is using a Popsicle stick to guide one into a worm corral made of dirt and pebbles. She is not really fond of worms, but doesn't want Colleen to think she's chicken of them either.

"She's just using you to get to your brother," says Marjorie.

Colleen doesn't take the bait.

"Shut up," says Madeleine nonchalantly to the pair of boots, and concentrates on her worm, placing the Popsicle stick now on one side of it, now on the other, watching it slowly slime along—short-long, short-long—into the paddock we go.

Marjorie stamps her yellow boot. "It's true! She told me."

"It's twue," repeats a voice behind her.

This time Colleen chuckles, because it's hard not to find it funny, how Grace says her "r's", especially if you aren't used to it. Grace's rubber boots are now in view—too big for her, swamp-green.

Madeleine watches Colleen pull a long worm from the ground with the expertise of a robin. She waits for the worm to snap but it doesn't, merely releases and recoils softly from the earth. Colleen drops it into her coffee can with the rest of her churning harvest, *good to the last drop.* Madeleine tends to her worm and sings softly in a cowboy accent, "'I'm an old cowhand, on the Rio Grande. . . . '"

Marjorie almost shouts, "You should just shut up Madeleine McCarthy because Ricky is mine and you know it!" Madeleine laughs. Marjorie persists—"He asked me on a picnic to Rock Bass, so there."

Madeleine nudges her worm as it makes the final endless centimetre into the corral, which she is just about to close with her Popsicle stick, and she is thinking about Popsicle sticks and their myriad uses, for example you can sharpen them to make knives, you can also make beautiful pagodas and lamps—when the yellow boot smacks down, obliterating the worm, the corral, a world. She looks up.

Marjorie says, "I'm sorry Madeleine, but you deserved that."

Colleen rocks back on her heels and looks up at Marjorie. "My brother wouldn't touch you with a ten-foot pole."

Marjorie starts backing away, even though Colleen doesn't sound angry, nor has she made any move to rise. Marjorie has backed halfway across the street, and Grace has followed, when Marjorie shoots it like a spitball—"You're a dirty Indian!"—then turns and runs, screaming as though she were being chased and pounded, although the only person following her is Grace, flopping away in her too-big boots.

Madeleine is on her feet. "Aren't you gonna slug her?!" Shouting after Marjorie, "*Mange d'la marde, Margarine!*"

"*Ci pa gran chouz,*" says Colleen. And, as though she has just tossed back a fish, "She's not worth it."

Madeleine looks down at her smashed worm, bluish in the middle, still writhing at either end. Colleen takes the Popsicle stick, scrapes the worm up off the ground and drops it into the can.

"Still good," she says.

Jack has sent his admin clerk out on an errand. Now he leans over the man's typewriter and pecks out Oskar Fried's name and address onto an envelope. He folds an empty sheet of foolscap into the envelope, licks the flap, seals it and affixes a stamp. He adds it to two others of different sizes and shades and heads out to mail them. Oskar Fried must be seen to receive a normal amount of mail. Oskar Fried must be seen to be normal in every way, and therefore not seen at all. Jack tucks the letters in his inside pocket and steps into the rain.

Cars drive slowly past, careful not to splash him; the parade square is shiny black. In spite of himself, Jack is comforted by the drizzle, the sky blanketed in grey. A groundless comfort, he knows—today's aircraft and missiles don't need visibility to do their work. Tensions have not eased, but they have not worsened. Khrushchev has diverted some ships away from the blockade zone but has speeded construction on the missile sites. The Canadian air force and navy are tracking Soviet subs off the east coast. The U.S. has intercepted its first Soviet cargo ship without incident. Jack stops in at the phone booth.

"How's the view from Washington, Si?"

"Well, from what I can see out my window through the welter of monuments, I'd say no one's letting out their breath quite yet."

"We're all just waiting for Khrushchev to blink."

"He's batted his eyelashes once or twice, but who knows, he may just be flirting with disaster."

It's odd how quickly we become accustomed to crisis. We ought not to be capable of desultory conversations to do with imminent annihilation. But we adapt. Blessing or curse? Jack wonders.

"You Canucks certainly took your time," adds Simon.

Jack knows he is being needled. "Hail to the chief, eh?" Dief has finally gone public with the alert, and made a statement in the House supporting Kennedy. "It's hard to believe that in this day and age a Canadian prime minister waits to take his orders from Whitehall."

"Yes, but you lot are always caught in the middle. And the Americans have an unhealthy obsession with Cuba."

"I'd be obsessed too if I had a whack of nukes parked ninety miles off my coast."

"Perhaps, but this crisis is a predictable outcome."

"You sound like my neighbour," says Jack.

"Really? Intelligent chap."

"At least Kennedy's got the guts to go eyeball to eyeball with this character."

"He'd do better to put a leash on his brother," says Simon casually.

"What's that? How do you mean?"

"It's not just Robert, of course, they're all irrational when it comes to Cuba. Almost a form of hysteria, really. Fidel turned down the New York Giants when they scouted him and the Americans never forgave him."

*Fidel.* "You're kidding me."

"Pukka gen, mate."

"Holy Dinah!" Jack laughs as much at Simon's use of the old expression as at the thought of Castro pitching for the Giants. *Pukka gen—* very RAF.

"And any self-respecting Latin American leader would take offence at plots aimed at making his beard fall out."

"What?" A cadet is waiting politely to use the phone. Jack turns away—out of lip-reading range. "Who's making his beard fall out?"

"Who do you think would come up with a cockamamie scheme like that? The CIA have had a mongrel assortment of agents down there, spookin' about for ways to discredit and/or kill Castro and trigger an uprising, for years. The Americans lost a cash cow, they want it back."

Jack can hear him inhale—he's smoking one of his Camels. He leans against the glass. "What's going to happen, Si?"

"Oh, I think it's happening. Khrushchev will back down and Kennedy will look good at home and to NATO. It's one for us, mate."

"You old cynic."

"I'm utterly sincere." Simon's tone is breezy. "Kennedy will remove the worthless Jupiter missiles from Turkey so Khrushchev can save face, but it'll mean a tremendous loss of prestige for the Russians. Brilliant stroke of *realpolitik* on Kennedy's part. If we don't all go up in flames over the next twenty-four hours, chances are we won't any time soon." Simon exhales. Jack can almost smell the smoke. "Before I forget, Fried's going to need mail—"

"Done."

"Oh, had I mentioned—?"

"No, but I figured."

"You've got a feel for tradecraft, old man," says Simon, in a send-up of his own accent.

"When are we going to see you up our way? Mimi would love to meet you."

"Is she aware of our little operation?"

"No, but she knows I ran into you the summer before—"

"How's the *Deutsches Mädchen?*"

"Oh she's grand, she's a spitfire."

"Chip off the old propeller, eh? Cheers, Jack."

"Cheers." Jack hears the click, and hangs up. He heads to the mailbox outside the grocery store and posts Fried's "letters."

Tradecraft.

The next morning, Jack picks up the paper from the front steps. He walks slowly back up to the kitchen, eyes on the front page: *SOVIET, U.S., AGREE TO HOLD PRELIMINARY TALKS ON CUBA.*

"Didn't the milk come?" asks Mimi.

"I guess not, I didn't see it," says Jack. Mimi slips past him, down to the porch, and gets the milk.

At the table, Madeleine reaches for a fresh-baked banana muffin. Her father lifts his paper to turn a page. She freezes. Towering over the breakfast table on the front page is a photograph of children ducking and covering under their desks. It's the exercise group. Her stomach closes.

*"Madeleine, qu'est-ce qui va pas?"*

"Nothing."

"Then pass your brother the butter."

"I only asked you twice," says Mike.

She has the odd sense that if she reached for the butter her hand would stay where it is, and that a phantom hand would reach out. She lifts her hand and it works perfectly, but before picking up the butter she obeys the impulse to sniff her fingers quickly. Mike bursts out laughing.

"What's so funny?" she asks.

"Old Smeller."

"Stop it!"

The newspaper comes down.

Mike is still giggling. "Well she's always doing that." And he imitates her, furtively sniffing his hands, fingers curled.

"Quit it!"

"Simmer down now," says her father. "Mike, don't tease your sister."

Madeleine's face feels like a heating pad, she has to go to the bathroom. Her parents are looking at her. "That's Diane Vogel," she confesses, pointing at a girl with her head buried in her arms, on the front page of the newspaper.

Her father says, "Those kids are down in Florida."

American kids. That's not a picture of our class at all.

He clicks air through his teeth and gets up. "Well, looks like tensions are easing, eh? Have a good day, fellas."

The grade four class recites in unison, "'For want of a nail the shoe was lost, for want of a shoe the horse was lost, for want of a horse the rider was lost....'" Art is always on Friday afternoons. The best pictures have been selected for the wall and for the window in the door. "'... for want of a rider the battle was lost, for want of the battle the war was lost....'" Madeleine has her eyes on the clipboard on Mr. March's desk, as though her gaze could fix it there, preventing him from picking it up and reading off the names. "'... and all for the want of a horseshoe nail.'"

He reaches for the clipboard. "The following little girls...."

After supper, the hum and rattle of Mimi's sewing machine competes with *Sing along with Mitch*. Madeleine watches the bright fabric passing beneath the pistoning needle, her mother's foot working the pedal like an accelerator. She is lengthening Madeleine's clown costume. Sewn from an old set of drapes, their indestructible muslin patterned with tropical flowers in crimson, emerald and canary-yellow, pleated and pompommed. Madeleine looks longingly at the hat—she is not allowed to wear it till Halloween. Constructed of *Life* magazines rolled up, shellacked and upholstered, it's pointed like a dunce cap. She recalls that Anne Frank is somewhere in there, smothering. She takes a deep breath and looks away.

"You'll get a job at Barnum 'n' Bailey in a costume like that," says her father. "You've got the smartest *maman* in the world."

On Saturday, a U-2 spy plane is shot down over Cuba, killing the pilot, and they all put their clocks back an hour, for daylight saving time. Madeleine endures figure-skating lessons at the arena, where the torment of picks and figure eights is mitigated by the presence of Auriel, who looks like a self-described "velvet sausage roll" in her tutu—and the sight of Marjorie, dander bouncing with every forward thrust, keeps them in silent stitches. Madeleine is stalwart through swimming lessons in the echoey indoor pool, survives the churning fug of the change room and emerges gratefully to watch Mike's hockey practice, hot chocolate steaming from a paper cup in her hand, swinging the heels of her boots against the scarred bleacher boards. Mike plays defence. She relishes each crisp swoosh and slice of his skates, admiring the look of concentration on his face, his cheeks pink with exertion. Afterwards, she watches, mesmerized, as the Zamboni heals the surface of the ice. Her brother and Arnold Pinder emerge from the locker room with Roy in tow, lugging his heavy goalie equipment, and the four of them watch as the big boys power onto the ice with graceful strides, sticks pivoting from their gloved hands: passing the puck, turning on a dime to skate swiftly backwards. Ricky Froelich is among them, skirting the boards easily, dangerously, flicking his hank of hair out of his eyes with a toss of his head. He was suspended last year for fighting, but it hasn't happened again.

In the afternoon the McCarthys go shopping in London, and at the crowded entrance to the Covent Market, Madeleine sees a young man and an old lady parading with signs, *Ban the Bomb* and *Insects Shall Inherit the Earth.*

That night, Jack sits with his wife and son on the couch and watches the *Newsmagazine* special on CBC. Knowlton Nash talks with White House press secretary Pierre Salinger in Washington, and a succession of officials line up to praise Khrushchev's "statesmanlike decision" to dismantle the missiles. The relief is palpable.

"It pays to stand up to a bully, that's what history teaches, Mike."

Madeleine sits cross-legged on the floor, waiting for the news to be over. Jack called them in to watch "history in the making." The main anchor, Norman DePoe, sums up: " . . . men are still dying in the rice paddies of Vietnam, the steaming jungles of Laos and the high thin air of the Himalayas. The little wars go on, but at least we're not going to have the big one. At least not yet anyway, and suddenly at last there's hope that we may be able to settle the little ones too."

"Where's Vietnam?" asks Mike.

"It's in south-east Asia," answers Jack.

"Is there a war on there?"

"There's always a bit of a one."

They stay tuned for Ed Sullivan.

That night, Jack tells Madeleine, "It's all over, little buddy, nothing left to worry about."

There will not be a nuclear war in our lifetime.

"You can wake up tomorrow and go to school feeling free as a bird," he says. "So much for Mr. Marks."

He turns out the light. And Madeleine's eyes stay open.

# TRICK OR TREAT

OCTOBER 31 IS THE BEST DAY of the year: Halloween. Everyone goes to school in costume. Doing normal schoolwork in a costume makes everything including arithmetic seem easier. Each class has its own Halloween party; the grade fours have bobbed for apples, and devoured a cake with orange icing brought in by Mr. March. But Madeleine is itching for the main event: nightfall. Trick or treat. She watches the clock, poised to flee with the bell.

"The following little girls. . . ."

It never crossed her mind that they would have to do exercises with their Halloween costumes on. It makes no sense. She stands against the coat hook, her head sweating under her pointed pompom hat, and waits.

"I don't want to be a clown."

It's almost dark out. Younger children are already making the rounds, accompanied by parents and older siblings. Jack is up in Madeleine's room, where she stands, clown hat in hand, her face glum despite her big painted smile, and framed by the ruffled collar. He wants badly to laugh but he stays solemn. "Why not, sweetie?"

Madeleine thinks. "I grew out of it."

"I think it fits you fine."

She looks down.

He asks, "What would you rather go as?"

"A golfer."

"A golfer? How come?"

"I don't know"—which is the truth.

"Well now, I have a set of golf clubs and a golf bag and we could fix you up with a cap and a moustache and whatnot . . ."

Madeleine brightens—*a moustache?*

" . . . but do you think that might kind of hurt maman's feelings?"

Oh. Madeleine hadn't thought of that. She feels suddenly terribly sad for Maman, when she thinks of how Mr. March touched the beautiful clown costume she sewed. She says, "I could be a clown going golfing."

Now he laughs. "Yeah, you could."

"With a moustache."

"Sure."

They go into the bathroom and Jack wipes the red lipstick from her face—grinds it off with a face cloth, then takes one of Mimi's eyebrow pencils and draws a handlebar moustache on her upper lip. She goes into her room and gets her pillow. Stuffs it under her costume, then enters her parents' room and stands in front of the full-length mirror. She is Mr. March dressed up as a clown disguised with a moustache going golfing. She smiles. "Thanks Dad."

She shoulders her golf bag and sets out with Auriel and Lisa. Auriel is a Hawaiian dancer with a coconut bra, and Lisa is Judy Jetson with go-go boots. Madeleine has taken only the putter so the bag won't be too heavy—she will use it for candy. Her Unicef box jingles already with pennies that Dad put in "to get the ball rolling." The PMQs are aglow with grinning pumpkins, alive with ghosts and skeletons, cowboys, Indians, pirates and fairies. Mike is dressed as a bedraggled soldier of fortune, despite his father's offer to help rig him out as Billy Bishop. Arnold Pinder wears his dad's camouflaged hunting outfit and totes a BB gun. Both boys have streaked burnt cork under their eyes. Roy Noonan is dressed as a hot dog.

After trick-or-treating at a couple of houses, Madeleine drifts away from her friends, drawn by a sudden urge to try out her golf swing in the park. "Fore!" she yells, and swings into the darkness. The iron weight pulls her around full circle. Grace and Marjorie scurry past. Marjorie is a pregnant lady, Grace is a teenager with a stuffed bosom and smeary lipstick. Marjorie turns and spits, "Watch what you're doing, Madeleine!" Madeleine swings and swings until she is dizzy, and discovers a new kind of crazy laughter as a runaway ventriloquist puppet—opening and closing her mechanical jaw, head jerking back and forth in time with her evil laughter. She laughs out of the park and down St. Lawrence Avenue, past Claire McCarroll in her bunny costume holding her dad's hand.

At the bottom of St. Lawrence she runs into a bear—just someone in an old raccoon coat, a paper bag over their head, with eyeholes. As Mr. March might say, this individual has not made much of an effort.

"What brings you out this evening?" inquires Mr. March with an English accent disguised as a clown with a moustache going golfing.

"Free stuff, what else?" Colleen Froelich. Who would have thought she would stoop to something as fun and normal as trick-or-treating?

They are at the schoolyard. Madeleine dropped a bar of soap into her golf bag before she left home, so she must have known she was going to do something bad, though she'd no plans to use it. She tips the bag over and some rockets and crappy candy kisses tumble out along with the soap. She has lost her Unicef box. She takes the soap and writes *PEAHEN* all over the grade-four windows, staggering, scrawling and calling out like a parrot in a pirate movie, "Peahen! Peahen! *Grawk!*"

Colleen says, "You're crazy."

Madeleine collapses on the ground beside her, giggling uncontrollably. "Why thank you, Peahen."

"What's 'peahen' supposed to mean?"

"Hmmm, *qu'est-ce que c'est la 'peahen'*?"

Colleen leaves. Madeleine lies on her back in the schoolyard in the dark, the laughter tapering off to no more than a dark trickle out the side of her mouth. Then she rises, slings the golf bag over her shoulder and follows Algonquin Drive up behind the houses, taking slapshots, whacking pebbles with the putter as she goes. She hears one hit a garbage can. She wonders what would happen if she heard the smash of glass, and keeps on whacking. She cuts through the park and takes a swing at the oak tree. Bark flies up, exposing a slash of white. She chops and chops, each metallic blow an ache that numbs her palms, travels to her shoulders and rattles her head on its post; she chops until her bangs are slick with sweat, until her arms have turned to rubber, and she figures she has just about chopped that tree right down.

Mimi is surprised to find no candy in Madeleine's golf bag. "What did you do all evening if you weren't trick-or-treating?"

"We gave our candy to a little kid who lost his."

It doesn't feel like a lie because she didn't think about it before she said it. She hides the bent golf club behind the furnace, and goes to bed with a stomach ache.

"You have a stomach ache because you ate all your candy, don't tell me *des petites histoires* about poor little boys losing theirs."

The next morning the grade-four windows are perfectly clean. Maybe she didn't soap them. Maybe it was all a dream. But after the national anthem and the Lord's Prayer, the principal, Mr. Lemmon, comes on the PA system and announces that there has been vandalism—"wanton vandalism"—in the park, and that school property has been violated. "The offenders are invited to come forward and confess. Otherwise, shame on you."

Madeleine feels prickly, and clammy as though she had wet her pants, and her head feels set to burst like a smashed pumpkin.

Before supper.

"Dad, say someone commits vandalism, do they get sent to training school?"

"That depends on what they did and how old they are."

"How old is a juvenile delinquent?"

"Under twenty-one."

"Oh."

"And over twelve. Why?"

"If a person was my age they wouldn't send them to training school, would they."

"Well, what did this eight-year-old person do?"

"I'm almost nine."

Jack refrains from smiling. "What did this almost-nine-year-old do?"

"Nothing. But what if they broke something or something?"

"Well. I'd have to say that, unless it was something of great value, something that couldn't be fixed"—it can be fixed. Windows get washed, tree bark grows back—"or unless it was a person who was harmed . . . I'd say it would be sufficient for the guilty party to apologize."

"But no one knows they did it."

"All the more reason they should come clean."

"Confess?"

"Yup. Do the right thing."

She feels as though there's a smell coming off her, and she sniffs her fingers to make sure they are clean.


## AMERICAN THANKSGIVING


SHE KNOWS THAT the smell will go away if she confesses to Mr. March about the windows. Then she must go to the principal and tell about the tree.

Mr. March's eyes get big and round, he looks at Madeleine as though he is seeing her for the first time—like an elephant noticing a mouse.

"I'm sorry, Mr. March."

It's weird because he says, "Just forget about it, Madeleine." He doesn't say, "Forget about it, little girl," he uses her name, which he never does unless he is reading it off his clipboard.

It's lunchtime. They are in the hallway outside the classroom. She has confessed to soaping "Peahen" all over the grade four windows. She has also confessed to dressing up as him as a clown going golfing.

Throughout, he has not taken his eyes from hers. For once she can see them through his glasses. They are large and grey. As she confessed, she felt cool water pouring over her head, even though her voice was shaking.

Mr. March glances down the empty corridor and asks, "Have you told anyone?"

"No."

"Well don't."

"I have to tell Mr. Lemmon."

"No you don't."

She is surprised, then reflects that he probably wants to tell on her himself. Then he will phone her parents and tell them. "I'm going to tell my own parents," she says.

"What for? What they don't know won't hurt them."

She goes to walk away down the hall because it's lunchtime, but he says, "Wait a moment, Madeleine."

She stops, and as she turns back to him, she gets the I'm-not-hungry-any-more feeling, because she realizes that he is going to make her do exercises even though it's not after three. Just as she had never imagined the possibility of doing exercises in a Halloween costume, she is now ambushed by the prospect of doing them at lunchtime. *You can do them in a box, you can do them with a fox. . . .*

She follows him back into the classroom, arms limp at her sides, but he just nips over to his desk and takes something from the drawer. He writes on it, then hands it to her. "You got a hundred percent on your reading comprehension, what do you think of that?"

At recess she knocks on Mr. Lemmon's door. She tells him about the tree. He doesn't say anything at first, and she thinks, oh no, I'm going to get the strap.

Then he says, "Come here, Madeleine." He is sitting behind his desk, and she thinks, I'm not going to get the strap after all, he is going to make me do exercises. She feels tired because this means she will have to start feeling sorry for Mr. Lemmon too. She approaches his desk and sighs—she ought to have known that this is what happens. She stands close enough for him to reach out and squeeze her arm muscle, and he does reach out, but he takes her hand instead. He shakes it. "I'm impressed, Madeleine, very impressed."

That I hacked up a tree?

"Most children would not have the courage to confess as you've just done."

*Courage.* A hail of bullets. Saving a dog from rapids. Being a juvenile delinquent. Confessing to it.

"Run along now, Madeleine."

Mr. March doesn't call the exercise group for a week after Halloween. And then, in the second week of November: "The following little girls will remain after the bell: Diane Vogel, Joyce Nutt, Grace Novotny . . ."

Madeleine waits for her name, the hot feeling in her underpants, the sick feeling in her stomach.

" . . . Marjorie Nolan . . . and Claire McCarroll."

What?

The bell goes. The clatter of chairs as everyone but the exercise group gets up to flee for another day. Madeleine remains at her desk and glances over at Claire, who has turned pink. When the room is clear, the members of the exercise group rise from their desks and line up shoulder to shoulder along the back wall, against the coat hooks. Claire follows them and fills the empty place next to Marjorie. From her desk, Madeleine can see that Claire's knees have turned pink too. What does Claire think is going to happen? She is in the cave now. From outside it looks like an ordinary mountain.

"What are you waiting for, Madeleine?" asks Mr. March.

She rises from her desk, walks to the coat hooks and stands at the end of the line beside Claire.

Mr. March rolls his eyes. "For heaven's sake, little girl, did you hear your name?"

"No sir," says Madeleine.

"Well then?" Someone giggles. Madeleine walks back to her desk and reaches in for her homework—"Slow as molasses in January," says Mr. March.

She leaves. Marjorie giggles again. Diane Vogel looks straight at her, with a solemnity that Madeleine has seen in a photograph in a book. It reminds her of Anne Frank, and that explains why she loves Diane Vogel. Claire is looking out the window.

Madeleine does not go straight home. Kids pour out of the school, yet the air around her feels quiet, muffled mohair. The kids stampeding past seem far away, as though they are in a movie. She traverses the throng and reaches the swings. She feels flushed, as though she has done something bad, and she knows that when she gets home Maman will take one look at her and say, "Do you have a guilty conscience?" Her head is hot and hazy, as though she has been up to something shame-ful—like watching a boy after he has offered to pee in front of you and all you have said in reply is, "If you want to." She has watched Philip Pinder pee. That was a sin. But she has not sinned today.

She sits on the swing. Stupid Claire McCarroll, if she hadn't been picked Madeleine would not feel so guilty now. Like Adam and Eve when God banished them from the Garden of Eden. *And they knew they were naked.* How dumb did they have to be not to notice in the first place?

She pushes off on the swing as the schoolyard shrieks and empties around her, kicking the scuffed dirt with her Buster Browns, picturing Mr. March, his floppy grey cheeks; how she does her backbends for him and he feels her "sweat glands" between her legs. She closes her eyes and sees Jesus' face, so sad. Jesus is sad because you have hurt him. Jesus often looks as though someone had just farted. She folds her arms across her knees and rests her forehead there, staring down between her dangling feet at a tiny patch of world.

Only yesterday, she was at home on the couch with her brother and Bugs Bunny, watching *The Beverly Hillbillies,* and it seemed then that there was no such thing as exercises. All that stuff remained in its own place. As if those eleven minutes after the bell were sealed and stored separately—the way you wrap leftovers in plastic so they won't go bad. The bag may have leaked a bit before but now it has broken and the smell is everywhere. Because today she was expelled from after-three, and now she is watching this patch of world move back and forth, back and forth. . . .

The toes of her shoes are badly scuffed now. She sits up and stretches her legs out in front. She thinks, everyone thinks I'm just a little girl with white ankle socks. They don't know that I know about after-three. About the coat hooks, how you can press your spine against one while you wait to see if he will call you up to the front. You try to press so hard against the hook that you will keep feeling it all the way through your exercises. They don't know that I know about Mr. March. About his smell. Like Javex. But I will go like the wind until all his smell is off me. She starts pumping her legs to get the swing going.

"We ha-ad chocolates, and you-ou di-dn't"—chanting—"nyah nyah-nyah, nyah nyah!"

Marjorie and Grace are holding hands, swinging them back and forth. Marjorie has chocolate around her mouth, as if to prove to Madeleine that she really did have it after the bell.

"So?! What's so big about that?!" Madeleine grips the chains of the swing.

"You di-dn't get a-any!" Marjorie sticks out her tongue, smeary brown.

Madeleine decides to ignore them and keep swinging.

"Where's your friend, Madeleine?"

Madeleine pumps and swings higher, the air feels good against her hot legs, her hot face.

"Yeah!" says Grace, which is quite a lot for Grace.

"Who?" demands Madeleine from a furious height.

"You know," Marjorie replies, then starts batting her hand against her mouth, whooping like an Indian in a cowboy movie. Madeleine lets go of the swing and sails softly through air, lands like a bullet, then *pound, pound, pound!*

"That's for you, Marjorie Nolan!"

Marjorie is screaming, blood has poured from her nose to join the chocolate mess around her mouth.

"I'm sorry!" Madeleine hollers into Marjorie's face, almost in time with the last blow.

And she is sorry. Boys do this all the time. Beat each other up. Madeleine is amazed because when you hurt people they are so pathetic, how could you want to keep on hurting them, or ever do it again to anyone? She pats Marjorie's head. "Here, Marjorie." She takes off one of her shoes, peels off her ankle sock and dabs Marjorie's nose with it— poor Marjorie, who is so revolting and can't keep anything in, her blood, her snot, tears and tongue. She is still sobbing urgently. Madeleine is suddenly terribly sad.

Marjorie gets up. "I'm telling!" She turns and flails toward home, head thrown back, hands flapping, wailing past the point of really crying, Madeleine can tell, but that's even sadder, because how horrible to be Marjorie.

Madeleine looks around for Grace Novotny, but Grace has run away. Grace peed her pants in school last year, and that's all you need to know about Grace.

"I'm sorry," repeats Madeleine softly to herself.

She still doesn't feel like going home. She can't put her ankle sock back on, it has Marjorie gunk on it. She removes her other sock, then puts her shoes back on. She plucks at the dark November grass until she has muddy roots in two fists, and rubs them onto her bare ankles. She rubs the earth in rings around her wrists and stripes her cheeks with it. She sees Claire McCarroll walking slowly from the side door, head down, knees still pink. She is carrying her art.

"Hi Claire."

Claire stops but doesn't look up.

"What's your art?"

"A turkey," Claire replies.

"Can I see?"

Claire stays looking down but holds the turkey out to Madeleine. It is smiling, wearing a pilgrim's hat and a white neck ruff.

"That's really nice."

"Thank you."

"How come you made a turkey though?"

"We're American."

Madeleine had forgotten. Americans celebrate Thanksgiving in November. Claire's other hand is clenched in a fist.

"Watcha got?" asks Madeleine.

Claire opens her hand. Her palm is a dark smear, in the centre a melting nub. Madeleine reaches out, dips a finger in Claire's palm and tastes the chocolate.

Mr. March makes Claire stays after school with the bad kids. This is just a worning. Do not seek my true identitty. I am your friend. I d'ont even know Claire. signed,
The Human Sowrd

Mrs. McCarroll shows the note to Mr. McCarroll. "It was on the porch with the milk."

"Claire." Her father beckons gently.

Claire is seated on the McCarrolls' living-room couch. Her mother stands with her hands folded, her father sits next to her, stroking her head.

"Claire, honey, are you in any trouble at school?"

Claire turns very red.

"It's all right, lamb, you can tell Daddy and me."

Claire looks down and adjusts her hairband with one finger. Blair and Sharon look at one another.

"Hey, pet?" asks Blair.

"Is Mr. March not happy with your work, darlin'?" asks Sharon.

But Claire will not look up and she will not say anything. She sits on her hands and big tears fall into her lap.

Madeleine waits for the Children's Aid to arrive in a kind of ambulance and take her away "for violence," but nothing happens. Marjorie Nolan has not told on her. And up at the front of the class, on the big felt bulletin board, she sees that she has become a hare in all subjects. She is even a hare in arithmetic. *Now I've hoid everything, doc.*

She helps her father rake the leaves, and confesses to having attacked the tree. He asks if she owned up to it at school and she answers yes. He tells her that she was taking out her anger at her teacher for scaring them with duck and cover, and possibly her anger at the entire grown-up world for having brought us so close to the brink of war: "Sometimes when we're frightened—when we feel powerless— we do irrational things. Do you know what 'irrational' means?" She does not. He tells her.

It was wrong to damage the tree, it was "not constructive" and it was not rational. But it was courageous of her to tell the truth—"You did the right thing, sweetie." He is proud of her.

She says, "I hurt the tree," and weeps inconsolably.

She wakes herself up screaming. She was punching the tree and her hand was full of chocolate blood.

She finishes out the night in Mike's room.

"But what if there isn't a war on?" she asks him, savouring the canvas smell of the hard camp cot. "How can you fight in one?" They are discussing the future.

"There's always a bit of war on somewhere," Mike replies in the dark. "And there's assassin jobs that are so secret, you never even hear about them."

"And that's when you're a missionary?"

"Mercenary."

It sounds like someone going around being merciful to people, but it's just the opposite, thinks Madeleine. How can you go around killing people you're not even mad at, who aren't even your enemy?

"It's nothing personal," says Mike, "you're a professional soldier, you work for pay. Anyhow, mercenary's just my third choice—like if something happens to me, say I lose an eye like Daddy."

Madeleine can just make out the framed photo of an elegant airborne CF-104 on the wall over Mike's bed. The pilot is looking at the camera from the window of the cockpit, but his face is not visible because he is wearing an oxygen mask—corrugated snout and goggles.

"What's your first choice?" Madeleine knows the answer but she doesn't want him to fall asleep.

"No question about it," he says. "Fighter pilot. That's what I'm going to be doing six or seven years from now."

"What's your second choice?"

"NHL."

"What position?"

"Forward."

"I'm defence."

"You're not on the ice, you're a girl."

"Let's say I'm a boy."

"Yeah, but you aren't."

"Yeah, but let's say."

"Well. . . ."

"Yeah, and my name is Mike, I mean Mitch, okay? And I'm really a boy."

"You're stunned."

"Pretend I'm really your brother, okay?"

"Mitch?"

"Yes Mike?"

"No, I mean are you sure you want your name to be Mitch?"

"What should it be?"

" . . . Robert."

"Okay."

He doesn't say anything for a while and Madeleine figures he has fallen asleep. Then he whispers, "Hey Rob?"

"Yeah?" Her voice feels slightly different. Not deeper, really. Lighter. Like a basketball off the driveway. Like red jeans. Madeleine waits for him to continue. After a moment he does. "What do you think of Marsha Woodley?"

Madeleine is so embarrassed she wants to squeal and pull the covers over her head, but she remembers she is Rob. "Gee, Mike. I don't know. Why?"

"Do you think she's. . . . You know. Special?"

"Yeah." Madeleine nods in the dark. "She's a real lady."

"Yeah, that's what I think."

She hesitates, then says, "And Rick is a real gentleman."

"Yup."

In the silence that follows, she waits for him to continue, but hears his breathing change and knows that he really is asleep this time. She falls asleep and has no nightmares. Rob never has nightmares.

Captain and Mrs. McCarroll are relieved when Mr. Lemmon calls their daughter's teacher into his office, and Mr. March is able to assure the worried parents, "Claire is a bright and pleasant student but she is a little given to daydreaming."

Captain McCarroll blushes and Mrs. McCarroll smiles, saying, "She gets that from her daddy."

Mr. Lemmon shows Mr. March the note. "Do you have any idea who might have written this?"

Mr. March takes a moment to consider, then shakes his head. "I can ask my pupils," he volunteers.

"Oh please don't bother." Sharon blushes.

Captain McCarroll says, "We don't want to embarrass her."

Mr. Lemmon asks if Mr. March has had occasion to keep Claire after three, and he replies that he did keep her and one or two other children for a few minutes to go over some spelling exercises, "but certainly not as a punishment for bad behaviour."

Mr. Lemmon thanks the parents for coming in, and Mr. March for clearing the matter up.

Claire is never again required to remain after three.

It is Marjorie Nolan who first feels his hands around her neck. Then Grace Novotny brings home bruises that no one asks her to explain. And that is all you need to know about Grace's mum and dad.

*Part Two*

# FLYING UP

# INDIAN SUMMER

*Which sentence is correct? (a) Smoking Days are the same as Indian Summer. (b) Indian Fall is the same as Smoking Days. (c) Indian Summer is Smoking Week. (d) Smoking Days bring Indian Autumn.*

Developing Comprehension in Reading, *Mary Eleanor Thomas, 1956*

THE WREATHS HAVE WILTED at the base of the cenotaph in Exeter, felt poppies have fallen from lapel pins and washed up against curbs softened by autumn leaves, damp and exhaling the last earthy smell before winter puts all scent and soil to sleep. Overhead, the remaining leaves have lost their lustre, clinging sparse and ragged to trees revealed magnificently complex against a hard orange sky at five in the afternoon. November. Two minutes of silence at the eleventh hour of the eleventh day of the eleventh month, to mark the end of the war to end all wars in 1918— and all the others since then. It seems also to have marked the setting in of the deep hibernation that muffles the land like a blanket. Shhh, winter is coming. In the air is the unmistakeable smell of snow.

Madeleine can smell it and she supposes Colleen can too. In the park it's cold and growing dark. Cold enough for mittens, but until the first snow comes who thinks of wearing them? Colleen's feet are still bare inside her tattered runners. Madeleine has turned nine. A wily number, able to look after itself. She had a pajama party and felt guilty for not inviting Colleen, but she couldn't picture her with her other friends, in baby dolls and curlers, levitating and talking about boys. And Madeleine would not have known which self to be. There is also a sense that the time she and Colleen spend together is something separate. Private.

They are crouched now at the far end of the park behind Colleen's house. It borders a number of backyards, including Philip Pinder's, where, this evening, there is a deer hanging upside down from a tree. Cold blood drips out of its mouth into a metal pail. Its eyes are staring open and a drop of liquid hangs from its nose. It's draining. As it turns slowly from its rope and pulley you can see where it has been slit open as though it had just unzipped its deer suit, like in a cartoon. All of its insides are piled green and brown and pink in a plastic bucket. It's an evil thing. Not the deer. But what has been done.

From the teeter-totters in the park, it seemed as though the deer might not be real. Or at least you could say, "That's a deer that Philip's father shot," and feel almost normal about it, because hunting is normal.

But when Madeleine came closer and saw the deer slowly rotating by its hind ankles, legs stretched so that it seemed they must snap and recoil any second, it was different. It did not feel normal. But Philip, his older brother, Arnold, their father, their mother and their Uncle Wilf are all out in the yard, working on the deer and behaving normally; although with an added air of seriousness, the way a person might if they were, for example, practising backing their new Airstream trailer into the driveway: "It's not that I'm trying to show off. This is work."

A neighbour comments, "That's quite a deer, Harve." But Madeleine can see that the neighbour is a bit embarrassed, trying to be polite, saying something about a dead deer that you would normally say about a garden. "That's quite a rhododendron, Harve."

As Colleen and Madeleine linger, however, a couple of other dads arrive and smile openly, wanting to know the whole story. They have a look in their eyes that Madeleine has seen on television shows—the look just before the wolf whistle at the pretty girl walking down the street. Philip's father keeps working and more or less ignores the other men. He tells the story briefly, quietly, accepting a beer almost as an afterthought. "Son of a gun!" they say and gaze at the deer. "She's a beauty, Harve." Philip is grinning in a strange way, fetching things for his dad. He picks up the pail of guts, pretend-vomits into it and offers it to Madeleine and Colleen.

"Philip," his dad warns softly. Philip puts the bucket down and looks up at his father, who has begun to chop meat off the deer. "Are you giving me a hand or are you playing with the girls?"

Philip turns red and proceeds to ignore Madeleine and Colleen. So do all the other men and boys—there are no women out here now that it's getting dark. The sky is sad and beautiful, stained orange where the sun splashed down. Someone's hi-fi is playing, music drifts from a window two or three doors away, "Bali Hai" is calling. . . .

Arnold Pinder is up in the tree now, with an extension cord, positioning a light bulb over the deer. The men have forgotten that Madeleine and Colleen are present. Spying.

Madeleine knows that no girls are allowed here. No women either. They will cook the meat and serve it, but it is not decent for females to be out here. Not because of the hacked-up deer—they're taking off its head now—"Hang on. Got it, okay. . . . Weighs a ton"—but in the way it's not decent for an older girl or a woman to go into a barbershop. Never mind a tavern. Those are men's places. Madeleine knows that her days of accompanying her father to the barber are numbered. This backyard has become a men's place.

They let out a short whoop as they cut down what's left of the deer, take the weight and lay it on a tarp. Philip's dad leans over the carcass with a hacksaw. The girls can't see past the men and boys, gathered and relaxed now around the tarp with beers and Cokes, but they see Arnold Pinder come around the side of the house. He's got his dog, Buddy, by the collar, and Buddy is practically walking on his hind legs, pulling Arnold toward the tarp. Mr. Pinder straightens up and tosses a stick to Buddy, who lunges and carries it off. It is not a stick, it's a leg.

Madeleine pokes Colleen, but Colleen just shrugs. Madeleine knows that deer was murdered. But Colleen would never say that. She rarely gives her opinion—even though it is clear to Madeleine that she always has one. Not just an opinion, but the right answer. Trouble is, she refuses to say it. "If you don't know, what's the use of me telling you?"

"That's a stupid answer," Madeleine recently got up the nerve to say.

To which Colleen raised her eyebrows and smiled slightly with a corner of her mouth.

Colleen can fire a neat and tidy round of spit off the tip of her tongue. She does this after she has given an opinion, silent or otherwise. She does so now, and says, "My brother shot a deer once."

For a moment Madeleine wonders who Colleen means, because the images of Ricky Froelich and shooting a deer don't go together.

"Ricky?"

"How many brothers do I got?"

Madeleine knows that Roger and Carl don't count. They're babies.

She swallows. "How come?" Colleen doesn't answer. Madeleine asks, "For food?"

Colleen has risen and is walking off. Madeleine follows. They slip into the chill of deeper shadows, up the gentle incline through grass that has begun to feel sinewy underfoot with the coming of frost.

She follows Colleen to where the monkey bars and merry-go-round glint glamorous and strange in the night. Through the gloom, the bare patch in the oak tree glows white, and she reaches out to stroke the wound as she passes—*Get well soon*.

The darkness makes the swings look bigger—giant metal A's at either end supporting gallows in between. The teeter-totters tilt astride their hitching post like bucking broncos, the slide gleams sly and skinny, everything says, "I dare you." Madeleine experiences a thrill at the lateness of the hour, only now realizing that she has stayed out long past when she is allowed. Her parents must have left by now for the Woodleys'. She lost track of time, what with the sunset and the electric light in the tree, the music, the men, the boys. And the deer.

"He had to shoot it," says Colleen, walking up the teeter-totter till she is balanced at the centre.

Madeleine follows. "Why?"

"It was suffering."

They stand back to back at the fulcrum of the teeter-totter and walk slowly toward opposite ends, as though about to fight a duel, trying to keep the board perfectly stable. Then they turn carefully and face one another. The object is to jump off with no warning, causing your opponent, should she not be quick enough, to come crashing down. They take turns. The darkness shines around them. The only light is from the houses and street lamps beyond—and from a wedge of moon that looks more remote than ever in the black sky. Certain questions may now be asked that would be impermissible during the day. Madeleine hears her own voice in the cold clarity of night—like the sound of a rifle being broken open. "Are you guys Indian?"

Colleen appears not to have heard the question. She stands at her end.

Madeleine swallows and says, "I don't care if you are, 'cause anyhow I like Indians." She cannot read Colleen's expression. Her skin is darker, blue eyes paler in the night.

Colleen says, "We're Métis."

Madeleine waits for more but Colleen is silent, watching her. Playing the game.

"What's that?"

"You know what a half-breed is?"

Madeleine nods.

Colleen says, "Don't ever use that word."

Madeleine waits.

"Ever hear of Louis Riel?"

Madeleine shakes her head.

"He was a rebel. He fought the settlers."

"What happened to him?"

"He got hanged."

Madeleine is poised with the keen anticipation of a hunter, or a deer, about to jump—

"*Dieu merci!*"

She turns at the sound of her mother just as Colleen jumps, sending her slamming to the ground, but she doesn't yelp. She is instantly caught up in a tight embrace. She feels her mother's chest, soft and cushiony, heart pounding beneath silk, she smells hairspray and perfume. The next instant, she is swung out at arm's length, spun round, whacked on her bottom and yanked by the hand toward home. Her mother crying and promising Madeleine "a good beating from *ton père*"—an empty threat, as Madeleine well knows, but one that gauges the degree of her mother's upset—"sick with worry!" Her ivory high heels sink into the earth with every step, spearing little clumps of mud and grass.

They reach the sidewalk and she turns to look back but Colleen is gone.

Five days later the weather has changed. Flurries in the morning. Thick flakes have swirled outside the windows of J.A.D. McCurdy all day, and in the afternoon a dark cloud moved in and the wind picked up. The snow blows like sand across the schoolyard and gathers in miniature dunes against the slide, the pitcher's mound, the bicycle racks and car tires. The class makes snowflakes in art. Take a piece of white construction paper; fold it neatly in two; draw one half of a snowflake; cut it out, then carefully poke the sharp end of the scissors through to make numerous tiny holes; unfold the paper. Miraculous.

The first snow is always a surprise. It comes overnight, and in the morning parents wake their children, "Come look out the window!" It covers everything—trees, houses, backyards and bikes. It brings everything and everyone together, even sounds—a fresh white muted world where the roll of tires is intimate, every whisper and bird call part of the same story. Houses and cars peer out from beneath white coverlets that pleat at eaves and headlights, and trickle into icicles. Across the lawns, now just one great lawn, curves and contours take shape, mysterious sudden swellings.

After breakfast, kids put on snowsuits and toques; padded oblong figures with penguin arms tread out into the winter sunshine, eagerly yet regretfully making the first marks. The birds have been there before them with their three-pronged prints, but otherwise the snow is pristine. Soon it will be pitted and dirty, rolled into snowmen, piled into snow forts, swished into angels, the grass exposed in patches and green slashes. There is the particular scent of soil filtered through the damp wool of scarves beaded with breathcicles, the taste of snow on woollen mittens.

By afternoon, steam rises from shining black driveways, the last white slabs slide heavily from a mailbox, a porch railing. Overheated children unzip as they swaddle home, galoshes unbuckled, hats in hand.

"This will confuse the birds," says a lady at the PX, where Jack is buying charcoal. The McCarthys are having a barbecue tonight. "The last one of the season," says Jack.

It is a mild evening. And although Madeleine is embarrassed to be the only family barbecuing in the shrinking snow, the chicken does smell irresistible turning on the rotisserie just outside the back door. The way her parents behave whenever they do some crazy thing like this compounds her mortification and completes her happiness. Her mother laughing unaccountably, her father winking back; Maman slipping her arms around his waist from behind, the way she does whenever he cooks or does something that is usually women's work. He boasts that all the great chefs of the world are men, and she bites his earlobe. Madeleine and Mike exchange looks, rolling their eyes.

## Housecalls

*One day Willie writes a note to the milkman, and is alarmed to read what she has written: the single word 'Help.'*
TV Guide *promo for* The Trapped Housewife, *with*
*Michael Kane as "the Voice of the Doctor," 1962*

JACK HAS BEGUN to feel rather like a chauffeur. "Errand boy" is too negative a term, especially considering that he is Oskar Fried's only contact. But it would help if the man were more forthcoming. Jack has put miles on the Rambler. Even in the city. Fried will not walk anywhere and he will not take a cab. He has done his best to badger Jack into allowing him to take the wheel, but Jack is not about to let Fried drive without a licence—what if they were stopped by the police?

Driving is conducive to conversation, but Fried rarely speaks. Jack endures his silent profile across the monotonous miles . . . Niagara Falls, the Botanical Gardens, the greenhouse at Storybook Gardens; an outing one or two afternoons a week, even dinner and a Leafs game in Toronto one night—he told Mimi he was at a function at the university. Tim Horton was in fine form and Gordie Howe at the top of his game; it might have been fun, but Fried is a dull date and Jack wished bitterly that he were there with his son instead. He provided play-by-play commentary worthy of Dick Irvin, while Fried watched his first hockey game with the rapt attention of an iguana. It was impossible to know whether or not he was enjoying himself. On the drive back to London, Fried said, "I keep this car." "I beg your pardon?"

"You borrow this car to me." "No sir, I'm sorry." And Fried's silence deepened.

Fried puts away a bottle of wine, tucks into a New York strip, but nothing loosens his tongue. Jack picks up the tab—Fried seems not to carry money. And he never fails to place his grocery order over the phone, so that Jack invariably arrives at the apartment laden with bags. Cognac, fresh pouch of tobacco . . . it adds up.

Simon has reimbursed him, but Jack was faced with a short-term quandary that Simon could not have foreseen: Jack's salary is deposited directly into the bank by the station accounts officer, and he and Mimi have a joint account. Not every married couple has one but every true partnership does, and that's what Jack and Mimi have. For Jack to spend close to a hundred unaccounted-for dollars would raise a question in Mimi's mind.

He got around this hitch by asking the flight lieutenant in the accounts office for an advance. Not unusual, not questioned. Not a problem. A week later Simon wired him the money, and Jack was able to deposit it in his bank on the same day as the rest of his pay. But when Mimi was reconciling the accounts two weeks later, at the dining-room table—he is the MBA, but she is the chief financial officer at home—she looked up and asked why there were two deposits on the same day adding up to his usual pay. He told her the accounts officer had made a mistake—shortchanged him by a hundred, then corrected it. She accepted that, and why should she not?

But it didn't sit well with him.

When he came home from his first afternoon with Fried, he was speechless when his wife inquired over supper what he had been doing at Storybook Gardens. How did she know? Had she been in London? Had she seen him with Fried? He felt his face flush. She answered his question before he could ask. It turned out there was a wretched sticker on the rear bumper of his car. Black silhouette of a castle turret against a bright yellow background. He hadn't noticed it when he returned to the parking lot, having waited while Fried stood silently, endlessly, before a series of potted plants in the greenhouse. He told Mimi he had grabbed a sandwich and gone there to stretch his legs between meetings. She didn't question him, and her subsequent behaviour betrayed no suspicion. And why would she be suspicious?

Yet Jack is annoyed to have felt himself squirm guiltily at his own supper table. It didn't feel like a "tactical" lie, it simply felt . . . shabby. He's angry at Oskar Fried for steadfastly refusing to visit his home, to get over the clandestine nonsense and meet his family under a plausible and congenial cover so that Jack can reasonably be seen to be helping the man out from time to time. To "normalize relations." He has considered confiding in Mimi but that would mean clearing it with Simon first, and he'd feel like a damn fool asking Simon permission to tell his wife because he's feeling like a sneaky schoolboy. And Mimi should not have to worry about a Soviet defector on the run from the KGB—not after what they've all just been through with Cuba.

He has drawn the line at weekends and his work isn't suffering, but he missed his son's first hockey game of the season. When he went to Winnipeg for his meeting with the AOC of Training Command, he was relieved—four whole days without a call from Fried. Without a grocery list, or a lie. He was no one's servant. No one's chauffeur.

Scientists are supposed to be curious. Fried has not asked Jack a single question about his work or life in North America, beyond bare utilitarian queries. Jack feels invisible. He reflects on the brief paragraph he read about scientific employees. *Non-social, non-participative.* He has begun to smell something unpleasant in Fried's manner. What at first seemed like fear has resolved into something resembling arrogance. Perhaps it's mere resentment or frustration at having spent so many years in grinding servitude to the Soviet system. Perhaps the poor bastard is incapable of happiness. Jack reminds himself that Fried is a rocket scientist, not a candidate for Miss Congeniality.

But if only he would talk about bloody rockets, even in the most general terms. Jack asked him about USAF but all Fried said was, "I prefer NASA." Jack was momentarily uplifted—here was a scientist who dreamt of working with the civilian space agency, a purist with his heart set on sending a man to the moon because it was there. But that was short-lived. Jack couldn't pry another word from him on the subject. When Simon told him that he would be acting as a "housekeeping agent," Jack had not realized he meant it literally. What did you do in the Cold War, Daddy? I delivered groceries.

Throughout November, Jack juggles family, work, and Fried on the side. He begins to tire, not so much from the activity as from the petty lies. They leave a residue. When Mimi massages the back of his neck out of sympathy for his extra workload in the evenings, he is unable to give in to her soothing touch. Again he feels vaguely guilty. Yet it's not as though he's transgressing in any way—not as though he's having an affair. Still, he is aware of fulfilling every condition necessary for the conduct of an affair—all the trouble and none of the perks. That last thought is unworthy of him, and he resents its intrusion.

Being as adept an observer of his own behaviour as he is of others', he is aware that his thought process has changed. He knows he is creating grooves and patterns, pathways of deceit that he has sworn to use once only and only for this purpose—yet the pathways will remain. How long before they are grown over with grass and disappear? He shrugs it off by diagnosing himself as perfectly healthy. A normal man with a decent conscience. He simply does not enjoy lying to his wife.

Finally Jack hits on a partial solution: television. He tells Simon that Fried could use one, if only to improve his English, not to mention mitigate the loneliness. He doesn't mention that Fried seems as self-sufficient as his orchids—except in the area of transport. Simon wires the money and Jack delivers a new RCA Victor to Fried, who carefully untwines an orchid from the rabbit ears. Jack leaves him watching *The Beverly Hillbillies,* as impassive as ever. "See ya, Oskar, call if you need anything." Jack smiles to himself as he pulls the door closed. Fried has not even bothered to get up and slide the deadbolt behind him.

The phone rings after midnight. Mimi gets downstairs before he does. He asks who it was but she doesn't know. "They hung up." It rings again. Jack grabs it and tells Oskar Fried he has the wrong number. Then he tells his wife, "That's it for me, I'm wide awake. Think I'll stroll around the block."

"At this hour?"

"Sure. Nice and peaceful."

He pulls on his trousers and heads over to the station, breaking into a run once he has rounded the corner, and returns Fried's call from the phone booth by the parade square.

Fried has called to tell him that there is something wrong with his new television set. A picture of an Indian has appeared and will not go away. Any other time, Jack would laugh. "It's called a test pattern, Oskar. There will not be any more television programs until morning. Go to bed now."

# FRÖHLICHE WEIHNACHTEN

*If an athlete gets athlete's foot, what does an astronaut get? Missile-toe?*

Schwarzwald Flieger (Black Forest Flyer) *magazine of RCAF 4*
*Fighter Wing, West Germany, 1962*

IN THE PARK behind the Froelich house, the slide is only half as high
because of the snow, and the swings are lodged in drifts. In backyards,
small children skate, ankles collapsed inward, on postage-stamp rinks
that their fathers have flooded. Claire McCarroll is among these, gingerly walking on her new blades toward her father's outstretched
hands—this is her first Canadian winter. In the McCarthys' dining
room, the heat from the Advent candles causes the brass angels to rotate
on their wheel above, spinning a little faster every Sunday as one more
flame is added. Madeleine and Mike take turns opening the tiny cardboard doors on the dog-eared December calendar that Mimi has stuck
to the fridge for the fifth year in a row. The chocolates that came with
it, hiding behind each day of the month, are long gone, but the tiny
pictures remain: a dog, a candle, a Christmas tree.... All leading up to
the twenty-fourth, when the Baby Jesus will be revealed. Across the top,
in medieval script, are the words *"Fröhliche Weihnachten."* Merry
Christmas, from the land of *"O Tannenbaum."* Mimi has tried to replace
the calendar with a new one but the children will not hear of it.

Jack goes to the parent-teacher interviews with Mimi and feels
lighter than he has in months. Mike is doing satisfactorily but is capable
of more. "He needs to apply himself," says Miss Crane. She is concerned
that he is spending more time with Arnold Pinder than is perhaps
advisable. But she likes Mike. She's not supposed to have favourites, but
he is definitely one. A nice boy. A good-hearted boy. Jack glances at
Mimi. She's beaming.

Madeleine may have got off on the wrong foot but she has come
up from behind to excel—her report card was worth framing. Jack
looks from the officious felt animals on the bulletin board to the bland
teacher sitting before him. A limp grey man with watery eyes—a walrus
moustache would not be amiss. He is the type who gets picked on in the
schoolyard, then grows up to take his revenge in the classroom.
Somehow Jack's daughter is managing to learn from this clown. It only
makes Jack more proud of her.

By the second week, Christmas cards have accumulated on strings
hung between living room and dining room, and the stockings go up

over the fireplace, their names embroidered by Mimi years ago in Alberta: *Papa, Maman, Michel, Madeleine.* On the mantelpiece the nativity scene is set out, nestled in cotton-wool snow. Bought in Germany in '58, it is a tableau that Madeleine never tires of contemplating. An angel watches over the wooden stable, its floor strewn with straw; in and about it, painted ceramic cattle and sheep sleep and graze while Joseph and Mary kneel at either end of the empty manger—the Baby Jesus is hiding in the drawer of Maman's sewing table until Christmas Day. Shepherds hover outside the stable, and Madeleine changes their positions daily, along with the animals. She is sorely tempted to add an army man or two of Mike's to the scene. The Three Wise Men make their way on camel-back from the far end of the mantelpiece, but Madeleine improvises, making them cover vast distances across the dining-room table, the desert of the kitchen floor; stranding them on top of the fridge, the North Pole—*musta taken a wrong turn at Albuquerque.* Sorry, God. One of the Wise Men is black with a beard and a purple robe. He is her favourite. *We three kings of Orient are, smoking on a rubber cigar, it was loaded, it exploded, now we're on yonder star....* It's impossible not to think of those words when contemplating the nativity scene. Madeleine banishes blasphemy by thinking of the Baby Jesus, for whom she is filled with a fervent love. She kneels before the sewing table, bows her head against the drawer where He lies waiting to be born, and tears come to her eyes as she prays that this time no one will hurt Him.

The house begins to smell a lot like Christmas. Mimi has been busy baking: shortbreads, icebox cookies, sugar cookies, "porkpies"—iced date tarts that resemble their millinerial namesake. The kids use the cookie cutters to make bells, stars and snowmen, decorating them with bits of green and red maraschino cherries. Festive tins pile up on the counters, wax paper peeking out from beneath the lids. Mimi takes the first of *les meat-pies* from the oven—spicy and mouth-watering, the Québécois call them *tourtières*—then gets to work on *les crêpes râpées.* At some point she will call everyone down to the basement to take a stir of the Christmas cake batter—it has been fermenting since November.

Mimi and Jack read Madeleine's letter to Santa Claus and laugh out loud. Their little girl wants a cap gun and holster "or any kind of gun," a skateboard and a walkie-talkie. There is a polite PS reminding Santa that she has enough nice dolls which he has been kind enough to bring her in the past.

Jack puts up the Christmas lights with a minimum of swearing under his breath, borrowing a ladder from Henry Froelich and counting the burn-outs to see how many bulbs he'll need to pick up at Canadian Tire. He takes the kids to get a tree from the temporary pine forest set up at the Exeter Fairgrounds. Thick flakes fall as though on cue from Frank Capra. They pick one that is not quite perfect, pained at the thought that this brave yet blighted tree might not be taken home and loved this Christmas. The bare patch can always go against the wall.

Jack digs out the tree-stand, which he threatens each year to throw away, it clearly having been designed "by a Frenchman" for maximum frustration, and, enlisting his son's help, performs the annual feat of engineering—shimming, trimming, sawing and straightening. "Careful, Jack, I don't want you looking like a pirate again for Christmas." He shakes his head, mock-rueful, as they recall the time he was poked in his good eye by a spruce needle and wound up wearing a patch till New Year's. That was the year they all had the flu and Madeleine was teething. "That was one of the nicest Christmases ever, remember, Missus?" He kisses her. She says, "It's still too far to the right." He puts the electric star on top, strings the lights, plugs it all in and his wife and kids applaud.

Two Saturdays before Christmas, the family goes into London. They have split up, Jack taking Madeleine to buy a present for her mother and Mimi taking Michel to buy for his father. They are to meet up again across from the Laura Secord's in front of Simpson's, and trade. Madeleine buys a ceramic frog for her mother, its mouth open wide to hold a pot scrubber.

The street lights come on and, with them, the electric stars and giant candles that arch overhead and cast a multicoloured glow on the crowds below. Carols play over a loudspeaker mounted at the entrance to the market building, *Hark the herald angels sing.* . . . Madeleine holds her father's hand in its huge black glove, and the two of them gaze in the Simpson's window, where toys ride a train through a winter wonderland, teddy bears skate on a frozen pond, and a jazz combo of cats plays beneath a Christmas tree.

She chooses her words carefully. "Some kids in my class don't believe in Santa Claus."

Jack knows it's a test. "Oh? Why not?"

She presents the case against Santa: one sled could not hold all those presents, one person could never cover the globe in a single night. Jack responds by asking her to speculate as to the nature of time. Perhaps what we think is the present is really the past. Perhaps we can only perceive reality after it has happened, and in this way we are like the stars: reflections of what has already been. "That's why some people are clairvoyant—able to see the future. And it's why others are able to time-travel. Like Santa."

"So . . . we could be already dead now?" asks Madeleine.

Jack laughs. "No, nothing like that, what I mean is. . . ." He looks down at her. She's got him. He is suddenly pierced by the memory of a day long in the future—or perhaps already in the past—when she will grow up and leave him. No longer his little girl—the one who believes he has all the answers. Moisture gathers in the corner of his bad eye; he blinks it away and says, "I think we have to conclude that anything is possible. But that, if there isn't a Santa Claus, we should make one up anyway, and enjoy the idea."

"Do you believe in him?"

"I believe in the idea."

"Me too," she says, relieved—Christmas still intact, no need for her to lie.

At the clang of a bell nearby, they turn from the window to see a Salvation Army man. Jack reaches into his pocket for change just as Oskar Fried comes out of the market building, a newspaper under his arm, smoking his pipe. So the sonofagun does go out, he just prefers not to carry his own groceries. Jack is about to call out a greeting when his wife and son arrive—"No one is to look in any bags from now till Christmas," Mimi says, pretending to be stern, and he smiles. "How'd you fellas make out? Mission accomplished?"

Fried is crossing the street, he sees Jack and looks away. Jack is surprised by his own flush of anger. It feels like a slap, this rejection of Jack's goodwill, his entire family here on the Christmas sidewalk. It's an unreasonable reaction, Jack knows, but he is tempted to call out, "Merry Christmas, Oskar, *Fröhliche Weihnachten!,*" forcing the man to respond. Fried walks right past him, so close Jack can see his newspaper, the *Frankfurter Allgemeine Zeitung,* bought at the German deli. Jack says nothing. He allows Fried to disappear into the crowd.

Mimi says, "What is it, Jack?"

"Oh nothing. Thought I saw someone, but I didn't."

At home the four of them begin their tree-trimming party. The spruce has stood for a week with its lights strung and now it's time to dress it up. Mimi has brought the boxes up from the basement, and they sit open on the coffee table, their contents glittering. The decorations are like a core sample of McCarthy family history—old tinsel from three postings ago that the kids refuse to part with; delicate birds with feathered crests from the first year Jack and Mimi were married, bulbs with skiers etched in frost.

Jack is fixing an eggnog for Mimi when the phone rings. She answers it. "Another hang-up."

"Some crank." He hands her the drink. He makes no move to "go for a quick walk" and phone Fried back, but as he reaches for a decoration, he feels his wife looking at him. More of a glance, really. It's fleeting—his sense that she is waiting to see whether he will find a reason to leave the house. He feels himself colour and avoids turning around, saying to his son, "Flip the record, eh Mike?"

Jack selects a bulb in the shape of an acorn and repairs its tin hook. That miserable bastard has phoned again, despite Jack's request, his clear explanation, regarding using the home number only in an emergency. If he is lonely, facing a blue Christmas, all he has to do is agree to come home with Jack and meet the family. No, he prefers to behave like a thief in the night, a pervert skulking in the shadows. "Ouch!" Jack manages not to swear, but he is bleeding, a shard of the fragile acorn wedged in the tip of his thumb.

Mimi runs upstairs for a bandage, and Madeleine hands him one of the unbreakable snowballs to which she and Mike were restricted when they were little. "These are my favourite," she says, and he rubs her head.

Bing Crosby dreams of a white Christmas and soothes away the dregs of Jack's anger.

The next day, Jack calls from his office to find that Fried is out of pipe tobacco. "That's why you called my home?"

Silence.

"But you were at the market yesterday, Oskar, why didn't you pick some up?"

Fried says nothing and Jack can almost see him shrug. What's he playing at? Last week Jack found himself carting the guy's laundry down to the basement of the apartment building—Fried claimed not to understand how to use the coin-op washer. "It's not rocket science, Oskar." Jack had to time his shopping for Mimi's gift to coincide with the rinse cycle.

"I'll bring some by tomorrow," he says, and hangs up. He has to go into town anyway—for an honest-to-goodness meeting with an actual guest lecturer—he'll drop off the tobacco on the way.

The phone rings again. He grabs it, irritated. "McCarthy."

"Jack."

"Hi, sweetheart."

She asks him if he is going into London and at first he says no, then maybe, then "Do you need me to pick something up?" She needs marzipan for a torte she is baking for the Wives' Club charity bazaar, but it can wait. She asks him what he wants for supper and he responds genially, "*Macht nichts.*" It's a normal conversation, but he can't help wondering if she has called to check up on him. How many times has she phoned when he has been away from the office? How many times has she told his admin clerk, "It's not important, no need to tell him I called"? How many times has his admin clerk said, "I believe he's in London this afternoon, Mrs. McCarthy"?

He tries to focus on a stack of course reports. He will be taking work home again tonight. This is not what he's getting paid for. He has begun to feel as though he is cheating the government, not working for it.

Jack's Christmas leave starts next week. It has been a logistical nightmare tending to Fried under the cover of office hours; it will be virtually impossible during the holiday week. Something has to give. He doesn't bother to slip on his rubbers over his shoes. He walks out over a fresh dusting of snow, across the parade square toward the phone booth.

The last day of school before the Christmas holidays. The classroom is gaily decorated, windows are stencilled with aerosol frost, Rudolph's nose gleams at the head of Santa's sleigh, and cutouts of children celebrating Christmas in other lands adorn the wall above the blackboard. Mexican children flail blindfolded at a piñata. Dutch children overturn their wooden shoes in search of gifts. German children in lederhosen and dirndls light candles on a pine tree, normal-looking British children decorate a yule log and, somewhere in Canada, Indian children kneel reverently over a luminous manger in the forest.

Mr. March conducts with his pointer as the class sings "The Huron Carol." "'Twas in the moon of wintertime when all the birds had fled, the mighty Gitchee Manitou sent angel choirs instead. . . .'"

The song is beautiful, haunting, and happily Madeleine will not have to sing it with the school band. She prevailed over her mother in the battle about joining the Christmas choir, explaining that they practised with the band on Wednesday afternoons, thereby adding to the burden of Brownies in the evening as well as taking valuable time away from her accordion. She backed this up by practising tirelessly three days in a row. The result is that she is slated to play "Jingle Bells" in the Christmas concert, but it's a small price to pay.

"'Jesus, our king is born, Je-sus is born. . . .'"

Madeleine is being assailed faster and more furiously than ever by unbidden thoughts. For example, the word "ass" is in Christmas— unavoidable. What if she went home and threw the Baby Jesus in the garbage? Such thoughts are shocking, and she buries her face in her hands at her desk.

"Sleepy, little girl?"

She looks up sharply and turns to the assigned page.

"'O little town of Bethlehem, how still we see thee lie. . . .'" What if she took the Baby Jesus and touched her bum with it? What can she do about these thoughts? Pray. She tries, while singing, to ask God to remove the evil thoughts, but instead of white clouds and angels, the image of herself smashing a baby's head in with a hammer appears. Rudolph saves her. The sight of his bright red nose like a clown's; the memory of his fearless stand against the abdominal snowman, his humility and triumph on Christmas Eve. . . . She knows it is not right to pray to Rudolph, but the thought of him calms her mind, soothes it like Vaseline on a burn and renders it impervious to the assault of ter- rible thoughts.

"You should join the choir, little girl, you have good pitch," says Mr. March.

Jack was surprised how good it felt to hear Simon's voice. He put it as casually as possible—careful to keep any hint of complaint from his tone—that it might be wise to brief McCarroll at this point. Make Fried feel a little more secure, knowing there was a second car on hand, another number to phone. Or if not McCarroll, it might be time to bring Mimi into the loop—in fact she could help. She could visit Fried during the day, do a little shopping, cooking . . . as Jack spoke he began to like this idea more and more.

Simon said, "Bugger's driving you mad."

Jack laughed.

"I didn't warn you, Jack, because I didn't want to prejudice you, but I'm not surprised. He's working you like a bloody housewife."

"That's about the size of it."

"Look, you don't need to put up with it, I'll have a word with him and—"

"Forget it, Si, I think I know what his game is."

"Oh? What's that, then?"

"He wants a goddamn car."

"Christ." Simon groaned. "It's what he's been after from the start."

Fried had asked Simon for a car when he defected. "I told him, forget it. Too risky, too complicated. He could drive it into a ditch—"

"Or get pulled over for speeding."

"It opens up a whole new can of worms. An expensive one."

Jack surmised a series of false documents: driver's licence, registration, ownership, insurance, plates. "Who will you register it under?"

"I won't, simple as that."

"What about—?"

"Not your headache."

"Look Si, why don't I brief McCarroll? It's what he's here for anyhow, and between the two of us—"

But Simon preferred to take on the chickenshit task of wangling a car for Fried, rather than allow the Americans in a moment before it was absolutely necessary. He said it was because he wanted the operation to remain airtight. Briefing McCarroll would mean making it porous. That would mean air pockets. "And you know what that means."

"Turbulence," said Jack.

"Don't say I never gave you a Christmas present."

Midweek, Jack catches a quick flight on a Beechcraft Expediter to Toronto. He has lunch with his counterpart, the OC of the Staff School up on Avenue Road, and makes plans for an exchange. Then he takes a taxi out to Toronto International Airport. Following Simon's directions, he walks to the far northeast corner of the parking lot. Simon has worked quickly as usual. The 1963 metallic blue Ford Galaxy coupe is there waiting, just as Simon said it would be, with a brand-new set of Ontario plates. Jack opens the door, lifts the mat and finds the keys. It's a spiffy set of wheels, the kind he would like to buy for Mimi when they can afford a second car.

He gets in, puts on his sunglasses and pulls into the brilliant December day. He makes good time back to London, and when he arrives at Fried's apartment at dusk and drops the keys into the man's open hand, Fried actually forms a small smile and says, "*Danke.*"

"*Fröhliche Weihnachten, Oskar.*"

"*Fröhliche Weihnachten, Herr McCarthy.*"

He has the taxi drop him in the village of Centralia, just beyond the station and out of range of inquiring eyes, and gives the driver a decent tip.

The street lights come on, dispelling the five o'clock gloom as Jack rounds the corner, the snow squeaky cold beneath his rubbers. He fills his lungs with clean crisp air. Tomorrow is his first day of leave. He sees Henry Froelich out hammering a nail into his front door. Elizabeth is bundled up in her wheelchair, a pyramid of snowballs in her lap. She is throwing them at unpredictable angles for the dog, who leaps to catch them between his jaws, where they explode.

The words escape Jack's lips: "*Fröhliche Weihnachten, Henry!*" He feels himself redden instantly. Time to take the bull by the horns. He walks up the driveway.

"Hank, I'm sorry."

"For what?"

"Being such a . . . knucklehead."

"What do you mean?"

"I mean. . . ." He reddens again. He can't apologize for his stupid "You're a typical German, Hank" remarks because that gets too close to a painful, private subject—Jack knows about Froelich's tattoo only by accident.

"Jack, are you okay?"

"Yeah, Henry, I'm just—look, I only recently realized that—I realize you don't celebrate Christmas, so I'm sorry for—"

"But we do celebrate." Froelich hangs a wreath on his door. "My wife likes to celebrate the solstice."

"The solstice?"

"Festival of light. Like Chanukah."

"Oh. Happy Chanukah."

Froelich smiles. "Jack, I am a Jew. But I am not religious. You worry too much."

Jack relaxes. The scrape of a shovel catches his attention; he turns and notes with approval his son shovelling his driveway across the street. In Froelich's front yard, the big dog rolls on his back in the snow. Jack is ambushed by a rush of pure happiness. "Henry, I don't give a damn if you're pagan, Moslem, Hindu or from Mars, you and Karen are coming to the New Year's Eve formal with me and Mimi as our guests."

"No, no, this we do not—"

"*Aber ja!*" exclaims Jack, counting on his fingers, slapping them into his palm. "You've fixed my car, my lawnmower, filled me up with good homemade wine, it's time I had a chance to pay the piper."

Froelich is about to object again. The two men stand, eyes locked, and a twinkle of amusement enters Henry's. He shrugs. "What the heck. I mean, thank you."

When he tells Mimi the Froelichs are coming to the mess for New Year's, she gives him a Mona Lisa smile and turns back toward the kitchen.

"What is it?" he asks.

"*Rien du tout.* I think it's lovely you invited them."

He follows her. "You do not, what are you thinking, woman?"

She pauses at the stove, bites her lower lip—a touch of malice just enough to be sexy—and says, "I'm curious to see what she wears, *c'est tout.*"

"You're bad."

She lifts her eyebrows briefly, then turns and bends, a little more than she needs to, to check the mincemeat pies.

On Saturday the twenty-third, chaos reigns in the rec centre as the children's Christmas party gets underway, to the helium strains of *The Chipmunks' Christmas Album.* Flushed faces bulge with candy canes, grown-up voices cry above the din, "Don't run with that in your mouth!" A mountain range of wrapped gifts surrounds the towering Christmas tree, each package bearing a tag marked "girl" or "boy." Madeleine knows better than to bother opening one marked "girl" but she also knows not to court public humiliation by taking one marked "boy." She joins in the ecstatic mayhem of chasing and screaming. Every kid in the PMQs is there, and so are many from the surrounding community—including a busload of orphans who arrive with a detachment of nuns, all of whom seem to know Mrs. Froelich. For once, Madeleine plays with all her friends at once, including Colleen. She experiences a moment of trepidation when a genuinely rotund Santa Claus enters. But it isn't Mr. March, it's Mr. Boucher. "Ho ho ho, Merry Christmas, *Joyeux Noël!*"

On Christmas morning, Mimi opens a big box from the St. Regis Room of Simpson's and says, as she always does, "It better not be a you-know-what." It isn't a mink coat, but Jack has nonetheless courted her wrath with an extravagant silk negligée. Mike receives the supreme gift of walkie-talkies. Madeleine doesn't receive a weapon of any kind, but neither is she burdened with more dolls. Her booty includes a Mr. Potato Head, an Etch a Sketch, a toboggan, yo-yo, puppet theatre, *Alice's Adventures in Wonderland* and other treasures too numerous to mention—chief among them a psychology kit complete with white goatee, glasses, and ink spots.

Only one gift requires acting. It comes in a little blue Birks box, and Maman looks so pleased as Madeleine unwraps it that it makes her feel plungingly sad. The kind of sadness that is possible only on Christmas morning; your dear mother, smiling and hoping you will like the special present she has picked out.

A sterling silver charm bracelet. With one charm on it already— "That's just for openers," says Dad, pleased to be giving his little girl a young lady gift. *"Merci maman."* Madeleine compresses her lips into a smile, swallowing the lump in her throat.

Her mother fastens the bracelet onto Madeleine's wrist and her family admires it. She keeps it on for church, then takes it off to go tobogganing, returning it to its blue box on her dresser. Wondering how long she can go before having to wear it again, she closes the lid on the silver bracelet and its single charm—her name.

## FOR AULD LANG SYNE

On New Year's Eve, Jack is shaved, showered and Brylcreemed by five. He wipes fog from the mirror, dries the walls of the tub, sets out a fresh towel and hollers, "It's all yours, Missus."

Mimi is in her slip, taking curlers out of her hair, when the phone rings. Jack calls, "I'll get it!" and grabs it before either of the kids can answer. "Hello? . . . Oh . . . oh, that's too bad, Vimy. Yup, yup, not to worry, I'll tell her."

He puts his head in the bedroom door and says to his wife at her vanity, "That was Vimy Woodley. Martha's got the flu."

Mimi's hands fall to her sides, a freshly liberated curl droops and bounces. *"Merde!"* Without a babysitter, at the eleventh hour. She glares at him and says, "Marsha."

"What?"

"Oh never mind, Jack," and lets slip the ultimate Acadian curse word: "Goddamn!," smacking her thighs. She starts yanking out curlers and pitching them among the silver combs and brushes on her table.

"Wait now, sweetie, just keep doing what you're doing, I've got an idea." He kisses her bare shoulder. "Wear the No. 5 tonight, it's my favourite."

Jack hands Mike the Kodak Instamatic and a flash cube, and the boy positions his parents in front of the fireplace and the oil painting of the

Alps. Jack is in his formal mess kit—short blue coat with black bow tie, blinding white shirt front and black cummerbund. Blue pants with gold stripes down the sides, tapered at the ankle, where concealed stirrups cause them to fit snugly over the high-polish ankle boots that lack only a Cuban heel to render them utterly hip. Mimi is in an off-the-shoulder gown of silk in shades of green and gold, with a shimmering satin stole. Her hair is done, her face is radiant, eyelashes long, décolletée within the bounds of good taste and off the scale of sex appeal. *Flash*.

Then Mike snaps a picture of his parents with the Froelichs: Henry in a freshly pressed brown tweed jacket with suede patches at the elbow, his usual white shirt and black tie. Mimi discreetly observes every detail of Karen's attire: an open-weave shawl over a dress that appears to be essentially a floor-length turtleneck. The shawl is lumpy black, but the dress is composed of several dull reds and purples that seem to have bled into one another. She has brushed her long hair and applied two horizontal lines of red lipstick. Beaded earrings dangle from her lobes. On her feet, a pair of embroidered Chinese slippers. The dress manages somehow to be both dowdy and clinging. The woman is obviously not wearing a girdle; her slimness is no excuse, slimness is not the point, shape is.

Mimi had handed Karen a sherry when they arrived. "That's a very pretty dress, Karen."

"You think so? Thanks, Mimi," she replied, as though Mimi had just given her a present. "I got it at a thrift shop in Toronto." She nervously tucked a strand of hair behind her ear. Nice hands, short unpainted nails.

Henry kissed Mimi on both cheeks. "*Aber schön,* Frau McCarthy, you look ravishing."

"He's right, Mimi, you do," said Karen and, try as she might, Mimi could detect not a drop of malice in her tone.

"'Night-night kids," Jack says now and, in his most jovially man-to-man voice, "Help yourself to anything and everything, Rick."

"Except the liquor cabinet," jokes Karen.

Mimi hopes her smile doesn't look too pained.

The men help the women on with their coats, carry their shoe-bags for them, and the four of them bundle into the Rambler. Mike, Madeleine, Colleen, Ricky, Elizabeth and Rex look at one another in the living room. The twins are already sound asleep up on Jack and Mimi's bed, behind a barricade of pillows. Ricky says, "What do you guys want to do?"

No one says anything at first—Colleen and Elizabeth may be used to having Ricky around, but for Mike and Madeleine it's as though a god has descended from Mount Olympus.

They feast on hot dogs and Kraft dinner. Ricky and Mike play table hockey, violently jerking the handles while commentating from high above the Montreal Forum: "Hockey Night in Canada!" Ricky has brought a stack of forty-fives. Madeleine and Colleen make popcorn as Jay and the Americans blast. Ricky ransacks the upstairs closet for blankets and drags them down to the basement, where he empties the bookcase and tips it against the wall to form a lean-to. Madeleine looks at Mike, who stands by, hesitant, then says, "My dad doesn't let us do that."

"Do what?" asks Ricky, opening the duffel bag where the camping equipment is stored.

"Make shelters."

"It ain't a shelter, it's a fort." He drapes blankets and sleeping bags over the bookcase and the basement furniture. "'Sides, you're going to clean it all up before they get back." He tosses Mike a flashlight, says, "You're it," and turns off the lights. Madeleine yelps in spite of herself. They play hide-and-seek in the dark all over the house—except in Jack and Mimi's room. Madeleine has to change her pajama bottoms due to a slight accident brought on by terror and mirth. They jump on the beds and take turns shooting each other with Mike's cap gun, dying spectacularly; they try one by one to tackle Ricky but he is invincible, hurling each assailant onto a mattress. They have a pillow fight in the dining room; the oil painting of the Alps is knocked askew, the couch cushions are on the living-room floor. Rex, exhausted from rescue attempts and the vain effort to herd everyone into one room, yields finally to temptation and, as intoxicated as the others, chews one of Mimi's rubber spatulas. Through it all, Elizabeth sings, drops off, wakes up, listens while Madeleine reads aloud her Cherry Ames book, and falls out of her wheelchair reaching for an Orange Crush. "Lizzie, you're drunk!" says Ricky, mopping up the mess, opening another bottle of the best— Mountain Dew. "It'll tickle yore innards!" he howls.

The party is just getting started.

In the officers' mess, logs blaze in the great stone fireplace. The crystal chandelier glitters, reflecting light from candles on the dining tables, where sterling gleams on white linen amid opulent flower arrangements. Next to each place setting is a complement of noise-makers and a sparkly cardboard fez with a tassel. The buffet is resplendent. Lobsters in top hats perch on their tails, ice sculptures depict the Old Year and the New, platters of elaborately carved tropical fruit alternate with steaming chafing dishes; cooks in white chefs' uniforms and hats stand ready behind hips of beef and racks of lamb. Cocktails flow from the mirrored bar, waiters circulate with wine, there is punch from crystal bowls and, on the polished dance floor, a slow spin of silk butterflies and air force blue as couples swirl to the big band sounds of Gerry Tait and His Orchestra, all the way from Toronto. "'Pennsylvania Six-Five Thousand'!" Above the bandstand arches a silver banner: *Nineteen Sixty-Three*.

"You smell nice," says Jack. He can feel her smile, his chin touching the top of her hair.

It's all worth it. The constriction of his starched collar, the slight cinch of his waistband, for which he has no one to blame but himself—this monkey suit was nice and roomy only last year. He is already formulating a New Year's resolution to do with medicine balls and running shoes when Henry Froelich cuts in.

Mimi smiles and sweeps away with him. All the other civilians are dressed formally. But so is Hank, thinks Jack, admiring his neighbour's Old World deportment on the dance floor. True formality comes from within, and Henry Froelich outclasses everyone with his patched elbows. Jack watches them disappear into the crowd, then moves to the bar, buys a drink for Blair McCarroll and asks Sharon to dance.

He guides her onto the floor and it's like dancing with a pretty girl in high school to whom you are mercifully not attracted. She smiles shyly as Jack leads her in a samba, answering his questions with diffident charm and brevity; a light creature, pliable but not fragile, her laughter blithe when he spins her back to her husband. A sweet woman.

Jack raises his glass to Blair.

"Merry Christmas, sir."

"Call me 'Jack' tonight, son."

Jack tries to picture the look on McCarroll's face when he finally tells him why he is here. Will he be offended not to have been briefed sooner? Jack places his empty glass on the bar and scans the dance floor. McCarroll will probably just nod and do his job.

The band heats up: "In the Mood." Vic and Betty Boucher show what they can do and a space clears around them. Jack makes his way toward his wife as the number ends but Vic beats him to it. "She's my prisoner for the next five minutes, Jack."

He spots Steve Ridelle, looking just as relaxed in his mess kit as he would in a golf shirt and slacks. Elaine is glowing; her blonde hair is curled in a flip, and the pale blue folds of her satin gown do nothing to minimize her eight-month pregnancy. She looks like too much of a kid, even in that gown, to be pregnant. She is sipping a Bloody Mary, "Loaded with vitamins," she says to Jack, patting her stomach, as he comes up to greet them. He swings her onto the dance floor, over Steve's laughter and her protestations. "No! Jack! What'm I supposed to do? The Dance of the Baby Elephants?" He spins her and she is just as nimble as if she were in a pair of dungarees, minus the weight of the new world she's carrying.

Steve intercepts Mimi for the next dance and Jack concedes defeat. "I'm never going to get near my wife with you fellas circling all night."

"Take a number, Jack," says Hal Woodley.

Jack extends his hand to Hal's wife. To dance with Vimy Woodley is to dance with a real lady. She converses graciously but easily, and makes him feel special—an up-and-coming young man. He knows that her attitude is an extension of her husband's, and he can't help feeling gratified.

When Jack returns to his table, Karen Froelich is there nursing a Coke. Her lipstick has worn off. He has formulated a chivalrous invitation to the effect that he can't sit this one out when there's a beautiful woman right here in front of him, but says simply, "Would you like to dance, Karen?"

"Sure, Jack."

He holds out his left hand for her and slips his right hand around her waist. She is thin. But strong. No Playtex armour—he almost wonders whether he ought to be touching her. Gerry Tait sets aside his trumpet and sings, "Fly Me to the Moon."

They dance. She smells like soap. And something else . . . sandalwood? From this angle her mouth looks sad, the faint bracket at its corner, the trace of a smile. The beaded earrings are her only adornment. Along with the faint lines at the corners of her eyes. Nordic.

"Are you Icelandic?" he asks.

"Finnish. Somewhere back there."

"I can see you on a sled. With reindeer." Must be the Scotch talking.

She says, "You've got me confused with Santa Claus."

He laughs.

She says, "Nice work if you can get it. Hip to kids, live forever, have lots of helpers."

He laughs again.

He leads Karen back to the table just as Henry arrives with plates of food for the two of them. He watches Froelich bend and kiss his wife.

Henry sits and raises his glass. "Jack, this is a wonderful party. Thank you." Jack smiles and leaves them to eat, side by side, looking years younger in the candlelight.

Mimi looks at him over the rim of her martini glass and asks, "What were you and Karen Froelich talking about?"

He pulls her close, feels the crinkle of her dress against his stiff shirt front and whispers in her ear, "Santa Claus." She pinches his earlobe between thumb and fingernail. He takes her glass, sets it aside and steers her onto the floor, his palm against the warm small of her back. The band plays the song Jack requested. She relaxes into him and they dance. "Unforgettable, that's what you are. . . . "

He whispers, "I love you." Her scent, the softness of her hair, her dress, her breasts, even the chafing of his starched collar against his neck—"I want another baby," he says in her ear.

She lifts her hand to stroke the back of his neck.

Just before midnight, Mimi bows to popular demand. It seems her reputation has followed her from 4 Wing. After a suitable display of resistance, she mounts the stage, confers with Gerry Tait, then takes the microphone and sings. "'*Bei mir bist du schön,* please let me explain. . . .'"

Applause, laughter. Henry Froelich sings along, dancing in skater-size strides with Karen in the centre of the floor.

" . . . '*bei mir bist du schön* means you're grand. . . .'"

Mimi gets into it, head moving, fingers snapping: "'I could say *bella, bella,* even say *wunderbar!* Each language only serves to tell you, how grand you are! . . .'"

In the McCarthy living room, Elizabeth and Rex are sound asleep. Colleen, Madeleine and Mike are huddled cross-legged on the floor, a sleeping bag around their shoulders. Not once throughout the entire evening has anyone thought of turning on the TV. The Advent candles cast a magical glow as Ricky Froelich strums and sings softly, "'So hoist up the *John B.* sail. See how the mainsail sets. Call for the captain ashore, let me go home. . . .'"

The others join in. They sing so quietly it's as though they are in the middle of a forest, silent but for the scurries and hoots of busy night hunters. They sing softly so as to soothe but not wake the bears in their caves, the wolves in their dens, the rabbits in their holes. They sing so as neither to douse nor fan the glowing campfire, or shake more cold from the blue-black winter sky.

"'I feel so broke up, I want to go home. . . . '"

Ricky outlasts them all, picking out a tune while the others sleep in a pile of blankets and pillows on the floor. But by the time the wheels of the Rambler crunch slowly up the snowy driveway, only Rex wakes at the sound.

Jack and Mimi tiptoe up the stairs with the Froelichs right behind. They glimpse the clutter of the kitchen, where every pot and pan has been hauled out to help bang in the New Year, and stop in the living-room doorway. Mimi gestures to Karen to "come here." She slips her arm through Karen Froelich's and the women look in on their sleeping children. Flushed and tangled, Orange Crush moustaches, popcorn ground into the carpet, sleeping hands still clutching toys. Ricky is flaked out on the easy chair, his guitar across his knees. His eyelashes flutter; he raises his head, glances around and says, "Sorry 'bout the mess."

A week after New Year's, Jack drives to London with his daughter. They take a walk in Storybook Gardens. The animals have left for the winter and only the greenhouse is still open to visitors. The castle draw-bridge is closed but they slip in through snowy hedges and walk among the silent frolicking effigies. Humpty Dumpty teeters on his wall, wearing a pointed hat of snow; the witch beckons, her palm full of white powder—Madeleine takes care to avoid her eye. Icicles grow from Little Bo-Peep's staff, the Cow jumps over the Moon and the Dish runs away with the Spoon, heedless of the change of weather, still in their fairy-tale finery.

On the way home, Jack takes a detour through a winter-postcard neighbourhood, cruising slowly round the cul-de-sac of Morrow Street in the twilight. He hasn't been summoned here in weeks. In the third-floor corner window, the curtains are open, blue light plays on the glass and ceiling. On the street, one among a line of parked cars, is the bright metallic blue Ford Galaxy—on its rear bumper, a yellow sticker from Storybook Gardens. Jack pulls away. Let sleeping dogs lie.

REX FOUND HER. She was in a field beyond the ravine at Rock Bass, halfway between the cornfield and the woods. German shepherds are natural trackers. It's terrible what happens to a face after death by strangulation. He recognized her scent as being hers and not hers. The sight of her made him bark because, for Rex, it was as though she had put on a Halloween mask.

On her back, beneath a criss-cross of last year's bulrushes, clumps of bluebells, wildflowers, April showers. Hairband not askew. Eyes closed. Eyes do not naturally close in death by strangulation.

There is nothing peaceful or natural about the faces of people who have died that way. They look terrifying. A child's peaceful body, soft pixie cut, and a monster face. It's as though the evil of the person who killed her has leapt onto her face. She does not look like anybody's child. She does not look like anybody any more.

By MARCH IT SEEMS as though winter will never end. But the earth knows when spring must come, and already the unseen bluebells and lily of the valley are tipped with green, tenderly curled but stirring beneath the soil. Deer can smell the trickling water, and they paw the banks for new shoots; in their nests, birds await the miracle of the first beaks to breach their shells.

It is two and a half weeks before Easter but you can still feel winter. Yesterday was warmer and it rained, but Jack Frost is back today, that's what March is like. On the road there are still a few worms but they are frozen. Wormsicles. There is a certain kind of ice on the puddles at the side of the road, the thin glass kind, fracturing like a sugar pane when you delicately press your boot, smashing like a windshield when you jump. Later in the day, when it gets warmer, you will be able to push the puddle's barely frozen surface and see it wrinkle and fold like a sheet. Where there is bare earth and bumpy old grass, the clumps glitter cold, fine-crunching beneath your boot, grains of glass melting from the faint heat of your foot. These are the things of March.

In the park, Madeleine notices green spears piercing the brown and yellow patches amid the receding snow, tough little crocuses; and there is the whiff of thawing dog-doo, reappearing now in wells of granular old snow. It is still cold, but not so cold that you couldn't eat an apple outside and taste it. Not so cold that snot will freeze on your nose. Grown-ups say that March comes in like a lion and goes out like a lamb. What does that mean?

Today is the last Thursday in March. In two weeks it will be Holy Thursday. Then it will be Easter Sunday, and that means chocolate bunnies and hunting for Easter eggs—the end of Lent. Maman has been very impressed by Madeleine's abstinence from candy, especially chocolate. But she'd had plenty of practice with the Mr. March candy. In a way Madeleine has cheated, because Lent is supposed to be hard. It occurs to her now that if she had really wanted to give up something important, she could have put her Bugs Bunny away for forty days.

She stops halfway down St. Lawrence Avenue, on her way to school, and takes a deep breath. Bugs would smother, because where would he be? In a closet? In a drawer? In the dark. No. After forty days of suffocating on his own, having no one to tell his jokes to, how could Madeleine expect they could ever be friends again? Now that would be something. To give up Bugs entirely. To give him away to a needy child overseas. To love Jesus more than Bugs. Oh no.

She crushes some icy mud into chocolate milk with her galoshes. She has never thought about it in this way before. If she is not willing to give up Bugs, does that mean she loves him more than Jesus? More than God? Who is God? He is an angry person who loves you. Does He want her to sacrifice Bugs? God sacrificed His only son, that's why we have Easter. It is blasphemy even to compare Jesus to Bugs Bunny. Bugs on the cross. *Now I've hoid everything.* Turning bread into carrots. Madeleine walks on, trying not to think these thoughts, *sorry dear God.* Jesus is supposed to be the one at your side, the one you talk to, not Bugs. Just as your guardian angel is always at your side. A huge silvery person who hovers, waiting for you to be run over or fall off a bridge. Madeleine knows that even though they are supposed to protect you, your guardian angel would like nothing better than to take you straight up to heaven while you are still a child with a pure white soul. God loves the souls of children best of all. They are his favourite. Yum. Like the giant in "Jack and the Beanstalk," and that is another bad thought because you should not think about God in that way. *Fee-fie-fo-fum.* Think of kind Jesus—*suffer the little children.* Madeleine slows down, out of range of her own house, still too far from the school—maybe someone's mother will let her use their bathroom. All of a sudden she has to go.

What if God wants her? There is nothing you can do if God wants you. There is nowhere to hide, it's like an air raid only worse because God is everywhere, especially in an air-raid shelter. When people get a vocation, they hear a voice saying, "Be a nun"—or if they are a boy, "Be a priest"—and there is nothing they can do, they have to be one. Because it's God's voice speaking. Forget it if you wanted to be on Ed Sullivan instead of in a convent. Forget it if you are too young to die, there are plenty of child martyrs, they perform miracles all the time, creepy little happy dead kids.

Madeleine starts to run.

Down St. Lawrence Avenue she runs, toward the schoolyard, where the crowd of kids jumbles like a plate of Smarties in an earthquake, running with her schoolbag banging against her back, listening to the March wind in her ears, straining to hear the playground screams that will drown out the Voice of God; running so fast that her throat begins to ache, outrunning her guardian angel winging behind now in pursuit with his or her huge sad face at the thought of how Madeleine will be run over in a minute, and how her pure white soul will be carried lovingly up to God. At this thought she stops running. Sputters to a walk, her heart still pounding. Unzips her quilted jacket— even though you might get pneumonia if you open your jacket in the cold while you're sweating.

She catches her breath and does not even turn around to see if her guardian angel is there. Because she is in no immediate danger of death or even a vocation. It's okay. She has just remembered that her soul is not pure white. It's yellowish. Like an old sheet. Because of the things from last fall. When she was little. The exercises. Don't think about them, just remember, it's okay. Your soul is not pure white.

She walks toward the school, her heart beating normally now. Her underpants feel wadded and damp and she hopes it is just sweat. The bell goes as she steps from the street onto the squishy field, and she sees the lineups filing in. She starts skipping, because when you are out of breath from running it's amazing how easy it is to skip and never get tired, and it's almost as fast as running. She arrives just in time to join the end of the grade four line as it files in the front doors past Mr. March, who says, "You're looking particularly blithe this morning, Miss McCarthy."

Up ahead, Auriel turns around and plugs her nose, and Lisa makes a Mr. March triple chin, so that Madeleine has difficulty keeping a straight face. She says, "Thank you Mr. March," and recognizes in her own voice an echo of Eddie Haskell's on *Leave It to Beaver*.

Once in the classroom, Madeleine sits at her desk and is relieved to note that her underpants have dried already—that's how you can tell if it's just sweat and not pee. Up at the front, an immense single-layer chocolate cake sits on Mr. March's desk, dotted with eleven candles that look as sparse as trees on a prairie.

"My wife made this cake."

Mrs. March. Picture him lying on top of her.

He removes the Saran Wrap and licks his thumb. "Would the birthday girl please rise?"

Grace Novotny gets up, tastes the corner of her mouth and grins at the floor. The class sings "Happy Birthday" with the gusto of nine-year-olds who know they are about to have cake. Philip Pinder and a couple of other boys sing, "You look like a monkey and you smell like one too."

Mr. March lights the candles. "Would the birthday girl please proceed to the front of the class?"

Grace has gotten tall. You don't usually notice how everyone has grown until after the summer holidays, but Grace had a growth spurt over Christmas—at least now she is growing into some of the clothes she has to wear.

Madeleine is grateful to be herself. How could anyone bear to be Grace Novotny? She has grown breasts, Madeleine can see them, like little dunce caps on her chest. Tits. She has already been given a titty-twister by Philip Pinder. She cried. Titty-twisters are very painful, boys give them to each other all the time, grabbing the flesh around each other's nipples and wrenching. Grace's new breasts are another thing that makes everyone else in the class, even Marjorie and Philip, seem clean. Whereas something swampy is happening to Grace.

The vast cake blazes on Mr. March's desk. "Well don't just stand there, little girl. Blow."

Grace blows and blows until her germs have covered every inch of the cake.

Mr. March cuts it into thirty pieces, remarking, "Mrs. March has never had to make such a big cake before." Madeleine wonders what his wife looks like. Is she fat too? Could she eat no lean?

Everyone files up to receive a slice on blotting paper. They eat silently. Some don't eat their icing and it's obvious why: germs. Madeleine can't bring herself to eat hers at all. Two rows over, Claire McCarroll is eating only the icing.

Madeleine closes her eyes and tries not to smell cake.

"What's the matter, little girl, don't you like chocolate cake?"

"I'm not hungry," replies Madeleine. Besides, it's still Lent.

He is standing over her. "Since when has hunger ever had anything to do with it when it comes to chocolate cake?" The class laughs politely.

Mr. March takes her cake, breaks it in two and gives half each to Marjorie and Grace.

A half-hour later, they are in the middle of a spelling exercise, working quietly at their desks, when Grace gets up to sharpen a pencil and Madeleine sees blood on the back of her skirt.

"Grace," says Madeleine, out loud.

Mr. March looks up.

Grace turns around to face Madeleine. "What?" And Mr. March sees what Madeleine saw, so does the front half of the class. A gasp goes up.

"You hurt yourself," says Madeleine, trying to be polite.

"Little girl," says Mr. March. Grace knows he is talking to her so she turns to face him, and the whole back half of the class gasps. She turns again quickly, as though stung by a bee, loose pleats flying; craning her neck, she sees the back of her skirt and screams. Wails. Some other girls start crying too and a couple of boys start laughing. Everyone else just stares. Blood. From someone's bum. Lisa Ridelle has dropped her head between her knees—her father is a doctor, he has told her what to do when she feels faint. Grace sobs, her mouth wide open, clear saliva spilling down the corners, eyes veering from the bloodstain to Madeleine, as though Madeleine had something to do with it.

"Silence," says Mr. March, then a shocking *smack!*—the yardstick across his desk. Grace is silent. "This little girl belongs at home," he says. "Hands?"

He is asking for someone to walk Grace home with her bleeding bum, why doesn't he just call an ambulance? Grace is staring at Madeleine as though Madeleine were a speck on the horizon, a ship. Oh no. Madeleine can feel it. She is going to raise her hand. *See? You should have given up Bugs for Lent, now you must make a sacrifice and walk Grace Novotny home.* Madeleine feels her hand rising from the desk—

"Marjorie Nolan," says Mr. March. "Walk this little girl home."

Everyone looks at Marjorie. She doesn't move. No one does. Grace is whimpering, walking slowly toward the coat hooks, clutching the back of her skirt to hide the spot.

"Slow as molasses in January," says Mr. March. Grateful laughter from the class. "Miss Nolan?" says Mr. March.

Marjorie gets up and walks briskly to the back, puts on her jacket, zips it up and waits with folded arms while Grace removes her cardigan from its hook and ties the sleeves around her waist so it will hang down and hide the stain.

"All right grade fours, the show is over, turn to page forty-one in your Macmillan spellers."

Madeleine sneaks a look back. Grace will freeze with not even her cardigan on. Madeleine gets up without permission, gets her own jacket and gives it to Grace. Grace puts it on without a word, like a sleep-walker, and leaves.

Madeleine walks back to her desk. Now everyone is looking at her. Mr. March says, "Behold the good Samaritan."

Laughter. Everything feels normal again. Madeleine takes a bow.

"Thank you Miss McCarthy, you may sit down now."

He doesn't sound angry. He sounds the way he always does. As though compelled to mock something that makes him very weary indeed.

Grace returns to school after lunch with a different skirt on. At recess she stays in and feeds the gerbil a piece of lettuce—Sputnik almost died because Philip Pinder drove him across the floor like a Dinky Toy.

Grace has been looking after him ever since. At two minutes to three, Mr. March picks up his clipboard. "The following little girls. . . ." They have all started to fish out their homework from their desks—everyone except Joyce Nutt, Diane Vogel, Marjorie and Grace. He has started calling them "monitors." No one wonders any more what they do, it is just a fact of Mr. March's class.

Madeleine puts away her speller and hauls out her arithmetic book, dreading tonight's homework—they have progressed from the purgatory of word problems to the hell of integers. "Joyce Nutt"—gone the friendly disguise of narrative. How could a word story describe what these numbers do? They go through the looking glass. The ghosts of real numbers, they live underground—"and Diane Vogel." Madeleine looks up. Something is different. Mr. March sits down. The bell goes. Ecstatic scraping of chairs—

"In an orderly fashion, boys and girls."

Madeleine zips up her jacket and sees that Marjorie and Grace have remained at their desks. Mr. March didn't read out their names, that's what is different. Still, Marjorie waits with her hands folded in front of her. Grace's mouth hangs open slightly, she is twirling her hair and looking at Marjorie.

Madeleine is pulling on her rubber boots when Mr. March says, "Little girls, did you hear your names?" Grace giggles. Marjorie's profile turns pink.

"Well?" says Mr. March, his voice droll. "Run along then. Your presence is not required."

Madeleine watches Marjorie rise slowly from her desk. Grace follows. As Marjorie turns, her gaze meets that of Madeleine, who is surprised to see that Marjorie's customary smug expression has deserted her. In its place is a look of pure bewilderment. Madeleine experiences a pang of sympathy, but the next instant Marjorie's eyes narrow maliciously and she sticks out her tongue. Madeleine leaves quickly by the side door.

The sun feels so warm, suddenly it's like summer. Over on the swings is Claire McCarroll. She has folded her pink raincoat on the ground next to her schoolbag. She is swinging, not high but happily. Madeleine ditches her own jacket and schoolbag on the ground. She has made a decision. Do not try to be nice to Marjorie, and do not try to be mean. It all backfires. The trick is not to be anything to Marjorie Nolan. Something slips away as Madeleine climbs onto the swing next to Claire's.

"Hi Madeleine."

"Hi Claire."

Madeleine swings higher, and as she does she kicks off one of her red boots. Claire laughs and kicks off one of her pink ones. Madeleine kicks off her other boot. Then so does Claire.

Grace and Marjorie scuttle past, looking pointedly at Madeleine over their shoulders, whispering behind their hands. Marjorie has her Brownie notebook out and is writing in it, but Madeleine doesn't care. Why did she ever? She tilts back and hangs upside down, pumping her swing higher and higher, feeling her hair flying at the nape of her neck like grass. Claire McCarroll follows suit, and soon they are laughing, because it is so easy to laugh when you are upside down.

## Sleeping Dogs

*Anyone who has been tortured, remains tortured.*

*Primo Levi,* The Drowned and the Saved

"Dora!" Henry Froelich cries out the word that springs, not to mind, but straight to his mouth. The man turns and looks at him, past him, unrecognizing, searching the crowded marketplace for the source of the single word that forced him round. Froelich was showing his baby boy the puppies asleep in a heap in the window of the pet store when he turned and saw the face. "Dora!" Again the word flies from his throat, as though dislodged by force. This time the man looks straight at him. No flash of recognition, but fear in the pale eyes. Then he turns and hurries away.

Froelich follows but loses him in the crowd—no matter, he knows where the man must be heading, so he hugs his baby closer to his chest and fights his way upstream toward the wide entrance of the Covent Market building in London. By the time he gets there, the man is already across the street, head down under his fedora, getting into a blue car—a 1963 Ford Galaxy coupe. Froelich can tell that much without his glasses, but what about the licence number? He grabs for his glasses, clawing his breast pocket, the left, the right, frantic at the inside one— and almost drops his child.

Across the street, he sees the car climb the sidewalk in reverse and come to a sudden stop against a parking meter before jolting forward again. Froelich gives up on his glasses, leaves the building, trots along the sidewalk parallel with the traffic and the car, which is gathering speed. The baby starts crying. Froelich runs faster, slipping in his shoes on the icy sidewalk, cupping his hand around the child's head— screaming now—straining for a glimpse of the licence plate. Cars pass, punctuating his view like frames in a reel of film, making him dizzy. He glimpses a blur of blue numbers and letters—an Ontario plate—is that an O, an X? or is it a Y?—and next to it, folded in the brand-new dent, is a bumper sticker. He doesn't need his glasses to recognize it. Bright yellow, etched with the silhouette of a castle. Storybook Gardens.

The car picks up speed through an amber light. Froelich stops in his tracks; he has found his glasses. They lie broken on the sidewalk at his feet. They were pushed back on his head the whole time. His baby is red-faced, tears and mucus streaking his face. "*Shhh, shh, kleiner Mann, sei ruhig, ja, Papa ist hier.*" But it's no good. Froelich is weeping too.

On his way back to his own car, he makes a decision. He will tell his wife about seeing this man. But he will tell no one else. This means he will not tell the police, even though it's clear this man must be in the country under false pretences and therefore illegally—but so are thousands of others. The government has turned a blind eye and, in some cases, recruited such men as immigrants—for whatever else these men are, they are not Communists. Henry knows; he waited years for a chance to emigrate to Canada, while men with SS tattoos under their arms received passage and the promise of jobs. But he has enough—his children have enough—to cope with, never mind taking on the past. To report this man would not only be futile; it would be to exhume what is cold and can never heal. To haunt his new family with the inconsolable griefs of his old one.

He places his baby, asleep now, into the basinette in the back seat, and tries to remember where he was going next. The orphanage, to pick up Karen. He gets behind the wheel. His wife, his children—he himself—living monuments to hope. The only possible response. Heinrich Froelich is an atheist. He pauses before he starts his car, still weeping, to thank God for his blessings.

Diefenbaker's government was brought down in February, over his refusal to take American nuclear weapons, and Monday, April 8, is election day. Jack has just been to the rec centre and voted. He has a feeling of vindication, as though by a single vote he has struck a decisive blow.

He is fresh from a weekend, just he and Mimi. They stashed the kids with the Bouchers and went to Niagara Falls for their anniversary. He is relaxed and happy, spring has rolled in and, like a Hollywood studio team, Mother Nature has worked overtime, transforming the dregs of dreary winter into vivid spring, seemingly in the space of a day. In the poplars overhead, fat buds are ready to yield to the next warm breath; tulips bloom on the grounds of his building; and on the parade square, a flight of cadets in gym shorts jogs by. Soon there will be a wings parade and the cadets will leave the Centralia nest. This weekend Jack will see whether or not his fitness regimen has paid off, when he squeezes back into his mess kit for a formal dinner in honour of a visiting air vice-marshal.

He enters his office to find a message on his desk. "Mr. Freud called. Call back ASAP," and Fried's telephone number. He shakes his head— "Freud." That's about the size of it. He finds himself looking forward to hearing old Oskar's reedy voice, it's that nice a day, and as he picks up the phone he wonders to what he owes the honour of a call. Freud would say it was all Fried's mother's fault. He dials. Pictures what Fried's mother must have looked like—like Fried in a bonnet.

The phone is answered on the first ring. The cautious voice. "Hello?"

"Hi Oskar, it's Jack."

He enjoys annoying Fried by calling him Oskar. Not only has Fried never invited him onto a first-name basis; Oskar, being an alias, is bound to be a double irritant.

"I have been recognized," says Fried.

"What?" says Jack. "Recognized? By whom?"

"I do not know."

"What do you mean?"

"Search *me,*" he says earnestly.

Jack almost laughs aloud—Fried has been watching too much television.

"Where, when?"

"I was to the market on Saturday and I call you immediately and all throughout the *Wochenende*—how says one—?"

"Weekend."

"*Ja,* but you are not at home."

"Just tell me what happened, Oskar."

"I get away, I do not hesitate."

"So someone saw you and you have no idea who he is or where he's from?"

"I know where is he from."

"Where?"

"I don't tell you this."

"Oskar, how am I going to help you if—"

"Tell Simon I am recognized."

"Did this man call you by name?"

"He calls me by a name."

"What name?"

"I recognize this name, this is how I know—"

"Is it your name, or not?"

Silence.

"Sir," says Jack, "I don't care what your real name is and you don't have to tell me, just tell me if this fella called you by your real name."

"No," says Oskar, and Jack can almost see him licking his dry lower lip. "He does not say my name."

Jack can feel the fear through the phone. He speaks gently. "Good, that's good, now tell me, what was the name by which he called you?"

Silence again.

Jack is worried, but he is also weary. Oskar Fried does not understand the chain of command; the fact that, in the absence of Simon, Jack for all intents and purposes *is* Simon. Not merely the delivery boy.

Fried hesitates, then says, "Dora."

"'Dora?' Why would he call you that?"

"He is from Dora."

"Dora sent him? Who is Dora?" His wife? A KGB agent? Jack waits for Fried to answer. "Oskar? Who is Dora?"

"You are not qualified me to—you are not qualified to interrogate me."

Jack bites his tongue and squints. Stay cool. Fried is frightened. Terrified of being taken back to the Soviet Union.

Fried says, "Tell Simon, 'Dora'. He understands this. You tell him to call me on the telephone."

"Fine. Meantime, just sit tight, Oskar—"

"Sit—?"

"Don't leave your apartment. No drives."

"I do not drive, he sees the car."

"The car?"

"I am running to my car, he follows, he sees."

The licence plate. Whoever saw it may see it again. May go looking for it. May find it on Morrow Street, in front of Fried's apartment building. . . . "Where's the car now, Oskar?"

"I park behind the building."

"Good. Now don't worry. You were spotted—you were recognized on Saturday. That's two days ago. If anything were going to happen it would've happened by now—"

Jack speaks with more certainty than he feels, but it is not an unreasonable deduction. He feels a stab of guilt—he should not have allowed himself to be lulled by the silence of the past few months. He ought to have stayed sharp. On alert. He ought to have given Fried the phone number of the honeymoon suite at the Holiday Inn in Niagara Falls.

Jack is about to hang up, he has to call Simon—

"I need food," says Fried.

Jack drops his head to his hand. "Weren't you just at the market on Saturday, sir?"

"Yes, I am recognized before I buy."

Jack sighs, reaches for his pencil and a pad of government foolscap, reflecting as he does that Simon will probably instruct him to move Fried immediately, straight over the bridge to Buffalo—there may be no time for groceries. He is already thinking of excuses for Mimi as to why he has to drive to London tonight as he says, "Fire away."

"I beg your pardon?"

"What groceries would you like me to bring?"

On the other hand, Jack may not have to do another thing but brief McCarroll. It's typical, he thinks ruefully; the American gets to ride in at the last second and take the credit. McCarroll will spirit Fried away to Wright-Patterson Air Force Base and receive a hero's welcome. No matter. The main thing now is to keep Fried safe. And calm. He listens and writes. "Butter, yup . . . mustard, yup I know, hot. . . ."

The list is lengthy and detailed—Fried's encounter with "Dora" seems to have done nothing to blunt his appetite. Jack scribbles. "Slow down, now. . . . Camembert and . . . what? Where am I going to find cherries? They'll cost a fortune this time of—okay, what else?"

He glances up to see Vic Boucher standing in the doorway with a grin on his face, how long has he been there?

Jack winks at Vic and says into the phone, "Yeah I'll make sure they're fresh. . . ." Vic wanders in, a sheaf of papers under his arm, and idly glances at Jack's grocery list upside down. Jack writes "celery" instead of the brand of pipe tobacco Fried has asked for, and wishes he had closed his door.

On the other end of the line, Fried says, "Caviar."

Jack reacts in spite of himself. "Caviar?"

Vic looks to the ceiling and mimes a whistle. Jack grins and shakes his head in response.

"That is all," says Fried, and hangs up.

Jack maintains his smile, and says into the phone, "Me too. Bye-bye sweetheart," and hangs up.

"Gotta hand it to Mimi," says Vic. "That girl's got champagne taste."

"Goes with my beer-bottle budget."

Vic asks Jack's opinion on the best case study to wrap up the semester, and Jack regrets his annoyance—this, after all, is his real job. Fried is the intrusion, not Vic. When Vic leaves, he takes the list from his pocket. Celery? He doesn't recall Fried asking for—oh yes, celery was code for pipe tobacco, but what was the brand again?

He pockets the list, grabs his uniform jacket and leaves his office, going over the situation methodically in his mind so that he will be able to communicate it clearly and simply to Simon. He can think of a number of reasons not to be unduly alarmed. If the unknown man at the marketplace was KGB and the Soviets have had Fried under surveillance, why call out to him in public? And, having done so, how likely is it that a KGB agent would lose Fried so easily in the market crowd? As he trots down the steps, he takes a deep breath of April air and looks up past the treetops into the blue puffed with white that might still turn to snow. Likely it wasn't KGB. Unless the grocery delivery is a trap. The poplars rustle the way they do, making the most of the slightest breeze. Jack's face has become hot but he considers it coolly. "Dora" could be anybody. Or anything. What does Jack know about this operation? Very little that's concrete. Simon has told him that Fried is a Soviet scientist, and Jack has surmised that his specialty is rockets. He realizes that he has likewise assumed that Simon is MI6, but it dawns on him now that Simon has never been specific: subtly fostering those assumptions while neither confirming nor denying them. The only thing he has spelled out is the necessity of keeping Blair McCarroll in the dark.

Jack reaches the open asphalt of the parade square and sighs inwardly, digging in his pocket for dimes. This adventure comes too late. All he can think is, what will Mimi and the kids do if anything should happen to him?

"British Embassy, good morning," the polite female voice with the Queen's English.

"Good morning, may I have First Secretary Crawford please."

"May I ask who is calling please, sir?"

"Major Newbolt." Jack feels foolish using the code name, but it's according to the procedure Simon laid down. "Newbolt" means urgent. This qualifies.

"How's she going, Jack?"

"Si, we got a bit of a gremlin."

"You at work?"

"I'm at the booth."

They hang up and Jack waits for the phone to ring. It is mid-morning, the parade square is deserted—everyone is in classrooms, of either the concrete or the cockpit variety. He glances up through the glass of the booth and watches three Chipmunks bank in formation. McCarroll is probably up there right now, in the instructor's seat of one of those little yellow kites. The phone rings, giving him a start. He picks it up. "Hi."

"Fire away, mate."

"Our friend has been recognized."

"By whom?"

"A man at the marketplace, he doesn't know who—"

"Did he call Fried by name?"

"According to Fried, whoever it was called out the name 'Dora.'" Jack waits for a response, but continues when none is forthcoming. "That's all I could get out of him. He wouldn't tell me who 'Dora' is, he said you would know."

"When was this?"

"Saturday."

"Well," says Simon, "whoever it was, it wasn't a Soviet or we'd know by now so that's one for us, although it is rather important our friend sit tight for the moment."

"I told him that."

"Good. Now we may have to accelerate the process somewhat." Jack is reassured by Simon's light, even tone, rapid but not rushed.

"You want me to brief my opposite number?"

"Mm."

"When?"

"Oh, now's as good a time as any."

Jack can feel Simon about to end the conversation so he says, "I guess you're not worried about this woman?"

Simon laughs. "Dora was a factory, mate."

"A factory? Where, in Germany?"

"Yes."

"During the war?"

"That's right."

"Never heard of it." Jack wishes he could take that back, aware it sounded defensive, even suspicious.

"Well you wouldn't have, it was a code name, as it happens. For their rocket factory."

"The V-2? That was Peenemünde."

"We bombed Peenemünde, so they took it underground and called it Dora."

Jack is pleased. Assumption confirmed. Fried is a rocket scientist.

"By the way, who's winning?" asks Simon.

"Who's—?"

"Will Diefenbaker hang on?"

"Oh," says Jack. "Naw, I think he's had it. Least I hope so. Look, Fried wants me to bring him groceries, should I tell him to pack his bags instead?"

"Don't tell him anything, I'll have a word. I think I know what's happened. Just bring what he wants as usual, no panic."

"Simon."

"Yeah?"

"How can you be so sure this fellow from Dora isn't Soviet? The fact they haven't moved on Fried might mean they're biding their time. Watching him."

There is the merest hesitation, then Simon says, "Because the Soviets don't realize Fried has defected. They think he's dead."

" . . . Oh."

"That's how we got him out and closed the loop behind him. If the KGB were looking for him despite that, I'd've heard from our people in the East by now. There'd have been a bit of fall out. Canaries in the coal mine."

" . . . So everything's still basically in working order," says Jack.

"Everything's tickety-boo."

And they hang up. Simon didn't sound perturbed. But he never does.

Jack leaves the booth but doesn't head back to his building; he walks in the opposite direction, toward the Primary Flying School—where he will find McCarroll.

So he was right, Fried worked on the V-2 rocket—the first ballistic missile, precursor to the Saturn rocket that is the West's best hope of propelling the Apollo astronauts to the moon "before this decade is out." He shivers—a surge of energy intensified by the raw spring air. Oskar Fried must have worked side by side with Wernher von Braun. This more than makes up for any minor annoyance Jack may have endured at Fried's hands. He nears the massive hangars that border the airfield and heads for Number 4, which houses the PFS.

Dora. An underground factory. The Germans had several of them—

twelve-storey palaces beneath the pines, turning out Messerschmitts till the bitter end. Feats within feats of engineering. Even greater feats of pure management—the genius of Albert Speer. Jack strides into the hangar; steel rafters arch high overhead causing him to feel suspended as he glances up. Underfoot is the smooth certainty of concrete. He follows a makeshift corridor between prefab classroom walls.

Has Fried been recognized by someone from Dora? A fellow scientist? Fried is paranoid, trained by the Soviet system to be constantly looking over his shoulder, but it's entirely possible that the man who called out to him did so innocently, at the sight of a familiar face whose name had escaped memory with the passage of years. It might have been intended as a friendly greeting—knowing Fried, he likely couldn't tell the difference.

Through open doors Jack sees aircraft parts laid out on tables, blackboards scrawled with meteorological terms and, in another room, the good old Link Trainer—sawed-off little simulator with its hood for blind approach training. Not all that much has changed since Jack's day. He stops at McCarroll's office door and taps on the glass.

An admin clerk looks out of the next office. "Sir, if you're looking for Captain McCarroll he's gone till Wednesday."

"Gone, eh? Where's he gone to?" What's the good of having an opposite number if he's not here when you need him?

"He's in Bagotville, sir."

"Bagotville?"

"I believe he's getting his time in on the Voodoo, sir."

Of course. Bagotville is an operational station with a training unit. McCarroll is keeping his flying skills honed at a thousand miles per hour. A great deal has changed since Jack's day.

"Good enough," he says to the clerk.

Back at his own building, Jack walks down the hallway, hearing the blunted sound of his heels along the linoleum. He could be anywhere. No doubt the halls of the Pentagon are paved with the same drab flecked squares. Not to mention the Kremlin. Someone has made a fortune.

He is no longer in a hurry, and as he tosses his hat onto the hook he's aware of feeling slightly crestfallen. He had looked forward to briefing McCarroll. Seeing the young man's eyes light up at the mention of rockets; his sense of vindication when he realizes that this posting was not in fact a lateral move, but an honour. It will have to wait till Wednesday.

He calls Fried and the man sounds calmer, having just spoken with Simon. Jack asks if he can possibly wait till Wednesday to get his groceries—Jack has remembered his son's first baseball game of the season this evening, and tomorrow he has back-to-back meetings followed by a bridge night out for Mimi. Besides, McCarroll will be back and he can take him to meet Fried. Kill two birds. . . .

"Yes, Wednesday is fine," says Fried.

Jack is taken aback. Fried sounds not just polite but friendly. He is either tremendously relieved, or scared silly.

He leans back in his oak swivel chair, rests a foot against the edge of his desk and looks out the window. High above, a jet stream coils and comes undone. McCarroll is somewhere up there. Getting his time in.

Grace is not the quiet type any more. Ever since she and Marjorie were kicked out of the exercise group, they have been thick as thieves. Marjorie no longer even attempts to skip with Cathy Baxter's group, and Grace has acquired the disgusting new habit of sucking her fingers, stroking her tongue and smearing the wetness around and around her mouth. Her lips look permanently sore, too red, as though they would taste tangy to her, and her eyes swerve as though she has been caught at something and is in a panic to pin it on someone else. She cries if a grown-up so much as says, "Grace," in a questioning tone of voice.

Marjorie has her Brownie notebook and pencil out. "We're reporting you, Madeleine."

Madeleine replies scornfully, "Reporting to who, pray tell?"

"None of your beeswax," replies Marjorie with a toss of her stiff yellow ringlets. Grace giggles. She is carrying Marjorie's baton.

By noon the clouds had rolled in and by three o'clock it had started to rain. Everyone else has run for home, but Madeleine doesn't want to give the impression that she is running away.

"I'm warning you, Madeleine McCarthy."

Just ignore them.

"Yeah," says Grace.

Madeleine is taken aback at that. How can someone you felt sorry for, and were recently so kind to, suddenly be so disrespectful of you?

"You stink, Madeweine."

"Do you hear me?" says Marjorie.

"Do you hear me?" repeats Madeleine.

"You're in big trouble, Madeleine."

"You're in big trouble, Madeleine."

"Shut up!"

"Shut up!"

Madeleine knows she should resist the temptation to torment Marjorie. Poor Margarine, with a sleeve full of Brownie badges and a retard for a friend. If you really want to be a good person, you will seek out those you can't stand and befriend them. That's what Jesus did. Bad women, and money changers. Madeleine is contemplating the radical notion of turning and extending her hand with a holy smile on her lips when she hears Marjorie behind her, "Get her, Grace."

The blow strikes her across the shoulder blades, knocking the wind out of her and causing her to stumble forward. She turns to see Grace holding the baton like a baseball bat, swervy eyes lit with excitement. Marjorie stands with her arms folded, a resigned, even regretful expression on her face. "It's your own fault." Madeleine's mouth is open but she is silent, and for an instant so is the whole world. The air looks sharper. It's as if the shock of the blow has propelled the three of them to a different place.

Grace glances at Marjorie, as though waiting for the order to strike again. Madeleine looks from one to the other and the words slip through her lips like a letter through a slot: "Nyah, what's up, doc?"

Grace giggles.

Marjorie says, "Quit it Madeleine."

"Quit it," says Grace.

Madeleine bobs and weaves like a monkey: tongue jammed behind her upper lip, eyes bugging out, limp fingers scratching her armpits.

"Stop it!" yells Marjorie.

Grace swings the baton and connects with the back of Madeleine's calves. It stings and Madeleine feels tears spring to her eyes. She straightens, points her finger aloft. "Of course you know, this means war."

Marjorie flies at her face, scratching, grabbing handfuls of hair. Madeleine shields her head between her elbows and is suddenly laughing like Woody Woodpecker—it feels automatic, flying from her like bullets from a machine gun: "He-he-HAH-ha!"

Marjorie screams, "Shut up Madeleine!"

Madeleine screams back, "Shut up Madeleine!"

Grace jumps on her before she can straighten, tearing at her raincoat, her schoolbag, trying to yank her to earth. "Do you want us to kill you, Madeleine?!" cries Marjorie.

"Kill you, Madeleine?" pipes back Newton the fawn, "Kill you Madeleine?" Her legs are heavy with Grace's weight, as though she were caught in quicksand. *Whatever you do, don't fall down.* She starts barking like a dog and laughing, growing weak with it. She feels a bright wet spot form under her eye, warmer than the raindrops, then suddenly she is weightless again. Grace has let go of her and started crying. Marjorie runs at her chest with the heels of her hands, but Madeleine stays up like an inflatable clown.

"You're gonna get it," cries Marjorie, out of breath.

Madeleine leans forward and shrieks, "Yabba dabba doo!"—hair and blood in her eyes.

Grace and Marjorie back away, lobbing exhausted threats and tearful imprecations. Then they turn and run.

Madeleine stands still to catch her breath. It seems to be taking a long time. Finally she realizes that she is not panting, she is making little sounds. She is crying—that is, her eyes are crying, her body is. She lets it. It's raining anyway. Her own tired sobbing sounds like a little kid in her ears—one she feels sorry for. Then the pain surfaces and begins to reverberate like an echo of the blows. Pain is clean and manageable. It allows her to focus her eyes on the houses across the field and start for home. It allows her to stop crying.

"I was chasing a dog and I fell."

Lying is second nature.

"What dog?"

"I think it was a stray."

"How did you manage to scratch your face like that?"

"I had my arms inside my raincoat when I fell."

"Oh Madeleine, *pourquoi?*"

"I was being a penguin."

And, because her mother still looks worried, she adds, "*Ci pa gran chouz.*"

" '*Ci' quoi? Qu'est ce que tu dis?* What kind of French is that?"

"It's Michif."

" '*Mi'-quoi?*"

"Colleen taught me."

"Is that what happened to you? Did Colleen Froelich push you down?"

"No!"

Maman puts on two Steri-Strips, one over Madeleine's right eye and one under it. There may be the tiniest scar. Then she calls the MPs and reports a vicious stray.

Jack picks up the late edition of *The Globe* for news on the election and uses it to shelter himself for the quick jog home—it didn't look like rain this morning. Mike's game will be cancelled. Perhaps he should make the trip into London this evening after all. But the shops will be closed, and how will he find a ride into town at this point?

He rounds his corner to see Henry Froelich out with an umbrella, gazing under the hood of the patchwork car, nursing his obsession. Jack calls out a greeting and Froelich raises his pipe. "Hank, what's the name of that poison you're puffing?"

"Von Eicken. You want you should try it?"

"No, thought I might get some for a friend."

"You buy it from the Union Cigar Store across from the market."

"Thanks," says Jack. He turns up his driveway and opens his front door. "Mimi, I'm home." Trots up the steps. "Boy, something sure smells good!"

"Where are my cherries?" she asks, kissing him hello.

"What cherries?" He smiles down at her, taking off his hat, shaking off the rain.

"Betty asked me where you found cherries and how much they were."

*Vic Boucher.* Jack keeps smiling and says, "I couldn't find any."

"Vic told her not to bother even asking about the caviar."

"What's Vic up to, anyhow, Missus?" His arms still around her. How much did Vic tell Betty? That he had overheard "Mimi" dictating a grocery list to Jack? What did Betty tell Mimi? Did Betty catch herself when she realized Mimi had no idea what she was talking about? Do Vic and Betty think Jack has a secret from his wife?

He gives her a peck on the lips.

She says, "Well you better not bring me caviar, Mister, I have a *ragoût* on the go," and turns back to the stove. She doesn't seem concerned— she seems normal.

"I don't know where Vic gets his ideas." He leans over her shoulder, lifts a pot lid and takes a sniff. "Wishful thinking, maybe. Mmm." She takes the lid from him and replaces it, lifts another and dips in a spoon.

He says, "Caviar's no great shakes compared to this, I'd rather have a good *bouilli* any day."

"Cassoulet," she says, blowing on the spoon, tasting.

"If you want caviar, Missus, all you have to do is snap your fingers."

She cups her palm under the spoon and holds it out to him. "I know that."

"'I know dat,'" he mimics her.

"Don't be saucy, monsieur."

He tastes. "Pinch more salt."

He pours himself a short Dewar's and takes the paper into the living room—*RECORD TURNOUT IS PREDICTED.* It looks as though a lot of Canadians are determined their vote will count. He sips his drink and glances out the picture window. The sky clearing in a blaze of orange—Mike's game will be on after all. He is doubly glad he put Oskar Fried off till Wednesday.

ON EITHER SIDE of the county road, the newly sprouted corn rippled
away green and gleaming, black furrows of earth still visible between
the rows. The road was baking, bending the air. Too hot for April. A
boy in red jeans was on the road, running. Seen from a distance, he
was a splash of scarlet, wavering and growing smaller. Heading
toward a willow tree that trembled in the visible heat and swept the
crossroads where the Huron County road met the road to Rock Bass.
Light flashed at the boy's feet, spun from the steel wheels of his sister's
chair which he pushed before him at a clip. A little friend pedalled
beside him, her blue dress rippling at her knees, while his dog kept
pace, harnessed to her bicycle.

She never came home. They found her eventually. And although
the boy did come home as usual, along with his sister and his dog, he
disappeared into that spring day completely, never to be found.

# WEDNESDAY'S CHILDREN

*A pale yellow butterfly flew here and there to taste the honey of the jungle
flowers. It flew with careless ease over the back of a crocodile stretched out on
a dry bank and taking a quiet nap. . . .*
  "Butterflies and Crocodiles," The Pupil's Own Vocabulary Speller, *1951*


THERE IS A YELLOW BASKET on Mr. March's desk, brimming with
bright foil-wrapped eggs on a bed of paper straw. Even to see such a
thing before Easter, while it's still Lent, is like peeking under your
parents' bed to see your Christmas presents. It's exciting, you want to
play with them, you want to laugh. Then by the end of the day you wish
you had not looked.

Easter is not as crucial, still you look forward to it. Painting the hard-
boiled eggs the night before, and there, in the morning, the giant
chocolate bunny waiting on the coffee table, smiling merrily with his
beady candy eye, a basket on his back. Madeleine always gets a bunny
and Mike gets a rooster. Hidden throughout the ground floor are
chocolate eggs—in shoes, in the fold-out speakers of the hi-fi, under
the base of the lamp. . . . Then the great hard-boiled egg battle to see
whose egg can crack the others while remaining intact. But remember,
all these treats are because, on Good Friday, Jesus was crucified, died
and was buried, and on the third day He rose again. The idea of having Easter treats in class before He has even been nailed to the Cross is
just not right.

It seems, however, that the grade fours are to have an Easter party
despite the fact that today is only Wednesday—not even Holy
Wednesday, there is no such thing. Things don't get holy until tomorrow, Thursday.

But first, a spelling test. Mr. March reads out the words, clearly, pon-
derously, giving each syllable a chance. "Crocodile . . . butterfly . . .
danger . . . nap . . . hatched . . . awfully . . . swamp . . . group . . . surface
. . . honey . . . escape . . . taste . . . puff . . . quiet."

The only difficult word is "quiet." Madeleine writes "quiet," then
remembers the little devil symbol pointing his pitchfork at the word on
the page to indicate difficulty, and amends it to "queit."

Mr. March collects the spelling tests, then pretends to be surprised at
the sight of the Easter basket on his desk. "It would appear the Easter
bunny has been here early."

An obliging "ohh" from the class.

"Who knows how to hop like a bunny?"

Hands shoot up. Who cares if hopping like a bunny is a kindergarten thing to do, everyone wants to control the basket—most of the girls, that is, and Philip Pinder. Once he puts up his hand, other boys follow suit, because if Philip is doing it, it's not sissy.

Mr. March raises his eyebrows. "I wish I could count this many hands when it's time to name the ten provinces and their capitals."

Even Auriel and Lisa have their hands up. So does Gordon Lawson, elbow resting politely on his desk. Madeleine is the only one without her hand up. And Claire. And Grace. That's because Grace knows she'll never get picked.

"Bunnies are nothing if not quiet and small," says Mr. March in a story-time voice, not at all sarcastic, which is how you know that he can be nice sometimes. "Who is quiet and small enough to be a bunny?"

All the hands go down and the class becomes very quiet. They all start curling up at their desks, covering their heads like duck and cover. Madeleine rests her chin on her desk and blinks. She doesn't want to hurt his feelings, but she doesn't want to be picked and have to eat his chocolate. Claire McCarroll is the only other one not acting like a bunny.

"Claire McCarroll," says Mr. March. "Hop to the front of the class, please." No one can be mad at Claire for getting to be the Easter bunny. She is the quietest, after all. And the smallest. She hops to the front of the class with her hands curled under her chin like paws and everyone laughs, not meanly, happily. Claire looks solemn. She has become a bunny. When she arrives at his desk, Mr. March reaches down and pats the bunny's head.

"Hop onto my lap, bunny."

And the bunny does.

Mr. March smiles at the bunny. He is often kind to the gerbil too. "Now Easter Bunny, I want you to distribute one egg per pupil, do you think you can do that?"

The bunny nods.

"Can you wiggle your ears?"

Claire turns her paws into tall ears and wiggles them. The class claps.

"Can you twitch your tail?"

Claire wiggles her bottom and everyone laughs, but Madeleine feels her face prickle. She pictures Claire's underpants from the day long ago when she saw them by accident while they were doing somersaults. Mr. March puts the basket into Claire's paws. "Hop along down the bunny trail."

She slides off Mr. March's lap and the skirt of her light blue dress rides up. Madeleine closes her eyes and a pattern appears against her lids, smudged so she can't make it out. Yellow blotches, chicks maybe. . . .

While Claire hops up and down the aisles, Mr. March conducts the class as it sings: "'Here comes Peter Cottontail, hopping down the bunny trail . . .'" She pauses at each desk and deposits a chocolate egg. Madeleine feels hot at the pit of her stomach, her palms are moist, her fingers cold. She places them against her forehead to cool it.

She feels better by the time Claire gets to her desk, because everyone is being kind to the bunny, thanking her, even patting her. Claire's charm bracelet gleams as she hands Madeleine the egg, and Madeleine remembers her own bracelet sitting scorned in the blue box at home. Perhaps she should wear it to Brownies tonight. She takes the egg and whispers out of the side of her mouth, "Thanks, doc, us wabbits gotta stick together," and the bunny smiles.

"All good things must come to an end," says Mr. March, and Claire hops back to his desk with the empty basket. "Did the Easter Bunny remember to save an egg for herself?" he asks. The bunny shakes her head. "Why ever not?" he says.

Claire looks down and murmurs, "I only like the real kind," in her soft sweet accent.

"Of course," says Mr. March. "How could I forget: our resident ornithologist." He scans the class and says, "Then who, pray tell, was the lucky recipient of two chocolate eggs?"

Gordon Lawson raises his hand, smiles and shrugs. The whole class goes, "Ohhhhhh!" and both Gordon and Claire blush. Auriel whispers to Madeleine that Marjorie looks as though she has just sucked a lemon, not a chocolate, and it's true, she does.

"Aren't you going to eat your chocolate egg, little girl?"

Madeleine looks at the coloured tinfoil oval on her desk. "No thank you, Mr. March."

"And why not? Am I a stranger?" Obliging laughter from the class. "No."

"Well?"

"I gave it up for Lent."

"Oh. We have a devout Christian in our midst." More laughter. "I'm not aware of having said anything amusing," he says, looking around. "Your self-discipline is admirable, Miss McCarthy, but Easter is just a few days away. What's wrong with celebrating the occasion with your classmates?" She swallows. He says, "Methinks you are splitting hairs." He waits, then rolls his eyes. "That was a pun. Hairs, h-a-i-r-s, or hares, h-a-r-e-s." Tentative laughter. "And what do we call two words that sound alike but mean different things? Miss McCarthy?"

"Twins."

"Incorrect." He writes the answer on the blackboard, which makes his bum jiggle. "Homophones." He underlines it, then turns to face them. "Class?"

All: "Homophones."

Philip Pinder shouts, "*Homo*-phones!"

Few people laugh because few get it.

"Jeez," says Auriel as they spill out the side door, "whoever heard of getting in trouble for not eating chocolate?"

"Yeah, that's religious prosecution," says Lisa.

"Hey you guys," says Madeleine, "want to roll all the way home?"

But they can't. Lisa and Auriel have band practice. Madeleine rolls like a runaway log, as fast as she can, because tonight at seven o'clock in the schoolyard the Brownies are flying up to Guides. There will be refreshments and parents, Miss Lang's fiancé will be in attendance, and if she hurries and changes into her play clothes right now, then rushes back, she will be able to help set up the giant toadstool and benches, and roll out the carpet of yellow crêpe paper that she and her friends have come to think of as the "golden pathway."

In the vestibule of Fried's apartment building the buzzer sounds. Jack hurries across the lobby, unchanged but for the addition of a new *Look* magazine. The cover catches his eye: two photos side by side—Fidel Castro and the Canadian flag—or rather, ensign.

The elevator begins its glacial ascent and Jack wishes he had taken the stairs. He manoeuvres his wrist around the grocery bag and peers at his watch: three-fifteen. The shopping took longer than he expected; he had to wait in line while the Bavarian shopkeeper and his wife chatted with each and every customer. Jack was fuming but contained his impatience so as not to draw attention. As it is, he will have to find a way to keep Mimi from the market for a week or two—long enough for the shopkeepers not to remark, "Back already? Your husband was just here," yet not so long that they'll say, "We haven't seen you since before your husband came in." How do people conduct extramarital affairs? They become travelling salesmen.

On the third floor, Jack walks along the swirly carpet toward the end of the hall. He planned to get a drive with McCarroll, but when he went to find him, the clerk said McCarroll was not expected home until the dinner hour. Simon was unconcerned by the delay in briefing McCarroll. He said Fried was in no immediate danger as long as he stayed in his apartment. "The chap who saw him hasn't a clue where to look for him."

Jack wondered how Simon could be so sure, but wasn't going to lose any sleep over it—he had other problems, chief among them transport. Jack had assumed that he wouldn't need the Rambler so Mimi had taken it into Exeter for groceries this afternoon and—what else?—to take Sharon McCarroll to get her hair done because her husband was coming home this evening. Well, there was the information about the exact timing of McCarroll's return, if only he had known how to decode it. He reflected on the vigour of the female grapevine, wondering if any man had ever managed to tap its potential.

Jack had turned his steps toward the ME section, intending to sign out a staff car, only to find that the entire fleet had been pressed into service for the visiting air vice-marshal. The flight sergeant in charge told him, "Squadron Leader Boucher is heading into town for a meeting, sir, if you run you might catch him." Jack didn't run. He could not begin to imagine the web of petty deceit he would have to weave to convince Vic that he too had a meeting—not at the university, of course, that was where Vic was going—where? With whom? Someone Vic had never heard of? What was more, he was irritated by his own irrational certainty that Vic was then bound to catch him at the market with an armload of guilty groceries. He had already become more finely attuned to Vic's manner since the "caviar and cherries" incident—trying to assess whether Vic thought he had lied to his wife. A midday trip to London on a flimsy pretext . . . Vic would surely tell Betty.

He left the ME section, sweating by now in his woollen uniform—too hot a day for April—and had just decided to scrub the journey into town altogether when a black staff car rolled up alongside him and a military policeman inquired if he needed a lift. The MP would not be returning until late that evening, and with a full car at that, "so I can only offer you a one-way ticket, sir."

"I'll take it," said Jack, and hopped in the back. A stroke of luck. He had just remembered Fried's Ford Galaxy. He could drive it back to Centralia. "What's your name, corporal?"

"Novotny, sir."

A bruiser of a fellow. Jack sat back and asked him who he liked for the Stanley Cup this year.

Now, Jack knocks at Fried's door. And waits. Finally, the shuffling, the pause during which he feels Fried's eye on him through the peephole. Slide of the safety chain, thunk of the deadbolt and the door opens. Fried turns without a word back toward his darkened living room and the blare of the television. The odour of stale tobacco greets Jack. He would love to go straight to the window and open it but light is verboten on account of Fried's orchids—vampire orchids, as Jack thinks of them. There are five now, growing up their coat hangers, dark delicate flesh, thriving.

Jack dumps the bags on the kitchen counter. In order to shop today, he had to get another advance on his pay. He has to hope that Mimi doesn't question the old "accounts-payroll mistake" excuse when she sees the double deposit on payday. At least he needn't worry about lipstick on his collar.

Jack has never considered adultery. Now it crosses his mind unbidden, because of the absurd situation in which he finds himself—sneaking away from work in the middle of the day, purchasing luxury items in secret, keeping a furtive rendezvous in dim rented rooms. As he puts away groceries in the refrigerator glow of Fried's tiny kitchen, he finds himself picturing sex with a woman not his wife—right here in this cramped kitchen. Up against the counter. He takes the cognac from the bag, sticks it in the cupboard next to an identical half-full bottle, annoyed and now inconveniently aroused. He is conducting a clandestine affair. With NATO.

Jack walks back into the living room. Fried is watching *Secret Storm*. Jack shakes his head; after all, you have to laugh. He would love to tell Mimi about Fried, she'd get a kick out of it, and one day soon maybe he will be able to. A commercial comes on for Ban deodorant but Fried doesn't take his eyes from the screen. Jack feels suddenly, oddly affectionate toward him. This is the last time he will see the man before he leaves to start working for USAF—and eventually, if Fried gets his way, NASA. He is a true eccentric, and what he lacks in charm, he clearly makes up for in courage and commitment. *It's been a slice,* Jack wants to say. "How about a game of chess, sir?"

Fried appears at first not to have heard him. Then, as noxious strains of organ music signal the resumption of the soap opera, he says, "Shhh."

Jack is stung. He feels himself flush and he takes a quiet breath. He would like to come away from this mission with more than a sour taste and a lot of unanswered questions. Fried's profile looks imperturbable in the light and shadow of the television. A woman's voice stutters, "Because I—I'm . . . the other woman," and she breaks down weeping.

This is Jack's last chance. The next time he sees Fried, it will be with Blair McCarroll, and after that he will likely never see the man again.

So he says, "Too bad von Braun didn't pick you to come to America with him in '45, you'd be at NASA by now."

Fried turns his head and glares. Bingo. He forms his words with unexpected precision and fluency. "You know where is Kazakhstan? You know what is Baikonur? You know who is Helmut Gröttrup?" He raises his voice above the tears and recriminations on the screen. "We are years ahead, we launch, we orbit, we beat you and do you know why?" He gestures with disgust toward the television. "Because you care more for this than you care for that," and he points at the ceiling. Jack assumes he is referring to the moon, and the cosmos in general. "The Soviets come when the war ends. With guns we are ordered to them and we work—" Thin cords stand out in Fried's neck.

Jack sits down, carefully, as though trying to avoid waking some-one—

"They take me and many others."

Jack has guessed right: Fried didn't make the first cut. At the end of the war, Wernher von Braun had the good sense to flee the Russian advance and surrender to the Americans, who had the good sense to recruit him. Von Braun had hand-picked his team from among those he had worked with on the German rocket program—including his brother, along with his managerial right hand, Arthur Rudolph—the brightest and the best, who now form the core of NASA. But he didn't pick Fried, and Fried fell into the hands of the Russians. Fried must have had a lot to prove in the Soviet Union.

Fried continues. "Gröttrup also is a scientist from Dora. He is of high rank. Not only von Braun knows how to make V-2, Gröttrup knows, I know. We work in the Soviet Union, many of us, and no luxury. Not like America." He mutters at the man and woman on the screen, entan-gled in an illicit embrace. "I have been the only German left now in the Soviet Union program. They dispose—how do you say . . . ?"

"Kill?"

"*Nein,*" says Fried impatiently, displaying more animation in one moment than Jack has witnessed in months, "throw away. Like garbage. They say, 'We have Russians now to do your job.'"

"Ah," says Jack, "Struck Off Strength."

"*Wie?*"

"Like obsolete—worn out—aircraft. Tossed aside."

"Just so. Tossed aside."

"Except for you."

"*Ja.*" Fried nods, his lower lip rising to displace the upper in a show of determination or self-satisfaction.

"Why, Oskar?"

Fried jabs his own narrow chest, where grey hairs stray from the open neck of his shirt. "I work. I watch the others. I see when there is sabotage, I know who is a traitor." His face is taut.

"But you're a traitor now."

Fried takes a deep breath but makes no move. Finally he says, "I don't care for money. If you have made something for your whole life, you wish only to continue. To work with the best. I do not care who wins this race to the moon. I care to participate. Russians will not allow me to go farther. By them I am always a foreigner."

Jack nods, somewhat touched by Fried's honesty. He says gently, "You must have made a major contribution to the Soviet space program." Fried betrays no emotion, but Jack can tell that, like a child, he has heard and is savouring. "No wonder the Soviets leapt ahead," Jack adds deliberately, "what with scientists of your calibre working for them." Fried leans forward and switches off the TV. Reaches for his pipe. Jack hands him the fresh pouch of tobacco. "You fellas were launching Sputnik while we were still blowing up on the test stand."

Fried shrugs—expressionless, delighted—and lights his pipe, passing the flame back and forth across the bowl, puffing.

"I guess you're looking forward to seeing some of your old friends down there, eh? There's bound to be some familiar faces at Wright-Patterson Air Base . . . over in the R and D facility?"

Fried says nothing. Maybe he doesn't know where he's going any more than Jack does.

Jack says, "Not to mention Houston."

Fried smokes, calm once more.

"Did you know von Braun?"

"*Natürlich.*"

"At Peenemünde?"

"And after, at Dora. He would come to inspect."

Jack recalls reading somewhere that von Braun always made a point of visiting the shop floor at the U.S. Army Ballistic Missile Agency. A visionary with a feel for hardware. "So you worked right in the factory. What did you do?"

"I am the superior to make certain the rocket is properly builded," says Fried.

"You oversaw production standards."

"You can say this."

"So you helped manufacture the actual rocket. The V-2."

Fried nods. Jack gets a chill. "Wow."

"This is a beautiful machine."

Jack nods. "Hitler's 'secret weapon.'" He wants to smile broadly—he has waited so long for this.

"Guidance and control," says Fried, "this is like the brain of the machine. Delicate. It is taken years. The rocket is fifteen point two metres long, perfect mixture for fuel, this also is taken years. We produce three hundred each month, but they are not all perfect. The SS does not know what is needed properly to produce this rocket."

"The SS?"

"This rocket could have winned the war."

Jack knows enough not to argue—the V-2 could never have won the war for Hitler, regardless of how efficiently they were produced. The world's first ballistic missile was an effective instrument of terror, but in terms of destructive power it was conventional ordnance. A glorified artillery shell. Hitler would have had to have a parallel track of atomic research going, then married the nuclear bomb to the V-2 rocket. Jack recalls what Froelich said—that Hitler rejected atomic research on the grounds that it was "Jewish science."

But Fried is probably like Wernher von Braun, whose passion for rockets was born of the dream of space travel. He couldn't have cared less about weapons. "Do you think we'll do it, Oskar? Will Americans get to the moon and back within the decade?"

Fried taps his pipe. "Is possible. If Soviets do not arrive first."

"Yeah, but we've got you now." Jack grins and sees Oskar Fried smile for the first time. "Maybe that's who spotted you at the marketplace?" He can see Fried clam up again but he presses on. "An old colleague? Maybe an engineer who worked for you?"

Fried shakes his head, no.

"I thought you said you didn't know who he was?"

Fried takes the bait. "I do not know who, I know what."

"Oh," says Jack innocently. "Well, Simon says this fella doesn't know your name so what's the problem? Maybe he just wanted to say hello—"

"He wants to put a rope about my neck." Fried has gone pale. He taps out his pipe.

Jack says gently, "Why, Oskar? What did you do?"

"My job." Fried gets up, takes a spray bottle from the windowsill and begins spritzing his flowers.

Jack was unable to get more out of him. Now, as he walks down the stairwell, he runs his finger along the serrated edge of Fried's car key in his pocket. "Simon asked me to move it," he lied. He heads out the side door of the building and squints against the blaze of afternoon, wondering, why should Fried be afraid that he will be hanged for the job he did? He was a scientist. He worked on the V-2, so did Wernher von Braun and half of NASA. Fried has laboured under the pitiless scrutiny of GRU— the Soviet secret police—for the past seventeen years. If he's paranoid, perhaps it's because he is like a bird that has been caged for too long— the door is open, but he has no idea he can fly out. Freedom takes getting used to. Like daylight for a miner. Fried would know, having worked underground at the rocket factory, and now Jack understands the orchids; they thrive in darkness. As he rounds the building, he feels a twinge of compassion. He finds the Ford Galaxy parked in back between two dumpsters, gets in and checks his watch. It's just after four.

Earlier, at three-fifteen, Colleen and Madeleine are in the schoolyard along with several other children and adults.

"What do you want to do now?" asks Madeleine. Colleen is leaning against the bike rack. Madeleine is sharpening a Popsicle stick on the ground.

"I don't know," says Colleen, "what do you wanna do?"

"I dunno. Wanna go to Rock Bass?"

"Maybe."

Across the schoolyard, Cathy Baxter and a number of other girls are busily helping Miss Lang prepare for the flying-up ceremony that will take place after supper. Glancing over at Colleen, Madeleine tries to quell her excitement.

She intended to be one of the helpers, but she lost the inclination when Colleen showed up. It's not that she is ashamed of being a Brownie, it's just that she would rather not be one in front of Colleen.

"I might quit after I fly up," she says, testing the point of her new Popsicle knife. The day is soft and the sun sits lightly on her bare arms and legs. "Unseasonably warm," said the weather man—in other words, perfect.

Through the open windows of the gymnasium, the sound of the band practising reaches them in fractured phrases. Madeleine recognizes the melody, and the lyrics run through her head involuntarily, *It's a small world after all, It's a small world after all....* If she had been forced to join the band, she would be trapped in there right now.

Colleen chews a piece of long grass and narrows her eyes at the giant toadstool being set up in front of rows of benches on the baseball field. Like an altar, thinks Madeleine. The Brown Owl's altar. Tonight the Brownies will receive the sacrament of their wings and fly up to Guides.

Except for Grace Novotny, who will walk, escorted by a Sixer, up along the roll of yellow paper. And except for Claire McCarroll, who, having just joined as a Tweenie this year, will be pinned as a full-fledged Brownie. *Too-wit, too-wit, too-woo!*

"Are you coming tonight?"

"No, I got other plans," says Colleen.

Good.

Here comes Claire McCarroll on her bike with the glorious pink streamers. She is still in her light blue dress that she wore to school.

"Do you like butter?" she asks, plucking one of the tiny yellow flowers that have so recently sprouted up like magic amid the grass.

Claire is very frisky for Claire. It's a big day for her—being the Easter bunny in school, and about to get her Brownie pin this evening. She holds the buttercup under Colleen's chin and says, "Yup, you like butter." It's impossible to imagine anyone else doing that to Colleen and getting away with it. Then Claire does the same thing to Madeleine, giggling, "You *love* butter, Madeleine."

"He loves me, he loves me not. He loves me—" Oh no. It's Marjorie Nolan, loudly plucking the petals from a daisy, with Grace Novotny in tow. Marjorie overheard Claire with the buttercup and just had to do something with a flower of her own.

Claire says to Madeleine and Colleen, "Want to come for a picnic?"

Madeleine watches Marjorie cheat, counting the final two petals as one, tearing them off. "Ricky loves me!" She is standing a little too close and speaking a little too loudly while pretending to ignore them.

"Where're you going?" asks Colleen.

Claire replies, "For a picnic at Rock Bass with Ricky."

Madeleine hums "Beautiful Dreamer" under her breath and catches Colleen's eye. Colleen grins ever so slightly. Neither wants to be mean, but they both know it's wishful thinking on Claire's part. No big deal. *I can dream, can't I doc?*

"Want to come too?" says Claire. "We can look for a nest."

Colleen and Madeleine decline politely so Claire lifts her Frankie and Annette lunchbox from the basket of her bike and opens it. She shares her picnic with them then and there. A red wax-covered disc of Babybel cheese, a chocolate cupcake with blue icing, and some apple slices. She is careful to save some "for the animals." Madeleine makes a pair of red lady-lips with the Babybel wax, and Claire laughs.

"I seen some baby rabbits at Rock Bass," says Colleen, wiping her mouth with the back of her hand. "They got a den right under the maple tree."

"Thanks Colleen."

Claire rides off.

"'Thanks Colleen.'" Madeleine teases. Colleen headlocks Madeleine and scrubs the top of her scalp fiercely with her knuckles. "Ow!" Colleen always decides when Madeleine has had enough and stops, in this case calmly walking away.

"Hey Colleen, wait up!"

The final strains of the song straggle out the windows of the gym, but Madeleine outruns them. *It's a small world after all, It's a small, small world.*

Ricky is washing the station wagon when Claire rides by. Elizabeth is beside him in her wheelchair and Rex trots to the foot of the lawn to greet her.

"Hi Ricky."

"Hi pal."

"Hi Elizabeth," says Claire.

"Ay." Elizabeth is nestled in a light yellow blanket. She has a plastic cup wedged between her hands, the kind babies use, with a lid and a spout.

"What have you got?" asks Claire.

"Ehhhm-oway," says Elizabeth with her weightless voice and big loose smile.

"Lemonade," says Ricky to Claire.

"Is it good?" asks Claire.

Elizabeth nods in all directions.

Ricky is wearing his red jeans, a white T-shirt and sneakers.

"You look nice, Ricky."

"Oh yeah? Thanks."

"What are you doing?"

"Washing the car."

"Want to come for a picnic?"

"I can't, pal, I promised Lizzie we'd go for a run."

"Oh."

"Want a drink?" he asks.

"Yes please."

Ricky gives her a drink from the hose. The best drink of all, rubbery water, it tastes like summer. Then he has some. Claire watches him drink. Then she rides off. "Bye."

Rex flops to the ground at Elizabeth's feet, in the shade of the wheelchair, grinning up at her, panting. Her hand slips down and wavers over him, finding his fur, giving him a knuckly graze on the head.

"You ready to roll, Lizzie?"

"I Rek umming?"

"I don't know, think it's too hot for Rex?"

"Ing sah wah."

"Good idea," says Ricky, heading into the house for a canteen which he fills with icy water from the hose.

It takes Claire ten minutes to make her way up the street and around the corner to the Huron County road, because after she leaves Ricky and Elizabeth, she stops to watch some boys and dads trying to make a miniature go-cart go. She can smell gasoline and see little puffs of white smoke every time they start its engine.

She stops again just out front of the Bouchers' house, at the corner of St. Lawrence and Columbia, because she thinks she hears someone softly call her name. She looks down in the direction of the voice, but all she sees is the ditch and the metal drainpipe. So she gets off her bike, carefully lies on her stomach and peers into the darkness of the pipe to see if anyone, perhaps an elf or a small creature, might be caught in there and in need of her help.

"Hello," she whispers into the gloom. But there is silence. She speaks a little louder, "Is everything okay?" But there is no answer. She sees a ladybug crawling up her wrist. She bends close and whispers, "Was it you?" And by the way Claire listens, it's clear that she has received some sort of answer, for she says in reply, "Don't worry ladybug, your children are safe. Now fly away home." And it does.

That was at 3:45.

By the time Claire reaches the Huron County road she has forgotten that she is not permitted to leave the PMQs alone. She was not intending to leave alone, it was her intention to go for a picnic with Ricky Froelich, and so convinced was she of this plan that, when it turned out he couldn't come, she saw no reason not to continue on alone. It's important, however, to return home in time for supper and to change into her Brownie uniform. She begins pedalling with all her might. She has passed the first farm and entered the corridor of tall trees when Ricky Froelich catches up to her, jogging along with Elizabeth and Rex. She is a little out of breath from her exertions. Ricky stops, removes his belt and hitches Rex up to her bike, and the little convoy gets underway again, proceeding at a good clip up Huron County Road Number 21, toward the willow tree that marks the intersection where if you turn left you head for Highway 4, and if you turn right you head for Rock Bass. If you keep going you hit the quarry—it's warm enough to swim today.

Madeleine and Colleen have decided to head for their willow tree. They have opted to travel cross-country, which means cutting through people's lawns and farmers' fields. Darting from poplar to poplar, over a fence and across the railroad tracks—stopping at Pop's to buy a grape pop. Colleen pays and Madeleine asks if she gets an allowance.

"My brother gives me spending money from his paper route."

They don't pause to use the bottle opener on the Coke machine; there is no time for that, their lives are at stake. They escape into the open field and hit the dirt flat on their stomachs, cautiously peering through the grass to see if they have been followed by enemy agents.

"Phew, that was close."

"What'll they do if they catch us?"

"Arrest us."

"Throw us in the clink."

"Firing squad."

Colleen pries the cap off the bottle with the blunt edge of her knife and hands it to Madeleine. Madeleine takes a sip, wipes the spout with her T-shirt and hands it back to Colleen, who likewise drinks but doesn't wipe, because it's her drink and her germs.

"Coast is clear."

"Come on, we gotta keep moving."

They hike parallel to the Huron County road, over rough terrain, watching out for land mines—patches of hard gritty snow persisting in shade.

"Duck!"

They roll into the ditch and Madeleine aims her imaginary rifle at the enemy convoy: Ricky is pushing Elizabeth in her wheelchair and Rex is pulling Claire on her bike. "Hold your fire," says Colleen.

It looks as though the wheelchair is a chariot and Ricky the charioteer in his Roman red jeans, Rex a horse out in front, Claire in her sidecar. Madeleine and Colleen lie unseen, mere feet from the road, and when the little party arrives level with Madeleine she lobs a pebble that twangs off the spokes of Elizabeth's wheelchair. Colleen punches her in the arm.

"Ow! I wasn't aiming." And she wasn't. "Now I've seen everything," says Madeleine.

"What?"

"Claire really was going for a picnic with Ricky. A Ricknic, *nyah dat's de ticket.*"

"Doubters," says Colleen.

"There's one way to find out," says Madeleine. "We just wait and see if he turns down the road to Rock Bass with her or not."

"I got better things to do." Colleen gets up, picking off the straw.

"I'll bet you a nickel he turns down the Rock Bass road."

"Jealous, eh?"

"No! I just betcha, that's all!"

"I don't take money offa small fry," says Colleen.

"I'm not a small fry."

"Plus you got a crush."

Madeleine turns beet-red. Colleen snickers, "*T'an amor avec mon frer com tou l'mand,*" corks the half-empty bottle of grape soda with her thumb and takes off, dodging cow-pies, following a gully to the next woodlot. Madeleine lingers. It's true, everyone *is* in love with Ricky Froelich. The dust still hangs in the air behind him and Claire and their little gang, and they are far enough up the highway now that they have begun to shimmer in the unseasonable heat. She watches the splash of red that is Ricky's jeans as it pulsates and recedes toward the willow tree at the intersection. Then she turns and runs off after Colleen.

They never do see whether Rick stops, unhitches Rex from Claire's bike and turns left with his sister and his dog; or whether he turns right down the dirt road to Rock Bass with Claire McCarroll.

On either side of the Huron County road, the earth sprouts green beneath the brash April sun. Light flashes at the boy's feet, spun from the steel wheels of his sister's chair. Beside him runs his dog, harnessed to the little girl's bicycle, her light blue dress and pink streamers lifting in the breeze as they head for the willow tree that sweeps the intersection where the county road meets the road to Rock Bass.

It was shortly after four, judging from the sun, but no one was ever able to say, for sure, the exact time.

By the time Jack has passed north of Lucan on Highway 4 and is nearing Centralia, he has thought better of driving the Ford Galaxy to the station. It would only draw attention. He can hear Vic Boucher now: "That a new little bomb for the wife, Jack?" He decides to carry on past the air force station up to Exeter, call a cab and have it drop him at Centralia Village, a quarter-mile from home. He'll walk back from there. He has enjoyed the drive—it's a sporty rig, too bad about the dent Fried managed to put in the rear bumper.

The afternoon sun tilts over Rick's shoulder. He and his sister and his dog are travelling alone once more, along one of the dirt roads that criss-cross the county. The vibrations from the handles of the wheelchair travel up his arms. He can smell Elizabeth's hair, freshly shampooed. Rick knows she is smiling. Rex trots in front, his tongue slipping to one side—Rick will stop in a minute and give him a drink, it's too hot for a fur coat today.

He turns onto Highway 4 where it veers east a couple of miles from the station—he will enjoy the jet-smooth pavement for a hundred yards or so, then find another back road above Lucan and make a big circle back to the PMQs. Rick likes the dirt roads, less traffic and better scenery. Often he doesn't see a single vehicle—like today. But he is on the highway at the moment and here comes a car. He can tell right away that it's a Ford. The car veers toward the centre of the road as it approaches in order to give Rick and his chariot more room and, as it passes, the sun bounces off its windshield, obscuring the face of the man behind the wheel, who raises a hand and waves. Rick waves back. Even though he isn't able to recognize the man, Rick knows it can't be a stranger. He recognized the outline of an air force hat.

Rick stops, pulls off his singlet and wipes his face and chest. He takes the canteen that is looped over the back of the wheelchair and shares the water with his sister and his dog. He could turn north and head for the quarry. Kids are sure to be swimming there today—it's against the law but everyone does it. Elizabeth is tugging at his arm. She has a problem. She has had a bit of an accident.

"That's okay," says Rick. He turns the chair around and they head for home the way they came. The dirt roads weren't such a great idea after all, he realizes—shook the piss right out of her. "No big deal," he says.

"Oh bih geal," she says.

That was around 4:45, judging from the time it took Rick to jog home. But this was never proven.

Jack walks into the PMQ patch just this side of five-thirty. Normally he arrives closer to five, but there is nothing too out of the ordinary about a difference of half an hour. As he turns from Columbia onto St. Lawrence, he makes a mental note to arrive at work an hour early tomorrow and catch up on this afternoon's paperwork. Between the multicoloured houses, he glimpses laundry billowing white from clotheslines. The grass is greener than it was this morning. The walk from Centralia Village has been quite pleasant, although he wishes he'd had his sunglasses. The air is fresh but the sun beats with an exuberance that is almost belligerent. He turns up his driveway and wonders if there is time to have a word with McCarroll before supper. He thinks better of it when he approaches his own front door and smells supper cooking—let McCarroll reunite with his wife and enjoy his dinner. Plenty of time to talk over a cup of coffee later.

Jack opens the screen door stealthily and enters his house like a thief, not pausing to flip his hat onto the halltree, three silent steps up to the kitchen. There she is. Lipstick-kissed cigarette drifting in the ashtray, CBC on the radio, she is doing something at the sink. He sneaks across and slips one arm around her waist, she jolts, yelps, turns—"*Sacrebleu! Don't do that!*"—laughing, whacking him on the chest.

He brings his other hand out from behind his back—

"Oh Jack, *c'est si beau!*"

"I got them in the village."

"You walk all the way to Centralia Village to get me flowers? *T'es fou.*"

"Think how far I'd walk to get you into bed."

She presses against him. "I'm making the supper, go away."

"No."

She kisses him. "You think you can burst in here and get your way in the kitchen?" Taking his tie in her hand.

"Just give me a little taste of what you're cooking—" her hips between his hands, the flowers slipping headfirst to the floor.

"You have to wait till after supper, then you get the dessert—" stroking his tie, slipping her finger in the knot.

"No way."

"*Lâche-moi les fesses.*"

"Oh yeah? Make me. Say it in English, come on."

"Get your hands off my ass—" sliding her hands over his.

He kisses her. "Where are the kids?"

"Out playing." She tucks her hand behind his belt buckle, pulling him. "Come on." She heads for the stairs, reaching behind to unzip her dress on the way up.

Look at what she's got on underneath. White but perfect, the right amount of lace, the right amount of everything. Jack probably thinks all wives wear exquisite underwear. He follows her up the stairs, drops his uniform jacket in the doorway, undoes his pants, she pulls him down, opens his shirt, lifts his undershirt, presses her palms against his chest. He slides her panties down, her fingernails in his biceps, draws up her legs, spreads her knees. She is every girlfriend, every picture in every men's magazine—he's fast and she wants it that way—she is the woman who seduces you from an open car and doesn't ask your name, the one you can forget you love or even know—he is going to come like a kid, she makes it so hard, so easy—she is the woman you love more than yourself, she has had your children, she always wants you—

"Oh Jack, oh . . . oh baby, oh, you're big, oh give me. . . ."

Oh God.

"Oh God," he breathes, and eases off, rolling away, slow motion. "Man," he says.

Lying on her side, her fingers trailing across his chest, perfect red nails—*"Je t'aime."*

*"Je t'aime, Mimi,"* he replies.

He floats. Soon the screen door will bang. The kids will be home. Suppertime. "Something sure smells good," he says, turning his head to face her.

"You got an appetite now?" She smiles. *"Passe-moi mes cigarettes."*

He reaches to the bedside table and takes a cigarette from the pack. Lights it, passes it to her. He gets up and she watches him change into civvies. She exhales and winks at him, her bra straps halfway down her arms. Kicks her panties off her right ankle and crosses her legs. "I'll be right down. Turn the heat off under the potatoes."

She doesn't want to stand up right away. She wants to stay lying down, help what's inside her to do its work. She is reminded of what the fast girls—*les guidounes*—in her hometown used to say: "If you do it standing up, you won't get pregnant." Her own sister Yvonne was caught that way, and it would be interesting to know how many eldest children were conceived vertically. But although Mimi knows it's nothing but an old wives' tale, she waits a good half-hour before getting up, until she hears the screen door bang downstairs—the kids are home.

She pulls on her skirt, buttons her blouse, and picks up Jack's uniform trousers, in a heap on the floor. Before folding them over a hanger, she removes his keys, change—a fortune in dimes—pencil stubs, paperclips, chalk—the amount of debris he manages to accumulate in the space of a day, he is still like his boyhood hero, Tom Sawyer—and a crumpled piece of paper. She is about to place it on his dresser—God knows it might contain one of his diagrams, a plan for restructuring the COS—but first, on impulse, she smooths it and reads: *cherries, cognac, caviar. . . .* She feels her face grow hot and places a hand at her neck.

She doesn't try to create a story for herself to explain the piece of paper. She puts it in her jewellery box. Part of being a wife is knowing when to say nothing.

The flowers are in a vase on the kitchen table, *"comme un beau* centrepiece,"* says Mimi, handing Madeleine a basket of *biscuits chauds* for the table, fresh out of the oven.

Jack is listening to the six o'clock news and reading *Look* at the same time. Mike has his baseball cards at the table, Madeleine is waiting for someone to notice. How come he gets to sit there and she has to help her mother?

*"Tiens, Madeleine,"* handing her the butter.

Mimi switches off the radio and Jack snaps out of his news trance, tosses his magazine aside, rubs his hands together and says, "Look at this, oh boy."

*Râpé,* a delicious Acadian concoction of pork roast, grated potatoes and onions. Jack pats his stomach under the table and resolves to eat no more than one biscuit. If he'd had his gym gear with him today, he could have stuffed his uniform into a rucksack and run the three miles home from Exeter this afternoon, rather than taking a cab. He picks up his knife and fork. A woman like Mimi should never be taken for granted.

She smiles at him as she sits down, and Jack realizes he has been staring at her. He smiles back and sets down his knife and fork again as she makes the sign of the cross and starts grace. *"Au nom du Père, du Fils et du Saint-Esprit . . ."* He joins her and the kids, speaking rapidly, "Bless us O Lord and these Thy gifts which we are about to receive through the bounty of Christ Our Lord amen, pass the butter Mike, what did you kids learn at school today?"

Halfway through supper the phone rings. Jack looks up, mildly put out. Mimi answers and he waits. If it's a hang-up, he will have to find some excuse to leave and get to the phone booth.

"Oh hi Sharon," says Mimi.

Jack relaxes and resumes eating.

"No, she isn't," says Mimi. "No, I haven't. . . . Oh that's all right, Sharon, no, no trouble, let me just ask her."

Madeleine looks up.

Mimi asks, "Do you know where Claire McCarroll is?"

"No," says Madeleine.

Mimi turns back to the phone. "No I'm sorry, Sharon, have you tried the Froelichs? . . . Oh well then, I bet she's off playing at someone's house. . . . That's right. . . . Will do, Sharon. . . . Okay, bye-bye."

She sits down again and Jack says, "Well madame, you've outdone yourself this time, they're going to have to wheel me out of here on a stretcher."

"Keep your fork, prince," says Mimi. "There's pie." *Tarte au butterscotch.*

"Yum!" says Mike.

Jack loosens his belt. "Do your worst."

"Madeleine, *aide-moi,*" says Mimi, handing her the kettle.

"How come I have to make the tea? How come Mike never makes the tea? How come he never does anything around here?"

Mike laughs. Mimi says, "He's a boy, he has other jobs."

"Like what?" retorts Madeleine, and feels the burn of her mother's red nails pinching her earlobe.

Her father grins and winks at her brother. "He'd only burn the tea, right Mike?"

Mike grins back at him. It makes Madeleine furious. "You can't burn tea!"

"Don't talk back *à ton père,*" says her mother, sharply.

"Come here," says Jack, and Madeleine climbs on his knee. Mimi leans against the counter, lights a cigarette. "Tsk-tsk-tsk, my papa would have given me a good slap."

He strokes Madeleine's pixie cut. "Maman needs your help," he says. "Me and Mike aren't any good at that sort of thing. Did you know it's a special treat for me every time you bring me my tea?"

Madeleine shakes her head. She doesn't dare speak, she might cry.

It wasn't a stranger. It was horrible because she thought she was going to see a bird's nest. Robin's eggs, the colour of her dress. There are boys who smash robin's eggs, but there was no danger of that here.

There was the egg, held gently in the outstretched palm. It was hollow.

"I know where there are more eggs, little girl."

You could see the hole in the shell where a snake had poked its tooth and sucked it out.

"Alive ones."

So she leaned her bike against the maple tree at the bottom of the ravine at Rock Bass, and followed.

# FLYING UP

*A Brownie gives in to older folk. A Brownie does not give in to herself.*

Brownie law, 1958

IT IS THE SOFTEST PART of the day; pillowy shadows have begun to gather, warm like a cashmere sweater, shapely and perfumed; the grass is still wet with the moisture of snow so recently soaked up by the soil. The days are getting longer, still light at six-thirty. The sun's rays have turned from linen to flannel, even the gravel is painted smooth. The schoolyard is bathed in glamour, the white stucco of J.A.D. McCurdy powdered pink in the long laze toward sunset. Swings are at rest, the teeter-totters poised like a lady's legs about to put on stockings, *Hey, big boy.*

Tonight, the Brownies are flying up to Guides. Benches have been set out on the baseball diamond next to the schoolyard. Madeleine is seated already, her hair tucked neatly under her brown beret. Sewn down her sleeve are numerous badges—some hard-won, such as that sporting a needle and thread. Sacrifices have been made. And this evening, she and her friends—not including Colleen—are getting their wings. That will make two sets of wings in the McCarthy household.

The occasion is tinged with poignancy; Miss Lang is leaving to get married. It is unlikely that an equally beautiful, kind and laughing Brown Owl will take her place. There is only one Miss Lang. She too is in her uniform this evening, her sash, emblazoned with crests and badges, across her chest.

Madeleine arrived conscientiously early, and sat in fervent contemplation of the giant red and black toadstool set up on the batter's plate. She watches now with equal fervour as Miss Lang chats with her fiancé. Madeleine swallows a lump in her throat, and blinks. Miss Lang lowers her eyes and smiles at something the fiancé says. He moves to hold her hand but she gently withdraws and reaches for her clipboard behind the toadstool. Madeleine observes him; dark crew cut, forearms muscular and lean, the cool lines of his cotton shirt, ivory chinos and desert boots. His back pocket bulges slightly over his wallet.

Madeleine turns to look for her mother—there she is, placing a platter of pink-and-green sandwich rolls on the refreshment table. Mike has arrived as well, with Roy Noonan. They are playing catch. But Dad is not here yet. Brownies and their families mill about. Even Grace's mother is here. Madeleine expected Mrs. Novotny to be a big fat lady from having had all those babies, but she's skinny, with ropey arms and sunken cheeks.

There is excitement in the air. On a long folding table, the yellow paper wings sit ready to be pinned to the backs of the successful Brownies, and along the aisle, the golden pathway extends to the toadstool. Madeleine drifts into a daydream wherein she is Miss Lang in her Brown Owl uniform, with a long train attached. She walks down the aisle to where the fiancé waits at the altar, dressed in a tuxedo, smiling at her with his clean square face. "You may now kiss the bride," intones the minister. Madeleine is startled out of her reverie by the realization that at the moment of the kiss, rather than being Miss Lang, she is kissing Miss Lang. She reverses things in her mind until she is kissing the fiancé, but the fantasy dissolves and her mind wanders.

"I promise to do my best, to do my duty to God and the Queen and my country, and to help other people every day, especially those at home." The Brownie Pledge. Forty-two girls between the ages of eight and ten have spoken it in perfect unison, their senses sharpened by the solemnity of the occasion. "Too-wit, too-wit, too-woo!"

Miss Lang takes attendance. "Sheila Appleby."

"Present."

"Cathy Baxter."

"Present."

"Auriel Boucher."

"Present."

Each voice is a little more earnest tonight—there is no girl whose heart remains untouched by Miss Lang. She checks off the names on her clipboard. Madeleine looks around again but her father is still not here. . . .

"Claire McCarroll."

Miss Lang looks up. Heads turn, everyone looks to see where Claire is, but she is not present. Madeleine looks out across the field, but Claire is not on her way either. Up on the table, along with the wings, is a pin; it is for Claire, who will become a full Brownie tonight when Miss Lang attaches it to her chest. Claire is getting pinned.

"Madeleine McCarthy."

"Present, Miss Lang."

Miss Lang pauses ever so briefly, with a smile, and Madeleine's heart is pierced.

"Marjorie Nolan."

"Present."

I will never forget you, Miss Lang, as long as we both shall live. . . .

"Grace Novotny."

"Present."

"Joyce Nutt."

"Present."

Grace has failed to earn her wings, but there is no such thing as a Brownie uniform big enough to fit her next year, so she will "walk up" to Guides wearing the specially issued fairy slippers made of crêpe tissue paper. Madeleine looks down the row at her—she is sucking on her fingers, sliding them in and out of her mouth. Grace Novotny— Marjorie Nolan's bad pet.

"Grace?" says Miss Lang.

Grace gets up and shuffles along the row, looking down at her paper feet—they go *swish swish*. Marjorie joins her in the aisle. It ought to be the Sixer, Cathy Baxter, leading Grace, but Miss Lang has made an exception because the two are best friends. Grace takes Marjorie's arm and they walk slowly up the yellow paper path—almost as though Grace were an invalid. Like in *Heidi,* thinks Madeleine. Grace breaks away and runs the last few steps, hurling herself at Miss Lang who, once she has regained her footing, gives Grace a big hug.

As the Brownies begin flying up one by one, Madeleine looks toward the road, hoping to see her father drive up in the Rambler. Will she miss her wings parade? At the turn-in to the schoolyard there is a concrete stormpipe that runs under the road to the field on the other side. You can shout down it but entry has been barred by a metal grid, hung now with grass and weeds, remnants of the water that has been gushing through with the melt—if you get caught in there in spring, you drown. Everyone says a kid drowned in there one year and that's why they put up the bars. A dog is sniffing around it—a beagle—Madeleine wonders if he is lost. She watches him squeeze through the bars.

"That dog is trapped."

Madeleine has spoken it aloud, and the Brownie in front turns and draws an imaginary zipper across her mouth. Cathy Baxter, you are not the boss of me.

The dog barks and Madeleine raises her hand. But Miss Lang doesn't see her; she is pinning paper wings between Auriel's shoulder blades. Auriel runs up the golden path. Madeleine lowers her hand. One by one they fly up, like proud butterflies. The dog barks a second time. Madeleine can no longer see it in the shadows of the stormpipe. The barking becomes a muffled yelp, retreating farther and farther, and she puts her hand up again, about to call out, "Miss Lang," when a car swerves into the school-yard and just keeps coming across the playground and onto the grass, bouncing toward them till it stops right next to the toadstool.

Captain McCarroll arrived home from his flying trip with a new charm for his daughter's bracelet, but he went straight back out again and began going door to door at ten to six.

"No, dear," said Mrs. Lawson in her doorway. McCarroll had removed his hat when she came to the door. "Wait now, I'll ask Gordon. . . ."

To the Pinders. "Yes sir," said Harvey, tucking his newspaper under his arm, "we saw her, why? Has she gone AWOL on you?" but his tone was not joking.

"When did you see her, Mr. Pinder?"

"Oh, some time before supper. We were out with the little go-cart when she came along, hang on"—he called over his shoulder—"Arnie! Arnie, Philip, get up here, boys!" The boys ascended the basement stairs wearing expressions of all-purpose guilt. "You know Claire McCarroll?"

"Who?" said Arnold.

Philip said nothing, eyes darting. Harvey flicked him on the ear. "She came by while we were working on the go-cart. On her bike. Did either of you see her after that?"

"No sir," grunted Arnold. Philip shook his head.

"Sorry sir," said Harvey.

"Around what time was this?" asked Captain McCarroll.

"Oh, this afternoon, three-fifteen, three forty-five? Four?"

"Thanks." McCarroll was on his way.

Harvey grabbed his windbreaker and headed for his car, telling Captain McCarroll he'd have a look around the area, "in case she's off on a little adventure."

To the Froelichs.

He knew his wife had already phoned. None of Karen Froelich's children were able to help him—Rick was off playing basketball in London and Colleen had taken her sister to the station library. Karen called down the basement stairs, "Hank." Henry Froelich emerged from the basement, toolbox in hand, and when Karen told him why Blair McCarroll was there, he took off his apron and proceeded to search for his car keys among the stuff on the kitchen table. McCarroll hurried home on foot to see if his daughter had returned in the meantime.

And so it went, until the streets of the PMQs were full of dads behind the wheels of crawling cars, going door to door, playground to playground, peering between houses, eventually with an eye on the ditch.

Jack had raised the window on his screen door to get the warm spring air flowing through the house, then he set out walking down

St. Lawrence Avenue a few minutes behind his wife and children. On the way, he saw McCarroll's car parked in the driveway. He was back. He'd be going to the schoolyard too, with his little girl, and Jack would take the opportunity for a private word. He would need only to say, "I have a special task for you, McCarroll, concerning a mutual friend." McCarroll would know that Jack was the "officer of superior rank" who was overdue briefing him, and Jack would have fulfilled the favour he had promised Simon. Over and out.

As he neared the little green bungalow, Jack saw McCarroll come out of his house—still in uniform at ten to seven—toss his hat onto the passenger side and get into his car. He drove up the street toward Jack, who waved. McCarroll jerked to a stop alongside him. Jack bent to the open window, about to deliver his simple message, but the words died on his lips. McCarroll was chalky white.

His little girl had not come home yet. Jack got in the car beside him, tossing McCarroll's hat into the back seat. The police had told Blair that they could not consider her "missing" after merely three hours. Jack did not remark on the stupidity of this, not wanting to stoke McCarroll's distress. Instead, he asked, "Have you called the service police?" They drove to the MPs' office, where Corporal Novotny climbed immediately into his patrol car and radioed another to join the search.

They had just driven past the willow tree, crawling south along the Huron County road, when Jack suggested Blair turn back and head for the schoolyard where the Brownies were gathered. They could ask Claire's assembled friends if they knew where she might be.

The driver's door opens as the car lurches to a halt beside the toadstool. Madeleine watches as Mr. McCarroll gets out, along with a second man from the passenger side. Dad. A winged Brownie has stopped short on the golden pathway; everyone waits while Mr. McCarroll speaks quietly to Miss Lang. Behind the two of them, the sun is setting fast. It will be dark before the Brownies have their refreshments. Madeleine waits to catch her father's eye, but he looks past her at her mother.

"Attention Brownies," says Miss Lang. "Mr. McCarroll would like to know if anyone has seen Claire recently?"

*Recently.* When you are nine or ten years old, "recently" means a minute ago. Certainly it refers to nothing that occurred before supper or in the remote reaches of this afternoon. No hands go up.

Mr. McCarroll turns to them. "Girls and boys—"

Madeleine looks at Lisa Ridelle, Lisa looks back and they burst into stifled giggles. *Boys?!* There are no boys in Brownies! Madeleine looks up. Her father is staring at her now, one eyebrow slightly raised. She stops giggling.

"I would appreciate knowing," continues Mr. McCarroll, unaware of his gaffe, "if any of you saw Claire today at any time at all."

Several hands go up. She was seen by almost everyone at school today. She was seen afterwards in the schoolyard by Madeleine, Marjorie—who jogs Grace's memory with a jab—and by Cathy Baxter and the other girls who were helping Miss Lang. Diane Vogel saw her out her living-room window, talking into a drainpipe in the ditch near the corner of Columbia Drive and St. Lawrence—it must have been between three-thirty and four because her mother was watching *Secret Storm*. Madeleine's hand is still up and Miss Lang says, "Yes Madeleine?"

"Me and Colleen—I mean Colleen and I—saw her on the county road."

"Walking south?" asks Dad.

"Um," says Madeleine, "she was going to Rock Bass."

Claire's father walks so suddenly toward Madeleine that she starts. He drops to one knee, his face a bit too close to hers—is she in trouble or something? No, it's Mr. McCarroll who is in trouble. There are lines between his eyebrows, his Adam's apple looks raw as he swallows and says in his soft southern voice, "Where's that at, honey?"

"Um, you turn at the dirt road."

"What dirt road?"

"At the willow tree. Before the quarry."

"Quarry?"

"Where kids swim."

"Oh my God—" Mr. McCarroll gets up and places a hand over his mouth.

Dad is there suddenly. He leans in and asks, as though making himself perfectly clear in a foreign language, "That's where you would turn right if you were going to Rock Bass?"

Is he mad at me? "Yeah."

Miss Lang and Maman have joined them now, they are standing over her; all the Brownies are staring. Madeleine starts to feel strange, as though she were hiding something—Claire in a sack. Why are they leaning so close?

Her father says to Mr. McCarroll, "Rock Bass is about half a mile west of the county road, if she was going there she'd've turned long before the quarry, Blair, she's nowhere near the water."

Mr. McCarroll nods and frowns. Her father continues, "That puts her there at around four, four-thirty, eh? We can be there in ten minutes."

Madeleine says, "Ricky might know."

Everyone looks at her again. Mr. McCarroll, his lips no longer stiff but parted now, kneels back down. Madeleine can see his five o'clock shadow; his face, bony and almost as young as Ricky Froelich's, white scalp visible through his brush cut. He looks at Madeleine in a way that no adult ever has. Supplicant. Like the faces at the foot of the Cross.

She says, relieved to have come up with the right answer, "She was with Ricky and Elizabeth. And Rex."

The adults look somewhat reassured at the mention of Ricky's name. If Claire was with him, she is bound to be all right.

Dad pats her on the head. "Good girl," he says, moving to follow Mr. McCarroll back to the car.

Marjorie Nolan pipes up, "She was going for a picnic with him." The men stop and turn again.

Madeleine says, "No she wasn't, Claire probably just made that up," and looks at Mr. McCarroll, concerned lest she has been rude. "Sometimes she just likes to pretend." Mr. McCarroll smiles at her and goes to his car. Jack follows.

The car backs over the grass, then fishtails a little as it accelerates out of the parking lot, onto the road, and they're gone.

Marjorie Nolan raises her hand. "Miss Lang, could I please have my wings now?" she says, in a sarcastic voice that is intended to be funny. Several girls laugh, and Miss Lang smiles. There is a general sense of relief. They'll find Claire. If she was with Ricky Froelich, then no harm can have befallen her.

The two men drive to a spot where the fence has been left unrepaired, and Blair follows Jack along the path to the edge of the ravine. They skid down and walk for a mile in opposite directions along the stream. It is deeper and faster at this time of year, but it wouldn't come above the waist of a nine-year-old, and it's well furnished with logs and stepping stones. Still, both men look not only to left and right, they look also into the water as they go.

Darkness falls and Jack rides with McCarroll well into the night, at a snail's pace, the headlights of the Chrysler illuminating stark fields on either side of one dirt road after another, in an ever-widening circle that takes in the Huron County seat of Goderich and grazes the eastern shore of the great lake glimmering beyond the dunes. Inland once more, past the lights of farmhouses, pulling in at a gas station to call again— has Claire turned up yet?—the look on McCarroll's face as he hangs up and walks back to the car: disoriented, as though he had only recently arrived on this planet. Driving, driving, between columns of trees whose shadows grow more animated with the passing minutes, until Jack is able to persuade him, "for your wife's sake," to head for home.

Jack doesn't mention having seen Ricky Froelich out running shortly after four-thirty this afternoon on Highway 4. At this point, it doesn't seem necessary to discourage McCarroll by telling him that Claire was not with the boy.

## MORNING

AT NINE P.M., the Ontario Provincial Police had a local radio station broadcast Claire's description, and every squad car in the area was alerted; this despite the fact that she was not yet officially missing. For anyone who knew Claire, her failure to show up at the most important Brownie pack meeting of the year was enough to indicate that she was missing. But the OPP didn't know her. They were able to say things like "You never know with kids, they get strange ideas, she may turn up at a relative's place."

"All our relatives are in Virginia."

"Oh. Well, Mrs. McCarroll, it's a bit soon to jump to conclusions. Our officers are keeping a sharp eye out. Why don't you get some rest and give us a call in the morning."

*The morning.* It is a far-off country reachable only through night, and Mrs. McCarroll does not know how to get through this one. Sit still, and the night will pass through you and around you. Then it will be morning. And Claire will be "missing."

That first night leaves a residue of cold ash within the mother. The light has been on in Claire's bedroom and the mother has sat on the chair by the bed with her hands folded, looking at the bed. She has smoothed the bed. She has looked in the closet where her child's clothes are hung, at the bookcase lined with dolls and fairy tales and stuffed animals—Claire's things are here, it is impossible that Claire should not return to them. Already Mrs. McCarroll has thought, "Why did I close her book?"—*Black Beauty*—"Why did I pick it up off the floor? I should not have done a wash this morning, I should have saved her crusts from breakfast." Crumbs are alive and immediate, they say, "The person who ate this toast cannot be gone from the earth." The clothes, the dolls, the crumbs, the laundry basket all say, "She'll be right back." This is her life, in progress, this is a pause only. These crumbs, this turned page, this undershirt in the laundry basket, these are not final things.

When is morning? Is it morning when you can see the dew on the grass? When the paper lands on the front step? When the lamp by the small bed is drowned in the tepid light from the window? Turn it off. The bedspread remains unwrinkled. Already, life is ebbing from the room. All that was poised, just put down or about to be picked up, appears a little more static; the afterimage of movement fading from objects, the leaves of books exhaling softly, clothes hanging more quietly in the closet. Like a multitude of small scarves flowing from the sleeve of a magician, the room and everything in it is being gently deserted by the spirits and currents that move things. The earth wants it. When is morning?

If you are waiting for enough light so that the authorites can thoroughly search for your child, morning doesn't come until six A.M., and right now it's only five-thirty. Sharon McCarroll didn't know how she would get through the night, but now the darkness seems gentle in retrospect, because during that empty night it was fewer hours since her daughter had left the house this afternoon—yesterday afternoon. And now another morning has arrived, taking the place of the previous one, blowing over it, depositing grains, beginning a slow obliteration.

"Don't worry, hon."

He is in his bathrobe. He put on his pajamas last night, in order to comfort his wife with the appearance of normalcy. At midnight he chose to stay home with her rather than roam the countryside in his car—that would only have alarmed her, and lit up the roadside, the damp ditches. Instead he panicked quietly in the living room, looking in on his wife from time to time in Claire's bedroom to say, "Do you want some tea, hon?"

She remained fully dressed, but each time he looked in she did her part to reassure him by smoothing her hair, forming a smile and saying, "That's okay hon, why don't you get some sleep?"

They have both prayed throughout the night but they have yet to pray together. They have swallowed the retch of emptiness that lunges from the gut, swallowed it back, the howl of something bottomless. Be careful, it smells your despair. Too much prayer can awaken it. Insufficient prayer can awaken it.

How can she have dozed off? For forty minutes in the chair. Fresh pain of surgery upon awakening, this is not a dream. Rising from the chair, empty bed, *my child is not at home.* The brief hallway to the kitchen; one hand grazes the wall, her feet hurt, she has slept in her heels that match her scarf because her husband likes her to look nice and now a chorus starts up in her head, it whips through all the acceptable reasons why her child is not at home, patters through lists of what-I-have-to-do-today, what-I-will-do-when-my-child-gets-home, this Christmas we are going home to Virginia, my mother and sisters will not believe how Claire has grown, take the meat out of the freezer for tonight. All staving off the sound of something deeper still—the bass line, slow-wave, the only reassuring voice because the one that promises an end to all this waking and waiting; deep and patient in its refrain until the mother is ready to make out the words it sings so regretfully: "Your child is dead."

She rode her bike down the dirt road to Rock Bass. She got off and pulled it through the opening in the wire fence left cordially unrepaired by the farmer, and walked it along the semi-path to Rock Bass.

She carefully descended the ravine, traversing the slope, holding her bike, skidding a little with its weight. She laid it on the bank, mindful not to crush the sparkly pink streamers, and crossed the water on the stepping stones.

Claire sat under the maple at Rock Bass, in the worn place where everyone always sat, opened her Frankie and Annette lunchbox and scattered the remains of her picnic in a semicircle at her feet. There was always one chipmunk bold enough to come up and snatch a morsel, but Claire imagined the other little creatures watching and trembling until she had left, when finally they would approach and nibble. She imagined they knew her now and might one day come to visit her at home. They might talk to her and be her friends. Or merely perch on her windowsill and watch while she slept, chattering away softly about the magic gift they were preparing.

She wiped her hands on a paper serviette which she then returned to her lunchbox. She looked at Frankie and Annette, each beaming brunette head framed in a pink heart. Ricky and Claire.

She began making her way up the other side of the ravine. This was a good place to look for fallen eggs that needed rescuing. She got a burr in her ankle sock and stooped to pick it out.

When she straightened up, there were the familiar feet.

"Hi little girl."

"Hi."

"Look what I've got."

"What?"

"Come here a minute."

Claire walked up toward the open hand. When she arrived, she looked into the palm and saw a pale blue egg.

"A robin's egg," she breathed. It was so rare to find one whole.

"You can have it."

The egg weighed nothing in Claire's hand, because it was empty.

"I know where there are more eggs, little girl."

You could see the pinprick where a snake had sucked out the insides.

"Alive ones."

And so Claire set off. She would never have gone off with a stranger.

"The nest is on the other side of the cornfield." And when they had passed through the cornfield—

"Across the meadow, just inside the woods."

And when they got to the woods, Claire said, "No." Her mother would not let her enter the woods.

"The cornfield is worse than the woods, Claire."

But it turns out that the meadow is worst of all.

When the squeezing started, Claire said, "I have to go home."

"It's okay, Claire."

And she didn't know, right away, that it wasn't.

# Holy Thursday

It was very late when Madeleine's father came home. She had placed her new brass wings on her dresser for him to see. He came into her room and she woke up when he sat on the side of her bed, but she pretended still to be asleep. He tucked the covers up around her and smoothed her bangs back from her forehead. "My good old buddy," he whispered.

She sighed "in her sleep."

He kissed her forehead and crept from the room. She considered calling him back and asking where Claire had been and what she had said when they found her. But she didn't wish to wreck the moment of being tucked in by Dad when he thought she was sleeping. She would find out tomorrow. She would ask Claire.

Madeleine pours puffed rice into her bowl, tolerating the dry fodder for the sake of the plastic sword and sheath that come with the bomb-shelter–sized bag. Mike spoons sugar onto his Cap'n Crunch as well as his egg.

"There won't be a tooth left in your head by the time you're twenty," says Dad behind his newspaper.

Mike's eyelashes are crinkled. He has told his parents he singed them "at Scouts" but Madeleine knows better.

"*Maman,*" he says, "*j'ai besoin d'une chemise blanche pour ce soir, c'est le banquet de hockey.*"

"*Oui, Michel, je sais, mange tout, c'est ça le bon p'tit garçon.*"

"Maman." He groans. "I'm not a little kid any more, okay?"

She squeezes his face between her hands. "*T'es toujours mon bébé, toi, mon p'tit soldat,*" she says in a kitchy-koo voice to tease him, and covers his cheeks with kisses. He writhes away but he's grinning, wiping off the lipstick.

"Dad?" says Madeleine.

"Yeah, sweetie?" He turns a page of his paper.

"Where did you find Claire?"

The newspaper stays put.

Mike says, "They didn't."

The newspaper is lowered to the table. Her father gives Mike a look, then says to her, "We're still looking." Adding in his reassuring tone—the one that sounds slightly amused—"She probably hid out from the rain somewhere overnight and she'll turn up all waterlogged and hungry."

Mike stares at his plate.

Jack gives Mimi a peck on the lips, pats Madeleine on the head and heads for the door. "Have a good day, fellas."

Mike speaks in French to his mother, so fast that Madeleine can't follow. Maman replies but less rapidly, so Madeleine is able to ask her, "How come Dad doesn't want me to worry? How come I would worry?"

Mimi looks at her daughter and reaches for her pack of Cameos on the counter. She says, "I want you to say a little prayer for Claire McCarroll," and lights a cigarette. "You too Michel."

"Why?" says Madeleine.

"Don't 'why' me, Madeleine, why is it always 'why'?" She inhales the cool menthol. "Because it might be difficult to find her. But they will. Now go get dressed. *Attends, Michel, je veux te dire un mot.*"

Oddly enough, Madeleine is more reassured by her mother's testiness than by her father's gentleness. And yet fear forms in the pit of her stomach, the way it does whenever her mother tells her to say a little prayer for someone. It means they've had it.

Madeleine was delighted when Mike told her to walk with him to school. Now she hurries along beside him and Arnold Pinder and Roy Noonan, taking two strides for their every one. Roy said, "Hi," to her for which he received a swift punch on the arm from Arnold. Mike gave up Arnold for Lent. Maman and Dad thought that was a very mature decision. They have no idea that he "broke his fast" yesterday, and that his eyelashes got burned when Arnold lit a frog on fire with gasoline in a jar.

"Mike?"

He ignores her, going on with what he was saying: "Ricky Froelich's got one made out of balsa wood, we could easily make our own."

Roy says, "Yeah, all's you do is adjust the scale upward and—"

"We could just go to the scrapyard and steal one," says Arnold.

"Mike," says Madeleine.

"What?" he says, exasperated.

"Where do you think Claire is?"

"How should I know?"

Arnold Pinder says, "Kidnapped, my dad says—"

"Shut up, Pinder," says Mike.

Arnold bristles, his fist retracts. Mike indicates his little sister with a glance and Arnold clams up. Mike says, "She's lost."

"Oh," says Arnold, "yeah."

Roy Noonan says, "Don't worry, Madeleine."

"You guys must think I'm retarded," she says, slowing her pace.

Mike reaches back without looking and grabs her by the wrist.

"You're walking with me," he says, dragging her.

"Why?"

"And you wait for me after school too."

"As if!"

"Maman said."

At least she has found out what really happened to Claire McCarroll: *kidnapped*. At this very moment, she is sitting in a cobwebby shed somewhere with her hands tied behind her back and a gag around her mouth. If Madeleine were kidnapped she would get away. She would rub the ropes against a rock like the Hardy boys. She would knock the kidnapper out, or jump from a speeding car and roll into the ditch, then hitchhike home. But it's impossible to imagine Claire doing anything but sitting there politely with her tied-up hands.

Madeleine doesn't consider anything beyond that. There is nothing beyond that. She does, however, wonder when the ransom note will arrive. Do the kidnappers think Claire is rich because she's American? Maybe President Kennedy will pay the ransom.

By the time Jack got through to the office of First Secretary Crawford at the British Embassy in Washington, it had begun to rain again. Grey streaked the glass and obscured the view from the phone booth. The McCarrolls' little girl was still out there somewhere. At best, she had fallen and broken a limb, was frightened and disoriented and unable to make her way back to the PMQs. It was possible.

"Crawford here."

"Si, McCarroll's nine-year-old daughter has gone missing."

A pause, then "Poor bastard." Simon agreed that Jack ought not to brief McCarroll until and unless his daughter turned up safely. "Call me at the night number the moment you hear anything." He sighed. "This operation has been plagued by more gremlins. . . ."

"What do you want me to do with the car, Si?"

"Oh right, the bloody car. Keep it."

"What am I supposed to tell my wife? That I robbed a bank?"

"I'll have to have someone pick it up, or . . . Christ. Where is it now?"

"I moved it to Exeter. I'll have to move it again at some point or it'll be towed for scrap."

"Let it be. Finders keepers."

"CIA's budget, I hope."

"I'm going to miss you, sunshine."

Jack was still smiling when he left the phone booth, but his smile faded when he saw an OPP cruiser pull up to Number 4 Hangar.

McCarroll came out and got in the car. Jack was wearing his government-issue rain poncho and rubber overshoes. He made his way quickly to the hangar to join one of the search parties. All male personnel, including kitchen staff, were out looking.

Miss Lang is taking Mr. March's place while he talks to the police. They are interviewing the staff, trying to find clues. He has been gone for half an hour already. There was a knock at the classroom door and Mr. March went to open it, singing, "'Who's that knocking at my door?'" But he stopped when he saw the police officer standing there, and said, "Just let me get my glasses." He returned to collect them from his desk, took his hanky from his pocket and cleaned the lenses. It was the first time Madeleine had ever seen him use his hanky for anything but his wiener.

Miss Lang asks what the class would like to do and the choice is unanimous: art. Never before has the grade four class had art on a Thursday afternoon; one good thing has come of Claire McCarroll getting lost. Even Grace puts up her hand and votes for art, although it's difficult to see how she will be able to hold a crayon with her hands bandaged. They are bound in thick white gauze that has frayed and turned grey with the passage of the day. Mr. March seemed not to notice, but Miss Lang asks if Grace has hurt herself. Grace manages to explain that her father has had enough of her with her fingers always in her mouth. He gave her a choice: "I'll break them or bandage them."

The class is quiet. Miss Lang is allowing them to draw anything they like as long as it's on an Easter theme. They are permitted to use any kind of medium—pastels, water colours, anything but fingerpaints. Madeleine has chosen to work with pencil crayons, drawing a day in the life of the Dynamic Duo. In the cocoon of the classroom, with its school smells, the comforting fug of orange peels, pencil shavings, damp wool and chalk, with the soothing rain against the windows, Miss Lang puts on an LP she brought from home. The Mantovani Strings release their magic in a slow waterfall of sound, *The-ere's . . . a sum-mer place. . . .*

Madeleine bends to her drawing, her tongue toying with a molar that has come loose, concentrating on the Boy Wonder disguised as a baby in a rocket-powered pram in pursuit of the Joker. The afternoon glows grey outside although it is not yet two-thirty. The patient rain embroiders the puddles that have formed in the shallow depressions at either end of the teeter-totters, beneath each swing and at the foot of the slide. Beyond the baseball diamond, the bungalows and duplexes of the

PMQs are hunkered down but cheerful in their rainbow colours, all the brighter against the pewter sky.

Madeleine directs her gaze across Algonquin Drive, to the farmer's field—the farmer with the fabled shotgun. There is activity over there. Cars are pulling up and parking on the shoulder of the road—ordinary ones and several black-and-white OPP cruisers.

She recalls the poor dog trapped in the stormpipe. Did it get out? Did it drown? She feels a terrible sorrow coming on, and consoles herself with the prospect of asking her father what happened to the dog. He'll know. She returns her eyes to her drawing and remembers that they were supposed to do art on an Easter theme. She draws a speech bubble for Robin and in it she prints, "Holy Thursday, Batman!"

She lifts her eyes from her drawing with satisfaction and studies the back of Grace Novotny's head and shoulders. Grace's profile is partially visible, contorted as she is over her desk in the manner common to all when colouring. She is licking her chapped lips, breathing through her mouth because her nose is plugged. Grace doesn't usually do anything without her eyes wandering a great deal, but today she is concentrating extra hard, perhaps because of the bandages on her hands. Madeleine can see the yellow pencil crayon sticking up from Grace's filthy fist. What can she be drawing?

Madeleine looks out the window again and sees cars parked on both sides of the road now. In the field, a line of men in rain ponchos comes into view, walking slowly, shoulder to shoulder, across the field. They are looking for something very small, thinks Madeleine. And valuable. A watch, or a diamond.

Beside the window, Claire's desk sits empty. It's as though she were away sick with the flu. She will be back tomorrow.

Madeleine raises her hand. "Miss Lang, may I please sharpen my pencil?"

"Yes, Madeleine, you may."

On her way back from the pencil sharpener, Madeleine slows when she gets to Grace's desk and gazes in wonder on Grace's picture. A storm of yellow butterflies.

There are so many, so many it's dizzying, each one perfectly drawn and coloured in, each wing intricately outlined, no two the same, like snowflakes. It's so good, you could probably make wallpaper out of it.

Miss Lang lifts the needle from the record and it's as if the whole class has been in the court of Sleeping Beauty. Everyone looks up groggily, tousled and calm. They hand in their work, and it turns out there was some very good art done that day.

"They were looking for Claire," says Colleen. "I seen them too."

"That's a dumb place to look," says Madeleine. "Right out in the open? In a field?" They are walking up St. Lawrence Avenue. While they never leave the schoolyard together, they have taken to drifting toward one another at some point if Madeleine is on her own.

"No it isn't," says Colleen.

The world is suffused with rain glow, the air soft and scented, all so vivid and promising; as though the three o'clock bell had heralded a widening of the world, a release into the future, unknown and yet contained within a frame, like a movie screen. Madeleine savours a keen anticipation. Something is going to happen. Something wonderful.

She says, "It is so, Colleen, it's dumb, because if Claire was in a field in broad daylight they'd see her right away, unless she was hiding, and who would hide in a field, and besides she's lost and you can't get lost in a field right across from the school." Madeleine takes a breath and adds, "Stunned one." She steps back, hoping for a reckoning. But Colleen neglects to take the bait.

Madeleine glances over her shoulder to see Mike and his friends following at a secure distance, like bodyguards. She is about to point them out but Colleen has said something. "What'd you say?"

"That's because they don't expect to find her alive," Colleen repeats.

It takes Madeleine a moment, and then it's as though she had stumbled down an unexpected step. And the world is a different colour. Metallic now, no longer lambent. The warm feeling of being in a movie is gone. Now she is not in anything. Except the rain. And it has no borders that mean anything at all.

That night, she requests *Winnie the Pooh*. There is no shame in returning to old favourites. And her father says one is never too old to appreciate great literature. She opts not to do the voices, requesting that he read it all. She contemplates the stick in the water rushing beneath the bridge and it soothes her mind. But when it comes time for him to turn out her light, she asks, "Dad, do they expect to find Claire alive?"

Jack pauses, his hand on the switch. He returns and sits on the edge of her bed.

"Sure they do."

"Then how come they were looking for her in a field?"

He turns and glances around the room. "Where's old Bugsy?" He finds him under the bed, plucks the nap off his ears and tucks him in beside her, saying, "They figure maybe she dropped something in the field and that'll help them find her."

"Maybe she left a trail."

"Maybe she did." Jack leans down to kiss her and she puts her arms around his neck, as she often does, refusing to let him go. He tickles her and she releases him. He makes it halfway to the door.

"What if she got kidnapped?"

" . . . Well there'd be a note."

"I thought so."

"Don't you worry about Claire, she'll be home before you know it." He turns off her light.

"Dad?"

"Yeah?"

"Are you going to die soon?"

He laughs. "Are you kiddin'? Tough old roosters don't die in a hurry."

"Everybody dies."

"You know what, Madeleine?" and his tone is no longer mollifying, it's factual. "That day is so far away it's not even worth thinking about."

"What if there's an air raid? Would the siren go off like in October?"

He looks her in the eye. "You know what NORAD is?" He leans in the doorway, framed by the hall light. "It's a big early warning system that would kick into action long before anyone could get over here with a bomb. We'd send one of our fighters up to blast it out of the sky and that would be it."

"Dad?"

"Go to sleep now, old buddy."

"Is Claire dead?"

"Nooo!"—he chuckles—"don't you worry, now. You know what?"

"What?"

"There's an old saying: 'Don't shake hands with the Devil before you meet him.'"

Madeleine lets him believe he has comforted her. "'Night, Dad."

Jack heads downstairs and out the door, telling Mimi he needs a breath of fresh air. He's not lying. But he also needs to make a phone call.

Madeleine strokes Bugs's long ears back from his merry forehead. "Don't worry, Bugs." She doesn't repeat her dad's comment about the Devil, however, because, while it's meant to reassure you that the Devil is nowhere near, implicit is the idea that, sooner or later, you will in fact meet him.

# GOOD FRIDAY

CLAIRE'S PHOTO IS ON the cover of the *London Free Press*. Madeleine sees it when she opens the door to get the milk from the front step. The photo is a little smudgy because it's a black-and-white reproduction of Claire's school picture—the one everyone had taken in the gym last November. But it is unmistakeably Claire smiling up from the front porch next to the milk. And the caption: *Missing Child*. Claire is famous. Madeleine carries the paper up with the milk, exclaiming, "Extra, extra, read all about it!"

Her mother takes the paper and thrusts it at her father, saying, "I don't want any of these in the house"—as though she were talking about getting rid of all the spinning wheels in the kingdom.

Jack is neither surprised nor offended, he merely folds the paper into his briefcase, and when Mike comes down and turns on the radio for the news, Jack shuts it right back off. They eat breakfast, Mimi dressed and made up as usual, leaning against the counter with her coffee and cigarette. It is as silent as it was during the missile crisis. This time, however, there is not even the crinkle of newspaper pages. Just the sound of crunching. Madeleine looks at Mike. He is wearing the same innocent expression as her father. She pokes her toad-in-the-hole and the yolk streams out.

Today is a holiday. But it's Good Friday, which means you are not supposed to have too much fun. There is to be no television tonight—Jesus is on the Cross, this is no time to be watching the Three Stooges. Mike is not even allowed to play road hockey. Maman lays down the law every year. And for supper, fish. Not fish 'n' chips, but a piece of watery white flesh on the plate next to pallid canned peas and boiled potatoes. No dessert. Offer it up for the suffering of Our Lord. When He was thirsty, all they gave him to drink was vinegar. Remember the poor starving children in Africa. It is raining, because it always rains on Good Friday.

Madeleine leaves to call on Auriel, but sees Colleen out in front of the Froelich house in a rain poncho. She is crouched with her coffee can, parting the grass with her fingers. Madeleine quietly retreats and cuts through several backyards before emerging farther up and crossing the street to the Bouchers' house. They are going to listen to Auriel's mum's Vera Lynn records and let the budgie fly around. Then they'll go next door and play with Lisa's new baby brother. They will continue to speculate about Claire's perilous adventure. Auriel has suggested that she may have run away to Disneyland. As Madeleine knocks on the

Bouchers' door, she glances down the street to where Colleen is making patient progress across her front yard.

"Hello pet, come in out of the rain," says Mrs. Boucher. Madeleine smells cinnamon buns baking—Mrs. Boucher is Anglican, they don't have to suffer as much on Good Friday. Something in her expression changes as she looks over Madeleine's head toward the street. Madeleine turns to see a police car coming up St. Lawrence Avenue. It crawls past them, then turns into the Froelichs' driveway. Colleen Froelich stands up with her coffee can.

Mrs. Boucher says, "In you go, love," turning to call up the stairs: "Auriel, Madeleine's here."

## HOLY SATURDAY

AN OPP HELICOPTER chops across the grey sky over the PMQs and kids stop what they are doing and look up. By now, everyone knows that the helicopter is searching for Claire. So are the bright yellow Chipmunks that have been flying low, tracing an aerial grid, each with a pilot and an observer to peer down through the rain. The grown-ups can no longer hide their fear. Kids openly speculate that Claire has drowned in a ditch, fallen down an air shaft—although there were never any mines around here—or been chopped to bits by a maniac with a hook. *The Exeter Times-Advocate* has urged farmers to check their barns and out-buildings, and to shine flashlights down their wells.

On the way back to the car after Holy Saturday Mass, Madeleine sees again the rows of men in rain gear, fanning out from the airfield into the meadows and woodlots. A brace of German shepherds strain on their leashes and sniff the ground frantically. Madeleine knows they have been given something of Claire's to smell. Just like Dale the Police Dog who found the little girl asleep in the corn. They should get Rex to help.

Jack makes no secret of going out to search again with the other men, and Mimi gets her children to kneel down in the living room and say the rosary with her for the safe return of Claire McCarroll.

Ricky Froelich has been helping with the search. He brought Rex along at first, but the policemen asked him to take the dog home since he was not a trained search-and-rescue animal. Rick wanted to say, "How do you know?" because Rex's origins before he wound up at the Goderich pound are unknown. But he didn't want to be smart to the cop. Those days are behind him.

On Friday a couple of policemen whom Rick knew from the search came by the house to ask him the same questions a couple of others had on Thursday. He didn't mind. If they were overlapping their efforts it meant they were working overtime to find the kid. He told the officers what he had told their colleagues: he had been out running with his sister and his dog when he met Claire McCarroll heading south down the Huron County road. She had told him she was going to Rock Bass. He had hitched her up to the dog and they had continued together to the intersection. When they had got to the willow tree they had stopped and he had unhitched Rex. She had turned right down the dirt road, heading for Rock Bass on her bike, and he and his sister and his dog had turned left toward the highway.

Rick has just returned home from searching all morning, and is in the middle of making and devouring sandwiches, when the same two cops arrive again on Saturday afternoon.

This time they ask him, "Did you meet anyone on the road after you left her?" This is a new question and Rick realizes that they now suspect someone may have harmed her.

"No, I didn't, sorry."

They ask him to come for a ride with them this time and point out precisely where it was he left her. As he is on his way out, his mother comes to the door and says, "Wait Ricky, I'll call Papa to go with you."

"It's okay, Mum, I'll be right back."

But she says, "Hang on a minute, honey, Papa's just down the basement."

Rick smiles, a bit embarrassed in front of the cops. One of the officers—the one who has asked most of the questions—says, "Mrs. Froelich, we just want to borrow your boy for a few minutes to show us exactly where he let the little girl off at, it might help him to remember if he saw anyone else in the vicinity."

Karen pauses, looking at the policemen, then turns and calls again, "Hank."

But Rick leaves with the officers, saying, "I'll be right back, Ma."

Karen watches them pull out of the driveway with her son in the back of the police car.

But they don't turn south on the Huron County road. They turn north, toward Exeter. The windshield wipers thunk back and forth and Rick says, "It's back there."

"Yeah, we're just going to make a circle, you said you were out running, is that right?"

"Oh yeah," says Rick, and leans back. He directs them in reverse along the path he took on Wednesday afternoon. The police radio crackles unintelligibly.

"If you remember seeing anyone or anything at all, you just sing out, young fella," says the cop in the passenger seat.

When they reach Highway 4—the stretch that doglegs west just north of Lucan—Rick says, "I saw a car."

The officer looks at him in the rearview mirror.

Rick says, "Going west, yeah, like we are now. He passed me, right around here."

The cruiser slows, pulls over and stops. The cop looks at Rick in the mirror and asks, "What kind of car?"

"Ford Galaxy."

"You could tell, eh?"

"Oh yeah, went right past me, eh, brand-new."

"You like cars?"

"I love cars."

The cop chuckles. "Me too. What colour was this Chevy?"

"It was a Ford," Rick corrects him politely. "Galaxy, brand-new. Blue."

"Brand-new, eh?"

"Yeah, '63, I could tell 'cause it has the new fastback."

"What else could you tell?"

"Well I could see where it had a dent in the rear bumper."

"Oh yeah?" The officer digs his notebook from his chest pocket and starts writing it all down. The one behind the wheel seems not to be taking any notice. The back of his head, his wide neck, impassive.

Rick leans forward between the two blue hats and searches his memory for any stray detail that might help. "It had a bumper sticker."

"What kind of sticker?"

"Yellow. You know, like from Storybook Gardens."

The policeman smiles slightly and nods, slowly repeating Rick's words as he writes: "Story . . . book . . . Gardens."

Rick feels suddenly a bit guilty. "I don't think it's going to help you much."

"Why not?"

"Well, whoever it was was wearing an air force hat, so. . . ."

"Yeah?"

"Yeah, I couldn't see who 'cause of the sun, but he's prob'ly not the guy you're looking for."

"Who are we looking for, Rick?"

"Well"—Ricky hesitates—"whoever, you know. Took her."

"Is that what you think happened?"

"Maybe. I don't know."

The cop smiles in the mirror, "Well we're in the same boat then, 'cause neither do we." He returns his eyes to his notebook. "Let me get this straight," he says, pen poised. "You couldn't see his face, but you saw his hat."

"Like the outline of his hat," says Rick.

"Right." Then to his partner, "Rudy, how do you spell 'silhouette'?"

"Don't ask me."

Rick laughs with them and says he can't spell it either. The cop clicks his tongue thoughtfully, then says, "I'm just trying to calculate. . . . How long would you say it takes to jog from here back to the intersection where you left her?"

"Oh, uh. I got home around five-thirty, quarter to six, so . . . and that's about the same distance, so I guess an hour or so?"

The cop raises his eyebrows companionably and writes it down, saying, "How can you be so sure when you got home?"

"I had a game. Basketball."

"Who you play for?"

"Huron County Braves."

"Good stuff."

No discernible signal passes between the officers, but the car pulls away from the shoulder once more and gathers speed. They travel in silence through the rain until the cop behind the wheel says, "You sure it was an air force hat? Could've been a cop."

"Naw," says Rick.

"How do you know?" asks his partner.

"He waved."

"Thought you said you didn't know him," says the driver.

"I couldn't *see* him," says Rick. "But I must've known him."

"I guess all the air force guys know all the air force brats, eh?" says his partner with a smile.

"I'm not an air force brat."

"I didn't mean it in a bad way."

"No, I know," says Rick. "I just mean my dad's not personnel, he's a teacher at the school."

They drive on and the officer behind the wheel says, "Just because a man is in uniform doesn't make him a saint."

"You can say that again," says Rick.

"What do you mean by that?"

"Nothin'." And the other cop winks at him in the mirror.

When Rick gets home, he taps the roof of the cruiser as it backs out of the driveway and touches two fingers to his forehead, the way the air force men do. The cop on the passenger side does likewise.

Upstairs, Colleen holds Elizabeth steady in the tub while Karen Froelich washes her. The door is closed to prevent the baby from crawling out and getting into everything. The other baby is down in the living room, sound asleep on Henry Froelich's sleeping chest, serenaded by Joan Baez.

Karen hears the front door and says to Colleen, "Everything's fine, baby." Elizabeth reaches for her mother, Karen catches her wrist and kisses the back of her hand. "See? Ricky's back already."

Though television is permitted on Holy Saturday, *Perry Mason* is strictly verboten at all times, but Madeleine is not deriving as much guilty pleasure as she should because things are out of joint. When Dad came in from helping with the search, her mother turned on the television herself, and told her to watch something. Now, Perry's theme music comes up, sexy and swaggering, but her parents continue to confer, oblivious, at the kitchen table.

Madeleine catches the tail end of her mother's sentence. " . . . they'll go to pieces."

"Who's going to pieces?" pipes up Madeleine from the living room.

"Never you mind, go back to your program."

Ordered to watch *Perry Mason*. Things are coming apart. She curls up on the couch with a cushion in her lap and resists an atavistic urge to suck her thumb.

Perry, Paul, Della and a "B-girl" with fishnet stockings and brassy hair are in a bar. The B-girl flirts with Paul, batting her eyelashes, chin raised to emphasize her industrial-size chest—bosom. This is supposed to be Holy Saturday, doesn't anyone care? Madeleine looks imploringly toward the kitchen, but her parents are huddled in the gathering darkness. Twenty-five minutes later, the B-girl winds up murdered and we are in court. "What in the name of time are you watching?"

"But Dad, Maman said I could watch it."

"Maman said you could watch TV."

"It's almost over."

"You mean to tell me you've digested most of this garbage already?"

"We're just about to find out who did it."

"Oh," he says, sitting down. "Well, let's see."

They watch, Madeleine curled in the crook of his arm. After two minutes, Jack says, "The gardener did it." Twenty minutes later, Perry points to a bony-faced man on the stand who is clutching a crumpled hat. "The hose you used to water the grounds; the hose you used to strangle Miss Delaney; the hose you then disposed of at the Fairmont Country Club!"

Madeleine gasps, "How did you know?!"

"You can't fool the old rooster. Now let's go get some supper."

Rick has taken his sisters to see *Kim* at the movie theatre on the station. On their way home, he tells them to wait while he stops in at the search headquarters set up in Number 4 Hangar.

He looks at the enlarged wall map of Huron County and sees that the search has been expanded to include the route of his Wednesday run. He wonders if the police are wasting their time—how likely is it that an air force man could have had anything to do with Claire's disappearance? On the other hand, there's over a thousand personnel on the station—Rick doesn't know them all. No one does.

It is turning out to be an excellent Holy Saturday. Madeleine piously reminds herself that it would be better if Maman were enjoying it with them, but she is down the street "keeping Mrs. McCarroll company." It wouldn't be very nice to say so out loud, but sometimes it's more fun to be on your own with your dad.

After they paint the hard-boiled eggs for Easter Sunday morning, Madeleine and Mike drive into Exeter with their father to pick up Dixie Lee fried chicken. *Aroma! Flavour! Tenderness!*

At the counter Jack leaves the kids to wait for the food. "I'll be right back." He drives down the main street, past the empty fairgrounds on the outskirts, to the old train station. It's boarded up, weeds flourishing between the tracks. He drives around the back. The Ford Galaxy is still there.

Too bad he can't simply keep it as Simon suggested. The police will auction it off. If this were a big city like New York, the car would have been lifted by now, or stripped. But this is Exeter—not exactly the crime capital of Canada. As Jack pulls away again he thinks of the McCarroll child and revises that last thought.

The day's festivities are capped with Mike tying one end of a string around Madeleine's loose tooth. He ties the other end to his doorknob, then slams the door. "Presto! That's worth a dime at least," he says, presenting her with the dangling, bloody molar.

Mimi is waiting for Karen Froelich to arrive before leaving Sharon McCarroll. It will be dark soon. The casserole she brought remains untouched in the oven. She has not been able to persuade Sharon, but hopes Blair will eat something when he gets home from the day's search. It's not right that routine should have entered into this picture to make it at all recognizable—"home from the day's search." As if looking for the body of his child were his job.

Steve Ridelle prescribed some pills and Elaine brought them when she came to do her shift with Sharon. Just three doses. Better she shouldn't have too many on hand. Mimi saw the bottle by the bathroom sink—Valium.

"Works wonders," Elaine told her.

Mimi has just turned the heat down on the casserole when there is a tap at the door. It's a small stab in her heart to see how Sharon looks up with a moment's hope, before the door opens and Karen Froelich appears.

Mimi exchanges a word and a squeeze of the hand with Karen and leaves—she is still not someone Mimi would pick for a friend but, as Jack says, it takes all kinds. Outside, the clouds have begun to part, revealing a star or two, but the darkness is still too complete, too close. She walks up the street toward the lights of her own house. Blair McCarroll should be home by now. They can't search in the dark.

When she gets in, Jack rises from the couch. "I'm going over to the station. The police called off the search till Monday and Blair lost his cool."

Madeleine is in Mike's room, at his desk by the window. He's sitting on his bed tying a baseball into his new glove. He has allowed her to stick a decal onto his model Lancaster bomber and told her not to breathe in the airplane glue. She sniffs it surreptitiously, then replaces the cap and ponders the snarled snout of the Lanc. Dad would have sat right there, behind the tiny plastic window of the cockpit. She picks it up and, as she flies it past the window, sees her father heading for the car. "Dad's going out," she says.

That means Maman is home. Madeleine remembers that she was supposed to have a bath. On her way down the hall, she pauses to hear something so unfamiliar that it takes her a moment to recognize the sound. Maman is crying.

THIS MORNING there was no money under Madeleine's pillow, just the tooth still, with its straggly root. She said nothing; it would be churlish to complain about the Tooth Fairy when the Easter Bunny has outdone himself. She and Mike have found all the chocolate eggs, Dad has won the hard-boiled egg battle and Madeleine has eaten the ears off her chocolate bunny, able to savour the dark richness for the first time since before the exercise group last September. This morning, chocolate has been redeemed along with all of us by the sacrifice of Our Lord Jesus and the miracle of His resurrection.

Mike has just decapitated his rooster when the phone rings. Mimi answers, and a second later Madeleine sees her mother sink into a kitchen chair, then glance over at her and Mike in the living room and make a gesture as though reaching to draw a curtain. Mike pauses, chocolate beak halfway to his mouth, but Madeleine plucks out a bunny eye and eats it, her warning systems jammed by sugar.

"When?" their mother asks into the phone.

Their father joins her. She looks up at him and he bends to put an arm around her, obscuring her from the children's view. A moment later he strides jauntily into the room. "Upstairs now and get ready for Mass."

They obey. Madeleine wonders what is wrong. They were supposed to fast for an hour before Mass but Maman forgot. Madeleine licks melted chocolate from the palm of her hand and steels herself for the ordeal of getting into the scratchy strangulating dress of tulle with matching pillbox hat.

Madeleine thinks she's in trouble for something when Maman says to her after Mass, "Your father wants to talk to you." On the way home from church, in the Rambler, Mike won't look at her. He is quietly examining a stack of baseball cards. She watches the back of her father's head for a sign, but he is silent and still. Maman's white chapeau with the grey silk roses is likewise inscrutable.

Mike nudges her. He is holding a card so new it still has bubble-gum dust on it. Roger Maris at the bat, his signature scrawled across his Yankees uniform. Mike nods to her—*it's yours*. She hesitates in disbelief, then takes the card. Mike has waited over a year to open that pack of bubble gum. It's gold. It's hers. Why?

They pull into the driveway and the butterflies wake up in her stomach. Mike and Maman go inside but Dad waits and says, "Let's you and I go for a little walk."

This can only be about one thing, Madeleine realizes as she gets slowly out of the car. They have found out about Mr. March. What she thought was so far behind her as to have been a dream has risen up whole and reeking. They have found Claire McCarroll and she has told them everything. Madeleine knows now that's why Claire ran away. She was afraid, when Mr. March made her be the Easter Bunny, that he would put her back in the exercise group. And Madeleine knows that Claire never would have gotten into the exercise group in the first place if Madeleine hadn't gotten out of it. It is all her fault. Her insides melt like chocolate, her thighs feel suddenly heavy. She looks up at her father and takes his hand with her small white gloved one and says, "Okay."

Everyone is being so quiet and gentle, it can only mean that they will send her away—for how can they continue to live with her now that they know what she has done? They will cast her out of the family. They walk. Up St. Lawrence Avenue to Columbia Drive.

It's a crisp day, but Madeleine's dress of salmon tulle, her hat tied with a ribbon under her chin, all of it is a hot, choking mass of burrs. This is the outfit she will be wearing when the Children's Aid comes to take her away. The sun is too bright, so much light she can barely squint to see, the buildings of the base like blinding snow across the county road. Her father puts on his sunglasses. "You want to walk over to the airfield?" he asks.

When Snow White's stepmother wanted to be rid of her, she sent her off with a woodsman who took her by the hand. He had an axe. "Bring me back her heart," said the Queen. But when they reached the forest, the woodsman took pity on Snow White and abandoned her in the woods. He returned to the Queen with the heart of a deer. "Okay," replies Madeleine.

Maman said, *Take Madeleine to the airfield.* Then what? *Put her on a plane.* They cross the county road. To one side of the gates, the crows' nest, still atop the wooden pole, bristles against the sun. It is sparser but intact after the winter, the rusted mouth of the siren protruding more rudely now. On the other side of the gate, the old Spitfire throws back the sun in sheets.

Madeleine walks into the shade of its wing and says, "I'm tired."

"Well, we don't have to go all the way to the airfield," says her father.

She is relieved. It wasn't part of the plan after all, to send her away by plane. She sits on the grass with her back against the pedestal.

"Madeleine," says her father, "I have to talk to you about Claire McCarroll."

She looks down. Drops fall from her eyes. She was right, they know. They know about the coat hooks and the exercises and all the bad things she has done. Too many ever to be forgiven. Her hands feel clammy, and she longs to inhale the bad smell off them before it reaches her father's nostrils. "It's my fault he picked her," she says, barely audible.

"What?" says Jack. "Who?" He squats down beside his daughter. She won't look at him. She's upset. Deep down she must know what he is going to tell her.

"That's how come I wrote the letter."

"What letter?"

"The Human Sword. To save her."

He shakes his head slightly. She's in a world of her own, an innocent world. And he is about to shatter it. He doesn't know how to say what he must tell her. "Madeleine"—he speaks as gently as possible—"something happened to Claire McCarroll."

Madeleine nods and starts to cry. "I know. I'm sorry."

Jack strokes her head and says, "It's okay, sweetie."

Madeleine says something but Jack can't make it out. It's garbled through her sobs. "Listen now," he says, wishing Mimi were here. Madeleine cries with her forehead against her crinolined knees, shaking with grief.

"Madeleine," he says.

"I'm—sorry—Daddy—" hiccupping.

Jack takes her face, shining with tears and mucus, between his hands. "There's nothing for you to be sorry about, old buddy. . . ." He holds her chin and reaches inside his suit jacket for his hanky. He wipes her face.

The pressure of Dad's hand, the scouring of the hanky, is comforting. He holds it against her nose and she blows, feeling ragged with sorrow, but calmer now.

"Listen, now," he says. "Claire died."

Madeleine stops crying.

He waits. She looks up at him, lips parted. Big brown eyes taking it in. He would give anything not to have to tell her, so soon, that the world can be such a terrible place.

"Dad?" says Madeleine.

"Yeah old buddy?" He has his answer ready. He knows he can't protect her from it, the whole country will know with tomorrow's news. But he can at least choose the words with which to tell her. *Claire was taken away by a sick man. She was killed.*

She asks, "Want to go home now?"

He looks at her a moment to make sure, but she seems fine. Perhaps it helped, coming from her dad. He thinks better of telling her the rest of the story. There will be time for that tomorrow morning. Besides, Mimi will be on hand to comfort her. "Sure." He rises, pocketing his handkerchief.

They head back across the county road into the PMQs again.

"I'm starving," she says, taking his hand.

He pats her head. She's a kid. They bounce back. Thank God.

Madeleine feels as though she has been away from home a long time when she follows her dad up the steps and through the front door. In the dining room, the table is set for Easter brunch. Bacon and eggs, pancakes and maple syrup, and blood pudding for Dad. She has never been so happy to be home. "Something sure smells good!" she says.

But Maman and Mike are still quiet, and Madeleine remembers, of course, someone has died, I have to be quiet. But she is hungry nonetheless, and happy: no one knows about Mr. March. She takes her place at the table, feeling as clean and fresh as the linen tablecloth.

The others join her but, moments after Maman has served Mike, he says, "May I please be excused?" Her parents exchange a sympathetic look and her father nods. Mike gets up from the table, kisses his mother. *"Merci maman, j'ai pas faim."*

He goes upstairs and Madeleine says, "Can I have his bacon?"

Maman looks as though she's about to reprimand her, but Dad says, "Sure, sweetie, eat up." And he piles it onto her plate.

At six o'clock this morning, Rick was out running with Rex before it was light. He would be home by eight, in time to hunt for eggs with the kids. Time to shower, then over to Marsha's house for Easter brunch. He left the PMQs and turned south down the Huron County road, Rex loping at his side.

It was a good time to run. The world soaked from three days of rain, the unvarnished sun coming up and the countryside steaming like a wool blanket. He got to the big willow tree and continued straight through the intersection, pale mud spritzing from his heels, flecking his bare calves, cresting Rex's belly fur with clay.

Rick wasn't looking for her, he was just out for a run.

When he got to the quarry the sun was on it like a veil, gauzy except near the centre, where light floated crisp on the last delicate breath of ice, blacker and brighter than the surrounding water, which was already taking on the haze of early summer, the first insects skating on its surface. Still too cold for leeches. Perfect.

He lifted off his singlet, pulled off his denim cut-offs and runners and dived.

A shock of pure life—he hooted and pelted toward the centre; Rex had run the perimeter and found a manageable spot on the far side to zigzag down. He splashed in and swam, they would meet in the middle. Rick reached the edge of the fragile crust. He knew he shouldn't stay in too long. He breaststroked into it, an ice breaker, his chin the prow; the ice parted like a curtain, shimmered in his wake like a robe.

Rex panted and swam in a circle, biting at the surface, bearding his chops with light. Rick turned onto his back, squinted up at the sun, spread his limbs and made an angel in the crinkling water. Then he arched backwards, diving so as not to destroy his silhouette, and surfaced several feet away. Rex's head turned like a periscope, scanning the surface for him. He saw Rick and surged toward him, whimpering, as Rick began his powerful crawl toward the bank.

His arms were numbing, his hands like bricks, shoulders heavy hinges by the time he grabbed hold of a hunk of stone and hauled himself out. Rex dripped at his side, his mass reduced by his drenched fur coat fringed already with ice. Rick stood, his flesh burning with cold, and saw at the centre of the quarry his angel drifting and distending, one wing higher than the other now. As though it were waving.

He jammed his feet back into his sneakers, hauled on his shorts, grabbed his shirt and they trotted up the jagged face of the quarry. His lungs wide open like a grassy prairie, every pore on his scalp singing, Rick started to jog, turning tight circles like a boxer. Rex leapt, nipping his forearms, growling, boxing back.

Rick turned and ran into a lumpy field of collapsed grass and new milkpods, heading for the woods. He would travel through the trees, across the fallow field beyond, and skirt the newly planted cornfield that bordered Rock Bass, where he would pick up the road back to the PMQs.

He ran, shaking out his tingling hands, lifting his face, craving the speed of twigs strafing his bare legs, the bob and weave of branches coming at his face, dodging stones and deadfalls.

He was not quite out of the woods when he saw his dog stop up ahead, a little ways into the meadow, and begin sniffing busily around a pile of vegetation. Under a big elm tree. Ricky's pace slackened. He was about twenty-five feet away when he saw her hand, the light blue of her dress through the mound of rushes and dry wildflowers. He went closer, drawing shallow breaths through his mouth, almost panting, he knew she was dead. But there was no question of the pull, like a force of nature, the necessity of making sure. Part of him was already running away across the marshy field, but that part was too insubstantial to make it very far. He came closer. She was dead. There was something covering her face. Cloth. He heard a faint sobbing—the sound of his own breathing as he bent, lifted the fabric, then let it drop again.

Rex began to bark.

Mimi lifts the ham out of the oven and places it sizzling on a trivet. Tilting her mixing bowl, she stands at the counter in front of the window and stirs biscuit batter. She sees a police car pull into the Froelichs' driveway. They have driven Ricky home. It's about time. A boy of his age shouldn't have to dwell on tragedy. It was Steve Ridelle who called this morning to tell them that Ricky Froelich had found her. Mimi went down the street to be with Sharon, but Sharon insisted on accompanying her husband to Exeter to see their daughter. The police are not going to lay charges against Blair; he broke someone's nose last night when they told him they were calling off the search.

The Froelich boy gets out of the cruiser, raises a hand in leave-taking, then turns and goes into his house, his head hanging. *Pauvre p'tit.*

Madeleine is at the Froelich house when Ricky returns from helping the police. She and Colleen have made a fort out of Lego. It's strange that, when Claire was here, Madeleine barely noticed her. Now that she has gone, Madeleine keeps expecting to turn and see her, and when she doesn't, it's as though there's an empty space, like a page torn out. Where is Claire? It is not possible that she will never be here on the Froelichs' rug, playing with Lego, ever again.

Ricky comes in and goes straight upstairs to his room. Colleen tells Madeleine why: "He saw her dead body." Madeleine goes home soon after Colleen tells her that. There is death in the Froelich house. Darkness and the smell of last fall, although she can't tell why—the smell of shame, as though dead were the most shameful thing you could be. She needs to be back with her own clean family.

The police arrived to pick Rick up at nine o'clock this morning, a half-hour after his father made the call on his behalf. The boy was chalk-white and his father wanted to accompany him, if not in the cruiser, then following in the old station wagon, but the officers asked him not to: "Sir, we could be dealing with a crime scene. The fewer people the better."

Henry Froelich understood. But when he re-entered his house, Karen said, "I thought you were going with him?"

Rick sat in the back of the cruiser. The radio crackled and this time the driver spoke into the mike, using a series of numbered codes to relay the fact that they had just turned west off the Huron County road and were proceeding toward the scene with the witness.

By the time they pulled over at the spot with the break in the fence, Rick heard a siren approaching. He looked in the sideview mirror to see another cruiser pulling up and, behind it, a plain Ford sedan. Last came the wan, daytime flashing red of an ambulance.

He led them to the ravine, down and across the stream, past the maple, up the other side of the steep bank, between the furrows of germinating corn into the meadow beyond, and stopped just short of the elm tree.

He pointed and felt suddenly faint. He dropped to his haunches and allowed his head to sink between his knees. They left him and walked toward the pile of clothes mixed up with the withered bluebells and last year's bulrushes.

When Rick opened his eyes he saw a pair of black brogues, and looked up. The man was in plainclothes, beige raincoat and hat. Sharp planes to his face. A lean man, but one who gave the impression of weight. Like a steel rail.

"I'm Inspector Bradley, Rick."

Ricky stood, shook hands, then lurched off to one side and threw up.

The inspector watched. This was the boy who had last seen the child. This was the boy who had found her body, after a legion of police and air force personnel were unable to. These facts did not make the boy guilty, but they made him worth questioning.

Ricky returned and apologized.

The police were cordoning off the area. Dr. Ridelle arrived and made his way to the elm tree. Rick saw him bend to look, then nod. A man in a trench coat started taking pictures and Rick was asked to move to one side. Then the medical examiner arrived and everyone stood back.

Rick followed the inspector to an unmarked car and got in. Bradley offered him a cigarette but Rick told him he'd quit when he was twelve, he was an athlete. He couldn't stop shaking, however, so he asked the inspector for a smoke after all. The nicotine soothed his nerves. Like old times.

He told the inspector what he told the other police officers. Bradley was especially interested in the Buick. "Ford," Rick corrected him. He readily agreed to drive with the inspector up to Goderich, where they could speak in the comfort of his office at the OPP station.

Rick had been waiting for over an hour in a plain green concrete room, nursing a Coke, by the time the inspector returned and asked if he would mind repeating his story for the benefit of a stenographer. He made no further mention of the comfort of his office.

Rick told the whole story again, the Coke gnawing at his empty stomach, and it was the hunger that reminded him. "Sir, I just remembered, I should call my parents."

"Oh we'll do that for you, son, what's the number?"

Inspector Bradley and the stenographer stepped out. For another hour. Finally, a cop—the passenger-side one—came in, "just to say hi." He was curious and wanted to hear all about the morning too, "if you don't mind." So Rick told him. The cop asked if Rick had caught sight of that Chevy again since Wednesday, and Rick said, "Ford. No sir. Do you know if they've called my parents?"

"They shoulda by now, by jeez, I'll check."

The cop returned five minutes later. "You're sprung, kid, let's get you home."

Throughout the PMQs, the mothers have been in touch in person and over the phone, assuring one another that they will be looking out their windows, tracking each child as though he or she were their own. The fathers have made themselves perfectly clear, and the kids have listened without interrupting while being told what the standard operating procedure will be until further notice. Siblings are never to lose sight of one another. If a child is visiting another's house, he or she must call immediately upon arrival and before setting out again for home. "I don't care if it's right across the street." It's to be straight home from school after the bell, no playing outdoors after dark and, above all, do not leave the PMQs.

"They just wanted to know how I found her, and all about the other day when we went to the intersection together," says Rick.

Karen has persuaded her son to come downstairs and eat something. Colleen joins them, squeezing into a chair between the wall and the kitchen table. "That's all, Ma, no big deal. I told them what I saw."

"For four hours?" asks Henry from the stove. He was on the phone all afternoon, but the *dummkopf* constable at the Goderich police station was deaf, dumb and blind.

Karen says to her son, "You've told them that fifty times already."

"I was just sitting there staring into space most of the time, Ma, they're pretty busy."

Colleen says, "*J'mi fi pa a ci batar la.*"

The parents ignore the curse word, but Ricky reprimands her, "*Sacri pa a la table.*"

Karen says, "So what did they want to know?"

His parents' concern prompts him to downplay the whole thing. "They gave me a Coke and we pretty much just shot the breeze while I waited for the head honcho to show up." He obliges his parents with a detailed account of what he told the police. When he gets to the part about the blue Ford Galaxy with its dented bumper and yellow sticker, his father slumps back in his chair and shakes his head, squeezing his eyes shut a few times. "Hank, what's wrong?" asks Karen.

"Karen, that is the man—the car of the man I saw, that is his car."

Jack uses the night number to call Simon. No clicks, no succession of lackeys, just Simon. "Christ," he says, when Jack tells him. A sigh. "And our friend?"

"Fit as a fiddle." Jack can see the moon, high and cold through the glass. McCarroll's daughter would be alive now if he'd never been posted up here.

"Jack, you still there, mate?"

"Yes, I'm here."

"It's not feasible to have a grieving father in the loop."

McCarroll doesn't know why he was posted to Centralia. He never will.


## EASTER MONDAY


INSPECTOR BRADLEY has offered the man coffee and invited him to be seated in the comfort of his office in Goderich.

"Cigarette, Mr. Frolick?"

"No thank you."

Bradley lights up and inhales. The man is clearly agitated; his son was detained for hours, then sent home hungry and scared—he's bound to be irate. Bradley is prepared to be patient.

Henry is sitting at attention. "Inspector Bradley, I come because I have information about a murderer in this area."

Bradley blinks. "In connection with what, sir?"

"In . . . ? In this, this, the child, Claire."

"You think she was murdered?" Froelich is taken aback. He starts to answer but Bradley asks, "Did your son tell you that?"

Froelich hesitates. "He found her in the field, yes? The police—"

"We haven't got the coroner's report yet."

" . . . You think it was an accident?" The inspector says nothing. Henry nods. "I understand, you cannot tell me. Who am I? But I am telling you of a murderer in this area, I have seen him."

Bradley resists the urge to lean forward. "Who have you seen?"

"A Nazi, a—war criminal."

"A war criminal?" Bradley reaches for a pen. "What's his name, sir?"

Froelich's tone implies that the answer is self-evident. "I don't know his name."

"How do you know he's a war criminal?"

"Because I am a—I was a prisoner!"

"Where was this?"

"First Auschwitz, then Dora—"

"I'm not familiar with Dora."

"It was a factory—"

"You say you saw this man in the area?"

"Yes, yes, this is what I am saying." Froelich leans in now, trembling. He tells the inspector about the man he saw getting into the blue Ford Galaxy outside the marketplace in London; of seeing him back into a parking meter, then speed off. He tells of the yellow sticker, of the partial plate number, and pauses for breath as the inspector writes it down. "And this is the same car that my son sees on this afternoon, on that afternoon that the child is—that she becomes lost." He is having difficulty keeping hold of his English. "*Ist klar* now, *ja?*"

"Your son said that an air force man was behind the wheel. He saw the hat."

"Yes, this I don't understand, he could . . . it could be another kind of hat, no?"

"Your son seemed pretty sure. And he said the man waved."

"Maybe . . . there are two men."

"An air force man and a Nazi with the same car?"

Froelich shakes his head, his eyes straying down to the desk.

"What's this war criminal doing in Canada in the first place?"

"Ach, there are thousands here," says Froelich with a wave of his hand.

Bradley licks his lower lip and puts down his pencil. Froèlich alters his tone. He doesn't want to discredit his information by impugning the Canadian government and its law enforcement agencies. "In some cases, perhaps, a war record is overlooked because we need scientists."

"What kind of scientists?"

"Atomic or rocket, for instance, this man—"

"I didn't know we had a space program here."

"We have nuclear power, weapons-grade uranium—"

"Why didn't you report this at the time, sir?"

Froelich chooses his words carefully. "Because I think maybe he is like ... some others. A Canadian citizen now. So what is the point? And it's the past. I"—he finds the expression—"press on."

Bradley watches the man, pale behind his shaggy beard. His eyes are bloodshot, clothing rumpled. Has he been drinking?

Henry's hands are like ice, but he is heartened. The policeman is interested, and the possible involvement of an air force man is starting to make more, not less sense of the situation. "The British and Americans, they have often screened refugees for Canada, in DP camps, Displaced Persons, *ja?* Many of refugees have committed crimes but are valuable with information—intelligence—or many only are young and strong, these are rewarded with coming to Canada."

"How do you know this, sir?"

Henry tries to keep the emotion from his voice. "I also was a refugee, I also try to immigrate and am not permitted."

"Why not?"

Henry shrugs. "I am a Jew. I am too old, too educated, I cannot cut wood, I cannot operate sewing machine, I have no family any more and the authorities want only anti-Communists—"

"Are you pro-Communist?"

"*Nein, nein,* I am Canadian, I mean only to say the authorities prefer sometimes a fascist background instead of socialist—"

"Do you have a socialist background?"

"This is a socialist country."

Bradley doesn't smile.

Henry says, "The Communists were the only ones to stand up to Hitler when—"

"And Canada. We stood up."

"*Ja, genau,* Canada, *natürlich,* but at first—Inspector Bradley, were you in the war?"

"I most certainly was, sir."

"Then we both understand to take nothing for granted."

Bradley is silent. Spittle has collected at the ends of the man's moustache. Bradley can smell his breath—corrosive. Finally, he asks, "What does this man look like, sir?"

"Ordinary. Brown suit." The inspector's pen is still. Froelich searches for something concrete. "Glasses. Pale. Perhaps sixty, not too tall. Grey hair. *Ja,* grey. And thin. Thin hair as well."

"Eyes?"

"Pale . . . perhaps blue."

"Thank you for coming in, sir."

Froelich gets up reluctantly. "Inspector Bradley, you must ask the commander—Woodley is a good man—you must find if the air force knows this man. He is a sadist, he enjoys, you see. I feel sick that I have not come sooner to tell you."

After Bradley has seen the man to the door, he finishes writing his notes on the interview with—he checks the spelling on the typed report—Henry Froelich. He lights another Player's and ponders his next step. He has already ordered a check on all '63 Ford Galaxys with Ontario plates, and now he can narrow it, thanks to the numbers provided by Froelich. Bradley will have the medical examiner's report tomorrow, but the pathologist has already estimated time of death as between four and five P.M. last Wednesday. The time the boy claims to have seen the car.

There are three possibilities. Froelich is telling the truth and an air force man is, knowingly or not, involved with a war criminal whose car was seen around the time and in the vicinity of the murder. Or Froelich is mistaken—he is Jewish, he was in a concentration camp, this may not be the first time he's convinced himself that he's seen a face from the past, and exaggerated the horrors associated with that face. Or he's lying.

If the first is correct, what should Bradley do? War crimes are an RCMP matter, he could simply pick up the phone. But this murder is in his jurisdiction; he's not about to pass the buck, nor does he relish the thought of muddying the waters by inviting another organization on board before he has to. He could talk to Group Captain Woodley, ask him straight out if he knows of any air force involvement with a German scientist. But what if the government has indeed knowingly recruited a war criminal for some highly classified purpose? Is Woodley likely to admit it? In which case the RCMP may also be in the know—so much for calling on them. Bradley couldn't care less about stepping on toes; if Froelich's war criminal is out there, then he's a suspect, and Bradley intends to track him down; for, much as he dismisses Froelich's extravagant claim of "thousands," he knows it's inevitable that a few

Nazis did slip through the net. There was a recent sighting just down the road here in Oxford County: Josef Mengele picking tobacco. And, whether Mengele has since fled or was never here to begin with, his case is not unique. There are still many of them on the run. Bradley smokes and leans back. He needs to figure out how to broach the subject with Woodley without tipping him off. . . .

Finally, Bradley locks his briefcase and leaves. He is the last one out, the night shift has already arrived. He's looking forward to his supper. As he gets into his car, he asks himself why, if Froelich is lying, he would come up with a "war criminal" story, of all things. The obvious answer is that good liars stick close to the truth, and it's probably true that Froelich was in a concentration camp. Perhaps he is something of a Communist sympathizer too—the Soviets like to inflate the number of war criminals said to be at large in the West. In any case, he strikes Bradley as a bitter man; he didn't want to cut wood, didn't want to run a sewing machine—Bradley's own father worked in an asbestos mine—if these people don't appreciate the freedom we fought for in this country, they're welcome to find another. But that is subjective and has no bearing on the case.

As Bradley drives across Goderich's town square—coming into bloom now around the courthouse—he entertains a simpler scenario: Froelich came up with this story because he knows that his son is lying and needs an alibi for the time of the murder. And how could the boy possibly know the time of the murder unless he committed it himself? Froelich has also provided an excuse as to why that alibi can never be corroborated, for if the alleged air force man were involved with a war criminal for some shadowy purpose, he would have good reason not to come forward. Doesn't Froelich know that he risks looking like a crackpot? A liar? Or is he crafty enough to have come up with a fairy tale that, by its very outlandishness, is not entirely self-serving and is thus plausible? He is supplying a red herring that can never be traced, and hoping it may serve as "reasonable doubt."

Bradley respects doubt even when he doesn't share it. His job is to parse doubt. To reduce it to a level below reasonable. Like a good scientist, he is skeptical, especially when it comes to his own leanings. He switches on his brights as he leaves the town limits.

A child is dead. But Bradley has decided that, before he sets a fifteen-year-old boy on track for the gallows, he will consider very carefully how to investigate Froelich's story as discreetly, as thoroughly, as if he believed it himself.

Bradley is a father too.

# Helping the Police with Their Inquiries

*Write "bicycle" and "terrible" in syllables. Draw a line under the last syllable in each word. Write the two words again.*

Macmillan Spelling Series, *1962*

On Tuesday morning the children come into the classroom after the long weekend to see whose art Mr. March has put up on the wall, and which one among this anointed group is marked with a gold star. The usual suspects are represented: the bossy girls, Gordon Lawson and Marjorie Nolan. Marjorie's picture is all-purpose religious and she has driven home the point by affixing a caption, "Moses Among the Cattails." What is shocking, however, is that Grace Novotny's art is not only up on the wall, it is the proud bearer of the coveted gold star. This is shocking not because the butterflies have been deemed the best—they are the best—but because they were done by disgusting Grace. With her bandaged hands like the Curse of the Mummy's Tomb. They are still swaddled. Filthy and frayed.

Just before recess, the principal, Mr. Lemmon, announces over the PA system, "Girls and boys, I have a very sad announcement to make. One of your schoolmates, Claire McCarroll, has passed away. Let us all observe two minutes' silence now for Claire and her family. Feel free to pray quietly to yourselves."

Mr. March makes them all stand and bow their heads. Two minutes. Like on November 11. It seems the silence goes on forever. Then finally, when it's over and the normal sounds trickle back into the day, it's difficult to remember what the island of silence was like. And Claire is gone. Washed over. A blank spot that will be worn down by the tide until the water runs smoothly again. Madeleine tries to picture Claire's face but it keeps stretching and distorting in her mind's eye.

Her face was covered with her underpants. Inspector Bradley has gone over the photographs, the autopsy report and the lab results. *Peculiarities of . . . (d) Skin: intense cyanotic lividity of face and neck; intense cyanosis of the nails and extremities of fingers. . . .* Although no semen or acid phosphates were found in her, there has clearly been what the pathologist noted as "a violent and very inexpert attempt at penetration." There may have been ejaculate on the ground, he may have forced her to watch him masturbate—common pedophile behaviour—but it would have been washed away by the rain. The killer tried to rape her, then he strangled her.

*Stomach: unremarkable*
*Intestines: unremarkable*
*Pancreas: unremarkable*
*Liver: unremarkable . . .*
*Hymen: destroyed . . .*
*Lower vagina: contused . . .*

He is a sexual deviant, that much is clear. A pervert with an under-developed sexual nature. And then there is the way he left the body: decorated, almost. As if she were only sleeping and it had all been a game—although the bulrushes in the shape of a cross hint at an awareness that she was dead.

The police are looking for an immature man with access to little girls. An inexpert sexual practitioner, known to the child, for there is no evidence that she was abducted, no sign of a struggle. He could be a teacher. Or a student. A friend. Bradley has already interviewed the victim's teacher and, now that the time of death has been confirmed, will interview him again tomorrow along with all other male staff, regardless of the outcome of today's search for the alleged air force man in the Ford Galaxy. Then he will draw a circle around the murder scene, and interview every farmer in a five-mile radius.

*Note on time of death: This opinion would place the time of death between 4:00pm and 5:00pm Wednesday, 10th of April 1963, based on the following observations and assumptions:*

*1. the extent of decomposition . . .*
*2. the extent of rigor mortis . . .*
*3. the limited degree of digestion . . .*

If Richard Froelich had been out on Highway 4, waving at an air force man between four and five, he would not have had time to murder the child, and arrive home when several people—not just his family—have said he did.

Bradley has set himself up in the office of the recreation director overlooking the curling arena at RCAF Centralia. He will question each man individually, that is how thorough he is prepared to be. He has not shared Froelich's story of a war criminal with his staff or his superiors, and certainly not with Woodley or any RCAF personnel.

Bradley is scrupulous. He and his team will interview upwards of twelve hundred air force personnel. They will start at eight A.M. Bradley is scrupulous, but he has told someone about the war criminal connection. He has told the father of the murdered child. Mr. Froelich's story has turned out to be doubly useful; Bradley was able, without lying, to tell Captain McCarroll that he was looking for a war criminal in connection with the death of his daughter. McCarroll has already assaulted a police officer. Who knows how he might react if he found out that the boy up the street is under investigation for the rape and murder of his child?

"Everybody's been very kind, very Christian," says Blair McCarroll.

"Very Christian," says Sharon McCarroll, smiling.

Jack says, "I'm glad." He is on the couch in the McCarrolls' living room, because they insisted he sit for a moment.

"Especially you and your good wife," says Blair.

"Oh Mimi's been an angel," says Sharon.

Jack has put Mrs. McCarroll's boarding pass and itinerary on the coffee table. McCarroll is in civvies. Jack is in uniform; it's just before ten A.M. He has used his rank as a senior officer to scrounge a more direct flight to the States for Sharon. The least he can do.

Sharon is staring down at her coffee table. She seems lost in its glossy surface, her smile only now beginning to fade. No one says anything. Jack wonders if he ought to leave after all. Tears fall on the glass tabletop. A moan, childlike, comes from somewhere—from her. Her face is half hidden by the forward fall of light brown hair. The moan rises, patient, relaxed even, until it's a wail; she doesn't cover her face, she is past that. Jack glances from Sharon to her husband, but Blair just watches her for a moment before putting an arm around her and taking her hand in his. The top of her head touches his chin. He stares down and off to the side; only one can cry at a time.

Jack hesitates, then gets up carefully. But Blair has done this a hundred times now, so has his wife; their movements are practised, her grief is shocking and intimate only to an outsider. Jack waits for an appropriate moment to exit. Why does the earth open and take some lives and leave others intact? The earth opened and took their child. My child happened not to be taken. He reaches for his hat on the couch—

"Would you like some coffee, Jack? I was just going to make some," says Blair.

Jack is taken by surprise, uncertain how to answer—surely he should not stay a moment longer. But Sharon blows her nose, looks up and, with a smile to her husband—"I'll make it, hon."

Jack has an interview with the police at ten-thirty, but he is not about to run out on these two if company is what they want. Sharon turns and walks toward the kitchen, only a step or two away in the tiny bungalow, and Jack hears the tap go on. He sits down again. The police have everyone filing one by one into various offices at the Mess, the language school and the curling arena—something to do with the investigation. Whatever it is, it must be pretty straightforward; the interviews are spaced a couple of minutes apart. He checks his watch discreetly—it's five past ten.

From where Jack is sitting he can glimpse Sharon's movements, bare arms, dark A-line dress, hair falling back from her face as she reaches up to the cupboards. McCarroll's wife is so pretty it breaks your heart. He feels his throat constrict, he leans forward, coughs. "So Blair, you'll be joining Sharon soon, I take it."

"That's right, her folks'll meet her and I'll join her later with Claire."

The fragile refraction of a normal conversation. *With Claire.* A man joining his wife, bringing their child. Jack is very careful. Blair is very careful.

"It's a decent flight she's on," says Jack.

"Yeah, thanks Jack."

"Oh don't thank me, you're lucky, that's all," and so that his foolish words don't hang in the air, he adds quickly, "Virginia is beautiful, I hear."

"It's God's country."

Silence.

There is a packing box in the corner of the room. Labelled "Toys" in red felt-tip pen. Soon the McCarrolls will be gone. Jack sees the room empty, white and waiting, the way it was before they arrived. The way it will be when the next family moves in, their temporary things anchored to the walls, the floors.

Their conversation is in disguise. It drapes itself in the tones and emphases of a different type of conversation—one you might have at the water cooler—in order to give manageable shape to . . . what? A ghost. Grief.

"Keepin' us informed," says Blair, nodding.

"What's that?" says Jack.

"The police. They've been real good about keeping us informed."

The disguise is slipping. *Keeping us informed.* Jack can't think what to say. Behind the mask of their conversation is what has been in this room all along: absence. They are keeping her alive with their chat, with the promise of coffee in a moment, with the box marked "Toys." The police, the investigation, all the tasks—even accompanying her body down to the States—it all amounts to a busy scaffolding, a sturdy context for her continued existence. Soon the tasks will be finished, and the whole skeletal structure will stand empty. Silent. *Keeping us informed.* Impossible for the father to talk about what the doctor found—what the police informed him the doctor found. And yet impossible for the father not to talk about his daughter. Last week she baked brownies for show-and-tell, she got eight out of ten on her spelling test and he helped her with a book report on *Black Beauty*—the teacher has not yet marked the book reports but the father is sure she did well. Two days ago she exhibited vaginal bruising and bleeding sustained just before she died, as well as thumb marks on her neck; she was listed as a "healthy normal prepubescent female" on her autopsy report. That's what's new. That's what she has done lately. He has to talk about his child. He has to be careful, that's all.

"They've got some good men there, the OPP," says Jack.

"Oh yeah." Blair nods. "They're sharp."

"That's for darn sure."

"I just hope they find their damn war criminal so they can get on with finding. . . ."

Jack has been feeling slightly disoriented. He realizes it now as he blinks at McCarroll and says, "What's that?"

"Police told me the Froelich boy saw a car on the road that afternoon, a blue Ford, and Henry says it belongs to some war criminal he saw last week, or—I can't make it out, it doesn't matter." His voice drops off and his head droops.

Jack parts his lips—they stick as though with glue. "I haven't heard anything about a war criminal."

"I think it's on the QT."

From the kitchen comes the sound of the fridge door opening, something being poured, milk.

Blair says, "I thought Henry might've mentioned it."

Jack's face is on fire. He looks down at the smear on the coffee table from Sharon's tears, and clears his throat. "What's Hank saying exactly?"

"Well," says Blair, relaxing back in his chair—it's a relief, this part of the story, it's clean, not obscene, interesting even. "He's saying this car, this brand-new blue Ford—you know the new Galaxy coupe—came down the road the boy was on—he was out running like he does with his sister and his dog, you know? And he says this car come along with an air force man in it who waved, but the boy couldn't tell who it was on account of the sun was on the windshield—"

"How do you take your coffee, Jack?" Sharon is here with a tray. Her eyes are puffy but she's smiling. Jack makes a move to help but she sets the tray down. "You men just sit and relax."

Claire would have grown up to be just as pretty, thinks Jack, just as much that rare find, a sweet and happy wife. They will have more children, surely. Jack says, "Cream, two sugars, thank you Sharon."

"Thanks hon," says Blair.

Both men watch Sharon fix the coffees, her wrist stirring, fingers clinking the spoon against the rim. They each take a mug and she turns and walks back toward the kitchen with the tray, but pauses halfway, as though she has forgotten something. She stands for a moment, her back to them, unmoving. They watch her. After a moment she continues into the kitchen.

Jack says, "What about this—war criminal? Is that what you said?"

"Yeah, I don't know," says Blair. "Henry Froelich says he saw this character in London a couple of weeks ago, same car, same dent, right down to the bumper sticker and a number or two on the plate. Told the police about it, that's how come I know. Said this fella was a Nazi. Knew him in a camp in the war."

"Poor bastard." Jack's heart is pounding but his tone is even.

"Yeah," says Blair, and sips his coffee. "So he doesn't know who it was waved, but he knows it was an air force type 'cause of the hat."

"Then they'll find him."

Blair shrugs. "I don't know. All sounds a bit funny to me. Like they're after frying bigger fish, what with looking for some damn war criminal. What would he want with a child?"

"They're just doing their job, they got to follow up every lead. Every stranger in the area," says Jack, reaching for his hat. He has a foul taste in his mouth.

Blair gets up to see him out. They walk to the front door.

"I don't want to disturb Sharon. Would you say goodbye for me?" Blair nods. Jack puts on his hat, glancing, as he does so, at his watch. Twenty past ten.

"Jack, I want to thank you for everything." Blair offers his hand; Jack shakes it. "You know, I was only supposed to be up here for a year."

Jack nods. Waits.

"I can't help thinking, if we'd never come here—" He breaks off, takes three or four quick gasps, but manages not to cry. He says instead, with a force and bitterness that shock Jack, "I hate this goddamn useless country." He squints, his chin trembles and he smacks away tears first with one hand, then with the other, and gets hold of himself. "I'm sorry sir, I didn't mean that."

"Blair, I'm sorry. We all are."

Jack walks quickly from the PMQs. It was Froelich. Jesus Christ. And why is he calling Fried a war criminal? A Nazi? Froelich was in a concentration camp—the number on his arm proves that; Fried was a scientist in a rocket factory; how is it possible they even crossed paths?

And yet Froelich called out the name of the factory, Dora. *He wants to put a rope about my neck.* Jack recalls how Fried looked when he spoke those words: blanched.

The sun is glaring again today, its harsh light unmitigated by heat. Jack marches up Canada Avenue; he has five minutes. He'd assumed the police were asking for alibis today from all male personnel, but now he's certain that what they're really after is that bloody Ford Galaxy and Oskar Fried. He will phone Simon right after his interview and break the news. He'll also ask Simon why a perfectly reliable man like Henry Froelich would identify Fried as a war criminal. Jack reminds himself that he is hardly in a position to demand explanations; this mess is his fault. *If I hadn't used that godforsaken car for my own convenience. . . .* He knows what Simon will say: make it disappear.

He crosses the parade square, heading for the curling arena. Steve Ridelle is standing outside—Jack didn't know he smoked. They exchange a brief, grim hello, and Jack recalls that Steve officially identified the body, assisted at the autopsy. He pushes through the big double doors, feels the chill off the ice and hurries up the steps to the recreation director's office, but the door is closed. The police are running ten minutes late and there is a man waiting ahead of him: Nolan. They nod. Today Nolan's silence does not seem out of place.

At recess there is not as much noise as usual and some girls are in little groups, crying. Madeleine leans against the crossbar of the teeter-totters and feels strange, as though she were looking at her friends from far away. Another space has opened up; only now is she aware that she is missing something—something Auriel and Lisa and the other crying girls take for granted. And she wonders if anyone else has noticed: the crying kids are normal, and she is not.

"Wing Commander McCarthy, how do you do, sir, I'm Inspector Bradley." The inspector is seated behind the rec director's desk. In a corner of the office, a uniformed police officer stands poised with a notebook. "Sir, I don't want to take up too much of your time, can you give me an idea of your whereabouts last Wednesday afternoon?"

"Sure, I would have been right here at the station, in my office most likely."

"Did you leave your office at any time, sir?"

"I think I stepped out to the PX at one point."

"Did you leave the station at all?"

"I can't say I did, no."

From the corner of his eye, Jack can see the constable writing down his answers. Inspector Bradley says, "Have you been out driving in the area recently, sir?"

"I've been back and forth to London once or twice, and my wife has—"

"So you've been on Highway 4 in the past week?"

"Oh sure."

"You see, we're hoping that someone may have noticed something or someone unusual in the area. You understand that we're looking for a killer."

Jack nods.

"Do you have children, sir?"

"I sure do."

"It's vital that we hear from anyone who was anywhere in the environs of the station that afternoon. Sometimes people see something and they don't realize its significance; that's my job. Of course, I can't do my job without the help of everyone here. Did you see anything, or anyone at all, when you were out on Number 4 last Wednesday?"

"No, I—I wish I could help you, inspector, but the fact is, I was right here all afternoon."

"Thanks for your time, sir, and again, sorry to trouble you."

"Not at all. Good luck." Jack starts to go.

"Wing Commander McCarthy." Jack turns, his hand on the door. "Please tell no one about the content of this interview."

"You got it," says Jack. And leaves.

He stops outside the phone booth next to the PX and takes a deep breath. Simon isn't going to like this. He enters the booth and hesitates—what if someone sees him making a phone call immediately after his interview with the police? He glances over his shoulder to make certain there is no one to see him feeding the phone with enough dimes to cover a call to Washington.

"Major Newbolt here, give me First Secretary Crawford, please."

Jack waits. People come and go from the PX; cadets enter the arena, skates slung over their shoulders—no one takes the slightest notice of him.

Simon's voice startles him—"Jack, call you right back." They hang up and Jack waits again, feeling conspicuous. He flips through the phone book—Exeter, Clinton, Crediton, Goderich, Lucan—looking for what, if anyone should ask?

A tap on the glass. It's Vic Boucher. "Mind if I make a quick call, Jack?"

Jack vacates the booth too promptly. "Go right ahead, Vic, I was just looking up—looking for riding stables, for Madeleine."

"Oh yeah?" says Vic, digging for a dime, stepping into the booth. "The wife said either cabbage or lettuce, and darned if I can remember which."

Jack smiles, hands him a dime and says, "Lettuce. They never want cabbage."

Vic dials and Jack checks his watch—Simon will get a busy signal and call back, that's all. And there's time; chances are, while the police are interviewing personnel, they're not out looking for the car. He wonders if they have contacted the RCMP. Froelich must have given a description of Fried—will police sketches go up at post offices across southern Ontario? Christ.

While Vic speaks intently into the phone, Jack's mind returns to Fried. *What did you do, Oskar?* Jack had asked. *My job.* How could that have included crimes against humanity? The Germans used forced labour in their factories during the war: Volkswagen, Zeppelin— Auschwitz itself was part munitions factory, Krupps etc. . . . It makes sense that there would have been forced labour at Dora too. Froelich could have gone from one to the other. Still, Fried's "job" would have been entirely technical, and while some workers did die, the intention would have been to keep them alive and healthy enough to do their jobs.

Vic hangs up and squeezes out through the folding door, grumbling heartily. "Sonofagun, how did you know it was lettuce?" The phone rings. He raises his eyebrows. "You expecting a call?"

Jack chuckles at the joke before he registers that it was one. A good reflex. How do people train for this type of work? Or are they born liars? Liars with unshakeable loyalty.

The phone rings a second time. Vic reaches back into the booth and picks it up. "Hello, dis place," he quips, then hangs up. "Nobody there." And leaves. Strolling toward the PX.

Jack re-enters the phone booth and resumes peering at the yellow pages. The phone rings. Vic turns, his hand on the door of the PX. Jack catches his eye, shrugs, picks up the phone and puts it right back down on its cradle. Vic disappears into the store.

The phone rings again and Jack grabs it. Simon says, "Bit of a snafu?"

"A lineup, that's all."

"What's shaking?"

"Si, it was my neighbour who recognized Fried, he's calling him a war criminal."

"Christ." Simon sounds almost contemplative. "When did he tell you this?"

"He didn't, I found out by accident—Si, is there any truth to it?"

"All I can tell you is, I cleared him for security myself."

Jack is already relieved but he has to ask: "Then why was Fried so scared he could be hanged?"

"No doubt that's exactly what would happen if word of his defection got out and the Soviets got hold of him."

Of course.

It's time for Jack to grit his teeth and make his report. "Si, the police are looking for Fried in connection with the murder of McCarroll's daughter."

Silence. Then, "How, by name?"

"I don't think so."

"Is there any truth to it?"

Jack is unprepared for the question. "No, he was—I left him at the apartment—the fact is, Simon, it's my fault." He explains how the car was identified when he drove it to Exeter and passed Froelich's son on the highway on the afternoon the child went missing. "Now the police hear the words 'war criminal' and figure there could be someone in the area capable of . . . this kind of thing."

"Fantastic," says Simon, as though surveying a marvel of engineering.

"They don't know it was me driving. I waved at the boy but the sun was on the windshield, all he saw was my hat."

"That's one for us, then."

"Simon, I'm sorry."

"My fault, mate, I ought never to have agreed to the bloody car in the first place. Ought to have trusted my instincts."

"Don't worry, I'll make it disappear."

"I take it your neighbour doesn't know that you know Fried?"

"No one does."

"What did you say his name was?"

"Froelich. Henry Froelich. He hasn't the faintest. I got all this dope by accident from McCarroll. The police told him. That's why I was able to head them off when they asked what I was doing last Wednesday."

"Well, at any rate, McCarroll's been good for something."

The comment pings like a pebble from a speeding tire but Jack presses on. "What about Fried?"

"What about him?"

"Where do we go from here?"

"You don't go anywhere, your job's done."

The sun splinters the booth as if through a magnifying glass, heating the interior. Jack squints. "Well, I thought what with McCarroll out of commission. . . . Should I drive Fried to the border? What do you want me to do?"

"Not your problem, mate."

It's over. Jack should feel glad. "I'll give him a ring after we hang up."

"I wouldn't," says Simon. "His phone may be tapped at this point."

"I'll drop down to London and check on him tomorrow then."

"I'd rather you didn't." Jack swallows his disappointment silently. Simon has every right to question his competence at this point. "Ditch the car and it's mission accomplished, lad, over and out. I'll take it from here."

"Simon, when you're passing through—"

"Several drinks are in order."

Jack walks from the phone booth feeling oddly bereft. Fried will cross into the U.S. and Jack will never hear of him again. Fried will have a new name and a new life. He will use his talents to help the USAF space program rival that of his old colleague, Wernher von Braun at NASA.

Jack hurries to the accounts office and gets a cash advance of one hundred dollars. Then he heads toward the ME section to sign out a staff car. It's entirely possible Froelich is mistaken—after all, he must have suffered terribly during the war. Every face from that time must conjure up horror.

"Did you decide on some lessons?"

Jack looks up. Vic Boucher, laden with grocery bags, a lettuce poking out the top of one of them, is standing with Elaine Ridelle, likewise encumbered with groceries and a baby carriage. They are watching him, expectant. What is Vic talking about? *Lessons.* . . . Something rumbles from the back of his mind, coming closer, like a dump truck carrying the information he needs. "Yeah, I found a place on Number 4, out Goderich way. Hicks' Riding Stable." Too much information.

"Have you spoken with McCarroll today?" asks Vic.

Jack feels the redness creeping into his face. "I'm going to look in on them later. Drop off Sharon's boarding pass." He changes the subject, bending to look in the carriage. "What've we got here?"

The baby looks as though he has just swooned into sleep, fingers splayed and stirring slightly beneath his chin, whitish residue on his puckered lips—a flower.

"He's a bruiser." Jack grins. "Looks like Steve."

"Well that's a relief." Elaine winks.

There is no way not to register her cleavage now that she's nursing. Jack feels himself stir, stiffen a little, and sticks his hands in his pockets. Elaine is a flirt but harmless. His response is harmless too—a polite nod to Mother Nature. What is more stimulating than a woman pre, during, and post pregnancy? It makes the world go round. He says, "Well, I better go do a tap of work."

He takes his leave and walks down Nova Scotia Avenue, back toward his building. He is losing valuable time but he doesn't want Vic Boucher watching him drive off in a staff car. He thinks longingly of his wife. He has an impulse to head straight home.

When he gets to the next corner, he looks over his shoulder to see that Vic is pulling away in his orange van and Elaine is following, pushing her pram. Jack does an about-face and cuts between the barracks where he lived so many years ago as a pilot in training, and heads for the ME section.

He looks at his watch, calculating how much time he will need, for he knows where he must take the Ford Galaxy if it is truly to disappear.

The tinted windows of the staff car take the edge off the bright hard light. Jack touches the brim of his hat to the guard and drives out through the main gates, past the Spitfire, and turns north on the county road.

He does not enjoy lying, and the thought that the police are wasting time chasing a phantom war criminal when they could be out finding whoever did this thing is making him feel unwell. He passes through the old Village of Centralia, then picks up speed toward Exeter.

On the other hand, whoever did kill the child is probably long gone by now. A drifter. Unless it's some sick bastard living alone out here on one of these farms. As he surveys the fields on either side of the road, it crosses his mind to wonder if the locals know something, and whether the police are questioning them. The civilian population. There could be a homegrown pervert among them, some known village idiot who might not prey on a local child, but might consider the transient children of the air force station easier game.

The first streaks of green have begun painting the naked soil. In gullies and along the roadside there remain scabs of dirty snow, but the cows are out and their brown hides have the look of summer already, as though they themselves were a source of sun and heat. Up ahead a tractor lumbers along the shoulder, raising early dust. He wonders if the police have gone door to door up and down these endless driveways. Who lives here, really? They are his neighbours; who are they? Would the police treat this investigation differently if the girl were not an air force child?

It's eleven-thirty. With luck he'll be home before dark.

The Kinsmen, the Rotary Club and the Royal Canadian Legion welcome Jack to Exeter on a freshly painted sign. If the Ford is not where he left it, at least he can be sure the police haven't got it. He half hopes it has been stolen—a thief would be unlikely to come forward with evidence of his own crime in order to help solve another. Crocuses are up around the cenotaph, and two folding chairs have reappeared out front of the barbershop, setting the scene for a summer-long game of checkers. He follows the main street out past the edge of town and pulls in and around the back of the old train station, to see the blue Ford Galaxy, gleaming, untouched but for its dented rear bumper. So much for any hope of a convenient thief. He pulls into the shadow of the boarded-up building and steps out into the winter of the noon shade. From the trunk of the staff car he takes a box of tools, a crowbar and a jack. He brings them to the Ford, gets in, removes his uniform hat, jacket and tie. He is banking on the idea that the police will not put out a bulletin for the Ford until they have finished questioning personnel late this afternoon. By that time, he will be on his way back home and this car will be as good as scrap— halfway to its next life as a washing machine. If he is pulled over, he has Simon's telephone number. And if, in spite of everything, the lid blows off the entire mission, well, *c'est la guerre.* Don't shake hands with the Devil before you meet him.

They have found Claire's bike. Madeleine can see it in the trunk of the OPP car parked in the driveway of the little green bungalow. Mr. McCarroll is standing on his front porch. One of the policemen takes it out of the trunk and holds it up. Mr. McCarroll nods.

Mike has been tailing Madeleine as usual. Now he says, "Quit staring, come on."

The policeman puts Claire's bike back into the trunk.

"I'm not staring, I'm just walking slowly," says Madeleine, catching up with him. "How come they're taking her bike away?"

"'Cause it's evidence," says her brother.

"What do you mean, evidence?"

"Against whoever did it."

"Did what?"

"Murdered her, what do you think? What are you doing now?"

Madeleine has sat down in the fine sharp gravel at the side of the road. *Murdered.*

"Well, what did you think happened to her?" asks Mike.

Madeleine doesn't know.

"Come on, get up."

Claire died, Madeleine knew that. That's what happens when children go off by themselves for too long. To the woods, after supper. Sometimes they don't come home. They stay out after dark and, when you find them, they are dead. *Passed away.*

"Madeleine."

Madeleine had not thought about how. Something terrible had happened and Claire was dead; "something terrible" had seemed specific. But it wasn't. Otherwise, Madeleine would not be cut down by the side of the road like a daisy.

"Come on," says Mike. "Okay, don't come on." And he keeps walking toward home, glancing back over his shoulder to make sure she is not getting murdered.

Madeleine stays in the cindery gravel, her bare legs folded under her. Her hands have disappeared. Her head is turned and she is looking and looking down the street at Claire's house, where the OPP car is backing out of the McCarrolls' driveway. *Claire got murdered.*

*Whatever will become of me?* cried the little girl when the birds had stolen the last of her food. Evil has become of her. Madeleine has the sick smell feeling. Like before, only worse. As if she has done a bad thing—*but I haven't done anything.* As though she has seen Claire lying dead in her blue dress—*but I didn't.* Just lying there, that's the most shameful thing for a little girl to do, to lie there dead and anyone could just pull her dress up. Oh it is a bad smell.

The policeman touches the brim of his hat and Mr. McCarroll raises a hand. Mrs. McCarroll is inside the house somewhere, Madeleine knows. She is in there with Claire's Brownie uniform and all her ankle socks and unbroken toys. There is nowhere for Mrs. McCarroll to go, the whole world is sore.

The cruiser comes slowly up the street in her direction. When it passes, she sees the handlebars of Claire's bike hanging out between the bouncing jaws of the trunk. "She only have one streamer," says Madeleine to nobody. "She only has one streamer," she corrects herself.

A pair of hands wedges under her armpits and pulls her up. "Hop on," says Mike. She climbs on and he piggybacks her home. "Sack o' potatoes," he says as she slides off his back onto the front porch.

Maman comes to the door, takes one look at Madeleine, feels her forehead and says, "Straight to bed."

Jack has made a loop west from Exeter, zigzagged south through a series of uncharted dirt roads until he knows he is below Centralia, then veered east again to pick up Highway 4, which he will follow south to London, and thence Highway 2 all the way to Windsor, where so many cars are born and go to die. He realizes he is squinting and tries to relax his eyes against the noonday sun. He knows exactly where his sunglasses are: on his desk.

Maybe it's time Simon had a word with someone in Ottawa—filter it down to the OPP that they are barking up the wrong tree, going after so-called war criminals. Get them back on the scent before it goes cold. Jack wishes he had thought to suggest this to Simon over the phone; he'll call and do so this evening.

He shades his eyes with his hand and longs to put on his hat with its merciful dark brim. But he leaves the telltale hat where it is, on the seat beside him, and points the Ford Galaxy west.

Madeleine convinced her mother that she was not sick. She is surprised at herself, passing up a legitimate opportunity to miss an afternoon of school. But she had a morbid feeling—as though, if she lay down on her bed or even on the couch in front of the TV, her eyes would go glassy, her head would heat up like a furnace and she would never get up again. So she has returned to school after lunch but, apart from the brief respite from monotony afforded by Grace Novotny's shrivelled-looking hands, she has been unable to concentrate on anything but the window.

Grace returned from lunch without her bandages. Her fingers are white and wrinkly, as though she has just got out of the tub. Someone called Children's Aid. Grace's dad would like to know who.

Jack squeezes his eyes shut once or twice, and increases his speed, driving into the afternoon sun. If the police do their job and come up with an honest-to-goodness suspect, the war criminal story may never be reported; left to fizzle at the local level. He is watchful, glancing frequently into his rearview mirror. He curbs his speed as he sails toward Chatham—the last thing he needs is to be stopped for speeding.

At recess, Madeleine leaves her friends and drifts over to the stormpipe, intending to look inside once and for all but she sees Colleen sitting on the sunny side of the school, where the white stucco prickles back the sun; she is bent over a piece of glass and a page from a discarded newspaper that has blown up against the wall. Madeleine sees a puff of smoke rise from the page, and approaches. Suddenly the paper levitates and curls inward, consumed by a brief orange flame.

Madeleine doesn't say anything and neither does Colleen, but soon they have strayed round the back of the building, leaving the charred headlines to blow away, *Ban-Bomb Trekkers Storm Secret Haven*.

They have never spoken on school property during school hours. They don't speak much now. Madeleine proposes a plan.

By two o'clock the report has come in on the registration search Bradley ordered on Ford Galaxys. It turned up eleven possibilities: five in Toronto, two in Windsor, two in Kingston, one in Ottawa, one in Sudbury. In ten cases, the owner was at work between four and five P.M. last Wednesday, with his car. In one he was out of the country altogether.

Jack accelerates. The police will be wrapping up their session at the arena right about now. Just east of Windsor, his heart leaps at the sight of a black and white cruiser in his rearview mirror. Gaining on him, tailgating. He's had it. He waits for the flashing light, even now preparing himself to pull over, to say nothing and insist on making a phone call. But the black-and-white pulls into the passing lane. Jack keeps his eyes on the road. What is more natural—to glance at the passing driver? Or to keep his eyes forward? His face feels like a beacon. The cruiser takes forever to pass—is the cop on his radio right now? Finally it pulls past Jack, steadily gathering speed, widening the distance between them. He breathes again.

*Welcome to Windsor.* Jack heads for the waterfront. Smoke rises from the GM factory across the river in Detroit—you could almost skip a stone to it. He finds what he's looking for on the edge of town.

Stretching before him are acres of bodies, some rusting, others wrecked—jagged windshields, gaping hoods, crumpled snouts. One great tumbling car crash. At the far end, stacks of neatly pressed chassis loom near a shack that sits in the shadow of a crusher, its magnet like a giant pendulum. Henry Froelich and his boy would be in heaven here, thinks Jack, as he takes the tools from the trunk. He gets to work, calm now. Maybe he is cut out for this sort of thing after all. He removes the hubcaps and sends them saucering in four directions. Then the tires. He unscrews the steering column and yanks it by the wheel, dangling wires and ignition. Uproots sparkplugs, pries off the bumpers, and hurls them.

He funnels dirt into the gas tank, removes the fan belt, the battery, and, holding the crowbar like a baseball bat, goes at the exterior. Finally, he smashes the windows.

There are bound to be bigger wrecking yards in Detroit, but he didn't wish to risk being stopped at the border, now that a bulletin has surely gone out on the Ford. Not to mention having to walk back across the bridge an hour later—although the guards are unlikely to pay much attention to him on either side of this point on the world's longest undefended border. Four thousand miles of freedom.

He drops the plates in the river.

In the recreation director's office at the curling arena, the last uniformed, hatted air force man goes out the door, closing it behind him. Constable Lonergan folds his notebook away, turns to his superior and asks, "Should I put out a bulletin on that Ford Galaxy now, sir?"

Inspector Bradley looks at the man, his face betraying no opinion as to the merit of the question he has just been asked, and says, "There was no Ford Galaxy."

If Mr. March wonders where Madeleine is when the rest of his class returns to their desks after recess, he doesn't show it. He neither informs the principal nor phones the child's mother. Has he thought ahead to what he will say when the parents ask why they were not alerted to their daughter's absence, now of all times? Or is he counting on Madeleine to make sure her parents don't find out, thus sparing him the ordeal of answering their questions as to why she would choose to avoid his classroom?

Perhaps Mr. March doesn't care what happens to Madeleine. Or maybe he doesn't believe her to be in any danger.

Jack directs the taxi to the Hertz dealership in downtown Windsor—he'll be able to get most of the grease off his hands there. His head has begun to ache, the pain radiating from his left eye. He decides not to take the time to find a drugstore, he'll grab a couple of Aspirins when he gets home. He rents a car—no need for back roads now. He'll bomb straight up the 401 to London and, with luck, be back before dark, although he knows his family will be safe at home. He can hardly bear to think of his daughter; her face becomes overlaid with the face of the McCarroll girl and he feels almost terrorized by his good fortune. His child is alive and happy. And right now she is in one of the safest places of all. School.

# REQUIEM

*Find in the story and explain: "Her thoughts were miles away."*
Developing Comprehension in Reading, *Mary Eleanor Thomas, 1956*

THEY HAVE TO FIND her other streamer. That is the mission. But Madeleine knows that what she really needs to find is where Claire was for three days and nights. Rex found her. "Good boy, Rex."

The two of them hid against the windowless exterior wall of the gym until the recess bell rang, then slipped away. Madeleine waited at the railway tracks by Pop's Candy Store while Colleen went home and got Rex, then they took the fields all the way to Rock Bass.

Madeleine doesn't feel she is doing anything wrong by playing hooky. This is like missing school for church. Or the hospital. Anyhow, they haven't taken off in order to fool around. There is something solemn about risking getting in trouble for the sake of finding Claire's other streamer. And visiting the spot. It's a necessary sacrifice. Colleen follows her through the gap in the wire fence.

They have brought Rex in case the murderer is still there. Murderers always return to the scene of the crime. Perhaps they ought to have brought weapons. Don't worry, Colleen always has her knife. And Madeleine can pick up a stone if necessary. She did think fleetingly of Mike's rifle, but that's a toy, and this is not a game.

Colleen leads the way down into the ravine. They have brought no food; this is not a picnic. They remove their shoes and socks and wade through the icy stream, ankles aching, then climb up the embankment, their frozen skin numb to the thistles, and into the newly sprouted corn-field. *Be careful.*

They put their shoes back on and walk for a long time, single file, between the furrows, feet growing heavy with mud, Rex in front, the lope of his hindquarters, his reassuring fur shining in the sun. They don't speak. The cornfield becomes the meadow.

Oh it is Tuesday, bright and sunny, but inside Madeleine's stomach it is chilly. Everything is so quiet, school-day quiet. Look for some-thing pink and gleaming in last year's fallen-down grass, or draped perhaps across a sticky milkweed pod or bulrush—furry brown spike bursting fluff. Maybe they will see it blowing across the tops of the lacy stinkweeds that are scattered like dropped napkins across the meadow—the entire countryside is a tablecloth laid for a banquet—or down among the dull burrs snagging their ankle socks—something winking back the sun, that will be her streamer. We have to find it because it was hers. And it is still out there, all alone. Keep walking. Rex knows the way.

He zigzags out in front, looking over his shoulder from time to time, stopping, letting them go ahead for a while. He is herding them. The lily of the valley release their scent, crushed underfoot in the new grass.

The ground becomes marshy. Up ahead, standing alone, announcing the woods, is a stately elm.

There, stop. Don't step in. Stay at the edge. Like stumbling upon a pond, you don't want to get a soaker. If this were a pond, you might see your own reflection and wonder if there was a tiny world down there looking back at you. But it's not a pond, it's a circular patch of tamped-down grass and weeds, as though someone had a picnic there. A spot the size of a puddle. Big enough for one to curl up in. That is where she lay. But already the tender grass is springing back. Soon there will be nothing to see. Around the edges, bluebells and dandelions have been plucked, the milk dried in their severed stems, their blossoms tossed among broken bulrushes. There is no sign of her pink streamer.

Madeleine says, "Maybe they're going to bury her one streamer with her, or else keep it as a souvenir."

When Madeleine is grown up, Claire will still be in a box in the ground. She will still be little, still in the same dress they buried her in. *No matter what I am doing, no matter where I go, Claire will be there in that one spot.*

"They can't do that with evidence," says Colleen.

*Evidence.* Imagine your bike, or your running shoe, or any old thing; one day it's just your stuff lying around, and the next day it's *evidence.* Police. Do Not Touch. Top Secret.

They search the area around the spot carefully without touching anything. They speak sparingly, in whispers. They walk lightly. This is a grave.

"We should have a funeral."

"Yeah."

Mike and Madeleine had a funeral for a fly once. They put it in a matchbox and prayed for it and Madeleine composed a poem, "Goodbye fly, the time is nigh. You flew too high, goodbye, good fly." A poem is coming to her now, "Claire, you were fair, but it was no fair. . . ." She can get no farther because all she can think to rhyme with it is "underwear." "But where is your underwear, fair Claire?" Lost and gone forever.

"Her underpants were off," says Colleen.

"How do you know?" asks Madeleine.

"I heard Mrs. Ridelle tell my ma."

"That's sick."

"Yeah."

They stand in silence, gazing down at the fading circle. Rex stands next to them. On guard.

"Maybe the murderer got her other streamer," says Madeleine.

"She coulda just lost it."

"No, she had it," says Madeleine, "'cause remember? We saw when she was going to Rock Bass with Ricky and Elizabeth."

"She wasn't going with them."

"I know, but I saw she had both of them then"—Madeleine looks back down—"and that was the day." She moves to pluck a weed to chew, then stops herself, not wanting to chew or eat anything from around here.

"We were the last ones who saw her," she says. Everyone in the world will have a last person who they see, who sees them. Who will mine be?

"No, Ricky and Elizabeth and Rex saw her after we did," says Colleen.

"Oh yeah."

"And someone else." Colleen has taken out her knife but she doesn't open it, or flip it and catch it, the way she usually does.

Madeleine says, "Who?" Colleen narrows her eyes and doesn't answer, doesn't look at Madeleine. Madeleine gets it: *the murderer, that's who.*

She can hear grasshoppers fiddling, insects crawling up blades of grass. Sun burns the centre part in her hair. Nearby, the woods are dark and cool. Rex sniffs the edge of the tamped-down circle, but he doesn't venture in either. Colleen reaches out and passes her hand over it. "To feel if it's still warm."

"Is it?"

"A bit. Feel."

But Madeleine doesn't want to. "Wanna go home now, Colleen?"

"No, I wanna tell you something, and if you ever tell, I'll kill you." Rex's ears prick up and he lifts his head. "What is it boy?"

They follow Rex's gaze, toward the woods. A crash—Madeleine's heart leaps, she grabs Colleen's arm, Colleen doesn't push her away, they stand stock-still. Heavy footsteps. The leaves are shaking. Madeleine sinks her fingers into Colleen's arm and Colleen says, "Shhh."

There, amid cool green shadows—light brown jacket through the branches—a doe. Huge brown eyes. She looks at them from behind the jigsaw green and black of the forest fringe. Like a creature up from an underwater world, about to sample oxygen, that dangerous and irresistible nothing.

Rex goes into a crouch, growls softly. His shoulders move, he inches forward. "It's okay Rex." He stops.

The deer steps from the woods into the meadow. Bends her head and starts to graze. They watch her, the three of them, oh for a long time, for five minutes, until the deer lifts her head and bounds away like a wave, diving back into the dark pool of trees.

That was Claire's funeral.

"What were you going to tell me?" asks Madeleine.

They have turned away from the woods, from the small circle, they are leaving the spot. Madeleine sees a piece of blue shell in the grass—it looks like a piece of robin's egg. She stoops to pick it up but, before she can, Colleen seizes her wrist and turns her face-on. In her other hand she holds her knife, open. She slaps the handle flat into Madeleine's palm and closes Madeleine's fist around it. Then she holds out her own palm and says, "Do it."

"What?"

"Cut me," says Colleen. "Then I'll do you."

"Why?"

"'Cause I won't tell you a goddamn thing if you don't, that's why."

Madeleine feels the carved weight of the knife handle and looks at Colleen's open palm. "Don't make it deep," says Colleen, "just enough for blood."

Colleen watches her. Madeleine hesitates. Colleen looks gritty as highway dirt, but her palm looks so soft. Madeleine lets the sharp edge rest across the fleshy part of Colleen's palm. Then she presses, and pulls the blade toward herself. The skin parts and a row of red seeds sprouts, then seeps into the hollow of Colleen's hand.

Colleen holds out her other hand for the knife. Madeleine gives it to her. Colleen waits, her cupped palm collecting blood. Madeleine extends her own left hand, palm up, clutching it around the wrist with her right as though to keep it from running away.

Colleen lifts the knife. Madeleine shuts her eyes and gasps. Then opens them. Colleen is looking at her, her mouth in a sarcastic tilt.

"You ready, Mighty Mouse?" Madeleine nods. She forces herself to watch, but before she can put on a brave face it's over, and she has barely seen the knife move, neither did she feel it, but the red stripe has appeared like magic across her palm, widening, gracefully overflowing its banks. Colleen slaps her palm into Madeleine's, holding tight, smooshing them together. Madeleine pushes back; it still doesn't hurt. Colleen lets go. "There," she says. "*On ai seurs de san.*"

Their two hands are smeared as though with fingerpaint. They let Rex lick their wounds, because everyone knows that dogs have antiseptic spit.

Colleen resumes walking and Madeleine follows. Colleen seems to have forgotten about her. They walk in silence.

"Hey Colleen, what were you going to tell me?"

"Not here," she says.

At Rock Bass, Colleen sits next to the flat stone by the stream and reaches down her white school blouse for the leather string she wears around her neck; tawny brown, softened with age. It's almost the colour of her skin. She lifts it out, its end enclosed in her palm— the unscathed one.

"I'm going to show you something," she says. She opens her hand to reveal a tiny deerhide pouch closed with a delicate leather drawstring. She opens it, picking the fragile knot. She reaches in with thumb and forefinger and takes out the secret. A crumple of paper.

"What is it?" asks Madeleine.

Colleen smooths it out. "It's from a catalogue."

The once glossy fragment is flannelly with age. Madeleine can make out part of a red bicycle—a boy's bike—and underneath, a caption, "Pony Express."

"I'm adopted," says Colleen.

The earth tilts soundlessly, the maple tree lists, suddenly rootless. *Adopted.* Madeleine concentrates on the charred flat stone between them. Behind Colleen is a blank. No—behind her are dead parents. That's why kids get adopted. "Are you an orphan?"

"No stupid, I got parents."

"I know, I mean . . . before."

"My blood parents are dead."

Madeleine feels dizzy. Colleen has had the thing happen that everyone is so afraid of, that your parents might be killed in the car without you—for that is how parents die.

There is a shawl of death everywhere, it seems to Madeleine. And trapped in its folds, a smell. It is the smell of the McCarrolls, of Colleen, of the exercise group, of Madeleine and Mr. March. Most people don't have the smell and don't even notice it on others. They are the lucky ones. *Like Dad. He thinks I am sunny and light.* Her mother has sniffed the air once or twice as though at the scent of smoke, then dismissed it, the way you do when you figure it's someone else's house on fire.

"That's how come your mum volunteers at the orphanage, eh," says Madeleine, seeing her own words like neat black writing on a clean page. Words are clean. The paper-thin scar at the corner of Colleen's mouth has paled, her lips turning mauve. "Yeah, that's one reason."

"You were just a baby when you were adopted, though, eh," says Madeleine.

"No, I was a little kid."

"But you don't remember."

"I fuckin' well do so remember, I remember everything."

This is not the time to ask what "fuck" means—not the time for questions that splash and ripple, but for words that go softly *plop.*

"I don't care if you're adopted."

Colleen just stares off.

"Your parents don't care."

"I know."

"No one in your family cares if you're adopted."

"We're all adopted, tithead." Colleen plucks a blade of grass and sticks it between her teeth.

Madeleine sees all the Froelich kids again, as though for the first time. It's true they don't look alike, but neither do she and Mike. Although Mike looks like Dad and Madeleine looks like Maman. "Even Elizabeth?"

"Yeah," says Colleen, turning to look at Madeleine. "You think that's funny?"

"No"—biting the inside of her cheek to kill a grin, not because it's funny but because it isn't.

Colleen hugs her knees and begins to rock slightly. "Except for Rick. He's my blood brother."

"You mean like—" and Madeleine indicates the fresh wound in her palm.

"No," says Colleen, "for real."

That makes sense. When you think about it, they do look alike, but the resemblance is beneath the surface. They are different colours— Rick's black hair and eyes and white skin in winter, the opposite of Colleen with her husky-dog eyes and dusky skin. Not to mention Rick is a gentleman. But their eyes and their cheekbones are the same shape, their lean builds.

"Our name was Pellegrim," says Colleen.

*Pellegrim.* Sounds like *pilgrim,* thinks Madeleine.

She and Ricky were on the floor in the back of the car when it crashed. They were looking at an old Sears, Roebuck Christmas catalogue.

"That's my rifle," said Ricky. A toy rifle with a white silhouette on the stock, of a horse and cowboy at full gallop.

"That's my two-wheeler," said Colleen. A red "All American Pony Express" with a shiny bell and crossbar.

"That's a boy's bike," Ricky told her.

"That's what I want."

"Sure, why not, you're pretty tough for a girl." He was nine, she was six. They survived because they were on the floor. Colleen's face was cut by the catalogue page, a bad paper cut. Ricky got a concussion and had his neck in a brace afterwards but he was all right. Their parents went through the windshield. The front end of the Plymouth was stove in but the engine stayed in place.

Colleen got herself out of the car and went to her mother. There was no other car. There was a half-dead deer. There was a rifle in the trunk of the car. Someone should get it and kill the deer, thought Colleen. She couldn't look at the deer because it was still alive and suffering. And she couldn't look at her mother because her mother was dead. She couldn't see her father. He had been thrown into the woods. She walked in a little way, found him, but she didn't go near. She returned and rocked on her heels next to her mother for a long while. In one hand she still clutched a crumple of catalogue pages.

Ricky woke up and got out of the car, and saw that the deer was still kicking. It was so sad, its terrible brown eyes, Colleen wondered what would happen to the baby deer off in the forest somewhere. Ricky got the rifle out of the trunk and shot the deer. He covered his mother with a blanket she had sewn. He found his father and covered his face with leaves. Then he took his little sister by the hand and they started walking down the highway, dragging the rifle along behind them.

The car engine kept running until it ran out of gas.

"What do you wanna do now?" says Colleen, getting up.

"I dunno," says Madeleine, "what do you wanna do?"

They rinse their feet in the stream. The water is so cold that their feet dry almost immediately. They put their shoes and socks back on,

Madeleine her Mary Janes, Colleen her scuffed loafers with the empty penny slots.

"Come on," says Colleen. "I could use a smoke."

Life began again in an orphanage. But soon, Colleen's brother disappeared. Memory survived as imagination, and after a while she forgot she had a brother—a real one. They gave her a new name, Bridget. Perhaps she'd had an Indian name and they'd changed it when she arrived; that was what happened to many of the children there. They were Indians. So was she, as far as the staff were concerned, but she was a half-breed in the eyes of the other kids. She didn't come from a reserve, she didn't belong to a band—her mother's people had had a beautiful cabin on a road allotment, but it was gone and they had scattered. She came from a car.

First they called her "mute," then "mentally retarded." None of the children were permitted to speak their own languages, because they were heathen. When she broke her silence to speak in Michif, that was considered even worse. Michif was not a language, and the Métis were not a people.

Finally, she was "uncontrollable." Social Services intervened when she was admitted to hospital, and sent her to a training school outside Red Deer, Alberta. It was a place for retarded, delinquent and discarded children. Many were Indians or somewhere in between. If you were good, you got to work on the farm. She was tied to the bed, for her own safety and that of the other residents. But she wasn't sterilized, she didn't stay there long enough. One day someone called out from the boys' side of the fence, "Colleen!" and she turned, knowing her name when she heard it. He was her brother.

Karen Froelich had realized that she could no longer volunteer at this place. It didn't need help, it needed closing. When she and Henry adopted the two "hard cases," they signed a paper requiring them to live within the province and report regularly to an officer of the juvenile court. Karen had been an aid worker with the U.N. Henry had been a refugee. They knew something about bureaucracy. They packed the children into the Chevrolet and drove east two thousand miles. Henry found work on an air force station in Ontario where everyone was rootless and no one stayed long enough to look too deeply into anyone else's past.

Rick is picked up on his way home from school that Tuesday afternoon. Jogging south from Exeter on Highway 4, his books in an army surplus knapsack, school shoes looped through the straps and bouncing. The OPP cruiser slows alongside him. He recognizes the two officers and salutes them casually. The one on the passenger side leans forward and says, "Hop in, son."

Rick keeps jogging, "No thanks, I'm in training."

"Get in the car," says the one behind the wheel.

Rick stops. "Why? What's happened?" His parents, the kids. Is Elizabeth okay?

The cop in the driver's seat says, "Get in the goddamn car."

Rick hesitates. The passenger door opens and his friend emerges like a bull from a pen. Rick turns and runs. Into the field, obeying an ancient reflex. It's crazy, he hasn't done anything, but he's running like hell across newly sprouted rows of beets, over ridges of earth hardening in the sun, books slamming his back, shoes whacking his side, throat burning. The cop is way behind, Rick can see that with a glance over his shoulder. He keeps pelting, there's a woodlot up ahead, if he can make it to the trees—another shoulder check reveals the big cop hunched over, hands on his knees, winded—an old glee pulls at the corners of Rick's mouth, unreasonable surge of triumph, "Try and catch me, *maudi batars!*" He starts to laugh, chin up, chest out, not tired, never tired, could run forever—another glance, the cruiser is rocking toward him over the furrows, tearing up a dirt cloud in its wake. It picks up speed, coming straight at him. He stops.

Jack pays the cab driver and gets out in front of the cenotaph in Exeter at 7:20. There is still light in the sky when he makes his way on foot to the staff car waiting for him behind the old train station.

He has never felt so comfortable behind the wheel of any car, relieved to be off the pins and needles that seemed to upholster the Ford Galaxy. He got a couple of Aspirin from the cabbie who drove him here from the Hertz drop-off in London, and now, as he cruises south, he feels his headache draining away and settles back to enjoy the cushioned suspension and the clean sense of having accomplished something—despite the grease under his nails. His hands look like Henry Froelich's.

The blue Ford was the only thing the police had to tie Oskar Fried to the area. Soon it will be no more than a metal envelope. Jack has done his bit for Queen and country, and now he analyzes in his mind the benefit versus the cost. The benefit: Oskar Fried is safe and free to contribute his expertise to the West's fight for military and scientific supremacy. The costs: the police have been allowed to waste precious time in the hunt for a child-killer, and Jack has lied to his wife. The latter need never be repeated. The former doesn't sit well with him, but he reminds himself that maybe Simon can pull strings from his end and get the authorities back on track.

He turns in at the gates, eager to ditch the staff car, wash up, then dash home. He phoned Mimi from Windsor, telling her he was stuck at a meeting in London. The last lie.

"I have to call my parents sir," Rick says again.

The inspector says, "I'll get someone to phone them for you. What's the number?"

Rick's stomach growls. He is in the same green concrete room, seated at a wooden table. The inspector sits across from him. Rick is cold. They took his knapsack with his windbreaker in it and have yet to give it back.

The inspector asks, "Why did you do it, son?"

"Do what?"

Rick is not all that aware of the attention he pays kids. They hang around him, like birds. He doesn't always notice, but when he does he may acknowledge them. A push on the swing if he happens to be in the schoolyard and a little kid says, "Push me, Ricky." A couple of shots on goal, sure, you can try on my jacket if you want to. He is like the person who happens to have a bag of popcorn when the pigeons land. So he doesn't know what Inspector Bradley means when he says, "You like 'em young, eh Rick?"

Jack heads down Canada Avenue, the white buildings of the station shining under the street lights. The air is as fresh as if it had just gone through the wash and Jack feels lighter than he has in days. He skipped lunch and he's looking forward to whatever Mimi will give him, eager to see his kids.

High pale clouds reflect the moon; it's possible we'll get one more snowfall this year, but it will be old man winter's last gasp. Soon it will be time to trade in his dress blues for the light khaki uniform of summer. He finds himself looking forward to New Brunswick this August—time Mimi saw her mother again, and Jack could use a good game of Deux-Cents, a real wingding with his brothers-in-law.

He passes the message centre on his left—had he not popped in there yesterday for Sharon McCarroll's boarding pass, had he not delivered it personally, he would never have found out about Froelich spotting Fried. So much of this game is about chance and making the most of it. Human intelligence. *Humint.* Simon is right, it's vastly underrated. When a U-2 spy plane is shot down, when an Igor Gouzenko surfaces, the public gets a glimpse behind the veil. But hundreds of men like Simon are working around the clock, fighting invisible battles, scoring silent victories, so that each morning the world can look the same as it did the day before. And we can continue to take it all for granted, and to have faith: the sun will rise, the sky will not be full of airplanes, will not be obliterated by an air-raid siren.

He passes the intrepid Spitfire, its nose tilted toward the stars, and crosses the Huron County road. He is among a quiet handful of people who know how precious and fragile it all is. Behind the tranquility of everyday life, something unstable is multiplying; something that wants to assert the primacy of chaos. Jack has, very briefly and quite unremarkably, worked behind the scenes so that his family and millions of others never have to find out. He enters the PMQs with an expansive feeling in his chest.

"Then why didn't your air force man come forward, if he saw you?"

"Maybe he got posted."

Rick is past hunger, feeling sick now, what time is it? They think I strangled Claire McCarroll. "Maybe he's not from the station, maybe he was just here on course and he left the next day."

"What servicemen do you know who have recently left the station?"

"I don't know."

"But he knew you—he waved, according to you—how do you explain that?"

"I don't know."

"You don't know much," says Rick's friend from the passenger side—the one who punched him in the gut when he stopped running. He is sitting on a chair tilted against the wall, taking notes.

"I want to call my dad."

"Trouble is, buddy," says the big cop, "there were no departures from the station that week. No courses finishing, no postings, no one away on leave. We checked, eh?"

Rick stares at the scarred tabletop.

"How do you explain that, young man?" asks Bradley.

"I can't."

"I can." Rick waits. Bradley says, "It never happened."

A bad dream. "I want my mother," says Rick and bites his lip, feeling himself redden with the approach of tears, ambushed by the potency of the universal phrase. He looks up. The big cop is grinning at him.

Jack runs up the steps and into his house. "What's for supper, I'm starved"—but the kitchen is empty. No dinner smells, the table not set. "Mimi? . . . Kids?" What's happened? *I went away and something happened.* The cuckoo clock startles him; he reaches for the phone, for Mimi's pop-up tin address book—although he hasn't a clue how to decode her filing system—and catches sight of the note on the fridge, "We're across the street at the Froelichs'." He breathes again. He wants a beer. Maybe Henry's got a good Löwenbräu on ice.

He is about to knock on the Froelichs' door when the bejesus police dog lunges at him through the screen—"Rex!" Colleen seizes his collar. "He thought you were another cop." She turns and disappears down the hall, and Jack enters. A record is blaring on the hi-fi. *Bambi.*

"Dad!" Madeleine scrambles from the living-room floor and runs to him.

"Hi old buddy."

"Hi Dad," says his son, absorbed in a Meccano creation.

The Froelichs' living room is chaotic—laundry hamper, newspapers, playpen, toys. The young gal in the wheelchair doesn't seem to register his arrival so Jack doesn't greet her. He finds his wife in the kitchen, feeding the two baby boys, one screaming. He grins at the sight; he'll tease her about it later, but it looks good on her, a baby at the end of each spoon, strained peaches in their hair. But she doesn't smile back, just says, "There's soup on the stove. Ricky Froelich's been arrested."

"What?" Jack hesitates, but the soup smells good. "What for?" He reaches toward the stove and lifts the lid on the pot.

"Claire," says Mimi.

The metal is hot but it takes a second for that message to get through, so that, by the time Jack replaces the lid on the pot, the pads of his thumb and forefinger are shiny and seared.

"Claire?" he says, his lips drying. The word dissolves like a capsule in his gut, spreading outward. *Claire.* He takes a breath. Sits at the kitchen table, the little boys racketing their fists against their high-chair trays. Mimi is sliding peach goo from their faces, folding it expertly into their mouths. He watches her lips move and struggles to follow what she is saying—the Froelichs have gone to look for their son, the police came and took away his clothes, claimed not to know where the boy was being held. She goes to the sink to rinse the bowls.

"Why?" says Jack. She hasn't heard him over the din. "Why?" he repeats.

Mimi says, "They don't believe his alibi."

Jack examines the word "alibi"—like a strange fish on the end of his line. He sees Colleen in the doorway. She says, "I'll put 'em to bed, I'll change 'em," barely moving her mouth, eyes more guarded than ever.

Mimi says, "You're a good helper, Colleen, let's you and me do it together."

Jack is alone at the kitchen table. In the living room, Shirley Temple's intimate tones boom from the hi-fi, a certain plaintive sexy catch in her voice. *His alibi.* How did he miss it? What he should have known. The boy on the road with his sister and his dog . . . a trick of perspective. Jack makes the realization that his memory of the event has been from Rick's point of view: the blue car, oncoming into the sun, bounce of light off the windshield obliterating all but the shape of a hat behind the wheel; a hand raised in greeting, a man waving. And as the car passes, the dent in the rear bumper, the yellow sticker.

Now Jack plays the same memory from his own vantage point behind the wheel. He sees Rick jogging on the road with his sister and dog, pushing the wheelchair. The boy lifts a hand to shield his eyes against the sudden glare of sun. Then he raises an arm, tentative, in response to Jack's wave. Wednesday afternoon. When the little girl went missing.

The police were never interested in what the boy saw. They were interested in whether or not anyone saw the boy. "On the afternoon of Wednesday, April tenth," is what Bradley asked. That must have been the time of the murder. Even thinking or saying "the time of the murder" seems to bring order to an obscenely disordered event. No one should call it anything; to name it is to include it in the world, and it should not be included.

Jack stares at the kitchen table; grey Formica sparkles blend with crumbs, a ring of milk. He folds his hands next to a wad of bills blotched transparent with butter.

He was just doing his job, it never entered his mind. . . . But who in his right mind could have imagined the police were after Ricky Froelich? He shakes his head—now that the "war criminal" is out of the picture, the picture is suddenly clear: *Rick was the last one seen with her. Rick found the body*—knew where to look for it, according to the police. And now, thanks to Jack, they can say, *Rick lied about his alibi.* The police were not impeded in their deductions by the knowledge of what a nice boy Ricky Froelich is. To them, he is just a male juvenile.

A sizzling—Jack looks up, the soup is boiling over. He gets up, turns off the heat. Warms his hands over the mess.

From the hi-fi a pert command, "Wake up, wake up! Wake up, friend Owl!"

Inspector Bradley's face is inscrutable, his voice as expressionless as if he were reading from an instruction manual. "You left your sister in her wheelchair and, accompanied by your dog, you lured Claire McCarroll into the field, where you attempted to rape her, and when she threatened to tell, you killed her."

"What's so funny, Rick?" asks the cop from the chair.

"Nothing."

"Something must be funny, you're laughing."

"It's crazy, that's all." He tried not to laugh, but it turned out that tears were easier to fend off. It is funny. It's eight-thirty and he has been in this room for five hours, he hasn't peed, he hasn't eaten, he has told the same story countless times, they are saying he would leave his sister alone in her wheelchair—"I would never leave my sister alone in her—" He is laughing so hard that tears trickle down his face. He lays his head down on his arms on the table. Heaving.

"What did you say?"

"You should ask her," says Rick, wiping tears.

"Ask who, Rick?" says Inspector Bradley.

"My sister. She was with me the whole time. She knows."

Inspector Bradley says nothing. The big cop sips his Coke and asks, "What good's that going to do, Rick?"

"She can tell you, I didn't do it."

"She can't tell us diddly-squat, Ricky."

"Yes she can, she was—"

"She's retarded."

Rick is so tired. He looks from the man in the suit to the man in the uniform and says, "Fuck you."

Madeleine reaches into the Lowney's candy tin that Mike brought from home and fishes out a green army man poised to hurl a grenade. Like a good book, it's impossible to tire of the Bambi story record. Shirley Temple's grown-up voice compels you to listen to the bittersweet end, her voice tearful yet brave, it's the sound of your own heart. "When

Bambi and his mother came to the edge of the meadow, they approached it with great caution for the meadow was wide open."

She surveys the impenetrable phalanx she has arranged around Elizabeth's wheelchair, repositions a prone sniper and feels a wet drop on the nape of her neck. Oh no, she realizes, Elizabeth drool. But you can't get mad at her, she can't help it. Madeleine looks up.

It wasn't drool. It was a tear.

"Don't worry, Elizabeth," says Madeleine, in the exaggerated kindly tone reserved for cats and toddlers. "Ricky will be home soon."

They have stripped him. They are searching his body for traces.

"How did this happen, young man?"

Rick says nothing. He looks down at the unknown doctor genuflecting before him. He has lifted Rick's penis with a wooden tongue depressor—a Popsicle stick.

"You stick it in a tree knot?" asks the cop.

The doctor gives him a look and the cop folds his arms, muttering, "This is making me sick."

A lesion on the side of the shaft below the glans, about the size of a dime. The doctor writes, then asks again, "What is it?"

Rick says, "*Ci qouai ca?*"

"I beg your pardon?" says the doctor.

"What the hell did you just say?" asks the cop.

Rick says nothing. Inspector Bradley waits impassively. A second uniformed officer takes a picture of Rick's penis. There is the sound of a commotion outside the room.

Rick knows the sore on his penis is from his denim shorts. From swimming in the freezing quarry on Sunday, then putting them back on without underwear. He says nothing as he zips his fly back up.

The doctor examines Rick's arms, face and neck with a magnifying glass. They are looking for evidence of a struggle. They have searched his clothes for an object, a mark, a stain, anything he might possess.

Inspector Bradley says, "Let's start from the beginning, Rick. Where did you go once you got to the intersection? Try to remember."

"*Asseye de ti rappeli.*" He remembers metal beds. Women with hard voices and white shoes, taking him along by the arm. Murky linoleum with white streaks, the smell of beans cooking, the smell of pee.

"What did you say to get the little girl to go with you?"

"*En pchit fee,*" says Rick.

"Cut that out," says the cop from his chair.

"We've got all night, Rick," says Bradley. "Try to remember, son."

He remembers the curious feeling of recollecting from time to time that he had a sister. It was as though the word "sister" had come to mean something that you used to have. Sisters were not things you hung onto. They didn't die, they just quite naturally disappeared. When brother and sister saw one another again, it was as if Rick had awoken from a spell. He swore he would never fall asleep away from anybody of his, ever again.

When he and Colleen turn twenty-one it will be up to them whether they go back to it their real last name—their first one—Pellegrim. His father played Cajun music and sang. Rick doesn't know where he was from, he never said, nor would he say whether he was Canadian or American, but he claimed Indian blood. He had fought in the Pacific. He had no passport, yet they were always crossing the border in the car—there were places then. Back roads across the Medicine Line. Rick's mother had long black hair, her features round and sweet. Her eyes dark and twinkly like Rick's. Genevieve.

They followed the rodeos. His father wore a cowboy hat and a fringed buckskin jacket with an eagle embroidered on the back in beads, the work of their mother's hands. She was from the Red River Valley, and one day Rick will go back and see if anyone is left. This is what he possesses. It fits into a very small bundle that you could hang on a stick if you had to up and leave. *Ousque ji rest? Chu en woyaugeur, ji rest partou.*

"Speak English," says the cop.

They are alone. The inspector and the doctor have left. Another noise in the hall—Rick recognizes his mother's voice. He turns and simultaneously doubles over in pain. The cop has kicked him in the nuts with his thick knee, still bent, blue fabric straining. The door opens and Inspector Bradley comes in before the officer can use his boot. The inspector places Rick under arrest for the rape and murder of Claire McCarroll and advises him of his rights under the law. Then Rick's parents come in. Rick is grateful that he is fully clothed when he sees his mother.

She takes one look at him and screams at Inspector Bradley, "What've you bastards done to him!" But the uniformed officer has left the room, and it's no good how loudly his mother insists she is taking him home, the arguments of his father, the professorial outrage in his voice, none of it makes any difference.

In his office, Inspector Bradley writes a memo to his chief, requesting that the officer who struck Richard Froelich be transferred to another unit. Bradley is not the "beating with a rubber hose" type. His job is to serve the justice system. This is a delicate case. Richard Froelich is a juvenile but he has committed an adult crime. He should be tried as one. Allegations of police brutality against a "defenceless child" will not help.

Jack crosses the street for home, following his kids, who are racing each other to the TV.

"Dad, can we watch 'The Flintstones'?" asks his daughter.

"Sure."

The small picture is worse. But Simon has control over the big picture. Jack will have to phone him from home this time, and tell him to talk to someone right away.

"Dad, can we have orange pop?" his son asks.

"Go ahead," says Jack and picks up the phone. Once Simon has adjusted the big picture, the small picture will come back into focus.

He goes to dial, then recalls that he will have to use the night number. It's in his wallet. Along with the key to the Ford Galaxy. He meant to toss the key into the scrapyard. He unfolds the slip of paper from his wallet, dials the number and listens to the ringing at the other end. When Simon answers, he speaks quietly. It's just as well the television is blaring in the next room.

"My neighbour's son has been arrested for the murder of McCarroll's daughter."

"Good Lord."

"Yeah. The police were never interested in Fried, it was the boy they were after."

"That's the boy you were mentioning," says Simon. "The one you saw from the car?"

"That's right."

"How appalling. Well, they've got him now, I suppose that's a relief."

"What? No, Simon, the boy is innocent. I'm his alibi."

The briefest pause, then "Oh."

From the living room, Madeleine sees her father facing away and leaning against the fridge. His head is bowed and his free hand grips the back of his neck.

Jack speaks with his mouth close to the phone. "The police ought to be out finding this pervert, not wasting time with—"

"Quite."

In the living room, the kids are squabbling. Jack moves farther into the kitchen, as far as the phone cord will allow. "The OPP need to know that I can vouch for the boy. We need to clear this whole thing up, discreetly, right away, Si. You'll have to have a word with someone."

"With whom?"

Jack feels faintly ridiculous. He licks his lips. "External Affairs; RCMP Security Service, whoever's got a back channel to the police here."

"The fact is, old friend, there is no one."

". . . What do you mean?"

"Just that," says Simon, almost breezy. "I've closed the loop on this one. The Soviets think Fried is dead. I've had to keep the points of entry to a minimum. You're the only Canadian directly involved. I told you that."

*You're the only one who knows.* He had meant it literally. "What about—well, how did you—?" Jack shakes his head. "How in God's name did you manage to get Fried a Canadian passport? How can you be operating here without Canadian authority?"

"Did you get rid of the car?"

"It's scrap by now. Simon, I asked you a question."

"We're not doing anything that contradicts our obligations under NATO."

"Bullshit. What's going on?" He has sworn like a cadet, right in his own kitchen. He glances over his shoulder but his kids are fixated, blue shadows dancing on their faces, bathed in undifferentiated racket.

"It's the truth," Simon is saying. "Politicians may prefer either not to know, or not to be seen to know, the details, but their policies implicitly authorize this sort of work, and they expect it to be done, otherwise we'd be part of the U.S.S.R. by now."

Is it legal? The job he's doing for Simon? What does Jack really know about Oskar Fried?

"Who are you working for, Simon?"

"It's time I bought you that drink."

Oskar Fried is a Soviet citizen, for pity's sake. And Jack has embraced him on the word of an old friend. A man he has seen once in twenty years. "You told me it was an American–Canadian–British operation."

"I never specified. I can tell you it ain't Soviet."

"You know there's a killer on the loose here, buddy?"

Jack's knuckles are white around the receiver. But Simon's voice, when he answers, is quiet. "Not a very happy place right now, eh? Centralia? I'm not keen on seeing an innocent boy punished, Jack. I'm not keen on child-killers going free."

A burst of gunfire from the living room.

Simon says, "That's not why I do my job."

Jack waits.

"That's not what we fought for, Jack." *We.*

Jack hears a sigh on the other end of the line, and feels ashamed. He takes a breath finally. Simon is not the enemy. The enemy is out there. He looks at the black shine of the kitchen window and sees a man, head bowed, on the phone. He steps forward and draws the curtains—the ones Mimi sewed in Germany.

"Your police are putting on a pretty poor show," says Simon. "They clearly haven't a fucking clue who's responsible."

"I'm sick about it, Simon. I've sent the police on a goddamn wild goose chase."

"Do you really think you've done that single-handedly?" Simon in the seat beside him. Asking the right questions. "We're taking some flak that's all. We'll ride it out. Don't shake hands with the Devil before you meet him."

Jack takes another deep breath, as quietly as possible, so as not to rouse his headache. Simon is right. They picked up Ricky Froelich because there are no other suspects. He wonders if there is any Aspirin in the house.

"What's the situation on the ground there, Jack? Has your neighbour. . . ."

"Froelich."

"Has he spoken to anyone else, any mention of Dora in the press?"

"No. The arrest will be all over the papers, but. . . . If I were his lawyer, I'd tell him to keep his war criminal story to himself. Just makes the boy look guilty."

"Good point."

"Simon, if this goes any farther, I'll have to come forward."

"I don't imagine it'll come to that."

An air-raid siren wails from the living room. Simon adds, almost as an afterthought, "Have you mentioned this to anyone at all? Fried? The fact you were in the car?"

"No—"

"To your wife—?"

"I've told no one."

"Good. You did the right thing, mate."

Jack's headache blooms. His left eye pulses, he sees a diagonal silver flash and loses a patch of vision. "I'll keep you posted." He hangs up and pauses, his hand still on the receiver. In the next room his daughter sings along with a commercial, "'You'll wonder where the yellow went, when you brush your teeth with Pepsodent!'" Where does Mimi keep the Aspirin? He begins opening drawers. In the cupboard under the sink he finds a ragged old housedress, not anything Mimi wears, surely, what's it doing here? Is it really possible that no one in the Canadian government is aware of Fried's presence? Or is Canada in the habit of granting carte blanche to the Americans and Brits? A grenade explodes behind him; he turns and is in the living room in two steps. "Turn that godforsaken box down!"

Madeleine looks up. Her father is standing in the doorway, staring at her brother.

"But Dad, I can hardly hear it," says Mike.

Her father looks strange. "What did you say, mister?"

"Nothing."

Madeleine sits hugging a couch cushion, while Mike drags himself to the TV and lowers the volume. Dad doesn't take his eyes from him. "What in the name of God are you watching, anyway?" Madeleine knew it was too good to be true—the half-naked Nazi, the chesty mademoiselle—

"*Combat,*" says Mike.

"Why are you letting your sister watch that garbage?"

"It's not garbage, it's good."

"American garbage."

"Well, we don't have our own garbage."

Dad clips him on the side of the head.

"Ow," cries Mike, and turns red.

Jack plants himself in front of the television. "I'll tell you something: the Americans entered both wars late and they like to take the credit, but you know who was in the front lines both times from the very beginning?" It's a question that requires no reply. "Canadians." His lips are thin and shiny. Bluish. "Do you know how many Canadian aircrew died in the last war?"

Machine-gun fire from the television—"I'm hit!" cries Sarge. Mike reflexively tilts his head to see past his father, who turns and switches off the TV. Mike punches his couch cushion.

Madeleine says, "Two out of three aircrew never came back."

Jack says, "That's right." He grabs Mike by the ear and yanks him from the couch.

Mike yelps.

"To bed!" he says through gritted teeth.

"Ow, Papa!"

Mike, following Dad's grip on his ear, looks suddenly very small and pink in his hockey pajamas and bare feet. Dad's neck has turned red. Mike is trying not to cry. Madeleine looks down.

"It's not my bedtime, Daddy!"—the last syllables get away from him in a sob that he fights to snatch back.

Dad pushes him to the stairs, releasing his ear, and Mike stumbles up the first step. Dad follows and grabs a close handful of Mike's brush cut, hauling him up. Mike is crying, "Daddy, please stop."

Maman says from the kitchen doorway, "*Qu'est-ce qui se passe ici?*" and drops her purse to the floor. Dad lets go and Mike runs upstairs— Madeleine hears his door slam shut.

Dad lifts his hand to his forehead and says, "Mimi, I couldn't find the uh"—he takes a deep breath and Madeleine hears a tremble in it. "Where's the Aspirin?" She sits perfectly still, clutching her pillow. Have they forgotten that she is here?

Mimi looks up at him and says, "Jack, what's wrong?"

"Headache," he says mildly, trying to smile. It's blinding him.

"Sit down a minute."

Jack returns to the kitchen, finds a chair and sits while Mimi goes upstairs to the medicine cabinet. Madeleine can see that her father is not moving. His forehead rests lightly on his fingers.

Mimi comes back down the stairs. "*Tiens,*" she says, handing him the pills and water.

He puts them between his teeth and attempts a grin for her. "*Merci,*" he says, and swallows.

The pain is there to smack him across the forehead when he stands, but he doesn't sit back down. The kitchen light trembles briefly above his head and he says, "I'm gonna go stretch my legs."

He walks past her, down the three steps, which have begun to narrow and grow dim, is the light still on? He will feel more relaxed in the night air, where he knows it's dark. He walks out the door, and the missing patch of vision is restored, replaced by a wavering arc, as though his eye were partially under water. It will pass. He wants only to walk out of the PMQs a ways, to where there are no street lights. Street lights burn, hard haloes expunging all other shapes, branding the insides of his closed lids, boring through to the back of his skull. The sun today on the drive, no sunglasses. No hat brim. No supper. It's just a headache.

He experiences a sense of "coming to" in the black freshness of night as he looks back upon the lights of the houses and the station buildings scattered at a gentle distance now, a spangled square mile. At the far end, a red light flashes unhurriedly from the airport control tower. Jack has walked north perhaps a mile. He smells the new fields. Earth and sky. Now that he is better, he realizes that he was close to keeling over as he left his house ten, twenty minutes ago. A slice of steel is wedged at an angle across the left side of his head, bisecting his eye. Soon it will begin to loosen, throb. He's fine. Couple more Aspirins and a Scotch. He turns for home. His eyes are watering. His throat is sore. Perhaps he is coming down with something. He stops, puts his hand out and rests it on a wooden fencepost soft with weather, he is weeping. It will help his headache. He is weeping and his nose is running.

It's amazing how a headache can undo a man, it's just as well he came out for a walk rather than inflict this on Mimi. She would ask him what's wrong, and although things are getting more complicated with the job he is trying to do, there is nothing so wrong that it can't be fixed. Except that a little girl is dead.

Jack's forehead rests on the back of his hand and he gives the weight of his head to the fencepost. A child has died. He sees in his mind's eye a little girl with brown hair tousled around her head, lying on her back in a field. She has his daughter's face. He cries. There is no one around. In his mind he hears his daughter's voice, *Daddy*. He sobs into his arm. *Oh God*. A child has died. His face in both his hands—*dear God. A child*.

"Oh God," he says, sniffing, wiping his nose with his forearm—the words coming up like crumpled paper. Breathing in through his mouth, both palms smearing his face. Not my little girl, but a dear child. Taken. Just like that. He slams his fist onto the fencepost, *Jesus*—and again, *Jesus*—let him alone with the likes of *that,* whatever it was that killed her—he wrenches the post in the earth like a bad tooth—*smash* him, *tear* him apart. *With my bare hands.*

He lets go of the smooth wood. His eyes still streaming, he starts for home, pulling his shirt out from his trousers to dry his face, blow his nose. His hanky is in his uniform jacket on the back of the kitchen chair at home, he has come out in his blue shirt-sleeves, and now he realizes that it's cold, April's sharp end.

He is grateful that no car has come along, for he is half out of uniform, no jacket, tie or hat. *LMF.* The initials come to mind—perhaps because he knows he is a poor sight at the moment. *Lack of moral fibre.* When he was in training, he knew a man who was turfed from the air force for that. It could mean anything. Usually it meant cowardice. Failure of nerve. Breakdown after a bombing run or, during training, the inability to go back up.

Madeleine stands still as a statue outside Mike's bedroom door. It is closed, but she can hear Maman softly singing. Her voice is muffled, but Madeleine recognizes the tune. "*Un Acadien errant.*" Mike's favourite song. Maman has not sung to him in a long while, not since they moved here. He has not required songs, he has required privacy for himself and his sacred airplane models.

Madeleine knows Maman is probably rubbing his back, warm beneath his hockey pajamas. Mike is lying on his stomach with his hazel eyes open, calmly gazing into the dark. Madeleine listens, standing so still she is convinced that, were she to move so much as a finger, it would creak and give her away.

It's like waiting outside an operating room to see if the patient will pull through. Mike is going to be thirteen in a week and a half. He would kill Madeleine if he knew she was out here spying. But he is too wounded at the moment to kill anyone. Maman is bandaging him up. Inside, her voice softly rises and falls—the tale of a wandering Acadian, far from his home.

Henry Froelich sees Jack rounding the corner of St. Lawrence Avenue. He is out on his front step with the porch light off. "Good evening Jack."

Jack squints at the Froelichs' house, shielding his eyes from the street light that spreads like a stain.

"Is that you, Henry?"

"*Ja.*"

"How's she going?"

"Not too good."

Jack has no choice. He walks up the driveway, his eyes still dazzled by the smear of light; he can see part of Henry Froelich at the edge of a yellow orb. "If there's anything I can do. . . ." His voice sounds high and reedy, does Froelich notice?

"Jack?"

"Yes?" He clears his throat.

"When the police have interviewed everyone today, they interviewed you too, *ja?*"

"Yeah they did."

"What do they ask you?"

"Let's see, they asked me if I was out driving last Wednesday. Out on Highway 4. Asked if I saw anyone." He coughs.

"You are ill."

"Some kinda bug floatin' around."

"Do they ask if you have acquaintance with a war criminal?"

Jack's surprise at being asked point-blank is genuine, no need to pretend and no need to lie, for the police did not ask him that. "No, they didn't." He half smiles, triggering twin throbs at his temple. "I'd've remembered that one. Why?"

"Do you wish a glass of wine, Jack?" Froelich's hand is on the door.

"Hank?" It's Karen Froelich from an upper window.

"*Ja, mein Liebling?*"

"Lizzie's asking for you, baby. Hi Jack."

Jack shields his eyes to look up and makes out her silhouette at the lit screen. "Hi Karen."

"This thing is so screwed up," she says, and he is struck again by how young she sounds. "The cops kept Ricky for hours before they even charged him, no lawyer, never even called us."

"That oughta be enough to get this thing thrown out right there."

"I've got a friend at the *Star,* I'm going to get him to come out here and—" A baby cries and Karen's outline withdraws.

Froelich says, "Sorry, Jack, I go."

"Get some sleep, eh?"

"You too, my friend."

"What does your lawyer say?"

"We meet him tomorrow morning. Before the bail hearing."

"Let me know if there's anything I can do."

"Mimi has been already very kind."

The yellow orb has shrunk to a splotch and Jack can see most of his neighbour quite clearly now. There are tears in Froelich's eyes. He extends his hand. Jack takes it.

"You are a good neighbour," says Henry Froelich.

Madeleine's foot has gone to sleep, crouched as she is outside Mike's door. Bugs Bunny is asleep too, his ears criss-crossed over his eyes to block the night light. The only good thing about Ricky Froelich being arrested today is that no one has noticed the cut in Madeleine's palm. She has kept it hidden, curled in her hand. It has scabbed over nicely and ceased to sting. She looks at it now in the semi-dark—a speck of moisture gleams at one end of the seam, she is tempted to see how far she can open her hand without causing it to bleed afresh. She hears the front door open downstairs, and steals back to her room as quietly as possible on pins and needles. Dad is home.

Mimi has left the kitchen light on. She has made him a meatloaf sandwich and placed it on the counter under Saran Wrap. Jack puts it in the fridge. He reaches to the cupboard above it and takes down the bottle of Scotch. A bottle lasts a long time in this house, it is still half full from last fall. Johnnie Walker Red. He pours a shot and swallows it. Puts an ice cube in his glass and pours another.

He takes off his shoes and creeps upstairs with his drink. The night light is on in the hall. His daughter's door stands half open; he looks in on her. She is asleep on her back, curved like a fish, halo of hair on her pillow. He wipes his left eye, which always seeps after a headache. It was good to cry, he's not made of stone. The ice snaps softly in his glass but she doesn't stir. The room is full of her child's breath, flannel, toothpaste and dreams. My little girl is safe.

*The Adventures of Tom Sawyer* lies on her bedside table next to a tattered Golden Book, *Pinocchio*. She is a scallywag. She will grow up to be anything she wants to be. My little spitfire. "Goodnight, sweetie," he whispers.

Madeleine doesn't answer, nor does she open her eyes when she feels his hand upon her forehead. He thinks she is asleep. She doesn't want to disappoint him.

Before he turns to leave, she thinks she hears him say, "I love you," and this is surprising because he always says, "Maman and I love you kids very much." But she has heard it, and it's one more reason to allow him to think she is asleep. Through the slits of her eyelids she sees his back silhouetted by the night light, and she moves her lips soundlessly— "I love you, Daddy."

This too is a little surprising because, although it's more often girls who call their fathers "Daddy," unlike Mike, she never does.

Lingering in his wake like a spirit, the smell of liquor from his glass, sharp amber, a new smell in her room. She adds it to her drawer of smells for Dad—cigars and blue wool, leather, Old Spice and newspapers, and his scalp after she has rubbed his head.

In his bedroom Jack undoes his pants, careful not to let his belt buckle hit the floor. He drains his glass, drops his socks and eases into bed; it feels like heaven. He smells her hairspray, warm remnants of the day's perfume—she turns. "Did you look in on Mike?"

He blinks in the dark. "Why?"

"He couldn't get to sleep, he was so upset."

Upset? Right, a fight with his son. Over what? Television. Blasted idiot box.

"Jack. Did you hit him?"

"What? When?"

"Tonight."

"No, no, lost my temper's all."

"Go tuck him in," she says, stroking his shoulder.

She must know something is going on. Everyone has taken the little girl's death to heart, everyone is upset about the boy's arrest, but she must know something is on his mind.

"Go on," she says, finding his lips in the dark, giving him a kiss.

He gets up from the bed. Jack has never brought his work home. He brings home his paycheque and his undivided affection. Men have to take things on by themselves sometimes, and not burden their wives— he finds his robe on the back of the door—their wives have enough to do. He knows she won't pry. Not if he's okay tomorrow.

He goes to his son's room. The moon filters through the curtains— spaceships and ringed planets. On the wall, the Canadian Golden Hawks still hold pride of place, but they have been encroached upon by a buildup of heavy armour clipped from magazines. B-52 bombers brood over a runway. A Sherman tank hulks amid tropical foliage, the cam-blackened eyes of a U.S. combat soldier peer through palm fronds. *The Few, the Proud. . . .*

He looks down at his son, curled in a snaggle of sheet and blanket, brow furrowed in sleep. Who is he like? Jack's own father? Maybe; Jack doesn't remember him that well. He was a little hard on the boy this evening. Well, he's a boy. Boys need to learn. Tomorrow we'll do something—what's tomorrow? Wednesday. We'll go to the rec centre, get out the floor hockey equipment.

He picks up a baseball cap from the floor—"4 Fighter Wing"—and hangs it on the edge of the mirror over the dresser. Before turning to leave, he glances back down at the bed. His son is an arrow that he can point, draw back and release. He wants to fire him off in the right direction. Mike is a strong boy, he loves his mother. Jack just wants him to do the things he never got a chance to do. *Don't disappoint me.*

"Did you tuck him in?" asks Mimi as he crawls back into bed.

"He's asleep," says Jack, reaching back to pat her. She curls against his back, slips her arm around his waist. Nibbles his earlobe. He doesn't stir. She kisses his neck.

"Jack?" she whispers.

"'Night, sweetheart," he mumbles. "Love you." And he's out cold.

In Goderich, Ricky Froelich is wide awake. Out his high window is a glimpse of branches against the blue-black sky. If he jumps, grabs the bars and hoists himself up, he can see the stone wall that separates the courtyard from the tree and the town beyond. On a sunny day or on a dark night such as this, the county jail is either picturesque or tinglingly Gothic. Either way, it is the oldest jail in Ontario, and one of the sights of Goderich, seat of Huron County, *the prettiest town in Canada.*

It has happened a couple of times now that Ricky has dozed off, then been awakened by the words "You still awake, son, feel like talking?" And they bring him out of his cell, give him a Coke and ask, "What did you do when you got to the intersection, Rick?"

Madeleine dreams of the Donnelly tombstone, but instead of the chiselled names, each followed by the word *Murdered,* there are the names of the Froelich kids and, after each one, *Adopted.*

Ricky Froelich: *Adopted*
Elizabeth Froelich: *Adopted*
Colleen Froelich: *Adopted*
Roger Froelich: *Adopted*
Carl Froelich: *Adopted*

Rex is there and he's licking an ice cream cone with his pink tongue, and someone's voice says, "Rex is an Indian." Madeleine doesn't want to turn around because she knows that Claire is behind her, and the voice says, "Look at my ice screamer," and just then Madeleine sees that it isn't an ice cream cone, it's a pink streamer—

She wakes up with a yelp still in her throat. She has wet the bed again, oh no. She gets up and feels the sheets—even her pillow is wet. She sniffs the damp patch, tamped down in the shape of her body. It's only sweat. She stares out her window at the placid moon. The moon has nothing against anyone. She stares at it, allowing it to cool the fear. There is kindness in that cool place.

ONCE UPON A TIME there was a mountain cave. It was deep and dark, as dark as outer space, and inside the cave was a treasure. Slaves worked day and night to mount up more treasure. They enlarged the cave with their bare hands, scooping the entrails of the earth, toiling on pain of death, out of sight of sun and moon, so that for them time was measured in hunger and fatigue. They were beaten and hanged, they died of starvation and disease, they lived with the treasure and they slept alongside it in that dank subterranean world. And although they were dirty, the treasure was clean. The cruel masters called the treasure Vengeance. All this happened in a land not so far away, the land of Goethe and the Brothers Grimm. The cave was called Dora. The name means "gold."

Meanwhile, in the world outside the mountain cave, a great battle raged. The evil masters were defeated; the good masters discovered the cave, liberated the slaves and claimed the treasure. So that none would associate the treasure with the impurities of the cave where it had been born, with the suffering of the slaves who had fashioned it, and with the cruelty of the masters who had abused the earth and her gifts in order to possess it, the new masters took the treasure to their own home and made it cleaner still. They took some of the evil masters, too, and cleaned them as well. But they took no slaves, since nothing could make them clean. They called the treasure Apollo, after the sun god. Nothing to do with the earth at all. Earth was written out of the story.

She may have become angry about this.

ON THE FRONT PAGE, next to the milk on the porch, two school photos side by side. Claire's—the same one they used yesterday—joined now by Ricky's. He too is smiling, his dark hair slicked back, crisp collar open at the neck. The dead and the accused are always pictured like this, in images captured at an unrelated moment, because neither is available for a fresh photograph just now.

Above the pictures, the headline: *Air Force Boy Arrested in Child Murder.* His name has been misspelled: Richard Frolick.

Jack picks up the paper before his daughter can see it, and returns to the kitchen, scanning the article. No mention of a war criminal. "Allegations" of a "mystery driver"—the details of the air force hat, "a late-model sedan" with a Storybook Gardens sticker. Just enough to send the blood up to Jack's face.

Mimi pours his tea. "*'tention, Jack, c'est hot.*" The radio news echoes in the kitchen: "A youth was arrested yesterday and charged with the murder of—" She switches it off.

Jack sits at the table and reaches, without looking, for his cup. The bail hearing is this afternoon. The boy will be home tonight. It crosses Jack's mind to wonder what will happen if Froelich goes public with his "sighting" once Ricky has been cleared. But that's Si's problem, not his.

"Papa," says Mimi. Jack looks up. She indicates, with her eyes, their son slouched over his cereal bowl, chin in hand.

"Elbows off the table, Mike," says Jack, and is surprised the next moment to see Mimi staring at him, eyebrows raised, trying to communicate silently over the boy's head.

Jack remembers and says, "Mike, what do you say to a round of floor hockey this afternoon?" The boy mumbles something in reply.

Jack refrains from reprimanding him and says simply, "What's that, pal?"

"Baseball tonight."

"That's right, the big game, good stuff." Jack is itching to remove the boy's elbow from the table himself, to say, "Look at me when I'm talking to you," but he catches Mimi's glance as she refills the kettle, and returns his eyes to the paper. A dog starts barking somewhere outside. It sounds like the Froelichs' dog, but it never barks like that—continuously.

Madeleine comes into the kitchen and says, "There's a police car in the Froelichs' driveway."

Mimi looks out the window. So there is. The dog is tied up, barking at the house.

Madeleine says, "Ricky must be home."

Her father glances up from his paper but says nothing. Rex keeps barking. Her mother switches on the radio and turns the dial till she finds music—a rock 'n' roll station! An escalation of saxophones and big echoey drum-throbs—Martha and the Vandellas are on fire with desire. Madeleine waits for one of her parents to switch the station, but it doesn't happen. Mike is making mush out of his Cap'n Crunch. She pours Rice Krispies and puts her ear close to the bowl to hear the *snap, crackle, pop*. Sexy music at breakfast, it's a mad, mad world. She starts moving to the beat in her chair. The song makes her think of Ricky and Marsha kissing on the porch that night, and she gets a hot liquid feeling in her chest.

The song ends and cheerful voices sing, "Let Hertz put you in the driver's seat, today!" Jack gets up, puts on his uniform jacket, folds the newspaper under his arm and, as he reaches for his hat, feels in his pocket for dimes, only to find the wretched key to the Ford Galaxy. He'll toss it away when he gets to work. "See ya, fellas."

"Jack," says Mimi.

"What, Missus?"

She turns to the kids and says, "Ricky Froelich is not home. Not yet. The police think—"

Jack takes over, using his most patient voice: "The police think"— speaking slowly, much better his children should hear it lucidly explained at home—"that Ricky Froelich may somehow be responsible for what happened with regard to—"

His son interrupts, "They think he killed her."

Jack takes a breath. He resumes speaking, his voice dangerously quiet. "The police are just doing their job, but they've made a mistake and pretty soon they'll realize that—" he jams his hat on his head— "and Ricky will be home." He is surprised at the sudden constriction in his throat. He hardly trusts himself to say goodbye to his wife, afraid his voice may have reverted to the reedy register of last night. What is that voice?

He kisses his wife on the cheek and she turns and kisses him on the lips—she doesn't want him leaving the house angry, or thinking that she is.

He is halfway down his driveway when the answer comes to him: it's the voice of an old man.

The police car is still in the Froelichs' driveway ten minutes later, when Madeleine leaves for school. Mike has not waited—he seems to have forgotten that he is her jailer. Rex is straining toward the Froelichs' front door at the end of his rope, still barking. "It's okay, Rex," she calls.

Foam has gathered on his chops, and Madeleine is worried lest the police mistake him for a rabid dog and shoot him. Perhaps she ought to wait until they come out, so she can tell them Rex is perfectly fine.

"Madeleine!" She turns. Her mother has called from the kitchen window. *"Va à l'école, tout suite!"*

She catches up with Auriel and Lisa. They have reassured one another with their dads' predictions of a speedy homecoming for Ricky Froelich, and she asks Auriel how she knows that her father is going to let her have horseback riding lessons. "Cripes, McCarthy, I hope I didn't ruin the surprise!"

Lisa has started riding and has quickly become horse-crazy. "Oh Madeleine, you should see Socks, he's so cute, and his mother is—"

Colleen's voice cuts in: "Madeleine."

Madeleine is shocked. To be addressed by Colleen en route to school, in the presence of her other friends. . . .

Colleen says to Auriel and Lisa, "Keep walking." Auriel is about to object, but Madeleine says, "It's okay, you guys."

Colleen waits until Auriel and Lisa are out of earshot, then asks, "What are you going to say if anybody asks?"

"Asks what?"

"If you saw him."

"Saw who?"

"Ricky, who else?" Colleen is looking straight at her.

"What do you mean?"

"Last Wednesday with Claire."

Madeleine doesn't want to talk about Claire any more. She wants to drive away from Claire like scenery she will never visit again. She starts walking, and Colleen walks backwards ahead of her.

"You got to say you saw him turn left at the willow tree."

"Yeah but I didn't," says Madeleine.

"Yeah but he did turn left."

Madeleine squints and curls her lip. "Why should I shay I sheen what I never shaw, shee?" asks Humphrey Bogart.

"'Cause they think he raped and murdered her."

Madeleine stops short. "What's rape?" The question escapes her like a weak bird, emaciated and able to slip through the bars. She looks down, because she doesn't want Colleen to answer. It's a dark, sour word. She knows what it means, she only wishes to go on not having a word for it. She smells tobacco and looks up. Colleen is lighting a cigarette, cupping the flame with her hand. Madeleine looks around; the street is full of kids, a mother behind every kitchen window.

Colleen funnels smoke out the side of her mouth and says, "You're so innocent, McCarthy."

Madeleine turns red. "My mum and dad say it's all a mistake, my dad says Ricky'll be home in time for supper," and as she says it she is aware that she is parting with something. Something just flew away, it will never come back. *My mum and dad are wrong.*

Colleen says, "Do you believe everything your mummy and daddy tell you?" Madeleine pushes her. Colleen stumbles back a step but doesn't flinch or retaliate. Madeleine takes off for school, running.

"Eee tuh neff! Eff! Oh dah highwayyy!" Elizabeth thrashes slowly in her chair, eyes rolling, spittle on her lips, sobbing, almost drowning out Rex barking himself hoarse outside. Henry Froelich lifts her from the chair and carries her from the room. *"Shh shh, Lizzie, ja, ruhig."*

Karen Froelich says, "You heard her, she said they turned left. Toward the highway. How many times does she have to repeat it?"

Inspector Bradley rises from the Froelichs' tattered couch and crosses one more loophole off his mental list. Even if the judge does allow this child as a witness, her testimony won't count for much—she's the boy's sister, after all. But Bradley has interviewed her so that no one will be able to accuse him of leaving a single stone unturned. This case is already national news; outraged letters to the editor have begun to trickle in. They will be a deluge by the time it goes to trial. People do not wish to believe that a child is capable of raping and murdering another child. In a perfect world, none of us would have to entertain the thought. But this is Bradley's job. And the boy is not a child, he is an adolescent male who has reached full sexual maturity. Still, though he doesn't share it, Bradley can sympathize with the disbelief of ordinary people. What annoy him are the bleeding hearts, safe in their ivory towers, far from the brutal realities of the modern world, who are ready to exonerate the worst criminals on the basis of an unhappy childhood and an assortment of half-baked Freudian notions. The truth is, many people suffer terribly in childhood but they don't grow up to be murderers. Bradley intends to get it right.

"I'm sorry to have upset the child, Mrs. Frolick."

"The name is Froelich, and she isn't a child, she's sixteen."

The woman is sloppily groomed. Maybe she couldn't have children of her own and now she's on a mission. Imagine choosing to adopt such a child. Not to mention the others. . . . Bradley looked for Richard Froelich's birth certificate and found an adoption file.

"Richard and his younger sister are both Indian, is that correct?"

The woman barely hesitates, but he can tell she is surprised. "No, it isn't, they're Métis."

Bradley knows what type the Froelichs are: holier-than-thou. He picks up his hat from amid the mess on the coffee table.

Karen Froelich says, "I'm going to press charges against the arresting officer."

"What are you accusing him of?"

"He beat my son."

"Your boy didn't sustain any real injury."

"He's a kid."

"He resisted arrest. That's tantamount to an admission of guilt," and before the Froelich woman can object, he continues, "Are you aware there's a court order outstanding in the province of Alberta regarding both Richard and his younger sister—" He looks to the constable in the doorway, who consults his notebook and says, "Colleen."

Bradley watches the woman pale. He isn't interested in making her life more difficult, but he would appreciate her attention. He seems to have it now. "I suggest you seek your lawyer's advice. My guess is he'll tell you to focus on your son's legal defence, and not go wasting money trying to bring the police to court."

They leave, making a wary arc around the snarling German shepherd. The constable turns and says, "Control your dog."

Karen Froelich says, "Control yourself."

Bradley's face remains expressionless, but Karen sees the uniformed officer smile and she curses herself. Her remark didn't do her son any good. Or her daughter—has this inspector already contacted the child welfare authorities in Alberta? Or is he just trying to blackmail her? She wishes she felt as optimistic as her husband—"This is Canada," he says. They are seeing the lawyer in London this morning, before the bail hearing. He has already told them that the police have very little to go on. Maybe she should keep quiet about the police assault—at least until Rick is out on bail.

She watches the cruiser pull from her driveway. She will let it disappear from sight before unleashing Rex; she is worried he may chase down the car. He's panting, his gums deep pink, muzzle wet, eyes bright with fear. She kneels and hugs him, only now looking up to wonder why the cruiser, rather than turning up the street toward the PMQ exit, has turned down St. Lawrence in the direction of the school.

Madeleine can see Colleen from the classroom window; she is sitting on a swing, rocking slowly, staring at her feet. Madeleine knows what that's like. She wishes now that she hadn't pushed her. Colleen's bowed head reminds Madeleine of the song "Hang down your head, Tom Dooley." Why hasn't the principal come out and given her heck? Perhaps he feels sorry for her because something has happened to her brother. Colleen lifts her head suddenly and looks toward the road. She slips from the swing and runs out of sight, and Madeleine sees a police cruiser pull into the parking lot.

"And what befell the hapless Father Brûlé?" asks Mr. March.

"He was burned alive."

"Correct." The grade fours are learning about missionaries among the Indians in the New World. The classroom walls are still decorated with Easter art. Everyone's is up now, but Grace's butterflies still reign supreme among the many bunnies and countless Easter eggs.

When the knock comes at the door, Madeleine is not surprised to see a policeman, but Mr. March seems to be. He looks down while the officer speaks quietly, then turns to the class and asks, "Who among you were special friends of Claire McCarroll?"

No hands. It's a difficult question. Claire didn't have a best friend, but she didn't have enemies either. And in some way, the question sounds like one that, in fairy-tale language, would mean "Who among you would care to accompany Claire into the mountain cave?"

Madeleine remembers sharing Claire's picnic last week, and the day on the swings when the two of them laughed upside down, and puts up her hand. All heads turn and she feels herself blushing as though she has been caught boasting, which was not her intention. Then Grace Novotny puts up her hand. It would be unkind to tell Grace that she was never Claire's friend. The only thing they had in common was their belief in Santa Claus. It is, however, a bare-faced lie when Marjorie Nolan puts up her hand. Madeleine expects Mr. March to say, "No you weren't, Marjorie," but he says nothing.

The policeman leaves, and Mr. March gets his hanky out and presses it to his forehead, then his cheeks. Tante Yvonne always talks about her "hot flashes"—maybe that's what's happening to Mr. March. The bell rings. Lunch.

Everyone mobs the coat hooks. Philip Pinder says Ricky's going to get the electric chair, and Cathy Baxter screams at him to shut up. No one can believe that Ricky has been arrested, but everyone is used to it already. Around and around the schoolyard swirls the story of Ricky's alibi: the "mystery driver," the air force man in a car with a sticker from Storybook Gardens. Some kids are saying it was a ghost car, others speculate that it was the real murderer, disguised as someone's dad.

This is all very different from last week, but is Madeleine the only one who notices the other difference? It has been eight days since Mr. March announced, "The following little girls will remain after three." Not since last week, when Claire was. . . . When there was Claire. Last Wednesday she was still here like everyone else. No one knew she was on the edge of a cliff. Who else is walking on the edge, on her way somewhere, her head full of thoughts like arrows pointed at the future, then—blank?

Madeleine looks up; she is halfway across the field but doesn't remember walking out of the school. She wonders if Mr. March has had enough of exercises. Perhaps he has given them up. Like in the story about the giant who used to eat children but found he would be much less lonely if he befriended them instead.

She sees Grace drawing a hopscotch with a piece of chalk at the foot of Marjorie Nolan's driveway. She is going to miss lunch. As Madeleine passes, she sees that it isn't chalk, it's a piece of old whitened dog poop. Behind her she hears Marjorie's voice calling from her door, "Go away, Grace. Shoo."

Lunch is Chef Boyardee. Maman was babysitting at the Froelichs' all morning and there was no time to prepare a *"ben bon déjeuner."* Madeleine finds the canned noodles revolting—like the slipped-off skin of a drowned dead body, although it would be impolite to say so. Maman has heated up some Campbell's cream of tomato soup with saltines for her instead.

The four of them sit at the table, eating. Mimi has fixed herself a Depression favourite, burnt toast and tea. Good for what ails you. The Froelich house is a depressing place and she would like to get the soiled laundry-old stew smell from her nostrils. The smell of misery. She says a silent prayer asking Our Lord to forgive her should any of her thoughts be uncharitable in that regard, and to guide the police in their search for the *maudit* crazy who is still out there. Then she drops her bomb. "Where were you yesterday afternoon, Madeleine?"

Madeleine freezes. Lowers her spoon. *Yesterday afternoon.* "In a field," she replies to her bright red soup.

"What field? *Dis-moi la vérité,* Madeleine." She doesn't sound angry, she sounds worried, which is worse.

"Answer your mother," says Dad.

Madeleine swallows and says, "I wanted to find her other streamer."
Maman says, "Whose?"

"Claire's." The word floats up like a tiny balloon.

Maman covers her face—she is crying, tears gush through her fingers, her red nails.

"I'm sorry, Maman."

Mike stops eating and looks at his mother. He rises from his chair, hesitates, then pours some tea into her cup, "*Tiens, maman.*" Mimi looks up, sniffs and smiles at her son, wiping her nose with her serviette.

Her father says gently, "Did you go to Rock Bass, sweetie?"

Madeleine nods. Maman seizes her, pulls her onto her lap, jams Madeleine's head against her shoulder and starts rocking.

Dad says, "Listen, old buddy, look me in the eye." Maman stops rocking but still has her in a headlock. "You know it was wrong to lie to your teacher and to play hooky from school, don't you?"

Madeleine nods.

"But do you know what's a hundred times worse?"

Madeleine shakes her head.

"You going to a dangerous place like that. A little girl has been killed. Do you understand what that means?"

"Jack," says Mimi softly.

"Yes," says Madeleine clearly, so Maman won't think that she too, like Mike, needs to be rescued from Dad.

"The worst thing you could do, to me and to Maman and to Mike, would be to put yourself in danger. How would you feel if Maman died?"

"Terrible," she whispers.

"What if I died?"

"Awful."

"Well, multiply that by a thousand and that's how Maman and I would feel if we lost you. Now, I want you to promise me, in front of your family, not to leave the PMQs without one of us. Ever. Swear it on your honour."

"I swear."

Maman kisses her head fiercely, then sets her on her feet, gets up and reaches into her purse for her compact.

Madeleine says, "I didn't go alone—" thinking that will make them all feel better, knowing in the next instant that it won't, when she is forced to say, "I went with Colleen."

Maman spanks her sharply—once, but it's enough. Dad makes a calming gesture with his hand and she lights a cigarette. "Eat up now," he says to Madeleine.

She returns to her soup. Maman turns on the radio. Soothing sounds of the Boston Pops mingle with the refreshing aroma of Cameo menthol.

After a decent interval, Madeleine says, "Dad, am I going to start riding lessons?"

Jack looks at his daughter.

"Auriel said you were going to take me for riding lessons. Like Lisa."

Mimi looks at him and he shrugs.

"Did I wreck the surprise?" asks Madeleine.

Jack says, "No surprise about it. Would you like to start riding?"

"Sure."

He would like to leave right now, get back to work; he can feel indigestion setting in. What is this junk he's eating, anyhow? Damn Vic Boucher for a miserable busybody. What else has he told his wife, his kids? That Jack McCarthy was seen driving a blue Galaxy? He stirs his tea with his fork—no sign of a spoon on the table—and reflects that he ought not to blame Vic. After all, if it hadn't been for the Boucher girl asking her mother if she could visit Madeleine, who was "home sick" yesterday afternoon, he and Mimi never would have known that their little girl was off hiking to the murder scene. Jack would like to punch Mr. Marks right in his foolish face. The idiot told Mimi over the phone that Madeleine had feigned a doctor's appointment. What's the good of teacher's college if you can't tell when a child is lying? Jack went over the miserable son-of-a-bitch's head and gave the principal a piece of his mind. Meanwhile his son is jabbering away in French. "In English, so the whole table can understand you."

Mike reddens and says, "I just want to know why he doesn't come forward."

"Who?" says Jack.

"The air force guy. How come he won't say he saw Rick on the road?"

"I've had just about enough of this subject, let's talk about something nice for a change. What did you learn at school this morning?"

Back at work, Jack circulates a memo to his department heads, and by three o'clock six air force hats have been delivered to his office and overturned on his desk. He is reminded of his early days in accounts as he rapidly totals the bills. He has four hundred and seventy-two dollars to plunk into Henry Froelich's hand. He adds another two hundred on Simon's account. Froelich has hired the best lawyer in London, and the best costs money.

"The following little girls will remain after three." Madeleine looks up. She is already taking her homework out of her desk, preparing to bolt with the rest of the class at the sound of the bell—

"Madeleine McCarthy . . ."

She freezes.

"Marjorie Nolan and Grace Novotny."

Has she time-travelled back to October? If she looks outside, will the leaves be red and gold? No, because Claire McCarroll's desk is empty. It's still April. Mr. March has put Madeleine back into the exercise group and there is nothing she can do about it.

Auriel turns to her with a quizzical expression but Madeleine can't move her muscles to return the look. Only her eyes can move.

The other kids leave forever, and Madeleine remains at her desk along with Marjorie and Grace. Mr. March is up at his desk, cleaning his glasses. A tap at the door. He answers it and the policeman comes in. The sight of his friendly uniform is a relief, but a second man follows him in. He wears a raincoat open over a civilian suit and he's holding a hat. He has a sharp face. Madeleine fears she has seen him in a dream, but how is that possible? Are they going to run the exercise group now, with Mr. March?

Mr. March says, "The police want to ask you young ladies a few questions about your friend Claire."

Madeleine feels her body return to life, like a leaf in water. Mr. March sends her out to wait in the corridor with Grace Novotny.

Marjorie puts the noose around his neck.

"Ricky asked me to go to Rock Bass."

"He did?"

"Mm-hm."

Inspector Bradley is seated beside the teacher's desk, facing the little girl. He has positioned the teacher behind her so that she won't look to him for cues. The man sits at one of the child-sized desks. Constable Lonergan stands by the door, taking notes.

"When?" asks Bradley.

"Um. On that day."

"What day?"

"The day that—the day when she got lost."

"Who? Claire?"

"Mm-hm."

"Go on."

Marjorie smiles and the serious man leans forward. Their knees are almost touching. "He was always asking me on picnics," she says, breezy.

The inspector lifts one eyebrow slightly. Marjorie looks down, folds her hands in her lap and adds, "Well, not always, maybe just once or twice."

"What did he say when he asked you?"

"He just said, 'Hey Marjorie, would you like to come for a picnic at Rock Bass? I know where there is a nest.'"

"And what did you say?"

"I said my mother wouldn't let me."

"Did you ask your mother?"

"No, because I knew she wouldn't let me."

"Why wouldn't she let you?"

"Well, for one thing," says Marjorie, "my mother is sick and she needs me to look after her. And for another thing," she adds gaily, "Ricky Froelich is way too old for me!" And she chuckles.

Inspector Bradley smiles and doesn't take his eyes off her. Marjorie smooths her hair and smiles back. "Marjorie," he says, resting his elbows on his knees, "has Ricky ever"—choosing his words—"behaved in such a way as to—"

The tiny desk chair creaks as the teacher shifts his weight.

The inspector smiles at Marjorie, just-between-you-and-me, and continues, "Has Ricky ever acted as though he were your boyfriend?"

"Oh yes," says Marjorie, solemn now.

"In what way?"

She turns to check in with her teacher, but Inspector Bradley says, "Look at me, Marjorie, not at the teacher. Can you answer my question?"

She starts crying.

Inspector Bradley hands her his hanky.

"I told him I couldn't." She wipes her eyes. "I'm too young."

"Did Ricky ever touch you?"

She pauses, her face in her hands. Then shakes her head.

"It's all right, Marjorie," says Inspector Bradley. "You don't have to say anything else. You've been very helpful."

Marjorie smiles up at the inspector and thanks him for the use of his hanky.

"Side door, little girl," says Mr. March.


Grace pulls the rope tight.

"Come in, Grace."

She hesitates in the doorway. Her plaid jumper, braids, white short-sleeved blouse—Grace is looking very fresh today. She enters the room in response to Mr. March's prompting, and looks up at the two strange men. Both are big, one is old; he looks angry already.

"Grace, the officers want to ask you one or two questions," says Mr. March, then sits at Philip Pinder's desk.

"Hello Grace," says the angry one, taking a step toward her.

Grace groans, her hand strays to her crotch.

"Grace," says Mr. March, and she clutches her hands together. "Sit down."

She obeys, entwining her fingers inwardly as though she were playing "Here's the church, here's the steeple."

The angry man pulls up a chair and sits. "How are you today, Grace?"

"Speak up, Grace," says Mr. March.

"Fine."

The man smiles and leans toward her. She can smell his face. What does he want?

"You knew Claire McCarroll, didn't you?"

Grace moans and hugs herself, begins to rock slightly.

"It's all right, Grace," says Mr. March. "Just a couple of questions, then you can run along." Grace nods, looking down, still rocking.

"Grace," says the angry man, "did you play with Claire last Wednesday?"

Grace groans, then cries, her forehead crumpling, her voice rising rapidly, mouth wide open like a much younger child—

"Grace," says Mr. March firmly. She grinds her fist into her eyes, wipes her nose on her wrist. Mr. March hands her his hanky. "Calm down now."

The other policeman, standing in the corner near the door, writes in a notebook.

Mr. March says, "Can you answer the officer now, Grace?"

It's silent in the dim green corridor. Kids only experience this odd aquarium feeling when they are excused to go to the bathroom in the middle of class, and they float down the empty halls.

"What are you gonna tell them?"

Colleen's face looks darker than usual; she is standing too close to Madeleine, outside the classroom where Grace has just gone in.

"Depends what they ask."

"Tell them you saw Ricky turn left toward the highway."

"But I didn't see him."

"Yeah, but he did turn left."

"Yeah, but I didn't see him."

Colleen licks her lower lip in the dry way she has and says, "You better say you did or they'll hang him."

Madeleine stares into Colleen's eyes—blue flints, narrow, almost slanted. She says, "They won't hang him," and sees a pale featherless bird slowly tumbling.

"Say it or you break our friendship," says Colleen.

"Did you see Claire last Wednesday?" the inspector asks.

Grace answers the corner of the big desk. "Yes."

"Did you play with Claire?"

Grace nods, her lips still parted, her nose red, eyes glazing.

"When was that, Grace?"

"On Wednesday," she tells the desk.

"When on Wednesday?"

"Um. At the schoolyard."

"During school? Or after."

"After."

"Go on."

Grace steals a glance at him from under her brows. He is leaning back in his chair; she pictures him with his thing out. "I saw her at the schoolyard 'cause me and Marjorie helped Miss Lang for Brownies." *Bwownies.*

"This was after school?" He is writing in a notebook now too.

"Yeah, after school, and Claire said, 'Want to come to Rock Bass?'"

"But you didn't go with her to Rock Bass?" He looks at her.

Grace looks away so he won't think she's looking at his thing. "No, I didn't want to go to Rock Bass."

"Did she tell you she was going to Rock Bass with anyone?"

"Yeah, Ricky."

"Ricky Froelich?"

"Yeah, everyone knows that."

"Do you know Ricky Froelich?"

"Yes."

"Has Ricky Froelich ever touched you?"

Grace looks up as though at the snap of a hypnotist's fingers. The teacher erupts in a fit of coughing. Inspector Bradley raises a hand to silence him. Grace whips her head around as though she has just remembered that Mr. March is there.

"Answer the question please, Grace," says the man.

*He isn't angry at me now, he's angry at Mr. March for coughing.*

"Yes sir," says Grace straightening in her chair. "He touched me."

The angry man smiles at her.

"I can't lie," whispers Madeleine.

"It's not a lie. They want to know if he turned left, and you know he did, so say it."

"You say it."

"I'm his sister, they don't believe me."

Madeleine glances at the classroom door. She sees a shadow move behind the Easter bunny taped to the window. She turns back to Colleen. "Did you see him turn left?"

Colleen doesn't answer. Instead she says, "We're blood sisters." *Seurs de san.*

"I know."

"So?"

"So?"

Colleen clamps Madeleine by the wrist. "That means you're his sister too."

"Where did he touch you?" asks the man. He smells like metal shavings, but it's not a bad smell.

"In the schoolyard."

"I mean where on your body, Grace."

"Here," pointing to the small of her back. "He pushed me on the swings."

Mr. March coughs again and Inspector Bradley says quietly, "Please, sir," but does not take his eyes from the child. "Has Ricky ever touched you as if you were his girlfriend?"

Grace hesitates. Her tongue finds the corner of her mouth.

"Just tell the truth, Grace," says the inspector.

But Grace has heard him the way you might hear someone speaking as he rolls up a car window. She tilts her head, her eyes wander over the floor. "Yeah . . . sometimes . . . we do exercises."

"What exercises?" He has a nice voice. He's kind, like a doctor.

"Oh—" Grace sighs. "You know. Backbends."

"What else?"

"And squeezing." Her voice is gentle, almost singsong.

"Squeezing what?"

Rocking again. "His muscle"—the linoleum is grey with queasy streaks—"he said to call it his muscle, but it's really his thing."

Inspector Bradley says, "Now Grace, I know this is all very difficult for you."

"No it isn't."

"Well"—his pen poised—"have you ever told anyone about the things Ricky did to you?"

She nods.

"Who did you tell?"

"Marjorie."

He nods and writes it down.

"And there's something else about Ricky," says Grace.

Inspector Bradley looks up.

"He strangles."

Bradley pauses ever so briefly before resuming his notes. Grace relaxes and, while waiting for him to finish writing, says, "He gave me an egg."

"An egg?" There is a frankly quizzical expression on his face at this point. He neglects to erase it—he is human, after all. "When?"

"That day."

"Wednesday?"

"Yeah."

"What kind of egg?"

Grace doesn't answer.

"A cooked egg?"

"No, a blue one."

"What kind of egg is that?"

"A special egg," she says.

Bradley looks up at the pictures lining the walls. The work of nine-year-old and ten-year-old artists. There are bunnies and chicks—even Batman and Robin—but eggs prevail, all gaily decorated with stripes, solids and polka dots in every colour of the rainbow and beyond—including baby blue. He looks back at the child. "An Easter egg?" he asks. She nods.

"Was it a chocolate egg?"

She nods again, then confides, "He said he knew where there was more."

"Thank you, Grace," says Inspector Bradley. He stares at his notes while the teacher escorts the child to the side door. The boy used chocolate to lure his victims. Every pedophile knows the power of candy.

Madeleine feels hot. She wants to get away from Colleen. *I'm not your sister, he's not my brother.* Colleen lets go of her wrist and takes her hand instead, pressing against it, palm to palm, until Madeleine feels her scab shift and moisten. The door opens. Colleen releases Madeleine and disappears down the hall.

"I don't remember. I think—I don't know if I saw him."

"Look at me, Madeleine." She does. "Did you see him or not?"

"Are you going to hang him?"

The inspector raises his eyebrows. "Do you think he should be hanged?"

"No!"

He leans back, tilts his head and regards her. Madeleine folds her hands. This policeman with his raincoat and his hat on Mr. March's desk, he is the boss of the nice one in the uniform standing writing in a notebook with a leather cover, like the kind the Brownies have. Inspector Bradley is like a teacher who already knows how you have done on your test and you haven't even taken it yet so what's the point? Madeleine knows she is going to fail.

"Does Ricky like to play with younger children?" he asks. It's a hard question. Ricky doesn't go around "playing," he plays sports and he fixes his car and little kids hang around sometimes and he doesn't care.

"He doesn't care," says Madeleine.

Inspector Bradley's face has tiny, faint red lines like on a map; it's square with two vertical wrinkles that run, one from each cheekbone, down to his jaw. Thin ginger hair. Hazel eyes, bloodshot; they say, *This is not a joke. Nothing is ever a joke.* He seems not to have heard Madeleine's answer. He asks, "Does he seek out younger children?"

Madeleine knows the inspector isn't talking about hide 'n' seek, but she is tempted to be a retard for him. "You mean like hide 'n' seek?"

"No." He just looks at her. She pulls her chin in so her face looks fat, raises her eyebrows and bugs out her eyes at the floor.

Mr. March says, "Madeleine," and she unmakes the face.

The inspector asks, "Has Ricky ever behaved toward you as though he were your boyfriend?" Madeleine chortles, but he isn't kidding. "Answer the question please, Madeleine."

"No," says Madeleine.

"I'm afraid you have to answer—"

"I mean no, he never. . . ."

Inspector Bradley proceeds methodically. He knows she has the thing he is looking for, she has hidden it in one of her pockets or her shoe, he will just keep frisking her until he finds it. "Did he ever ask you on a picnic?"

Madeleine shakes her head.

"Did he offer you a ride on his bike?"

"You mean his motor scooter?"

"Any bike."

"Once we were all down at the schoolyard and—"

"Did you ever go for a ride with him alone?"

"No."

"Has he ever touched you?"

"Pardon?"

"Has he ever touched you?"

"Um. He put his hand on the top of my head once and said try and punch him, but I couldn't reach."

"Has he touched you where he shouldn't, or has he made you touch him?"

Madeleine gets the glue feeling. Behind her is the glue man, Mr. March. What has he told the inspector?

Inspector Bradley resumes his search. "Has he done anything dirty?"

She sits very still. Shakes her head. Heat prickles up from her stomach to her face. She can smell the smell, can anyone else?

"Did he undo his pants?" The undertow tugs at her stomach— "Madeleine?"

Gravity is working at different rates on different parts of her, it will suck her insides out and her head will come off and float away.

"That day when you and Colleen Froelich saw Ricky and Claire on the county road—"

"And Elizabeth and Rex—" Her mouth feels very small, the words look very small in her mind.

"You say you saw him turn down the road to Rock Bass with Claire—"

"No," says Madeleine, and swallows. "I didn't see him go with Claire."

"Are you telling me you saw him turn left toward the highway? I'll know if you're lying, Madeleine."

"He didn't do it," she says.

"Did you see him or not?" He looks at her the way he has looked at her from the start: at a thing—at a broom in the corner.

"He turned left, toward the highway." She doesn't break her gaze or blink. "I saw him."

It's quiet except for the scratching of the policeman's pen in the corner of the room.

"Run along then."

She rises, and as she walks to the side door she resists the temptation to look behind her, to see if she has left a puddle of sweat or anything on the chair.

Bradley has asked all male staff to wait to be re-interviewed this afternoon, and he plans to follow through. He doesn't want any loose ends. He doesn't believe the McCarthy child's story, but a jury might.

## THE MORALITY OF ALTITUDE

*Missile building is much like interior decorating. Once you decide to refurnish the living room you go shopping. But when you put it all together you may see in a flash it's a mistake—the draperies don't go with the slip covers. The same is true of missiles. . . . That's why I go to the fabricating shop. I want to see what my baby will look like.*

Wernher von Braun, Life, 1957

MIKE IS LETTING HER run for grounders and pop-flies out in the grassy circle behind the house. Warming up for his game tonight in Exeter. This is his first year playing bantam. Madeleine wears his old glove, but avoids catching the tempting fastballs for fear her cut will open up again.

She keeps an eye on the house, wanting to waylay Dad before supper. She needs to ask him a question. Two questions: Will they hang Ricky Froelich? And is it all right to lie in order to make someone know the truth? Also, she wants to tell him about the policemen who asked her the questions today after school. Maman didn't notice she was late because she was babysitting at the Froelichs'. Madeleine spots her father between the houses, coming up the street, and calls out, "Dad!"

Jack turns and sees his kids, carefree, happy as clams, out in the field behind the house. He waves, then turns up the Froelichs' driveway. The patchwork hotrod is near completion, missing only a set of tires, but the old station wagon is gone—one of them must have driven to Goderich to pick up their boy. He taps on the door on the chance of finding Henry at home.

Betty Boucher opens it. Jack smiles and says, "For a second I thought I had the wrong house."

"I'm part of the bucket brigade. Mimi took the morning shift, they've neither of them been home all day." The women have snapped into action. Betty's own youngest clings to her skirt while one of the Froelich babies bounces on her hip. The other screams from inside. "It's beyond me how they do it, Jack. I thought I was a veteran."

"When are you due to be relieved?"

"I expected the lot of them home before this, what time is it?" She shifts the baby in an effort to glimpse her wristwatch.

"It's ten past five." Jack follows her into the front hall. "Hank told me reporters have been sniffing around."

Her expression says what she thinks of that. "Three of them this afternoon"—indicating with her fingers—"Toronto, Windsor and Detroit, if you can believe it, all wanting to know, did I think our Rick was a"—she glances down at her toddler—"suspect. I told them they wouldn't find a solitary soul on this station who thinks that boy is aught but a sterling young man."

"You better believe it," says Jack.

"Henry—" The baby spits up on her shoulder. Betty dabs her sweater with a tea towel and continues. "Henry called from the courthouse. They were about to go in for the bail hearing."

Bail hearing. Courthouse. Suspect. None of these terms were on anyone's lips this time last week—strange how seamlessly they have introduced themselves into neighbourly conversation. Life has stretched to accommodate the bizarre. Life has begun to run around it—the tragedy and now the mistake—like water around a rock, softening it till it's worn to a bruise on the surface that seems to change nothing. But nothing will ever be the same. The river has altered its course.

"Poor little bugger. . . ." Then, looking past him through the screen door, "Hang on, who's this then?"

Jack follows her gaze to a taxi rounding the corner, crawling toward them.

"What can have happened?" says Betty. There is only one passenger. Henry Froelich.

He pays the driver and joins them on the porch. Karen Froelich is still at the jail in Goderich. Ricky Froelich has been denied bail.

"Henry," says Betty, "I'm so sorry, love."

Jack lingers after Betty leaves. In the Froelich kitchen, Henry has his hands full and Jack is doing his best to help, holding one of the babies—it feels suddenly suspiciously warm against his uniform jacket. Froelich is heating milk. He rolls up his sleeve to test the baby bottle on his fore-arm and Jack sees the numbers tattooed there. "Where was your lawyer when all this was going on?" he asks.

"He was there."

"Well, is he any good?"

"He has letters after his name."

"QC? Queen's Counsel, that's good. He's appealing the bail ruling, right?"

"Oh yes, but he tells me this judge is known for this, so there is little to be done. All of them wait only for this judge to die."

"What about—the police detained your boy improperly, can't your lawyer—?"

"He tries but they say Ricky volunteered to talk to them. My lawyer says all he can do is get Ricky's statement ruled off."

"What's the good of that? There's nothing incriminating in his statement to begin with."

Froelich shrugs. Rolls down his sleeve.

"Henry, you were in a concentration camp during the war, weren't you?"

"Yes." He reaches for the baby and Jack passes him over.

"I wish I'd figured that out sooner. I wouldn't've made so damn many stupid remarks."

"Which remarks?"

"Ah well, about your work, and you being a typical German, and how it's such a beautiful country. . . ."

Froelich puts the bottle into the flailing hands and guides it to the mouth. The child begins to suck, gazing up into the dark beard, curling star fingers absently against his own soft cheek. Jack waits quietly. Finally Froelich nods in the direction of the second baby, already asleep in his high chair, head relaxed at an impossible angle, face closed like a flower. Jack picks the child up carefully, knowing it to be a volatile substance, and follows Froelich up the stairs.

They lay the babies side by side in a crib in the master bedroom, which is as messy as the rest of the house. No headboard on the unmade double bed, an unframed painting tacked to the wall—unintelligible blocks of colour—clothes, books, towels. The characteristic smell of the Froelich house—baby powder, urine and tobacco. He tries not to look closely, not wanting to glimpse anything too personal. Karen's underthings—a slip. . . .

On their way back, Jack notices the two other bedrooms. They are the only tidy rooms in the house. One is obviously Rick's—guitar in the corner, red bedspread, cowboy boots. And across the narrow hall, a room with twin beds—one with metal rails.

In the kitchen once more, Froelich is feeding Elizabeth, and Jack is trying to avoid the sight without appearing to do so. Froelich puts down the spoon. "You're not so hungry, bubby?" He wipes her mouth with a tea towel, takes her face in his hand and kisses her on the cheek. "Not too full for dessert, I think." Elizabeth's head moves diagonally from side to side. He puts his ear close to her lips, listens, then replies, "Soon, *ja,* don't worry, Lizzie, look at Poppy, do I look worried?"

"Yeahh," she groans, and Froelich laughs. "Okay, dizzy Lizzie"— and the girl smiles—"frizzy Lizzie," says Froelich, and scoops her up in his arms. Her hands find one another around his back as Froelich carries her from the room.

After a moment, Jack hears him put a record on the hi-fi. He recognizes the throaty alto voice, "*Du, du, du, macht mein kleines Herz in Ruh. . . .*" A popular German love song. It reminds him of what a beautiful language it is when women speak it. Like a woman in a man's shirt.

Returning to the kitchen, Froelich reaches into the cupboard under the sink and lifts out a bottle of red wine. He fills two odd glasses and passes one to Jack, who politely raises it to his lips, though he can feel the home-brewed tannins working on his gut already.

"What does your lawyer say?" he asks. "About the chances of this going to a—what are the chances of an actual trial?"

"I think I need a detective." Froelich leans back in his chair, cradling his wine against the crook of his shoulder. "I think this is a better idea."

"You mean a private detective? Why?"

"Because the police don't find this man from the camp."

Why does Froelich use the word "camp," Jack wonders. Dora was the code name for an underground factory, wasn't it?

"Is this the . . . the 'war criminal' you were mentioning last night?" Jack is startled by a hot breath on his hand under the table. The dog has come in.

Froelich begins to speak, staring at the kitchen wall as though describing a scene unfolding there, and he tells the story of seeing Oskar Fried at the marketplace. "If I had told the police immediately," he says finally, "perhaps the little girl would be alive today."

"Why?"

"Because he is a killer."

"You told this to the police?"

"Yes, but they don't believe me."

"Why not, why would anyone lie about a thing like that?"

"They think I protect my son's alibi."

Jack takes a deep, even breath, willing his face to stay cool, his voice merely concerned.

"Which camp was this, Henry? If you don't mind my asking?"

"Dora."

"Dora?" Jack repeats, as though hearing the name for the first time. And in a way he is.

Froelich bites his moustache where it straggles at the corner of his mouth, wine-stained. "The police have not find him—found him"—he reaches for the bottle again, pours—"and they don't find either the air force man—forgive me, Jack, my English suffers this evening."

"I wish my German were half-decent, Hank, you must get sick of speaking English all the time."

"Not so much. I miss my language, but it is dead in any case, *nicht wahr?*" And drinks.

"What do you mean, 'dead'?"

"You cannot use a language and make it to mean many things except the truth, you cannot—" Froelich stares at Jack then says, as though uttering a password, "*Deutsch.*"

Jack nods carefully in response.

"They torture it. The Nazis. And now there are many words that cannot any more remember themselves. The other meaning, the false one, is there always behind it like a coat, like a—*nein, wie ein Schatten. . . .*"

"A shadow."

"*Ja.* But I forget nothing. This is how I will help my son."

He tips the bottle over Jack's glass. "This man from Dora is here, and someone on this station knows this." He looks up. "But they do not say it. And I know why."

Jack refrains from swallowing. He waits.

Froelich says, "The West has need of these people."

"What people?"

"People who have worked on technologies such as the rockets." Jack keeps his gaze level. He knows the answers to the next questions, but it's advisable to ask them anyway. "This guy worked on rockets?"

"*Ja.*"

"What? The V-2?"

"*Ja.*"

"At Peenemünde."

"At Dora."

"Dora?"

"Peenemünde is bombed."

"That's right, we bombed it. Canadians did that," he adds, feeling foolish, like a schoolboy boasting. He wasn't there. He was in England behind a desk, managing supply at an RAF station.

"The factory moved underground after the bombs, inside a mountain. The Nazis called it Dora," says Froelich. "I was there."

"With the V-2s?"

Froelich nods and falls silent.

Jack's interest could almost douse his anxiety. If only he were simply sipping wine with Henry Froelich, listening to tales of a subterranean rocket factory. He pictures it: pristine concrete floor twelve storeys deep. A fifty-foot V-2 cradled on a rail car, its guts and brain exposed, triple gyroscope to guide it through space and time in a slow minuet. He sees the rocket roll up the sloping tracks to meet the night sky, through hatches camouflaged with rocks and pine trees; war is the grandmother of invention. Carefully the rocket is winched until it is erect on the test stand, pointing at the stars, tanks replete with the secret, crucial mix that will produce enough thrust to take it across the Channel to London in five minutes. Vengeance-2. Hitler's secret weapon. Yet this is what will take us to the moon. This is what will keep us free. And Henry Froelich worked there.

"Did you work on the rockets themselves?"

Froelich nods.

"Holy liftin'," says Jack quietly. Then, because he cannot resist, "Did you ever see one of them fired?"

Froelich shakes his head. Beneath the table, the dog groans and rests its chin on Jack's foot.

"When I saw Dora, it was no longer a mystery how the pyramids were built. The rockets are built by slaves."

"Slave labour," says Jack. Somehow the addition of the word "labour" blunts the force of the first word, and he wonders if this is what Froelich meant a moment ago when he talked about words losing their memory.

"Hitler's 'secret weapon,'" says Froelich, draining his glass, getting up. "Slaves only are trusted to work, because we arrive but we do not leave." He almost smiles. "We leave through the chimney." He makes an upward spiralling motion with his finger.

"They had a crematorium? At Dora?" Jack swallows. "I didn't know it was . . . a death camp."

"Not extermination, no, but many workers die, and they burn bodies, otherwise more disease." Froelich lifts the lid of a pot on the stove and stirs. "So you see they are not afraid that we will tell the secret, but they are terrified of sabotage. They are right, there is sabotage, but often they hang the wrong ones." He picks up the bottle, finds it empty and bends to the cupboard once more. "Mornings, when I finish the shift, there are men hanging from ropes. Do you know how they hang them?"

Jack doesn't answer.

Froelich twists the corkscrew into the bottle. "A piece of wood here between the teeth"—he indicates with his finger—"so no screaming. They tie with string at the back of the head. The rope goes about the neck, so, and the other end is tied to a plank that is attached to the crane. . . ." He describes the mechanics with the precision of the engineer he is. "We are ordered to watch or they will hang us too, it is to remind us of the reward for sabotage. The crane lifts them slowly . . . the SS have calculated this method. With hands tied behind, but the legs are free to move because this is the show, entertainment, *ja?* I heard once two secretaries from the office, one to say to her friend, 'Hurry up, you miss the legs.'" He proffers the bottle. Jack complies, pushing his glass forward.

"They hang at the entrance to the tunnel, perhaps a metre and a half—five feet?—from the ground, so we must pass among the legs—they have lost their trousers, you pass through like curtains, the SS enjoy to watch this." He lifts the lid once more and steam escapes. "Will you join me?" he asks, ladle poised over a bowl.

"No. Thanks, Henry, but I'm not hungry."

Froelich returns to the table with his bowl. "It was used to be a mine," he says, and eats.

"What?"

"Dora. In the Harz Mountains."

"The rocket factory?"

"In a mountain cave."

A secret, in a mountain cave, worked by slaves. It sounds like a fairy tale.

"Near Buchenwald," says Froelich. "Near to Goethe's home. They bring the *Häftlinge*—the prisoners—to dig to make the cave larger. With bare hands they have digged and many die. These are no Jews at first, these are French and Russian, German, English, Poles and Czechs and many others. They wear the triangle, many different colours, but all wear the stripes. And on our feet, the wooden clogs, bare in winter also. In the beginning, the slaves must sleep in the earth with the rockets and many die." Froelich raises another spoonful to his lips but pauses. "You see, the Nazis have two intentions and these did not go together, but they were efficient with each." Jack sees the professor again as Froelich raises two fingers consecutively. "*Erste:* to produce the weapons. *Zweite:* to kill the workers, *ja.*"

"Henry—"

"When I arrive to Dora from the other place—"

"What other place?"

"From Auschwitz *Drei*—Auschwitz Three, *ja?* I am not so strong but I have learned to say 'electrical mechanic' and so I do not die with carrying the skin, the shell of the rocket, how you say?"

"Casings."

He is speaking quickly now. "I am fortunate also because I have not terrible dysentery, only somewhat, but there are many children and they take them away and beat them to death. I am lucky because I have not marched all of the way from Auschwitz to Dora, I have been on a railway *Wagen,* it is open, no roof. This is good because it is winter and I drink the snow from my shoulders, you see? Also I can breathe. I do not freeze because many die around me so I crawl beneath their bodies. I am thin but when I arrive to Dora I am fortunate, I do not build my barracks, others must do this and many die."

The word "Auschwitz" sizzles like acid in the air around Jack. His home is across the street. His bed. His children in their beds. His wife. He feels heat on his face, but it is not comforting. He is too close to something. He should move back, but he cannot.

"We sing for the guards."

"What?"

"It is winter and I do not know the date, only that it snows and they make us to sing '*Stille Nacht.*'"

"'Silent Night.'"

"So I know this is December 1944."

Froelich tears off a piece of bread and feeds it to the dog, whose black nose glistens just below table level. A new layer is unfolding in Jack's mind. Fried worked in a criminal place, so it follows that Froelich would associate his face with brutality, but it does not necessarily follow that Fried personally committed crimes. Still, he must have known about the hangings. Does Simon know? *I cleared him for security myself.*

"So he was a scientist."

"Who?"

"This fella you saw, the man from Dora."

"A scientist? He was just an engineer. *Es macht nichts.* He is a criminal."

"Are you saying he was a—what? SS?"

"I never saw a uniform at Dora," says Froelich. "Only the guards wear uniforms. Von Braun does not wear his uniform."

"Von Braun?"

"*Ja,* he visits his rocket."

"Von Braun was SS?"

"*Natürlich.* But the other one, always brown wool."

"What?"

"The engineer—he wears always a suit of brown wool. And small glasses, round like pebbles. No face—I mean to say, no expression. His eyes do not change, his voice does not change, always quiet. With him, *alles ist normal.* This is what I remember." He pushes his bowl away and sits back. "An ordinary man."

Jack sips in order to wet his lips; they have gone dry.

Froelich continues, "Except for his flower. It was rare. It grows in the tunnel." He shakes his head. "People are not boring, Jack, do you agree?"

"What did he do, Henry?"

"He was an engineer in the tunnels."

"No, I mean, what did—?"

"He saw over production in his sector. He hated to see his rocket to be built by us. We were scarecrows. He looks for sabotage. He finds a great deal. He wishes to impress his superiors, *verstehen?*"

Jack leans forward. "What was his crime?"

Froelich likewise leans forward. "You know how many people are killed by the V-2?"

"No, I don't," says Jack. Their faces are only a foot or so apart.

"Five thousand." Froelich drops his palm to the table with a smack. Jack doesn't move. "Do you know how many die of building this rocket that is so fascinating you, Jack? *Mehr als*—more than twenty thousand." The palm slams down again and the empty glasses jump.

The dog barks, the back door opens and Madeleine's little friend comes in.

"*Colleen, Schatzi, hier zu Papa, bitte komm.*" The girl goes to him and he hugs her, stroking her rough hair. The narrow blue eyes stare at Jack over Froelich's shoulder.

"Hello, Colleen," says Jack. The child doesn't answer. Jack notices a faint scar at the corner of her mouth.

Froelich fills a bowl for her and she takes it from the room. The dog follows. After a moment, music comes from the hi-fi—a woman singing "Mack the Knife" in German.

"In the camps, I am not so young and strong but I know something. If you help another to survive, maybe you also survive. At Auschwitz, I take a boy's glasses when we are pulled from the train. There are dogs and lights and music very loud, and screaming of guards, all to confuse, but underneath is very organized, you can see this if you are not so terrified, and I am lucky, I am not so afraid because I know my wife is safe.

Also"—he looks at Jack as though imparting a secret—"I have a trick. I imagine that I have lived before these experiences."

Froelich looks expectant so Jack nods.

"This boy," continues Froelich. "A student, probably—I knock his glasses down and I tell him what to say, 'electrical mechanic.' They push him to the right. To right is work. To left is death. I have already been from Bühne so I know. Perhaps he has survived." Froelich closes his eyes. "Also, I do not realize the bombing until after the war, so this also helps me."

"What bombing?"

"Hamburg."

Jack remembers—that's where Froelich is from. "Your wife?" he asks quietly.

Henry breathes evenly, eyes still closed. Memory is lapping up. The whisper of shells, combings of silent seaweed and stray shoes, are they teeth or pearls that shine down there, pebbles or bones? The wash of lost objects, memories cut adrift from their owners, memories released by death. If he kept his eyes closed long enough, would all the lost memories find their way through Henry Froelich, as through a living portal?

"My wife was safe from the camps. And so was I, for a time."

Jack has the curious feeling that, if he rose to leave now, his body would stay behind, seated at the table, a shell.

"She was, according to Nazi classification, Aryan. Which is ironic because, when I brought her to meet my mother, my mother did not approve. My mother was *sehr rafiniert.*" He smiles. "Annie was a peasant."

"What was your father's view?"

"He was killed in the Great War."

"My father fought. My uncle was killed."

Froelich nods. Jack sighs. Something has been understood between them, so he feels he can ask, "Henry, why didn't you leave Germany when Hitler came in? Why did you stay?"

"I am *Deutsch.* This does not change. You are right, Jack, it is a beautiful country, it is *my* country. We were *Deutsch,* you see. Then slowly we find that we are not. This does not happen over one night, there is not an invasion. Friends—those one has eaten with, at the table, as you and I here. One realizes, too late, this is the enemy."

Jack feels the headache coming on. Like muffled footfalls on a metal staircase. Froelich is saying, "And my mother refused to leave Germany. When she died we tried to come to Canada but we were not admitted."

"You couldn't get into Canada?"

"We were admitted nowhere, and my wife refused to leave without me."

"But you were a professor or something, you should've had your pick."

Froelich shrugs. "I was a Jew. Not a very good Jew, but from 1933 it did not matter. Good or bad, when the knock comes at the door in the middle of the night, you are a Jew."

"How did you wind up at Dora?"

"We had a good apartment in Hamburg. The block warden did not have such a good apartment. He reported me for listening to the BBC. I was arrested and taken away in April 1942. In July 1943 came the bombs."

Jack recalls the name of the mission: Operation Gomorrah. British and Canadian bombers dropped nine thousand tons of explosives on Hamburg in three days. Forty-two thousand civilians died in the firestorm—incinerated, asphyxiated, crushed, swept away by thermal winds. Jack does not ask if Froelich had children.

"I love Canada," says Froelich.

It seems Oskar Fried is the farthest thing from Froelich's mind at this moment. Jack eases his chair away from the table, but Froelich is still talking. "So. I did not fight in the underground. But at Dora I do what I can."

At the mention of the factory, Jack sinks back onto the spent vinyl of the kitchen chair as quietly as possible.

"Nobody sees the entire rocket, only the piece he works on, but I am in the *Elektriker Kommando*. My job is to spot-weld the skin—the casing, and also to fix the welding machines, therefore the rockets are near to me and I have . . . opportunities."

"Sabotage?"

"You put a bad piece for a good, loosen a screw, perhaps you can urinate on some wires to make rust. Maybe you weld not always perfectly at the seam. This helps me to survive. I knew a Pole who was hanged for making a spoon. But I am more afraid of my *Kapo*."

"Is that who he was? A *Kapo*?"

"What?" Froelich shakes his head, impatient. "A *Kapo* is . . . a *Kapo*. He is a prisoner also, in stripes, rags, *ja*? But with a green triangle, for *criminal*. He has power. This one tries to kill me. Every day with the *Gummi*—this is a hose—black, thick. He says, 'No Jews on my *Kommando*,' he wants his squad should be *judenrein*. Not only guards and *Kapos*, the engineers also enjoy to beat the prisoners. It is not necessary to hang a man, most starve and the sick are selected for extermination."

"Did this man you saw in the market, the engineer—did he beat prisoners? Did he personally order any hangings?"

"I know this *Kapo* would have killed me if it had not been for him."

"He saved your life? How?"

"The engineer points at the *Kapo*. The guards take him and hang him over his machine." Jack waits.

"You see, the engineer knew I am skilled. The *Kapo* was sabotaging a valuable worker, so the engineer points at him. Whenever the engineer points, the guard takes the prisoner away, and one morning soon you will meet that prisoner again, at the mouth of the tunnel, when you walk beneath his feet. I saw him point many times. Once when a prisoner offered him a cigarette. Once when one said, 'Good morning.' So when he hangs the *Kapo*, I do not say thank you."

" . . . Henry? Are the police still looking for this man?"

"No. I told you, they don't believe me." Froelich's eyelids are heavy, his mouth stained purple.

Jack stands, reaches for his hat. "I believe you."

Froelich gets up and takes his hand. "Thank you, Jack. For everything. This is my country now. I will call up the newspaper, I will tell them what I have seen and who is living in this free country with us. I will tell how the police persecute my son, and I will have this man to prison."

"What does your lawyer say about all this?"

"My lawyer?" Froelich rolls his eyes. "He says, 'Keep quiet. You prejudice the case.' I don't think he believes me either."

Jack pauses halfway to the door, remembering the money, changed to large bills and weightless in his pocket. He puts his hand inside his jacket and removes a small brown pay envelope.

"What is this?" asks Henry.

"Please accept this—"

"No, no I can't."

"A lot of good men have contributed. I can't go giving it back to them." He places the envelope on the table, among the bills.

Henry stares at it. "My lawyer says, even if it is true, my son appears more guilty with this alibi since I have claimed to see the same car." He takes a big breath. "When I think through the eyes of strangers. . . . They do not know my son. They don't know me. We are from . . . elsewhere. His alibi, I think . . . it sounds like a *Märchen*—a fairy tale."

Jack clicks his tongue. "You're probably right, Henry." He sticks his hands in his pockets and with a shock he feels the lone car key.

"I think I take my lawyer's advice," says Henry.

"He's the expert."

"Then afterwards, I tell the newspapers what I have seen. And this air force man, whoever he is, I make him to feel it."

Henry walks Jack to the door. "I never forget a face, Jack. In April the Americans came. I remember a soldier who reached down his hand and I think every day, *I hope this boy has a good life. I hope he has children.*"

"Henry, I'm sorry."

"For what?"

"Making you—stirring up all these memories."

"*Ibergekumene tsores iz gut tsu dertseyln.* Troubles overcome are good to tell." Froelich smiles and the twinkle returns to his eye. "My grandmother used to say this. She was 'typical' Yiddish."

Jack steps out into the night, the key closed in his hand, digging into his palm. Across the street, he sees the light in his kitchen window. He feels suddenly sorry for his wife—pictures her at the table with a cup of tea, poised to turn the page of a magazine, waiting for him. As though he were away at war—although, if he were, the picture would not seem so sad. Add a child drinking cocoa at her side, and the caption, "What did you do in the war, Daddy?"

The lights of a car catch his eye as it turns onto St. Lawrence. Karen Froelich is coming home, alone. He turns and heads back between the Froelich house and the one next door—he will take a shortcut through the park to the station. It would be quicker with his car, but he doesn't want to alert Mimi, cloud the situation with explanations. She will assume he is still at the Froelichs'.

He jogs past the swings and teeter-totters. Is it possible Simon knew all about Fried? Jack quickens his pace, running as much to dissipate the adrenalin spurting in his gut as to reach the phone booth in short order. Fried is a killer, a man who concealed his past and switched loyalties when it suited him—why would he not do so again? How likely is it that Simon would knowingly recruit such a man on behalf of the West? Jack is about to emerge from the park when he notices something hanging from a backyard tree—rope and pulley. What's it for? He slows to a walk now that he is back under street lights.

A man like Fried would besmirch the jewel of Western science: the space program. He'd put into disrepute our fight for missile supremacy, and play into the hands of Soviet propaganda. The Soviets are ahead because they coerce their people—their entire country is a concentration camp. Jack loosens his tie, cooling his neck, and crosses the county road, passing under the wing of the old Spitfire.

Up Canada Avenue and past the hangars, he slows to a walk. The darkness thickens ahead of him, where the mown grass on the far side of the runway turns to weeds obscuring the lip of a dry ditch. He would rather not be out of earshot of his family at night—although whoever did this thing is probably miles away. Like the McCarrolls themselves, in Virginia now. Loved ones filling a suburban living room. Framed photographs. Sandwiches and tears. *So sorry.* He crosses the runway and takes the key from his pocket. He raises his arm, poised to throw, and is shocked by his next thought, which arrives without remorse: *better his child than mine*—because in this instant Jack is certain that it would have been his child, had it not been for McCarroll. As though one child was demanded by something. A sacrifice. To what? He hurls the key into the darkness.

The phone booth shines across the parade square. He runs, pushes through the glass door and dials zero. He hears the phone ring in the darkness at the other end of the line.

"Operator."

Jack takes the scrap of paper from his wallet, reads out Simon's night number and listens as the digits are dialled, clicking like the tumblers in a safe. He looks up at the frank sliver of moon through the glass of the booth and realizes something: Simon is still on active duty. He hasn't lived in peacetime since 1939. He has gone from one war to the next. Jack is grateful not to have his job—even if Simon is still "flying ops." And while this mission cannot now be called a success, it has not been entirely futile if Simon's task included depriving the Soviet space program of Fried's expertise. Even if Fried is shipped back when the truth is out, the Soviets are unlikely to return him to work. It's more likely he'll be executed. Jack feels no twinge of pity for the man, but his next thought chills him: perhaps Fried is actually a Soviet spy. He takes a deep breath—no point getting ahead of himself. He listens to the phone ring somewhere in Washington.

Madeleine tried to stay awake but sleep overcame her, invisible magic wand—why is it we can never remember the moment of sleep? Now she has awakened with no sense of what time it is, merely the knowledge that it's late. Her father must be home by now, and she needs to ask him the questions before school tomorrow.

She creeps into the hall. A stealthy push at her parents' door reveals the room. Bed made. Her heart leaps—her parents have gone away! Of course they haven't. They are staying up late, they are grown-ups, they are allowed.

She pads to the top of the stairs. There is a light downstairs, coming from the kitchen. She descends, one cautious step at a time, until she sees her mother alone at the kitchen table. She is still dressed, a cup of tea in front of her and the cards laid out. She is playing solitaire. Madeleine watches as her mother places one card on top of another. The kitchen is neat and clean. Her red nails stand out against the silver flecks of the tabletop. Smoke drifts up from a crystal ashtray.

"Maman?"

Her mother looks up and smiles. "*Eh, ma p'tite fille, qu'est-ce que tu as, viens à maman.*" And opens her arms.

Madeleine walks to her, aware that her back is arched a bit, stomach sticking out the way it used to when she was little, twining her hair around her finger. She climbs onto her mother's lap. Her mother has also forgotten that Madeleine is nine. She puts her arms around her and rocks her. Madeleine rests her head against her mother's shoulder and resists the desire to suck her thumb. "Maman, are you going to have another baby?"

Mimi smiles. "Maybe, if God sends one."

"What are you going to call it? If it's a girl."

"Oh, I don't know, what do you think? We could call her Domithilde."

"No!"

Her mother laughs. "Why not? After your Tante Domithilde, what's wrong with that?"

"Can we call her Holly?"

"Why?"

"'Cause it's kind of like Hayley, for Hayley Mills."

"Holly is nice, but there's no Saint Holly."

"Was there a Saint Claire?"

Mimi strokes her forehead. "Hush, *ma p'tite*. There is a Saint Claire and she is looking after our little friend. Claire is with God now."

Then why is everyone so upset? Madeleine pictures a trio walking away from her. Claire in between Saint Claire and God, holding their hands and looking up at them. Grown-ups in robes and a kerchief, solemnly taking her away, talking to one another over her head. Where were they when someone killed her? Watching?

"Say a little prayer now," says Maman, folding her hands. And they pray, "'Angel of God, my guardian dear, to whom God's love commits me here. . . .'"

As soon as the prayer is done, Madeleine says, "I have to ask Dad something."

"Ask him in the morning, okay?"

Madeleine closes her eyes as her mother rocks her to sleep. She puts her thumb in her mouth and ponders God and Saint Claire. Holy grown-ups who wait to meet murdered children at the airport in Heaven.

"Simon, I've just been talking to Froelich—my neighbour—he's told me about Fried, about what he did at Dora. He had people hanged, Simon, he ordered executions . . . Simon?"

"Go on."

"Well, if it's true—and I think it is—we *are* harbouring a war crim-inal. He'll have to be deported."

A click at the other end of the line—not electronic, the sound of a lighter. Then an intake of breath. "I'm afraid that's out of the question, Jack. Fried's war record is neither here nor there."

Jack thought he was prepared for this. He isn't. "Are you telling me that you knew?"

No reply.

"I can't be part of this, Simon."

"I knew he was no Boy Scout. Not unlike several of the others."

Simon's tone—unconcerned, the same one Jack has always admired so much—repels him now. He isn't ready for what he feels—not anger but a sagging disappointment. It's as though he were seeing the world transform around Simon, bodies piling up. But Simon remains the same—the same half-smile, relaxed stance—knee-deep in blood. Jack says quietly, "I'm going to tell the police that I saw the boy on the road. I'm going to tell them I was in that car and I'm going to direct their inquiries to you."

"Do you know what Project Paperclip is?"

"Did you hear me, Simon?"

"Ever hear of Operation Matchbox?"

Jack doesn't answer.

"They're related programs—classified, of course. The first is American. The second, Canadian. The Brits come and go as needed. Like Donald Maclean. You were right, Jack, I do have his old job. It involves liaising with the Americans, and targeting foreign scientists for recruitment by them. Although, in Maclean's case, he was serving the wrong master."

"And if these scientists happen to be war criminals, you turn a blind eye."

"It's true, a few required a little dusting off before they came state-side"—Jack hears him take a long drag off his cigarette, then exhale—"von Braun for one."

The night has turned cold. Jack can see his breath. "What about von Braun?"

"Well he was rarely photographed in his SS uniform, but he was a *Hauptsturmführer.* A captain."

" . . . A lot of them were forced to join."

"I can't picture anyone forcing von Braun to do anything."

"Did he commit an actual crime?"

"I've seen minutes of a meeting that took place at Dora, attended by senior scientific, management and SS staff, including von Braun." Simon speaks quickly but unhurriedly, a routine briefing. "They discuss bringing in additional French civilians to use as slaves, and they note the requirement that workers wear the striped concentration-camp uniform. No one is on record objecting. And if you look at the transcripts of the Dora war crimes trial, you'll find the general manager on trial for mass murder. He mentions that von Braun was a frequent visitor to the factory and knew all about its operations, including executions."

"The press should get hold of this."

"They can't. It's been classified."

Jack sees condensation from his breath on the black dial face of the phone. "But von Braun didn't order executions—" he hears a foolish, plaintive note in his voice.

"Well that's what they all said, but in von Braun's case no doubt it's true. Rudolph, however, is another story."

"Arthur Rudolph?"

"Project director of NASA's Saturn rocket program. He was head of production at Mittelwerk—"

"Mittelwerk?"

"Mittelbau. Sometimes referred to as Nordhausen, after the nearby town."

"What are you talking about, Simon?"

"Dora. It was called anything but. Still is. What better way to confuse the enemy than by layers of ever-shifting bureaucratic nomenclature?"

"You knew all this."

"It's my job to know."

Jack watches the fog gathering outside. Dimly visible beyond the aircraft hangars, the red light of the control tower blinks at regular slow intervals.

"The purpose of Paperclip is threefold," Simon continues. "To deprive the Soviets of scientific expertise. To provide the West—usually via America—with scientific expertise. And three: to reward individuals who have enriched Western intelligence."

"Reward Nazis."

"In some cases," says Simon. "Former Nazis. A number of them got to come to Canada. Lead quiet lives. You very discreetly welcomed them at the request of Britain or the U.S. "

"War criminals."

"The fact is, most are completely harmless now. Pruning their roses, paying taxes. And they have no sympathy for Communists."

"It doesn't change what they did."

"I quite agree. In a perfect world, they'd have hanged. Or gone to prison."

Jack says nothing, annoyed by Simon's exercise in relativism, and conscious that this imparting of classified information is a form of flattery aimed at co-opting him.

"It's also different from the rat line," says Simon. "The CIA ran that operation with the Vatican, funnelled a lot of these chaps, mainly to South America—genuine bastards. People like Barbie and Mengele. Their usefulness was purely intelligence, and I have my doubts about that, but there's a big military-industrial complex here in the U.S. with a vested interest in keeping the military on tenterhooks; jockeying among the generals for bigger slices of the budget, a lot of competition among security agencies to see who can bring in the scariest bit of intelligence, the best defector, cock-and-bull about who has the most missiles, and a lot of them believe it too, all grist for the mill, good for business. It's called threat inflation. But they damn well know who the enemy is and they do get things done, the Yanks."

"Who runs Paperclip?"

"The Joint Intelligence Objectives Agency. JIOA. Courtesy of the Pentagon."

"An American operation designed to thwart American immigration laws, operating illegally in Canada. You're subverting democracy."

"We're fighting to preserve it. At worst, we're skeletons in the democratic closet."

"You're treating the public like the enemy, that's what Communists do. And Fascists."

"A number of senior American officers feel as you do. I heard one say he'd trade the whole pack of these former Nazis to the Soviets for a dish of caviar. And American scientists resent the plum jobs going to foreigners. There are even a few at your National Research Council in Ottawa."

"Okay, Simon, I get it, but I'm not going to let that kid go to jail for a Nazi, I don't give a damn how many of them we've got on our side now."

"There's a Soviet spy at the Marshall Space Flight Center."

*NASA.* Jack waits.

"Fried has identified him. Fried will take up employment in the USAF missile program, then be seconded to Marshall. He'll make contact with this individual and pose as a Soviet agent himself. He'll feed the man false information to pass on to his handler."

If Jack had heard this a week ago, he'd have been thrilled. Now he says, "You're willing to let a boy go to jail so that we can confuse the Soviets?" Outside the booth an impenetrable fog has descended. Jack has lost sight of the red pulse of the control tower—he will be hard-pressed to find his way home.

"Our operation may involve American intelligence," says Simon, "but at least they're air force types. If the CIA get wind, they'll move in on the Soviet mole, bag him, and it'll be a notch on their belt, unless they decide to run him themselves as a means to get their foot more firmly in the door of the space program. No one wants that."

"Forgive me if I can't muster a whole lot of sympathy for your turf war, Simon. And even if I did keep quiet, I can't control what Henry Froelich does."

"If the cover is blown from our little mission, the Soviets won't be the only ones to sit up and take notice."

"What do you mean?"

"It'll be out of my hands."

"Who are you talking about? The CIA?"

"I'm simply saying that I can't predict the outcome."

What might the CIA do? Froelich is an immigrant. A Jew with leftist leanings. The McCarthy era is not so long in the past. Would they smear him? Get him deported? "The CIA isn't authorized to operate in this country."

No answer.

"Simon. It's murder. The boy could hang."

A hard silence at the other end of the line. The kind that takes a piece out of your fuselage in the night. Finally Jack adds, "That's the worst-case scenario."

"I'll tell you what the worst-case scenario is, Jack," and Simon's tone is still reasonable. "A number of our people—brave people, agents-in-place—begin dying in the Soviet Union, far from your precious conscience. Fried's information about Soviet intentions and capabilities vis-à-vis their strategic missile program—test results, blueprints, organizational structure—becomes worthless; the press has a field day with the story of Nazis at NASA and government funding is cut, crippling our bid for the moon, to say nothing of the implications for Western intelligence, and the fight for supremacy in certain technologies that keep you safely at your fucking barbecue."

"Yeah, well Simon, I'm here and you're not, and so is Fried. I just have to make one call and he'll be picked up so fast—"

"Fried is long gone, mate."

Of course. Jack takes the humiliation. "When?" he asks, adding, "I know you won't tell me that, just tell me, was he already gone the other day when I offered to look in on him?"

"Afraid so." Simon's tone is almost apologetic.

Jack reaches up and leans his hand against the cold glass.

After a moment, Simon says quietly, "Jack, the reason I came to you with this mission is that I've learned to trust very few people," and it's the voice of a friend again. "I don't care what their security clearance is or where they're from. Some of the worst offenders are among my own countrymen. I wouldn't ask you to cross the street for Oskar fucking Fried. We're not doing this for him." He sighs. "This war—the one we're engaged in now—makes me pine for the last one. Any fool can die for his country, Jack."

"I don't happen to think forty thousand Canadians were fools."

"I'm not belittling the sacrifice made by my friends and yours—by my younger brother, for Christ sake, I'm pointing out that you and I don't have the privilege of fighting and dying. We have to live, and we have to make decisions—we had to make decisions in the last war too but they weren't all secret. The guilt and the bullshit and the triumph were shared and we called it duty. . . ." Jack can't talk about the last war. He was and was not there. *I don't have the right to talk about it.* And those who do have the right almost never talk about it at all. "Then one day the shooting stopped and we called it victory. We demobbed and went back to work, got married, had children and we called it peace. But it isn't quite. And you're right in the middle of it."

"Simon, I manage an organization that teaches people how to manage organizations. I drive a station wagon, I love my wife, I'm not in the middle of a damn thing."

"You're in it, lad. You're on ops now, whether you like it or not." Simon's tone brightens. "You know we bombed the shit out of the German war industry. The Ruhr night after night—you should've been there, mate, you were robbed." Is he being sarcastic now? "You know I went to Peenemünde." *I went to Peenemünde.* Jack knows enough to translate: *I beat the odds and survived a bombing mission. Target: Peenemünde.* "We bombed the hell out of Hitler's V-2 rockets—"

"That's for sure."

"So they moved underground, got a lot of slaves, worked them to death at Dora, starved them, hanged them, bloody good show."

"That wasn't our fault."

Simon continues, his voice calm—Jack realizes he is furious. "When we bombed Hamburg, thousands of people died. I was in on that one, we dropped incendiaries, fluorescent bombs along with the old block-busters, and what was down there? Civilians. We killed them just as surely as if we'd lined them up and shot them into a pit, and we won the war either because of it or in spite of it, I suspect in spite because I know who rebuilt their cities, the bloody women did, brick by brick, and how are you going to defeat that? But we got rid of Hitler, didn't we, and what's bothering me, Jack, is that Stalin killed more civilians than Hitler did, but Germany is a different place now and Russia is not. And I'm ask-ing you—your country, your goddamn civilization, is asking you to maybe, perhaps, sacrifice the life of one boy—and very probably not his life, merely his freedom—in the interests of peace, in the interests of a number of scientific advances that could make the difference between survival and annihilation, in the interests of your daughter. You bloody fool." Simon falls silent. When he speaks again, he no longer sounds angry. Merely sad. "I killed hundreds and hundreds, perhaps thousands of people. But I didn't do it secretly and I never saw a single victim. You don't at that height, it's called the morality of altitude. And I got a medal for it. You are being asked to jeopardize one person. The difference is, you know him. I didn't know the women rushing to the shelters when the sirens went, I didn't know their children, who died under buildings or stuck to the roads when the tar melted, I didn't know the people in the hospitals and churches, or the ones who ended up in the canal, I don't delude myself that they deserved what they got and I don't indulge in a lot of pointless guilt and virtuous hindsight. I did my fuck-ing duty, Jack. It's time you did yours."

The fog has obliterated time and place. Jack could be anywhere—ten thousand feet above the earth, *trust your instruments. . . .*

Simon says, "There's an old Chinese proverb: once you've saved a man's life, you're responsible for him."

"You don't owe me anything, Simon."

"My colleagues know there is a senior Canadian officer involved, they know he is stationed at Centralia, and although I haven't men-tioned your name, they could track you quite easily, I should think. But here's the crux of it, Jack. So far, they've no inkling you intend to break silence."

If Simon thinks Jack is worried about his career right now, he's sorely mistaken.

"Are you threatening me, Simon?"

"No." He sounds genuinely surprised. When he speaks again, his tone is intimate, almost aggrieved. "I'm giving you my word that they'll not hear it from me."

Jack swallows and says, "Simon. I won't let that boy hang. He's innocent."

"Then he has nothing to worry about."

*I don't know what to do.* Jack has not said it aloud. But Simon has heard him. Simon is just across the table, a Scotch away. He leans toward Jack now and says, "Do the right thing."

The phrase stirs something in Jack's memory, just behind his left eye. . . . What Simon said when Jack awoke in the MRI to learn his war was over: *You did the right thing, mate.*

"Goodbye, Jack."

Jack takes his hand from the opaque glass and his print remains, black and transparent. He looks up and through it. Outside, the night is clear. The moon glistens through his palm. The fog was inside the booth all along, made of nothing but his own breath. He opens the door and feels the chill through the wool of his uniform. It has started snowing. Flakes graze his eyelashes, melt against his lower lip. He puts on his hat. His legs carry him over the silent white. Halfway across the parade square, he becomes aware of a set of muffled footsteps behind him. He quickens his pace but so does the follower—he can hear the catch of the stranger's breath, almost feel the clap on his shoulder: *You got rid of the car, Jack. Even if you did come forward, the police wouldn't believe you any more than they believed Henry Froelich. There never was an Oskar Fried.* He stops. Who would believe him? His wife. The Soviets. And the CIA.

Jack has never been afraid to do the right thing. But it's difficult sometimes to recognize it. *Show me the right thing and I will do it.* Where is up? Where is down? He longs to talk to Mimi, but he must not involve his wife. She didn't join the armed forces, he did.

He turns, though he knows there is no one behind him. Across the parade square, the empty phone booth glows, transparent once more. The snowflakes gather on his shoulders, thickening like feathers. He stands there as his hat grows a ledge of white, and his shoulders collect frosted epaulettes. He doesn't know what to do. He only knows what he has done.

> " . . . And it's not for the sake of a ribboned coat,
>      Or the selfish hope of a season's fame,
>   But his Captain's hand on his shoulder smote—
>      'Play up! play up! and play the game!'"
> *Sir Henry Newbolt, 1862–1938*

## FLEXIBLE RESPONSE

> *"Bobby?"*
> *"Yeah?"*
> *"I don't want to make it look like we're all fucked up here. . . ."*
> *Tape transcript of JFK to RFK during the*
> *Cuban Missile Crisis, October 23, 1962*

MIMI IS AWAKE before Jack. She gets up quietly and reaches for his uniform, crumpled on the floor—she will give it a quick press. As she picks up the jacket she catches a whiff of something. She holds it to her face and sniffs—urine. It takes only a moment to realize that he must have been holding one of the Froelich babies. She looks at him, pale and sleeping, his mouth open, and has a sense of the old man he will one day become. She needs to be gentle with him.

Last night she waited up for him, but when he finally came in he wasn't hungry and he didn't want to talk. She gave him two Aspirins; he downed them with a Scotch, and went straight up to bed. She looked in on Madeleine, and when she joined her husband he was already asleep. She waited for him to turn to her, to warm her feet, which were always like ice, but he was dead to the world. He had missed his son's game. Now was not the time to ask him what had happened over at the Froelichs'. Whatever it was, it had made him ill. Jack was thirty-six and it was important to remember that men bottled a lot up inside, that this could take its toll. Mimi knew how to relax him but he was too sound asleep for that. Her period was late. Maybe this time. . . . She heard his teeth grind together briefly. She wasn't sleepy. She stared at the white stucco ceiling, where the shadows of snowflakes fell across a stark moonlit rectangle. She could have got up for an extra blanket but she was too cold.

A baseball game was not the end of the world, but their son would only be young for a very short while. She worried that too soon he would cease to place such importance on his father's being there to cheer him on. Already Michel was pretending that it didn't matter—strolling in, announcing his win as though it were an afterthought and telling her he wasn't hungry; Arnold Pinder's father had taken them for hamburgers. That this should have caused tears to spring to her eyes, she could only put down to the emotional strain of the past week.

Mimi folds the uniform jacket onto the chair—it will have to be dry-cleaned—and heads for the bathroom. She recalls that the Froelichs' station wagon was absent from the driveway for most of yesterday evening, and it occurs to her to wonder which of them Jack was keeping company—Henry or Karen?

In the bathroom she pees, then sees on the toilet paper a streak of watery red. She is momentarily bewildered. There have been no cramps, no bloating. She tells herself lots of women have irregular cycles, but she knows better: she has never been one of them. That's why she and Jack have never had any "surprises." If her period is changing, it's because she is too, no matter how young she looks and feels. She splashes water on her face—she has no right to cry. She has two beautiful healthy children, and her neighbour has just lost her only one. It's wrong to grieve for a child who has not even been conceived. Besides, who knows, there's nothing to say it might not still happen. She lets the water run, and sits on the side of the tub with her face in her hands. Madeleine bangs on the door: "Maman! I have to go!"

At breakfast she persuades Michel to tell his father about the baseball game. The rain has washed away the freak snowfall and the grass is a new livid green. She dresses more carefully than usual, and kisses Jack goodbye with an extra love-bite on his ear to make him smile.

Madeleine didn't get a chance to ask her father the questions, because Mike monopolized breakfast with a play-by-play account of his game. Perhaps it doesn't matter, because the police don't return to the school. When Colleen corners her at recess, Madeleine tells her what she told the police, then runs to rejoin her school friends— her light cool friends—before Colleen can thank her or rub anything off on her. The scab in the palm of her hand has begun to flake, and Madeleine picks at it as much as she dares.

For the next three days Jack sits tight, in hope that the case will be dismissed, but on Friday a date is set for a hearing. The Crown is willing to move swiftly in consideration of the fact that some witnesses may be posted before the summer is out. Perhaps they also have in mind Ricky's extreme youth, and the fact that he has been denied bail, for the hearing is a mere three weeks away. The Froelichs' lawyer has welcomed the speed of events, in view of the scantiness of the prosecution's case. The Crown will seek to have Ricky tried as an adult, but editorials have already appeared in the major Toronto papers decrying this as inhumane and "an abuse of the letter, and a breach of the spirit, of the law."

Jack does not immediately go to the police. He reasons that the whole point of a hearing is to determine whether there is enough evidence to proceed to trial. And how likely is that? Jack will act, but he will act responsibly. And that means not blowing the whistle until, and unless, absolutely necessary.

Grace Novotny has one pink streamer in the handlebar grip of her beat-up bicycle. She stands astride the bike at the edge of the grassy circle that borders Madeleine's backyard. It's raining again. Some kids might chant, "Who rides a bike on a day like this?" the way kids do to try to make you feel like a weirdo. Grace has no raincoat on. She has her hand between her legs—she often clutches herself quite absently like that. She reminds Madeleine of an old rubber doll, naked but for one plastic shoe, hair uncurling, abandoned at the bottom of a toy box. It's after school on Friday and Madeleine is in her red raincoat and sou'wester. She has been dissecting a golf ball she found in the grass. Mike has told her there is nitroglycerine at its core; perhaps she will make a bomb.

"Hi Grace." Grace doesn't seem to notice the rain. The hem on her wet dress is uneven. Madeleine asks, "Hey Grace, where'd you get the streamer?"

Grace runs her fingers through the pink plastic strands and looks away. "Someone gave it to me."

"Who?"

"Someone."

Madeleine says, "You stole it."

"I did not!" Grace pelts the words, stamping her foot the way Marjorie does, as though expecting you to *scat* like a cat. When Grace does it, though, it's not sharp, it's just raggedy.

"Then where'd you get it?" asks Madeleine again.

"She gave it to me."

"Who? Claire?"

"I found it."

"Liar." Madeleine feels a little mean—Grace is an easy target. "Tell me, Grace."

Grace jumps on the seat of her bike, bouncing up and down on it hard on purpose as she rides away—that must hurt.

"Madeleine. *Viens, c'est l'heure du dîner.*"

Supper that night is quiet. Madeleine keeps waiting for something to happen, but nothing does.

"Pass the peas, please," says Mike. Her father doesn't criticize him for sprinkling sugar on them.

Madeleine wishes the radio were on, even the boring news. The rain is not comforting against the window, it's a monotonous reminder that there's nothing to talk about.

"You've got Scouts tonight, is that right, Mike?" asks Jack. Mike grunts in the affirmative, but her father doesn't reprimand him. Something is terribly wrong with this picture. Her father is being extra nice, covering something over, as if he's leading up to telling them some awful news—he has a terminal disease. What if he only has a year to live?

"Pass the butter, sweetie."

It's too much. Her face crumples, tears drop onto her tepid canned peas; even in the midst of her grief, she notices and wonders if she'll get out of eating them.

"What's wrong, little buddy?"

"*Madeleine, qu'est-ce que tu as?*"

Mike rolls his eyes.

"Shut up!" she screams at him savagely. Her father gives Mike a look, then opens his arms to Madeleine. She climbs onto his lap and weeps into his shoulder. "I'm sorry!"

"What are you sorry for, old buddy?" His amused voice, the one that tells you it's time to worry because he's reassuring you.

"Nothing!" She weeps, grinding her fist into her cheek. When she looks up, they are alone at the table.

"Tell me what you did in school today."

Today Madeleine watched for the police through the window. "Nothing," she says.

"Did you sing? Did you do arithmetic? Draw pictures?"

"We had art last Thursday."

"Well, tell me what you drew last Thursday."

"I didn't get a star."

"That's okay, art is subjective. Do you know what *subjective* is?"

"No."

"It means a matter of opinion. Art is a matter of opinion."

"The butterflies got a star."

"Butterflies. Not terribly original."

"They were yellow, they were really good."

"What did you draw?"

She tells him about Robin crying, "Holy Thursday, Batman!" He laughs. She feels better.

"Humour is often underrated," he says. "But it's the hardest thing of all."

He tells her about the old vaudevillians like Bob Hope working their way up, second by second, to a golden three-minute routine packed with reliable laughs. "Comedy is the brain surgery of the performing arts."

"Are they going to hang Ricky Froelich?"

"No, no, no, they won't do that."

"Um. How do you know?" She tries to make her voice sound polite, so as not to seem rude in questioning his judgement.

"Well, first of all, he's a juvenile."

"A delinquent?"

"No, no, juvenile just means that you're not yet an adult, so you can't be punished as an adult."

"Do they ever hang kids?" asks Madeleine, knowing that she will soon be ordered to "think nice thoughts."

He sounds a little insulted when he replies, "Of course not, the chances of that happening nowadays are virtually nil."

Like the chances they'll drop the bomb.

"First of all, the case probably won't even go to trial. You see, there has to be what's called a hearing, and that's when the judge'll say, 'Listen fellas, there's no direct evidence here—'"

"It's all circumstantial." The kind Perry Mason deals with.

"That's right, and he'll throw it out."

Madeleine says, "Want to watch *Rocky and Bullwinkle*?"

They watch as Boris Badenov and his evil Russian girlfriend, Natasha, try to sabotage a circus act, only to be foiled by J. Rocket Squirrel and his trusty moose companion. During the commercial, Madeleine asks, "But what if they don't throw Ricky out?"

"No jury in its right mind would convict him on no evidence."

"Yeah, but if they did?"

He looks her in the eye, and for the first time he speaks to her in the man-to-man voice. She feels her spine straighten, knowing it means he believes she can take it like a man.

"If they convicted Ricky Froelich of murder," he says, "the worst-case scenario would be life in prison."

She sees Ricky in black and white stripes, behind bars, a matching cap on his head, *go directly to jail, do not pass go*. . . .

He leaves his tea on the coffee table and goes to the kitchen cupboard over the fridge. He pours a drink from the bottle of Scotch.

*Candid Camera* comes on.

"But even that won't happen," says Madeleine, still in man-to-man mode.

"What's that, sweetie?" He returns to the couch. "Rub Dad's head, eh?"

She kneels beside him and rubs his head, saying, "He won't even go to jail."

"No, he won't," says Dad and takes a sip.

Cheerful voices sing from the television, exhorting the audience to smile—You're on *Candid Camera*!

"'Cause he didn't do it," says Madeleine. Her father gets up to raise the volume. "That's what I told the police."

"What's that?" He turns to her, still bent over the TV. "What about the police, sweetheart?"

"They came to the school."

He straightens up. "When?"

"Yesterday."

"What for?"

"To ask questions."

"About what?" She regrets bringing up the subject. How will she be able to confess to her father that she lied to the police? His face is red. "Who was there?"

"Just me," Madeleine answers. "And Mr. March."

"Who asked you the questions?"

"The one in the suit."

"Inspector Bradley?"

"Yeah."

"For the love of. . . ." He places his glass down on the coffee table in a measured way that Madeleine recognizes as fury. He goes to the kitchen and removes the phone book from a drawer—not banging anything, licking his finger and flipping the pages with deliberation. It seems he isn't angry at her after all. All the same, she has stepped through a weave of grass and fallen into a trap, it isn't possible to know where adults have dug them. She watches him dial.

"Hello, is this George March? Jack McCarthy here, I'm Madeleine's father. . . ." Madeleine is too shocked to reach for a cushion. "There's something I'd like you to explain to me. . . ."

She has the nervous giddy feeling of when Dad is mad at something but it isn't her—the godforsaken tent pegs! She watches the look of bewildered outrage enter his eyes. He is saying, "I'd like you to explain why I shouldn't drive over to your house right now and break both your arms."

She chomps the inside of her cheek and reaches for a couch cushion. ". . . Oh, I think you know why, mister."

*Mister!* She bites into the fabric.

"'Exercises'? I'm not calling about schoolwork, buddy, I'm calling about what happened yesterday in your classroom after three."

Madeleine's eyes feel as big as saucers.

"I don't care what the police said, the law says parents must be consulted before their children are interrogated." His fingers are white around the receiver. "I know she told the truth, I've raised her to tell the truth, that's not the point. . . ."

Madeleine grins into the cushion, laughter frozen in her throat.

"You'll be lucky if you still have a job by the time I'm through. . . . You're damn right it won't happen again." And he hangs up.

Jack has his finger on the number for the local OPP detachment, but reconsiders and flips back through the white pages to find a Thomas Bradley in Exeter—call the bastard at home, get him off guard and off his ass.

Before dialling, Jack turns to his daughter and says, "What did they ask you?" All the giddy thrill drains away. Madeleine takes the cushion from her mouth and tells the truth.

"If I saw Ricky and Elizabeth and Claire all going down the road."

"Which road?"

"Huron County road."

"Okay." He nods, poised to dial. "And what did you tell them?"

"I told them . . . I saw them."

"Did they ask you anything else?"

Madeleine answers truthfully again, "They said, 'Did you see which way Ricky went?'"

On the TV, a Volkswagen Beetle splits in two, drives around a telephone pole and comes together again on the other side. Laughter.

Madeleine concentrates. "And I said . . . yeah, I mean yes." That too is a truthful answer, for that is what she told the police. She's not lying to her father.

He waits.

"And I said he didn't go with Claire 'cause I saw him and Elizabeth and Rex turn left."

He looks different. As though he's not looking at his old buddy—yet neither is it as though he's looking at his little girl who has been naughty. She doesn't recognize this look, so for a moment she doesn't recognize herself. Who is he looking at?

Words have formed in Madeleine's head, they are floating down toward her mouth, *but that was a lie 'cause I didn't see which way Ricky went.* She opens her mouth to release them, but they are jolted back by the thunk of Dad's hand on her head. He ruffles her hair, the weight of his hand wobbling her head on her neck.

"You know what, old buddy?" he says.

"What?" She stares at his belt buckle, the fly in amber.

"You never have to answer a grown-up's question unless you're in the classroom and the teacher is asking you the capital of Borneo or something."

She looks up. He grins. She mirrors him.

"Pilot to copilot," he says, "do you read me?"

"Roger."

"Good stuff. Come on, let's hop in the car and go for a spin."

He doesn't comment when she takes Mike's windbreaker from the halltree and puts it on. The one with the plaid lining that matches his.

"When you go to school tomorrow, don't mention to anyone that your dad called up the teacher and dressed him down. He's had his punishment."

"I won't." Man to man. Wondering what her father would say if she asked him to call her Rob.

It has stopped raining. They drive to Crediton with the windows open; the smell of wood fires and fields reminds them of Germany. It is almost dark, a grey twilight is on the land—not glowering or hazy, a promising kind of grey—lucid, silvering up the barns, sharpening the fences. They pull in at the dairy outlet on the village's one street and her father goes to the counter. It's only too cold for ice cream if you are a baby or a wimp. Madeleine waits in the car, gazing out the window as Rob. Down the street is a neat little house—a bungalow—with flower boxes and a bird feeder out front. The door opens and Mr. March comes out with a bag of birdseed and fills up the feeder. Rob stays perfectly still. Mr. March has gone back inside by the time her father returns. As he hands her an ice cream cone, he says, "Do you know what 'discreet' means?"

"It's when you don't go around blabbing things." She has chosen good old vanilla.

"Yes," he says, licking the edge of his maple walnut. "But it also refers to a way of getting something done with a minimum of fuss and disturbance. We've dealt with Mr. March now, and we don't need to rub his nose in it."

"He's got his pride," replies Rob.

"That's right," says Dad. "Mission accomplished."

Each of them has an elbow out the window, matching sleeves rippling in the wind.

Is it a lie when you don't tell someone a lie but you let them believe one? Dad asked Madeleine what she told the police and she told him. Is that a lie?

"Just play it cool," says Dad.

Or is that "discreet"?

Madeleine takes a bite of her ice cream and holds it freezing in her mouth. Tears spring to her eyes, it's so cold it hurts. Her mouth will thaw out, and when it does, it's funny how the ripples on its roof will feel as though they have been burned.

Her father slows the car a little and lets her steer.

When Jack gets home to find that Mike was ejected from the Scout meeting for picking a fight with Roy Noonan, he is able to discuss the matter calmly. A great weight has lifted from him, and left him free to handle this minor crisis with his son. His daughter has provided Ricky Froelich with an alibi.

*Part Three*

# THE QUEEN'S MERCY

Family of the victim on the right. Family of the accused on the left. Strange wedding. Wooden benches, pews. Up front, on a large table, ranged like gifts, the exhibits:

Jar of stomach contents. Envelope containing cotton underpants. Left shoe. Right shoe. Lunchbox. Silver charm bracelet in envelope. Blue dress. Photograph showing Constable Lonergan at a position where body was found. Photograph of Claire McCarroll at autopsy. Bulrushes turned over to coroner. Container of larvae. Container of blood from Claire McCarroll. Bulrushes retained by Constable Lonergan.

Overhead, a ceiling fan turns slowly. Along one side of the courtroom large windows tilt open, but the air is still. It is hot for mid-June—feels more like July. Outside, the town square is tree-lined and spilling with roses. *Welcome to Goderich, the prettiest town in Canada.*

"My lord, I move for the trial of Richard Plymouth Froelich on this indictment." The Crown attorney sits back down and wipes his forehead with a hanky. It is ten A.M. The Supreme Court of Ontario is sitting in Assizes at the county courthouse.

"Place the prisoner in the prisoner's box," says his Lordship, the judge. His bench is flanked by two flags: the Union Jack and the Canadian Ensign. On the wall above his head, a portrait of Her Majesty Queen Elizabeth II. *Elizabeth Regina.* Rick's adversary.

Rick is led in in his new blue suit and handcuffs. His wrists protrude, bare and bony, from the sleeves—he has had a growth spurt in prison. The bailiff removes the handcuffs. Rick sits down.

The registrar says, "Will the accused please stand?" Rick stands up.

There is a scratch on his cheek and a speck of dried blood on his chin—the razor they gave him this morning had been used already by several inmates, the water was cold, his nerves did the rest. This has been duly noted in his file, because every injury must be accounted for. Mr. and Mrs. Froelich are seated behind him, with Colleen.

A few rows behind them sits Jack in his summer uniform. He has taken a day of leave in order to attend the first day of the trial. Leave is precious, but Mimi will understand. He leans back against the hard bench. He feels relieved already. It's almost over. The past couple of months have been calm, but not reassuring—*becalmed* is the word. The sun has shone, there has been nothing visibly askew—except that the boy across the street is gone. School ended a few days ago and he took the kids for ice cream. They have gone shopping, he has cut the lawn, set up the wading pool, he has barbecued—and he has made love to his wife.

But when he looks back on the last two months, the Froelich situation permeates everything—arcs like the sky over Centralia, the blue overlaid with a faint grey film that makes it a little harder to breathe, a little harder to move. Traps time. Time has passed around Jack and he has engaged in the motions but, like a man in a bucket brigade, he has not moved from his spot. He has even had a birthday but that was just a page on a calendar, candles on Daddy's cake. Inside, he knows he is no older than he was two months ago. Which is not the same as feeling young. He has been waiting for time to begin again. Today.

"You stand indicted by the name of Richard Plymouth Froelich," the registrar reads from a clipboard, "that Richard Plymouth Froelich on or about the tenth day of April 1963, at the Township of Stephen, in the County of Huron, did unlawfully murder Claire McCarroll, contrary to the Criminal Code of Canada. Upon this indictment, how do you plead, guilty or not guilty?"

The press is here—a row of sweltering men in crumpled suits at the back—but they are not permitted to report anything until it's over. There are no photographers—they have been banned from within fifty feet of the courthouse, unlike the public. Jack saw the police car pull up to the steps this morning but his view of Rick was blocked by the surge of a small crowd. He heard snatches, hurled insults. "There he is!" "You bastard!" "Burn in hell!" A reminder that, despite sympathetic editorials by journalists outraged that in a civilized country like Canada a fifteen-year-old could be tried in adult court, most people who have never met Rick have no reason to doubt the police. The boy is not from around here, not even an air force kid, he's adopted—that came out at the hearing—he is not really white. He is Métis. A "half-breed."

Jack was disgusted by the scene. And surprised—he is so accustomed to thinking of Ricky Froelich as the boy next door, it hadn't occurred to him that some might see the kid as a reassuring culprit. A stranger in their midst.

Across the aisle sits Inspector Bradley. Next to him are the McCarrolls.

"Not guilty," says Rick.

"You are appearing, Mr. Waller?" asks the judge.

A man in the black silk robes of a QC rises from the defence table next to Rick. "I am, my lord."

The registrar asks, "Are you ready for your trial?"

Rick replies, "Yes."

The jury is sworn. Jack is struck by the contrast between the formal—even theatrical—language, and the monotone voices. Most of these people have gone through these motions hundreds of times. For Rick it is a debut. And for the jury. There are no women among the twelve. There seems to be no one under fifty. *He's hanged*—the words obtrude upon his mind but Jack dismisses them, almost offended—perfectly decent hard-working men from the community. Each and every one of them reminds him of his father: tight view of a tiny world. And he dismisses that thought too.

The registrar says, "Would the accused stand, please?" Rick stands again. The registrar continues, "Gentlemen of the jury, look upon the prisoner and hearken to his charge."

Jack keeps his eyes on the registrar. Across the aisle, Sharon McCarroll folds her hands and looks down. As though she were in church. She is wearing a pale yellow twin-set that she got in Denver when Claire was alive. Everything about their lives up until two months ago can be summed up like that: "when Claire was alive." They have yet to say, "when Claire died." Because she did not die, she was killed, but who can imagine saying, "when Claire was killed"? People are killed in car accidents and floods. Claire was murdered. And there will never come a time when her parents can say, "when Claire was murdered." What they will say instead is, "when we lost Claire."

" . . . Upon this indictment he hath been arraigned, upon his arraignment he hath pleaded not guilty and for his trial has put himself upon his country, which country you are."

Sharon tucks a strand of hair behind her ear. She will testify today, then she will return to Virginia. Today is like the last day of school before the summer holidays. First there will be a quiz. She will describe precisely what she put in her daughter's lunchbox and she will describe the clothes her child was wearing. She will tell the story of Claire's last day: "Claire came in and asked me to pack a snack and I said, don't you want to help me make an apple pie for the Brownies? She asked if she could go for a bike-hike instead and I said, sure, but don't forget you have to change into your Brownie uniform before supper, and she said, 'I won't forget, Momma.'" Thinking of this brings a smile to Sharon's face. Claire is still here, in this courtroom. Along with her clothes and her Frankie and Annette lunchbox, exhibit number 23. And her charm bracelet. Blair puts an arm around his wife and bends to look into her face.

"Now, gentlemen of the petit jury," says the judge, "you have been sworn in this case and are therefore now seized with it. This young lad that we are about to try is charged with murder, which is the most serious offence known to our law. . . ."

A pathologist from Stratford is here. He will testify as to the medical evidence indicating that she died in the spot where she was found, and he will testify as to time of death. He sent the jar of stomach contents to the office of the Ontario Attorney General, where members of the biological analysis staff re-created Claire's snack, including the cupcake, which they baked according to a recipe provided by Mrs. McCarroll. They ate it, along with a piece of Babybel cheese, and apple slices, then vomited in order to compare it to the victim's stomach contents.

" . . . and if you have heard any gossip about this case, as I am sure you have," says the judge, "I don't suppose it is possible to have lived in Huron County in the last two or three months without hearing something about it. . . ."

A few rows in front of Jack, Henry Froelich's head is bowed—he is wiping his brow. Jack sees the back of Karen Froelich's head. Straight fly-away hair. Mousy, even. Then she turns, he glimpses her profile and something jumps just below his sternum. Some women have mouths that are actually better defined without lipstick. The faint line bracketing the corner of her mouth—lips parted, close to her husband's ear, whispering comfort.

"Please dismiss it from your minds now . . . ," says the judge.

Jack was at the preliminary hearing. It lasted a day. And given the little the prosecution could come up with, it's a wonder the case proceeded to trial. Rick found the body. Rick was the last to see her alive. Rick fled from an intimidating cop. Time of death. End of story. Proving nothing. " . . . I would ask that you avoid reading any newspaper reports about this case and that you likewise avoid any radio reports or television. . . ."

This is a farce. Two families are being put through hell because of a botched police investigation. The local civilian population may be sleeping easier in their belief that the murderer has been found, but most parents in the PMQs are still on alert. " . . . at the hotel in Goderich, where, if you are not comfortable, gentlemen, do not hesitate to make demands upon the county. . . ." The McCarrolls are among the few who now believe Rick may be guilty. And who can blame them for desiring a swift end to this aspect of their grief? " . . . if those chairs become hard, gentlemen, I have already requested that rubber cushions be brought in for your comfort, since it is important that you be able to give your full attention to. . . ."

Jack has put in for an early posting. He has gone over the head of the personnel officer at Centralia, straight to a superior officer he knew at 4 Wing in Germany. A couple of years ago Jack went out of his way to organize a last-minute flip to Canada on a service flight for this man's family, earning an "any time I can do anything for you, Jack. . . ." The group captain is now an air commodore at HQ in Ottawa—"What can I do for you, Jack?"

Jack will move his family the moment his posting comes through. In fact, he will take his leave the moment the trial is over, pack his family into the Rambler and point it east for New Brunswick—now that school is out, it will be difficult to keep Madeleine within the PMQs and out of the woods.

"May it please your Lordship"—the Crown attorney rises, his robes likewise black but heavier, woollen—"and ladies and gentlemen of the—pardon me, gentlemen of the jury. . . ."

Jack looks out the window at the tranquil square, picture perfect. Perhaps he should retire from the air force, hit civvy street. Go back overseas. As a consultant . . . for a big company . . . pharmaceuticals, widgets, it hardly matters. They'll buy a house of their own, they'll travel. Like old times. " . . . the time of death, to the time of finishing the last meal. Other times are also of importance—" Jack removes his jacket and straightens his back, wet now against the bench. The Crown attorney is outlining his case, such as it is. " . . . when she walked out of the house. That was the last time her mother ever saw her alive. But you will hear of her being in the playground of the school after that, where a Brownie pack—they are little girls commencing to be Girl Guides—was to gather. You will hear from two children who may be very important witnesses in your estimation, Marjorie Nolan and Grace Novotny. . . ." The one name is familiar. Friends of Madeleine? What have they got to say? They were not at the preliminary hearing, no children were. " . . . they are girls from the same grade as Claire McCarroll and they were playing together that afternoon, and you will hear better from their own lips. . . ."

The precise time Claire left the playground, the precise time she met up with Ricky and Elizabeth. Half the children in the PMQs will be called to establish for the prosecution that which is not even in dispute: Claire shared her snack with Madeleine and Colleen at such-and-such a time. She left the playground at such-and-such a time. She met up with Rick and left the PMQs, etc. . . . Why must the children be subjected to this?

The Crown attorney drones on, " . . . the place was a section of Huron County known to the children from the PMQs as Rock Bass. This is an invented name, you will not find it on any map, gentlemen. It is accessed by a dirt road called Third Line division road but you may expect to hear witnesses refer to it as 'the dirt road,' and it runs east-west between Number 4 Highway—that is the King's Highway, not to be confused with County Road Number 4, with which it intersects farther north—as I said, between the King's Highway and the Ausable River, this 'dirt road' is intersected—and this intersection may become important—by a section of road which is the southerly continuation of County Road Number 21, and which may be referred to in the course of this trial as 'the county road'. . . ." Is the Crown doing it on purpose? Is this strategy? Jack looks at the jury: twelve drowsy men. What follows is a baroque account of how long it takes to jog while pushing a wheelchair from the PMQs to Rock Bass, linger long enough to violate and murder a child, then jog back again in order to return to the PMQs by a certain time. The judge grimaces and shifts in his seat.

It is not physically possible for Rick to have committed the crime at Rock Bass, then returned to the PMQs via the route he claims to have taken, in time to arrive home when his mother and several witnesses will say he did—including his basketball coach, who received a phone call from him from a phone number that Bell telephone records will confirm is the Froelichs'. The time when Rick left for his run and the time when he returned are not in dispute. All that is in dispute is where he went and what he did in between. " . . . you will hear that the accused claims to have exchanged a greeting in the form of a wave with a passing motorist, an air force man, on the King's Highway Number 4, and you will hear a police inspector tell you that, despite a thorough investigation. . . ." Jack blinks twice rapidly, his eyes stung by salt sweat.

### SUNSHINE, LOLLIPOPS AND PUP TENTS

MIMI HAS TOLD MADELEINE that she would rather she didn't play with Colleen Froelich "for the time being," or spend so much time over at the Froelich house. She has been careful to explain to Madeleine that it's not because there is anything "bad" about Colleen or the Froelich family, it's just that the Froelichs have a lot on their minds these days. Madeleine was guiltily relieved. The Froelichs' house has become dark in her mind. So has Colleen—she is halfway to Claire.

Summer holidays. *No more homework, no more books! No more teachers' dirty looks!* Glorious June. Madeleine spent the morning with Auriel and Lisa, running through the sprinkler in their bathing suits, until the pool opened over on the base. Then they put on their bright new thongs, still springy at the heels, grabbed their beach towels, sunglasses and Auriel's transistor radio, and headed over for three hours of splashing, cannonballing, choking, and stinging water up the nose. "No running on the deck!" They sunbathed on the Riviera with Troy Donahue and shrieked with laughter when Roy Noonan's swim trunks ballooned in the water. When they returned to the PMQs, hungry for lunch and replete with sun, there was a moving van in Lisa's driveway.

Now the three of them sit in Auriel's pup tent, peeling her sunburn. They are so much older and wiser than when they last gathered in this enchanted orange twilight and watched the dust motes float across the triangular mesh window. Auriel's mother has allowed them to bring their pyramid of peanut-butter-and-jam sandwiches into the tent in honour of Lisa's farewell. The girls knew the moving van was coming today but it is still a shock to see it: the yellow ship rocking across the painted waves. The Ridelles are moving to B.C.

"Wow," says Madeleine, peeling a perfect strip of translucent parchment from Auriel's shoulder. "It's got like fingerprints on it, and little holes like for your hair and everything." They examine the gossamer moult, reducing it to powder between their fingers.

The three have exchanged comics and promises of undying friendship. They have agreed to write, and not to start shaving their legs or having a boyfriend without first informing one another.

"I know," says Madeleine, "let's meet in the schoolyard in the year 2000." Auriel's eyes widen, extra blue against her freckles, which are browner against her sunburn. Lisa opens her mouth in silent wonder, her hair almost white with summer.

Auriel stretches out her hand, palm down. Lisa places hers on top of it, and Madeleine places hers on Lisa's. *All for one.*

It is on the tip of Madeleine's tongue to suggest that they become blood sisters, but she hesitates. There is a whiff of disloyalty in the notion of being blood sisters with anyone but Colleen. There is also a corollary effect: the taint of knowledge—of some shame—that Madeleine associates with Colleen, even though she never told her about the exercises. Inside this pup tent, Madeleine is a normal, carefree girl. There is no need for blood.

They have brought out their autograph books. Madeleine opens hers and flips forward, looking for the first blank page after Germany—the printing from grade three looks glaringly childish. The name *Laurie Ferry* rises from the page but it's a moment before a face takes shape to go with it . . . *your best friend.*

Lisa writes in Madeleine's book, *Yours till the U.S. drinks Canada Dry, love your best friend (not counting Auriel) Lisa Ridelle.*

*Yours until Niagara Falls,* writes Madeleine.

And Auriel writes, *If you get married and have two twins, don't come to me for safety pins! Love Auriel Boucher.*

The smell of chlorine and canvas will forever be the smell of best friends and sweet summer.

Auriel and Lisa hug each other. Madeleine looks away, worried lest things start to get mushy—*parting is such sweet sorrow, doc.* She stares at the crumbs on the floor of the tent, feels the flattened grass beneath it—*this is the last time I will ever sit in this tent.* The Bouchers are moving too. Mr. Boucher will roll up this tent tomorrow and pack it into their VW van.

Lisa blurts out that she is in love with someone and now she will never see him again. "Who?" both Madeleine and Auriel press her.

Lisa shakes her head, then finally cries out, "Mike McCarthy!"

"You love my brother?"

Lisa buries her face in her hands and nods.

Then Auriel declares her love for Roy Noonan, "even though he's such a square!" Madeleine gapes in amazement and switches on the transistor. Like a sign that they really will remain friends forever, their theme song comes on, "It's My Party." They stare at one another, open-mouthed with delight and disbelief, and sing their hearts out along with Leslie Gore, crying if they want to. Tears sting Madeleine's eyes, still stripped by chlorine, and she sings louder.

That afternoon, the moving van heaves away round the corner like a huge beast and disappears, and the Ridelles' house sits empty and blank.

"WERE YOU ACQUAINTED with Claire McCarroll?"

"Yes sir. She lived four doors down from my house on St. Lawrence Avenue. My daughter Lisa attended Brownies with her, and they were to attend a flying-up ceremony together that evening."

Steve Ridelle is standing in the witness box. He is in uniform.

"During the happenings in question here, doctor, what appointment did you hold?"

"I was senior medical officer at the Royal Canadian Air Force Station Centralia."

Jack should be at work, but he has taken another day of leave. It is just after ten o'clock, the temperature outside in the square is eighty-six degrees today. Higher in here. In the row ahead of him, people have already begun to fan themselves slowly with hats and newspapers. In the back, the row of reporters bends to write.

"Dr. Ridelle, are you familiar with the place referred to as Rock Bass?" asks the Crown attorney.

"Yes sir, I am."

"Were you a quarter-mile west of there, between a cornfield and a woodlot, in a field lying fallow, on the morning of April fourteenth, Sunday?"

"I was."

"And did you see there a body?"

"I did."

"Will you describe the scene as you saw it?"

Jack is here because Henry Froelich told him that medical evidence would be presented today. He wishes to hear the total absence of direct evidence linking Rick to the scene. He is here because he cannot stay away.

Yesterday the Crown attempted to read out Rick's statement, which the police had taken immediately after his arrest, but the defence objected because neither a lawyer nor a parent had been present at the time. The judge sent the jury out while he listened. As Jack expected, apart from a couple of places where the boy was obviously rambling with exhaustion, there was nothing remotely incriminating. The jury returned and Jack watched their faces as they learned that the judge had ruled the statement inadmissible; surely they were bound to assume there had indeed been something incriminating in the statement—otherwise, why would the defence have objected? Couldn't the judge have anticipated that?

"The body was lying flat on its back with the lower limbs, the two legs, parted. Under a tree, an elm. The body was clad in a blue dress. . . ."

All the witnesses are repeating what they have said many times, and speaking as plainly as possible—the way one is trained to communicate in the military. No narrative inflections to lure the listener or to warn of a bump in the road.

"It was—the body was covered by reeds, I should say bulrushes, and flowers, wildflowers, although due to the rain and, I think, probably animals—"

"Was the face visible?"

"The face was covered."

"With what?"

"A pair of underpants."

"Cotton underpants?"

"Yes sir."

Steve Ridelle received his posting in May, and he has lost no time moving his family. He has returned in order to testify.

"Are these the underpants?"

"Yes."

Jack watches the Crown attorney return the patch of yellowy cotton to the table up at the front. Exhibit number 49.

Sharon McCarroll is no longer present. She has returned to Virginia to be with her mother.

Photographs are produced, the jury is sent out, a *voir dire* ensues, the jury is brought back in and the pathologist is called.

"The stomach was removed as a whole and was held over a sterile jar and was opened so that all the contents went straight into the jar which was then sealed and labelled. . . ." Jack glances across the room. Blair McCarroll is still here. It isn't right that he should hear this. ". . . the jar up to the light to see what we could see and we saw a small amount of brownish. . . ."

The next half-hour is taken up with parsing the contents of the snack. It is tricky, establishing time of death via stomach contents. Digestion is not an exact science. It can accelerate or it can slow, depending on circumstances—such as fear.

McCarroll is staring at the back of the bench in front of him, his expression neutral.

Blood was taken from her heart. Her heart was weighed. It was normal. Her height, her weight, everything was normal. "The patient had marks upon the neck. . . ."

The *patient?* Jacks looks up.

" . . . bruises on the windpipe but no sign of a ligature, and the face was grossly congested, was bluish black. Bluish, anyway. . . ." A pair of hands. Thumb marks on the windpipe. Her non-fatal injuries were examined. Steve is recalled.

" . . . there was no pubic hair, and on the right-hand side of the outer lip there was an area where the skin, the superficial topmost layer of skin, had been ripped right away over an area about the size of my fingernail. . . ."

His Lordship says, "The right-hand side, is that what you said?"

"I said 'the right.' As far as I can remember, it was the right."

"Is that the girl's right?"

"Yes, the girl's right, I'm sorry."

Jack knows from the press that the child was raped, and yet. . . .

" . . . and it was bruised and the whole of the entranceway was widely dilated."

"Pardon?"

"Widely dilated."

Is it a failure of his imagination that Jack never anticipated these details? He glances around and wonders if others did. Toward the back he sees a familiar face. The schoolteacher, Mr. Marks. He looks like an overgrown child. It would not have been worth beating the can off him. In the same row is the pretty young woman teacher who leads Madeleine's Brownie pack. Did either of these teachers imagine they'd ever hear one of their pupils described in this way?

" . . . masses of maggots about in this region, and on removing the maggots it was quite obvious this area was grossly bruised. . . ."

Jack has told Mimi to be prepared to move within weeks. She has already cancelled next fall's dental checkups for the kids. Madeleine will testify some time next week, and her testimony will put the kibosh on this travesty.

"Concerning the injury in the outer labium and to the vagina," asks the Crown attorney, "has that any significance to you?"

*Any significance?* "A female child at that age would have a hymen, which is something through which you cannot normally insert a little finger, and that was completely missing, it had been completely carried away. . . ."

Jack permits his mind to run elsewhere. He is expecting a call from his contact in Ottawa any day now. A teaching post has opened up at the Royal Military College in Kingston. He is a shoo-in for it.

Although just about any place will do.

The Crown attorney says, "In your opinion, Doctor, how were these injuries caused?"

"In my opinion—"

The defence says, "My lord I don't want to unnecessarily interrupt, but might I suggest that in view of the changes, post-mortem changes that this man found in this area, that it would be extremely dangerous for him to express any opinion at this time because he told us he found some very serious post-mortem changes in this area . . ."

Is the defence logic garbled or is Jack merely having difficulty concentrating? His mind drifts sideways again. *Changes*. A gentle word, yet not a euphemism. We change from the moment of conception and we do not stop changing until we change back into earth. It's a kind of miracle, thinks Jack. This return to earth . . . *to land a man on the moon, and return him safely to earth*. That indeed would be a feat, but to return a man to earth after he has died is far more complex.

"No, listen to the question as put—"

As miraculous as conception. The intricate particle-by-particle detachment and falling away of our bodies. It takes years. A longer gestation than birth.

"Are these lesions a type of injury you would expect to see with some large object dilating this area?" asks the Crown.

The defence attorney interrupts, "My lord, I suggest that it would be dangerous for the doctor to—the doctor is not a pathologist, my lord."

"You might demonstrate later on that it is of no particular weight," says the judge, "but I think the doctor is entitled to give his opinion as to what caused these changes, since he was at the autopsy, and we shall see what the pathologist says later."

Jack looks at the defence lawyer, expecting him to object again, but he doesn't. Things seem to have speeded up. Something is changing. . . .

The Crown says, "Dr. Ridelle?"

"Would you repeat the question, please?"

Why is Steve even up there? He's a GP, not a—

"Is it possible these injuries are consistent with a very inexpert attempt at penetration?"

Dr. Ridelle says, "Possibly."

"Such as by an inexperienced or immature male?" says the Crown attorney.

The defence attorney interrupts, "My lord."

The judge says to the jury, "Gentlemen, you are to disregard the Crown attorney's last question, you are to put it from your minds."

Lunch.

# The Home Front

JACK STEERS THE RAMBLER into the PMQs, hoping to get a glimpse of his kids before they head back to school for the afternoon. He has no more patience for the courtroom. Besides, he has heard all he needs to hear—or not hear—of the day's proceedings: there was no physical evidence to place Rick at the scene. There was not even semen, nor a trace of the chemical that semen changes into after it decomposes. The rain may have destroyed it. The maggots. But there would have been something left, inside her, and there wasn't. Had there been, the police lab could have determined blood type and ruled Rick either out or in. As it is, there is not a scrap of direct evidence. The defence will make this clear after lunch, surely, during cross-examination. How much is Hank paying that guy? He'd better start living up to those letters after his name.

He turns onto St. Lawrence and sees a moving van in the Bouchers' driveway. Perhaps it's time to pass his hat around the mess again, before everyone is posted away. As he slows toward his driveway, he notices that the Froelichs' front lawn is yellowing—he'll get the sprinkler out this afternoon and run it for them. After he mows it. He pulls into his driveway.

The absence of sperm makes it impossible to prove that she was penetrated by a penis at all. The child was raped, but perhaps with something else. Perhaps with a blunt object used by some sicko who turns to little girls because he can't get it up the normal way—or can't climax and therefore can't ejaculate. Neither would describe a healthy teenage boy. Surely that will not be lost upon the jury, who were all teenagers once. Teenage boys can be brutal, but only an older man could be that warped and impotent. He gets out and slams the car door shut, picturing some sorry specimen in his fifties, thick fingers, *thumb marks on the windpipe*—he locks the car door—then unlocks it, because he never locks his car, no one does—then locks it again, because Mimi may wish to use the car after dark and what if . . . ? Then he unlocks it, because this is ridiculous.

No one is home. Of course, they are across the street. He tosses his hat onto the halltree. It's Mimi's day to look after the Froelich kids. The women have been wonderful—although there are fewer hands since the Ridelles moved away, and now Betty Boucher is all but gone. Vimy Woodley has been good about pitching in but they're moving too. That leaves Mimi.

By September, a quarter of the PMQs will be filled with new families. They won't know the Froelichs personally. They will only know what they have read in the papers. Jack pours himself a Scotch and takes the newspaper to the couch.

Mimi is standing over him.

"What's wrong?" she says.

"What?" Where is he? On the couch. Must have fallen asleep.

"What are you doing home?"

He grins—his mouth is dry—and gets up. "Playin' hooky," he says, heading for the kitchen with his empty glass.

"You were at the trial."

"I dropped in this morning." He runs the cold water.

"You took another day of leave."

"We've got the whole afternoon to ourselves, what do you think, Missus?" He winks at her and gulps the water.

She joins him at the sink, pulls on a pair of rubber gloves, opens the cupboard below, bends, takes out that ragged dress and puts it on. Ties an old diaper around her head and kicks her high heels into a corner. He watches as she fills the bucket at the sink, clunks it to the floor, plunges a brush into the foam, then gets down on her hands and knees and starts scrubbing. "Move your feet," she says.

"Hi Dad." It's Mike.

"What are you doing home from school?"

Mike rolls his eyes, but Jack remembers as soon as he asks: it's summer holidays. "Don't be smart," he says. "Where's your sister?"

"How should I know?"

"What did you say, mister?"—his hand opening, lifting.

"Jack," says Mimi, and he stops himself.

Mike ducks out of the kitchen. A crescent of soapy water sloshes past Jack's shoes. "She was in the front yard this morning," says Mimi. "Mike took her swimming this afternoon, now she's in the Bouchers' backyard, I'm her mother, if you want to know where she is, ask me, not your son." And keeps on scrubbing.

Jack leaves. Winds up at the mess; it's peaceful this time of day. He settles in by a window overlooking shrubs and the green sweep down to the tennis courts. He sips a Scotch and reads *Time*. President Kennedy has committed sixteen thousand combat troops to Vietnam.

When he gets home, the table is set for two, the kids are nowhere to be seen and Mimi says, "I'm sorry, Jack."

He's tired and his head is aching, but she has made coq au vin and he must be hungry, he has had no lunch. "Holy liftin', a gourmet meal," he says.

She pours him a glass of wine. "Jack, I don't want to be a bitch, I'm just worried."

"I don't think they'll convict, honey, I really don't. Can I have a glass of water?"

"No, I'm worried about Mike."

"Mike?"

"He quit."

"Quit what?"

"Baseball. And he broke a window—"

"He—?"

"Don't be mad, it was an accident. Over at the rec centre."

Jack sighs, nods.

"And I'm worried about—" Tears fill her eyes.

"What's wrong, baby?"

"Our holiday." She weeps. "You're using up your leave and you— I want to see my mother."

He takes her in his arms. "We'll go right after the trial, I promise. I got plenty of leave left."

"Jack," she says. She has put on perfume, he can smell it. He feels silk brush his back as she gets into bed next to him—the emerald negligée he gave her for Christmas. "Jack." She strokes his shoulder.

She has rubbed cream into her hands to soften them. She feels terrible that she let him see her that way—in her work clothes—but he must have known the house doesn't stay clean on its own.

"Smell nice," he mumbles.

"Jack. . . ." She touches her lips to his ear.

"Where's the Aspirin, baby?"

She gets up, returns with a glass of water and two pills. "Is it bad?"

"Naw," he says, rolling to face the wall.

"*Pauvre bébé*"—massaging his neck.

He reaches back and pats her on the hip. "Thanks for dinner, it was great." He sleeps.

He is up and gone before Mimi wakes—there are his pajamas on the floor. She folds them, then goes into the bathroom. Someone is mowing a lawn nearby, she can hear the motor, and there is the particular smell of gasoline and cut grass that she associates with weekends, not Friday mornings. She brushes her teeth, and out of the corner of her eye she registers someone mowing the Froelichs' front lawn. She glances, then stares; it's her husband. Closing in on a shrinking square of overgrown grass in the centre of a perfect green carpet. The Froelichs' front door opens and Karen Froelich comes out with a steaming mug. She hands it to Mimi's husband.

Madeleine sits with Rex in the cindery strip between grass and street. She steers an ancient Matchbox truck through roads she bulldozed with a piece of roof shingle. She knows she is too old to play in the dirt by herself with someone's dog—maybe I'm retarded and don't know it.

There is a U-haul in the Froelichs' driveway. Her father saw it too, from the kitchen window, at breakfast, and said he was going over there to "see what's up." But her mother got the idea to go on a spur-of-the-moment camping trip, and told him to help her pack instead.

Madeleine is half hoping that Colleen may come out of the house and say hi. She is always at the trial, and when she comes home it's late in the evening, after visiting Rick. But today is Saturday, and the U-haul says that any minute the Froelichs will come out of their house and start loading something into it. Or maybe they are going to buy something. A new couch. Madeleine hears her name being called—"Madeleine, *on y va*"— and joins her brother and parents in the Rambler.

"No one ever asked me," Mike mutters under his breath at the back of his father's head. He spends the whole drive ignoring Madeleine and thumping his fist into his baseball mitt.

When they return Sunday evening, the U-haul is gone and so is Ricky's home-made hotrod. The Froelichs' house sits empty. "What the heck is going on?" says Jack, standing in his driveway, fists on his hips, looking across at the purple house.

At first, Madeleine thought her father was offended because the Froelichs had decided to move without telling anyone, or saying good-bye. But it turned out the Froelichs had lost their PMQ.

# How

*Ousque ji rest? Chu en woyaugeur, ji rest partou.*
*Where do I live? I am a traveller, I live everywhere.*

Métis voyageur, Minnesota, 1850s

"I CALLED HQ," says Hal Woodley, "but my hands are tied."

Hal is cleaning out his desk. The handover parade is next week. A new CO will take formal command of RCAF Centralia. The air force band will play, officers, cadets and other ranks will be in their uniforms—a dazzle of gold braid and, for the wives, new spring hats. Jack knows nothing about the new CO, but how reasonable is it to expect that he would lift a finger to help Henry Froelich? Hank is not even military personnel.

"Did they at least tell you why they turned him out on the street?" asks Jack.

"Froelich's no longer eligible for housing because he's no longer employed by the local school board."

"They fired him?"

"'Chose not to renew his contract' is the official word." Hal takes the framed photo of the Avro Arrow off his wall and places it in a box.

"How's your young gal—Marsha—doing?"

"Well, she's . . . she's young, she'll be okay. We've sent her to stay with her aunt out west."

Jack knows the girl was taken out of school before the end of the year. According to Mimi, she had to be sedated when she heard about Ricky; Elaine told her that Steve has since prescribed a mood-elevating drug. But time heals, and in just a month the Woodleys will be at NATO headquarters in Brussels. Jack feels a pang of envy, then remorse when he recalls the Froelichs. Stuck here and virtually homeless. "Hal . . . what are the chances that a well-placed phone call to the school board from someone like yourself might—?"

"Tell you the truth, Jack, it's probably for the best. What kind of life would the Froelichs have here after what's happened?"

"But the boy will be acquitted, don't you think?"

"Probably. But the damage is done."

Jack nods. Extends his hand. "Raise a good glass of German beer for me, will you, sir?"

"Will do, Jack."

Mimi and Mike have headed off to a movie together, over on the station—*The Sands of Iwo Jima,* starring John Wayne as a hardbitten Marine sergeant. Jack pointed out that "for a fella who never saw action, he sure gets a lot of credit," but Mike just shrugged. Jack had officially grounded him, but Mimi told her son that, although she was not usually partial to war pictures, she'd heard this one was good. Jack gave her a look—what's the point of punishing the boy if you're going to turn around and spoil him?—but she ignored him and the pair left the house.

Jack watches them walk up the street and, when they have disappeared around the corner, turns and calls over his shoulder, "Where's my little buddy?" Then, "Hop in the car, I'm going to get my ears lowered."

In Exeter, Madeleine chats with the barber and the men who play checkers outside, and they get her to do her impression of Sammy Davis Junior. The barber gives her a Crispy Crunch bar and they head over to the A&P to pick up a few things.

It's fun grocery shopping with Dad. He buys all kinds of things Maman never would: store-bought cookies, precooked ham in tins, a barbecued chicken, ready-made potato salad and Wink, the world's best lemon-lime soda. They shop quickly, without looking at any price tags, and Dad tells her to pick out a treat from the store freezer. She chooses a rainbow Popsicle, which she splits in half by cracking it against the curb in the parking lot.

"Where are we going?" she asks, because he has pointed the car north, instead of south toward Centralia.

"We're going to drop in on some old friends."

They drive fast up Highway 4, then veer left on Number 8 toward Lake Huron. "Are we going to Goderich?" she asks—*maybe we're going to visit Ricky at the county jail.* But they turn inland again just south of Goderich, crunching over gravel, then dirt, until they come to a farm— at least, it used to be a farm. The barn is in a state of slow collapse, its boards half consumed by the earth already, and the yellow brick farmhouse has had its eyes nailed shut with planks. In the field there are not crops but rows of trailers. A hand-printed sign announces "Bogie's Trailer Park." They drive slowly over ruts, Jack looking to left and right. They pass a shed with another scrawled sign, "Office," followed by a list of "Camp Rules," the letters jamming up toward the bottom of the board. Some trailers have flower boxes and paper lanterns. Some even have patches of grass. Others have rusty barbecues and no awnings. They pass the showers, equipped with another list of rules. Madeleine says, "There's Colleen."

She has had no time to worry about how to act when she sees Colleen again because she had no idea where they were going. Now she is unsure. Is Colleen mad at her? Is Madeleine supposed to talk about Ricky, or not mention his name? Is she supposed to act really serious? Or really funny?

Jack pulls up and Colleen sees them. She is carrying a bucket of water. "How do you like your new digs, Colleen?" he calls out.

"It's okay."

Madeleine decides to try to act normal, but not disrespectfully so. Like at a funeral; you shouldn't stare at the dead body, but you should remember it's there.

"Hi," she says.

Colleen leads them a short distance down a rutted "street" to where a wooden ramp zigzags up to the screen door of a dirty white aluminum box, rust stains bleeding from the eaves. Rex barks and gets to his feet.

"How come you got him tied up?" asks Madeleine.

"Rules," mumbles Colleen, as she hauls the bucket toward the trailer.

Madeleine hugs Rex and feels his warm breath down her back. Oh, it's good to feel his fur against her face and to smell him again. His fangs glisten in his pink gums as he grins at her.

"Don't put your face so close to the dog's," said Dad quietly as the screen door opens. "Howdy, strangers," he says.

"Jack," says Karen Froelich, and walks toward him with hands outstretched.

Henry follows and shakes his hand. "Come in, come in, have a glass of wine."

Karen says, "Let's sit outside, Henry, it's nicer."

"Yes, it's nice out."

"How are you, Madeleine?" asks Karen.

"Fine thank you, Mrs."—then blushes as she remembers Mrs. Froelich's long-ago request—"Karen."

Karen puts an arm around her, laughing. "Go in and find Colleen, she could use a good laugh, go on, babe."

Madeleine hesitates, then walks up and opens the screen door. Behind her she hears her father say to the Froelichs, "We can't stay long."

Jack takes the groceries from the car and piles them onto the wooden ramp, over Henry and Karen's protestations. He holds his glass as Henry fills it with red wine, and he tries to keep his eyes on him, aware they keep straying to Karen. Somehow, despite her dusty black flip-flops and the dirt between her toes, she manages to look oddly elegant, her long fingers pale and perfect, a beaded bracelet around her wrist. . . .

"How are you, Jack?" And he is struck by it again, that quality she has—alone among women, in his experience—of seeming to see him, to address him, directly, as who he is, without any accessories.

"Can't complain," he answers, and shifts his eyes back to Froelich.

Madeleine enters the trailer, and treads carefully amid the rubble of toys and clothes so as not to wake the babies, who are sleeping on a cot. The interior is positively neato, with miniature everything—a real icebox that uses a real block of ice, bunk beds and shelves that fold into the walls. A Coleman stove, a blackened pot. There is no electricity and no tap over the sink. The Froelichs are on a permanent camping trip.

"Hi Elizabeth."

"Ay Ademin."

"Watcha got?"

Elizabeth shows her. A paperweight from Niagara Falls. Shake it and snow drifts down over the *Maid of the Mist*. Naturally, as long as Elizabeth holds it, it is always snowing.

"That's beautiful."

In the dusk of the trailer, Colleen turns to Madeleine. "Want to see something?" She leaves the trailer through a low flap at the back, and Madeleine follows. It feels so good in the dying light, the cool of early summer, to be following her friend over ruts and ridges through the tall grass. Colleen is barefoot but Madeleine has on new plaid runners, her bare ankles already wet with "snake spit." She does not call, "Wait up!" because Colleen stays the perfect distance ahead, brown and bright in the last light like a copper penny.

Colleen stops at a wire fence and says, "Shhh." She slips between horizontal metal strands, careful not to touch them, whispering, "It's an electric fence." Madeleine ducks and slips between the wires, death three inches above and below her, thrilled with fear. "Don't worry, it won't kill you, just scares the cows," says Colleen when Madeleine is through.

But there are no cows in the field, which is rapidly shifting from gold to pink; only ponies. Three of them. Colleen walks toward them and, as though they have been expecting her, they turn and canter over. Serious tall dogs, they vie with one another to nuzzle her. She gives them something from her pocket and strokes their soft noses. She encircles the neck of one with her arms and, in a motion so effortless it could be from a film played in reverse, slides up and onto his back. She pats his neck. "Hop on."

Madeleine doesn't want to ask how. Colleen reaches down, Madeleine grasps her arm just below the elbow and jumps as Colleen pulls. "Hang on."

It hurts, but Madeleine would not choose to be anywhere else as they walk, then trot.

"Use your legs," says Colleen.

Across the field, onto a path between the trees, ducking branches, then out again onto a smoother meadow, tender green-to-mauve alfalfa. Madeleine hangs on for dear life, her legs around the pony's wide back, arms hooked around her friend's bony ribs, wondering how Colleen manages to stay on and steer at the same time.

"Rick showed me," Colleen says.

They slow to a walk and Madeleine turns to look back at their wake, a darker green gash already closing up behind them. They rock slowly toward a dip lined with trees and the most magnificent willow she has ever seen, a palace of a tree with a west wing, an east wing, turrets and a moat. "Here's my camp," says Colleen.

There is a small firepit and, under a rock, her tobacco, rolling papers and matches. She lights up. The pony drinks from the stream below. They lean back and look up at the first stars appearing in the intensifying blue. *This is the life, pardner.* "Hey Colleen. Is it an Indian custom— I mean, Métis?"

"What?"

"Being blood sisters."

"How should I know, I got it off a movie."

Colleen passes her the cigarette and Madeleine takes it, careful to betray no surprise. She holds it smouldering between index and middle finger, flooded with forbidden glamour—but she does not yield to the temptation to do Zsa Zsa or Bogart. She simply takes a puff and is immediately seized with a fit of coughing, eyes streaming, marvelling through the pain at how something so insubstantial as smoke can sear like a hot blade. When she can breathe again, she hands it back and says, "*Ci pa gran chouz.*"

Colleen laughs.

Madeleine reaches for a blade of grass. "We could light outta here," she says, chewing the tender pale shoot. "Head for the territories."

"What territories?"

"Well. You know, we could just ride away."

Colleen takes a drag from her cigarette. "You always run into something no matter where you go. Turns out you're someplace after all." She exhales. "Know what I mean?"

Madeleine feels her eyes widen in mystification, but she nods and, in a tone she hopes sounds both weary and comprehending, replies, "Yeah."

She is about to suggest that they make a fire when Colleen says, "That's what happened when we exscaped from the training school."

"Is that when you rode to Calgary?"

"Yeah." Colleen spits out a speck of tobacco, narrows her eyes and runs the tip of her tongue along her lower lip. "They brung us back."

"How come you . . ." Madeleine doesn't want to sound as though she is correcting Colleen, so she likewise says, "exscaped?"

"'Cause there was one or two sick fuckers there, eh?"

Madeleine's desire to build a fire dies even as it occurs to her to wish she had brought a jacket. When she speaks again she tries to sound casual, this time not in order to convince Colleen that she knows what Colleen is talking about, but in order to reassure herself that she does not. She forms a polite question. "What did they have?"

"Not a disease, *Dummkopf*," replies Colleen.

Madeleine swallows and waits. She doesn't know the way back to the car. She doesn't know where they are or how long it has taken to get here.

"They were sick in the head," says Colleen. "They liked little kids."

Madeleine stares at the cold firepit and doesn't ask.

Colleen says, "Know what I mean?" Madeleine shakes her head. "Good," says Colleen. "Hope you never find out." She takes a big drag.

Madeleine starts to shiver. She concentrates on the red ember glowing at the end of Colleen's cigarette. The world seems suddenly huge and chilly, a place where she might roll and rattle about endlessly, like a marble. She watches the red dot arc from Colleen's fingers down into the stream, where it sizzles and disappears. She wants to go home and watch television, she doesn't want to live in a trailer after all.

Colleen stands up and makes a clicking sound with her mouth, and the pony turns and shambles up to them. Madeleine gets up. She waits for Colleen to mount first, but Colleen says, "Hop on." Madeleine feels too heavy to jump up this time, but before she knows it Colleen is boosting her. She swings her leg over and lurches forward, grasping a handful of mane as the pony shifts his weight. Colleen says, "Hang on," and starts to run. The pony follows, and Madeleine does hang on.

By the time they get back to the trailer it's dark, the crickets are singing and Madeleine's legs are still trembling, her heart still ping-ponging.

Colleen says, "You can come back and ride any time you want."

The grown-ups are sitting out front on kitchen chairs, with glasses of wine, and Elizabeth is wrapped in a Hudson's Bay blanket, asleep in her wheelchair. A kerosene lamp burns on a stump and Mrs. Froelich is bent over Rick's guitar, strumming and singing softly, "'Where have all the flowers gone, long time passing, where have all the flowers gone, long time ago . . . ?'"

A lump forms in Madeleine's throat, and she hangs back in the deeper shadow of the trailer. She watches Colleen walk into the pool of light and Mr. Froelich's encircling arm. Madeleine skirts the light and comes up behind her father. She leans on the back of his chair and he says softly, "Did you have fun, sweetie?" She nods, even though she is behind him. They wait until the song has ended, then Jack gets up.

Karen puts her arms around him and says, "Thank you," in his ear. He feels her about to step back again, and holds her briefly. He feels her return the pressure of his embrace for an instant, then she turns away. It has taken all of a few seconds. Henry Froelich grasps his hand with both his own. "*Danke,* Jack. You are a *Mensch.*"

As they pull away, Madeleine folds her arms on the open window frame, rests her chin, and watches the Froelichs recede into the night. Colleen raises her hand so Madeleine does too, and waves goodbye.

But Colleen is not waving. She is simply holding her hand up, perfectly still. Like an Indian in a western: *How.* Confident that she will not be giving offence by following Colleen's lead, Madeleine stills her own hand. And in doing so, she realizes that Colleen is not saying *How.* She is showing Madeleine the scar in the palm of her hand.

The Rambler rounds a bend in the track, and the light of the Froelichs' patch of world disappears.

When they pull into the driveway, Madeleine says, "Dad, I just remembered something."

"What's that?"

"I'm not allowed to play with Colleen."

"You're not? Who told you that?"

"Maman."

Jack hesitates. The lights are off in the house, Mimi and Mike are still out. He says, "Well, I won't mention it if you don't."

When he makes love to his wife that night, he imagines a thinner woman—her hair less rich, her cheek almost gaunt, her body less supple—a woman less beautiful than his wife.

# To Tell the Truth

*"Huck, they couldn't anybody get you to tell, could they?"*

*"Get me to tell? Why, if I wanted that half-breed to drownd me they could get me to tell . . . "*

*"Well, that's all right then. I reckon we're safe as long as we keep mum. But let's swear again, anyway. It's more surer!"*

*"I'm agreed."*

*Mark Twain,* The Adventures of Tom Sawyer

THE BOUCHERS' HOUSE sits blank at the corner of Columbia and St. Lawrence. Like Lisa's and Colleen's and Claire's, it no longer remembers Madeleine or how she so often entered its front door and played in its rooms and backyard. Her footprints and those of her friends, the echoes of their voices etched in the air, all have disappeared. The houses are waiting for the next families to move in and to believe that they own them, that the things they do beneath those roofs and on those lawns, the games, the meals, Christmases and dreams, are tangible, indelible. Where do they go? All the remember-whens?

The night before Madeleine is to testify at Ricky's trial, Mimi makes her favourite supper: wiener schnitzel. She takes it straight from the frying pan and puts it onto Madeleine's plate, saying, "What would you like to wear tomorrow, *ma p'tite?*"

"Something not too scratchy," says Madeleine.

Mike says, "How come I can't go?"

"You've got baseball practice," says Jack.

"I quit."

"That's what you think," Jack says, and salts his schnitzel.

Madeleine looks up at her father to see how angry he is, and he smiles at her.

"Madeleine wants me come," Mike says gruffly. "Don't you?"

Madeleine looks from her father to her brother and mumbles, "Yeah."

"See?" says Mike.

Jack ignores the boy.

Madeleine says, "How come I have to testify when I already told the police?"

"That's part of our justice system," says Jack. "The accused and the public have the right to hear all the evidence in open court." It will all be over soon. "And you'll be under oath."

"Do I have to swear on the Bible?"

"Yup," says Jack. "Just tell the truth, like you did last Halloween," he tells her.

Madeleine's stomach closes.

Mimi says, "What about last Halloween?"

Jack says, "That's classified," and winks at Madeleine. She forms a smile with one side of her mouth. He reaches over and pats her on the head, saying, "We're right proud of you, sweetie."

"I've got a stomach ache."

"You've got butterflies in your stomach," he says. "That's natural." Madeleine sees butterflies—a storm of them—yellow. . . . "Just tell the truth."

Mike says, "You better or they'll hang him."

Jack slaps the table, and Mimi jumps along with the cutlery. "That's not true," he says. "Where'd you hear that?"

"Everyone's saying it."

"Who's everyone? Arnold Pinder's father? Answer me."

"Jack," says Mimi.

Jack takes a breath and says to his wife, "What's for dessert?"

Jack tucks her into bed next to Bugs Bunny and obliges her by kissing the rabbit's plastic cheek. "Why don't we read something?" he says, putting down his Scotch, reaching for the book on her bedside table, *Alice's Adventures in Wonderland*.

"Dad?"

"Yeah?" He flips through the book.

"Sometimes is it—? Can a lie ever be good?"

He glances up. "What that's, sweetie? What do you mean?"

"Like. Say . . . in a war."

"You mean when a soldier is being interrogated by the enemy?"

"Yeah."

"Well, the best policy is to say nothing at all—apart from your name, rank and serial number. If you lie, you might get caught in it."

"What if there isn't a war on?"

"Well, I'll tell you, it's almost never all right to lie. Lies are self-perpetuating, do you know what that means?"

"No."

"It means that one lie leads to another, until you have what's known as a domino effect."

Dominoes is a game. Everyone gets it for Christmas. No one knows how to play it. Now is not the time to ask about dominoes. "But Dad?" Now is also not the time to mention someone's life depending on a lie in a courtroom, because Dad will know she is talking about Ricky Froelich and she will have no choice tomorrow but to tell what she really saw— didn't see. Even Madeleine's questions are lies designed to hide what she is really asking. "What if you have to tell a lie to make people believe the truth?" she asks.

He lowers his glass and looks at her. From the mouths of babes. She can't possibly know anything. He sets the book aside. "Why do you ask that?"

Madeleine swallows.

"Have you been reading something, old buddy? Did you see some-thing on TV that made you wonder?"

She nods, yes—she is not really lying. She has been reading some-thing. She has seen things on TV. They often make her wonder.

He takes a big breath and smiles. "You're going to be a lawyer when you grow up."

"I don't want to be a lawyer, Dad."

"You can be whatever you want to be, you can be an astronaut, or an engineer—"

"I want to be a comedian."

"That's right." He laughs and rubs her head. "You've posed a very complex question. You've got a good head on your shoulders."

Madeleine feels sorry for her father. He thinks she has a good head on her shoulders. His *Deutsches Mädchen*. His spitfire. He doesn't know she is a liar. His sore eye looks sad. "Thanks," she says.

She sees him as though through the crack in the door of a dark clos-et. She is in among the coats and battered board games, and he is out there sitting innocently on the edge of her bed, tucking her in. When she comes out of the closet, the shadows follow her but he doesn't see them. Because he is good.

He says, "That is what's known as an ethical question." *Ethical*. It sounds like gasoline. He says, "Sometimes, the truth lies somewhere in between."

*The truth lies.*

"Sometimes, you have to assess the whole situation. Do what's known as a cost-benefit analysis, to see how the truth will best be served. That's also called diplomacy."

Sometimes, with Dad, you ask for one definition and you get the whole dictionary.

"Nine times out of ten, however, the truth is pretty cut and dried."

"Like at Halloween?" she asks

"What about Halloween?"

"When I hit the tree and wrote stuff in soap?"

"You wrote stuff in soap?"

Madeleine reddens. "Yeah."

"I don't remember that. . . . You soaped someone's windows?"

"Yeah."

"Oh. Whose?"

" . . . A teacher's."

"I see." He nods. "I don't think you mentioned that."

Madeleine shakes her head. "But I told on myself."

"Good. You told your teacher? And what did he say?"

"He said, 'I won't tell if you don't.'"

"Well, he was as good as his word. What did you write?"

Madeleine looks at her bedspread. Chenille highways, mountain paths leading in all directions. "A word."

"What word?"

"A bird."

"You wrote the name of a bird? What kind of bird?"

"Um"—she swallows—"peahen."

"Peahen?" He smiles. "What'd you write that for?"

Madeleine shrugs.

"Was that something you learned in Mr. Marks's class?"

"March."

"Was that part of your science lesson?"

"Health," says Madeleine.

"Health? What's that got to do with health?"

"Exercises."

"What exercises?"

"For muscles."

"What's a peahen got to do with that?"

"It's a girl peacock."

"I know what it is, I just don't see what it's got to do with health class."

Madeleine doesn't say anything. Jack looks at her. "No wonder you soaped his window."

Madeleine waits.

"It was wrong, but you owned up to it."

She nods.

"It takes guts to tell the truth sometimes. That's what you've got. Let me tell you something, old buddy. If you ever find yourself wondering what's the right thing to do—because, as you get older, you'll find the truth is not always what it seems—when you find yourself in a tough situation, just ask yourself, 'What is the hardest thing I could do right now? What is the toughest choice I could make?' And that's how you'll know the difference between the truth and a whole bunch of . . . excuses. The truth will always be the hardest thing."

His knuckles are white around his glass, with its slick of ice and amber at the bottom.

"'Night-night, sweetie."

### Regina vs Richard Froelich

*'Give your evidence,' said the King, 'and don't be nervous or I'll have you executed on the spot.'*

*Lewis Carroll,* Alice's Adventures in Wonderland

Madeleine is standing on a box in the witness box. It's like a penalty box for one.

"Speak up."

"Pardon?"

"I said, what is your name, little girl?"

Madeleine looks up at the judge. He has a big frog face.

"Madeleine McCarthy."

"These gentlemen want to hear you—" Off to one side, on chairs ranged like bleachers, a bunch of old men sit facing her. They already look disappointed.

"The jury needs to hear you," says the judge. "What is your name?"

"MADELEINE McCARTHY!"

He looks startled. Titters from the audience. Madeleine looks out; smiling faces. Where is Dad? Where is her mother?

"Well, Madeleine, how old are you?"

"NINE!" Laughter.

"Order, please."

She is not trying to be funny, only obedient. But the judge doesn't sound mad. "You don't need to speak quite so loudly, Madeleine."

"Sorry."

"That's all right. Do you know what it means to take an oath?"

"Yes."

"What does it mean?"

Ricky Froelich is sitting at a table in front. He is taller. Bony. He is looking at her, but it doesn't seem as though he is looking at anyone he knows. She smiles at him.

"I don't think I will swear this child," says the judge.

Madeleine looks up again—what was the question? She is in trouble now. A tortoise in the court of King Arthur.

"My lord, that is entirely up to your discretion," says Mr. Waller—he is Ricky's lawyer. He has bags under his eyes but his black gown shimmers and floats when he moves. "Though I would like the child to be sworn if possible."

"I know you would like it, Mr. Waller, but that is not why we are here. What grade are you in, Madeleine?"

"I'm going into grade five, your honour." Not too loud, not too soft, look at the judge, pay attention or you will not get to swear.

"My lord," says the judge to her.

"Pardon?"

"In Canada a judge is addressed as 'my lord,' or 'sir.'"

"My lord," trying not to do an English accent—*don't be smart.*

"We have television to thank," he says, and people titter again.

There's Dad. Sitting next to Maman, a few rows behind Mr. Froelich and Colleen. He winks at her. She smiles back as discreetly as she can, and feels like a puppet.

"What does it mean to take an oath, Madeleine?"

"It means you swear to tell the truth."

"To tell the truth," he says. "And what is that?"

Is this a trick question? Is he talking about the TV show *To Tell the Truth? Will the real Madeleine McCarthy please stand up?* What does he mean?

"What is *To Tell the Truth?*" she repeats.

"Do you know the difference between a lie and the truth?"

"Yes your ma—my lord." *Your majesty?!*

"What is the difference?"

"The truth is when you say what happened when someone asks you, and you don't leave anything out just to try and make them believe something else, and you don't act like they're only asking you only one exact thing, you have to tell everything and that's what 'the whole truth' means." She takes a breath. She feels clearer, as though she has just woken up.

The judge nods. "I wish more adults had a similar grasp. What grade are you in, Madeleine—rather, who is your teacher?"

"My teacher last year was Mr. March."

"Did you like him?"

"No," she says, and everyone laughs.

"Order please, ladies and gentlemen, I would ask you to remember why you are here." He looks back at her. "You are being truthful, Madeleine, that's good."

Halfway toward the back, Jack smiles and feels his face relax back into flesh. It had tightened across his bones like a burn; he was shocked, like everyone else in this room, by what a little girl said this morning under oath.

"You live in the Permanent Married Quarters with your family?"

"Yes sir," replies Madeleine.

"Do you go to Sunday school?"

"We call it catechism."

"What church do you go to?"

"We're Catholic."

"Roman Catholic, I see. I think this girl might understand."

Who is he talking to?

Jack licks the corner of his mouth. A young child, no older than his daughter—a friend of hers if he is not mistaken, pretty little thing; Marjorie. Where did she get her dreadful story? He watched the jury turn to stone as the child testified. But if Madeleine is sworn, her testimony will count. All Rick needs is reasonable doubt. And Madeleine will provide that. She will corroborate what Elizabeth Froelich so painfully tried to communicate to the jury this morning. Karen was there to translate. The Crown turned this to his advantage, claiming the mother was putting words in her daughter's mouth, since she was the only one who could understand what the poor girl was saying. It ended with Elizabeth in tears, her testimony struck and Mr. Waller—and, by extension, Karen Froelich—chastised by the judge for subjecting a "poor crippled child" to such an ordeal.

The judge turns to Madeleine again. "Do you know you are under obligation here to tell the truth?"

"Yes, my lord," says Madeleine.

"Do you understand that?"

"Yes."

"What is that brooch you are wearing?"

"It's a lighthouse."

"Where is it from?"

"It's from Acadia"—this poor brooch was touched by Mr. March— "my mother is Acadian." Mr. March never would have touched it if I weren't ashamed to speak French. "We speak French," she says.

"I think we should swear this little girl."

*I passed.*

Jack wipes a trickle of sweat from his temple. It's almost over. He longs to undo the top button of his shirt but he doesn't wish to worry Mimi, sitting next to him; he's been a little short of breath lately. The little girl, Marjorie, was convincing. And the statement taken from the absent one, Grace. . . . Jack shivers. Innocent children. How could they know of such things?

"Bailiff?" says the judge.

A pot-bellied man in a uniform approaches Madeleine. He looks like Mr. Plodd, the policeman in *Noddy*. He has handcuffs on his belt and carries a big book in his hands.

Jack stares at the back of Froelich's head, then Rick's. Froelich is a good man, but naive. Where is the boy from? Where was he before the age of twelve? In some institution. Terrible things may have happened to him there. Children learn what they live. Jack knows Rick is innocent of the murder charge, but is it possible that what those little girls said is true? Has he interfered with children? With Madeleine?

"Place your right hand on the Bible."

Jack watches as his daughter is sworn. If anyone has touched her. . . . He feels—almost hears—something bend, like a twig, in his left temple. He blinks. He sees his daughter suppressing a grin as she listens to the bailiff—he can tell she is trying not to laugh. She's fine. This experience will roll right off her back. He would know if anyone had touched her—Mimi would know. . . . But something must have happened to those other two little girls. Where were their parents? Jack glanced at Squadron Leader Nolan's face while his daughter gave her testimony. Where was he? If Ricky Froelich molested those children, he deserves to be up there. With that thought, something releases at the base of Jack's skull. His headache—the low-grade one he has ceased to notice—unlocks and begins mercifully to seep away, like runoff down a grate.

" . . . so help you God?"

Madeleine says, "I do." *You may now kiss the bailiff.* She looks out, expecting Dad to be beaming, but he is just watching her steadily. So is Colleen. And Mr. Froelich.

She is ready. *To Tell the Truth,* with Kitty Carlisle and your host. . . .

"Did you know Claire McCarroll?"

She feels hot again. "Yes."

It's Ricky's lawyer. He is on our side.

"Were you a friend of Claire's, Madeleine?"

"Yes."

*Then why didn't you take care of her?* Madeleine's stomach goes gluey.

Mr. Waller says, "Do you know Ricky Froelich?"

"Yes."

"Was that a yes?"

The judge says, "Yes, yes, it was a yes, the witness nodded, please proceed, Mr. Waller."

"Were you in the playground with Claire and the other children on the afternoon of April tenth?"

"Yes." She has to go to the bathroom.

"Speak up, please."

"Yes."

"Did Claire tell you—?"

The judge says, "None of that, Mr. Waller."

Mr. Waller continues, "What did Claire tell you?"

"She told me she was—"

"Speak up, Madeleine."

"Pardon?"

"What did Claire tell you that afternoon, the afternoon of the tenth of April, in the schoolyard?"

"She said she was going for a picnic with Ricky Froelich."

Mr. Waller's shimmering silk robe has begun to look like the uniform of the losing team. He says, "What exactly did Claire say?"

"She said, 'I'm going for a picnic with Ricky Froelich.'"

"And what did you say?"

"I said—I sang—I hummed 'Beautiful Dreamer.'"

"Why did you do that?"

"'Cause everyone knows—"

The judge says, "Only say what *you* know, Madeleine."

"Because I knew she made things up. Not lies, just . . . her imagination."

"Why did you think she made it up?" asks Mr. Waller.

"Because she wanted to go for a picnic with him."

"No, let me—what I mean is, Madeleine, what made you think that it might just be Claire's imagination?"

"Well, one time she told me they went to a dance together at Teen Town."

"And had they?"

"No. Only teenagers are allowed. And she said she was going to marry him."

Madeleine smiles to show that she isn't criticizing Claire, but no one else is smiling. There is a table full of things over there in front of the jury. A jar of something brownish. A rag with yellowy spots. Bulrushes. Claire's Frankie and Annette lunchbox. It's like show-and-tell. What's in the jar?

"What did you say, Madeleine?"

Did she ask it out loud?

The judge says, "Cover that table back up, and keep it covered."

Someone coughs. Mr. McCarroll is sitting on the other side of the aisle from Ricky. He is wiping his lips with a hanky. Seeing him gives Madeleine the idea to call on Claire when she gets home this afternoon. Then something jumps behind her eyes—like when you turn a light switch off and on really fast—and her brain flicks on again and says, "You can't call on Claire, she's dead." Madeleine knows that's true, but there is something else underneath her brain that wants to walk her feet down the street and call on Claire. Something that knows Claire is still there in the green bungalow, if only someone would go and call on her.

Mr. Plodd covers the table with a white sheet.

"And who else was there when you said—hummed, rather—'Beautiful Dreamer'?" asks Mr. Waller.

"Um. Colleen."

"Colleen Froelich?"

"Yes. And Marjorie and Grace."

"So they overheard Claire say that she had received an invitation—"

The judge says, "Mr. Waller."

"My lord, I am establishing that Marjorie Nolan and Grace Novotny had a basis for concocting—"

"I know what are you doing, Mr. Waller, and you will refrain from it."

Jack works through the logic of the two girls' testimony this morning and finds it flawed. Their story hinges on the claim that Rick asked them to go to Rock Bass that day, presumably to do what he had done to them in the past—namely, molest them. And that when they refused, he asked Claire and she obliged—she must have, because she went with him. But Jack knows that Rick didn't take Claire to Rock Bass. Therefore, it's reasonable to conclude that he didn't invite her. Thus the claim that he only invited her because the other two little girls turned him down falls apart. Rick never invited any of them, because he had no intention of molesting anyone at all.

His neck begins to tighten again. The idea that he could have breathed a sigh of relief at the notion of his friend's son being a child molester—when did I become that kind of man? All the little girls had crushes on the boy, it's that simple, and that innocent. Jack is relieved to have unflinchingly faced the most unpleasant part of himself. There is no necessity for Ricky Froelich to be guilty of anything. Besides, he will go free because Madeleine will say which way he turned. Jack reaches for Mimi's hand and squeezes it to reassure her.

Mr. Waller says, "When did you last see Claire McCarroll that day, Madeleine?"

"Me and Colleen—Colleen and I went to Pop's—"

"What is 'Pop's'?" says his lordship. "I don't recall 'Pop's.'"

"It's where we got grape pop," says Madeleine.

"'Pop'? Is it Pop or Pop's?" says the judge.

*Pop goes the weasel!*

"My lord, 'Pop's' is a local variety store," says Mr. Waller.

"Is it relevant?"

"No, I don't believe it is, my lord."

"Then keep moving through, Mr. Waller, you're taking five steps when you could be taking two."

Madeleine has tucked her chin in to keep from laughing, but that always makes her eyes bug out. There is nothing safe you can do with your face except forget about it.

"Where did you go after that, Madeleine?" asks Mr. Waller.

"We were going to the willow tree—"

"The willow tree at the inter—? Where is the willow tree, Madeleine?"

"At the intersection."

"And which direction would you turn if you wanted to go to Rock Bass?"

"Right."

The judge says, "Do you mean to say you would turn right to go to Rock Bass?"

"Yes, my lord." She didn't mean to use the English accent, but the judge seems not to have noticed.

"Good," says Mr. Waller. "And you and Colleen were on your way to the willow tree at the intersection."

"We were going cross-country." She looks out and meets Colleen's eyes.

"And you could see the willow tree?"

She looks back at Mr. Waller. "Yes."

"And you had a clear view of the intersection."

"Yes."

"And what did you see?"

"We saw—"

"Only what *you* saw, please."

"I saw Ricky and Rex and—"

"Who is Rex?" asks the judge, sounding exasperated.

"The dog, my lord," says Mr. Waller. "Go on then, Madeleine."

"And Ricky was pushing Elizabeth in her wheelchair, and Claire was on her bike and Rex was towing her up the road."

"And they were travelling toward—in which direction were they travelling?"

"Toward the tree."

"The willow tree."

"Yes."

The judge says, "The willow tree and the intersection are one and the same for your purposes, gentlemen." He is talking to the jury. He turns back to Madeleine. "And then what did you see?"

"We—I saw, um"—Madeleine swallows—"a red-winged blackbird." And her throat dries.

Mr. Waller doesn't say anything. He is waiting for her to remember her lines. But Madeleine is silent. Like the frog in the cartoon, who can sing opera but, at the moment of truth, opens his mouth and says, *ribbit.*

You can hear the creak of the ceiling fan, but you can't feel any breeze.

Mr. Waller says, "Yes, and what did you see then, when you looked at the intersection?"

Madeleine's chest is pounding, it has started to do that on its own. She is breathing through her mouth even though that dries her throat to the point of paper—it will hurt to swallow. Like the time she had her tonsils out and could eat only ice cream.

"Madeleine?"

The judge is looking at her. "What did you see?"

"Look at me, please, Madeleine," says Mr. Waller.

The ceiling fan grows louder in her ears. Where is Dad?

He is looking at her, his face tilted slightly. Pale and shiny. *Guts, that's what you've got.* He crashed his plane. *That's what you're made of.* The right stuff. *The truth will always be the hardest thing.* Stab right through, like the coat hooks going straight through your back. Stab through and you will never have to go back there again. Nothing will ever press at your back again. *Do the right thing.*

Dad nods gently. *Pilot to co-pilot.* Do it your way, sweetie. Tell the truth. And she does.

Her parents are quiet in the car. Up ahead, a pink plywood ice cream cone tilts toward the highway, but she knows they will not be stopping, because of the silence. She is relieved because she doesn't feel like ice cream. Maman is angry. She yanked Madeleine all the way to the car, and Dad followed.

The Rambler slows and her father pulls in. "How about an ice cream?" He glances at Madeleine in the rearview mirror.

"Jack, I don't think it's a good idea."

"She's earned it, don't you think?"

Madeleine forms a smile for him. He is not disappointed. He wants to get her an ice cream. Her mother says, "Jack," but he is already getting out of the car.

She waits in silence with the back of her mother's head.

After she told the truth, Mr. Waller sat down and the other lawyer came up to her in his gloomy black robes. "Why did you lie to the police, Madeleine?"

"I'm sorry," she said.

"You've been a very good witness, Madeleine, you've told the truth. No one is going to be angry with you here today, but it is important for us to know why you told the police that you saw Ricky turn left, when you didn't."

"'Cause I—" Her throat was no longer dry, but neither were her eyes, they were filling up like dishes, yet she didn't know what was so sad. As though she had just heard about a dog dying.

"Speak up, Madeleine."

"I was worried that he would. . . ."

"What were you worried about?"

"That he would get hanged."

There was a sound in the room. "Order," said the judge. "Let this child finish her testimony. You're doing very well, Madeleine," said the king of the frogs—he was not unkind.

"Now Madeleine," said the winning lawyer, and Madeleine was on her guard, for he sounded as though he was trying to coax something out of her. "Who told you that?"

"No one," she said.

"You're under oath, young lady," said the judge.

And suddenly it no longer counted that she was a little girl. Perhaps she wasn't any more. Perhaps twenty years had passed and she was a grown-up, she felt her neck begin to stretch effortlessly like Alice in Wonderland's, and her head begin to rise—soon she would be at the ceiling, getting her head chopped off by the fan.

"Who told you he would be hanged, Madeleine?" asked the lawyer.

She returned to her normal size. "Everyone says it but it's not true."

"Can you give me an example of a particular person?"

"My brother said."

"Your brother?"

"Yeah, Mike said."

"And who else?"

" . . . My friend."

"Which friend?"

Dad returns and hands Madeleine a triple-scoop Neapolitan, but he has not bought himself one to share with Maman. The car pulls from the gravel back onto the highway. Madeleine wishes she could accidentally drop the ice cream out the window, but that's out of the question. So she eats the whole thing as quickly as possible.

The courtroom was as hot as an oven. Everyone was perfectly still. They were all being baked into gingerbread boys. Madeleine's tears didn't fall, they evaporated. She looked at Colleen. *When the oven door is opened, she will leap from the pan and run away. We will run away together.*

"Colleen," she said.

"Colleen Froelich?"

Madeleine nodded.

"Was that a yes?"

Madeleine nodded again.

"Yes, the witness nodded yes," said the judge. "Go on, Mr. Fraser."

"Did Colleen tell you to lie, Madeleine?"

Madeleine didn't answer.

The judge said, "Answer the question, Madeleine."

But Madeleine didn't speak or even move her head.

"Madeleine," said the judge, "look behind you. Who is that lady?"

"Our gracious queen."

"Do you know that we are here today in her name? When I or this gentleman asks you a question, it is exactly as though our queen were asking. Would you answer the queen?"

Madeleine nodded.

"Would you lie to our queen?"

Madeleine shook her head.

"Now, Madeleine," said the judge, "did Colleen Froelich tell you to lie?"

Madeleine said, "I told myself."

Dad stops the car outside Exeter so she can be sick.

Maman says to him, "I told you."

"I don't think you're going to get much more out of this witness, Mr. Fraser," said the judge, and he seemed to forget all about her once he said, "You may step down, little girl."

Mr. Fraser turned away from her and went back to his table. Madeleine waited. There was something not finished. *He didn't do it.* That was what she had been waiting to tell them. Ricky Froelich turned left, he did not do the murder. *Ask Elizabeth.*

She said, "Elizabeth—"

And the judge said, "The queen has finished with you for now, young lady, please step down."

"Not the queen—!" she cried.

"Bailiff?" Mr. Plodd came walking toward her.

"Stop!" A woman had spoken, and she was making her way down the aisle. Maman.

The judge said, "Madam, please be seated."

"*C'est assez,*" said Maman, clicking toward the witness box on her high heels.

"Madam, please! Bailiff."

Mr. Plodd reached out his hand to Madeleine, but it was slapped away and Maman's hand was there, with its red nails. It took Madeleine by the wrist and pulled her from the box and up the aisle. A jumble of faces bobbed by—Colleen looking straight ahead, Mr. Froelich with his head down, and Dad looking at her and Maman as though they were the last two people in the world he expected to see here.

"We'll have a short recess," said the judge behind her.

"Jack, *allons-y!*" called Maman from the door of the courtroom.

Madeleine ran to keep up with her mother's grip, down the waxed corridor, between the paintings of men in robes, past a name on a door that leapt out at her, F. DONNELLY, QC.

Maman wipes Madeleine's face with a wet-nap and they get back into the car. One good thing about stopping for ice cream at that roadside place in the middle of nowhere: it means they didn't stop for ice cream in Crediton, where Mr. March lives.

"I want us to leave tomorrow, Jack." She unzips her dress, steps out of it, takes a hanger, sticks it into the dress as though she were handling a boning knife and jams it into the closet.

"We can't just up and leave." He is standing, still dressed, with his arms folded.

"Why not? You up and go to that trial any time you want."

"It'll be over in a few days."

"Are you going back?" yanking off her earrings.

"I'm not leaving before it's over."

"Why not?"

"I can't do that to Henry, I can't—they're going to have to appeal."

"So?" She pulls her slip off over her head, turns her back to him and removes her bra.

"The guy's broke."

"We don't know that." She pulls on a nightgown.

"You haven't seen where they're living."

She turns to him. "And you have."

He hesitates, but why should he? "Yes I have, I visited them, so?" He instantly regrets the defensive *so?*

"So? So what, you tell me what's so?"

Normally he would tease her about a turn of phrase like that, but not tonight. "Nothing," he says. "What are we talking about?"

"They're not our family, Jack. That's not my son."

"The kid is innocent."

"Maybe not."

"He is."

"How do you know?" She looks at him. He doesn't answer. "Madeleine was sick to her stomach because she knows you wanted her to lie."

"I didn't want her to—"

"What's going on!" She has screamed at him.

He says very quietly, "Mimi," making a calming gesture with his hand.

She screams in a whisper, "I want to know!" Slaps her hairbrush against her thigh. "Why do you care so much about that family?!"

He waits.

"You care more about that boy than you do about your own son."

"Mimi, that's not—"

"And you don't want another baby." Her face trembles, but she compresses her lips and doesn't take her eyes off him. "Do you?"

"What are you talking about?"

"That's why you hardly ever—" She bites her upper lip and takes a deep breath, tears standing in her eyes.

"Mimi, what could possibly give you the idea—?" He moves to her, opening his arms.

"Don't touch me." Her voice has cooled. "That family, they're having terrible trouble, but it has nothing to do with us. Does it, Jack?"

He says nothing.

She opens her jewellery box and says, "What's this?"

A scrap of paper. "What is it?"

She hands it to him. "That's what I'm asking to you."

He reads: *cherries, cognac, caviar.* . . . Fried's shopping list. He looks at her.

"For how long?"

He's cautious. "What do you mean?"

Her voice is trembling. "You cut their grass, you're at their house, you leave your office in the day—I know, I call and they can't find you. You go in a staff car to God knows where; I answer the phone, there's no one there." Her voice lurches up but she catches it, poised at the edge of tears. "Goddamn, if I'm going to cry, you're not going to see."

"Mimi. Do you think—?" He smiles in spite of himself, knowing he sounds guilty. She turns away from him. He laughs. He sounds stupidly fake to himself; think how he must sound to her.

"Mimi, that list was for Buzz Lawson, he forgot his anniversary and I was going in to London anyhow so he asked me to pick up some—you know Buzz—Mimi, look at me."

"I don't believe you."

"You think I'm interested in Karen Froelich?" He chuckles, but she turns and stares at him.

"You see? I didn't even have to say her name."

He feels his face suspended in jovial bewilderment, the picture of masculine guilt—he doesn't need a mirror to know it.

She gets into bed. "We have to go tomorrow, Jack."

"Mimi—"

"I'm going to sleep." And she turns out her light.

His grin corrodes and his throat begins to rust. His eyes sting salt. If only she would turn and look at his face now. He wouldn't try to hide it. She would say, "Jack, what's wrong?" And he would tell her. *It was me. I waved.*

He waits, motionless, but she doesn't turn or open her eyes, and he has lost the power of speech.

Madeleine takes a long time to fall asleep. Her parents have been fighting. She has never heard them do that before. Not for real. Maman must be terribly angry at Madeleine for lying to the police. And even angrier at Colleen for telling her to. She will never be allowed to play with Colleen Froelich ever again.

She hugs Bugs and rolls onto her stomach, where it's safer. She remembers that Colleen will probably not want to play with her ever again anyway. And she is relieved.

She wakes up screaming and spends the rest of the night sleeping in her parents' bed with her mother. A dog was barking in her dream. It woke her up, but she knew she must still be dreaming because, when she went to her window, her curtains lifted in a breeze she couldn't feel. At first she thought her curtains had a new pattern, because they were covered in yellow butterflies. Then the butterflies began to move and she saw that they were real ones.

Dad picked her up out of bed and hugged her. She asked him, through hiccups, what had happened to that dog that was trapped in the storm sewer the night of flying up. At first he didn't seem to remember, then he said, "Oh yeah, I remember. I think the fire truck came and they got him out."

"They did?"

"Oh yeah. They brought him home, he's fine."

And she didn't ask any more questions.

Dad put her in bed with Maman and left the room. He was not in his pajamas yet. She whispered, "Maman?"

"What is it, Madeleine?"

"Can you tell me the story of Jack and Mimi?"

"*Non, pas ce soir, Madeleine. Fait dodo.*"

"Sing '*O Mein Papa.*'"

"Go to sleep, Madeleine. Think nice thoughts."

Madeleine has a sore throat. She stands on her front lawn, staring across the street at Rex's old front lawn. Mimi says, "Get in the car. Madeleine. I said, *viens. Main-te-nant!*"

She gets into the back seat, alone. Mike is riding up front. Dad is staying here. It will be the back of Maman's head all the way to New Brunswick. The Rambler reverses out of the driveway. Slowly, because it's her mother driving. She watches out the rear window as her house recedes, along with Colleen's and Lisa's and Auriel's, and Claire's; like the word repeated on the Donnellys' tombstone, *Empty, Empty, Empty, Empty. . . .* Until they turn the corner and her white house with the red roof is out of sight.

"Goodbye Rex." She says it very softly because her throat is sore. She asks, "When are we coming back?"

"When the holidays are over," says her mother, annoyed.

"I never said goodbye to Rex."

"Come off it," says Mike in the front seat, and Maman doesn't reprimand him.

Her tears feel hot as hot water from the kettle. Her mother and brother don't see her crying. She lies with her face wedged in the crack between the seat and the backrest and feels her tears slime onto the plastic. *Poor Rex.* She whispers the words through her tears, dark and thick as woods and she can't find her way out of the Black Forest, *poor Rex.* She takes a deep breath but she's careful to make it smooth, so that, if her mother or brother happens to glance back, they will think she is sleeping, *poor Rex will think I went away without saying goodbye.*

She sobs quietly. Just before they get onto the 401, they pull over and Mike buys her a Nutty Buddy. He climbs into the back seat beside her. "Here you go, Rob."

She is more grateful to have him hogging the back seat again than she is for the treat, which she takes with a stoic smile.

But all the way to New Brunswick, all the way to their next posting and the one after that, all the way to the day when Madeleine left home and got her own place and decided not to finish university, she could still cry fresh hot tears from the kettle every time she pictured Rex's face. Even though he had already moved away with his family to the trailer park by then, she pictured him—and in future would insist to Mike that Rex had been—standing there on the front lawn of the purple house that day, watching as she drove away in the Rambler, wondering why she left without saying goodbye.

## THE QUEEN'S MERCY

IT TOOK THE JURY all of two and a half hours to find him guilty, "with a plea for mercy."

The judge said, "Richard Plymouth Froelich, the sentence of this court upon you is that you be taken from here to the place from whence you came and there be kept in close confinement until Monday, the second day of September, 1963, and upon that day and date you be taken to the place of execution, and that you there be hanged by the neck until you are dead, and may the Lord have mercy on your soul."

Jack has no memory of leaving the courtroom. Henry Froelich was mobbed by reporters the moment the verdict came down, Jack couldn't get near him. Nor did he seek out the inspector, the judge, the Crown attorney. . . . He needed to tell Simon first. He drove the staff car back to Centralia. He parked it at the ME and walked, out of habit, toward the phone booth at the edge of the parade square—but there was no need. His wife and children had left him three days ago, no one would be home to overhear his conversation, so he passed the phone booth and continued toward the PMQs as the evening sun sank behind him.

There was a moving van in the Froelichs' driveway—a new family arriving. A man and woman waved at him but Jack didn't wave back. It was as though he were seeing them from behind a transparent barrier thick as ice; it didn't even occur to him to wave back. He entered his empty house. His empty kitchen.

Now he picks up his phone and dials the night number but there is no answer.

He is alone. It is dusk. He reaches to the cupboard above the fridge and takes down a fresh bottle of Scotch. He will keep trying the night number. Failing that, he will wait until morning, call Simon at the embassy and ask how long his people in the Soviet Union will need to get themselves out of harm's way, if they haven't done so already. Then he will tell Henry Froelich the truth; he will put on his uniform and go to the police. He considers heading over to the airfield now, to see if he can find the key to the Ford Galaxy in the tall grass, but thinks better of it and pours himself a drink. The police will have plenty of time to get out there with metal detectors in the next few days.

He tries the night number every half-hour.

At three A.M. he opens the drawers of Mimi's dresser, then her vanity, to find only winter things remaining. He buries his face in her sweaters but it's no good, they have been dry-cleaned. He kneels at her side of the bed, not to pray but to smell the sheets. It's useless, she changed them before she left. He returns to the kitchen and rifles it until finally, in the drawer beside the phone book, he finds something useful. Her recipe box. He opens it and up wafts vanilla, butter—he takes out a card covered in her indecipherable hand, the ink brighter in places where grease has stained it. He stares—a recipe for bran muffins, as far as he can make out—and begins to weep.

He fell asleep at some point, on the couch. When he opens his eyes, the morning sun is blaring through the living-room window. He sees with relief that the bottle of Scotch on the coffee table is only half empty—it's safe to stand up, so long as he does so slowly.

He doesn't open the door to get the paper off the front step—he knows what the headline will be. He waits until nine o'clock, when the British Embassy in Washington is open for business, and reaches for the phone, but it rings, startling him.

Karen Froelich's voice asks, "Jack, has Henry been out to see you?" Henry drove off in their car last night with a reporter.

"Henry called a reporter?"

No, the reporter was present throughout the trial. After the verdict, he helped them to their car, escorting them through the crowd of other reporters and photographers. He got in and drove to the trailer park with them. He said he had heard through his police sources that Henry had spotted a war criminal, and he wanted to know why it hadn't been brought up at the trial. When Henry told him, the reporter said he believed Rick had fallen victim to a grave miscarriage of justice. He said the investigation might have been tainted by anti-Semitism.

"Our lawyer said not to say anything before the appeal," says Karen, "but Henry was so relieved that someone finally—"

"Where's he from, *The Globe?*"

"No," says Karen. "The *Washington Post.*"

"The *Post,* that's great."

So it will all be coming out soon. Jack will have only to fill in the missing piece of the puzzle, and this thing will be all over the American and Canadian papers in a matter of twenty-four hours. He's relieved.

"Don't worry, Karen, it's going to work out, I guarantee your boy will—"

"Jack, he isn't home yet."

"No, but he'll win on appeal—"

"No, Jack. Henry. He hasn't come home. I told you. Last night. He hasn't called, I'm—" He hears her voice catch, but she sounds calm again when she continues. "I called the police but they told me they can't consider him missing until—"

"Karen, don't worry. He probably stayed out all night with this reporter—you know Henry, once he gets talking. . . ." He can almost hear her smile, eager to believe him. "This is great news about *The Washington Post.* Did he tell you where they were—?"

"No, I figured they'd go into Goderich for dinner, but—"

"Have you been to—?"

"I don't have the—"

"Right, Henry's got the car. Listen, don't worry. I'll drive up to Goderich right now, if you like, and—"

"No, you don't have to—"

"I'll come out to the trailer park—"

"No, Jack. Don't come out."

He pauses. She's right, he shouldn't go out there. "Karen, keep me posted, okay? Okay?"

"Okay."

"And if Hank turns up across the street, three sheets to the wind and looking to get into your old house again, I'll drive him straight home to you."

"Thanks, Jack." Her voice already sounds far away, as though she is diminishing, like the picture on a television screen, toward a vanishing point.

He calls Washington.

"British Embassy, good morning."

The same pleasant female voice—she'll put him straight through when she hears who's calling. "Major Newbolt here for First Secretary Crawford."

"I'm sorry, sir, there's no Crawford here."

"This is the British Embassy."

"Yes sir, but—"

"Then give me Crawford, this is urgent."

"Sir, I'm afraid you have the wrong—"

"Like hell, you tell him Jack is on the line."

"I'm afraid I can't help you, sir."

And she hangs up. He calls back and gets a busy signal.

He stays by the phone all day in case Karen calls, in case Henry calls, in case Simon calls, in case Mimi calls. But it's silent. He doesn't sleep that night. He lies on the couch, attuned to every sound, every car headlight panning across the ceiling.

In the morning he picks up the newspapers from the front step; he throws yesterday's away and unfolds today's. In the bottom left-hand corner of the front page, just above "Your Morning Smile," a reproduction of Henry Froelich's school board photo and three inches of print. *The father of convicted sex killer Richard Froelich is missing and feared dead. Henry Froelich's station wagon was found parked on the U.S. side of the Peace Bridge yesterday morning by New York State Troopers. No suicide note was found, but. . . .*

Jack reads and rereads the brief article. There is, of course, no mention of a mysterious war criminal. No mention of a reporter from *The Washington Post*. He pictures the row of sweltering men at the back of the courtroom, in wrinkled suits, notebooks in hand. Reporters—except for one of them. And he was there from the beginning. When did Simon tell the CIA about Froelich? When Jack threatened to come forward with the alibi? Or earlier? When Jack first mentioned Froelich's name? Is that what happened to Froelich? Is Jack next? The question doesn't frighten him; it makes him weary.

He puts the newspaper down and calls the movers. He will pay out of his own pocket to have his household put in storage at a warehouse in Toronto. Either his contact in Ottawa will come through with the posting—any posting—or Jack will retire from the air force. Regardless, at the end of this week, he will fly to New Brunswick and get his wife and children back.

He doesn't tell himself that he won't let Ricky Froelich hang. Anything he says now will be like shouting into a storm at sea. And if someone actually did hear him, where would that leave his family? Without a provider? Like the Froelichs?

He goes down to his basement and rummages until he finds the cardboard moving boxes neatly collapsed and stacked by Mimi last August. He begins unfolding and reassembling them.

*Part Four*

## What Remains

*"My father told me that in whatever tunnel or cave you may dig, you find the bones of the dead."*

*Primo Levi, "Lead,"* The Periodic Table

When stories are not told, we risk losing our way. Lies trip us up, lacunae gape like blanks in a footbridge. Time shatters and, though we strain to follow the pieces like pebbles through the forest, we are led farther and farther astray. Stories are replaced by evidence. Moments disconnected from eras. Exhibits plucked from experience. We forget the consolation of the common thread—the way events are stained with the dye of stories older than the facts themselves. We lose our memory. This can make a person ill. This can make a world ill.

In 1969 a rocket piloted by men reached the moon. Men walked there. They were changed by the sight of the milky blue jewel of Earth across that vast darkness. But we were not changed. If anything, the story of flight and the dream of space were treated to a cold shower of the "it really happened" variety. We had moon rocks for a while, parades, and a sense of Western military superiority extrapolated from the physical feat of reaching an impressive target. Then we forgot about it. On to the next.

We continued, however, to have faith in Armageddon—a myth that will never disappoint, because either it will never happen or, if it does, we will not be around to puzzle over the pieces of the shattered story. Space race was outstripped by arms race. Our weapons became even more terrifying because they could now be delivered anywhere, any time. And there were so many more of them. The Bomb was like democracy—only a few countries could be trusted with it. This fact justified our preference for tyrants, and the contained wars that kept the dispossessed busy buying weapons and killing one another, far from our doorsteps. It made us rich.

In the meantime, we lost interest in the moon. We have some difficulty now in looking up to her for inspiration, or for confirmation at the moment of a kiss, because, after all, we've been there. We've had her. She put out. We think we know all about her, we think we know how NASA did it. How Apollo, the sun god, got to her. But the fuel, the thrust, the heat shield, they are not the whole story, they are just the evidence, part of which is missing. Not hidden—the facts lie scattered and dismembered. In plain sight. Perhaps, if we collected all the pieces where they lie snagged like bits of Lego, tiny army men in the grass, and laid them all out, they would turn back into a story and we could discern its meaning. We could begin, once more, to care that three brave men went to the moon in 1969.

"To tell" means to count. Like a bank teller. Even an accountant deals in narrative, and the storyteller too is a kind of accountant. Each provides an audit of events and their cost, and it's for the listener to decide—was it worth it?

The price of the rockets is the account of how they were born, not simply of how they flew to the moon. The latter account—on its own—is a story with its feet cut off. Lame, like the child who was spared the mountain fate when the Pied Piper led the children away. Until we listen to the story, we have not paid the Piper. And he will continue to take our children.

The evidence shows that the rocket was launched from Cape Canaveral, but the story tells us that it was fired where it was forged, deep within the earth—illuminating a giant grotto, its ceiling lost in shadow, its floor littered with bones and rust, embedded with the vertebrae of train tracks. And that when it rose, clean and white, to breach the mouth of the mountain cave, it trailed flames and blood and soil as it flew all the way to the moon.

The cave is yawning open still. Emitting a draft, exerting a pull.

We were supposed to think it all began with NASA. But it began with the Nazis. We knew this, half remembered it, but a great deal was at stake and we put it from our minds. Events without memory. Bones without flesh. Half a story—like a face gazing into an empty mirror, like a man without a shadow.

What do shadows do? They catch up.

# And That's the Way It Is

*These fragments I have shored against my ruins. . . .*

*T.S. Eliot,* The Waste Land

WHERE IS JACK? He's reading his newspaper. Please do not disturb him.

He left something back there in 1963. Stepped out of it like stepping from a stream, and the current that had borne him along went on without him, water disappearing round a bend.

When you are in it, the current feels inevitable. When you step out of it and have to walk, nothing is inevitable. You notice time, bowed closer and closer to the earth by the weight of what you carry on your shoulders. The newspaper is a soothing companion, filled as it is with pieces of time presented to the reader pebble by pebble, but never as a bird's-eye view. Turn the page and the pebbles collapse into dust, to be replaced tomorrow: *Scientists Track Chernobyl Cloud. Afghan Freedom Fighters Repel Soviet Invaders. Prehistoric Fish Discovered.* Crinkle of the turning page. A woman's voice reaches him, as though through parting mists. "I said, Jack, do you want some hot?"

"What's that—? Oh, *merci.*" *Crinkle.*

To see Jack reading the paper, edges gripped, is to see Jack for the past twenty-some-odd years. Not that he hasn't been busy. He got his posting and moved his household from Centralia in August '63. He taught leadership and management to the officer cadets at the Royal Military College in historic Kingston, with its antique forts and cannons still aimed at the Americans across Lake Ontario. He retired from the air force when they moved to Ottawa in the early seventies, and opened his own management consulting firm. "I'm a glorified accountant," he liked to joke. He did well. They put in a pool. And until the heart trouble, he had every intention of pulling up stakes and moving with his wife to Bahrain or Saudi Arabia or some other friendly foreign part. Run an oil refinery. A hospital. Managerial skills are endlessly transferrable nowadays.

There is no longer an RCAF anyhow, the yahoos on Parliament Hill have seen to that. Jack hates the vulgar synthetic green uniform that all personnel now have to wear, obliterating the distinctions among land, sea and air. In summer, a cheap white version shows off the contours of jockey shorts, foolish in the extreme—as if the military hasn't come into sufficient disrepute, tarred with the brush of American folly in Vietnam.

But he has no patience with young people who take their freedom for granted, whining about "American imperialism." Where do they think their "free this" and "free that" come from? We like to blame the Americans, but we like to spend the dividends too. Who do we think invented Agent Orange? The baby boomers have yet to produce a single real leader—where is their Churchill, their Roosevelt, their Mackenzie King? He enjoys it when his daughter argues with him—"Oh yeah? What about your Stalin, your Hitler, your Mao?" She is the best of a poor lot—a generation of draft dodgers and potheads. *Crinkle.*

This facile anti-Americanism is, at best, naive—like so many Americans themselves, wide-eyed and trembling yet again in shock at their "lost innocence." They never had it. What they had was a sandbox and a long neck. That's why they fail to notice when their security agencies traipse around the planet shelling out weapons like Halloween candy, overthrowing elected governments, training religious fanatics, death squads and drug dealers. Contra, my foot. Does the poor bastard on the shrinking production line in Flint, Michigan, have a clue what's being done in his name? Or why he may be called upon to donate a son or two to the cause? The Soviet Union is crumbling from within, creating a power vacuum; the world is flooded with arms, most of them American-made; Eisenhower's military-industrial warning is playing out; it's more likely than ever that we'll all go up in a mushroom cloud; meanwhile, the president is consulting astrologers and singing "When Irish Eyes Are Smiling" with our own sorry excuse for a prime minister. *Crinkle.*

On the other hand, it's important not to lose sight of the big picture: the West appears to be winning the Cold War and, whether because of or in spite of that fact, it's still free. Still democratic. More or less. We must be doing something right.

Mimi took his old blue uniform and hung it down in the rec room closet in a garment bag. He doesn't recall what he did with the green abomination—that was only one of the many things that went crazy in the world after Kennedy was killed by a "lone gunman" in Dallas. That must have been some bullet, able to change direction in mid-air. Maybe it was designed by Wernher von Braun.

Jack barely allowed himself to register relief when, in November 1963, he read in the paper that Richard Froelich's death sentence had been commuted to life. Relief was not for him. He pressed on, piece by piece: the next house, and the next, and the next school for the kids, and automatic car windows and microwave ovens, from black-and-white to colour, from split-level to Tudor style; picture frames from wall to packing box to wall again, "a little to the left, that's good there." The same wall only different, the same only different, the same only different, and the next desk and the next, a backyard pool, an empty nest and then a condo with a minimum of stairs. Jack and Mimi.

Like many men of his generation, Jack doesn't really have friends of his own. His wife organizes that side of things. It would be nice, however, of a summer evening, to light a cigar, smell the grass, watch the sun go down through the incline of the sprinkler and talk about this crazy world. About the possibility that we may someday discover another one. Solve the world's problems over a good German beer. But when he allows himself to picture this, only two men join him on the lawn under the hot blue of evening, and they are now much younger than he is. Sealed in memory, protected from the decaying effects of oxygen. Forever young. Simon and Henry. *My friends. I lost them in the war.*

He reaches for his tea.

He gets *The Globe and Mail,* the *Ottawa Citizen, The Times* of London, *The Washington Post* and the Sunday *New York Times.*

In May 1966, he read that Ricky Froelich had been transferred to a medium-security prison in Kingston, set on a working farm across the highway from their suburb. A job came up in Ottawa and Jack grabbed it. He knew his wife didn't want to risk running into Karen Froelich at the Kmart.

He sips—"Mimi!"—scalding his tongue.

His son was arrested for possession of marijuana, but the sentence was suspended and the record later expunged. He experimented with LSD, joined the air cadets, quit, was expelled from high school. He quit hockey and took up football. An overrated game. An American game.

In July 1966, Jack read in *The Washington Post* that a senior American army officer had been arrested for selling atomic, missile and bomber secrets to the Russians. The man—Lieutenant Colonel Whalen—had been deputy director of the Joint Intelligence Objectives Agency, JIOA. Simon had mentioned it only once, but Jack had a military man's head for acronyms, and he instantly recalled that the JIOA had run Project Paperclip. Lieutenant Colonel Whalen had hand-picked foreign scientists for recruitment by the U.S. God knows how many spies posing as defectors he had knowingly imported into American military R & D programs. There was a photo of him emerging from his office at the Pentagon: a craven look in his eye, the big head, skinny arms and soft gut of the career alcoholic. The highest-placed American officer ever convicted of espionage. Simon's boss. *Crinkle.*

Jack becomes absorbed in an article on the next page about the new supertankers, marvels of technology. Reads all about a new artificial heart. Just think, the day is not too far off when we'll be able to cure diseases before they even start, with just a flick of a genetic switch. History in the making.

Jack has never told his wife about what he did in Centralia. She still thinks his strange behaviour had to do with Karen Froelich. What would she think if he told her the truth now? With the passage of years there have been fewer and fewer reasons not to tell her. But he has become so accustomed to keeping the secret that he is wary now of dislodging it. Like an old piece of shrapnel adhering to tissues and vessels— removing it might cause more harm than leaving it to rust and seep. Things have a way of changing when exposed to the air—they rot.

Assassination upon assassination, demonstration upon riot, black power, flower power, power to the people. Students shot dead on campus, people's sons and daughters face down on the grass. In '69 we got to the moon. We beat them. *Crinkle.*

In late 1970 the McCarthys were informed that their son, Michael, was missing. That same year, FLQ terrorists tried to bomb, kidnap and murder their way to civil war in Québec, then fled to Cuba. Prime Minister Trudeau invoked the War Measures Act, suspending Canadian civil liberties. Mrs. Trudeau sang a made-up song to Fidel Castro and began dating Mick Jagger.

In 1973 he read in *The Globe* that Ricky Froelich had been "quietly paroled under a new name." It was over.

That day, he gave some thought to what he had done back in 1963. The events rose in his memory, separate and solid as cinder blocks. The facts. He saw them float and find one another, the pieces arranging themselves in his mind's eye until he could have drawn them as a flow-chart leading to a deliberate and foreseeable outcome. This he called taking responsibility. The accompanying cost-benefit analysis took shape so that, twenty-three years on, if he were to tell what had happened in spring 1963, he would report on how he had made a decision. He would not tell the foolish tale of how he allowed a decision to happen to him. How he desperately ran to catch up with, then tried to outrun, a decision. How he feared he had betrayed his duty as a Canadian officer. How he feared for his life. How a family was destroyed. He salvaged what he could and did his best to believe it: I did not come forward because I knew that the life of one boy was less important than the cause of freedom, even if I was not able to perceive, from my limited vantage point, precisely how that cause would be served. Or if it would be served. I did my job.

"Jack?"

*Crinkle.*

Piece-by-piece living is hard to do. It may even feel like the hardest thing. But it has this going for it: you never need to know what it is you're carrying on your shoulders.

Jack had his second heart attack in the driveway, turning to see if he had locked the car door. He had his third in the hospital, while waiting for bypass surgery.

IN NOVEMBER OF 1963, Richard Froelich's sentence was commuted from hanging to life imprisonment. He found out from the newspaper.

He was moved from the death cell to the Provincial Training School in Guelph. There were boys his own age, and sports. Two and a half years later, at the age of eighteen, he was transferred to the maximum-security prison in Kingston, where he was raped. He was then transferred to a medium-security facility on the outskirts of town, called Collins Bay Penitentiary—a grand Victorian pile in the neo-Gothic style, set amid the acres of a working farm.

Collins Bay Pen also comprises the farm annex, a minimum-security facility where inmates work in the fields and tend the animals. Escape would be easy, but is rare. If you are an inmate of the farm annex, chances are you will soon be paroled. In time, Rick was transferred there. Parole, however, was a thorny issue for the authorities, because Rick would not admit his guilt. How, then, could he be rehabilitated?

He raised rabbits and worked in the fields. His father was gone but the rest of his family visited as often as possible, although they were not permitted to bring his dog. He avoided close friendships within the prison because everyone always left eventually. The staff of guards, janitors, cooks, social workers and psychiatrists got on well with him. He was not raped at Collins Bay.

He had many sessions with many psychiatrists. In those days the concept of wrongful conviction had yet to gain currency. But there was psychology. And there was pharmacology. Some of Rick's psychiatrists admitted that they could not tell whether he was guilty. His chief psychiatrist had come to like him, and to believe that Rick had repressed the memory of raping and killing the little girl. Like his colleagues, he pointed to Rick's murky childhood—a defenceless Métis child, parents unknown, an institutional upbringing to the age of twelve, when he might have been subject to sexual interference at the hands of his keepers, finally adopted by an unconventional couple. Not surprising that, as an adolescent, Richard Froelich had experienced a psychotic break during which he attacked and killed the little girl.

The consensus among the doctors was that the best they could do for the young man was help him remember his crime. And come to terms with it.

He was given truth serum—sodium pentothal, administered intravenously—and lysergic acid diethylamide, administered orally. LSD had been developed by the CIA via a course of illegal experiments, with the help of German scientists who had been imported in the postwar period. The fact that the drugs were still experimental was no impediment to Canadian prison authorities, who may or may not have known that their development had been funded by a foreign intelligence agency. This course of innovative drug therapy was part of an effort to help Richard Froelich recover his memory, thus allowing him to rehabilitate to the point where he could be safely released back into the community.

Eventually, Rick had difficulty remembering details of the days leading up to and following these drug treatments. And having recounted repeatedly the events of April 10, 1963, while under their influence, he found that aspects of that day which had always been stable in his mind, began to shift and disappear in patches, as though consumed by moths, and he became uncertain how to match up the tatters that remained.

He was diagnosed by a panel of psychiatrists as egocentric, grandiose, guarded, impersonal, defensive, narcissistic, schizoid and characterologically psychopathological.

A few years into his sentence, there was something called a "reference." Queen Elizabeth II summoned Richard Plymouth Froelich to present arguments to the Supreme Court to assist them in deciding whether or not there was a legal basis on which to order a new trial.

This time, Ricky testified on his own behalf but showed no emotion. He impressed some as arrogant and overly controlled. A "chilling absence of affect" was noted. The panel of judges was not favourably impressed by his claim that he could remember little of what had happened on April 10, 1963, when he had left the PMQs at RCAF Centralia in the company of the nine-year-old victim.

The original evidence of the child witnesses was upheld. No new evidence was brought forward.

There had never been a subsequent similar murder in Huron County.

The court found insufficient grounds to order a new trial.

# After-Three TV

*"Even a joke should have some meaning—and a child's more important than a joke, I hope."*

                      *Lewis Carroll,* Through the Looking-Glass

MADELEINE REMOVES a flesh-coloured bathing cap from her head—it sports a glued-on grey comb-over and a permanent sprinkle of dandruff—and places it on a Styrofoam head that stands, impaled and impassive, on the makeup counter of her dressing room. She takes off a pair of thickly rimmed men's glasses, lenses fogged with dulling spray, and adds them to the blank face. Loosens and removes a narrow black tie with a mysterious smudge—egg?—then sloughs off a vast grey suit jacket purchased at Mr. Big & Tall. She slips shirt and suspenders from her shoulders in one motion, and the trousers—sixty-five-inch waist—drop to the floor. She steps out of a pair of men's size twelve brogues—brown, permanently dusty—then reaches behind to undo the snaps of her prosthetic torso. The opposite of a corset, it encases her in sculpted foam-core fat. Being constructed of a non-breathing synthetic, it's hot, especially under television lights. Good night Maurice. She steps into the shower.

Madeleine is entering her prime—like the moment known to film people as magic hour, that fifteen or so minutes in which there is no sense yet of the approaching evening, even though the sun has breathed its first sigh of descent. No one has died of cancer yet. No one has given up. Early sorrows feel like ancient history, and current crises are manageable. Madeleine's father has heart problems, but they are under control—it turns out he doesn't need the bypass. There is AIDS, but that's a terrible aberration, and even it seems to be a plague of the young. Most straight people still feel safe, and lesbians feel safest of all.

Madeleine stands under the shower, allowing her short hair to melt and her shoulders to drop. She starts to sing. Assisted by the burbling of water past her lips, she does Louis Armstrong, "what a wondahful woild. . . ."

She was a tragedian between the ages of eleven and seventeen. It began at the Grand Theatre in Kingston, with an inspired Saturday-morning drama teacher called Aida. Aida was from the north of England—big-eyed, thin-lipped, with a raspy voice, a stricken expression and dyed red hair. She had been to RADA. She was Madeleine's first grand passion after Miss Lang. It wasn't a sexual attraction with Aida, however, but a passion of the soul. In Aida's classes, Madeleine survived Auschwitz, a shoe her only companion; resisted cannibalism in a stalled elevator; decided who should live and who die in a rowboat adrift on the South Seas—"Wahtah wahtah everywheh, nor any drop to drink." Aida didn't reprimand her for using accents.

Madeleine lifts her face to the water. She always goes slow after a show, whether live or taped or somewhere in between. At all other times she is a moving target. It's not possible to walk on water, but it's possible to run. Just as it's possible to dance on thin air. Keep talking and don't look down. Move at the speed of thought, uncatchable as a wascally wabbit, swifter than a Road Runner, *meep meep!* She stands still, eyes closed, lips parted, allowing the water to love her.

When the McCarthys were set to move from Kingston, Aida took Madeleine aside, lit a fresh Gitane, inhaled and rasped, "Madeleine, you have a great gift, darling. But you're funny. In the words of the immortal Dietrich, 'you can't help it.' Don't ever let anyone disparage you for it. Laughter bubbles from the well of tears, my cherub, and at the bottom of your well there is blood."

Aida was the second person in Madeleine's experience to invoke the top-hatted Deutsche Diva. Her inner eyes remained wide as saucers in awe-filled contemplation of the oracle. By the time she was a teenager, however, irony had loped in, lithe spike-collared beast, to ridicule the Aidas of this world. But when the mists of adolescence retreated, she recovered her memory and, though she still did not fully comprehend Aida's prophecy, she recalled what she had always wanted to be when she grew up, and pursued it through her twenties. Funny. It runs on a harsh diet and requires a strong stomach. Popeye eats spinach to get his strength. A comedian eats the can.

"You coming for a drink, hon?"

Shelly stands in the doorway. She is reassuringly forty.

Madeleine pokes her head around the plastic curtain. "I thought we were doing notes."

"We'll do them at the bar."

Shelly wrangles comedians. Makes them focus until something gets written, then shot on set. Like many producers, she seems not to have an iota of patience, but she could get a Chihuahua to double-ride a cat on a bicycle. She is trying to get Madeleine to write a one-woman show.

"Hurry up, McCarthy."

"Order me some of those deep-fried—those fried—something fried, okay?"

It's Friday. Dress rehearsal, then shoot in front of a live audience, then drink, debrief and start hatching next week's show. Friday is fun, the peak of the week. It follows marathon Thursday, which is about rewriting, rehearsing, starting over, envying the misery and terror of the set and costume people, who are envying the misery and terror of the performers, and being grateful for a private dressing room with a bathroom of one's own. Monday is full of laughter at new sketch ideas, Tuesday you work on the new ideas and no one laughs at them any more, on Wednesday only Shelly can tell if anything's still funny. Saturday and Sunday are the days off, and the only ones free of gastrointestinal disturbances. Madeleine has the same mixed feelings about it all as the others do: she loves it.

Shelly leaves and Madeleine puts on an iridescent blue polyester bowling shirt with "Ted" stitched on the pocket, a low-slung pair of vintage pinstripes, a pair of battered orthopedic Oxfords so square they're hip, and an Indian Motorcycle jacket of expensively distressed leather—she pictures a supermodel, clad only in the jacket, being dragged behind a Harley over gravel to achieve the fashionable patina. She feels what she often feels after a show: that she has removed one costume in order to don another. She spikes her hair, despikes it then gives up. Switches off the lights around her mirror, turns off the overhead and closes the door. It locks behind her.

The pieces of Maurice remain in her dressing room, ready to be reassembled and restored to life next time. But the flesh-tone bathing cap with the stuck-on grey hair that she fashioned herself—not with great craft, but with conviction; the black-rimmed glasses, perched now on the bridge of the rudimentary Styrofoam nose, smudged lenses obscuring blank eyes; the wide grey suit hanging limp from the rack next to the foam-core carapace of guts; and the big empty brogues, yawning caverns just right for hiding Easter eggs; these pieces of Maurice seem never to deanimate completely, no matter how far apart they are kept.

On some nights, when Madeleine pulls the door of her dressing room closed, she enacts a small ritual that she has never tried to explain to herself or anyone, because it is so trivial: she makes certain not to turn her back on the room until she has closed the door. She looks from the slack grey suit to the Styrofoam head, making certain to exhale through her nose as she does so, and to refrain from blinking as she pulls the door to. Then she tries the lock three times, *click click click,* turns, breathes and leaves. A harmless tic.

She performs similar rites when leaving her house: touch the doorknob three times, this assures her that she did indeed turn off the stove—an indispensable prerequisite to road trips, which are otherwise interrupted by a U-turn halfway to Buffalo, and it's back to Toronto to find, "Of course I turned it off." Her footfalls between the cracks of sidewalks are at times subject to baroque calculations, and when drinking a glass of anything she is careful never to exhale onto the liquid before sipping, and is often compelled to inhale first. If you say these things out loud, you sound nuts.

She looks more like a tired twenty-year-old than a thirty-two-year-old, which goes to show that low-grade obsessive compulsive disorder is good for the skin.

The television studio is located way up in the 'burbs of Toronto. She is the last one out, as usual. She says good night to the security guard and exits into the street-light sharpness of the April night, the hard gloss of manicured grounds, newly green. She jaywalks to an island in the middle of the six-lane suburban "street," makes it to the other side and sets out across the parking lot of an immense mall which, like a mountain, seems to get no closer with her approach, as though she were moonwalking in place, until suddenly it's on top of her and she can no longer see the entrance. She looks right, then left down the massive exterior, which might as well be featureless, its endless illuminated signs an optical cacophony. Light bleeds into the black sky and she closes her eyes, squeezing the yellow orb that appears on her inner lids like a lemon. Then she opens them again and sees it: the giant pickle.

Madeleine started stand-up by accident, when she was twelve. It was Jack's idea. She was in a public-speaking contest. He had helped her write her speech, on the topic of "Humour: Its History and Uses." She forgot her lines halfway through at the intramurals and had to improvise. He said, "Let's build it in."

As she advanced toward the provincial finals, he would identify some point at random within the speech and, depending on what was in the news that day, or what they saw from the car windows on their way to the hall, she would pitch a topical reference and see how far out into left field she could go before bringing it all back home. "Just get up there and do it your way, Sweetie," he said. She was eventually disqualified for "extemporizing", but they went out for ice cream afterwards and he did a cost-benefit analysis of her public-speaking career on a napkin. She came out ahead because experience was worth its weight in gold. "If you want to be an entertainer," he said, "you have to take every opportunity to hone your craft." He always said "entertainer" and, even after she came to know it as a hopelessly outdated term, she never corrected him.

She majored in Classics at McGill University in Montreal, and moon-lighted in a Québec-separatist guerrilla-theatre troupe. This involved terrorizing law-abiding citizens in public places from a leftist perspective, and "exploring her sexuality" with a mandolin player named Lise who was into iridology. Her French improved, along with her tolerance for *dépanneur* plonk, and though she was welcomed by the Québécoises as a quaint and feisty Acadienne, Madeleine felt like an imposter. Something had to give. She moved to Toronto, where she could comfortably resume her long-time disguise as an Anglo.

She quit university with her father's blessing. "Anyone with a decent brain and self-discipline can make a living as a doctor or lawyer or glori-fied bean-counter like me," he said. "It takes a gift to make people laugh."

Comedy. The brain surgery of the performing arts.

They went out, just the two of them, for dinner at a Swiss Chalet. He spread out a paper napkin. "What business are you in?"

"The funny business."

"What are you selling?"

"Laughs."

"No. You're selling stories. Every joke tells a story. Every laugh is the result of a combination of surprise and recognition—" he wrote the two words down on the napkin, then enclosed them in boxes each with an arrow pointing to the blank middle of the napkin. "The unexpected and the inevitable"—two more boxes—"that's what stories are made of, whether they're happy or sad—" two circles, one smiling, one frowning, separated by a slash, connected to the blank centre by a wavy line. "It's no good just making fun of things, even though it's important to have all that mimetic talent and wit"—two more circles—"you have to have a point of view"—overarching heading—"and that's what you've got." He tossed the pen to the table. "A little different way of seeing the world. And the ability to let other people see it that way too. You take the familiar and tilt it. The ability to see things from multiple simulta-neous points of view is a sign of genius."

He had left the centre of the napkin blank, so she filled it in— STORY—and drew a circle around it.

He grinned. "That's right. There's your feedback loop."

She looked at the mini-solar system. "It's like a consolation," she said.

He nodded. They had both heard her say "constellation."

In those days, Toronto was a hair shirt, despite the best efforts of Yorkville with its coffee houses, its folk singers, and radicals; still Toronto the Good, WASP bastion. This was before pad thai, before spritzers and "Beemers," when "pasta" was still spaghetti, before anyone "did" lunch, and when career women wore chiffon scarves with their pantsuits. But she found an apartment on Queen West, over a textile store run by an unsmiling Hungarian couple, and stumbled upon a rich vein of counterculture. A bar called the Cameron was a hothouse of art, music and theatre, a multimedia mecca where hipsters of all races drank side by side with honest-to-goodness Sally Ann hobos. She had a brief but pivotal affair with an intense alcoholic feminist, the publisher of an underground Marxist-Leninist newspaper, whose phone was tapped by the RCMP—it would have reflected badly on her if it hadn't been.

She performed wherever she could, developing the gourd-like rind that every comic needs, and that a woman couldn't live without if she was crazy enough to do stand-up. Phyllis Diller stood at the edge of the known world; beyond her were sea monsters. The new generation of brilliant funny women worked mainly in ensembles or in story-based one-woman-show contexts. Gilda Radner, Lily Tomlin, Andrea Martin, Jane Curtin. . . . There was safety in numbers, whereas stand-up was strictly kill or be killed.

*How'd it go tonight?*

*I killed/I died.*

In the clubs, comics were like indentured servants, clawing their way onto the stage in exchange for a kidney, their first-born child, their left testicle, but the women comics—wait a second, *women* comics? At Yuk Yuk's, the hook was used liberally and literally. The safest stuff was "blue," mean and macho, but Madeleine couldn't have pulled that off if she'd tried.

What business are you in?

*The funny business.*

What are you selling?

*Stories.*

She died at Yuk Yuk's, then auditioned at the Old Fire Hall for the Second City touring company. She hit the road, and often the Fire Hall stage itself, when the main company took a night off. It was almost as rare to cross over from stand-up to improv as it was to be a female stand-up in the first place. But she loved having a gang, she gloried in high-speed improvisation, doing sketches that were "about something"—politics, pop culture, the hostile grocery clerk this morning, processing whatever had happened in her day, working it all out at night on stage. In between sketches, ransacking the flea-bitten costume pile backstage; the exultation that accompanied the appearance of a new character courtesy of that red shirt, that hat, those boots, without which

you would never be able to do that character again—"where the *fuck* is
that red shirt?!" The bizarre and strangely ritualized behaviour that preceded every performance, jokes among themselves so gross they'd have
had to import earth-moving equipment to go any lower. Big huge Tony
prancing nearly nude through the dressing rooms like a Las Vegas show-
girl, seizing and humping the company dry-cleaning with great graphic
gusto when it arrived, then hitting the stage with a wholesome smile,
ready to entertain the Rotary Club. They toured relentlessly, *Welcome to
Kingston, Gananoque, Chatham, Hamilton, Windsor, Sudbury, North Bay,
Timmins.* They played roller rinks where punchlines took ten seconds
to hit the back of the arena. They did benefits—once for a Holocaust
museum where the emcee brought out a child's shoe from Auschwitz
before introducing them, "Now here to entertain us . . ."

She bought a vintage VW Bug and retraced the tour on her own,
doing stand-up in every burg with a university or bar. *Alone, alone, all,
all alone. Alone on a wide wide sea.* She did the club-sandwich circuit and
graduated from seedy motels to Holiday Inns. She honed her craft
before rooms where half the tables were empty and the other half full of
lonely guys waiting for the stripper to come on. She survived a stag
party of drunken engineers who tossed a blow-up doll around the room
throughout her act—"isn't it a shame when cousins marry?" She performed for musty nickel miners and their dates, who had turned out in
the misprinted expectation of singing along with Stompin' Tom
Connors. She learned to love the beehived silhouettes that came to pack
her return gigs in the taverns and "cabana rooms" of borscht-belt north.
Make the women laugh, put the guys at ease, then turn up the heat
until, by the end, she had come out as a burly nickel miner trapped in
the body of a muff-diving lezzie. It helped that she was cute.

It was after Stonewall but before "gay pride." If she wasn't murdered
in the parking lot, she would be taken into countless gnarly normal
hearts. It helped that she met Christine—a Women's Studies major
whose father was a cop in Timmins. Madeleine didn't have to explain
contradiction to her. Christine wore batik dresses with police boots,
kept her hair long and drove standard. She regularly rescued
Madeleine, turning up in Sarnia with a cooler full of pesto and wine, a
pillow from home, and a willingness to have sex that involved nothing
but sleep afterwards.

She quit the touring company before she could be fired or promoted,
and focused on in-town. Christine told her what to read and Madeleine
sharpened her mental knives late-nights in Toronto at a boozecan-
cum-salon called Rear Window. She started out as The Astonishing

Elastowoman. She branched out with The Astonishing Elastowoman's Introduction to Classics of Western Civilization. She branched and branched and branched. She became known for her bendy body and bizarre male characters, including Anita Bryant. There was Lou, a powder-blue-polyester-leisure-suited lounge lizard who accompanied himself on accordion and sang with an outrageous French accent. There was Roger of Roger's Room, a fifteen-year-old boy obsessed with *Soldier of Fortune* magazine, prone to tears and fond of his pet turtle. At the end of every sketch, he would look down the sights of an AK-47 and name all the people he saw there the way the chick on *Romper Room* used to do with her magic mirror. And there was Maurice.

She began to headline in places with air conditioning, and graduated to concert halls across the country and to venues in Chicago and New York, where people bought tickets with her name printed on them. She crossed over into TV, into film, she crossed over and over and over. She merged feminism with humour, she merged being out of the closet with being in the mainstream, she merged and merged.

It helped that she was used to moving.

Jack and Mimi saw many of her shows. Jack saw most of them. She wished her brother could have seen one.

Propelled by the feeling of juggling, of entering a time-space continuum where she could see thoughts coming and pluck them from the air the way Superman plucks speeding bullets; by the revelation that everything is connected—start anywhere, go go go, you will inevitably wind up back at this spot, because space is curved and so are thoughts, a thousand boomerangs—she couldn't focus on one thing, so she focused on everything.

She did it where it was safe: on stage, in front of many strangers who had paid good money and expected a good time. In person she remained shy well into her twenties.

If Madeleine stopped: all the balls would drop. The atoms would disperse. She would look down, see the void beneath her feet, the precipice just out of reach; hear the tin-can sound effect of feet racing for purchase on thin air—*Mother!*—and zoom straight down to the Wile E. Coyote bottom with a powdery *pok!*

She arrives at the faux-rustic double doors of the Pickle Barrel Family Restaurant and pushes them open. The reassuring aroma of ketchup and fried food greets her, along with a blast of "Crocodile Rock"—all oldies, all the time. She spots the others at a big round table loaded with beer, nachos, burgers and wings. This is After-Three TV. She, one other woman and four men, all thirty-something, have been together for seven years. A combination of Second City alumni and renegades. When they first got together, they realized that each, at one time, had been the "bad" kid at school, the one required to remain "after three."

They are crowded around the table with Shelly and two of their regular directors, who look as though they haven't slept in a week, along with an even more haggard-looking script editor and Ilsa, She-Wolf of the Pretty Department—hair and makeup Überfrau—who just broke up with her boyfriend and doesn't want to drink alone. Hands crisscross the table, helping themselves to every plate but the one directly in front of them. At a distance of a table or two, the group looks perfectly at home up here in the land o' malls. They don't appear bohemian—even if Madeleine's personal style tends toward urban-lesbian-warehouse chic. On the whole, they resemble nice generic white people; a Judeo-Christian cross-section of North Americana, somewhere between university student and middle management, and there, but for a small yet crucial quirk, went they all.

When you look closely, however, you can see that they all have the thing in their eye. The result of an accident or a gift. Perhaps God dropped each of them on the head before they were born. Light seems to reflect at an odd angle from their irises—the visible effect, possibly, of information that, having entered the brain obliquely, exits the eye at a corresponding tilt. Something, at some point, smote or stroked them. Each lives in genial terror of being found out and exposed as a fraud. Each is fuelled by a combustible blend of exuberance and self-loathing, informed by a mix of savvy and gullibility. None was cool in high school. Denizens of the great in-between of belonging and not belonging; dwellers in the cracks of sidewalks; stateless citizens of the world; strangers among us, familiar to all. Comedians. These are Madeleine's people.

She starts toward them. She is not the only one to harbour a pool of perfectly black water at her core, still as onyx, unreflecting of any light at all, whence, if comedy occasionally bubbles up, it is either hysterically funny or just plain ill. Or right on the line—like Maurice.

Ron waves, Linda makes room, Tony asks if she got lost again; Madeleine adjusts her balls and says, in Tony's voice, "I stopped on the way to drain the peg," and they laugh. They have been meeting here for over a year and she still can't find the place. Someone pours her a glass of draft.

This watering hole of choice is loud enough for them to be able to hear themselves think. Madeleine squeezes into the banquette and yields to a bone-crusher from Tony, who outweighs her two to one. Good for a laugh, better than hours of therapy. Tony could make a fortune. He almost has; so have some of the others at this table—like Madeleine, poised at the brink.

"You're not finished that wing, eat that wing," Maury says to her.

"I ate it."

"You didn't, look at all the meat you left, here, give."

"Take."

"I'll show you how to eat a wing, you're so obviously a goy, eating a wing like that."

Early thirty-something existential moment of truth, when you first realize that not everyone you worked with in your twenties is a genius, that some people are "wild and crazy" and others simply have a substance problem, that the alluring sexy-sad people are just depressive, that depression is rage slowed down, that mania is grief speeded up. The first great winnowing.

Ron says to Linda, "The haunted house bit was funnier the first time—"

"It was shit."

"No it was funny when you came on after I did the—"

"When you do that thing with the lamp, it screws up my—"

"No, you got a laugh!"

"That was not my laugh."

"Shelly, she got a laugh, am I right?"

These are the last immortal days, racing toward that next great good place, Your Life. Last days of travelling light, before slowing, turning and, with a hand shading the eyes, espying the moving van heaving into sight with all your stuff on it, finally being brought out of storage. Stuff you forgot you owned.

They drink and eat and talk all at once; the men talk the loudest because they have bigger larynxes and millennia of entitlement. The women tell them to shut up and they do, chastened like terriers but, like terriers, only briefly. No one ever resents Tony for hogging a scene because he somehow seems generous even when he's pulling focus; everyone knows Ron is a genius but Tony is the only one who can really deep down stand him any more, and everyone is in love with Linda. She has a strange beauty and is severely gifted at coming in under the radar, but her brand of comedy is easily trampled by a Ron. Maury is solid, especially in drag, Howard is the Art Carney guy, Madeleine walks a tight rope between writing for the company and taking too much space with her low-staus characters that nonetheless command centre stage. The six of them love one another, are suspicious of one another, can't stand one another—they are a company. They can anticipate who's going to bite whom next and how hard.

"We should take Linda's newlywed thing and—"

"We should make a sequel—"

"We should do the sequel *first*—"

Out of this come the sparks for next week's show, charted by Shelly on a tablet of lined paper in the form of squiggles and diagrams. The boxes and arrows remind Madeleine of her father. There is method in this madness. A map for improv that will lead to a script that will remain fluid until past the final take. Writing is a hellish task, best snuck up on, whacked on the head, robbed and left for dead. Tonight, among the munchies, the beer and the noise, writing is what they are doing.

"Someone should write this down," says Howard—someone always says this at some point.

"Madeleine, this one reeks of you," says Ron—this is a devious way of sticking her with the actual writing. Writing. Opening a vein in your wrist with a spoon. No one wants to do it—

"He's right, it stinks of you, McCarthy," says Tony.

—the sit-down kind, the stuff you do alone, Marlborough-man writing.

"I'd rather apply this salsa to an open wound," she replies.

Shelly writes on her tablet. "Madeleine . . . 'Breaking News'".

"How come, when it comes to writing stuff down," Madeleine snarks, reaching for a napkin, "you're all dylsexic?"

Howard says, "I'm a hemophiliac, if I slip while writing I could die."

It sounds flippant, but it's a delicate negotiation: Madeleine taking on the "dirty work", while the others play down their need of her, keeping resentment in check. In turn, she plays down her ability and pays her dues, contributing to the ensemble to make up for her star-turns. It may not be fair—Ron doesn't pay dues—but the truth is Madeleine can write and, like many writers, will only write with a gun to her head so it's just as well . . . plus, this way she gets to be a solo act in the bosom of an ensemble. The best of both worlds. She makes notes on the napkin, then reaches for another. Shelly knows better than to offer a sheet of paper. That would be too much like writing.

Shelly has three kids. Madeleine wishes at times that she were one of them. In a sense, though, she is. All six of them are.

On the way back to their cars in the parking lot of the silent studio, Shelly asks her, "What've you got for me?"

"A shameful craving to see you naked but for a clipboard."

Shelly is like a hard-nosed version of dear old Miss Lang. There are really only about five people in the world.

"I'm not going to talk you into this, Madeleine."

Shelly has brokered a U.S. network option on Madeleine's idea for a one-hour special. A pilot for a series starring a real live out-of-the-closet gay comedian called Madeleine. *This could be my big bweak, doc.* So far she has written three words. The title: *Stark Raving Madeleine.*

"The others've got their own stuff going too, you know," says Shelly.

"I know."

It's inevitable that the After-Threes will evolve careers in their own right. Some have already soloed, and hived off in various combinations for film, TV and live gigs in New York and L.A., making life backstage at After-Three tense, and life on stage even more of a feeding frenzy. Madeleine has wangled a coveted green card, thanks to a recent stint on *Saturday Night Live* after Lorne Michaels saw her at Massey Hall in Toronto. She entered the bear pit for three adrenal weeks. She wrote and grew pale like the other crypt-dwelling writers. She lost ten pounds and Christine told her she had an eating disorder, but it was pure speed—the metabolic kind. She had an affair by accident—bold production assistant, empty office—but virtuously avoided the coke, the only recreational drug she has ever truly enjoyed. She told Christine about her stalwart abstinence but not, of course, about the headset-wearing drug-substitute who, in the scheme of things, mattered not at all. Really.

Lorne is putting together a new "less famous" cast for next season and has asked her to come back, and bring Maurice, Roger and Lou—lose weight *in front* of the cameras this time, which, when you're writing, always seems easier. Her producer, Shelly, has congratulated her but warned her about trying to join "the boys' club." You're a dyke," she says, "so it helps you get buddy-buddy, but you're not going to sleep with any of them and, no matter how good you are or how much they like you, you'll never be one of them. You've got your own stuff going on, like Lily, except . . ."

"Except what?"

"She doesn't need all the crutches and bullshit you do." Shelly has been pressuring Madeleine to shed the props and costumes.

"What about one-ringy-dingy, what about Edith Anne, the hair, the chair, gimme a break!"

"She doesn't need that stuff to do them."

"Well I don't need the costume to do Maurice—"

"So do him that way."

"My point is, you can't do The Cone Heads without cone heads."

"So do cone-headesque stuff for the rest of your life."

Regardless of which way Madeleine goes, she is poised to join the "Canadian invasion." Funny Canucks who head south of the border because, while it's no longer impossible to get anywhere at home—Canadian-content laws having begun to pay off, not to mention tax breaks that have turned Toronto into Hollywood North—there is no limit to how far you can go by leaving. This makes sense, Canada being small, but performers are also targets of the Canadian syndrome: the cultural inferiority complex that prompts their fellow citizens to confer authenticity on those who blow this northern Popsicle stand. Because, if you're so great, why are you still here? And its inverse: what kind of lousy Canadian are you, up and leaving like that?

English Canadians; stealth Yankees. Yanks in sheep's clothing. People who seem perfectly American but who know that Medicine Hat is not an article of apparel. People who can skate, holiday in Cuba and speak high-school French; people who enjoy free health care, are not despised abroad and assume that no one in the restaurant is armed. Cake-eating-and-having Americans. After-Three is straining under the pressure of its own success. Madeleine has no reason to feel guilty.

"It's not that I feel guilty."

"Then what?" says Shelly. "Shit or get off the pot."

"You're so sensitive and nurturing."

Shelly's hand is on the door of her station wagon; she looks exhausted, her kids will be up in six hours, she says to Madeleine, "You're my pony, you're the one, I want to see you go for it."

Madeleine hugs her, wishing she harboured a shameful craving to see Shelly naked but for a clipboard. The fact that Shelly is straight and Madeleine is in a long-term relationship are details they could work out later.

"G'night Momma."

"G'night Mary Ellen."

Madeleine gets into her old Volkswagen Beetle. Dirty white eggshell with red interior. She turns the key, coaxing it to life with a prod of the gas pedal, tender release of the choke. She pats the dashboard, "good little car." She turns on an oldies station and heads home to Christine.

On the way, the thing happens again. When it first happened, a week or so ago, during a live performance, she wrote it off as nerves or flu, or—most reassuring—a small stroke. But what does one call "the thing" when it happens during a drive on a quiet city street, toward home in a light rain?

## THE STORY OF MIMI AND JACK

THE OVER-ARCHING SHAPE OF TIME is always there, like the unseen sunny day above the clouds. And above that endless day, an infinite darkness into which our warp of time loosens and drifts, the slow dispersal of a jet stream.

Ruptures in time. When they lost Mike. When their daughter announced that she was gay. "I know, it's a horrible word," said Madeleine, grimacing. "*Lesbian*. All snaky and scaley."

Mimi was crying, Jack had compressed his lips and was looking down. Their daughter made a living out of being different, being flippant.

"I'm not taking this lightly," Madeleine said, biting her lip, grinning. "I feel sick."

"You feel sick," said Mimi, "you *are* sick."

That was 1979, Mimi remembers the date, two weeks before they got the kitchen redone. Her son ate standing up at that counter, hugged his mother goodbye standing on that spot. Retiled now.

It's important for Mimi to be able to take responsibility so she can cope. One child gone, the other blighted. Mimi is a modern Catholic mother. She knows it's all her fault.

Copers also need to cherish what remains. My husband. The part of my daughter that still shines. Faith that the damage is not irreversible. "*Viens,* Madeleine, I'll take you shopping."

"It'll end in tears."

Scrabble. Food. Shopping. The things they can share.

"Maman, why don't you come to Toronto one weekend and we'll go shopping?" But Mimi cannot set foot in that apartment. Not while her daughter is living that way with another woman. That is not a home, that's . . . not a home.

Something must have happened to my daughter to make her like that. Jack is no help there. He refuses to discuss it with her.

After all those years of unwrapping Jack's gifts to her, saying, "It better not be a you-know-what," one Christmas it was. But she no longer wanted a mink coat. She wanted what she'd had. She wanted to *want* one.

For years she longed for him to confess his stumble. She didn't know how to tell him that, if anything, she would love him more if he shared it with her, took it away from that woman in Centralia, made it theirs alone. She longed to say, "It's not your fault we lost our son. I forgive you." But those two sentences didn't add up. And he never mentions Michel's name.

Sometimes she fails to tell him when she has topped up his cup with hot tea, or fails to readjust the driver's seat if she has used the big car, fails to notice that he has immaculately trimmed the hedge and ingeniously solved the bird-feeder-versus-squirrels problem. On these occasions, he takes her out for dinner.

He teases her about how she always makes friends with the waiter or waitress, but in fact she does it for him. He'll end up talking about everything under the sun with the chef, the owner, other diners. The old Jack—the young one. Otherwise, he reads his paper. Pretends not to hear.

Mimi does a lot of volunteer work. The Heart Fund, the Liberal Party, the Church. She took a refresher course and went back to work, too, and she still plays bridge. She enjoys Ottawa, the fact that she can shop and get her hair done in French, enjoys the outdoor concerts in summer and skating on the canal in winter—she even gets Jack out now and then. She has a lot of friends, but that's just it: they're hers not theirs. Numerous ex–air force people, old friends from previous postings, have retired in Ottawa, there are card parties, dinners, curling. But Jack declines to "live in the past."

They used to go to Florida every year. He had his first heart attack down there, on the golf course. It was expensive; thank goodness for Blue Cross. Mimi goes to New Brunswick two or three times a year to visit her family in Bouctouche, but her husband hasn't come with her since Mike went away. Her sister Yvonne is widowed now, she spends most Christmases with them in Ottawa, and Jack likes being spoiled by her. But Mimi rarely has people over any more. It takes too much out of her. Placating him, dreading that he may withdraw into himself once the guests arrive, enduring his criticism of them in advance, his muttered hope that "Gerry won't plunk himself down at the head of the table again, and foist the photos of his latest trip to the Galapagos on us," and that "Doris won't rattle on about her grandchildren." "Not Doris, Jack—*Fran*." Then the guests arrive, and Jack laughs and chats and teases Mimi about being uptight when she brightly directs the guests to their place cards at the table—interrupting her to say, "Sit anywhere you like, Gerry." He has a wonderful evening—and is irritable for days afterward.

They are still an attractive couple. Jack hit sixty with scarcely a grey hair. Mimi still has a twenty-six-inch waist when fully dressed. She dyes her hair, having no intention of looking older than her husband. Fine lines are visible through the makeup but she has avoided the full extent of the smoker's crenelated upper lip by forty years of careful puffing and moisturizing. Calves still very good, hands still soft, nails perfect. Extra folds of skin at the elbows and knees—that's what sleeves and hemlines are for.

She has never told anyone about her daughter's "lifestyle." She hasn't had to. Everyone's read about it in the national newspaper—the Entertainment section.

She has a job as staff nurse at the National Capital Commission downtown. She is the confidante of the entire department. A woman in accounting recently "came out" to her; "You're the only one I can talk to about this, Mimi." She gave Mimi a coffee mug with a Chagall print on it, in gratitude: "I could never talk to my mother like this."

Mimi knows that had she never left New Brunswick; had she never entered nurse's training and earned money of her own; never married a handsome *Anglais,* learned to give cocktail parties and wear clicky high heels; had she never danced beneath a chandelier, and had her wedding dress remained her only ballgown; had she remained Marguerite—God would have blessed her with a third child, who might in turn have had children by now.

At least He would have allowed her to keep the two she had.

Eventually, there comes a time in Jack and Mimi's life when the television is always on, even when they are not watching it.

# HAVE YOU EVER CONSIDERED THERAPY?

*Italian patient, circa 1890s: "Doctor, I'm suffering from melancholy. I've lost my joy in life, my appetite for food, for love, I don't care if I live or die. Please, tell me what to do."*
*Doctor: "Laughter is the best medicine. Go see that wonderful clown, Grimaldi."*
*Patient: "I am Grimaldi."*

WE ALL NEED to look under the rock from time to time. We are all afraid of the dark, and drawn to it too, because we know that we left something there, something just behind us. We can feel it now and then, but fear to turn lest we catch sight of what we long to see. We wait that critical moment, allowing it to flee before we turn, saying, "See? It was nothing." We are scared of our own shadow. A good comedian scares the shadow. Aided and protected by speed, comedians can turn so quickly that, from time to time, they actually glimpse the shadow as it flees. And so we do too, from a safe distance. If you had to make Dante's trip into the Inferno nowadays, would you go with Virgil or John Candy?

"Incomplete classic migraine," the eye doctor tells Madeleine. "Visual phenomena unaccompanied by pain."

An ophthalmologist is not going to tell you that you are seeing your shadow. This kind of doctor will not say, "Don't be afraid. Turn around slowly. Talk to it. It wants to tell you something."

Comedy slowed down is terrifying. This is what is happening to Madeleine.

She was afraid to pull over because that would have been to admit there was something wrong. It was raining, her face was too hot against the cool window when she pressed her cheek to it, her heart was light and rapid like a propeller and she didn't understand where she was going. She knew in her head where she lived, that she was going home in her car after the Friday night taping; she had all the knowledge of life that she'd had one second ago; but something had receded like a transparent layer. The thing that allows us to agree on all the pieces of the world. The thing that make things one thing. She was seeing everything separately, piece by piece. A street light nothing to do with a street. A sidewalk nothing to do with a curb. She didn't understand why anything was anywhere. She saw what was behind everything—nothing.

Her heart accelerated, a creature trapped in her chest; was she going to die? An inky feeling like shame in her stomach. A person was hurrying toward her car from the gas station on the corner. Had he realized that she no longer knew how to be? No, he continued past.

Her heart slowed to a walk. The windshield wipers smeared light around the glass and she looked away, but the yellow smear followed her gaze.

"Maybe I just need glasses."

"Has this kind of thing ever happened before?" asks the therapist.

The room is panelled in fabric and wood, soothing terracotta tones, spatial sedative. On a side table is a pitcher of spring water, a shallow box of sand with a miniature rake, and a box of Kleenex. There is a couch with a big pillow for punching, there are seashells, a crystal, an air purifier, several degrees on the wall, a Georgia O'Keeffe print. Madeleine takes a deep breath and mumbles, "Few weeks ago."

She hears in her voice the sullen muffle of adolescence. Regression proceeding on schedule.

The therapist waits, serene in her swivel chair. Some sort of handmade-without-cruelty earrings dangle discreetly from her ears. Nina. Madeleine sits crunched in an armchair opposite. She is cottoning onto the therapy game: therapist oozes impersonal compassion until client can't take silence any more and blurts, "I killed my mother!" But first the disclaimers: "I'm exhausted. After-Three is in production, plus I'm doing a workshop of an original alternative-theatre piece for no money—why? Because the director has pink hair."

The therapist waits. At a dollar twenty-five a minute.

Madeleine tells what happened the last time she did stand-up:

The old Masonic Temple in downtown Toronto is packed. Light spills from the stage onto the heads and shoulders of the standing crowd. Ceiling fans spinning overhead do nothing to dispel the heat generated by hot bands, arid performance art, flaming flamenco and The Diesel Divas, a choir of heavy-set women in plaid shirts and brush cuts who sing a repertoire of sacred music by Bach. A sold-out benefit for a downtown battered women's shelter.

Madeleine looks out over the mass of heads silhouetted and shading into darkness toward the back. Physically loose and mentally coiled, with her usual blend of butterflies and focus, this is the one place she feels thoroughly at home. The safest place on earth.

She banters with the audience, tailoring bits for them. Riffs on various news items: the search for the gay gene—"Why not search for something really useful like the stupid-driver gene?"—Reagan's waxy nuclear buildup, Margaret Thatcher's iron handbag, Prime Minister Mulroney as auctioneer. She takes shots at political correctness and Jerry Falwell alike, whips through Orgasms of the Rich and Famous, and Virginia Woolf Writes an Episode of *Love Boat*. Fizzy stuff, fun. They keep calling for "Maurice! Do Maurice!"

"You're sick!" she calls back.

"Maurice!"

Now she knows how the Beatles felt. Bearded, high and tie-dyed, the crowd clamouring nonetheless, "'I Wanna Hold Your Hand!'"

"How'm I supposed to do Maurice? The outfit alone, come on."

"Do the puppet! The puppet!!"

She is agile in a pair of U.S. Marine Corps surplus jungle boots. On top she wears a West German Army singlet with the eagle of the Bundesrepublik emblazoned on the chest, under which she is braless. Official Überdyke-wear.

She glances up at the neo-Gothic mouldings of the Masonic Temple. "I think it fitting that we are gathered this evening to raise some filthy lucre for a feminist cause here in a former bastion of the patriarchy."

Applause.

Her hair is soaked and she can feel sweat trickling down her back, but someone must have switched on the air conditioner because she is suddenly chilly. She listens for the telltale laugh-killing hum of the cooling system but can't hear it over the crowd. She takes a sip of water from a plastic bottle.

She allows her eyes to unfocus and bulge. Her chin retracts, gut swells. The audience laughs and chants, "Mau-rice! Mau-rice! Mau-rice!"

You never know what people are going to fixate on. Maurice isn't even that funny. Someone throws a pair of panties onto the stage, but Maurice doesn't take the bait. She releases him, puts the underpants on her head like a balaclava, then slingshots them into the wings.

She takes another sip, allowing the water to trickle down her neck, and showers with the rest, removing her shirt with masculine insouciance and using it as a towel. It's easier to take your shirt off if you have small breasts—Madeleine wonders if she'd have the nerve to do it if she were stacked, rack and pinion. It's also easier to come out as a lesbian if you look like the girl next door, and have a prime-time television show—it's not like you're going to lose your job and your apartment.

Madeleine has a long list of why it's easy for her, she keeps no account of how it's hard.

Taking your shirt off is a cheap shot but it works—the rubber chicken of feminist comedy. She squeakily unscrews, polishes and oils her nipples, then screws them back on. The audience goes hysterical and she takes the opportunity to catch her breath—she must be tired. She doesn't do a lot of stand-up any more, and she didn't really have time to do this gig but was reluctant to say no to a good cause.

She paces herself. Happily this is a smoke-free venue; since it's a feminist event, the organizers have tried to make it a hospitable environment for the smoke-intolerant. Feminism is as yet only ankle-deep in the new wave of "intolerances," which include perfume, lactose, yeast and the presence of others enjoying a beer—part of the inevitable splintering of a movement that has achieved so much—perhaps because it has achieved so much.

Friends are here tonight. Olivia—she of the pink hair. She is an alternative-theatre director, tastefully pierced, whom Madeleine met when Christine got her to direct a Komedy Kabaret for International Women's Day. Also out there somewhere is Madeleine's high school friend Tommy, as is her main After-Three man, Tony, along with friends from many of the circles that overlap and proliferate to make community. Christine is not here—"You don't mind, do you, sweetie? I've seen that material before and I've got a paper due."

Madeleine waits till the crowd is quiet, then breaks into her trademark evil-out-of-synch-ventriloquist-puppet laughter.

They are still laughing when she experiences an odd sensation: as though she has just come to. She wonders how long it's been since she did the puppet-laughter thing. It can't have been more than seconds, because the laughter is just peaking, but she feels as though it were ages ago. She continues grinning demonically and takes the opportunity to look for a square of light under the exit sign. There must be a door open, admitting the sharp April night—it's freezing in here, her sweat has turned icy; then she becomes aware of a collective motion out there among the dark heads and shoulders, small shapes fluttering like leaves—people are fanning themselves with their programs.

She blinks the sweat from her eyes and feels the salt sting. "If these walls could talk, eh? I wonder what the Masons talked about that was so secret. Or maybe it's the idea of secrecy, it gives you power. That'd be so typical WASP, not even to have any secrets, just let the rest of us keep jamming our ears up against the wall with a glass, hoping to hear how to invest or which judge is going to hear our case or how to get our Yorkshire pudding to come out right. Maybe they just bowled in here. Did the secret handshake." She does a secret handshake that takes over her whole body.

"Masons aren't the only ones to have a secret society. The Vatican is loaded with secrets. And they've got money too, right? They've got everything, they got an army, a bank and a passport office for war criminals. . . ." She peers down her nose at a passport in her hand. "'Hmm, Dr. Mengele'"—stamps it with a *kchunk*, then, smiling— "'have a nice trip sir.' I don't get how it's like this whole country—the Vatican—run by these guys in robes and tall pointed hats with crosses and no women or Jews, like are we talking Ku Klux Klan?"

She wipes her forehead with the heel of her hand while they laugh. Squeezes her eyes shut and sees yellow trails, the lights have lost their edges, making a shadowy mess of the audience.

"I'd be so pissed off if I were Mary," she says, suddenly too aware of her own voice. "First of all, she gets married to a really sensitive guy, a 'feminist man' with like no money, can't afford a hotel—at Christmas!" It's as though there were a slight delay between the time the words leave her mouth and the moment she hears them. It's fine, they're laughing, she'll power through this, then go home to a Neo Citran.

"So she gives birth in a barn and all these guys keep barging in with useless presents—myrrh? 'What'm I gonna do with that?!' Not to mention the presents are all for the baby. Then the Church comes along and says Joseph wasn't even the father. God was. Plus, she was a virgin. Hello? The worst part, though, is that the Church Fathers—the pointy-hat guys—sit around all grizzled and serious and holy, debating whether or not it *hurt* when Mary had the kid." Numbskull anchorman voice— "'What do you think, Augustus?' 'Well Fluvius, I don't think it hurt a bit. What do you think, Farticus?' 'Oh I don't think it hurt, what about you, Thomas?' And Thomas Aquinas says, 'Oh, um, what he said. Didn't hurt.'" Madeleine takes a beat, then "It did-n't hurt?" Gapes at the audience. "It hurt!" Manic—"*She was in the stable pushing out a baby the son of God he was bi-i-i-ig! He had a big holy head he was Go-od! It hurt! It fuckin' hu-urt!*"

Normally at this point the laughter is drowned by Iggy Pop, who blasts over the speakers while Madeleine pogos and improvises a series of *lazzi*—an old *commedia dell'arte* term meaning physical comedy turns: schtick. She'll trip over the microphone cord until the series of falls escalates to a mad imbalancing act with no longer a bone in her body. Gumby and Pokey on bennies.

But tonight she stands frozen. The darkness, the laughter, the clapping and hooting are no longer friendly or warm, they are not anything. Out there, the silhouettes and lights are as strange as a landing strip at night. Numbness travels from her hands to her elbows, the smear of lights begins to waver and she loses a piece of the world to her left. A wedge from her field of vision is gone, sealed over as though it had never been there, the exit sign has simply disappeared.

She gets home somehow. Driving slowly, trying to stay alive, fearing not an accident but something she cannot name.

"Maybe it was just stage fright."

"Is that what you think it was?" asks the therapist.

"That's what Christine said it was." And in answer to Nina's silent question, "She's my girlfriend. Partner. Thingy."

"Panic attack" does not describe it, although that's probably, officially, what it was. The total and complete loss of the known. The sudden inarticulable strangeness of the familiar; the appalling observation that one foot goes in front of another. The realization that one thing is not related to another. A finger bewildered by a hand.

Madeleine continues, thinking all the while, this rinky-dink therapist is going to tell me I'm having panic attacks and I'm going to tell her to fuck off. She finishes by saying, "Panic attacks, right?"

Nina says, "Is that how you think of them?"

*Clever, doc.*

Nina asks if anything has occurred recently in Madeleine's life, any kind of change.

"You think I need an excuse to go off my rocker? I'm a comedian, I'm halfway there at any given moment."

"Is that true?"

"That's the cliché."

"Is it useful?"

"Chicks love it."

Nina says, "I'm wondering if something triggered the . . . thing."

"I'm probably just burnt out, wouldn't be the first time. It's how it's done; you work yourself into the ground and you make it look easy and you get somewhere."

"Sounds as though you have to be pretty stable in order to do that."

Madeleine shrugs, gratified but unwilling to show it.

"Why are you here, Madeleine?"

Madeleine summons irony but it falls back like a vampire at a whiff of garlic. She fights the sensation that she is turning into a velvet painting, brown eyes going treacly, throat swelling with tears—why? *Oh no. Emotion taking hold . . . got to . . . swim away. . . .* She looks at Nina and says reasonably, "I keep having these urges to skin puppies and violate young children."

Nina's calm, attentive expression doesn't change. She waits.

"I cried at Loblaws."

"Which aisle were you in?"

Madeleine laughs. "Ethnic foods," she replies and weeps. "Holy shit." She chuckles. "See? This is weird, is this like . . . really early menopause or something, should I be shopping for yam extract?"

She explains her recent bouts of incontinence: ambushed by tears at the sight of a woman in a sari putting a can of chickpeas into her cart. The yelp of a dog reaches her on a breeze, her hand flies to her eyes, she stops as though struck by a stray Frisbee, and weeps. Plummeting sorrow at a child's anguished resistance to a sun hat; at an old man in a soiled tweed vest behind her in the bank lineup, as he keens the words, "Northrop Frye, Northrop Frye." At cooking shows, at special offers of twenty-five golden hits, *These magic moments can be yours for only . . . !*

"Is that why you're here?" asks the therapist.

"Yes, I need to curb my daytime TV intake." Nina waits. Madeleine hears herself say, "My dad had another heart attack."

She feels her face tighten in the smile of grief. She reaches for the Kleenex and plucks several. "Few months ago. It's not like he's dying."

And he isn't. *I'm lucky,* he told her in January. *It's the rich man's disease. The stuff they can do nowadays, they don't even have to open me up. . . .*

"Are you close to your father?"

Madeleine nods, opens her lips, tries but fails to get out the words. Nina waits. Madeleine says, "He's my best. . . ."

"Your best what?"

Madeleine shakes her head. "It's stupid. Don't know why I can't say it, so corny." She straightens in her chair, inhales and says, "My best old buddy."

There.

But her cheeks contract again and her eyes continue to weep. She shakes her head. She is in worse shape than she thought. Or maybe she is just too good a performer—I'm sitting in a therapist's office, I must be cracking up, therefore: crack-up. Do I get the part?

"What's the pain, Madeleine?"

"Well." Madeleine sighs. "It's not as bad as having a pubic hair caught in the adhesive strip of your panty-liner. But it's worse than a fork in the eye."

Madeleine made the January drive from Toronto to Ottawa's Heart Institute in four hours and fifteen minutes, door to door.

"Holy Dinah," chuckled Jack, "what'd you do, fly?"

He was sitting up in bed reading *Time*—she was immediately reassured. Electrodes led from his chest beneath the blue hospital gown to a heart monitor, intravenous tubes ran from his wrist and an oxygen mask was slung casually around his neck. He winked and gave her the thumbs-up, past two young nurses who were joking and making a fuss over him as they changed the IV bags—one of fluids, one of blood thinners. Madeleine smiled, worried her face would shatter and fall, proud for one unreal moment of having the handsomest, youngest-looking dying father on the ward.

The nurses introduced themselves, told her not to make her father laugh too hard, said they loved her show and "your dad is so proud of you."

They left, and Jack continued smiling so broadly she could see his gold tooth.

"How are you doin', Dad?"

"Oh I'm fine, they're turnin' me loose tomorrow."

"What about—? You're having surgery—"

"Naw." He waved his hand. "Don't need it. Witch doctor shook some rattles over me and said, go on, get out of here."

"How come they're not operating?" Her voice dull and metallic like flatware.

"'Cause I'm better off without it," he said, jaunty.

"Is that true?"

He chuckled, incredulous. "'Course it's true." *What snake under the bed?*

Mimi was down the hall in the washroom. Madeleine took a slow walk along the corridor with her father and his IV stand. His blue gown gaped in the back, exposing his white Stanfields. He lowered his voice discreetly—it didn't need lowering, it had thinned along with his blood—saying, "These people are *really* sick." Patients who looked much older, cadaverously thin or mountainously fragile, moving gingerly as though lodged deep within their bulk was a bomb.

She told him about the option on her one-woman special. He laughed at the title—carefully. There was a bomb in his chest too. But apparently it was getting better. They returned to his room. She sat on the edge of the high hospital bed and he sat in the armchair, one hand relaxed around the IV stand as though it were a fixture of long standing, no big deal. As usual, he asked her how she was fixed for cash, and she consulted him on whether she ought to move to the States. He reached for the napkin under his plastic juice cup and drew two columns, *Pro* and *Con.* As they made the list, she said, "Sometimes I feel like I'm not doing any good in the world."

He motioned with his head toward the door. "That cardiologist, he can tell me what's going in here"—he pointed with his thumb to his chest—"they could even give me a new heart if they had to, and that's no mean feat. But a fair number of people could study and learn to do that. Try as they might, though, very few people can open their mouths and make a roomful of total strangers laugh. And that's the best medicine in the world. Just keep doing it your way."

She smiled and looked down at her feet dangling over the floor.

They finished the list. *Pro:* world's biggest English-speaking market/close cultural-political affinity/job satisfaction/fame/more money. *Con:* your Canadian identity/Maman.

"Maman?"

"I think she might miss you something terrible."

Madeleine raised her eyebrows but forcibly drained the irony from her voice. "Really?"

He nodded—stoic, complicit—then sipped his juice through the jointed straw. His blue eyes widened and his mouth worked carefully, drawing in the liquid. He looked so innocent—like a child. She held her face immobile, weathering the rise of sorrow in her throat. She knew what the biggest Con of all was—that she would miss him something terrible: *what if Dad died while I was far from home?*

He asked about Christine, and she set to rubbing his head the way he liked it. "She's great, Dad, thanks. We're thinking of buying a house—"

She caught his warning look, and turned to see her mother entering the room. They hugged and Madeleine smelled the familiar mingle of tobacco and Chanel, feeling comforted in spite of herself.

His voice took on a boyish quality. "Hey Maman, I told Madeleine I've been sprung out of here. No need for surgery."

Madeleine gauged her mother's expression. Sour. She must have overheard them referring to Christine. She told herself to be nice. "Maman, did you bring the Scrabble game?"

Mimi smiled brightly, and reached for the shelf under Jack's bedside table. Madeleine saw her shoot him a "significant" look and wondered what was up, but he pulled the portable black-and-white TV down on its hinge and turned on the news: the great escape.

Madeleine pulled a handful of letters from the old flannel Crown Royal bag. Mimi pulled out hers and said, "*Voilà,* I pulled out seven without counting."

"Me too, weird eh? Do you think the tiles have soaked up the energy of the game after all these years?"

"Ask your father."

But he had his taut news face on. The picture of a certain species of masculine contentment.

Madeleine looked down at her tray and saw the inevitable. Amid the other innocuous letters, the word, scrambled but unmistakeable, popped out at her: CUNT. She sighed and made CUTE.

The sound of a countdown . . . *we have liftoff.*

"Holy Dinah," breathed Jack.

"What is it?" said Mimi.

"Wait now," he said, "they're going to replay it."

They huddled around the tiny screen and watched the *Challenger* explode.

"Your mother hasn't come to terms with your sexuality?"

"You might say dat, doc."

"Are you an only child?"

"No." Madeleine has heard the truculent note in her own voice.

Nina waits.

"I have a brother."

Nina waits.

Madeleine says, "He went away."

"When?"

"Nineteen sixty-nine." Madeleine feels her face simmering as she stares at Nina. Go ahead, ask. *Make my day.*

But Nina asks a different question. "What's the anger about, Madeleine?"

Madeleine changes the expression on her face. Friendly. "Remember moon rocks?"

Nina waits.

Two can play this game. Madeleine smiles, unblinking, blank as a coin-operated dummy waiting to receive a dime through the slot in the palm of its hand.

Nina says, "We have to stop now, Madeleine."

"Had enough, eh? Wimp."

"No, our time is up for today. Would you like to come back next week?"

"Would you like to sit on my face?" Nina's expression doesn't change. "I can't believe I said that."

Nina nods.

"Clearly I need therapy."

Nina waits.

"Yes, please may I come back next week?"

In the summer of '69, the three of them gathered in the rec room in front of the television. Mimi sat perfectly still, not ironing, not smoking, Madeleine sat next to her on the couch. Jack was in his leather La-Z-Boy and Mike was long gone. But he would be watching too, wherever he was. The whole world was watching. Walter Cronkite, "the voice of space," was standing by to bring them live footage from the moon. "History in the making," Madeleine expected her father to say, but he just watched, tight-lipped. His grim profile trained on the screen reminded her of something but she couldn't place it. Another broadcast, years ago. . . . The late John F. Kennedy's voice came up under photographs of the smiling astronauts, " . . . this nation should pledge itself, before this decade is out, to landing a man on the moon, and returning him safely to. . . ." And she remembered: crouching on the landing in her pajamas, listening to the sound of the television, hollow and mushrooming up the stairs to reach her where she sat hugging her knees. *Anyone who thinks the Russian missiles can't reach Centralia from Cuba is sorely mistaken.* Her memory wants to attribute this to Kennedy, she can hear it in his Boston tones, but she knows Mr. March said it. Mr. March explaining the domino effect: *For want of a nail the shoe was lost, for want of a shoe, the horse was lost. . . .*

Walter Cronkite brought her back. " . . . live, from the moon." On screen, the *Eagle* landed, spindly and impossibly fragile, more insect than bird. Neil Armstrong's boot hit the surface and raised a puff of moon dust. "That's one small step for a man—"

Jack said, "Well, we beat them."

Mimi threw up her hands. "What did he just say?! *Bon D'jeu,* Jack, you talked over him."

"They'll rerun it."

They saw the earth reflected in the glass of a NASA helmet. They watched as the astronaut lumbered weightlessly, as blunt as a child's drawing—his glossy round head; the rudimentary movements of arms and legs encased in white, segmented at the joints; a slow bounding caterpillar poised with the American flag, which he planted in the Sea of Tranquility. It was really happening. Up there. While we were watching down here on earth, in the rec room.

Jack shifted his chair to the upright position with a *thunk,* rose and headed from the room. Mimi ignored him but Madeleine called, "Dad, aren't you going to watch?"

"What for? He did his job, over and out."

Madeleine was shocked.

"It's a sideshow," said Jack.

Mimi reached for a cigarette, and Madeleine tensed. She hated it when they bickered. Her mother was like one of those Hitchcock birds, pecking, pecking at her father's head with red talons. No wonder he had no patience with her. She's going through menopause—like one giant endless "time of the month," thought Madeleine uncharitably, staring at her mother's tight face. Things had been calmer since Mike had left home, but constricted, too. Arid.

Her father continued, referring to the television so Madeleine would know he wasn't directing his bitterness toward her. "These guys'll splash down—if they don't burn up on re-entry—and they'll get a big tickertape parade and all that good stuff, and we'll all pretend to be interested in moon rocks, but no one wants to know the real story."

"What do you mean?" Madeleine could hear something in his voice—either it was new or she was recognizing it for the first time. A self-pitying note. It repelled and embarrassed her.

"No one wants to know what it took to get them up there." He jerked his thumb at the ceiling, dry red patches appearing on his cheeks. "While the hippies have been moaning and bellyaching about police brutality and free this and psychedelic that, it's all been happening right under their noses."

This voice didn't belong to her dad. Her dad gave opinions, sometimes adamant, but always with an expansive quality, inviting argument. This man was whining. "You want to know where the rocket program started?" he asked, thin-lipped.

Madeleine was confused. "Okay."

"Ever hear of Dora?"

"Who?"

"What do they teach you in school anyhow? Sociology and basket-weaving, God help this generation—"

Mimi said, "Shhh."

Walter Cronkite had established contact with the Marshall Space Flight Center, where Wernher von Braun was standing by. Jack left the room.

Later that evening Madeleine asked her father who Dora was, but he waved his hand dismissively. "Ancient history."

"Dad, are you mad at me?"

He laughed. "Naw, what gave you that idea? I'll tell you something, you're lucky to've been born into a generation of yahoos. You'll be able to set them all straight." He asked if she wanted to go to a movie. *Butch Cassidy and the Sundance Kid.* Mimi didn't go with them. She never did.

When they got home, Mimi was in bed. Jack made them a snack of sardines on toast and a cucumber broken in half and doused, bite by bite, with salt. Food of the gods. They talked about the origins of life; about whether or not there was a purpose, a design for it all; about the nature of time and the illusion that it moved forward. He poured her a Scotch, taught her to sip it. The Scots were the most civilized people on earth, second only to the Irish, from whom they sprang; they gave us golf, single malt and accounting. He laughed and she could see his gold tooth. He asked her where she wanted to be in five years.

"On TV," she answered.

He reached for a napkin, found a pencil stub in Mimi's coffee can next to the phone, licked the tip and drew a flowchart. "What's your first step?"

The man who whined reappeared from time to time, but she kept him separate from her dad. It never occurred to her that the woman who criticized and complained was anyone other than her mother.

Madeleine walks her bike home through Kensington Market after her session with the therapist. She has chosen not to ride, aware of carrying something that ought not to be jostled. She pictures a collection of old wooden blocks painted with letters of the alphabet—faded red A, blue M, stolid D. . . . They are in a precarious pile, as though they have recently been played with and may collapse at the slam of a door, an adult footfall.

The sights and sounds of the market envelop her, she is comforted by the ramshackle opulence of it all. Feathers lilt up with the breeze of passing feet, narrow streets are gridlocked with cars at the mercy of pedestrians as disregarding as pigeons. Madeleine looks up; buds are on the trees, and the thousand market smells have begun to blossom too, in the warmth of the April noon—empanadas, chicken shit and Brie. West Indian, Portuguese, Latin American, Granola, Punk, Dowdy Artist, Old Lady Who Has Lived in That House since 1931, Korean, Italian, Greek, Vietnamese, South Asian. . . . Toronto's politicians are on a "world-class" kick, and monuments to eighties prosperity have been going up—gold-plated bank buildings, the CN Tower. But this is where Toronto is truly world-class, because so much of the world has chosen to live here.

She turns from Augusta onto Baldwin Street, already appreciating the shade of musty awnings. Even if most of the live animals are destined for the chop, at least you can hear them squawk, see them strutting freely in courtyards. In the fishmonger's, giant turtles stir like living rocks; doomed lobsters crawl over one another in their tanks; bright trout and tuna bask on their beds of crushed ice, united in their one-eyed stare across the great fresh/salt water divide; in the window of the butcher shop a stencilled trio of smiling pig, calf and chicken preside over the pledge *Live and Fresh Killed;* bunnies hang upside down, stripped of flesh, resembling cats; there is no pretence here. Nothing comes in a Styrofoam shell emblazoned with a logo, history of hoofs and ears erased. The most processed thing you can buy is a jar of Kraft Sandwich Spread, wipe the dust from the lid first. Vegetables tower, the bins of nuts and rice could suffocate a grown man if they ever tipped over, and you can buy a complete wardrobe of Doc Martens, plaid flannel jacket, orange safety vest and polyester sundress for under fifty bucks.

Kensington is bordered on the east by a Chinatown that's advancing up Spadina Avenue, following the prosperous retreat north of the first wave of Eastern European Jews, kosher delis giving way to Peking duck, bolts of textiles to embroidered dragons. Bagels are now toasted and draped with lox by women fresh from Hong Kong. Businesses and dwellings are tucked in tight, their painted signs abrupt translations of the mother tongue—restaurants, funeral parlours and weight loss clinics, "Eating Counter," "Danger Figure Centre," "Wing On Funeral Home." And a curious concentration of driving schools.

On the corner, a wooden telephone pole bristles with staples, some biting into nothing more than dog-eared wads, the corners of flyers long since torn away to make room for fresh chatter—*Refuse the Cruise, A Woman's Right to Choose, Learn to Think in Spanish! Reg Hart Retrospective, Sunny Basement Apartment, Have You Seen Our Cat? The Vile Tones at the Cameron, Hamburger Patty at the El Mocambo, Abortion Is Murder! Thursday Is Dyke Night.* A glossy new poster catches her eye—three women in matching power suits, stylish, almost film-noirish, the thrusting semicircle of city hall in the background. The race for mayor is on. The favourite to win is a politician called Art Eggleton. The women in the poster are part of a multimedia alternative theatre company called Video Cabaret. They are running as one candidate. Their slogan: *Art versus Art.*

Toronto is a big dresser with big drawers, and this is a golden time when there is room for everyone to fight for room, enough funding for the arts to seem as though there is not enough funding for the arts, and massive immigration in flight from an increasingly dangerous world.

Down Spadina and along King Street, old textile factories—ex–sweat shops years away from loft conversion—are presently incarnated as cavernous rehearsal spaces and illegal live-in artists' studios, where thousands of straight pins can be found in the cracks between the floorboards. It's in one of these—the Darling Building—that Madeleine is working with Olivia on a piece called *The Deer*. A bewildering, glacial process called collective creation. She feels as foreign to it as those women from Hong Kong must feel when rumpled regulars of The Bagel set themselves down at the counter and ask for knishes.

Olivia asked Madeleine to be part of a group of actors with whom she is creating this feminist revision of the Greek tragedy *Iphigenia*.

"Why don't you call it *Death in Venison?*" said Madeleine.

"I think it's about colonialism," said Olivia, and Madeleine nodded sagely.

The "alternative theatre" is about as far from the comedy scene as you can get, but Christine encouraged her to do it, and Madeleine jumped in, if only because Olivia has a piquant way of both idolizing her and disagreeing with everything she says. *The Deer* is set on a shifting landscape evocative of the fence at Greenham Common and a rainforest. Olivia is working with a composer on a score inspired by baroque music and Latin jazz which incorporates text from *Dr. Strangelove*. Last night they improvised a scene in which the deer was caught in car headlights and interrogated in Spanish and English. "Are you now or have you ever been a member of the Sandinista party?" "Are you tired and listless? . . ." It all makes a strange sort of sense to her, but she is reluctant to admit this to Olivia. The deer itself—Madeleine—is an entirely physical role.

"Why do you want me to be in this?" Madeleine had asked.

"Because you're good with story and character."

"I thought it was supposed to be avant-garde, non-narrative, non-fun theatre."

"You see why I need you."

They had gone to the Free Times Café and Olivia had bought her a beer and was asking her opinion on everything despite Madeleine's protestations that "I don't know much about art, but I don't know much about art." Olivia is a gorgeous, if slightly punked-out, egghead. The reverse of the classic 1950s secretary whose boss says, "Miss Smithers, take off your glasses. Now remove that bobby pin from your bun." And *voilà,* bombshell. Madeleine listened and allowed one eye to cross toward the other—her way of declaring herself allergic to the kind of intellectualizing that Christine and Olivia love to get up to.

"But Madeleine, you *are* an intellectual."

She responded with her best puppet face, and Olivia laughed but didn't back down until she had drawn out and dismantled Madeleine's most dearly held prejudices. "You deal with ideas all the time, your work is *about* something." Olivia's eyes are hot crystal-cut blue, the irises limned in black, they make her olive skin glow.

"I hate arguing, why am I arguing with you?!"

Olivia countered reasonably, "We're talking, I'm asking you questions about yourself, you love it."

At the corner of her mouth there is an indentation—not so much a dimple as a bracket—that lingers after she smiles. Shades of the face she will age into, eroded by happiness.

"What."

"What 'what'?" says Madeleine.

"You just zoned right out."

"Oh yeah? Well . . . you're not the boss of me, kid."

Madeleine decides to stop for a coffee. Olivia resides in the top two floors of one of these festively decaying houses, over a bar and grill. Christine is a TA at the university and Olivia was one of her students. Being a few years younger, she has enjoyed waif status, Christine insisting on feeding her, even at times dressing her—"Here, you can have these, I plan never to be that thin again." But Olivia has a fixed address now, and last month she had them over for dinner. She cooked a vegetarian chili, and they sat at a long sawhorse table with the five grungy housemates. Madeleine has never understood the appeal of communal living and, although Christine respects vegetarianism, she woke up starving in the middle of the night, made BLTs and teased Madeleine, "Olivia's got a crush on you." Madeleine knew better. "She's way more interested in you, babe. Besides, she's not my type."

Madeleine finds a nice birdshitty table outside at the Café LaGaffe and orders a cappuccino. She discovered, during the vegetarian feast, that Olivia's mother is Algerian and her father is a United Church minister. She has blue eyes and speaks French with an Arabic accent. Madeleine doesn't have to explain contradiction to Olivia.

Marianne Faithful croaks over the speakers, "It's just an old war, not even a cold war, don't say it in Russian, don't say it in German. . . ."

Madeleine reaches down for an empty matchbook from the pavement and wedges it under one wobbly wrought-iron leg. *Success without Colleen* promises the cover. She blinks. *College.* "Say it in bro-o-oken English. . . ."

She can see the CN Tower over the shingled roofs and between the skyscrapers beyond. She can smell the four corners of the earth. The old guy whose pet parrot rides on his head and swears walks by.

"Hi George," she says.

The parrot swivels his head and replies genially, "Fuck off."

Madeleine laughs, asks the waiter, "Have you got a pen?" And reaches for a napkin.

In Jack's hospital room, the cardiologist told him and Mimi, "In these cases, we have three options. One is to extend the life of the patient through surgery. Two is to improve the health of the patient through drugs. Three is to stabilize the patient and increase his comfort through drugs and . . . oxygen . . . et cetera. In your case, Mr. McCarthy, the first two options are not open to us."

The doctor looked about twelve.

Jack's face felt tight. He thought, *You're sending me home to die, thanks for nothin', buddy.* He nodded and said, "Fair enough."

Mimi said, "You can do better than that."

"I'm afraid we can't, Mrs. McCarthy. But there's no reason your husband can't enjoy—"

Mimi said, "*C'est assez, merci,*" and turned her back on him.

He flushed. Jack winked and gave him a complicit smile. "Well. We'll see you soon, sir," said the young doctor, and fled.

It was not a case of getting a second opinion. This was the third opinion—Mimi hadn't stopped until she had pulled every string and found out who was good, who was the best and who was a butcher. She turned back to Jack and said tartly, "Well Monsieur, what am I going to do to you?"

He grinned at her; she almost managed a smile, squeezed shut her eyes, clenched her hands until she felt the nails dig into her palms and, just as tears breached her lids, felt his arms around her.

"You're not supposed to get up."

"Who told you that?" He chuckled in her ear, holding her as close as he dared, careful of the intravenous tubes at his wrist. She felt warm. Hairspray and Chanel. Still so soft.

What is it to end a love story after forty years? So many nice times. So many remember-whens. Remember, Missus? I remember—*je me souviens.*

What is it when so much of what is precious is so far past? Like a drawer sealed for so long. Open it, up wafts memory, love, no sorrow or recollection of hardship. How can this be? They lived through the Depression. They lived through a war. How is it that it was so sweet? How is it that the scent rises fresh as lilacs and cut grass? That sunny place. Post-war. Let's have kids. Let's be the ones who do it right.

They sway ever so slightly. *That's why, darling, it's incredible that someone so unforgettable, thinks that I am unforgettable too.*

They stood like that for a while. From outside the hospital room, through the big window that looked onto the corridor, it would have been difficult to say which one was weeping. Jack held his wife and experienced such a powerful sense of déjà vu, it felt like a blessing, and he had never been so grateful in his life.

Mimi wanted to tell Madeleine the truth. Jack said, "You're the boss. Let me do it, though."

When Madeleine arrived at the hospital later that day, Jack told her, "They've sprung me. No need for surgery."

When Mimi returned to his room after fixing her makeup, she could see from her daughter's face that her husband had told her nothing at all. She got out the Scrabble. She pressed on.

They discouraged their daughter from visiting again too soon. Jack didn't want to alarm her with the sight of an oxygen tank—she was busy, she was young; better that he and Mimi should get used to his new "lifestyle" first. "Wait till I'm back on my feet," said Jack over the phone in February, "and we'll go for a big juicy steak. That is, if Maman lets me."

In March they said they were driving down to see her in Toronto, but at the last minute Jack phoned to say Mimi had the flu. In April they said, "We're thinking of going to New Brunswick next week, why don't you plan on a weekend in May?"

# Scenes from a Marriage

*"Who am I, then? Tell me that first, and then, if I like being that person, I'll come up; if not, I'll stay down here till I'm somebody else."*
                Lewis Carroll, Alice's Adventures in Wonderland

When Madeleine got home last Friday night after the taping—the night the "thing" happened in her car—Christine had cooked eggplant parmigiana. Madeleine wasn't hungry but she said, "Boy, something sure smells good."

She ate a slice and Christine ran her a scented bath. Madeleine was still fresh from her shower of a couple of hours ago, but Christine had put flower petals in the water.

"Thanks, babe."

Christine handed her a glass of wine and began gently, sensuously, to wash her back. It felt like someone stomping around, rattling the things on Madeleine's dresser. Something was going to fall and break.

"Um. I think I'm getting a cold."

"Oh yeah?" said Christine sympathetically, brushing back a lock of her long wavy hair where the tips were trailing in the water.

"Yeah, my skin hurts."

Christine dropped the washcloth into the tub with a plop and exited the bathroom.

Madeleine called after her. "It felt . . . great, babe, really—thanks. . .," her voice sounding robotic in her own ears.

The death of desire is a bottomlessly sad thing. Books are written, documentaries are made and counsellors are paid to help people want each other again. Perhaps it's just a momentary ebb in the tide of our relationship, let's take this opportunity to see what treasures have washed up on the beach in the meantime. Get to know one another again. Take a holiday.

And perhaps it comes back, or perhaps it does enough for one party but not the other. Desire can be detected at such low levels that it's difficult to say when it's dead. The patient is on life-support "but she can still hear you." When do you pull the plug?

Madeleine waited until the apartment was silent before getting out of the bath. If Christine was already asleep when she came to bed, Madeleine would be relieved. But it would be all she could do to resist waking her to find out if she was mad at her. If Christine wasn't angry about the small "empathic break" in the bath just now, she was sure to be angry at having been awakened. Madeleine would exert a good deal of energy getting Christine over her anger; this might involve Ovaltine and cognac. Then, once Christine had reassured Madeleine that she was no longer angry, Madeleine might use the opportunity to punish Christine for having had the gall to be angry over nothing. This punishment would consist of a silent, innocent distraction—an absent glance toward the curtained window as she set down the steaming mug.

"What is it, Madeleine?"

"Wha—? Oh, nothing. It's just . . . never mind."

And Madeleine's actual grievances would rear, not their heads, but a few hairs, apropos of nothing. Christine would never see what didn't hit her, but she would intuit it all. At three A.M.

"You hate me, why don't you just say it, Madeleine?"

"Christine, why are you so mad at me all of a sudden?"

And the cycle would begin again.

In fact, Madeleine loves Christine dearly, would feel gouged and left for dead were she to lose her—feels everything but the abiding sexual interest that allows two people to grapple happily and hotly, then take each other for granted, in the nicest possible way, over breakfast. And to allow one another what is now called personal space, but is really just a new spin on an old virtue—privacy. Privacy is sexy.

They got together in their twenties; privacy was hypocritical then, a form of patriarchal frost. Madeleine is learning the difference between secrecy and privacy. With Christine she has no privacy, but plenty of secrets. Christine can smell them, like bones buried all over the house, and it drives her crazy. Madeleine has hidden them so well that she has no idea they are secrets. Mice dying behind the walls, dreadful smells wafting up the drain.

Christine will walk away and slam the bedroom door. Madeleine, in a rage at being shut out, will punch the wall, then her own head. She may, depending on the ferocity of leashed but ungrounded anger, open the cutlery drawer, find the sharpest knife and carefully wrap her hand around its blade, slowly squeezing up to, but not past, the point of laceration—because how did her life take her, step by step, into the domestic clutches of such a bitch? Then she will open the fridge to get a glass of water, and the sight of the leftover eggplant parmigiana will cause her to weep, because poor Christine cooked it innocently and with love.

As they played out a version of this that Friday night, it never occurred to Madeleine to tell Christine what had happened to her in her car on the way home.

"I'm not into 'healing,' okay?" says Madeleine at her next appointment, and places a cheque for six sessions in advance on Nina's desk, next to a conch shell. "I don't want you turning me into a vegetarian or—and I don't want to be straight when I walk out of here, I want be exactly like I am now except able to drive again. And, you know, work." She sits in the swivel chair, leans back and folds her hands.

Nina says, "You don't want to be a vegetarian and you don't want to be heterosexual—"

"I wouldn't actually mind being vegetarian, I'm kind of interested in that, just not the hairy-leg kind."

Nina narrows her eyes.

Madeleine says, "You suppressed a smile just now. Either that or you're offended 'cause beneath your hemp-and-linen leisure suit you're sporting a pelt like a Sasquatch."

Nina smiles, says, "Madeleine, I'm going to take a chance and guess that you're not here about your diet or your sexual orientation, or your profession. Or even your driving habits."

"So why am I here?"

"That's what I'm hoping we'll work toward."

"No, can you please just take a wild therapeutic guess?"

Nina says, "You want to go forward. But something is stopping you. You feel as though you should know what it is, but you can't make it out. It's like trying to identify an elephant when all you can see is one square inch of it."

Madeleine is tempted to yield to something. Repose. The promise of it makes her newly aware that she is fatigued. "Or looking at a mountain from an inch away," she says.

Christine had mixed feelings about Madeleine going into therapy.

On the one hand: "Good."

"Why?" said Madeleine. "You think I'm that fucked up?"

"I think you have . . . issues."

"*Gesundheit.*"

On the other hand: "Is this just an elaborate way of leaving me?"

"What? Christine, what are you—?" If Madeleine were Christine she would say, "Why is everything always about you?" But Madeleine never thinks of the right thing to say in the moment. Unless she is in front of hundreds of strangers.

"Christine, have you seen my keys?"

"Where did you leave them?"

*That's not what I asked you.*

"They're right in front of you, Madeleine."
*So they are.*

"Why do you think you're here, Madeleine?"

"Gee doc, if I knew dat, would I be here in de foist place?"

"That's very good."

"Thank you."

"You sound just like him."

"Want to see me do Woody Woodpecker?"

"I've seen you."

"Oh. Right, you've seen After-Three."

"I've seen you live too."

"Are you stalking me or what?" Nina just smiles. Madeleine says, "Want to see my evil-out-of-synch-ventriloquist-puppet laughter?"

"I've seen it."

"Want to see me do it naked?"

"I've seen you do it topless."

"Oh. Terrifying, eh?"

"It was very very funny. Madeleine—"

"Nina, are you American?"

"Originally, yes."

"Where you from?"

"Pittsburgh."

"My condolences."

"It's actually quite nice."

"Got you."

Nina smiles. "A little."

"I'm just saying that our relationship, as it grows and matures and . . . deepens, will inevitably . . . change."

"Just say it, Madeleine, you're leaving me."

"What? No! Christine, we can still—we can live together, we can still go camping."

Christine rolls her eyes, pours herself another glass of wine and doesn't bother to set the bottle down. She is defending her thesis next week. Madeleine hates herself for wishing Christine would shed ten pounds, feminists are not supposed to feel that way.

"Why are you looking at me like that?"

"Like what?" asks Madeleine, innocent distraction, reminding herself of someone—

"Like you hate me."

—her dad. "I don't hate you."

Christine glares over the rim of her wineglass. Madeleine feels like a weasel, knowing she is lying but unable to say exactly where the lie is, frisking herself to find it. "I just think we should each be free to—"

"Fuck around," says Christine. "That's what you want, just say it, you get paid for saying horrible things all the time." Here we go. "Go ahead, Madeleine, say it in a funny voice."

Christine is right. But Madeleine doesn't know how to deviate from the script.

"Where are you going?"

"Out to get cream."

"Bullshit, Madeleine, do you ever not lie? 'Hello,' she lied."

"We're out of cream."

"We're out of a lot of things."

Madeleine feels as though she's leading a double life. Loathsome guilty troll at home. Successful ray of sunshine to the rest of the world. The one who makes it look easy. The person who looks "exactly like my cousin/my best friend in high school/my boyfriend's sister, maybe you know her." Photos are produced from wallets and purses; Madeleine never fails to be amazed at the total lack of physical resemblance, and she never fails to smile and say, "Wow, that's amazing." Madeleine is familiar. Maybe that's why she gets away with so much. Why the audience is willing to follow her so far from home. Why there seem to be so many of her. While she fears there may be none at all. Pied Piper without a pipe.

Nina balances a smooth pink stone the size of an egg in the palm of her hand and asks, "Who's Maurice?"

"Don't do that."

"What?"

"Don't pathologize my work."

Nina waits.

"I made him up, that's my job, I make up weird shit all the time, it's what I get paid for."

Nina waits.

"I kind of based him on a yucky teacher I had."

Pad thai will forever taste of conjugal discontent.

"You've got so much to say to everyone else, pretend I'm a stranger, Madeleine. Pretend I'm the goddamn waiter."

She has never told Christine about Mr. March. She has never told anyone, not really. Not much to tell. Dirty old man she never thinks about any more.

Madeleine is a flirtaholic. Everyone has to have a disorder nowadays, like Brownie badges sewn up the sleeve, and that's hers. If she were a guy she would be an asshole, but she is "endearingly feisty," a "high-octane pixie," and has the press to prove it. She tells herself that as long as she does most of the flirting right in front of Christine, it doesn't count. And it never leads to anything serious like an affair. Except for that one time, which definitely didn't count. Plus the New York thing.

Deep down, Madeleine knows that what she is addicted to are escape clauses. Backdoor rabbit holes. Flirting: the long wick that leads to the stick of dynamite that can reliably blow up your life and land you in a new one. This is for people who are terrified of being trapped—and more terrified of being abandoned. This is for people for whom sex with a familiar other becomes more and more like having their wounds probed while splayed across the gutted upholstery of a midsummer car wreck.

Some say we keep repeating patterns until we figure out what they are. Madeleine is too busy to find out. It's all fun until someone loses an eye.

"Christine, where's my—"

"It's right in front of you."

Christine doesn't even have to look to know it.

"Is it just me or are you incredibly bored too?"

Nina is silent.

"Want to play Parcheesi? Have sex on your hand-knotted Bolivian rug?" Madeleine puffs an imaginary cigar. "Don't worry, you're not my type."

"What's your type?"

"Oh, you know, masses of pre-Raphaelite hair, tad of a drinking problem, an overdue thesis and a violent streak."

"Is Christine violent?"

"Naw, just when I drive her insane she's been known to"—Madeleine grins—"lose it somewhat."

"What does that look like?"

Madeleine pauses, then springs, hands outstretched, toward Nina's neck. "Like this!" Nina doesn't flinch.

Madeleine laughs.

Nina asks, "Has Christine tried to choke you?"

"Well," says Bugs Bunny, "to know me is to stwangle me."

Nina waits.

"Look, I'm not here about my relationship, no one's is perfect. I didn't come here so I could leave my partner of seven years. Is that like an itch on your belt? Nice work, you must be proud."

Nina says nothing.

"I mean 'notch.'"

Nina waits.

"Strangle is an overstatement."

"Does she put her hands around your neck?"

"Maybe once or twice."

"Did she squeeze?"

"Briefly. But it's not like I'm in any danger. She's the one who gets upset by it. And it's my fault anyhow, I know where all her buttons are."

"Can you give me an example?"

"Well. This one time. . . ." She takes a deep breath. She has never told anyone this before, and now that she has accidentally grazed the subject, it looks different. It looks ugly. "Well. . . . I criticized her bean dip and she lost it."

"Her bean dip?"

Madeleine nods. She sees something flicker across Nina's face—a smile—and feels a grin stretch the ends of her mouth. She tells the rest of the story through tears of mirth.

Christine was under a lot of pressure with her thesis. She screamed in Madeleine's face, "You're completely insensitive!" The demon entered Madeleine on cue and she began riffing—*provoking,* said Christine—"Madeleine, just grow up!"

"'I'm ony two and a half yeahs owd,'" said Tweety Bird.

"Shut up, Madeleine, please!"

Madeleine laughed like Woody and kept going—*some o' my best woik, doc.* The hands clamped around Madeleine's neck and Christine cried and throttled her for a matter of seconds. There is psychodrama. This was psychocomedy.

Madeleine sums up, in her manly broadcaster voice, "It's never just about the bean dip."

"What did you do when she began to throttle you?" asks Nina.

"I just went . . . you know . . . really calm."

"Calm?"

"Yeah. Kind of neutral, you know? Like waiting for it to be finished."

"As though it was familiar."

Madeleine stares at Nina. Feels her hands growing cool. "Why would you say that?"

"Because of the way you describe your reaction. You don't seem to have been surprised."

Madeleine takes a deep breath. "In a way I felt relieved—" she didn't know she was going to say that.

Nina nods.

After a moment, Madeleine says, "So what do you make of it, doc? Am I, like, some kind of masochist? Apart from deciding to make a living as a comedian, which, it goes without saying. . . ."

Finally Nina says, "I don't think labels like 'masochistic' are very helpful. Especially for women—or anyone for that matter."

"It's my own fault, I press her buttons."

Nina pours a glass of spring water from the pitcher.

"What do you think?" asks Madeleine.

Nina takes a sip, "I think Christine has a lot of buttons."

Madeleine laughs.

"Have you ever told anyone about the assaults?"

Madeleine looks up as though she has been slapped. It has never occurred to her that the force of Christine's grip around her neck, the thunk of her own skull against the wall, constitutes anything like abuse. Madeleine does benefits for women's shelters. She is a grassroots feminist hailed by counterculturalistas and mainstream alike, a liberated lipstick lesbian in expensively distressed leather. "They're not assaults," she says.

"What do you think of them as?"

Madeleine's mouth is dry but she doesn't want to reach for the spring water. "Wow," she drawls, "talk about a *scandale*," and, resuming her news voice, "'Feminist Egghead Assaults Funny-Girl Gal-Pal No Laughing Matter!'"

"Madeleine—?"

"'Intrawoman Violence: The Hate That Dare Not Speak Its Name.'"

"Did I upset you with my choice of word?"

"Isn't that why you chose it?"

Madeleine is aware that she is behaving predictably: denial, grandiosity, self-pity, self-loathing. The whole textbook. She rises and grabs her knapsack, muttering, "I don't need this shit," and leaves.

Madeleine has always admired Bugsy's ability to escape down convenient rabbit holes and traverse the earth underground. That is what work has been for her. Always a number of things on the go, escape routes and connecting tunnels; head popping up in the midst of a field of carrots, gorging until she is shot at, then ducking in a puff of white smoke and speeding off, looking for that left turn at Albuquerque. It worked, professionally and personally, for quite a while. Then the "things" started happening, and therapy was supposed to be another rabbit hole. But it turns out this one wasn't dug by Bugs. It belongs to the March Hare.

Maurice is seated at a dainty escritoire. He exudes a bland intensity. Beside him hangs a gilded cage from a stand. In it, a stuffed bird. His movements are small and lead nowhere, compelling and pointless. It becomes clear, however, that a decision has been accumulating behind his smudged glasses. Unhurriedly he opens a drawer in the tiny desk, withdraws a pair of panties, sniffs them, then returns them to the drawer.

That is the long and short of Maurice.

Sometimes he appears in historical garb—as a pilgrim on the *Mayflower,* or blinking tortoise-like from among the famous faces on Mount Rushmore. Combat soldier, Elmer the Safety Elephant, hippie. Always the glasses and grey suit predominate, with one or two touches —Quaker Oats hat; machine gun and reefer; stop sign, peace sign.

His inertia prevails regardless of what is occurring around him: the fall of Rome, the butter scene from *Last Tango in Paris,* the assassination of John F. Kennedy. And whether facing a high-noon duel or bounding weightlessly over the lunar surface, glasses glinting through the window of his helmet, Maurice always knows where to find the panties—in Ben Cartwright's saddlebag, under a moon rock—and, invariably, he sniffs them.

He has become a cult figure. One of those characters who break free of their creators; Madeleine recently overheard a teenager on the subway say in tones of delighted disgust, "Ooo, that's gross, that's so Maurice!"

A BOY IN RED JEANS disappeared into a sunny day long ago, in 1963. In 1973 he was quietly released from prison. He was not exonerated; he was granted parole. He had been a model prisoner and the authorities had determined that he posed no danger to the community, despite his steadfast refusal to admit guilt.

Oceans of ink were spilled on the Richard Froelich Case, which divided professionals and lay people alike. It became the subject of after-dinner speakers at coroners' conventions and police conferences. The pathologist from the trial published articles and gave lectures; Inspector Bradley was promoted and addressed meetings of law enforcement agencies from across Canada and the U.S. Both men tirelessly shared their experience of the investigation and trial, intensifying their efforts when books and articles began to appear accusing "the system" of having failed a possibly innocent boy.

Over the years, whenever there was a story about a miscarriage of justice or debate about the death penalty, the Froelich case would be cited. Newspaper articles would appear alongside old school photographs of the boy and the victim. Eternally paired in grainy reproductions, their smiles more and more remote in time—his slicked-back hair from a bygone era, her Peter Pan collar. Older and older, and younger and younger.

As time went by, the case acquired the air of legend. Articles never failed to include certain "haunting details" such as the wildflowers and the cross of bulrushes found over her body. Her underpants over her face. And "the mysterious air force man," the passing motorist who supposedly had waved from a blue Ford Galaxy, then failed to come forward. Journalists speculated that he might have been the real killer. In the late seventies, a weekly news magazine ran an article that featured an interview with a retired police officer who had been a constable on the case. Lonergan revealed for the first time that the boy's father, "a German Jew named Henry Froelich," had claimed to have seen a war criminal driving that same car in downtown London.

In the eighties a commission of inquiry was set up by the federal government to investigate the presence of war criminals in Canada.

Parts of the report were never published, available only via the Access to Information Act, for it turned out that there were possibly thousands of war criminals in Canada—among them, concentration camp guards and an entire SS unit from Eastern Europe, members of which had claimed "conscription" and a healthy hatred of Communists among their credentials in their quest for Canadian citizenship.

Eventually a few cases were brought to trial, and although public opinion was divided on whether these law-abiding senior citizens should be prosecuted after all these years—whether it was justice or "Jewish vendetta," whether it was democracy at work or playing into the hands of "Soviet propaganda"—Henry Froelich's story began to look less far-fetched. Journalists, authors and documentary filmmakers theorized about the fate of Henry Froelich, whose body had never been found. Had he stumbled on—to use a term that had become common currency—a "covert operation"? Was he a victim of RCMP dirty tricks? Was the CIA involved?

Sporadic attempts were made to find Richard Froelich and interview him. But he had changed his name, and his whereabouts remained a mystery.

# WILD KINGDOM

*Everything that is now in space had its origins here, not in America or Russia.*

René Steenbeke, speaking of Dora

ONE MORNING, Madeleine saw their pictures in the paper. Under the headline "Supreme Court Turns Down Bid for Appeal." She was seventeen at the time. But Ricky was still fifteen, and Claire of course was nine.

She glimpsed the pictures when her father turned the page at the breakfast table, then they disappeared when he folded the paper. He took it to work with him. She knew he hadn't wanted to leave it lying around. She got up from the table.

"You leaving already, *ma p'tite?*"

"Yeah, I want to get to school early. I'm meeting Jocelyn." Unnecessary lie, but harmless. Her first class that morning was a spare.

"*Qu'est-ce que tu as,* Madeleine?"

"Nothing's the matter."

"You're flushed, come till I feel your forehead."

"I'm fine."

She left, forgetting her lunch. She needed to go outside, where it was cool and normal. She didn't need to read the article, the headline said it all. She didn't want to read the fine print, to see again the words *child witnesses.* When her Man In Society teacher, Mr. Eagan, asked the class how many of them were familiar with the Richard Froelich case, Madeleine and two other students—one from Pakistan and one from Uganda—were the only ones who didn't raise their hands. She drew cartoons in the back of her scribbler while the class discussed the possible miscarriage of justice.

After supper she asked her father, "Dad, do you think it really was an air force man Ricky saw in the car?" They were in the family room, watching the new colour TV. A nature show. He didn't seem surprised by the question.

"If it was, you have to ask yourself why he didn't come forward."

"Why do you think?"

"Well, assuming Ricky wasn't mistaken, I'd have to say that this air force type, whoever he was, must've been up to something fairly confidential."

"Like what?"

He shrugged, eyes on the screen. "Government business?"

She stared at the lurid greens and shifting blues of the television.

"Do you think there really was a war criminal?"

"I wouldn't be surprised," he said, getting up to adjust the colour.

"So you think Mr. Froelich was telling the truth?"

"Knowing Henry Froelich," said Jack, "there's no doubt in my mind."

She started to ask another question, but they heard Mimi coming in through the garage door and Jack warned her with a look. They stopped talking and concentrated on the screen: an unspoiled tropical paradise—white sand, azure sea.

In the kitchen, Mimi began rattling around. Emptying the dishwasher, putting away groceries.

"He was in a camp," said Madeleine quietly. On the screen, a sea turtle glided underwater. "I saw his tattoo once."

"Did you?" His profile was impassive.

"He must've been at Auschwitz." She had studied the Holocaust in History. She never used the term "holocaust" at home, however, because her father objected to it: *the Second World War was about a whole lot more than that.* She watched the turtle sleeping on the ocean floor and heard her father say, "At first." She looked at him, perplexed, but his gaze was on the TV and he kept it there as he spoke. "He was at a different place later."

"Another camp?"

"This was no ordinary concentration camp."

She waited. *You mean there's such a thing as an "ordinary" concentration camp, doc?*

"Dora," he said.

"Who?"

On the TV, hundreds of baby turtles flailed across the beach toward the sea. Birds dropped down, leisurely, picking them off one by one as the narrator, in measured manly tones, asserted that "only a handful" would make it.

"Dora. Where the rockets were built."

"What rockets?"

"Ever hear of guided missiles? Ever hear of Apollo?"

She heard the note of grim sarcasm, the one usually reserved for politicians, the school system and—before he left home—Mike. She wondered if her father was about to get angry again, the way he had at the moon landing last summer. His anger never frightened her, however. It gave her a pang in the pit of her stomach. Something was wrong. Someone should fix it for him.

In the kitchen, Mimi turned on the Cuisinart. It sounded like a jet engine.

Jack said, "Dora is where it all started." Eyes fixed on the South Pacific. "Henry Froelich was there."

She pictured Mr. Froelich in his white shirt, skinny tie and thick glasses, bearded and conspicuous in a row of clean-shaven scientists and engineers hunched over their computers at Mission Control, Texas.

"It was a concentration camp," said Jack.

In Houston? Madeleine was beginning to feel as though she were a little stoned. A mother sea turtle began the near-futile task of digging a hole in the sand with her flippers. "Where was Dora?"

"It was in a mountain cave." His voice changed again. It took on the dreamy quality she recognized from childhood, his once-upon-a-time tone. "During the war," *a long time ago,* "in what would later become East Germany," *in a country that no longer exists,* "Hitler's secret weapon," *there was a treasure,* "built by slave labour" *they toiled out of sight of sun or moon. . . .*

The sea turtle excreted her eggs into the sandpit, hundreds of them. Buried them. And split.

"The V-2 rocket," said Jack. "V for Vengeance."

" . . . and the cycle of nature continues," said the narrator. She recognized the voice. Lorne Greene. Pa from *Bonanza.* She turned to her father again, but he was focused on the screen, features etched in concentration, he could have been watching the President, *Good evening my fellow citizens. This government, as promised, has maintained the closest surveillance of the Soviet military buildup on the island of Cuba. . . .* The surface of the sandy nest stirred. Cut to predators wheeling above. Cut back to sand, where a tiny ancient leather face breached its shell.

Mimi called from the kitchen, "Madeleine, I need your help."

"I don't suppose they've taught you who Wernher von Braun is at that high school of yours," said her father, his shoulder twitching.

"The NASA guy."

"That's right. Director of the Marshall Space Flight Center, father of the Saturn rockets that went to the moon." Model for Donald Duck's uncle, Professor Von Drake—but Madeleine kept mum. "Von Braun and his colleagues ran Dora during the war. Before it went underground, it was called Peenemünde."

*Pain Amunda.* "Uncle Simon was there—I mean he bombed it."

Jack looked at her. "That's right."

"Whatever happened to him?"

"Haven't a clue." He turned back to the screen. "Here's something I don't expect you to have learned about in school: there was a government program a few years back, in the States. The British were involved as well. So were the Canadians . . . to a degree. Still happening, for all we know."

"What was it?"

"Project Paperclip."

She waited but he was silent. A commercial came on. "What did they do?" she asked.

"They got us to the moon."

On TV, the Man from Glad bagged a housewife's leaky garbage.

"How?"

"By importing German scientists after the war. Nazis, some of them."

"Was von Braun a Nazi?"

"Darn tootin'. So was Rudolph."

"Who?"

Rudolph, Donald Duck, Apollo . . . like something out of *Mad Magazine*. But he wasn't joking. He wasn't even using his man-to-man voice, he sounded different. Constricted. The aural equivalent of looking through a telescope from the wrong end. "That must've been illegal." She knew that much from school, despite what her father liked to call the Mickey Mouse curriculum.

"It sure was, and it's still classified," he said. "So not a word."

"Madeleine." Maman was in the doorway with her yellow rubber gloves on.

"How do you know about it?" she asked her father.

He winked, and sounded like himself again. "You better go help your mother."

Madeleine was graduating high school in three weeks. In three weeks her life would begin. She slouched into the kitchen. Behind her she heard the TV switch off and the patio doors slide open. A short time later, she and her mother heard the roar of the old lawnmower, and as they chopped rhubarb and peeled apples for the church bazaar they saw him through the window, crossing at intervals back and forth, closing in on a shrinking border of longer green around the swimming pool.

She felt sorry for her father. Trapped in a suburb. With a wife incapable of discussing the subject that fascinated him most. She looked at her mother, pricking the pie crust with a fork before sliding it into the oven. Mimi could not tolerate even the mention of the name Froelich.

"My mother's way of dealing with difficult subjects was to bury them."

Nina asks, "How did your father react when you came out?"

"Oh, he was—he wasn't nearly as bad as Maman—my mother. He always asks how Christine is—unless my mother's in the room, because she'll throw a fit—"

"What does that look like?"

"Oh, oh it's all pointy and shrill and hysterical. My dad, on the other hand, takes us for lunch when he comes to Toronto."

"How does your mother feel about that?"

"We don't tell her."

"You keep it secret?"

"Not a secret, we just don't . . . well, yes, okay."

"Whose idea is that?"

"It's not an idea, we just don't want to deal with her freak-out."

Madeleine recalls strolling back to her father's hotel with him after that first visit: "How do you think Maman might feel if she knew the three of us had had lunch?" he asked.

"She'd freak."

He smiled. "You know, when I met your mother she wasn't much younger than you are now. Full of beans. Real little spitfire, like you. She's never been afraid of anything. I've been afraid of plenty, but she . . . would've made a good officer. She's been through a lot, your mother." Eyes on the sky, compressing his lips. "She's a real lady."

She felt suddenly ashamed—sad and full of guilty love for Maman.

"Her feelings might be hurt," she said.

Dad nodded and made his mild wincing expression. "That's what I'm afraid of."

"I won't mention it if you don't."

He smiled and winked at her. Pilot to co-pilot.

"So it was your father's idea," says Nina.

"He's the one who has to live with her. At least he supports my relationship."

Nina is silent.

"What?"

"So you knew Richard Froelich."

Madeleine nods.

"Did you know the child who was murdered?"

Madeleine shrugs. "Kind of."

Nina waits.

Madeleine is silent.

Nina asks, "Did your father do intelligence work?"

Madeleine almost laughs. "He's a management consultant."

"How did he know about Project Paperclip?"

"I don't know, he . . . reads a lot. Well, he reads newspapers. And *Time*. And *The Economist*. . . ." She can almost feel the lightbulb over her head when she says, "Uncle Simon."

"His brother?"

She shakes her head. "His old flying instructor. This glamorous David Niven kind of guy, you know? British—the ascot, moustache, the whole bit. He offered to train me as a spy." She hits the arm of the swivel chair in delight. "Any bets he was an intelligence type!"

"Where is he now?"

"I don't know. Maybe he's dead."

They sit silent for a few moments. Then Madeleine asks, "Have you ever heard of Dora?"

"No."

"What were you thinking just now?"

"Oh, just that it's an odd name."

"The Nazis liked to give pretty names to horrible places."

"Yes, but Dora was also the name of a patient of Freud's."

Christine has told Madeleine this story. Dora was a famous "hysteric." She told Freud that her father had interfered with her sexually, and Freud believed her at first. Then he started hearing so many rape and abuse stories from so many women that he decided they were all deluded.

"Your father believed Henry Froelich."

"Yeah. He was about the only one who did." Madeleine looks at the ceiling, compressing her lips. "My dad is like that. Loyal."

WHAT HAPPENED in a cave long ago. What happened in a classroom. What happened at a crossroads, in a meadow, on a bridge.

When the Piper was not paid, he treated the children as he had the rats. Led them away. They disappeared into a mountain. All but one who was lame. What was in the mountain?

They never found Henry Froelich's body. Jack never heard from Simon again. He never heard of Oskar Fried again. All the children disappeared into adults, all but one who returned to the earth and remained there. Forever young.

The cave called Dora remained part of East Germany, borders shifting around it. The Berlin Wall began to crumble from within. One side could no longer afford the arms race and, like a homeowner taking the precaution of opening windows before a hurricane, parted the Iron Curtain and called it glasnost. The wind reawakened a babel of nations, and they wanted borders that followed bloodlines.

Oil crises, hijackings and environmental disasters. "Terrorism" arose to rival "Cold War," and "covert action" entered common parlance. Security required secrecy, and so did its crimes, but all was worth it if we managed to avoid "the big one." As it turned out, the small ones were very profitable, waged by "freedom fighters" or "terrorists," depending on who had last sold them arms. The trick was to spread the weapons and the cash around in such a way as to keep the Third World, the Arab world, all the "other" worlds, at each others' throats. The West was winning.

Rockets bred anti-ballistic missiles and spawned dreams of Star Wars—safety nets in the sky, life imitating entertainment to lull the prosperous into forgetting about the danger lurking in human hearts; the same anger that triggered a holocaust in 1914 with a simple assassin's bullet, its trajectory traceable through a century. Fanaticizing anger. Anger that requires no bullets. Anger that consumes empires.

Still the cave waited. Gaping, sore and empty. As time went by, it mattered less and less that in 1969 a rocket went from Florida to the moon and men walked there. Good men. People's dads.

These were only events, scattered in time. Draw them close, rub them between thumb and finger till they roll like larvae, soften like silk, distend to knot, to weave.

It takes a village to kill a child.

## Bambi Meets Godzilla

In pop culture and folk tales, ghosts haunt creepy houses at night, appear in old photographs of church picnics, are glimpsed in the rain-lashed beam of a headlight on a country road amid endless fields of corn. In life, they arrive when you are emptying the dryer at ten A.M.

The shadow is the same. It chooses mundane moments. Like most ghosts, it does not wish to scare you off. It needs to be seen. That's why it has come. Imagine the sheer exhaustion of making the journey up from the shades time and again, only to have your long-lost one shriek and run away. That's why it learns to approach in the open, when you are engaged in familiar tasks, guard down. Doing the dishes. Driving. It doesn't necessarily want you to crash, but it does want your attention. It gets this by making the familiar shockingly unfamiliar.

Madeleine can no longer drive on the 401 where it proliferates into sixteen lanes across the top of Toronto. She can no longer see the whole road all at once, only one piece at a time—broken line, section of guardrail, whoosh of a passing car, another, another, another. These days she has to take the slow city streets all the way up to the After-Three studios in the northern suburbs, adding forty minutes to the trip. Life is too short, but she has no choice. That place from which we perceive the world—the cockpit behind the eyes, the *me-ness*—fragments into a multitude of formerly autonomic tasks that suddenly require volition: breathe now, blink now, beat now, steer. *Trust your instruments*. Her only real choice is to wrench the wheel into traffic. Not to do so is to prolong the terrifying paralysis of entrapment. The terrifying insanity of no choice. You have a choice. Wrench the wheel. This will make something make sense.

With multiple lanes shooting past her on both sides, Madeleine repeats random phrases, ads—"'You deserve a break today, so get up and get away'"—until she is able to pull over or exit. Then, forehead resting against the steering wheel, parked in front of a mall where there is nothing to buy but water purification systems and barbecues that roast whole steers and bake cakes: "'You'll wonder where the yellow went, the yellow went, the yellow went. . . .'" Okay. It's okay now.

"I've become neurotic. I'm going to be one of those irritating middle-aged women who's got to have the aisle seat and can't be trusted next to the emergency exit. I'm afraid all the time, a total coward."

Nina is silent. Madeleine takes a breath; her eyes wander to the Georgia O'Keeffe print—bleached skull of a steer—then over to the clock, distended Dali-like through the glass water pitcher.

Nina says, "Fear isn't the opposite of courage."

"What?"

"It's the prerequisite to courage."

Madeleine dismisses this with a raised eyebrow.

"You said 'the thing' first happened when you were performing," says Nina. "But did it remind you of anything? Was it familiar in any way?"

Madeleine is surprised because the answer is so close at hand—lying on the surface, like a sealed envelope on a stack of mail after the holidays. She opens it:

It was during *Bambi*. Part of a double bill with *Bambi Meets Godzilla* at the Rialto Cinema in Ottawa. Her best friend, Jocelyn, had smoked half a joint but Madeleine, being a failed druggie, hadn't had any, so it wasn't that. She was fifteen, Joss was sixteen.

"Wake up, wake up! Wake up, friend Owl!" cried Thumper.

At the sight of the cheery rabbit Madeleine felt her extremities cool. At the same time her face grew hot. "Are you hot?" she asked Jocelyn.

"No, it's freezing in here."

"I mean are you cold?"

"Are you stoned or what?"

Madeleine felt fear rise like a tide to her chin. Her heart began to ripple, then race. She became convinced she was about to die. She had in fact been diagnosed with a heart murmur—mild, the doctor had said, no impediment to athletic activity or a normal life, just have it checked as you get older. But this rippling didn't feel familiar. Was this what a heart attack felt like? A "murmuring" heart—what was it trying to say?

"If you can't say something nice, don't say nothin' at all!" chanted the stoned audience along with Thumper.

If I think about my heart, my heart will stop. If I don't think about my heart, my heart will stop.

"Bird!" Bambi's first word.

"Want some?" Jocelyn passed Madeleine the popcorn.

"Butterfly."

Madeleine obeyed an old impulse and smelled her hands. Jocelyn didn't notice, she was gazing up at the screen, giggling, glassy-eyed.

Madeleine rose from her body. She gripped the armrests but this only caused her to rise more swiftly.

"Wait here," said Bambi's mother. "I'll go out first, and if the meadow's safe, I'll call you." A shot rings out.

"Faster, Bambi! Don't look back!"

She hovered in an elastic curve high above her own hands, she could see them lying limp on the worn velvet armrests below. She must have grown, for she was stretched over several rows of seats now. It was not entirely unpleasant. Winter comes and goes. In the meadow, new grass pierces the snow. Crows sound the alarm. . . .

"Mother! Mother!" cried Bambi. The audience laughed.

Jocelyn said, "Here, you can have the rest." The condensation of the cold paper cup against her hand jolted Madeleine in her seat and, now that she was back, she was terrified of having left her body. Her heart beat rapidly, panting like a tongue, stinging like a cut.

She stared at the floor—sticky splotches, the popcorn tar pits. She chewed the plastic straw. She was okay.

"So . . . ," says Madeleine, "what? Don't just tilt your head attentively. Give."

Nina half smiles.

"Come on, Mona Lisa."

"The psychiatric term is 'depersonalization.'"

Madeleine allows her gaze to rest on the bleached skull. How did O'Keeffe manage to capture an image of serenity rather than morbidity? "So how come people get depersonalized?"

"Any number of reasons," says Nina. "Abuse, for example."

Madeleine feels her body temperature drop. The breath drops from her body too. She has to go to the bathroom.

Nina continues. "It's a survival mechanism. It can feel crazy, but it originates as a pretty sane response to an insane situation. The ability to 'leave your body' when what is going on is intolerable."

Madeleine feels her face grow hot. Shame is a physical condition, there ought to be an over-the-counter spray to control its embarrassing effects—so much worse than leaving your dentures in an apple.

Nina pours Madeleine some water.

Madeleine says, in a Viennese accent, "Very interestink."

Nina picks up the pink egg and asks, "Does Maurice ever speak?"

Madeleine doesn't answer.

"Why don't you do any women characters?"

"Why don't you buy a new pair of Birkenstocks, those are getting on my nerves."

# A Dozen Muffins

From on top of the fridge Mimi takes a bowl of muffin ingredients that she prepared earlier today, before driving her friend Doris to the doctor. Doris is widowed and has osteoporosis. Mimi is one of the lucky ones.

She removes the shower cap from the bowl, adds milk and eggs and stirs with the wooden spoon. She holds the phone receiver in the crook of her shoulder and talks to her sister Yvonne long-distance while she works.

"Doris, she's the one with the stutter," says Yvonne. Mimi can hear the clickety-click of needles—Yvonne is knitting.

"Yvonne! She has a slight speech impediment."

"She turns everything into a shaggy dog story, that one. I'm always half-dead and totally starved by the time she gets to the point."

Mimi laughs. "She wants to know when you're coming up again."

"Don't tell her!"

"She's going to give you a card party."

"No!"

When Yvonne asks what she's doing, Mimi replies that she is making muffins but doesn't say that they are for her daughter. It's not because Jack is close by, in the living room, that Mimi doesn't broach the subject of Madeleine—he wouldn't understand her in any case, because of course she and Yvonne speak in French. But Mimi doesn't discuss Madeleine with anyone; not with her husband, because he doesn't share her feelings about what he calls their daughter's lifestyle; and not with Yvonne, because Yvonne does. She and her sister both believe that the way Madeleine lives is a mortal sin and a total rejection of her parents and everything they taught her. Yvonne is more graphic: "She shits on it." Yvonne feels the anger and the disgust. Everything but the love.

So when Yvonne asks, Mimi replies, "Making muffins."

"How's my little prince?" *Mon p'tit prince?*

"He's himself."

"Put him on."

Jack is in his La-Z-Boy. The condo is designed so that the kitchen opens onto the dining and living area. She can see the top of his head but she doesn't want to wake him if he's napping. The TV is on. She puts down the phone and goes to his chair; his eyes are closed. She turns off the TV; he opens his eyes.

"Just restin' my eyeballs."

"Want to say *bonjour* to Yvonne?"

"Sure."

Within moments he is laughing. She can see his gold tooth, and a healthy colour enters his face. She spoons the batter into the muffin pan. Yvonne loves Jack as if he were her baby brother. Nothing has ever been too good for him. *Un vrai gentilhomme, Mimi, ton mari.*

The last time Mimi and her sister discussed Madeleine, it was likewise over the phone. Yvonne said, "What happened to her?" She shared Mimi's belief that the blight must be the result of something. "Did someone touch her?"

Mimi felt sick in the pit of her stomach. Something had happened to her child. Because she had failed to protect her.

Yvonne said, "She always had a secret, that one."

*Like her father,* thought Mimi.

"Did you ask her father?" Yvonne continued.

Mimi was startled because at first it was as though her sister had read her mind. Then she realized what Yvonne might have meant, and she went icy. She didn't want to have to lose her sister, so she pretended not to have heard. And perhaps Yvonne had meant something quite innocent. The line was silent for a moment, then Yvonne said, "Men are men." She always said this in English—the way some people reserve the foulest words for a foreign language.

Yvonne must have sensed what hung in the balance, because she never again broached the subject of "what happened to Madeleine."

Mimi stands, muffin pan in hand, poised to open the oven when the red light extinguishes. Jack laughs and says, "I don't know, I'll ask her"—and to Mimi, "Yvonne wants to know how come you never bring me down home any more."

"You tell her I don't want *les belles de Bouctouche* stealing you away." The light goes out and she slides the pan into the oven.

Dark, dark, far back in the back of her mind is a shadow. She never turns to look. It wafts from time to time toward the front, where it settles momentarily, like a veil, before retreating once more. The breath that lifts the veil and carries it is shaped into words as it passes through the lacework. The words must never be spoken and she does not heed them: *did my child's father touch her?*

In Centralia, the look on the child's face when she played—wrestled—with her father. The blood on her underpants, the little lies she told. *No.* Mimi squeezes her eyes shut and keeps busy. This is the kind of thought sent by the Devil. In whom she does not believe—a heresy for which, perhaps, she is being punished. So she has never asked her daughter, "Did someone touch you when you were small?"

Mimi is looking forward to meeting God. He will have some questions for her, but she has a few for Him. He doesn't know everything, He can't. He's not a mother.


## When Do I Find Time to Write?
## I'm Writing Right Now

"What on earth is this?" asks Christine.

"It's a barbecue." Madeleine is on the balcony, tilted back on a kitchen chair with the phone and a mongrel accumulation of notes, trying to write.

"Really?"

"Yeah, it even bakes cakes."

Christine stares at her. "Why would anyone want to bake a cake on a barbecue?"

"I thought you might like it."

"I'm not your bloody wife, Madeleine."

If you are an aspiring alcoholic, if you were abused by your parents, if you have a mysterious chronic condition and wish to find a reason for it, move in with someone who is trying to write. You need never look farther for the source of your pain.

Madeleine says, "I'll cook supper, I'll make paella." She gets up, lifts a rounded lid in the centre of the barbecue. "See?"

Christine turns and goes back inside. Madeleine experiences guilt, fear, pathos—the food groups. The beaded curtains sway provocatively in Christine's wake, a housewarming gift from Olivia.

Madeleine has spent the afternoon writing, having promised to come in with a revised shape for the "Breaking News" sketch. She's working on an idea for a war criminal thing—it's all over the news, a recent rash of decrepit Nazis arrested while pruning their rose bushes in suburbs across Canada. She has also sworn to give Shelly a paragraph for *Stark Raving Madeleine,* and has a good excuse to figure something out because she told her friend Tommy she'd do five minutes at an AIDS benefit next Monday—*Love in the Time of Latex.* Conveniently, she has no time to write because evening workshop sessions have been scheduled this week on *The Deer.*

"Bring Olivia over after," said Christine this morning.

"We're working till midnight."

"I thought you were finished at nine."

"The schedule changed. I'm sorry, sweetie, it'll all be over soon."

Christine smiled. "Wait, stay in bed, I'll bring your coffee." She paused at the door in her burgundy robe. In the light filtering through the blinds, she looked just as she had when they met. For that first date they had planned to go to a film festival movie— Madeleine had already bought the tickets—but they didn't make it out of Christine's apartment for three days. They saved the movie tickets. Put them in the album with the photos that traced seven years. Holidays, birthdays, friends. The Story of Madeleine and Christine. "You know what?" said Christine. "Everything's going to be okay. All your work. This project with Olivia is exactly what you need right now. It's going to feed into the thing you're working on for Shelly. It's going to help give you your new show. And that's going to change everything."

"Come here."

Christine snuggled back next to Madeleine.

But that was this morning. And who knows by what series of incremental snags and toe-pinching minutiae the day progressed to the point where they fought over a wretched barbecue?

Madeleine is due at the Darling Building in ninety minutes. No time for paella—what was I thinking? Having no time to write is almost as important as having all the time in the world. She had all day. She procrastinated elaborately, virtuosically. While cleaning the fridge, she noticed an overdue bill stuck to the door with an Emma Goldman magnet. She dutifully wrote a cheque, and stepped out to the post office for stamps.

She and Christine live in the top half of a Victorian house in the Annex, a leafy downtown neighbourhood of artists, students, immigrants and lefty yuppies. On her way down Brunswick toward Bloor she breathed deeply of spring, and noticed that the sidewalks were packed with look-alike couples. There were identical lesbians with neatly pressed sweatshirts and big glasses. There were gay men with matching sideburns. There were straight couples in khakis and windbreakers— stick a canoe on their heads and it's anyone's guess. Twinsexuals. At the post office in the back of the pharmacy, she reached into her pocket for money to buy stamps and found a "Final Notice" for a delivery—funny how one never receives a "First Notice." She handed it across the counter and the elderly Korean lady gave her a brown-paper package about the size of a cereal box. She opened it—a bran flakes carton, mummified with masking tape. Inside, a dozen stale muffins and a note in her mother's hand, "Ma chérie, bon appétit. No news, love and prayers, Papa et Maman. P.S. Remember Mr. McDermott across the street? He died. Papa bought a new Olds." Madeleine smiled in private oblation to love and absurdity.

She doesn't really have time to do the AIDS benefit, but doesn't want to say no to a good cause. And Tommy is persuasive. She went to her high school graduation prom with him. Tomasz Czerniatewicz. She'd had paralyzing crushes on two people—Stephen Childerhouse and Monica Goldfarb—but was too shy to approach the former burnished god, and her desire for the latter dark lady simmered behind a fire-curtain of denial. It was not hip to be queer, it was perverted, and not a single rock star had yet admitted to bisexuality. She tried to escape the "bad feelings" but it was like outrunning a cartoon bullet that passes you, skids to a stop midair, turns and nails you. She saw *The Children's Hour* at fourteen, while babysitting, and went home with a temperature and stomach flu. She had watched, bathed in shame, yet riveted by the desire palpable in the boarding-school air between Shirley MacLaine and Audrey Hepburn. Shirley felt so "sick and dirty" she hanged herself, freeing Audrey to seek solace in the manly embrace of James Garner. Madeleine sought solace in James Garner's manliness too, but couldn't quell the broken record of svelte Shirley sobbing, "I feel so sick and dirty!" Like George's parrot, "sick-and-dirty, sick-and-dirty, *grawk!*" Supposedly the film is a metaphor for the Communist witch hunts of the 'fifties. Tell that to the lesbians.

She had intended to boycott the prom and spend the evening scoffing at it with Tommy and the other marginals from the drama club, but she was so shocked by his invitation that she said yes. Her mother was thrilled and worked for weeks sewing Madeleine a formal. "*Ah, Madeleine, que t'es belle!* We'll take a picture to show your brother when he comes home." Tommy wore a baby blue tuxedo with a hot pink cummerbund, anticipating disco by a good few years.

They had bonded over the fact that Madeleine was not allowed to wear jeans to school and he was not permitted to grow his hair, even to a length acceptable in the Dutch army. He wore glasses that made him look like a physicist, which was what both his parents were at the National Research Council. The whole family wore identical Nana Mouskouri glasses, and they all had short hair except for the mother, who wore a scraped-back bun. Mr. and Mrs. Czerniatewicz were Polish immigrants, they had survived the war. So much for the sixties;

the older Czerniatewicz brothers listened to classical music, excelled at math, wore flood pants, and had pocket protectors and bone structure to die for. They were at university, but had played high school football with Mike and, like him, were all-star athletes. Except for Tommy, who'd been born with a hole in his heart—"that's why I got piano lessons."

He reminded Madeleine of Gordon Lawson—a perfect gentleman, with the hanky to prove it. But with a wicked streak of humour; when she went to his house after school and met his parents, he told them she was Jewish, and she could hear their chiselled smiles atrophy with a *clink*.

She suffered torments of guilt, but Tommy begged her to keep up the ruse and soon she was in too deep to back out. Mr. and Mrs. Czerniatewicz grew fond of her, queried her about her culture and beliefs, and it was all she could do to fend off their desire to meet her wonderful parents who had survived the camps and changed their name to McCarthy to facilitate immigration. Stymied in their efforts, the Czerniatewiczes struck up a friendship with a Jewish scientist at the stark lab where they hunted for particles, and wound up at a Passover Seder the following spring. Tommy pranced and clicked his heels together: "We're like the Littlest Hobo and Lassie, spreading love and understanding."

He tutored her in math, and they spent hours belting out Broadway tunes while Tommy pounded the piano and Madeleine danced like a Gumby Gwen Verdon.

Her best friend, Jocelyn, went to the prom with the captain of the football team, the impossibly good-looking, strong and silent Boom Boom Robinson. His sandy curls lapped at the collar of his midnight blue tux, and before dawn, when she and Madeleine ditched their formals and dived into the backyard pool, Jocelyn confessed that he was nice enough but he "didn't even try anything." They dried off and ate a loaf of Wonderbread fondue: take a slice of Wonderbread, squish it into a ball, dip it in a bowl of melted chocolate chips.

Tommy and Boom Boom ran into each other ten years later, at Woody's Bar in Toronto, fell in love and moved in together. Boom Boom died six months ago and Tommy has been raising funds and awareness ever since. That's how he and Madeleine hooked up again. His hair is even shorter than it used to be, platinum buzz-cut. He teaches at a high school for the performing arts.

"I had a huge crush on your brother, Madeleine."

# The Few, The Proud

To the tune of "The Colonel Bogey March":
*Hitler! had only one big ball*
*Goering, had two but they were small*
*Himmler, had something sim'lar*
*And poor old Goebbels had no balls at all!*

*Anon.*

MADELEINE IS STARING at a spot on the taupe carpet. Feels her mouth in the shape of an upside-down smile, her cheeks striped with tears, nose red with crying, is that the real reason clowns have red noses?

Nina puts a glass of therapeutic spring water into her hand.

She drinks, feels tadpoles in her stomach, contents of a swamp, thickening, things hatching. "I feel sick," she says, and drops her forehead to her hand.

"Madeleine. Can you close your eyes for a moment?"

She does. Tears seep out.

"What is it?"

"My brother," she says, and weeps.

"He died," says Nina.

"We don't say 'died,' we say 'missing.'" She reaches for the tissues and covers her face with her hands, sobbing. "My poor dad."

"Were they close? Your brother and your father?"

Madeleine shakes her head, blows her nose and almost laughs. She lobs the sodden wad into the wastebasket, pulls a fresh handful from the box and tells a story.

In the spring of '69, when Madeleine was fifteen, Mike came home to Ottawa in a United States Marine Corps uniform.

"What the hell are you wearing?" said Jack.

He was supposed to have been out west, working on an oil rig in Alberta. Instead, he had completed basic training at Parris Island. His head was shaved. He was newly muscled, neck straining against his collar.

"Have you got a brain in your head?" asked Jack, white around the mouth. "Are you that stupid?" Smacking his newspaper down on the kitchen table.

"I thought you'd be proud," Mike said.

"Why in God's name would I be proud?"

Mike had thought his father would be proud the way he had been proud of the comparatively few Canadians who had fought in Korea—

"They fought as Canadians, not Americans, they were part of a U.N. force!"

"They were fighting Communism," Mike yelled back, "it was the same!"

"You've pledged allegiance to a foreign power!"

Madeleine leaned against the kitchen counter, glazed with shock. Her mother didn't even light a cigarette.

*The Few, The Proud*—a slogan of the Marine Corps. Canadians were the few among the few. The invisible among the despised. While scores of young American males objected, stayed in college or fled to Canada to avoid an insane war, Mike was one of a hefty handful of Canadians who volunteered. Many came from Québec and the Maritimes—a preponderance of working-class boys, Irish, French and Native Canadians. They enlisted at recruiting centres located deliberately close to the Canadian border. Mike joined up in Plattsburgh, New York. *Shit, shower, shave!* This time next month he would be "in country."

Jack's hands dangled at his sides. "Go on, get out of here." He turned and walked away.

"Jack," said Mimi—Madeleine could hear the shock in her voice.

"He's Canadian, not American, it's a foreign war and it's a foolish war. It can't be won, they're not fighting it to win it, he'll be killed."

Mimi cried out and covered her mouth.

"*Maman*," said Mike, "*c'est pas vrai, maman, je reviendra, calme-toi, eh?*" He looked at his father. "See what you've done?"

Jack rolled his eyes.

Madeleine was rooted to the spot. She was wearing a pewter peace sign on a leather string around her neck. Last week she and Jocelyn had joined a protest in front of the American Embassy against the atrocities at My Lai.

Jack pointed at his son and said, "You're to stay out of it, mister."

"You're just jealous," said Mike.

"What?" said Jack.

Madeleine shared her father's incredulity, but she could not bear to see her brother's cheeks inflamed with humiliation. She was terrified he would cry. She bit the inside of her cheek.

"I'm going to be flying."

"Flying what?" said Jack.

"A chopper."

"A chopper." Slow disdain. "Killing a whole bunch of peasants. From a helicopter. I'm impressed."

Mike turned scarlet. "At least I'm fighting for something. At least I'm not flying a fucking desk."

Jack struck him across the face for speaking that way in front of his mother. Mike gasped back his shock—Madeleine could see tears in his eyes, what would be worse? If Mike cried? Or if he hit Dad back?

Mike turned to his mother and said, "*Excuse-moi, maman.* I didn't mean to swear."

Mimi was crying. She reached up and put her arms around her son, hugged him and said, "*Va avec Dieu, hein? Mon petit homme.*" Stroking his back the way she used to when he was a kid. "*P'tit gentilhomme.*"

Madeleine could see her brother's jaw and mouth working as he held their mother, but still he didn't cry. All she could think was, *You big idiot. Stay home.*

"You're to stay home," said Jack.

Mike turned and left.

Nina says, "Is that the last time you saw him?"

Madeleine smiles. "No. I followed him out of the house."

He is pulling away in a battered Chevy Nova, pockmarked where rust has been sanded off. She runs after him. He sees her in the rearview mirror and stops.

They pick up Jocelyn.

"Are you for real?" Jocelyn asks him, climbing into the back seat.

"Surprise, surprise, surprise!" bleats Madeleine in Gomer Pyle's voice.

They drive into downtown Ottawa. It's surreal—Mike's crisp summer uniform and bean shave in contrast with the jeans, frayed hems and split ends everywhere—the only people with hair shorter than his are the Hare Krishnas with their orange robes and tambourines.

They walk through the airy light of the early June evening, down Sparks Street Mall—thronging now with tourists, civil servants and hippies, past "Lucy in the Sky with Diamonds" piped from a record store, past buskers and jewellery vendors, through a gauntlet of stares.

Madeleine is in a cold and lucid dream, on a wagon en route to the stake, naked but for her hair and smock, the crowd may spit and jeer, she will not seek to justify herself. She holds her head up and walks in step with the U.S. Marine at her side.

"Where do you hang out?" Mike asks.

"A little place down on Sussex."

She doesn't really frequent the place, but the thought of walking in there with her soldier brother is mortifying, so that's where she will take him. They walk past the Parliament Buildings, turn left down Sussex Drive and come to a coffee house called Le Hibou.

He opens the door for them. "Ladies first." Jocelyn rolls her eyes at Madeleine, Madeleine rolls hers in agreement.

Jocelyn looks like an Arthur Rackham fairy in blue jeans. Madeleine wishes she could be ethereal too, but she is stuck being strong instead. A gymnast's body. The difference between a unicorn and a pony.

They enter and sit down; candles flicker in wax-withered Mateus bottles, on checkered tablecloths. Beneath the acrid smoke of Gauloises and Gitanes, an odour—Mike is wearing Hai Karate. It mingles with patchouli oil and incense. Oh God, why did we come here? People stare as they find a table and sit, Madeleine in the middle between Jocelyn and Mike.

Mike leans across and asks Joss, "Are you a women's libber?"

Jocelyn doesn't bother to look at him. "That depends," she says, smoothing her straight blonde hair behind one ear. "Are you a male chauvinist pig?"

Mike grins. "Nope, I'm a hippie, I believe in free love."

"You're a Neanderthal," says Madeleine. "Move over." Shoving him away.

Mike looks up and says, "Can I get a beer?"

The guy serving them pauses before answering, "We're not licensed."

"No problem," says Mike, "I'll have a coffee."

But the waiter lingers. He stares at Mike. "Do you enjoy killing people?" he asks.

Madeleine stiffens, can feel the wooden wheels of the cart rattling beneath her feet, how many more miles to the stake?

Mike chuckles. "I don't know, I haven't killed any." And turns away, unbuttoning his tunic.

"But that's what you're trained to do," says the waiter.

He has no discernible hairline or facial features, he is all black curly fly-away and pasty white skin. He stares at Mike. Mike smiles, big fist relaxed around the car keys.

Madeleine's long dark hair is parted in the middle; her peace sign, her tie-dyed peasant blouse, faded bell-bottom jeans and water-buffalo sandals—the sartorial reflection of her belief in passive, non-violent resistance. She says to the waiter, "Why don't you go fuck yourself and, when you're done, bring us three coffees and a spoon so I can shove it up your ass."

Mike bursts out laughing.

Jocelyn says, "God, Madeleine," and sinks in her seat, crossing her arms.

Madeleine has never noticed Jocelyn's breasts before but she does now, they are perfectly round under her saffron T-shirt.

Mike says to the waiter, "Don't worry, we're leaving. Thanks anyhow, what do I owe you for the table?"

"It's okay," says the guy, "I'll get the coffees."

Madeleine is possessed by remorse for her behaviour. As well as by a yearning to burn something down, blow something up. She often feels this way, and has no idea how to square it with her personal politics.

On the tiny stage, someone is playing bongos and a woman has started reading poetry in a slow downward cadence.

Madeleine's sociology teacher sent her essay on Canada's war guilt in Vietnam to the newspaper. In it, she calls for a boycott of Canadian companies that supply the American military-industrial complex, manufacturing everything from bullets to green berets, Agent Orange to ration packs, and employ one hundred and forty thousand Canadians. She entitled it "Workin' for the Yankee Dollar." It was published, and her father was proud, for even though he does not entirely agree with her point of view, "dissent is the wellspring of democracy."

"'The country beneath the earth has a green sun and the rivers flow backwards,'" reads the poet—

Burning huts and burning people, naked crying children. Her brother is going over there to do more of it.

—"'the trees and rocks are the same as they are here, but shifted. Those who live there are always hungry—'"

He will participate in the obscenity of war, even though he will not participate in war crimes—but this war is criminal by its nature, so where is the line? She looks at his hands. Will he kill someone with them? Someone's brother? She watches him sip his coffee and tilt his head the way Dad does, listening to the poetry. She is terrified for him. Disgusted. And envious. Nothing adds up.

—"'from them you can learn wisdom and great power, if you can descend and return safely. . . .'"

When the poet finishes, Mike applauds and turns to Madeleine. "That was great. I mean it."

Life is a series of random events, there is no such thing as morality, there are only collective delusions, occasional leaps of faith, and feats of self-interested discipline that prevent people from exploiting one another all the time. This is what she and Jocelyn talk about on Friday nights while listening to *Ladies of the Canyon.* By three A.M. they have dug out The Beach Boys and are talking about sex. Jocelyn has gone all the way. Madeleine has not.

Jocelyn winds the beads of her choker around her finger and leans her ear close to Mike's mouth to hear him above the bongos. She has a habit of covering her mouth when she laughs. She reminds Madeleine of Lisa Ridelle. There are really only about five people in the world.

"Is he your boyfriend?" the waiter asks Madeleine, appearing with a carafe of coffee.

"No, he's my brother," ready to go another round.

"Do you want to come home with me tonight?"

She looks at him. Guys are amazing. He's giving her the look she has noticed lately. The one that gives her no room to look back.

"I'm around," says the waiter, and moves off through the tables.

Mike takes Madeleine's cup from its saucer, slides it under the table and tips a silver flask over it. He does the same with Jocelyn's, then his own.

They wind up across the river in Hull. At two in the morning, on the Québec side, she jives with her brother to a rockabilly band howling James Brown in French accents. The lead singer is skinny with prematurely false teeth and a cowboy hat. He plays accordion—"Get up there and show 'im a thing or two," says Mike.

No one in this bar gives them any attitude about Mike's uniform, or raises an eyebrow at the sight of him with two underage hippie chicks. The clientele ranges in age from under to way over; guys from the pulp and paper mill, university students who chain-smoke and speak more intensely to one another than the students on the English side of the river—they're messier and sexier too. There are secretaries and factory girls in low-cut polyester party dresses and slingbacks—they may have heard of women's lib but they probably don't care. Above the bar, a portrait of the King in uniform: Elvis as a GI.

On their table, a forest of "gros Mols"—tall brown quart bottles of Molson's beer—and here and there an empty chaser of Jack Daniel's, "dead soldiers," Mike calls them. He doesn't say another word in English all night. Jocelyn keeps hollering to Madeleine above the music, "What's he saying?"

"He said, 'My girdle's killing me.'"

"No, come on, what did he say?"

Mike goes to the bar; the band plays "Havin' Some Fun Tonight," Madeleine grabs Jocelyn and they polka furiously.

Madeleine hollers over the music. "He said, 'Join the Marines. Travel to exotic far-off lands, meet interesting people. And kill them.'" Jocelyn screams with laughter. They hurtle into the table of empties; tall bottles topple and roll like bowling pins; a waiter with a Brylcreemed bouffant and the face of Methuselah springs into action, scooping them up, and they order another round.

Jocelyn lounges at the table wearing Mike's uniform hat as Madeleine jives with him, shooting at high speed between his ankles. He spools her back and forth to "Jailhouse Rock," compliant spaghetti at the end of his grip.

Mike is a good dancer; always out of step with his own generation but popular at weddings, those Sunday afternoons with Maman have paid off. His tie is loose, shirt untucked at the back and patched with sweat, his face aglow.

When the song ends he walks up to Jocelyn, leans over the table, extends his hand and she takes it. Madeleine watches from her chair, remembering Lisa in the pup tent, confessing her love for Mike.

She feels old, and world-weary too. The booze, the circumstances, her span of fifteen years all gang up on the moment to contain it. It means something. As though it were part of a story. Why is she thinking about Lisa Ridelle tonight? Where is Lisa now? She was hilarious. Or was it that she laughed a lot? Who was the funny one, me or Lisa? Auriel was; Madeleine feels a surge of warmth and longs to see Auriel again. That was only six years ago. It feels ancient.

She checks a beer bottle for butts, then takes a long pull.

The band is playing "Love Me Tender." Jocelyn and Mike lean into one another, swaying slowly. Madeleine bums a cigarette from a young woman with a beehive and cleavage. Leaning forward for a light, she gets a close-up of pencilled brows, liquid eyeliner, and a whiff of lily-of-the-valley perfume.

"Thanks," says Madeleine.

"*Garde les allumettes,*" says the girl and winks.

They have nothing in common.

They strike up a conversation in both languages, switching back and forth without noticing. Madeleine has never been drunk before and her French has improved mightily. They talk about the young woman's fiancé, who is off cutting wood in Nouveau-Brunswick. She tells Madeleine she'd be pretty if she'd just do one or two things—offers to take her to the bathroom and do her makeup. Madeleine follows her.

The ladies' room is a pukey pink and reeks almost as much as a gents'.

The Québécoise opens her patent-leather clutch and goes to work on Madeleine's face with a brush and several tubes.

"*Que t'es belle, ma p'tite, tu me fais penser à ma petite sœur.*"

"Oh yeah? How old's your little sister?"

"*Ben, chérie,* she died, *elle est morte.*"

"Shit," says Madeleine. "*C'était quoi son nom?*" and immediately regrets asking because she knows what the young woman is going to say—

"Her name was Claire."

"Shit," says Madeleine. "What happened to her, what the fuck happened to her?"

Madeleine never swears—she never drinks, either, or wears makeup or hangs around with tarty French girls who've probably never heard of Simone de Beauvoir.

The young woman answers, "She got sick, honey. The meningitis, she just goes like that," and snaps her fingers. "*Pauvre petite,*" she adds. "Oh you are sad, baby." Cupping Madeleine's cheek with her hand. "*Pleure pas.*"

"I'm not crying," answers Madeleine, lifting her chin for a topcoat of clear gloss applied by the girl's middle finger.

Madeleine feels the graze of a nail along her lip, then the French girl kisses her on the mouth—taste of chemical cherry, cigarette juice, and so soft, a wet pillow—"Don't be sad, eh?" she says to Madeleine, stroking her hair, and kisses her again.

Madeleine kisses her back, melting into her mouth. The Québécoise slides her hand down Madeleine's hip, around behind, and pulls her close.

"You want to come home with me, baby? *C'est quoi ton nom?*"

"I can't," says Madeleine, ducking out of the bathroom.

Back at the table, Mike and Jocelyn are resting. Jocelyn is flushed, laughing. Mike takes a haul of his beer, allows it to trickle down his neck and pats it on like aftershave, singing, "'There's something about an Aqua Vulva man.'"

Jocelyn turns and sees Madeleine. "Oh my God."

Mike takes one look at her and fumbles in his pocket for his hanky. "You look like a two-dollar whore." He wets the hanky with his tongue the way Dad used to. "I let you out of my sight for one second—"

He goes to dab at her face, but Madeleine escapes to the bar and checks herself out in the mirror—*sacrebleu.* Mike appears over her shoulder and laughs. She looks like a raccoon and her mouth is all smeary. She grabs his hanky, douses it in beer and wipes the lipstick off. The crotch of her jeans has gone smeary too, but thank goodness that's invisible, thank goodness girls don't get public hard-ons.

Madeleine sees the young woman in the mirror—she has returned to her table and is necking with a big guy with a dirty blond braid down his back. Madeleine thinks of the waiter back at Le Hibou. I should do it with him. Why not? Someone's got to be the first. At least he doesn't go to her school, and she won't have to let him be her boyfriend.

At three-thirty A.M. Mike requests a song from the band. Little Richard and the Big Bopper give way to a French Canadian folk song. The singer laments, close in to the mike, "*Un Canadien errant, banni de son pays. . . .*" Madeleine cringes—this is so corny. Any second now, a separatist is going to jump up and throw them out of here. "*Parcourait en pleurant, des pays étrangérs. . . .*" A simple tune, like the best folk songs the world over—I have lost my home, I long for my home, my home exists now only in memory.

Maman always sang the original, "*un Acadien.*" But Mike will soon be *un Canadien errant.* Vietnam—it doesn't get more *errant* than that. And where are he and Madeleine from, anyhow? *Say goodbye to the house, kids. . . .*

Mike puts his arms around Madeleine and slow-dances with her. His hair is wet with sweat, the back of his neck pink. He drops his head to his sister's shoulder. She laces her fingers together between his shoulder blades—he does have shoulder blades in there somewhere, beneath the muscle, soft and hard all at once, my big brother. He still smells nice even through the Hai Karate, the beer, the bourbon and sweat. He smells fresh—the freshness of hide 'n' seek at night in summer, the smell of grass stains, of swimming in the lake, and sun-baked sand dunes, their sleeping bags side by side—where have those times gone? *Qui peut dire où vont les fleurs?*

Madeleine is drunk for the first time in her life. She strokes the back of her brother's brush cut—stupid idiot, Michel, why do you have to go away? Why do you want to hurt anyone? I know that's not why you're going, why are you going? His buzzed hair is soft, a thick and delicate carpet. They will not know you are different from the others, Mike. They will not know you are kind. She bites the inside of her mouth but it does no good, she is drunk, her famous ability to go neutral has dissolved, mascara traces clown tears down her cheeks. *Sarge, I'm hit.*

Mike raises his head, beams into her face—kisses her on the cheek. "Stunned one," he says, and holds out his arm to Jocelyn to join them. The three of them sway in place, arms around one another, to the rest of the song.

They travel across the bridge back to Ottawa in the pockmarked Nova. Madeleine drives—she is the least drunk, and in no danger of losing her licence, because she doesn't have one. She turns along the river and follows the curving parkway past the prime minister's residence, past the governor general's and through Rockcliffe Park. Jocelyn's parents are divorced, she lives with her dad, she has no curfew—paradise. Madeleine pulls up in front of her house among the embassies.

"Pretty ritzy," says Mike. "I'll see you to the door."

He and Jocelyn stand under the porch light, kissing. Madeleine is shocked. Jocelyn reaches behind, opens the front door and slides in, Mike slides in after her.

Madeleine waits. She rests her head against the steering wheel, because she gets the spins when she leans back against the headrest. She falls asleep and Miss Lang, the Brown Owl, arrives in her wedding gown and Brownie beret. She smiles slyly and says, "Of course you know what *hibou* means in English?"

Madeleine replies, "It means 'owl.'"

Miss Lang winks. "And what do owls say?"

"Who."

"Who killed me, Madeleine?"

Mike wakes her, pulling her from the undertow. "Move over, Rob."

He drives them back to the suburbs as the sun comes up—big lawns dewy and rich in the morning mist, backyard pools slumbering under blue plastic covers. He drops her just as their father pulls out of the garage in his Oldsmobile, the automatic door closing behind, his wheels yielding, cushiony, over the curb of the driveway. Jack turns to Madeleine and touches two fingers to his forehead in the old casual salute. He doesn't look at Mike.

Madeleine says, "He's going golfing."

"Give Maman a kiss for me, eh?" says Mike. "*Je t'aime.*"

Then he drove away.

# MIA

His parents cannot say, "When Mike died," because if he is dead, he did not "die," he was killed. But they cannot say, "When Mike was killed," because they don't know for certain that he was. They don't say, "When Mike went missing," because that sounds as though he simply wandered off.

When is mourning?

When you are waiting, watching to see a flower open, a leaf unfurl, or attending the slow folding down of a dear, dear one who seems so much better today, the waiting is painstaking. This long blossoming, or extinguishing of a beloved face feels endless; each small movement gauged, exaggerated, compared or denied, but one thing is sure—the plant will open, your dear one will die, it is only a question of when, and of many acts of loving vigilance.

Absence is different. You can't watch over an absence. Care for it, help it on its journey, love it. You can only watch life flow around both hope and dread, softening edges, eroding grain by grain all expectation, awaiting the merciful time, which may never come, when one can say, *he is gone.*

The soreness deep in the chest. The falling asleep over a book, unable to keep one's lids open, only to reawaken deep in the night with a fresh release of sorrow. Slow, warm, adrenal. Like a gentle hand. *Wake up. Wake up, friend owl.* Sore, sore sorrow.

And still there is no funeral, no emptying of grief; no shaking droplets from the trees, followed by the steaming up of loss, gentle respiration of memory. Grief-in-waiting is a tap left dripping, the unstaunched hope, drop by drop, *perhaps, he might, what if, it could.* Friends can only do so much. Those who are experienced, unembarrassed by grief, know not to dispense bromides, wear long faces or chat with plastered grins. They behave like good dance partners. Life goes on. That's the way it is. You do not forget, neither do you dwell; be there, that is all. Stop with the casseroles and too frequent phone calls after a while, but do not disappear. Be there.

Waiting is exhausting. Like living in a language not your own. You translate continually, filtering the present through the hypothetical, *if Michel were here . . . when Mike gets home. . . .* Soul and sinews poised. Prepared for sudden joy, or sorrow. It does no good to wish you had appreciated life more before the misfortune, we are not made that way. We are made to desire; to cherish and to disregard by turns. Some of us have a talent for happiness—this has little to do with circumstance. Few have a talent for waiting.

Wincing at the sound of the phone, the knock at the door, the clank of the mailbox. But there is no news. No relaxation of soul or sinews. There is, instead, the loss of elasticity. The bow pulled back for too long, once released, sags or snaps.

Grief is a fulcrum. The joint in time between the vanishing of hope and the beginning of loss. Missing link. Allows the living to move forward, and the dead finally to return, smile and open their arms to us in memory.

There has yet to come a moment when his family has been able to say, *he is dead.* Instead, hope has shaded to the next phase, wherein his parents cannot recall when it was they began to say, "When we lost Mike."

"How did it go at the benefit Monday night?" asks Nina.

"Fine."

"No problem with the 'thing'?"

"The what? Oh. No."

"What are you feeling, Madeleine?"

"Absolutely nothing."

## HIS

*The other was a softer voice,*
*As soft as honey-dew:*
*Quoth he, "The man hath penance done,*
*And penance more will do."*
　　　Samuel Taylor Coleridge, *"The Rime of the Ancient Mariner"*

JACK IS A MAN without a shadow. It died of neglect. Like a puddle on a hot day, it grew smaller and smaller.

He listens to the news; reads and watches it constantly. More than a strategy of masculine retreat, it fends off curdling panic. He regards his wife warily. Like the keeper of one of a set of dual keys, she can trigger his grief. Her grief can end the world. But the news is soothing. Piecemeal and manageable, with a few sweeping arcs reminiscent of the narrative structure of soap opera—the world turns and nothing changes.

The occasional twinge pierces the anesthetic—Walter Cronkite declaring that the war over there was unwinnable, *And that's the way it is.* . . . Flick of the remote as Jack switches the channel.

He doesn't know what he doesn't know. He doesn't know how he has changed. How he looks from the car behind him, through the eyes of a driver he has just punished by slowing down. He didn't know his staff in Ottawa were afraid of him. He didn't know his son loved him.

The news allows you to forget. Tirelessly reordering the world, which crumbles daily. Reporters are the king's horses and men who put Humpty together again, every day, several times a day. News imparts the reassuring illusion of time passing, of change. No need to tap into the undercurrent, which is slower and so much stronger and costs us grief and knowledge. News is a time substitute, like coffee whitener.

He knows who killed his son. The Americans. Their arrogance, their false innocence. Their short-sightedness, their love of tyrants, their greed, their lies. As surely as if Richard Nixon had come into his home and murdered the boy. Because before Vietnam, everything was fine. *Crinkle.*

Now he is drowning slowly, sitting in his chair. His lungs have been filling quietly, like the North Sea rising over the land. Congestive heart failure.

When mines are abandoned, they often become flooded. Caves fill from within, water leaching from the earth that has been gouged and left for dead. This happens to lungs when the pump begins to fail.

The only way for the earth to heal itself is to flood or to cave in, or both. This is a slow process that begins immediately upon abandonment. Drip, drip, slight shift, crumble and line of scree. Millions of small changes underway, brought to bear suddenly one day in a great fall of earth and stone; or quietly, when the water in the cave finally rises to kiss the roof of its mouth.

> *The spirit who bideth by himself*
> *In the land of mist and snow,*
> *He loved the bird that loved the man*
> *Who shot him with his bow.*

# Hers

*Your children grow up, they leave you,*
*they have become soldiers and riders.*
*Your mate dies after a life of service.*
*Who knows you? Who remembers you?*

Leonard Cohen, You Have the Lovers

MIMI DOES HER BEST not to cry in front of her husband any more. In the months after they received official word that their son was missing in action, she cried. Jack comforted her and predicted a hundred happy outcomes, a hundred bureaucratic errors, a worst-case scenario involving their boy lost in the shuffle, lying wounded but alive in a field hospital. She endured the incoming tide of sorrow, and the slow draining away of hope. Emotional anemia. She kept busy around the edges, which were all anyone could see. At the centre was a bare patch—it could not be called a clearing. Nothing would ever grow there again. Like irradiated soil. Sterile.

She confides in a few good friends. New friends: Doris, Fran, Joanne. She leans, catches her breath, but never collapses on any of them. If no one ever says "poor Mimi" again, she will have done her job.

No one can keep up with her—the Heart Fund, the Cancer Society, the Liberal Party, the Catholic Women's League, her nursing job. She keeps busy, but Mimi has never had a talent for sidestepping time. She becomes aware of a metallic taste in her mouth—forty years of smoking has never interfered with her ability to season a sauce, this is new. Something has to change. Something does change. No one is able to tell, not her husband or her daughter. Here is her recipe for grief:

Keep busy. But care that the young couple on the corner have planted a new tree. Care that the woman whose husband died last year has a new dog—a mature mutt from the pound—Mimi doesn't even like dogs, "*Ah, mais il est mignon!*" bending to pat his bony head. Care that someone had a baby. Cook something, bring it over. Go for a walk every Thursday morning at seven with Joanne, who, what with her long grey hair and Greenpeace pamphlets, reminds Mimi of Karen Froelich, and therefore seems the unlikeliest of friends. When consumed by jealousy of Fran with her grandchildren, by anger at the number of worthless young men who are allowed to survive, sit in your car with the engine off and squeeze the steering wheel. Cry until your throat hurts and the steering-wheel is wet and it leaves a notched impression on your brow.

Think of the Blessed Virgin, she knows what you are suffering. If you have the presence of mind—in the way that an epileptic might look for a safe place to lie down at the first sense of a seizure coming on—remove your makeup first. Cry at night, careful not to shake the bed. Get up, empty the dishwasher, bake muffins for your daughter in Toronto. Wait until six A.M., then call Yvonne in New Brunswick, where it's seven. Gossip, judge, tell her not to judge so harshly, laugh. Look after your husband.

Upward tilt of the head for the morning kiss. Co-conspirators:

"When did you get up, Missus?"

"I've been up since six."

"Something sure smells good."

Look after him. Women live longer than men. Men are delicate, Mimi ought to have taken better care of hers. Both of them.

Put the kettle on. Look out the kitchen window.

Love what remains.

## And Now for Something Completely Different

*"'How puzzling all these changes are! I'm never sure what I'm going to be, from one minute to another!'"*

Alice's Adventures in Wonderland

SHE HAS FIVE MINUTES before meeting Christine for lunch, then she has an appointment with Shelly to show her material for *Stark Raving Madeleine*—a mere paragraph, but just add water. She is walking along Harbord in the direction of the university campus and Christine's office when a title in the window of the Toronto Women's Bookstore catches her eye. So she makes her way through the usual knot of demonstrators outside the abortion clinic next door, and goes in.

*The Pregnant Virgin: A Process of Psychological Transformation.* Feminist goddessy take on Jungian healing blah-blah. Nina stuff. She flips through—cocoons, butterflies. . . . She sighs. Do I have to heal now? Who's got the time? The whole idea makes her crave a dose of Dirty Harry. But she buys the book and lingers to chat with the cute dreadlocked girl at the cash, not leaving till she has heard the analysis behind every political button pinned to the bib of her denim overalls.

*Get your laws off my body!* shouts a pin on the girl's left suspender. *Bi now, gay later,* muses one on the right. She smiles at Madeleine and says, "Do you like reggae?"

"I love it." Overstatement.

"I'm at the Cameron House on Thursday."

"Are you a singer?" *Are you even of legal drinking age?*

"Yeah."

"Cool." *What a nerd. Cool. What a maroon!*

"I love your show," says the girl, leaning forward, elbows on the counter.

Madeleine flees. Hit and run, duck and cover.

She picks up a falafel and eats it on the way to meet Shelly—what a gorgeous day. When she gets home, she writes an inscription in the book and, before taking the phone out to the balcony to call Olivia, leaves it on the kitchen table, a gift for Christine. More up her alley. And God knows, if therapy has taught Madeleine anything, it's that Christine could use a little honest introspection.

Later that same week:

Madeleine stands stranded on her old Persian carpet in her empty living room. Her office is the only fully furnished room remaining, but she is avoiding it—rebuke of the blank computer screen, posters of past triumphs looming a merry reproach from the walls.

"Take the stuff," said Madeleine.

And Christine did.

Madeleine had forgotten their lunch date. She had had a terrible meeting with Shelly, who believes in her. Her peripheral vision had gone wavy in one eye, and pins and needles had consumed both hands up to her elbows when she was in the Bloor Supersave buying eggs. And Christine left her.

*Nyah, what's up doc?*

She has enough money to continue nervously breaking down for another eighteen months, if she buys bulk. That's the beauty of television residuals. Soon she will go to Ikea and fill up an oversized cart. Trawl the aisles, along with the other divorcées, and families with young children. Today is Saturday, she could get started this afternoon.

"What about dinner?" she asked stupidly as Christine unlocked her bike from the veranda.

"Cook it yourself."

*That's not what I meant.*

They had been going to go for Vietnamese food with friends. Friends of Madeleine-and-Christine. Christine-and-Madeleine.

"You call them," said Christine, dragging her bike down the wooden steps. "They were never really my friends anyway. You're the shiny one, Madeleine." Then she rode off on her beautiful old Schwinn Glyder with the generous gel-pad Drifter saddle.

She returned the next day, with a U-Haul and an undergrad. Madeleine helped. Now she has no furniture. She has a beach towel. A Melmac plate, bowl and mug; a knife-fork-spoon combination. At least she still has a bed. She has been to Honest Ed's and bought a complete set of pots and an ironing board. She brought it all home on her bike, having had no need for the car when she nipped in with the intention of buying bagels. She forgot the bagels. She is as pathetic as any deserted husband. More so, having no home-repair skills.

"Why don't you just go to her, that's what you're going to do anyway."

"Go to who?" asked Madeleine. "Whom?"

Christine just shook her head and went into the bedroom. Madeleine followed like a spaniel. Christine started yanking open drawers.

"What are you doing, Christine?"

"What does it look like?"

Madeleine said robotically, which was how she knew she was in trouble, "I love you, Christine, please don't leave. Don't leave, Christine."

"You're incapable of feeling, Madeleine."

The two of them had been drawn together by one another's sadness. Residue of childhood in the eye. The problem is, neither was particularly compelled by the other's idea of happiness.

"You hate it when I'm happy, Madeleine. You always choose that moment to stick the knife in."

That's not fair. Madeleine can't bear to hurt her, so she always waits until Christine is up before . . . raising issues.

"You're too cowardly to confront me," said Christine, folding, flinging clothes onto the bed.

Maybe she was right and Madeleine did prefer the sad Christine. The helplessly angry one. The one who strangled.

Christine slammed her drawers shut, eyes flaming. Madeleine wanted to laugh because Christine was so worked up, full face flushed with rage like an angry doll.

"What's so funny, Madeleine?"

Madeleine formed a serious expression, and Christine turned away in disgust.

*Not disgust,* says Christine, *sadness. I've never been so sad in all my life.*

Madeleine saw two dark splotches appear on the mauve duvet cover. *Don't cry, Christine*—but who the hell is Madeleine to say such a thing?

Why isn't love enough?

"I hate myself when I'm with you," said Christine, wiping the corner of her eye, still packing with the simple vigour of a hausfrau.

Madeleine clung to her for seven years because she believed Christine could really see her, right down to the bottom.

"You're so much fun with everyone else, but with me you're always in a crappy mood," said Christine.

With you I am myself, Madeleine would have replied at one time, but that was no longer true. With you I lead a double life. Chuckle and Hide. "Why are you leaving?"

"'Cause you don't have the guts to leave me." Christine almost spat it. "What are you waiting for, Madeleine? Go to her."

Madeleine, honestly stumped, stood—not rooted, but slumped on her strings.

Christine muttered to her gaping drawers, "That bitch."

What bitch?

Christine said, "She's been after you from the start, pretending to be my friend too, coming over for dinner. I cooked for her! Now she's got you in that stupid project and you're neglecting your own work."

*Olivia.*

"You think Olivia and I . . . ? She's my *friend,* babe." Madeleine felt the foolish grin of masculine guilt creep over her features, masking her already unreal face. "It's not true!" Then why does this feel exactly like a lie?

"I quit, Madeleine. I'm sick of this codependent bullshit."

But what will I do without you? Now that I am more and more successful and beloved. No one else will ever know how bad I am. No one else can possibly see me as you do.

Madeleine watched, immobilized, while Christine stuffed clothes into a knapsack. "Why don't you use the suitcase?" asked the robot. "It has wheels." Christine ignored her. Christine had never understood that when Madeleine was most "real"—feeling most acutely—she turned into a puppet. Painted wood. Christine was tired of sharing a bed with a grown woman who still perched a grimy old Bugs Bunny on the pillows.

Madeleine had been on the phone with her father when the final conflict flared. They'd been arguing and she had resorted to out-talking him, asking how he could object to American foreign policy, yet laud Reagan's bogus Star Wars plan, "the product of a cryogenically preserved brain! George Bush is actually running the country from a CIA desk littered with GI Joes and conversational Arabic tapes, *oil, that is, black gold, Texas tea!*" and Jack was laughing and egging her on. Christine came in with a pastry box and new highlights in her hair. She stood smiling for an instant, and Madeleine glanced up—"My dad says hi." When she got off the phone, Christine had already dragged the forty-gallon knapsack from the attic.

Madeleine was grateful for marathon Thursday, sailed through shooting Friday, laughed and heckled at the Pickle Barrel while Ilsa gave her a scalp massage with her blood-red talons, and filled three foolscap pages for Shelly. No one suspected that her life was falling apart. She felt like a high-functioning alcoholic: slithering down the drapes at three, greeting hubby, bright-eyed and breath-minted, at five.

For three nights she cried into her mattress. She wept for Mike at twelve, she wept for her smiling self at nine, she grieved the smack of a good catch, baseball arcing from glove to glove like a dolphin in the after-supper sun; she wept for childhood, and for anyone who had ever been a child. Amazed, even through tears, at the thematic sweep of her grief. Concentric bands of sorrow radiating outward from ground zero. Centralia.

At a quiet moment—tears on empty, not yet dawn—she pulled his string. He spoke, wise-crackling and unintelligible like a transmission from outer space. She hugged him and fell asleep. *Don't tell.*

On Saturday morning she went to Honest Ed's for cutlery and came home with a portable black-and-white TV, the kind they have in hospitals and taxicabs. She has spent the day cross-legged on the carpet, watching infomercials and *The PTL Club* and letting the answering machine take the calls. Shelly, her mother, Tony, Janice, Tommy, five others and Olivia. *Ring.* . . . She ignores it. She has ordered an all-purpose cleaning agent not available in stores, and responded with a hundred-dollar pledge to Goldie's plea on PBS. *Ring.* . . . She switches to *Secret Storm—klachunk.* "If you have a message for Madeleine, please leave it after the beep; if you're looking for Christine, call 531-5409." *Bee-eep.* A voice through the machine: "Good day Mrs. McCarthy? My name is Cathy? And I'm calling from Consumer Systems Canada? And I wonder if you would be kind enough to phone me back at 262-2262 extension 226 and consent to participate in a brief questionnaire concerning certain well-known consumer items—?"

Madeleine grabs the phone—"Hi, Cathy?"

"Oh, hello Mrs. McCarthy—?"

"Look, I've just been diagnosed with inoperable brain cancer."

"Oh my—"

"Yeah, so I drowned the kids in the bathtub."

Silence.

"Cathy?"

"Um . . . I—I can call back."

"Sure, why don't you do that, I'm just wrapping them in the shower curtain."

*Click.*

Poor Cathy.

On Sunday morning, by dint of supreme effort, Madeleine reaches forward and switches off the television. In a display of strong-mindedness, she decides to take a shower. She finds *The Pregnant Virgin* behind the toilet, its pages fanned into an accordion. Did Christine drop it in the bath on purpose? She sits on the porcelain edge of the tub and starts reading: "Analyzing Daddy's Little Princess." Oh please! Not to mention you can tell right away it's written mainly for straight women. Oh well, to be gay is to be on simul-translation from day one, finding the universal in the particular and ingesting the distilled nourishment; like any minority that hopes to eat from the big table. "Integration of Body and Soul. . . ." She starts reading. She reads until she has a crick in her neck and moves to the floor with her back against the tub. She reads until she is hungry. She reads until she has finished the book.

Madeleine knows that while she had Christine, she could be the unfucked-up one. Now, in the wake of Christine's departure, Madeleine's friends and colleagues will see through her crumbling facade, smell the bodies amid the rubble and turn away. Anyone foolish enough to stick around would have to be an idiot.

"No, McCarthy," says Olivia, "you're the idiot." They are on the phone. Olivia says she's coming over.

"No, I'll come over to your place."

Madeleine climbs the fire escape, past a cat or two. Dingy bricks cooking in the mellow light of five o'clock, peeling black of the iron stairs that ring out low like church bells; visible between the slats below, drift of garbage in the grease-slicked alley, old cushions, dog-torn plastic bags, smell of pot and lilacs; the bar and grill at the front is playing Annie Lennox. . . . Look up. Olivia is sitting at the top of the steps, on a milk crate, in a slant of sun, smoking Drum tobacco, roll-your-own.

"Success without college," says Madeleine.

Olivia reaches down her hand.

The housemates are out. There is half a bottle of bad white wine in the fridge, along with blocks of tofu, mysterious Asian greens and murky tubs of things.

"How many people live here?" asks Madeleine.

"That depends," says Olivia.

How can she bear communal living? The bathroom alone. Madeleine sips and is ambushed by a complete happiness. What are these unreasonable happinesses? Like the lilies of the field who neither toil nor weep. The way the light leans in from the balcony down the hall to lounge against the walls painted pale pink, the softness of a gust of air, one's sudden weightlessness. Ecstasy. State of grace in a friend's apartment on a Sunday evening in May. Everything is going to be all right.

Olivia walks past her with a watering can. After a moment, Madeleine hears music. Strings—attenuated, patient. Baroque strands like hair drawn through a comb, untangling the market sounds outside. She follows the music to the front room. Olivia is on the rickety balcony watering the plants.

Madeleine joins her. Olivia turns to her.

"No," says Madeleine, "it would be like kissing my sister."

"You don't have a sister."

Olivia's secret identity is revealed in the kiss. The amazing transformation works in both directions: she turns back into Madeleine's friend when they are talking. Colleague, critical, argumentative. They go inside. They kiss against the wall outside Olivia's bedroom. They stay standing for quite a while, in deference to Madeleine's desire to avoid a "rebound" relationship.

"We don't have to have a relationship," says Olivia, "we can just have sex."

"Is that what you want?"

"No, but I think it's better if we think of you as a swinging bachelor for the time being. You should date for a while."

Madeleine sees herself in a Matt Helm apartment—remote-control bed and bar, shag rug. "I don't think so," she says.

Olivia leans, one shoulder against the wall, shirt open, devastatingly sensible underwear. The Maidenform Woman—you never know where she'll turn up.

"'Date,'" says Madeleine. "I don't even like the word."

"Okay, then we can just have sex. And be friends."

"That's called a relationship."

Olivia kisses her again. "You're not ready for a relationship."

They lie down on the dreadful futon, field of lumps and crabgrass, and Olivia resumes her secret identity, pink-tinted titan.

"I'm actually in crisis," says Madeleine, looking up into the most familiar, most radiant face—most amused too. "In pain. I'm on the brink of a nervous breakdown. How come I'm having such a good time?"

"Because you're a happy person," says Olivia. "That's your guilty secret."

Madeleine smiles. Closes her eyes, tastes sweet water. "You're so sweet," she says. *You run so sweet and clear.* She opens her eyes, keeps them open. "*C'est pour toi.*" Don't talk. *Take what you want.*

In between, there is the guided tour of small scars. Have you ever noticed that many people have a tiny one over an eye? At the outer edge of brow, the bony orbit doing its job, taking the brunt of whatever was hurtling toward the eye—a branch, a ball, hockey stick, a paw—

"I got this playing badminton when I was nine," says Olivia. "My mother put a butterfly Band-Aid on it and I felt really important."

"Wounded in action," says Madeleine.

"Where'd you get this?" She holds Madeleine's left hand, palm up, tracing the lifeline and its pale shadow with her finger.

"*Ci pa gran chouz,*" says Madeleine. Olivia smiles but doesn't ask what kind of French that is. "A knife did it."

Olivia raises an eyebrow. "Presumably someone was holding it at the time."

*On guard!* "Colleen."

"Who was Colleen?"

"My best friend," says Madeleine. Says her heart. "We became . . . *seurs de san.*"

Olivia hesitates, then, "Blood sisters?"

Madeleine nods. "When I was nine. Colleen Froelich." *Pellegrim.* The name arrives from the back of her mind, dusty but intact.

"Where is she now?"

"I don't know."

"You have a sister out there somewhere."

Olivia smells like sand and salt, a tang of sweat and Chanel. Old-fashioned feminine. Skilfully juxtaposed with the pink hair and multiple earrings.

The aroma of smoked sardines floats in. Olivia joins Madeleine at the window, chin on the sill. On the next balcony over, small silvery bodies hang pegged like socks to the clothesline. Olivia calls, "Avelino! Hey, Avelino!"

A stocky, charred-looking man in car-greasy overalls steps onto the sardine balcony and squints in their direction.

"Toss me one, pal," calls Olivia.

*Pal.*

Avelino plucks two fish from the line, turns to her, rehearses a toss, then releases them. Madeleine ducks. Olivia catches one fish, the other lands on the floor. "*Obrigado!*"

They eat off a ratty bamboo placemat on the futon, with bread and olives and the rest of the bad wine.

Being lovers with Olivia is like wrapping the present and tying on the bow after you have been enjoying it for years. Backwards, perfect. Everyone should fall in love with a friend.

"Why did your parents call you 'Olivia'?"

A loaf of bread, a smoked sardine and thou.

"My father loved Shakespeare and my mother loved olives."

Here is love's guilty secret: it doesn't hurt. It has been right in front of her.


### Asseye De Ti Rappeli

*" 'If I don't take this child away with me,' thought Alice, 'they're sure to kill it in a day or two; wouldn't it be murder to leave it behind?' "*

Alice's Adventures in Wonderland


In my dream, I am travelling through woods at night. The vegetation is very green despite the darkness. Leaves and branches swish past with the intimate indoor clarity of movie sound. Rex is walking beside me, I can hear the crackle of his paws through the undergrowth, smell his breath, meaty and warm, feel his fur. I know the trees are watching. There is a level of dread but I realize it's part of the ordinary condition of dogs and trees. I think to myself, dogs and trees are very brave. We come to a clearing. A canopy of mist—no, light—over a child lying on the grass. A girl in a blue dress. Rex looks up at me. His face so kind and concerned. Expectant too. I recognize the child. It's me. The grass around her begins to bend and flatten. I wake up, terrified.

"What is it?" asks Nina.

"The blue dress," says Madeleine, and weeps.

Blue dress is one of those details that come alive only when they are released into speech. Like the princess in the glass coffin. Open the lid, remove the apple from her mouth, release the word into air. Watch it reunite with its companions, form clusters of meaning.

Blue dress might have remained preserved under glass, like the exhibits in a museum case—hollow eggs, pinned moths. Mute about meadows and nests and the warm hides of deer who bend to drink from a stream in springtime. Showing, but not telling.

The blue dress was Claire's, of course—Madeleine knows that, never forgot it—but it's surprising how information can lie quietly dispersed for a lifetime. She has never forgotten what happened in the classroom after three, but she has remained immune to its meaning. It has lain dormant in its cocoon of silence.

"What about the blue dress, Madeleine?"

"It was hers."

"Whose?"

This immunity to meaning is not amnesia, it is craftier and harder to "snap out of." Because you are awake and sane. There was no tornado, no looking glass or rabbit hole. There is just a room at the top of your mind with a lot of stuff that never got put away. Like toys that lie inert, waiting for midnight.

"Claire." The word is a small cry, a bird escaping her throat.

"What about Claire, Madeleine?"

She hears a moan, it has come from her but reminds her of someone else. . . . "She was murdered?" In her voice she hears the interrogative inflection of a child, cadence of bewilderment and fear, *whose fault is it? Mine?*

"I know," says Nina. "I'm so sorry."

"She was strangled?" She begins to rock.

"Madeleine?" says Nina gently.

Madeleine looks up and takes the box of tissues from Nina's outstretched hand. "I'm sorry."

. . . Reminds her of Grace, voice veering, eyes unmoored and swerving. Like a trapped dog.

"Why are you sorry?"

"I don't know," she sobs.

*Grace Novotny.* Why does Madeleine remember the names of kids from grade four when she can't remember the names of people she bonded with six weeks ago on a film set? *Marjorie Nolan, Grace Novotny, Joyce Nutt, Diane Vogel. The following little girls.* . . ."I testified at the trial."

She tells about Ricky's alibi, the air force man who waved but never came forward. She tells about her lie, and how she reversed it on the stand. About how her father revealed to her the secret of how to recognize the right thing. It was simple: the right thing would always be the hardest.

"Poor little thing," says Nina.

Madeleine stops rocking and allows her eyes to rest on the painting of the bleached skull, relieved to have told the story, and is rewarded with a realization: "I think I still feel a lot of guilt about Ricky." Once the words are out, she recognizes them as stunningly self-evident. "I guess I'm an open book to you, eh?"

"Perhaps, but I can only read one page at a time."

"Oh wow, was that, like, profound or something?"

Nina waits. Madeleine fiddles with the rake in the miniature sandbox, feeling very small. "Nina . . . what if I get better and . . . I'm not funny any more? What if I can't work? What if I have to go back to school and become a lawyer or a pharmacist or something?"

Nina holds the pink stone in the palm of her hand, gently weighing it, and says, "When did you first want to be a comedian?"

"Oh, when I was about, like . . . I was five or something. I stood on a kitchen chair and told jokes."

"When did your friend die?"

"We were—she was nine."

Nina says, "So you were funny before that happened."

Madeleine bites her lip, nods.

"Comedy is your gift," says Nina. "The other things . . . the pain. Your father's illness, your brother. And Claire and . . . all the things I don't know about—those are all, at best, grist. At worst, they make you want to go off the road. And that's not really funny."

Madeleine longs to thank Nina for this, but she can't speak. Like a dog, she will take this treat away to eat later, in private. "See you next week."

In a second-hand clothing store in the market, while shopping for a new old Hawaiian shirt, Madeleine sees Claire. In the next instant she corrects herself; that child couldn't possibly be Claire, Claire is my age, she wouldn't look anything like that now. In the next instant she corrects herself—Claire is dead. Let's not think about what she looks like now.

She is out doing normal Saturday afternoon stuff, unaware that a layer has advanced from the back of her mind to the front, like a slide in a kid's View-Master. The newly promoted layer is taking a turn filtering everything she sees, and distributing the information to the various lobes and neural nets that deal with face recognition, emotion, smell, memory. The layer is dated, however. It doesn't get out much. It hasn't been used since 1963. Like software, it needs to be upgraded.

She glimpses a dog out the corner of her eye—*Rex.* She looks again, it's a beagle. Besides, Rex must be long dead by now. *Good boy. Such a good Rex.* It happens all day, breaking in this rookie layer of mind. Thus Madeleine sees a kid squinting through the smoke of a cigarette, leaning delinquent against the convenience store at College and Augusta, and says, *Colleen.*

"I'm sorry."

"What are you sorry for?" asks Nina.

"I'm sorry I—I feel so sorry for my parents." She puts her face in her hands.

"Why?"

Plucking several tissues: "Well. That was their little girl. They didn't know what was happening to her. They loved her." She blows her nose.

"What about you, Madeleine?"

"I can see him, you know? I'm standing there, and he's got his hand up, you know? Up my dress. It's like their little girl came home to them all smudged and broken and they never knew it. They still treated her . . . as though she was precious." Sobbing, throat aching, she is beyond sarcasm. "My mother picked out those pretty dresses, and he touched them."

"You sound as though you feel . . . it was your parents who were violated."

Madeleine nods. This makes sense after all.

"What about you, Madeleine?"

She looks up. "What do you mean?"

Nina looks so kind, Madeleine feels a little worried.

"If you could go back to that classroom now," asks Nina, "what would you do?"

"I can't change what happened."

"That's true."

"I would"—sorrow comes like sighs, gusts of rain, no longer falling but blowing across fields, dirt roads—"I would say, 'It's okay, I'm here,' and . . . I would watch."

"Watch?"

Madeleine nods, tears rolling down. *Mum, Dad. Watch me.* "'Cause I can't change it. But at least, if I watched it, she wouldn't have to be alone."

"Who wouldn't?"

"Madeleine. Me."

Nina passes her a glass of water.

"Did you ever tell anyone what happened?"

Madeleine sips, shakes her head. "I kinda danced around it, you know? I didn't know. . . ."

"What didn't you know?"

"I didn't know it hurt. . . ." Madeleine cries into her hands. "I didn't know it hurt so much." She is raining, raining. She feels the box of tissues arrive in her lap.

After a minute, Nina says, "You've been alone with this."

Madeleine nods.

We think of "witness" as a passive role, but it's not, it can be terribly difficult. That's why we say "to bear witness." Because it can be so painful. *Watch me.*

"What would happen if you told your parents now?"

Madeleine stops weeping. "Oh I can't do that."

"Why not?"

"My dad's not well, I might—it could . . . kill him." She blows her nose.

"What about your mother?"

"I don't know. . . . What if she—?" Madeleine groans because here comes the sorrow again. "I don't want her to comfort me."

"Why not?"

"Because she hates what I am."

Nina waits.

"That's not fair, she loves me. I just don't know what she'd do with the information."

Nina waits.

"She'd—she'll say, 'So that's why you're the way you are.'" Something so precious and individual, put down to a crime, an obscenity. . . . No.

Nina says, "If surviving sexual abuse were a recipe for homosexuality, the world would be a much gayer place."

Madeleine smiles. "I'm all better now," she says.

"Glad to hear it."

"You don't believe me."

"Not for a second."

She dreams again of too much light. Too green grass. Legs so heavy she can barely walk, thighs like wet cement, pressed down to earth by yellow light.

### ABRACADABRA

*"You know," he added very gravely, "it's one of the most serious things that can possibly happen to one in a battle, to get one's head cut off."*
            *Tweedledee,* Through the Looking-Glass

MADELEINE BUYS TWO AVOCADOS for Olivia and, on her way past the butcher shop in Kensington Market, catches a glimpse of the clock between stripped rabbits hanging in the window; a hand-printed sign beneath them announces, "Fresh Hairs." She has a date with Christine for "some closure" in forty minutes—enough time to do a little writing.

While she's sitting outside at a guano-festooned table, making notes on a napkin, the ass of a big grey suit passes inches from her face. "Pardon," says the puddingy voice, like the cartoon hippo making his way down the row in the movie theatre. Restaurants and theatres: the only public contexts in which it is perfectly acceptable to have the ass of a stranger grazing your nose. Madeleine leans back to give the man room. It's Mr. March. Her stomach plummets. He has kids, a son and daughter. Foiled again, doc—Mr. March would be sixty-something by now, he would be . . . her hands go cold on the wrought-iron table, she gets the point. He would be sixty—maybe seventy-something. He has continued through time, just like Colleen and Madeleine and the clock in the butcher shop and the rabbits on their way to the pot. He is not a ghost in a classroom, playing out the same eternal scene. He has been teaching for the past twenty-three years. He may still be teaching. He is still out there.

She gets up and leaves. Goes to Olivia's apartment, finds the key under the brick, enters and calls the police.

She is referred to various departments within the OPP, and finally reaches someone who takes down her story of sexual abuse—"It wasn't just me, he had a group of us—" and promises to get back to her.

What else is right in front of her that she can't see?

Various roommates begin to arrive. Someone starts playing the banjo. Of course they don't mind if she hangs out. She curls up at the end of the heavenly collapsing couch, under a blanket that smells like years of laundry, and waits for Olivia.

Rape.

It's embarrassing to find out that you are like other people. Even if half of them are celebrities. Especially if half of them are celebrities. *It can happen to anyone. I am not special.*

"I feel like I'm making it up."

Nina says, "When we invest so much in denying the truth, it can feel unreal when we finally speak it."

"Wape," says Bugs.

Nina waits.

Madeleine can cope. People who can cope take responsibility for things. Which means they need to have had them coming. The alternative is too terrifying: that bad things can just happen to them. It will be you the icicle falls on from twenty storeys up. You waiting for the bus when a motorist has a stroke and mounts the curb. To have been available to disaster once means to be permanently without a roof. Unless it was somehow your fault.

"It's not like I never had a choice, even at nine," says Madeleine. "You always have a choice."

"And you're willing to drive off the road to prove it."

Sexual violation is a form of robbery. You arrive home to find your house ransacked. All items, the precious and the mundane, the priceless and the merely expensive, have been treated the same way. All items have been turned into the same item. Overturned, flung aside, the picture of your grandparents and the contents of the cutlery drawer. You can still hear the foot-stomps through your house. You can buy a new TV but only time will restore the cushioned peace of your home, heal the rent in the air on the stairs, the aftershock in the living room, all those places where emptiness has been allowed to leer obscenely into your home. *Why us?* Nothing personal.

"I feel sick."

"Would you like some water?"

Rape treats the victim like nobody, like everybody, like anybody, *bitch!* Up the ramp, through the door to the slaughterhouse. The uncountable qualities that make one individual different from another, shocked away; the soul, shocked from the body, looks on in sorrow and pity at what is happening to its sister, its brother—*bitch!* It will be very difficult for the body to allow anything to inhabit it after that. Very difficult for it to allow the soul to re-enter. The soul may have to be content to follow close, make common cause with that other lonely follower, the shadow. Very difficult for the body to know whether that light request at the nape of the neck, *please let me in,* is the soul or the shadow. It is the soul. The shadow's request is more humble, it asks only to be seen. *Please don't turn away, every time you turn away, I die.*

"I feel carsick."

"Put your head between your knees."

Sexual violation turns all children into the same child. *Come here. Yes, you.* Children heal quickly, so that, like a tree growing up around an axe, the child grows up healthy until, with time, the embedded thing begins to rust and seep and the idea of extracting it is worse than the thought of dying from it slowly. *I'm not hurting you.* Once pleasure and poison have entwined, how to separate them? What alchemist, what therapist, what priest or pal or lover?

"I'm not into that 'repressed memory' bullshit," says Madeleine and picks up the pink stone, weighing it in her hand, cool marble, satisfyingly oval. "But you know that story 'The Purloined Letter'?"

"Yes."

"I feel like there's stuff just lying around but I can't see it."

"Hiding in plain sight."

"Yeah. Or camouflaged."

"Like a frog changing colour to match its surroundings?"

"Yeah, or like um, you know, like speckled eggs that hide in the uh . . . in the. . . ."

"Grass?"

"Yeah." She is weeping.

"What is it, Madeleine?"

"I don't know, my eyes are crying."

"Why?"

"Search *me,* doc." She puts the stone back on the table, spins it.

"What were you saying when your eyes started to cry?"

"I don't remember." She rubs a tickle from the palm of her hand.

"You were talking about a speckled egg—"

"Not speckled, blue."

"A robin's egg?"

Madeleine takes a deep breath and looks down.

The grass is thick with neglected objects no longer confined to the room at the top of her head; she is finding pieces everywhere, strewn underfoot, collecting in the cracks of sidewalks, reflected in the blur of subway trains. The mystery is how they have managed to stay intact long enough to be found, these breakable things, fragile as butterfly wings, perishable as childhood, spilling like fluff from dandelions and cattails—catch one, make a wish, release it back onto the breeze—glittering like stolen silver in a nest.

It is as though she has hit upon the magic words to make these objects glow so that they can be found. But they are not "magic," they are just words. Not spells, just spelling. Names. Perhaps that is what magic is. *Claire.*

## Through the Looking-Glass

*"Oh dear! I'd nearly forgotten that I've got to grow up again! Let me see—how is it to be managed?"*

Alice, Through the Looking-Glass

"Did Georgia O'Keeffe ever do butterflies?" asks Madeleine, settling into the swivel chair, cross-legged, warming her feet in her hands.

"I'm not sure," says Nina.

"I dreamt I found a Georgia O'Keeffe print like the one you have here, and it made me so happy to know that you and I both had the same picture. Except in my dream it was this incredible butterfly. Huge and bright yellow like the sun." Madeleine gazes at the serene skull and horns.

She has grieved in the best therapeutic tradition. She has "come to terms with her abuse," she has wept and called the police. Surely her work here in terracotta-land is done. Me go home now.

"I'm seeing someone," she says.

Nina listens.

"I'm um . . . happy. Isn't that weird?"

Nina smiles.

"I feel like part of me is awake and that part's really happy. But it has to drag around this other part. This dead-weight like an unconscious patient. It's me. My eyes are closed, I'm in this blue hospital gown." She crinkles her face. "How transparent am I, doc?" She waits. "The girl in the blue dress. It's like she grew up in a coma."

"In your dreams your legs feel heavy."

As though something were weighing me down. A body. *Mine.*

The OPP have not been able to tell her anything but she has been assured they are on it. She doesn't intend to wait while the bureaucratic wheels grind, however. She has a meeting with a lawyer tomorrow. She is going to bring charges. It's the right thing to do.

"What kind of charges?" asks Nina.

"What do you mean? Sexual assault, of course."

Just as Madeleine had never been able fully to comprehend that people and places went on changing after the McCarthys were posted away, so a child's world, though crowded with fantasy, coloured by faith in talking animals and time travel, is in fact rigidly ordered and unchanging. Policemen are always smiling and uniformed—you never picture one in a lawn chair with a beer. Butchers wear white coats and stand behind counters, they do not shop themselves, or go to the doctor wearing an ordinary shirt. Teachers are unimaginable outside school—you may see them on their way to their car, but they fall off the edge of the earth when they leave the parking lot, only to rematerialize the next morning at the front of the class, appropriately attired.

It was a breach of reality when Mr. March did what he did after three, but reality healed around it like a mysterious nub in the bark of a tree. Part of being able to accommodate this breach—to dilate normalcy—meant applying to it the same rigid laws of childhood physics: this is what happens after three. It happens in the classroom. Up by his desk. Just as the butcher never shops for broccoli, the policeman never plays croquet and the milkman is never without his truck, the things that happen in the classroom after three could never happen anywhere else.

Through the earth-toned portal of Nina's office, Madeleine has returned to the classroom, she has watched the child, she has lifted the bandage and smelled how rank the wound, exposed it to air so that it too can re-enter time and begin to change, to seal itself. She has listened faithfully, but has yet to translate the child's story into adult language. So she has not truly heard it. She is just one more grown-up who nods and loves but can do nothing to help.

She cups her hands over her face and inhales.

"You feeling faint?" asks Nina.

Madeleine shakes her head. "I still have to do it sometimes. Smell my hands. Weird, eh?" She grins. "My brother used to razz me about it."

Something so simple will be gained in the translation. Something that adults take for granted as they freely walk the earth, unbounded by bedtimes and the reproach of vegetables uneaten on the plate: Teachers can leave the classroom. They can leave the parking lot in their car. They can drive along a dirt road to a place where the fence has been left cordially unmended by the farmer. They can descend to the ravine at Rock Bass with a fragile blue egg sheltered in the palm of one big hand, then up the other side and, in their brown brogues that the children have only ever seen on asphalt or school linoleum, they can walk across the newly turned cornfield to the meadow beyond, where an elm tree stands. . . .

"Why do you do it?"

"To clean them. To inhale a bad smell off them. Obsessive compulsive, right? You should be paying me."

"What does it smell like?"

"Well there isn't really a smell."

"What do you imagine it smells like?"

"You're good. Okay, it's uh, clammy. It's a yellow smell."

"Yellow? You mean like urine?"

"No, just . . . yellow."

She has yet to translate the bold text and pictures of her child's story into the fine print of adulthood. When she does, she will be able to tell it back to the child. Tell it gently. The terrible story that the child does not know she knows.

She flexes her fingers, closing and opening her fists, this is the way to feel that your hands will not be chopped off.

"Does that help the smell to go away?" asks Nina.

Madeleine notices her hands swivelling on her wrists. "No." She relaxes them on the armrests and they go ice-cold. She takes a deep breath and sits on them.

"I think maybe I did it."

"Did what?"

"Killed her."

"Why do you think that?"

"Because I can see her lying there."

"You saw yourself, we know that."

"But I have such a clear picture of her."

"Can you describe the picture?"

"I can, I can—I see the grass tamped down like someone had a picnic there, you know?"

"Madeleine. Can you see her face?"

"We saw a deer."

"Who did?"

"Me and Colleen and Rex."

"Can you see Claire's face?"

"Mm-hm."

"What does it look like?"

"She's sleeping?"

"Can you describe her hair? You said she was wearing a hairband."

"Barrettes, yeah, and she had on her charm bracelet."

"What about her eyes?"

"They're closed."

"What about the rest of her face, Madeleine? Her mouth, her cheeks?"

"She looks peaceful but she's pale because, well, she's dead."

"Madeleine?"

Madeleine looks up.

Nina says gently, "When people die of strangulation, their eyes stay open. They change colour, they don't . . . it doesn't look anything like your picture."

Madeleine feels tired suddenly. As though tired were her natural condition and she has been waiting only for something to fall—all the balls, stilled in air, to drop. *Am I dying?* A voice has asked the question from deep within the tiredness. From the heart of the woods where the eyes of animals shine, from a den where a bone-white girl crouches.

"I'm afraid," says Madeleine.

"Can you describe it?"

"I'm afraid I know something."

Pictures, even scary ones, can be reassuring because they are narratively complete, unlike memory, which lies around, some assembly required. Madeleine's picture of Claire lying peacefully dead turns out to have been a piece of painted scenery all along. "Like *Bonanza*," she murmurs.

"*Bonanza?*"

Yellow Shell sign, intact and filling the screen until Ben Cartwright and his boys burst through on horseback.

"I see," says Nina.

After a moment, Madeleine says, "I don't want to."

"Want to what?"

"See what's behind the picture." She blinks spasmodically but keeps her eyes on Nina, paying attention. *Concentrate, little girl.* "What if it was my dad?" she says, in a voice as small as a toadstool.

"Do you think that's possible?"

"It would be the worst thing."

"Madeleine? Why is it up to you to find out what happened to her?"

Madeleine looks up, bewildered—*you've lost me, doc.* "I thought you thought . . . I knew. Like I'm looking at a clue but I don't recognize it, because . . . I don't know that I know."

"Madeleine. You may never find out what happened to Claire. But there are things you can find out."

"Like what?" She feels her forehead wrinkle like a dog's, earnest and pleading, eyes growing puddly and round as saucers.

"Who you are in all this."

Madeleine stares at Nina, aware of a corrosive feeling in her stomach. "And anyhow, her underpants were covering her face," she says.

"I know," says Nina. Everyone knows that. One of the "haunting details." "You've been carrying a heavy load, Madeleine. Can you imagine putting it down for a moment? And resting?"

Something shifts, yields to gravity. Madeleine sinks without moving and, as though in answer to the new proximity of the earth, tears flow.

"I think I'm dying." Her words reach her as if someone else has spoken them. Someone she has known all her life but forgotten. A traveller returning. Shawl around her head and shoulders. Mourner.

She doesn't recognize this self. She has discovered a talent for grief—like walking downstairs one morning and playing Chopin, never previously having touched a piano. Is sorrow a gift? Tears are flowing from every place on her body, sprouting like leaves, she can hear them lightly singing back the rain, she is weeping like a willow.

"Give me your hands," says Nina.

She does.

"Nina, I know I didn't kill Claire. But my hands think I did."

"Why?"

"Because they know how."

Time stops for grief.

Deep and muddy green, ping of sonar, what is down there? Dark and drowned, keep diving, this is a dream, you can breathe underwater. Dive, dive until you know how terribly sad it is that a child was killed.

"What do your hands know, Madeleine?"

Madeleine holds her breath at the top of every intake, exhaling in short gusts. She says, "I—can't say it."

"What can't you say?"

She looks down at her hands. White dogs, dumb animals. She strokes one with the other, warming them. She inhales carefully, then walks out onto a narrow branch. "He used to make us strangle him."

This is the trick of telling. Objects fly together magically, pieces of a broken cup; or simply shift by one degree, kaleidoscopic, changing the picture entirely. Mr. March never strangled Madeleine, so Madeleine never thought of him as a man who strangled. She was nine. She didn't know how to turn the picture around. To draw its mirror image. The pressure of his thumb in the soft flesh of her arm, his grip tattooed in blue bruises, his hold intensifying as she placed her own small hands around his wide soupy neck. *Squeeze.* She is thirty-two now and all it took was to say it out loud.

She is aware that the colours in the room have brightened a notch. She looks at Nina and says, "He killed her."

She grips the armrests so hard she feels the wood giving way, melting, turning to chocolate.

*Part Five*

# HUMAN FACTORS

# THE GLIDER

IT WAS AFTER they had found out Mike was missing. It was before hope had begun to fade. It was years before Jack and Mimi moved into the condo. Madeleine was graduating high school in three weeks; in three weeks her life would begin. She surged with the dark and shining joy of imminent escape into the world, far from this suburb.

She was at the kitchen sink, resentfully peeling apples for her mother. From the backyard came the roar of the old lawnmower. Through the window, they saw her father crossing back and forth. "Look at your father out there mowing the lawn."

Madeleine said, sullen, "You want me to do it instead? He won't let me." Her mother always talked about her father as though he were some kind of invalid—*your poor feeble father, out there pushing the mower on his crutches*. Why can't anyone just be normal around here? Houses have lawns, men cut them. It's not rocket science and it's not a tragedy. There is nothing poignant about a middle-aged white man mowing his lawn. Especially when there's a big fat swimming pool in the middle of it.

Mimi turned and smiled and Madeleine got a stab of guilt in the heart. There were tears in her mother's eyes. *If Mike were here he would be mowing the lawn.* She felt horrible for her mother, horrible about what a horrible daughter she was, and she felt furious that her father never let her mow the lawn—as if the safe operation of a small engine with blade affixed required the presence of a Y chromosome. He told her she could be anything she wanted to be—politician, lawyer, brain surgeon, astronaut. He would send her to the moon but he didn't trust her with a *maudit* Canadian Tire Lawn-Boy: *These things are tricky, you can lose a toe before you know it.*

She slouched toward the front door. She heard her mother's voice from behind her, "Why don't you ask your father if he wants to go for a walk?" She hated it when her mother tried to "encourage" her relationship with her father. *We have one, okay? And you are not the boss of it.* So— annoyed at her mother for making her annoyed at the prospect of going for a walk with her father, which was something she otherwise enjoyed doing—she headed for the back door. "You have the nicest papa in the world," she heard her mother say, and let the screen door slam.

She stepped out into the backyard and said, "Hey Dad, wanna go for a walk?"

He looked up from where he was crouching with the mower tilted, wiping its green-stained blade. Tightening the nut. The smell of cut grass and gasoline reached her, deeply reminiscent, reassuring . . . and sad. Everything is fucking sad. It's sad to be conceived. We start to die the moment we are born.

"Sure, sweetie."

She followed him into the garage as he wheeled the mower across the concrete to its appointed place. The smell of cool concrete—another deep suburban smell, along with the chlorine whiff, mingle of roses and other people's suppers.

"How come you don't buy an electric mower, Dad? They're better for the environment. Or just get a push mower."

"That's not a bad idea, I like the sound of those things a whole lot better."

They've had this mower since Centralia. Dad calls it "the beast."

"I'm just waitin' for this one to die, but Henry Froelich fixed it so well, I'm afraid it never will."

They left the garage and walked.

It was one of those rich Ottawa sunsets. The humidity lent a ravishing quality, wet fire streaked an aqua sky. Leaves so shiny they looked waxed, sprinklers hissing, parked cars gleaming.

They talked about the future.

"Why don't you go to New York? Wait tables and work your way up through the clubs to the *Ed Sullivan Show*?" She had moved past Ed to *Laugh-In* but she didn't correct him.

"Or why don't you take a raft up the Yukon River?"

They walked past the high school. A group of kids were hanging out in the parking lot, music coming from the radio of someone's dad's station wagon. She glanced scornfully in their direction. The cool kids. Like I care. Dating, mating—all those girls soon to be trapped. She saw gorgeous Stephen Childerhouse. He looked up and she looked quickly away; he was holding hands with Monica Goldfarb. So what? The world doesn't exist anyway. Reality is subjective. We are all just in a dream, and probably not our own. Don't wake the red king. See? I don't have to get stoned to be weird.

They got ice cream cones. He took his first lick and she turned away, because he looked so young and she felt so old.

They walked out past the edge of the housing development to where the land was still shaggy and the trees lived for themselves, trailing their leaves in the Ottawa River. Out there in the middle was a Huck Finn–sized island; why had she never snagged one of those stray logs from the match company upriver and floated across? She had always meant to, but at seventeen she wasn't a kid any more. And it wouldn't be much fun to do it alone. Jocelyn wasn't that kind of friend. Madeleine had only ever had that kind of friend once.

They walked along the dirt path past a blackened spot where kids had had a campfire and she said, "Dad? Do you think it's possible that Ricky Froelich did it?"

"Absolutely not."

"How come they convicted him?"

"That was a travesty."

Madeleine felt the tang and churn of something deeper than guilt. Something she could not outrun; she had to wait for it to pass, like the recurrence of a tropical disease. Shame. Her father would know nothing about it. He was clean. She watched him from the corner of her eye, willing him to keep his eyes from her. If he looked at her now he would see the dark thing. He was squinting into the sky, licking his ice cream, so innocent and unconcerned. *This Book Belongs to John McCarthy.*

"Look at that," he said, and pointed up. She felt her darkness falling away. "Up there," he said, "see it?"

She looked up and saw a white airplane. Silent. Slow. Wings long and tapered, clean and unencumbered by engines.

They watched in silence. Unhurriedly she banked, dove, looped up and paused, offering her smooth breast to the sky before swooning back into the arms of gravity, her dance partner.

"Now, that's flying," said Jack.

## Le Grand Dérangement

*"That's the effect of living backward," the Queen said kindly, "it always makes one a little giddy at first."*

Through the Looking-Glass

NINA DIDN'T THINK she should be alone this evening. Suggested she call a friend, and gave Madeleine her home number "in case you need to talk." She asked if Madeleine was prepared to find out that Mr. March had died.

"That doesn't matter, I still have to tell what he did."

"I think you need to prepare yourself for the possibility that you may not find exactly what you expect."

"Why, you think Ricky did it?"

"That's not what I'm saying, Madeleine."

"Well what the fuck are you saying?!"

"I'm saying—I'm asking. Where are you in all this?"

But Madeleine didn't understand the question. And she was late, late for a very important date.

Out into the blinding street, people spilling across the intersection, light refracting off windshields and hoods. She can't seem to get an entire lungful of air. It's a beautiful day, not too hot, mid-June. Her eyes are up to their old tricks, this time seeing words that aren't there, shivering letters stencilled on a restaurant window, *It's Cruel Inside.* . . . She runs down the leafy Annex sidewalk. She wishes she had her bike, she runs faster—

"Hi Madeleine!"

"Hi Jim," she calls in return, but doesn't pause. He has a baby in a Snugli, when did that happen?

Her hands twist as though they could unscrew themselves, she gulps air, just north of Bloor now, still running, the heels of her *Quatre Cents Coups* sandals pounding—this is the way to feel that your feet will not be chopped off. . . .

There has been enough talking. It's time to do the right thing.

She runs up the steps of her veranda. Her bike is not there, that's because she left it locked to a parking meter outside Nina's. Up the inside stairs two and three at a time. On the carpet in the middle of the empty room, the red light of the answering machine is blinking. She picks up and dials.

It could have been me.

It would have been me.

It should have been me.

She has called 911 this time. " . . . only for genuine emergencies," says the female voice.

"This is an emergency."

"Call your local police division, I'll give you the—"

"I've already called them, they did dick!"

"I'm afraid you'll have to—"

Madeleine slams down the phone and dials 411.

There are places and moments that are definitive. Like old photos, they can tell us where we come from. . . .

" . . . thank you, here's your number—"

She is from a summer afternoon, the late August light that makes the corn glisten in the fields; her mother in the rearview mirror, lips arched to receive a fresh coat of red.

"You have reached the Ontario Provincial Po—"

"Hello, I'd like to report a—"

"If you have a touchtone phone, and know the extension of the department. . . ."

She is from a street of Technicolor houses where she pedals toward a man in a beautiful blue uniform and hat; he leans forward, arms wide to catch her. *Do it your way, sweetie.*

"I have information about a murder."

"Go ahead."

She is from the jab of a coat hook next to her spine.

" . . . the Froelich case, yes. . . ." She is from a secret. " . . . a teacher called Mr. March, he's retired now, but—" How is she to get back there? "I called last week, someone was going to—you should have a file. . . ." To the meadow in springtime. To Colleen and Rex . . . school-day quiet. "March. Like the month." As she follows Colleen across the field to the meadow on the other side. Watch for something gleaming in last year's grass. Something pink and winking back the sun, that will be her streamer.

"I don't have a record of your call, Mrs. McCarthy, can you hold, please."

Muzak in her ear. She sits cross-legged, gazing at the geometry on her carpet. She is gathering the facts, she can see them spread like pebbles before her, she wants to collect them in her hands but something keeps interfering, live loose ends of story snap and hiss around her, touching down, singeing the carpet. She hangs up, and stares at the phone as though it were a rat, capable of staring back. Through the beaded balcony curtain comes the sound of drumming several blocks away, the sun pink as Lik-m-aid, fizzing colour, the beads are so many candy necklaces strung end to end on shoelace licorice. She picks up the phone again and dials.

The universal voice: "Information, for what city, please?"

"Crediton."

"For what name?"

"March. George, I think. George."

"One moment. Here's your number."

It's that simple. That possible and near. What must it be like to go through your entire adult life with one phone number? She thinks of Mr. Froelich with his "old phone number" tattooed on his arm. His chalky fingers and kind face, blackboard full of hazardous fractions behind him as he bends to touch her forehead, *"Was ist los, Mädele?"* Why is that man no longer in the world? She keys in the area code, then the number—it plays a tune, "Camptown Races."

The beauty of the evening finds its way into her empty living room, touches the mouldings of the high Victorian ceiling, medallion at its centre. The phone rings at the other end of the line. So empty. The sound of a chain in a dry well.

"Hello?" An older lady's voice, tentative.

"Hello . . . Mrs. March?"

"Yes?"

"Hi, I'm an old student of Mr. March's."

"Oh." The guard drops, Madeleine can hear the smile.

"I wondered if I could speak with him." She hears her own voice trembling, as though she were speaking into the blades of a fan. She feels herself growing smaller and smaller, will he even be able to hear her when she finally speaks the words? And what will they be?

"Oh I'm sorry, dear," says the lady, "George passed away."

There are landmarks we use without thinking. You can never get lost if you can see a mountain. Now Mr. March is gone. And Madeleine no longer knows where she is; or how to get back to where she came from. *Oh dear!* cried the child when she realized she had lost her way, *Whatever will become of me?*

She could have got back through him. Through the bad time to the blessed, last good time. *Centralia.* But the door in the mountain closed before she could reach it, and she can detect no opening or notch in this implacable surface.

"Are you still there, dear?"

"I'm sorry."

The elderly voice aspirates, "Yuh, yuh," and there is a cherishing quality to her next words. "Eighteen months ago now."

Madeleine does not reply.

"What did you say your name was, dear?"

"That's okay."

"Oh, I wish he could have talked to you, he loved his pupils."

Mrs. March is saying something, her voice still fluttering from the earpiece, as Madeleine guides the receiver gently to its cradle and hangs up.

It's over.

She carefully lies down, curled with her head by the phone. She hears her own voice softly moaning, "Oh no-o-o, oh no-o-o-o," like poor Grace, poor Grace, poor Grace. She observes herself stroking her own forehead as though her curled fingers belonged to someone else—a grown-up, preoccupied but able to spare some absent comfort. She is grateful to be alone on the rug. She wishes it were the cool Centralia grass. The smell of earth, the tickle of an ant crawling up a curving blade, crackle of countless lives beneath her ear. She wishes she could feel a pink tongue, like a slice of ham, warm against her cheek, Rex panting, dog-laughing. Wishes she could smell the sun on her arm, hear kids' voices from many backyards away, watch the wheels of her brother's bike ride up. She would give anything to see his high-tops, one poised on his pedal, the other planted on the ground, to hear him say, "What do you think you're doing, stunned one?" turning to call, "Maman, she fell asleep in the grass."

Where are you, Mike? My brother. *Gone, gone to grass.*

The kind disinterested fingers press against her eyes, because Mike is dying now too, finally, and again. He is part of the earth, part of the lush forest that is slowly healing itself over there. His bones, fragments of his uniform, tattered green, the chain he wore, metal dog tags, one of them his name. I love you, Mike. *Rest.*

Where have all the children gone?

She lies weightless on the carpet, arms and legs, hands and head like a loose collection. If she got up, half might remain, scattered on the rug.

Once upon a time there was a mountain cave. The piper led the children into it, all except one who was lame and could not keep up. By the time that child arrived, the door had vanished and she was forlorn, never knowing whether she was lucky or just lonely. Who was that child? The lame one. The one who became a grown-up.

Through closed eyes, Madeleine can hear the voices of children from inside the mountain. Hers is among them. The wool of the carpet bristles her cheek, she keeps her eyes closed, listening.

How can a grown-up ever gain entry? *Unless you become as one of these. . . .* Not "innocent," just new. Raw and so very available to life. Why do grown-ups insist on childhood "innocence"? It's a static quality, but children are in flux, they grow, they change. The grown-ups want them to carry that precious thing they believe they too once had. And the children do carry it, because they are very strong. The problem is, they know. And they will do anything to protect the grown-ups from knowledge. The child knows that the grown-up values innocence, and the child assumes that this is because the grown-up is innocent and therefore must be protected from the truth. And if the ignorant grown-up is innocent, then the knowing child must be guilty. Like Madeleine.

She left something back there, dropped it in the grass.

*Where?*

*In the meadow.*

If she could go back and find herself at nine, she could ask and she would listen. The pieces would become a story and lead back here to where she lies on the rug at thirty-two. And she would be able to get up again.

*Claire McCarroll* MURDERED
*Madeleine McCarthy* MURDERED
*Marjorie Nolan* MURDERED
*Grace Novotny* MURDERED
*Joyce Nutt* MURDERED
*Diane Vogel* MURDERED

## BLUE EGG

AFTER JACK GOT HOME from the hospital, he gave his wife a gift. Unlike the mink coat, it was something she still wanted very badly. He passed it to her carefully. She received it as the precious and fragile object it was. Like a Fabergé egg, sapphire-blue in her hands:

*I never touched Karen Froelich.*
*Here is how you will know I am telling the truth.*
*It was I who waved.*

This is what a good wife could do for you if you were of that generation. She could take something terribly dark. Terribly heavy. Corrosive. And in her hands it could shine like a jewel, simply because you had shared it with her. Your Secret becomes Our Secret.

But few people are ever lucky enough to have such a marriage. And while his gift was not, and now never could be, the third child that Mimi had prayed for, it was precious nonetheless. And it made her weep because he was and always had been hers. Always would be. She longed to give him something in return. *It wasn't your fault our son went away. I forgive you.* But the two statements didn't add up, so she kissed him instead, stroked his face and put the kettle on.

HERE IS SOMETHING that will always make sense: it's my fault.

Take Highway 2 east out of Toronto. Through suburban sprawl interrupted by farmhouses stranded on shrinking arable islands, through towns where split-levels and monster homes crowd out or ye-oldify the gingerbreaded main street, which never ends but morphs into fast-food, new-and-used, superstore, multiplex and featureless buildings that have created a housing crisis for ghosts. *I saved myself from after-three, but that only caused him to claim Claire as my replacement.*

Back within sight of Lake Ontario on your right—so close yet inaccessible, because where there are roads leading down to it there are also housing developments and factories and fences. You could abandon your car and travel like a dog through the long grass over lumpy ground to the shore, where signs tell you what, precisely, is unsafe about this particular spot. This is North America, there are signs warning you of danger everywhere. Caution: Cliff. We are at the point where we risk walking off the edge of any precipice, however stark, that is not furnished with a sign. Caution: Children. *I saved Claire with the letter from the Human Sword, but that only drove him from the classroom to the meadow, where there was no door to close, no other little girls to see, no principal just down the hall. . . .*

Turn north on Highway 33. The landscape changes, highway slicing through limestone, exposed rock face on both sides, teeming with still-life, layer upon fossilized layer spray-painted now with graffiti. *If only I had told my dad.* Careful not to get into a mental groove or make a nursery rhyme out of your guilt, you will be lulled smack into KIL-ROY WAS HERE. *Claire wouldn't have died, I wouldn't have lied, Ricky wouldn't've needed an alibi, he'd never've gone to jail.* This is the land of Hidden Intersections and painted yellow signs with leaping deer. *Mike would not have gone away, Mr. Froelich would be alive today.* Take number 16, soon to be the Veterans Memorial Highway, Lest We Forget, *my dad would not be ill.* Welcome to the National Capital Region, *Bienvenue à la Région de la Capitale nationale. . . . and all for the want of a horseshoe nail.*

These two-lane, two-way highways are statistically more dangerous than the straight multi-lane 401, the difference being that these winding roads, with their scenery and their signs, are narrative. The 401 is just a series of facts. Armed with a Tim Horton's coffee, Madeleine feels no sense of dissolving from within, no dread that her hand will wrench the wheel into the Canadian Shield. The rain starts and she turns on the radio and windshield wipers. Leslie Gore sings "Sunshine, Lollipops and Rainbows." Everything is going to be okay. I'm going home. To my mum and dad.

*What will you do when you get there, Madeleine?*

I will tell my dad what happened to me. And my mother will make me a plate of food.

*Why must you tell now?*

Because there is a person who can save me, a perfect donor match, she is nine, I have to find her before it's too late.

I will say, Dad, someone hurt me.

I will say, Dad, please walk me to school today.

Watch me, Dad.

And I will never again have to wait my turn in the lonely lonely classroom where the clock is always set at five past three.

She is hungry and almost happy. She drives out of the rain and into one of Ottawa's unlikely tropical sunsets.

Sailing along the Queensway, glimpse of the flag atop the Parliament Buildings. Maple leaf. No emblem of war or victory or workers' solidarity. A leaf red as a crayon, the kind children collect in autumn.

There is a way back, after all. Through the front door of a new ground-floor condo in the suburbs of Ottawa. It opens onto all the modern conveniences and the one person in the world capable of taking her back there. Once upon a time there was a young air force pilot named Jack and a pretty Acadian nurse called Mimi.

Open Sesame.

ONCE UPON A TIME, there were magic words that soothed us. *In defence of democracy. Just say no. Resolve. Freedom. Justice.* We no longer liked the word *war* because it conjured up pictures of soldiers burning villages in order to save them. But *war* was potent if it was summoned against a concept or social condition. When we went to war against people, we preferred to call it by names that resembled movie titles, with their comforting implication of beginning, middle and end, as well as their expedient hint at a sequel.

Some of us conscientiously gathered proof to justify attacking tyrants, while others waited to examine the evidence duly laid out. But we all ignored the story of how we had helped to create them: the drug lords, the war lords, the nuts who, with our help or the help of our friends, had cut down the ranks of the moderate among them. This was an old story and we wanted to believe in a new world order, so we ignored it. But empires have always divided and conquered, tilted and tolerated. And prospered for a time. It's a question of balance, and the problem, in the end, is always greed. Like the story of the king who grew hungrier the more he ate. Like the aldermen of Hamelin, who, seeing their fair city cleansed of rats, refused to pay the Piper.

Once there was a golden age. Post-war, green dream, people raised families and there was more than enough of everything to go around. People from all over the world came to find freedom, peace and prosperity. The Great Experiment worked. Never have so many lived so peacefully, never has so much diversity thrived, never has dissent bred so much opportunity. This beautiful idea made gloriously concrete, this raucous argument, ungainly process, cacophony of competition and compromise; this excellence that emerges from disarray like a smartly dressed woman from a messy apartment in time for work. This precious mess. Democracy. How much can be done in its name before, like an egg consumed by a snake, it becomes merely a shell?

Once upon a time in the West.

# The Air Force Cross

*I was much too far out all my life*
*and not waving, but drowning.*

                    *Stevie Smith,* "Not Waving But Drowning"

When she arrives, her mother says, "What's wrong?"

"Nice to see you too."

*"Je suis ta mère,* you can't fool me."

She steps inside. "Maman, it's just spur of the moment, that's all, I had the day off."

Mimi raises an eyebrow, then hugs her. The condo is high-ceilinged, its foyer leading past the kitchen and opening onto a spacious dining and living room. The halo of newspaper around the gold La-Z-Boy lowers and her father's head appears around the side. "Whozat?" he says playfully, staring down his reading glasses.

"Hi Dad!"

Mimi closes the front door behind her—"We're not paying to air condition the outside"—and ushers her into the kitchen, which over-looks the foyer as well as the dining and living area from behind a waist-high wall and several decorative pillars. "Come and eat, you're too thin, what's that you're wearing? I'm taking you shopping."

Madeleine follows her mother, thoroughly annoyed, deeply reassured. She hugs her father, who joins them in the kitchen and laughs to see her so unexpectedly.

She eats a "heart smart" version of Maman's *fricot au poulet.* How's After-Three? How's *Stark Raving Madeleine?* Are you still planning on going to the States? "Jack, let her eat." He moves slowly to the fridge, fumbles in a compartment and, with a wink, brings out a foil-wrapped brick.

*"Mon D'jeu, qu'est-ce que c'est que ça?"* cries Mimi.

Crack cocaine, a human skull—a pound of butter. This house has become a cholesterol-free zone, but Jack has obviously been hiding a stash. He plunks the butter on the table in front of Madeleine with a wheezy chuckle—"For you. Some skin on your bones"—grins himself mauve and returns to the living room.

Mimi shakes her head and says, "You have the nicest papa in the world."

The kitchen is immaculate. The one patch of chaos flourishes around the phone: stacks of rubber-banded envelopes, a jumble of pens—most of which, her father claims, are out of ink—the old dented pop-up tin address book, whose entries he swears would flummox a Bletchley Park code-breaker, and a Maxwell House Coffee tin jammed with mysterious essentials impossible to inventory. It strikes Madeleine for the first time that her mother's filing system—her way of working—is not dissimilar to her own. In this kitchen, you don't dare throw anything away unless your name is Mimi.

Her mother is loading the dishwasher, effortlessly executing a spatial feat the equivalent of cramming twenty-five people into a VW bug. She pauses and holds up a mug stamped with some sort of impressionistic painting. "A lesbian gave me this mug."

Madeleine looks up, at a loss. " . . . That's nice." Is this the break-through? Are we going to have the Movie of the Week reconciliation now?

But Mimi asks, "What are you doing this summer?"

"Working probably."

"Why don't you come with your father and me to Bouctouche? Your cousins would love to see you."

"Maybe I will." Sure, I'm thirty-two years old, why wouldn't I take a holiday alone with my parents? By the way, Maman, I'm divorced and in love.

The Pope, Queen Elizabeth II, Charles and Diana and The Blessed Virgin Mary look down from a row of commemorative plates on a plate-rail that runs the upper perimeter of the kitchen, their ranks bolstered by the Acadian flag, the Eiffel Tower, the crest of 4 Fighter Wing and a New Brunswick lighthouse. The cuckoo clock is mounted over the stove as usual, the same faint apprehension hovering about its closed door.

Past the kitchen—at the far end of the living room, by the patio doors with their sheers—Madeleine can see that the television is on and muted—*Murder, She Wrote,* a rerun. On the coffee table the crystal roosters still duke it out and, above the door to the master bedroom, Dürer's praying hands preside. The stereo is playing a cassette of east-coast fiddle music, Grandmaman's hooked rug with the cooked lobsters in the waves hangs over the couch, and in pride of place above the man-tel of the gas fireplace is the oil painting of the Alps. *Plus ça change.*

Madeleine tries and fails to wedge her plate into the dishwasher, so rinses it in the sink and joins her father in the living room. He sits half reclined in his gold La-Z-Boy, newspaper fanned out in front of him, several more washed up around his chair. She sinks into the couch to his right and is tempted to turn up the TV, stretch out and veg. Why did she come here again? Wasn't it so she could rest? Regress? *Hey Dad, want to play Chinese checkers?* She pulls her eyes from the screen to the side table, about to reach for the remote when she sees it. Tucked under the table, an oxygen tank. Industrial green with a transparent plastic coil and mask, it hits her like an obscenity.

She finds her voice and asks casually, "When'd you get this groovy accessory?"

"What? Oh that, little while ago. Keeps me fit for my jog around the block."

She wills her smile to hang in place, like a picture too heavy for its nail. "That's good, so it helps, eh?"

He shrugs. "It's more for show. I take a little nip now and then to please Her Nibs." He grins and gestures with his thumb toward the basement stairs, where Mimi has gone to look for something.

Madeleine smiles back. She doesn't question the charade.

Why didn't her mother tell her that Dad is on oxygen now? That changes things. When you see the oxygen van pull up in front of a house, you know someone in there has had it. *Don't think that.* She swallows. "Just as well to have it on hand, eh?"

"Oh yeah," he says, picking up the paper.

"Dad?"

He drops the paper, looks up suddenly and says, "Wait now"—clears his throat of reediness. "I just remembered." And gets up.

She can tell he is moving spryly on purpose, for show. For her. What's worse is that she wants him to. She doesn't want to see him shuffle the way he did in the hospital, with his bracelet and gaping blue gown. Hospitals are where people go to shuffle, and when they no longer need to shuffle they go home. She doesn't want to see him shuffle here. It would mean he was sent home shuffling. Sent home to die. *Don't.*

She watches him disappear into the bedroom with the deliberate spring in his slippers. On the TV, Angela Lansbury talks to a nervous man with sideburns and confronts him with a titanium letter opener. Jack emerges from his bedroom and tosses her something. She catches it.

A silver cross suspended from a red-and-white-striped ribbon. The Air Force Cross.

"That's for you," he says.

She looks up. "Wow."

He says, almost sighs, "Thought you'd like that," returns casually to the La-Z-Boy and reaches for his newspaper.

This is all the conversation he will muster for another few moments. That's what the newspaper is for now. It helps to smooth over the patches when he no longer has breath for speech.

"Thanks Dad." She closes her hand around the medal until she feels its four points dig into her palm—this is the way not to cry when your father gives you something he wants you to have after he dies.

When she can open her hand again, she looks down at it. Silver thunderbolts and wings, a cross composed of propeller blades topped by an imperial crown. *For valour courage and devotion to duty whilst flying, though not in active operations against the enemy.*

"You got this in Centralia in, what? Forty-two?"

"Forty-three." He's reaching over the side of his chair, fishing in his newspaper pile.

"Can I help you find something?"

He shakes his head, going pink, his old irritation. "Maman puts my papers into the recycling before I've read half of them."

"Which one are you looking for?"

"Couple months ago." He reaches toward the table for his glasses, and finds them on his nose.

She rifles through and finds a yellowed two-year-old copy of *The Washington Post.*

"That's it." He looks at it accusingly. "She must've hid it on me," he says in his playful tone, leafing through it.

Madeleine says, "I was thinking of going back there. To Centralia."

"How come?" he asks, and clears his throat.

"I want to see if there are any bones in that stormpipe," she answers, blinking in surprise at her own words. He raises his eyebrows but continues skimming the *Post.* "Remember there was a dog trapped?"

He shakes his head, but she can see him taking a reading, getting a fix. . . .

"The night of flying up."

He locks on.

She takes a deep breath, but quietly, not wanting to worry him. She is already trembling, cold. "You told me the fire truck came and saved it."

He smiles and nods.

"Is that true?"

He opens his mouth and forms a word, then another, but no sound comes out. Then his voice kicks in, as though he were transmitting through radio static, and he continues without going back to the beginning of his sentence. She pieces it together.

He has said, with a convivial grin, "Why would I lie to you?"

"To make me feel better."

That sounded harsh—as though she were angry at him. She has no reason to be angry. Especially at him, especially now.

He shrugs as if to say, "Fair enough," then folds the *Post* and hands it to her. It's crumbling at the seam but the page is intact. A photograph of an old man walking down the steps of a building in Washington. He's flanked by a middle-aged woman and three men in suits.

*RUDOLPH RELINQUISHES US CITIZENSHIP.* She skims the article: *Nazi. . . . NASA. . . . War crimes come to light. . . .*

"Dora," says Jack.

Madeleine looks up. "The rocket factory."

"Bang on," says Jack, and she is glad to have pleased him. "Remember Apollo?"

*Rudolph, Dora, Apollo.* What kind of story is this?

She looks back at the article. Arthur Rudolph. Wernher von Braun's right-hand man. He has left the U.S. rather than face charges of crimes against humanity dating back forty years, to his time as general manager of an underground factory called Mittelwerk.

"They don't say anything about Dora here."

"They never do," says Jack, and she hears the old sarcastic note. "It was a code name."

She looks back at the article. Yet another old Nazi. "Took them long enough."

"Rudolph managed the space program, he and von Braun got us to the moon."

*Rudolph with your nose so bright. . . .* Concentrate.

"The Americans pinned a medal on him, and now they're finished with him they want to fling him in jail," says Jack.

"Isn't that where he belongs?"

Jack shrugs reasonably—"You're probably right"—and sighs reaching for today's paper: "Fella in Texas just got an artificial heart, how do you like that?"

She can feel her mind glazing, fights the pull of the news, the TV, the smell of baking. "Dora—that's where Mr. Froelich was."

"That's right," says her father. "He was a slave."

*Slave.* The word is like a wound. She watches his profile. Finer, the skin drawn more closely than before over the bones, the involuntary sadness at the corner of the eye that comes with age—exacerbated in his left eye by his old scar. His mouth still set against all odds, lips moving slightly as he reads—he never used to do that.

She wonders how to bring up the subject. What she has come here to tell him.

"Tens of thousands of them died, and some were hanged right in front of that fella's office."

Madeleine looks back at her father. "What?" Then at the photo again. She reads the caption: *Rudolph and daughter. . . .*

"He's trying to come to Canada now."

"We won't let him in, though."

"Probably not. Not at this point."

"Is that what—? Did he get into the States because of Project Paperweight?"

"Paperclip."

She returns the disintegrating *Post* to the newspaper pile as it dawns on her—what her father is telling her. "Is this the guy Mr. Froelich saw?" Maybe his hearing is going a little, because he doesn't answer. "Dad?"

"No," says Jack.

"What?"

"That's not the man Henry Froelich saw." He continues reading his Ottawa *Citizen.* "They just performed laser surgery on a man in Detroit"—he pronounces it "lazzer"—"zapped a blood clot in his brain, pretty soon we won't need surgery at all. They'll map the human genome and get in there and engineer everything at birth."

"Did Mr. Froelich ever tell you who he saw?"

Jack nods, and she waits as he lifts the clear plastic mask to his face and takes a drink of oxygen before she asks, "Who?"

"An engineer." He exhales through his mouth. "Henry didn't know his name." He looks at her for a moment, and she waits for him to speak but he returns to his paper.

"Did you tell the police?"

"Tell them what?"

"About the engineer?"

"Hank told them."

"How come they didn't do anything?"

"I don't think they believed him."

Because his story was tied to Ricky's alibi. The one she helped to undermine. She tightens her hand around the medal again.

Jack raises the mask toward his face, pauses—"It was a different time. We were after Communists then, not Nazis. Old war"—then inhales.

It takes her a moment to realize that he has said, "Cold War." He draws in the oxygen slowly, his lids half closing as though in prayer. He will be asleep soon. Then it will be too late in the evening. And if she waits till morning, the sunshine will persuade her that she's fine and ought not to burden him with her story. She knows now how to begin. *Dad? I have to tell you about something sad that happened to me a long time ago, but don't worry, the story has a happy ending. See? I'm happy.*

She watches his face fall—like a slackened sail, it abandons expression, and it's clear how much effort has gone into the rigging of an ordinary smile. Are we all making that effort all the time, unaware of what it costs?

He glances at the mask but doesn't reach for it. He turns his clear blue gaze on her. "What is it sweetie?"

It's suddenly painful to hear him. Not because his speech is faint or laboured but because it is not. She is hearing her father's voice for the first time in—how long? It has been eroding, crumbling like a shoreline. She feels tears standing in her eyes. Is it because of what she has to say, or because, at the sound of his voice, her father has returned? As though a younger version of him has been permitted to come up from the shades and sit here in the living room of the condo. If she closes her eyes she will see the back of his sandy crewcut, elbow out the car window, hairs on his forearm combed by the breeze. *Who wants ice cream?*

"I've been feeling. . . ." She wishes she had the excuse of an oxygen mask to hide the rise of sorrow.

She closes her eyes and hears him say, "Spit it out, old buddy."

She opens her eyes and smiles. "I used to feel guilty."

"Why, what for?" His blue eyes have sharpened. Even his left eye is awake.

"Because I made Ricky go to jail," she says, and feels her forehead wrinkle at the childish syntax. "Because . . . I think my testimony caused him to be convicted." Her face contorts, and she begins to breathe through her mouth.

Her father is looking at her hard.

"No it didn't."

It's his man-to-man voice. If she didn't know him so well, she might think he was angry with her. But she knows he's worried.

"I'm okay, Dad. It's just, you know, over the years, I'd read in the paper"—seeking refuge in a sarcastic tone—"'convicted on the evidence of child witnesses' and I'd think, 'Gee, maybe he actually was guilty and I don't have to feel so bad,' and that'd make me feel worse." She needs to say the words. About Mr. March. And then something will be all right. *Say it.* She opens her mouth but nothing forms except a pool of saliva under her tongue.

Jack says, "You weren't the only witness."

"I know."

"Those two little gals—one of them was a friend of yours, what were their names? Martha?"

"Marjorie."

"That's right."

"And Grace."

"Well, they did him in." His choice of words is like a bump in the road. She waits. Then asks, "What did they say?"

"A whole lot of nonsense." He reaches for the mask.

"I always thought"—willing herself not to cry, her face feels like a balloon full of water—"thought I disappointed you that day."

He juts his chin forward and his face darkens. "Let's get one thing perfectly clear," he says. "You have never—and I mean never, not *once*— disappointed me." *Do you read me?* He takes another breath.

He's fading. *Don't go, Dad.* Returning to the shades. *Wait.* It will be too late to tell him. About the silence of the school after three. The smell of orange peels and pencil shavings. The empty corridor she walked afterwards, past our gracious Queen, running when she got outside to make a breeze to soothe the sting, *it doesn't hurt.* I was so strong, I didn't know that I was small. *Dad, watch.* She opens her mouth to tell him and hears him say—

"I waved."

She blinks. Tears suspend. "What?"

"It was me. I saw Rick on the road that day. I waved."

She sits, lips still parted with what she was going to say, but it's gone.

"I was the one in the car." He holds the clear mask up to his face, closes his eyes and inhales through his nose. Exhales, opens his eyes and looks at her. True blue.

She shakes her head slowly, waiting, as though for Novocaine to wear off. She sees the shape of a man behind a windshield, sun splintering off it, the outline of his hat, his hand. Dust in the wake of a blue car on a country road in spring. . . .

"Why didn't you say something?" she asks.

"I was doing my job." And he tells her.

She leans her elbows on her knees, looks down at the white pile carpet between her feet and concentrates on breathing evenly. She slips her hands into her armpits to warm them. Something has fallen away. Quietly, with no fuss. The ground beneath her feet.

" . . . Oskar Fried, I don't know what his real name . . ."

*Uncle Simon and Mr. McCarroll*

" . . . my number two . . ."
*Joint Intelligence Objectives Agency*
" . . . a drunken U.S. Marine officer arrested for espionage a few years later . . ."
*NATO*
" . . . the space race . . ."
*NORAD*
" . . . threat from Soviet missiles . . ."
*USAF*
" . . . Cuba on the brink . . ."
*USAFE*
" . . . Berlin set to blow . . ."
*The Pentagon*
" . . . one individual can't possibly see the whole picture . . ."
*The Moon*
"She never would have been in Centralia," says Madeleine.
"Who?"
*The schoolyard*
"Claire," she answers.

His bad eye has begun to seep. He wipes it with his wrist. "That was a terrible tragedy."

Madeleine stares at him. *Who are you?* is the logical next question. It lasts less than a second, the glimpse of the strange man in the gold recliner, freshly defined as though by the flash of a camera illuminating a previously unseen shape in the dark. Then he is her father again. Smaller than he used to be. A little lost in his golf shirt. His white tennis shoes looking too new, too substantial, the way old people's new shoes do.

" 'Tragedy' is a word people use when they don't want the blame." she says.

*If Claire had never moved to Centralia, who would Mr. March have selected in her place? A little girl with a dark brown pixie cut. . . .*

" . . . imagine flying through a thick fog where you can't tell what's up or what's down. In a case like that, you have to—"

"It didn't make the world safer, Dad."

"—trust your instruments. And it worked, we beat them."

"Beat whom?"

"The Soviets. They're crying uncle." The expression on his face is obstinate. An old child.

She says, "Do you think the world's going to be safer when the wall comes down?"

He leans toward her. "I'll tell you a secret, old buddy, sometimes it's hard to know what's the right thing to do, but if you're ever in doubt, just ask yourself, 'What's the hardest thing I could do right now?'"

"Mr. Froelich died."

Jack sighs and reaches for a tissue to dab his eye. "I think he may have been killed."

"Who killed him? Simon?"

"More likely someone Simon told."

" . . . the CIA? Why, for the sake of Oskar Fried?"

"Presumably."

"You told Simon about Mr. Froelich."

"It was my job to tell him."

Everything has become granular. She can feel her lips, her face, the air around her; she can see the coffee table, the fighting roosters, the Alps, the television, all of it turning to sand, set to disintegrate at the slam of a door.

"I'm not saying it was right," says Jack. "I told Simon before I knew what could happen. That's no excuse."

She is struck dizzy by a jolt of memory—Maman dragging them to the car while Dad stood in the doorway, looking shell-shocked. The day after her testimony. Maman almost screeching at her to get in the car, *main-te-nant!* She got them out of there. Far from the place where a man lived who killed children.

"My involvement didn't change the fact that, if the police had ever had a hope of catching the man who did it, they never would have looked at the Froelich kid in the first place. Whoever it was had to be long gone by then. Because there was never another similar murder in the area." It's his last-word-on-the-subject voice.

Is this the voice Mike always heard? Is this the father Mike had? What would she have done if she had had this father? Would she have found a gun and a jungle? Kill or be killed.

From the basement Maman calls, "Madeleine."

"What?" she bellows back at the stairs.

"Come down here, I want to show you something."

"In a minute!" She turns back to her father.

*What did you do in the Cold War, Daddy?*

" . . . we beat them in space . . ."

*Why?*

To keep the world safe for you kids.

*Why?*

To make sure there would be a world for you to inherit.

*Why?*

"Everything we did was for your sake."

"Maybe you should have asked us for help," she says.

"Asked who?"

"The kids. We were born into it. The world that could be destroyed in a matter of hours. We were tougher than you."

"Look me in the eyes." She does. "What I did was one tiny part of a much larger effort. There were countless operations like it, and many were much more costly. Some were genuinely effective. Others you'd have to write off as sunk cost. The point is not 'Was what I did worth it in and of itself?' Look at the Second World War, look at the Dieppe raid. That was a travesty." His eyes narrow, along with his mouth, his voice—flinty. "A thousand Canadians killed, two thousand taken prisoner, for what? So the Brits could test out a bunch of tactical theories. But the bottom line is, we won, and no one's calling Churchill a war criminal. If our leaders today had one-tenth his guts and brains. . . . He'd never have got mired in the likes of Vietnam. . . ."

They are still for a while, their breathing audible. His lower lip is compressed against his upper one, lids drooping with every inhalation. On the TV, a new improved Mr. Clean visits two women in a toiletless bathroom.

"Dad?"

"Yeah, sweetheart?" Jack watches her carefully, gauging her expression. What will she do with what he has told her? She looks worried, but in her face is an appeal. It reassures him. It's the same look she always gave him when she knew something was wrong but she also knew she had come to the right place with her problem. *My little girl.*

"Do you remember my teacher in Centralia?"

" . . . Mr. Marks."

"Mr. March."

"Sure, I remember him, why?"

She doesn't reply right away. He reaches out his hand. "What's wrong, sweetie?"

Finally, she says, " . . . He died."

He watches her face crumple, and she weeps. He opens his arms. She comes to him, kneels by his chair.

"I'm sorry, sweetie," he says, stroking her head. "That's too bad."

Her face is hidden in her hands on the armrest of his chair, her shoulders begin to shake. Should he call her mother? "When did he die?"

She doesn't answer, she is crying too hard. He didn't know she was so fond of her old teacher.

"Was he very old?"

She shakes her head but doesn't look up. Keening softly, like a poor dog. "You know what, old buddy?" He thinks he hears her reply, "What?" so he continues, "I think maybe you're taking it extra hard because of all the sad things that happened in Centralia."

His throat tightens, helping lighten his voice to a tone that used to come naturally years ago, when she was a child—the once-upon-a-time voice. "But you know, it's a funny thing, 'cause even though some sad things happened there. . . ." He pauses, blinks and clears his throat. "We had some of the nicest remember-whens in Centralia." He feels tears on his cheeks. So as not to take his arms from around her, he raises his shoulder to his face and wipes them away on his shirt.

"Remember how you used to come with me into Exeter to get my hair cut and you'd entertain the troops? Remember going to the market in London for crusty rolls and good German wurst? Remember Storybook Gardens?" He strokes her head—hair so soft, still shiny like a child's. "Remember those mice in the Christmas window at Simpson's, and that little pussycat jazz band?" He chuckles. "Remember the first day of school, when you had me walk you there and held my hand the whole way? That's the last time you ever needed me to do that."

He pauses for breath. There is all the time in the world. . . . *You kids have your whole life ahead of you.* . . . "That's the funny thing about life, eh? Some of the nicest memories are mixed up with the saddest ones. And that just makes them nicer. You have to think of the good times. That's how I think of your brother. . . ." *And if we spoiled you, it was because we loved you so much. Wanted you to have what we never had, you and your brother. . . .*

Jack doesn't picture his son. He sees the blue dome over that place where it is always summer, where the white buildings bask in sunshine, the parade square shimmers and the little coloured houses wait for the men to come home at five. That's where his son is. Jack is there too, with his family. His beautiful wife. All he ever wanted.

He strokes his daughter's head and realizes that he is nodding in time to something. A vestige, perhaps, of an old impulse to rock his child. She seems calmer now. He was always the one she came to, and she always allowed herself to be consoled by him. Can a child know what a gift that is to a parent?

"It's okay, sweetie," he says, because she is still crying. "Hey, I meant to tell you. You know that dog in the stormpipe? Well, the fire truck came and got him out. Safe and sound, I saw him. It was a beagle."

He told her a hard thing today. Perhaps she will hold it against him, but he believes she will understand one day. He told her because she is his best. And she should know what she's made of. "You're my best," he says to her softly, "my best old buddy."

Madeleine weeps, water leaving her like darkness draining. She yields to this blessed respite. To what remains. Glimpsing once more—from her old hiding place, across the distance of years—her father gently comforting her for what he doesn't know hurts her.

After a while she feels his hand come to rest. She moves it carefully and stands up. He is asleep.

She wipes her face and blows her nose. Looks down at him. His head tilted, lips parted, hands lax on the arms of his chair; straggling fingers, ten spent soldiers. In his lap, the oxygen mask. Fighter pilots and invalids. *Per ardua ad astra. . . .*

She bends to kiss him. His skin soft as suede, faint capillaries and tributaries visible, traces of an old torrent. His cheek is wet, whiskers less dense now. Old Spice.

"See you, Dad."

*Through adversity to the stars.*

She is putting on her jacket in the front hall, but turns at the sound of her mother mounting the basement stairs.

"You're younger than I am, Madeleine, you could come downstairs." Mimi sees her reaching for her car keys. "Where are you going at this hour?" She arrives at the top of the steps a little out of breath. In her arms, a froth of yellowed satin and lace.

"What's that?"

Mimi smiles shyly. "I thought you might like this."

Madeleine stares. "Your wedding gown?"

Mimi nods, forehead crinkling bashfully.

It's on the tip of Madeleine's tongue to inquire pleasantly, "What for? Halloween?" But she has sunk below the comedy watermark, the calm of the almost-drowned is upon her. She sighs.

"*Madeleine, qu'est-ce que tu as?*"

"Nothing, I'm fine, I just . . . oh, I remember what I was going to ask you, *pourquoi tu ne m'as pas dit que papa avait besoin d'oxygène?*"

Mimi shrugs her shoulders, eyebrows rising in tandem—her old show of impatience. "Why would I tell you? You know anyway he has this pill, he has that pill"—counting on her fingers—"he has the glycerine, the beta blockers, he has the oxygen, it's the same."

Madeleine waits.

Finally Mimi drops her shoulders and her eyebrows. "We didn't want you to worry."

"I'm worried anyway, plus I'm the only one left, who are you going to worry if you don't worry me?"

Mimi says, "You're crying," and moves to touch her daughter's face.

Madeleine backs away reflexively and feels an immediate pang of guilt. "I'm okay, Maman, thanks, that was such a good *fricot* but I've got to get back, I'm working." She reaches for her keys on the hall table but they fall from her hand—when did she pick them up? She stoops to recover them.

"What were you talking about with Papa?" asks Mimi. Maternal radar. She meets her mother's eyes.

"He told me he waved," she says matter-of-factly, and observes the air go flat around her. "You knew, eh?"

Her mother's features tighten. "Of course I knew," says Mimi. "I'm his wife."

"Why didn't you go to the police?"

"He's my husband. He's your father."

"He's a criminal."

Madeleine hears the smack, feels her face burn with the slap she can see poised in the palm of her mother's hand. But no one gets slapped.

"It's okay," she says, "I'm leaving."

"Don't be silly, Madeleine," says Mimi, draping the wedding gown over the banister, turning toward the open kitchen. "Come," she says, lighting a cigarette, "I'm making a *poutine râpée* for you, you're too thin, then we'll play Scrabble."

Madeleine stares after her mother. *No wonder I'm so fucked up.* The smoke reaches her and she inhales the refreshing menthol difference, resisting its power to comfort her. "Mother, did you know oxygen is highly flammable? It is also highly inflammable."

"Madeleine, your trouble is you're too much like me."

"I am nothing like you."

Mimi turns on the tap, pulls on a pair of yellow rubber gloves and starts scrubbing potatoes. Her husband is dying.

Madeleine inquires reasonably, "Have you thought of cutting down to, say, three packs a day?"

"You call yourself a feminist, but you're not very nice to your mother."

Madeleine sighs. She notices the kitchen table, already set for breakfast for three. A cock-a-doodle tea cozy forms a quilted free-standing complement to matching napkins and placemats. Next to her father's plate sits a long, narrow plastic container with fourteen compartments stamped with the days of the week and "am" or "pm." In the centre of the table, the salt, pepper, sugar, toothpicks and napkin-holder cluster on a lazy Susan. *It's ten P.M. Do you know where your life is?*

"*Qu'est-ce que t'as dit, Madeleine?*"

"Nothing."

Madeleine stands immobilized in the spacious foyer, like something delivered by mistake from Sears. Around her rise the clean lines of the condo. On the wall that leads down to the rec room are framed family photos, starting with her parents' wedding, then descending, posting by baby by holiday, black-and-white to colour, The Story of Mimi and Jack. The pictures stop in 1967—the four of them at Expo in front of the American pavilion—a geodesic dome. Mike had long hair.

In the kitchen, water rushes and smoke coils up from the ashtray next to the sink. Madeleine watches her mother's busy back as she flays potatoes with her yellow-gloved hands, *so flexible I can pick up a dime.* In the living room, her father has not moved in his chair. On the TV, cartoon enzymes are eating dirt particles. *How many more miles, Dad?*

"I wish Mike were here," she says.

Mimi brushes her ear with the back of her hand, as though at a fly, and resumes scrubbing.

"Why can't we just say he's dead?" inquires Madeleine of the wall, uncertain whether or not she can be heard above the roar of the tap. "Why can't we have a funeral for him?" she says to the foyer, and her words float small and weightless up to the cathedral ceiling.

On the wall next to her mother, between the coffee maker and the microwave, is mounted a small plaque. It holds a pair of scissors on a magnet, and bears a painted verse: *These are my scissors, they belong on this rack / If you use them please put them back.* At the edge of the sink perches the old ceramic frog holding the pot scrubber in his big grin.

"I love you, Maman."

The tap thunks off, Mimi turns and, hands upraised and dripping like a gloved surgeon, comes quickly to her daughter, and hugs her.

Her mother's embrace. Small, hot and strong. Something dark beneath the perfume and Cameo menthol. Salt and subterranean. Unkillable.

Madeleine feels the old guilt. It comes of always knowing that Maman was hugging a different child, one with the same name. She has always tried to hug her mother back as that child—the clean one.

"Oh Madeleine," says her mother into her shoulder, with a squeeze like steel bands, "Papa and I love you very much."

She knows her mother's eyes are clamped shut. Like a medium bracing herself for the sheer force of love passing through her—this love that Madeleine has always believed to be general, directed toward "my child," never toward Madeleine herself.

She waits for her mother's grip to relax, then says as kindly as possible, "Maman, I have to go back to Toronto, but I'll come home next week, okay?"

"*Mais pourquoi?*"

She can't bear to see the bewilderment enter Mimi's eyes—why am I always hurting my mother? "I have so much work to do and . . . I have to move out of our—out of my apartment."

Her mother's face tightens again—prepared to repel the word *Christine*. Or any word that may be a synonym for *Christine*. Mimi lifts a hand in defeat, or dismissal—"Do what you want, Madeleine, you always do"— and returns to the kitchen.

"You know, the irony is, Maman, Christine and I might've broken up ages ago if you hadn't been so against us."

She watches her mother's back. Chopping now.

"It's not like a diagram of a cow in a butcher shop, you know," she says. "You can't cut out the part of me you hate and take the rest."

If Mimi were to turn, Madeleine would see that she is annoyed. She is annoyed because she is crying. She is crying because—perhaps you can understand, even if you are not a mother, what it is to have your child say, *You hate me.*

Madeleine waits, numb. Like a dead tree. If the earth were beneath her feet now, instead of the gleaming floor, she could lie down and commence that long return. This is the terrible kindness of the earth: she will always welcome us back, hers is a love that never dies, never says, "I will take this part of you, but not the rest."

The phone rings and Mimi answers it. Clears up a scheduling mistake regarding the Catholic Women's League, consults a list and confirms a bridge date.

Madeleine says, "You remember my teacher in Centralia?"

Mimi glances at her, then back to her list. "Mr. March."

"He abused us. Me and some other girls."

Mimi turns to face her daughter and hangs up the phone—then looks back at her hand as though surprised at its initiative.

"It's okay, Maman, I'm fine, I'm only telling you because—"

A sound like a chirping, it's her mother, hand cupped in front of her mouth; she looks as though she's about to cough something up, a feather.

"Maman?"

Madeleine is too much like her mother, she realizes, as she watches Mimi's mouth turn to an upside-down smile, red blotches appear on her cheeks, neck, nose—stricken, painted with the unreserved sorrow of a clown.

"Maman, it's okay—"

Madeleine would like to put this whole visit back in a bag under the basement steps, stuff it among the Christmas decorations and the card-table chairs.

All Mimi wants to do is remove it from her daughter, wipe it from her face like summer dirt, a little blood from a cut, all she wants is to offer her own flesh in place of whatever happened to her child, but she can't. It's too late. Her arm is powerful, but it can't reach her little girl leaving for school, any more than it can reach her son walking out the door seventeen years ago. She is left clutching air. Nothing she did was enough. *Ce n'est pas assez.*

Madeleine has never seen her mother cry like this. Not even when Mike went away. Fresh sorrows reactivate old ones. We go to the same well to grieve, and it's fuller every time.

She is amazed by what her mother says next:

"I'm sorry, *ma p'tite, c'est ma faute, c'est la faute de maman.*"

Madeleine holds her mother, and the embrace is still hot but not so hard now—flesh instead of wood—which one of them has changed?

"It's not your fault, Maman."

Everything is going to be okay. What is this dark feeling? Mortal happiness. Here is the wound. It doesn't smell after all. It hurts terribly, but it's clean. Here is a fresh dressing, let Maman do it.

"*Je t'aime, maman.*"

Mimi wipes Madeleine's face with her hands—thoroughly, like a mother cat—then digs a tissue from her sleeve and holds it to her daughter's nose. Madeleine blows and laughs.

Mimi smiles. "You're so pretty, *ma p'tite.*"

"I take after you."

Mimi glances toward the living room. The top of his head hasn't moved, he is still asleep in his chair. She lowers her voice. "Did you tell your father?"

"No."

"Good."

And Madeleine is certain now that it was good, is grateful not to have burdened him. Her mother can take it. *Women are stronger.*

Mimi kisses her daughter, and the pain is not mitigated by what she realizes next—in fact it's worsened because, like polio, what happened to her child could have been prevented. "Oh Madeleine, Madeleine. . . ."

Madeleine follows her mother's voice. In it she hears the cadence of comfort. What remains may not be a lot, but it's good. I have my mother.

She steps into the meadow unafraid, there are no hunters here. Basks in her mother's gaze, unashamed, so grateful finally to be seen.

"Oh Madeleine," says Mimi, and cups her daughter's face tenderly in her hands, "is that why you are the way you are?"

A sensation behind Madeleine's eyes as though a reel of film has skipped. She knows she has reached the end of something, and passed through it to something else, because her voice sounds robotic in her ears, as though she's speaking a new language. "I'm pretty sure that Mr. March killed Claire."

Her mother is still speaking the old language as Madeleine leaves the house. She can hear her voice but can no longer make out the words.

Outside, she reaches for the door of her car and hears something clink to the asphalt. It gleams silver in the porch light. The medal. She picks it up and gets into her car. Rubs her palm where the four compass points have gouged their temporary impressions, and sees the old paper-thin scar that shadows her lifeline.

Ricky Froelich *MISSING*
Henry Froelich *MISSING*
Michael McCarthy *MISSING*

## GRATIA

MADELEINE HAS PULLED OVER to the side of the 401 expressway across the top of Toronto. This time she couldn't make it to an exit ramp. Forehead resting against the steering wheel, she is praying. She doesn't believe in God, nor is she a non-believer. Belief has nothing to do with it. She's praying because there's so much pain. The living and the dead. The known and the unknown.

She can hear it—it has always been there. Like the chatter of a pebble beach. It grows louder, closer, until she hears a chorus of souls, mouths pulled down in sorrow. All those imprisoned in their minds; all those who are doing their best for their families; all who are struck with the vertigo of standing on two feet, all who live so bravely on four legs, so tirelessly on two wings, on bellies and between fins; the heartbreaking courage of animals; the lonely death of a dear brother, of a child long ago in Centralia, were they very frightened? Oh if only we could visit them at the hour of their death—not to intervene, because that is impossible, but simply to witness. To love them as they leave, not seek to make their suffering invisible. All they ask is that we picture it. *Watch me.*

"Pray for them," she whispers to the instrument panel of her old VW beetle. Sixteen lanes zip by. *Pray for them.* It is then—on the noisy paved shoulder, wondering if she will ever be able to leave her car—that she receives the gift: it fills her like a breath. It is not a knowledge of the mind, it simply arrives: the only thing in the world that matters is love.

After fifteen minutes she is able to start her car and gather speed along the shoulder. The little bug, dirty white eggshell, travels down the exit ramp. Designed for Hitler. Built by slaves. As recognizable as a Coke bottle. The sins of the father. Good little car.

She feels fine when she gets home, and knows she will never be the same. Nothing can ever frighten her out of her life again. As though she had survived a disaster. A plane crash. Something.

> *"That self-same moment I could pray;*
> *And from my neck so free*
> *The Albatross fell off, and sank*
> *Like lead into the sea."*

## Butterfly Effects

IN THE SUPREME COURT OF ONTARIO

REGINA
vs
RICHARD PLYMOUTH FROELICH
(murder)
Trial Evidence

A strange transformation is effected by the authority of the printed word in an official document. *The prisoner.* Ricky. *The victim.* Claire. The welter of information regarding where precisely the crossroads were, the words *willow tree* drained of colour, the numbing exactitude regarding where the body was found and in what position.

        The body was clad in a blue dress.

Thank goodness it's Wednesday. Shelly thinks Madeleine is still out of
town, and in a way she is. She got an hour's sleep on her carpet this
morning—Christine had returned for the bed.

        ...The body was lying flat on its back with the lower
        limbs, the two legs, parted. Under a tree, an elm.

Madeleine is wearing a baseball cap to shelter her eyes from the fluorescent lights in the windowless reading room of the Provincial Archives
of Ontario. Steps from the YMCA; she could have come here any time.

        ...the patient had marks upon the neck.

The patient? She reads on. The pathologist, the police, Dr. Ridelle—
Lisa's dad. This transcript is a 1,858-page list of what the grown-ups
knew. Legal size.

        A female child at that age would have a hymen which
        is something through which you cannot normally
        insert a little finger, and that was completely
        missing, it had been completely carried away....

She is sitting at one of several long wooden tables. Around her, a pallid
few others pore over genealogical records and municipal sewage blueprints. Insomniacs unite.

        ...masses of maggots about in this region....

For years she carried her unrevised child's picture of Claire lying peacefully on the grass, sadly dead. Babe in the wood, tended by swallows
bearing leaves and wildflowers to blanket her.

        intense cyanotic lividity of face and neck, intense
        cyanosis of the nails and extremities of fingers, the
        tongue protruded...

The picture is altering now. It's changing. Finally growing older.

        ...colour and pupils obscured by post-mortem glazing...

She is here because she can't come tomorrow, tomorrow is the regular After-Three Thursday marathon—she will have all this evening to write, the archives close at four. She is here because she can't tell anyone what her father did.

```
...large amount of uric acid on the legs but not on
the underpants, which would indicate...
```

She is here to bear witness.

```
...a type of injury you would expect to see with some
large object dilating this area...
```

She is here because she can't go forward. She has to go back.

```
...the whole of the entranceway was widely
dilated.
His Lordship: Pardon?
A: Widely dilated.
```

And when she gets there, she needs to listen to the children.

```
...the body was covered by reeds, I should say
bulrushes...
```

*Moses among the bulrushes.* We always called them cattails. Why have I thought of Moses? Moses was among the rushes, not bulrushes.

```
Q: Was the face visible?
A: The face was covered.
Q: With what?
A: A pair of underpants.
Q: Cotton underpants?
A: Yes sir.
Q: Are these the underpants?
```

Marjorie Nolan. She drew a picture with the title "Moses among the Cattails." Miss Lang corrected her gently.

```
A: Yes
```

I drew Batman and Robin, and Grace Novotny got a gold star for her picture—what did she draw? Madeleine sees the back of Grace's head—uneven part, messy pigtails constricted by bare elastics. She tries to look over Grace's shoulder but sees only her hands at work. Bandaged. Imagine doing that to a child. She can hear Grace's pencil crayon against the construction paper, colouring, colouring, colouring. . . .

There was a record playing—"A Summer Place," by the Mantovani strings. We didn't normally have Miss Lang for art. Art was normally on Friday.

Some things are difficult to see straight on. They can only be glimpsed by looking away, caught by the corner of the eye. Like phosphorescence in a cave; look away and you will see. Madeleine tries to look away but there is too much light coming through the big classroom windows. She squints but it's no good, the sun is up there, bright yellow, smiling and pulsating, obliterating Grace and her drawing. Madeleine squeezes her eyes shut and sees a yellow orb tattooed inside her lids. And yet, as she recalls, it was a rainy day. She returns her attention to her own drawing, *Holy Thursday, Batman*—and winces at the realization that this was the day after Claire went missing.

Some things stay in the containers we placed them in years ago, bearing the labels we wrote in an awkward childish hand: The Day Claire Went Missing. They stay that way and, even into adulthood, we may not question them. Until we have occasion, one day, to open the container, smell what has happened to the contents and revise the label: The Day Claire Was Murdered.

EXHIBIT No. 49: Underpants referred to

Madeleine's red boots flew off one by one, Claire swung so high that Madeleine saw her underpants, "I see London, I see France! I see—" *yellow butterflies*. On Claire's underpants. Madeleine looks up from the page, suddenly parched. Is there a water fountain in this room? *Archives*. The word itself is a desert.

She smells the polish on the oak table. It reminds her of her father, his various desks. She looks down again at the dry page.

HIS LORDSHIP: ...what is your name, little girl?
A: Madeleine McCarthy.

I can't remember what I was wearing that day. It was hot.

```
Q: You don't need to speak quite so loudly,
Madeleine.
A: Sorry.
Q: That's all right.
```

She remembers her father sitting halfway toward the back. Giving her the thumbs-up. She sees him in his blue uniform but she knows that's impossible, it was June. Like now. He'd have been in his khakis. Very important loved ones become, in memory, like cartoon characters—a definitive version is called up, always in the same outfit. One that survives burning, being run over, blown up, drowned and riddled with bullets.

```
Q: What does it mean to take an oath, Madeleine?
A: It means you swear to tell the truth.
```

Transcripts are spartan. Factual stage directions, lines of dialogue unembellished by emotional cues in brackets. But personalities come through. And Madeleine sees herself, still vulnerable, on the page. Like a butterfly, pinned. Forever nine years old.

```
Q: ...who is your teacher?
A: My teacher last year was Mr March.
Q: Did you like him?
A: No.
```

Madeleine reads on and it's like watching a series of calamitous events unfold in a movie. Don't go back in the house! Check the back seat! *Ask me the question!* Why did no one ask the right question? A sleeveless dress with a Peter Pan collar, that's what I was wearing. With a matching hairband.

```
Q: What is that brooch you are wearing?
A: It's a lighthouse.
```

It is the brooch Mr. March touched.

```
Q: Where is it from?
A: It's from Acadia, my mother is Acadian. We speak
French.
```

Bailiff: Place your right hand on the Bible.

But it's not possible to enter the page and alter what happened. It has been happening here, in four boxes housed in downtown Toronto, for twenty-three years, and it will go on playing itself out. A long-running show.

A: What's in the jar?
Q: Cover that table back up, and keep it covered.

The show-and-tell table. Madeleine flips back to the index of exhibits at the front of the volume to find out what was in the jar—there is no judge to stop her now, she is a grown-up, she is permitted to choose her horrors:

EXHIBIT No. 21: Jar of stomach contents

"Want a bite?" said Claire. And Madeleine and Colleen shared her chocolate cupcake, her apple slices and the little round of cheese in red wax. Madeleine made a pair of lady lips with them afterwards and Claire bubbled with laughter. She was a great audience. Her last meal. *Stomach contents.* One of a long list, like snapshots.

EXHIBIT No. 22: Bulrushes turned over to coroner
EXHIBIT No. 23: Lunch box

But salient information is often missing; e.g., it was not just any lunchbox, it was a Frankie and Annette lunchbox, priceless, coveted—

EXHIBIT No. 24: Pink bicycle

—again, the significant feature omitted: two luxuriant pink streamers. Except that when Madeleine saw Claire's bike in the trunk of the police car, there was only one. That's why Colleen and I went out to the field that day, to the tamped-down spot—to find her other streamer. But it turned out Grace had it.

Grace in the rain with no raincoat on, the bedraggled pink streamer transplanted into the handlebar grip of her beat-up bike, too big for her. Bouncing up and down on the hard seat, stark like the skull of a steer, *it doesn't hurt.*

*Hey Grace, where'd you get the streamer?*

*Someone gave it to me.*
*Who?*
*Someone.*

Madeleine's breath comes like a dog's breath. Grace got the streamer from Mr. March. A trophy, plucked by its roots from Claire's pink two-wheeler. A prize for his pet.

She swallows, her throat parchment. She glances at the archivist. At the other researchers. No one has noticed. What is there to notice? A dark-haired young woman sitting perfectly still, obscured from view by four cardboard crates of documents.

But she has something now. She can tell the police about the streamer. They will find Grace Novotny. Grace will tell who gave it to her. No one will need to know it was Jack who waved that day. . . .

She returns to the page:

```
EXHIBIT No. 25: Silver charm bracelet in envelope
```

Not just any charm bracelet; she had the *Maid of the Mist,* a heart, a teacup and many other things, including her name in silver cursive script, *Claire.* Madeleine wonders if the McCarrolls have kept it. She wonders if they ever had another child. Perhaps they would rather not know the truth. Reawaken their grief.

```
EXHIBIT No. 26: Photograph of Claire McCarroll at
autopsy
EXHIBIT No. 27: Container of larvae
EXHIBIT No. 28: Bulrushes retained by Constable
Lonergan
```

*Moses among the Cattails.* Madeleine flips ahead.

```
HIS LORDSHIP: Do you go to church, Marjorie?
A. Yes sir, and Sunday school.
Q. Do you know what it means to tell the truth?
A. Yes sir.
Q. Are you a Brownie?
A. Well,
```

Madeleine can hear Marjorie giggle, although the court stenographer didn't record it.

```
actually I flew up so I'm a junior Girl Guide now. I
have a babysitting badge.
```

You lie, Margarine! Why did no one check up on that?

```
Q. How old are you, Marjorie?
A. I just turned ten.
Q. These children are young, I don't know if I can
swear this child. Do you understand the nature of an
oath?
A. It means that you swear on the Bible to tell the
truth and not to lie in court.
Q. That's right, Marjorie. What happens to people who
do lie?
A. They get punished.
Q. Good. Swear the witness.
```

Madeleine wonders what she would make of ten-year-old Marjorie now, through adult eyes. Would she be taken in, the way the grown-ups were? Waxy curls. Blue doll-eyes. Polite and slightly, reassuringly, out of date.

MARJORIE NOLAN, sworn:

EXAMINATION IN-CHIEF BY MR FRASER:

```
MR FRASER: You live with your parents in the
Permanent Married Quarters of the Air Force Station
in Centralia, Marjorie?
A. Yes sir.
```

Mr. Fraser, the Crown prosecutor. In the gloomy black robe.

```
Q. And last spring were you in the same grade, four,
as Claire McCarroll?
A. Yes.
Q. Was Claire your friend?
A. Yes.
```

Another lie.

```
Q. And did you know Richard Froelich?
A. Ricky?
Q. Yes, Ricky.
A. Yes.
Q. And on Wednesday, April 10, did you have a conver-
sation with Ricky?
A. Yes.
Q. Will you tell what that conversation was please?
A. Well, Ricky said, "would you like to come to Rock
Bass? I know where there is a nest."
Q. And what did you say?
A. I said, "no."
Q. Why did you say no?
A. Well,
```

Madeleine hears another giggle, and the good-natured know-it-all tone.
Are some children transparent only to other children?

```
first of all, I had Brownies that night. So did
Claire, but she's only a Tweenie—
HIS LORDSHIP: Stop right there. Gentlemen of the jury,
Mr Fraser has already explained and the witness, Miss
Lang who is an officer of the Brownie pack, has
already explained what Brownies are. If you are not
clear on this, please feel free to request clarifica-
tion. Good. Go on, Mr Fraser.
```

It's strange to picture these grown men—1963 men—grappling with
the taxonomy of the Toadstool—Tweenies, Sprites, Elves and Pixies.

```
Q. And was there another reason you said no to Ricky?
HIS LORDSHIP: Was that a yes?
A. Yes sir.
MR FRASER: What was that other reason, Marjorie?
HIS LORDSHIP: The reason she declined his invitation?
MR FRASER: Yes, my Lord.
HIS LORDSHIP: Go on, Mr Fraser.
Q. Why else did you say no to Ricky, Marjorie?
A. Because I'm not allowed because I am too young.
Q. What are you too young for?
```

```
A. To go on dates.
Q. Why did you think Ricky was asking you out on a
date?
A. Because he said, "let's go on a date."
```

Dream on, Margarine.

```
Q. He said that on April 10?
A. Yeah, yes. And lots of times before that.
Q. Where did he say it on April 10?
A. On his front lawn. He was out with the hose.
Q. And what did he say on April 10?
A. He said, "Want a drink, Marjorie?" and then he did
something rude.
Q. What did he do?
A. He. He pretended like, you know.
Q. Yes?
A. Like he was going to the bathroom.
Q. Yes?
A. With the hose.
Q. Then what happened?
A. I said "I'm not thirsty."
Q. And what did he say then?
A. He said, "Would you like to come on a date with
me? To Rock Bass? I know where there is a nest."
```

Claire said that. No, not exactly, she said, "We can look for a nest."
Madeleine and Colleen were in the schoolyard, Claire had a buttercup.
Music was coming from the school, the band was practising . . . the tattered melody struggling out the windows of the gym at J.A.D.
McCurdy School—*It's a world of laughter, a world of tears . . .*—the
school band playing as Mr. March thumped time at the piano. Marjorie
was nearby with Grace, trying to butt in, she heard where Claire was
going and why. And with whom. Ricky, so Claire imagined.

```
Q. And you said no.
A. I said, "I will have to take a rain check."
```

Poor Marjorie. Terribly left out by everyone—except Grace and Mr.
March. Is that how he found out where Claire was going that day?
Mr. March's little fiend, running to him, reporting.

```
Q. Thank you, Marjorie.
A. You're welcome.
```

Show-and-tell. "I collect them, sometahms," said Claire, the weightless robin's egg cupped in her hands. Madeleine rubs her palm and looks
at it. There is the pale scar, but something else is there too—a piece of
shell. Pale blue. No, not in her hand, not yet, she is reaching for it in the
long last-year's grass but Colleen grabs her wrist, slaps the knife into her
hand, *Cut me*.

It was only a bit of blue shell, but perhaps it would have been bad
luck to take anything from the murder scene—yes, that's where she
found it. A foot or so from the edge of the tamped-down circle. Fairy
ring. Was it from Claire's blue egg? One she found that day?

```
EXHIBIT No. 50: Statement of Grace Novotny
```

What if Madeleine had accepted Claire's invitation and gone with
her to Rock Bass? Claire might still be alive. Or would they both be
dead?

```
HIS LORDSHIP: Have you read this statement, Mr
Waller?
MR WALLER: I have a copy of Grace Novotny's statement
My Lord, given to me by the Crown Prosecutor, Mr
Fraser, this morning. I had not seen the document
before, much as I did not know until last week about
the existence of the witness, Marjorie Nolan—
HIS LORDSHIP: We've been over that, Mr Waller.
```

Mr. Waller. The nice loser in the shimmering silk robes. Defending
Rick.

```
MR WALLER: My Lord, the question of the propriety of
concealing a witness—
HIS LORDSHIP: What do you have to say to that, Mr
Fraser?
MR FRASER: My Lord, there is no question of the pro-
priety here since Marjorie Nolan's testimony was not
exculpatory.
MR WALLER: My Lord, with the greatest respect I would
```

like to point out that there is a cumulative possibly
deleterious effect that could have the effect of causing this trial to become a mistrial—
HIS LORDSHIP: I'll be the judge of that, Mr Waller.
MR WALLER: Yes, my Lord, but in the interests of
avoiding a costly appeal—
HIS LORDSHIP: The Crown has not breached the law of
disclosure that I can see.
MR WALLER: No, my Lord, not the letter, but perhaps
the spirit.
HIS LORDSHIP: Gentlemen, we won't need you for a few
minutes.
---Jury retired.

IN THE ABSENCE OF THE JURY....

Many pages of legal arguments. Many cases cited by both sides, with
a kind of quiz-show virtuosity. Inspector Bradley has the statement he
took from Grace in the classroom after three. The defence wants the
statement ruled inadmissible. But the Crown says Grace's statement is
consistent with Marjorie's testimony and therefore ought to be read out
in court. All this because Grace is not here to testify in person. Her
mother left her father and took the younger children. No one knows
where they have gone.

It's not really a statement at all. It's a stitched-together series of
quotes: answers she gave to the policeman's questions, which he duly
recorded in his notebook. The judge decides that Inspector Bradley
will be permitted to read out the statement but, in deference to the
defence, only if the inspector consults his notes in order to reinsert
the questions "and every other detail" that elicited the responses that
became the statement. A short recess is called so that the inspector may
go over his notes and those of Constable Lonergan's, and revise Grace's
"statement" after the fact.

IN THE PRESENCE OF THE JURY...

Although Inspector Bradley will be sworn before he reads Grace's
statement, the statement itself may not be deemed by the jury to be a
sworn statement. The judge asks the jury to perform the mental gym-
nastics of listening and weighing, but not too heavily.

INSPECTOR THOMAS BRADLEY, sworn:

MR FRASER: Inspector Bradley, you are a member of the
Criminal Investigation Bureau of the Ontario
Provincial Police?
A. Yes sir.

The inspector had the type of face that made Madeleine feel she was
lying the moment she walked into the room. She would have felt guilty
no matter what she told him. He knew she was lying. Why did he not
know that Marjorie was lying? And Grace?

Q. Inspector Bradley, would you please read the transcript of your interview with Grace Novotny?
A. I said, "You knew Claire McCarroll, didn't you?"
At that the subject exhibited signs of distress, she
proceeded to rock and to moan audibly.

Grace's eyes rolling, face crumpling. . . .

I asked, "Did you play with Claire last Wednesday?"
Whereupon the child began to cry and to wail,

. . . that sound, peculiar to Grace, that rose from her throat or someplace
deeper, until you couldn't tell where it was coming from, steadily rising
like an air-raid siren.

so I gave the child a kleenex and attempted to calm
her.

No one could calm Grace.

I asked her if she had seen Claire that day in the
school yard and the child nodded, "yes." I asked if
she spoke to Claire and the child shrugged. I asked
if Claire had spoken to the child and the child said,
"Yes." I asked what Claire had said and the child
replied, "She asked me to go to Rock Bass."

Marjorie must have told her to say that.

```
I asked her what she said in reply to Claire and the
child said, "I didn't want to go to Rock Bass." I
asked, "Did Claire say she was going to Rock Bass
with anyone?" The child answered, "Yeah, Ricky."
```

Madeleine hears Inspector Bradley's measured monotone; it marries perfectly with the typed page. But Grace is there too, behind the page. Madeleine can hear her and see her—messy braids, the vague grin, chapped lips. She can smell her, too—old pee and Elmer's glue. . . .

```
"Has Ricky Froelich ever touched you as if you were
his girlfriend?" She answered, "Yeah, sometimes we
do exercises."
```

That's what happened to Ricky Froelich—Madeleine's guts go liquid —Marjorie and Grace happened to him. And Mr. March, and Jack McCarthy. How did those two wind up on the same side?

```
"Back bends. And squeezing," she said.
```

What has been left out of the inspector's cobbled-together "statement"? By how many sideways stepping stones did he herd Grace higgledy-piggledy across the stream? Because Madeleine knows Grace never got anywhere on her own.

```
I asked, "Squeezing what?" She replied, "His muscle.
He said to call it his muscle, but it's really his
thing."
```

Grace had the courage to say it. Cut from its moorings, but the truth nonetheless. Why was there no one to hear? How loudly must she have wailed it?

```
"And there's something else about Ricky," she said.
"He strangles."
```

And it was over.

```
I asked, "Have you ever told anyone about the things
Ricky did to you?" She answered, "Marjorie."
```

They only had each other.

> The child then offered the following statement: "He
> gave me an egg." "When?" I asked. "That day," she
> said. "What kind of egg? A cooked egg?" "No," she
> said. "A blue one..."

Madeleine remembers to breathe.

> "What kind of egg is that?" I asked. "A special egg,"
> she said. "An Easter egg?" I asked. The child nodded,
> yes, then said, "He said he knew where there was
> more."

A *robin's egg,* not an Easter egg. That's what "blue egg" means to a child. Why did Bradley not know that, why did he not ask someone qualified—another child?—Why did he not ask Madeleine?

But it was Easter time. There was Easter art up on the walls of the classroom where the interrogation took place. It was a natural assumption on his part. . . .

> "Was it a chocolate egg?" I asked. She replied, "Yes."

Again, a version of the truth. Mr. March gave out chocolate eggs at the drop of an Easter bonnet. *Blue eggshell in the grass.* . . ."I know where there is a nest" is all anyone would have to say, and Claire would follow—it's what Rick said, according to Marjorie. Perhaps someone did say it. Did Marjorie hear it? Did Grace?

Madeleine squints at the page. In the schoolyard, Claire said only that she was going to look for a nest. She didn't specify a robin's nest. And yet blue eggshell was what Madeleine found in the grass. . . . Why would Grace mention a blue egg in connection with that day? *Madeleine reaches into the grass for the pale blue fragment.* Was it from Claire's egg? One she was lured with? How could Grace have known that? Dear God . . . what did the child see?

The shiver runs up her spine—stinging her eyes, which have begun to water, escaping through her lips, and she is gulping air, flipping back to the beginning of Volume IV, to the index of exhibits—because Grace's art was also up on the classroom wall that day—the day after Claire was murdered. The drawing she had bent over and coloured so lovingly, Madeleine can see it with its gold star, in pride of place among the lopsided Easter bunnies and brightly coloured eggs—the beautiful picture that Grace made with her dirty bandaged hands that day, brilliant, abundant: a storm of yellow butterflies.

EXHIBIT No. 49: Cotton underpants with yellow moth
pattern

They were butterflies, not moths. Only an adult would have seen moths. *Oh Grace. What did you see?* Madeleine's tears will hasten the deterioration of these archival documents. *They were yellow butterflies, not moths.* Why didn't anyone ask? It was Moses among the Cattails, not Rushes, or even Bulrushes, because Marjorie was there too, in the field beyond Rock Bass. Both children saw what he did to Claire before he covered her body with what the grown-ups called bulrushes, and purple flowers. Both little girls saw how he laid her underpants across her face, which had gone blue with suffocation, oh God. What happened to the children? *What happens to children?*

Madeleine puts her head down, shielded by the boxes.

In the condo in Ottawa, Mimi taps out the pills from the plastic compartment stamped *Thurs pm.* Once you or a loved one are on this much medication, it's impossible to mix up the days of the week.

She fills a glass and sees the sunset through the window over the kitchen sink. She is fifty-eight. She is in perfect health and will probably live many more years, despite the smoking. She doesn't want to go on a cruise with a nice gentleman she meets a few years from now. She wants to go with her husband.

She places the water glass and a cluster of pills on the side table next to his oxygen tank. He doesn't wake up. She turns off the TV, he opens his eyes. "Wha—? Just restin' my eyeballs." And he winks at her.

Women live longer. Mimi knew she would have to do this part of the job eventually, she just didn't expect it so soon. She got a card from Elaine Ridelle the other day. They have retired to Victoria on the west coast, she and Steve still golf, they went on an Alaskan cruise last summer. Elaine has become diabetic but, since Steve is a doctor, *I'm his hobby now!*

Jack's eyes are watery with medication. He pops the pills into his mouth like peanuts, sips—brow rising, eyes widening like a child's, as he tilts back to swallow. "*Merci,*" he says.

*I love you, Jack.*

Hot gold pours in through the sheers on the patio doors. Remember those spring evenings in the square in Baden-Baden? Cobblestones and roses, the sound of the fountain. You and I and the kids would get dressed up and go out to look at the rich people, but everyone always wound up looking at us. Where have we gone?

Jack reaches for the remote and turns on the news.

Olivia is waiting on Madeleine's front step. A barrel-chested short-haired orange dog, with a head like a German Second World War helmet, is panting on a leash beside her.

"Whose dog?"

"Mine, but I'm leaving tonight."

"I thought you weren't leaving till tomorrow, I was going to drive you to the airport, I still will, hang on—"

"It's okay, I called a cab."

"Cancel it, I'll—"

"No, no, sit."

"Are you talking to the dog or me?"

Olivia laughs and takes her hand, pulls her down to the step beside her. "This is Winnie." Winnie is fresh from the Humane Society.

"He's a pit bull," says Madeleine.

"She. Winifred is an American Staffordshire terrier."

"Which is a fancy way of saying pit bull."

"Technically." Olivia kisses her. "*Je t'aime.*"

Olivia's kiss is like an electrical gauge. It lets Madeleine know that, against all odds, she is in excellent working order. "Then stay and have dinner with me, we'll roast wieners over the gas ring, I'll pop the Manischewitz and we'll make the beast with two backs, what do you say?"

"I can't, I got a grant to go on this trip."

"Give the money back."

"I want to go."

Madeleine strokes the dog's head and is assaulted by a tongue of bovine heft. She looks down and addresses the porch steps. "Why'd you adopt a dog if you were just going to ditch her right away?"

"I'm not ditching her, I'm giving her to you to look after."

"You expect me to look after her for three months?"

"No, she's going to look after you."

Madeleine looks at the dog and the dog grins back—fleshy mouthful of shark teeth, six hundred pounds of exertable pressure ready and waiting between those jaws.

Olivia says, "She loves kids."

"I don't have any kids."

Olivia smiles, raises her eyebrows briefly in a way that reminds Madeleine of someone.

"What does she eat? Cops? Drug dealers?"

"I had to take her," says Olivia. "She'd been there for six months."

"Really? Why?"

"No one wanted her. She's not a puppy. Plus she's a pit bull."

"She's a pussycat."

Olivia smiles. "I know." She puts the leash in Madeleine's hand, kisses her and gets into a waiting taxi.

In the condo in Ottawa, Mimi says, "Jack, do you want some hot?" and switches the TV off.

Madeleine and Winifred watch as the taxi disappears down the street and around the corner. Madeleine goes to rise and notices a drawstring bag on the step. In it, two dog bowls, a sample bag of kibble and a thick red candle with a scrolled note. She puts the note in her pocket for later and goes inside with the dog, feeling like a child of the universe. In the middle of the empty living room her wineglass, crusted red on the bottom, is where she left it by the phone on the carpet. It magnifies the red light blinking on the answering machine. She ignores the light and fills one of the bowls with water, the other with kibble. The dog laps promiscuously, great plashes of pleasure, then devours the food with a series of contented asthmatic grunts. More porcine than canine.

"Was that good?"

The dog tilts her massive head attentively, ears cocked, forehead wrinkled, panting.

"You're part alligator, aren't you, Winnie"—scratching her behind the ears, feeling the steel-belted wall of muscle beneath the neck fur—"Aren't you an alligator, aren't you!"

They play tug-of-war with the one remaining towel from the bathroom, Winnie growling in a lubricious and gratifying show of viciousness. Madeleine chases her all through the empty apartment, Winnie wiping out on the hardwood, biting air with her high-pitched play-bark, leaping back in delighted fright when Madeleine springs from a cupboard, from around a corner, snarling, "I'm gonna get you, oh you better run! Run run run run!" Until they are exhausted. Now that's therapy.

Winnie makes a beeline for the carpet and flops down the way dogs do, abandoning themselves to gravity as though they've been shot. She knocks over the wineglass, which breaks against the blinking answering machine. Madeleine shoos her from the broken glass, cleans up and, as an afterthought, rewinds and begins to play the messages. Nine from Shelly, five from Olivia, several from Tony. Rising urgency, common theme: Where are you? Where the hell are you? Are you okay?

Today is Thursday.

*Holy shit, Batman!*

The enormity of realizing that she has missed an After-Three Thursday is almost exhilarating. Like a shot of B vitamins. She will make it up to everyone. They will have scrambled and written her out of the Friday night taping, but she will scramble and squeeze back in, bursting already with generosity, ready to charge in with a bagful of one-liners to shower on her colleagues.

"This is bad," she says to the dog, "really bad." Winnie tilts her head. "Not you, you're good, me bad, bad Madeleine." She puts her hand on the phone. Make the hardest call first. Shelly. "Thufferin' thuckotash," she says to Winnie, lifting the phone to her ear, about to dial—but the line is dead. Not dead, someone is there—

"Hello? Hello, Olivia?"

*"Oui, allô?"*

"Oh hi Maman, it didn't even ring." She laughs, "We're psychically linked." If she didn't know better, she'd swear she had forgiven her mother for yesterday—why am I so happy all of a sudden? *Your guilty secret. You're a happy person.* "Maman?"

On the other end of the line, a pause to rival one of her dad's. Then Maman says, "Your papa is gone," and her voice breaks.

Madeleine's lips part. She leans forward slowly and drops her forehead to her knee. So this is the thing, when it finally comes. She cradles the receiver against her shoulder while her mother weeps.

*Your papa. Your papa. . . .*

Jack McCarthy *DIED OF WOUNDS*

When a parent dies, a planet disappears, and the night sky will never look the same again. It doesn't matter how grown up we are when we lose one. And when both are gone it's as though we are permanently without a kind of roof—invisible shield, first line of defence between ourselves and mortality, gone.

Madeleine's relief at seeing her mother was a shock to herself. She craved to be scolded for her choice of wardrobe, to be informed with asperity that she was too thin, but Mimi was coming undone. Not in the presence of friends, the priest, the relatives who had begun to arrive. Only with Madeleine. For so many reasons—because Madeleine is part of Jack, part of her son, part of her, because *"tu es ma fille,"* no matter what, and only a daughter can know. Long raking sobs, makeup-ruining grief. The sight of tears trickling through her mother's fingers, running down her hands—well preserved but older now, the polish a little starker—was the worst for Madeleine. But something surprising was happening. She had always feared she would go to pieces when her father died, but she was discovering an unsuspected reserve of emotional endurance. It felt involuntary, as though she had been born equipped with it, like the impulse to suckle, to walk, to run—standard mammalian features. The ability to remain supple while her mother held onto her and wept; to remain patient while being told how to boil water; to know when to run her a hot bath; to be able to say, "What about his clothes?" This while a tap within her gushed, profligate sorrow—how is it possible that this strength and this grief can go together? *My dad is gone.* "Have you chosen the flowers, Maman?" His empty chair, the newspapers in the blue boxes at the foot of the driveway. "You choose, Madeleine." His TV remote, his shoes, wrinkled across the instep, his slippers, his name on the stack of mail on the hall table. *Where is my dad?* She chooses daisies.

*"Qu'est-ce que c'est que ça?"* said Mimi when Madeleine returned to her car for her suitcase and the dog.

*"C'est une chienne."* Madeleine scrambled to catch the leash as Winnie bolted toward the front door.

"It's not yours," said Mimi.

"A friend's."

"It's not coming in the house?"

"Where do you expect her to sleep?"

"Sleep?"

Mimi adhered to a Depression-era view of dogs, according to which, unless they were earning their keep, they were classed as a form of vermin and, in any case, belonged outdoors. Within seconds she was upending dining chairs onto the couch, the La-Z-Boy—"*Aide-moi, Madeleine*"—in an effort to keep the filthy animal off the upholstery.

"She's not filthy, I gave her a bath."

"She's a dog," said Mimi, barricading the loveseat. "There. Now she can come in the living room."

Madeleine turned and called, "Winnie." Then—zero-to-sixty alarm—"Maman, you left the door to the garage open!" She was halfway out the front door when a shriek drew her back inside to the master bedroom, where Mimi stood frozen in the doorway. Winnie was asleep on her back and snoring in the middle of the white duvet.

"Get it off, Madeleine!"

Winnie rolled over and growled when Madeleine said, "Off, Winnie. Off. Off. Get off, now, there's a good girl. Off."

Lip curled. Wet snarl.

Madeleine stepped back.

Mimi put her hands on her hips, raised an eyebrow, and ordered, "*Bouge-toi!*"

Winnie hopped from the bed and stood gazing up at Mimi, tail wagging, big fleshy grin.

Madeleine sent her mother out to walk the dog.

"I'm not walking that thing."

"It's not a thing, Maman, it's a sentient creature and it likes you."

Mimi glared at the dog. "Well I don't like it. *Regarde moi pas, toi.*"

She heard the door close and got busy, working quickly, packing up as many of her father's clothes as possible for the St. Vincent de Paul so her mother would not have to do it. She had emptied his hanger rail and was working her way along the closet shelf when she was momentarily defeated by an old V-neck sweater. She stood, face buried in the moth-eaten wool, and breathed in his scent. When she came across his uniform in an old square garment bag, she placed one empty sleeve against her cheek and closed her eyes—the smell of mothballs and wool, its masculine scratchiness like a five o'clock shadow. She allowed her fingers to run down the jacket front, brass buttons embossed with wings.

She lost track of time, folding, sorting, crying, until finally she heard the door—rattle of the leash, clickety-click of Winnie's nails on the hardwood, clickety-click of her mother's high heels. Heard Mimi scolding, "*Non*. Go 'way, *va-t'en,* I don't want kisses from *les chiens.*"

When Madeleine emerged from the bedroom, she caught her mother giving the dog a piece of barbecued chicken.

"Not the bones, Maman."

"I wasn't giving it—I was—it's gone bad anyway."

"Don't give her rotten meat."

"It's fresh today!"

Madeleine's reflex impatience melted into something familiar, but not in the context of her mother. It was . . . amusement. She smiled.

The table was set meticulously for one. For Madeleine. She sat down to a chicken sandwich and asked, "What are you going to do with Dad's uniform?"

"It would have been your brother's," said Mimi and turned away.

Madeleine dropped the subject and picked up the newspaper.

Big Tante Yvonne flew in from New Brunswick with tiny ancient Tante Domithilde, the nun of the family. Together there was enough of them to fill two airplane seats comfortably, with the armrest up. Still, Tante Yvonne arrived with her back in spasm, a martyr to sciatica and her feet "*totalement* kaput." She brought a dozen lobsters on dry ice and a shopping bag full of knitted Phentex slippers in various stages of completion. Tante Domithilde started baking immediately. Mimi's brothers drove up with their wives in a convoy of Cadillacs and Continentals. Everyone but the aunts stayed at the Econo Lodge up the street, in a feat of logistics that had Madeleine on the phone for hours.

Tante Yvonne said, "What's that thing doing in the house?"

Mimi answered, "Her name is Winnie."

Jocelyn arrived with her husband and two kids—"We love your show, Madeleine." Shelly, Tony, Linda, Tommy and Ilsa made the trip from Toronto. They embraced Mimi and stayed up all night in the kitchen, talking and eating with the relatives; learning from the uncles on the first night how to play Deux-Cents, learning on the second night how to cheat. Yvonne had brought her accordion and ordered Madeleine to play while she sang in honour of "'ti-Jack" *Swing la bottine!* Shelly watched it all keenly, Madeleine could see the wheels turning.

"Don't you ever stop working?" she snapped, refilling Shelly's teacup, spiking it with rum.

"I got the money, hon, the network is in."

A U.S. network commitment to *Stark Raving Madeleine,* the pilot.

"Really?" said Madeleine. "Who're you going to get to write it?"

"How come you never told me you were half French?"

"Not French, Acadian."

"Tell me about it."

"*C'est assez.*"

Nina sent a card and flowers; Madeleine had cancelled her therapy appointment, and said why in a brutally curt message on Nina's answering machine. Olivia called; she had deduced via mental telepathy that something was wrong, and tracked down the phone number in Ottawa when she couldn't find Madeleine in Toronto. She introduced herself to Mimi over the phone and they chatted for twenty minutes in French before Olivia mentioned that she was calling from Managua. Mimi gasped—not at the thought of political peril, but at the long-distance rates—"*Madeleine, viens au téléphone, vite vite!*"

Tommy handed Mimi a letter from his parents—the McCarthys and the Czerniatewiczes had never met in person. "Oh how kind," said Mimi, opening it. "'May God comfort you among the mourners of Zion and Jerusalem. In sincere sympathy, Stan and Lydia.'"

Tommy was appalled and blamed Madeleine. Mimi told him he hadn't changed, "You're still saucy," and pinched his ear.

Company is what wakes and funerals are about, especially if the loved one has died "naturally" and was, at the very least, an adult. Noise, love, food, the clatter of cups and saucers—a seawall, notched with perforations to let manageable amounts of grief through at a time. For three days the condo was Grand Central Station. Madeleine took refuge in manning the rented coffee urn, and passing plates of squares to the endless stream of relatives, friends, neighbours and co-workers.

Fran: "We follow your brilliant career, dear."

Doris: "When are you moving to the States?"

Phyllis: "Don't be in a hurry to get married."

Doris: "Phyllis, she's gay."

Tante Yvonne: "You're not still, tsk-tsk-tsk."

Grizzled Tante Domithilde: "Don't let the bastards get you down, *ma p'tite.*"

Fran: "In our day we weren't allowed to be gay, dear, no one had a lifestyle then. You just keep doing what you're doing, you're grand."

Hugs and more hugs, fat-lady kisses like fresh-baked buns. The lesbian from Mimi's office showed up with her "partner"—Madeleine will never get used to that word—"We love your show." The priest, the mailman, the lady from Mimi's bank, the entire Catholic Women's League and half of Ottawa paid their respects, thank goodness it was

June and people could flow in and out through the patio doors. Nice men in light summer suits smelling of clean cotton, cigars and manly hair product. Firm warm handshakes. Old bomber pilots and retired management executives. Jack would have loved every minute of it.

It's the second evening in visitation room B of the Hartley and Finch Funeral Home. Flowers from the Ridelles, the Bouchers, the Woodleys and others from postings past. Even Hans and Brigitte have sent a card from Germany—Madeleine's old babysitter, Gabrielle, has five children now. Madeleine is avoiding the half-open casket resting at one end of the crowded but hushed room between two sprays of daisies; the flowers could not contrast more vividly with the morose Muzak piped at an annoyingly subliminal level—murky interfaith organ-noodling. Who authorized that? She is thinking of tracking down one of the sombre men who no longer call themselves undertakers, and telling him to play the Stones or something instead. This music, the waxy makeup on her father's face, his hands folded as though in prayer—who do these people think he was? None of it has anything to do with him. Except his blue air force hat resting on the lower, closed half of the casket. Like a fig leaf, she thinks. Then realizes that, despite her grief, she is still wadded in shock.

She turns away and finds herself facing the photo wall—arranged around a framed picture of Jack as a pilot officer cadet in training. Impossibly young in his uniform and wedge cap, left eye bright, unscathed. She and Mimi spent a day arranging reproductions on a large sheet of bristol board, displayed now on an easel. Wedding photo, a shot of the whole family on a picnic in the Black Forest. . . . They had several slides made into prints. The four of them at the Eiffel Tower, she and Mike in the waves of the Riviera . . . *that was the day you got lost, remember?* As she gazes at the photos, she can hear the hum of the slide projector in the dark. *So many remember-whens.* There is the picture of herself and Jack standing in front of the statue of the Pied Piper of Hamelin. A shadow spills across her father's trouser leg and the skirt of her dress—the silhouette of head and raised elbows. Uncle Simon. Mimi selected that one, and Madeleine wondered if she remembered who had taken it. Yesterday she was cleaning up between onslaughts of company and found a card in the garbage. She fished it out, figuring her mother had tossed it away by accident. On the cover was an old-fashioned pastel scene of an English country garden—quaint cottage spilling over with rosebushes. Inside, in a neat, efficient hand:

Dear Mrs McCarthy,

My one regret, in all my years of friendship with Jack, is that
I never had the opportunity to meet you. Jack did, however, tell me
enough about you to allow me to conclude that he was indeed a very
lucky man. I cannot begin to comprehend your loss, so I will say
only that I am so very sorry, and hope that you will accept this small
expression of what was, and always will be, my great regard for
your husband. Jack was a fine man. The finest.

   I read of his passing in your national newspaper to which
I subscribe via the post (retired as I am, I'm afraid I mount up more
than my share of newspapers. Some would say *The Times of India* is
rather pushing it, but I have—or rather, had—friends in so many
parts of the world that the obit. sections of the international press
have become my way of keeping up).

   This may seem an odd invitation coming from someone you've
never met, but I extend it with all my heart: should you ever find
yourself in England, please look me up. I live in one of the few
remaining unspoiled corners of what used to be the English countryside, and there is not a bird nor plant with whom (I refuse to say
"with which") I am not acquainted. It would be my very great
pleasure to "show you about". As the years advance, one finds that
old friends are the best friends, and I can't help but think of you
as a friend, valuing as I did so highly the friendship of your husband.

   Please give my regards to the "Deutsches Mädchen". I catch
glimpses of her brilliant career from time to time, thanks to a
dreadful satellite dish that I've done my best to conceal at the back
of my cottage.

   Yours very truly,
   Simon Crawford


There was a return address in Shropshire. Madeleine hesitated, then
tore it up.
   Out the corner of her eye she sees the parish priest threading his way
toward her across the room and she makes for the nearest exit. She is
longing for a drink. If only Mike were here with his flask—and then,
all of a sudden, he is. The photograph stops her in her tracks. She has
never seen it before. It sits on its own in a frame on one of the many

occasional tables that are otherwise covered with flowers and cards: Mike in uniform. USMC. Brush cut bristling beneath his hat. Dewy lips, full face, soft eyes. Lying in front of the frame, a single red rose. She reaches for more tissues, from one of several boxes strategically located throughout the room, as if it were one big therapy office.

She blows her nose, then looks up at the sound of her name. A plump but fit-looking woman with curly hair and freckles is standing in front of her. Some people don't change.

"Auriel?"

They hug as fiercely as ten-year-olds. Auriel's mother called her from Vancouver. "I'm so sorry, Madeleine. Your dad was always so nice."

"He died watching *All in the Family,*" says Madeleine. "At least he died laughing."

Auriel releases her, blows her nose and smiles. She looks the same only proportionately larger. Eyes still merry but steady now, perhaps she is a nurse, thinks Madeleine. Auriel's is the kind of face you'd hope to see if you were hooked up to an IV. She's wearing a pastel blazer over a print dress with a chiffon scarf. She looks like what she is: a suburban middle-class working mother. Backbone of the nation.

"You look fantastic," says Madeleine intensely.

Auriel replies, equally intense, "You're so cute on television I can't stand it," and they laugh and grip one another's hands.

Auriel has three kids, and a husband called Dave. They have just been posted to headquarters in Ottawa—he works for Corrections Canada. "He's a prison warden."

"Whoa."

"It's mostly social work."

Auriel has lived a life similar in its uprootings, its esprit de corps— and its marginality, according to mainstream society—to the one she and Madeleine knew as children.

"Auriel?" says Mimi, joining them. "*C'est pas possible!*" They hug.

"Hi Mrs. McCarthy." Then, tempering her big instinctive smile, "I'm so sorry about Mr. McCarthy."

"Thank you so much, chérie." Mimi goes to move off but her eye is caught by a floral arrangement. "*Elles sont très belles,* who sent these?"

Yellow roses.

Madeleine leans in, reads the card and blinks. "They're from Christine."

"Ah."

Madeleine says quickly, "I don't know how she found out, I didn't tell her."

"I did," says her mother, then turns on her spike heel and crosses the room to greet new arrivals. Madeleine is speechless.

"She looks great," says Auriel.

"It's the nicotine, it acts as a preservative."

Auriel looks at her for a moment before asking, "How are you, Madeleine?" Maybe she *is* a nurse.

"I think I may be having a nervous breakdown, but only because I can afford one."

"Really?"

"Naw, I'm just a bit burnt out."

"Are you with"—she glances at the roses—"Christine?"

Madeleine sighs. "No, we . . . parted like two mature adults. It was ugly."

"I was sorry to hear about your brother."

"Thanks. I don't want to be rude, but can we talk about you instead?"

Auriel was a nurse—"I knew it!" says Madeleine—at the National Defence Medical Centre in Ottawa when she met her husband. Military personnel and, at times, prison inmates from across the country were treated there. Dave was visiting a member of his prison population from Collins Bay Penitentiary, Kingston.

"Ricky Froelich was at Collins Bay," says Madeleine. The two women fall silent at the mention of a name embedded so deeply in their past.

*Small world,* thinks Madeleine, and the next instant regrets it because that old saccharine song enters her head and she knows it won't be banished in a hurry. Mr. March and his baton—*It's a world of laughter, a world of tears. . . .*

Auriel shakes her head. "That was before Dave's time, of course. But he knew the warden."

Madeleine holds Auriel's gaze a moment, then asks, "Do you ever wonder who did it?"

"Can I tell you the truth, Madeleine? I don't wonder any more, I just pray for them all."

"Do you pray for Marjorie and Grace?"

Auriel's forehead creases. "Why?"

Tears have filled Madeleine's eyes at her mention of the two girls, as if they are the ones she is mourning today. She shrugs. "I just wonder sometimes, you know? . . . Whatever happened to those two?"

Auriel is looking at her so sympathetically that Madeleine is tempted to tell her everything. She has fought so hard to find and reassemble the many pieces of the story, to make it and herself whole again. And now she must carry it, the information lodged in her like an unexploded bomb, a live shell left over from the war. *I waved.* Auriel is looking at her. Auriel is the closest thing to a real sister she's ever had. *Tell.*

But her mouth won't move. She has the old familiar sense of looking out from a dark closet, but this time she recognizes it as tunnel vision. Precursor to migraine or, in Madeleine's case, panic attack. She looks away from Auriel, and focuses on her father's hat.

"Margarine," says Auriel, but she says it sadly.

Madeleine smiles. "Poor old Margarine."

"They moved when we did."

"The Nolans? Where, do you know?" She is aware of trying not to sound too interested.

"Out west, I think. Winnipeg."

"Oh yeah?"

"No—nearby, you know there used to be an air force station, what's the name of that little place? Sounds like a pickle."

"Gimli."

"That's it."

"That doesn't sound like a pickle," says Madeleine.

"Then how did you know?" Auriel laughs. "I saw her name on a list at a nursing convention about five years ago. But she didn't show up. She's a geriatric nurse."

"Oh." Madeleine shudders.

Auriel gives her a pained smile. "Yeah."

She doesn't know what became of Grace. They stand silent for a moment, then Auriel says, "I hope he's been able to have some kind of life."

"Who?"

"Ricky. He lives with his sister now. What was her name?"

" . . . Colleen." *Don't tell me where they live.*

"She was scary."

"Remember Elizabeth?" asks Madeleine.

"Oh yeah. What a great family, really, eh? So sad. I don't think anyone really believed he did it."

With no warning, tears run down Madeleine's face.

"Oh Madeleine, I'm so sorry about your dad." Auriel hugs her again.

Madeleine sniffs. "Actually, I was thinking about Rex." She is wiping her eyes, feeling better—out of the woods somehow—when she hears Auriel say, "They changed their name." And she knows the thing she wanted very much not to know. Their name. How to find them.

The night after the funeral, Madeleine lies dry-eyed and sleepless with grief, on the pull-out bed in her parents' rec room. Surrounded by bookshelves, trophies—public speaking for her, sports for Mike—and framed photos of smiling squadrons of men in uniform. Such young men. She never realized that before. Today at the church she was unable to read the speech she had written. She had composed a eulogy of remember-whens—things that remain unchanged by what her father told her. She wrote it for her mother. She got out the first few words, "My father was a good man." And was destroyed. She pulled herself together, set aside the speech and managed to get through his favourite poem, "High Flight."

After the funeral Mass, the graveside. Madeleine's arm is still tender to the touch where Mimi gripped it as they lowered the casket. Gleaming mahogany. Rectangular excavation. Astroturf. Nothing to do with Jack.

Now, despite the soothing snores from Winnie, wedged beneath the covers, and the resonant purring of old Tante Yvonne in the guest room next door, the house feels too quiet. This is the true wake; the silence in the wake of departing mourners. An end to bright voices, the buoyancy of company keeping Jack afloat—he could walk in at any moment, it's his party after all.

Madeleine can hear her mother upstairs in the kitchen, unloading the dishwasher. She looks at the digital clock. Just after three A.M. The rattle of the dishes gives way to silence. She gets out of bed and creeps upstairs.

"*Tu dors pas?*" Mimi is flipping through a *Chatelaine* magazine— "*HOW TO TAKE THE MISERY OUT OF MOVING*" "*15-MINUTE WORKDAY DINNERS.*" She is in her pale pink quilted housecoat and slippers. Madeleine is in boxers and an old T-shirt with "Joe's Collision" printed on it.

Mimi puts the kettle on and brings out the Scrabble game. They each reach in and pull seven letters from the blue flannel Crown Royal bag. Madeleine looks down at her tray and sees, scrambled but unmistakeable, seven letters for a bonus fifty points: LESBIAN. She sighs and puts down NAIL.

"Tsk-tsk, Madeleine, you can do better than that."

Something is different tonight—beyond the immeasurable absence of her father. Something one doesn't notice until it ceases—like the sound of a refrigerator. Madeleine watches her mother's long tapered nails place two letters in the interstices of three words. "AI? What the heck is AI?"

"A three-toed sloth." For twenty-seven points. They always play in English—a way of handicapping Mimi so as to create a more level playing field between her and her daughter.

"Maman, you don't open up the board when you make mingy little words like that."

"No, but I win."

Mimi is eating day-old burnt toast—that Depression delicacy—and Madeleine has a cup of Campbell's tomato soup with saltines. *À chacun son snack.*

"Have you got the Q?"

"Yeah," sighs Madeleine, looking down at her tray: QUEER.

Mimi drapes POUTINE across the board. "*Voilà,* a nice long word for you."

Face value plus fifty bonus points for using all seven letters. Madeleine watches her mother totting up the points. "You're cheating, that's a French word."

"Poutine is universal language, look at the fast-food menus, it's right next to wings."

Madeleine lays down QUEER for a triple word score.

Her mother doesn't bat an eye, merely says, "That's more like," and counts, tapping each tile with a long buffed nail. "Forty-two points."

"Maman, you're not smoking." That's what's different about tonight.

"I quit."

"When?"

"Today." They play.

"XI?"

"It's an ancient Chinese coin."

They switch to speaking French at some point. At least, Mimi does; Madeleine limps along half and half. But she understands every word. A rough translation: "For years after we lost your brother I used to pray that I might receive a letter one day from a Vietnamese girl. I imagined that she would say, 'I have his child. Your grandchild. May I come see you?' And she would move here with her child—a little boy—and we would all live together. She would be my daughter-in-law. Very pretty. Long dark hair, sweet-natured. She would speak French of course, and we would become the best of friends. Her child would grow up with her and your father and me, and . . . we'd all live happily ever after. And then—I don't know, maybe only last year—after your papa had his heart attack"—here Mimi pauses to wipe her eyes and Madeleine hands her a box of tissues—"I realized that this young woman I was making up . . . this sweet girl with the long dark hair, she was my daughter. And that"—Mimi sucks in a breath through her mouth, unlipsticked at this hour—"I already have . . . a beautiful daughter."

Mimi holds the tissue to her eyes. Madeleine reaches across the Scrabble board and takes her mother's hand.

When she was set to return to Toronto the following week, Madeleine put her bag into the trunk in the front of her VW, closed the lid and called Winnie, who was leaning against Mimi's legs in the doorway of the condo.

Mimi reached down and stroked the helmet-head. "Madeleine, do you mind if I hang onto her for a little while?"

" . . . You want to keep her?"

Mimi began to rev up: "I'm a woman alone, a dog is good protection—"

"Maman, it's fine. But you have to give her back when Olivia comes home."

"Olivia? Oh yes, your Spanish friend."

"Not really, she's just in Latin America at the moment."

"Oh"—baby-talking to the dog—"then she won't mind, will she? Will she, *hein*? Will she, will she. *Ça ne dérange personne, non? Non, non, non, non*—"

"Maman?"

Mimi looked up again.

"I'll call you when I get home."

Madeleine pulled away, a cooler in the back seat filled with enough food to feed an Acadian family for a week.


## HIGH FLIGHT


WHEN JACK DIED, a large white bird rose and departed through the ceiling of the fully serviced condo in the suburbs of Ottawa. Camouflaged by cottony clouds, it caught a warm updraft and soared higher and higher. Wingspan of an eagle, ocean ease of a gull, white bird of great good fortune, it ascended. . . .

*. . . slipped the surly bonds of earth*
*And danced the skies on laughter-silvered wings;*
*Sunward I've climbed and joined the tumbling mirth*
*Of sun-split clouds—and done a hundred things*
*You have not dreamed of—wheeled and soared and swung*
*High in the sunlit silence. Hov'ring there*
*I've chased the shouting wind along and flung*
*My eager craft through footless halls of air.*

"Look at that," said Jack, pointing up. It was before he and Mimi moved into the condo. It was after they found out Mike was missing. It was before hope began to wane. Madeleine was surging with the dark joy of imminent blast-off into the world far from this suburb.

"It's a glider," said Jack.

A white airplane. Silent. Slow. Wings long and tapered, clean and unencumbered by engines. It banked and looped unhurriedly.

"Now, that's flying."

He licked his ice cream—rum 'n' raisin. Madeleine, hers. Neopolitan— best of all worlds.

"Want a lick?"

"Thanks Dad, that's really good."

They watched as the craft arced upward, decelerating, offering its smooth breast to the sky before swooning back into the arms of gravity, as trusting, as brave as an animal or a child.

"You know, old buddy, you can be anything you want to be."

And when Dad said it, she knew it was true.

*Up, up the long delirious, burning blue*
*I've topped the wind-swept heights with easy grace,*
*Where never lark, or even eagle, flew;*
*And, while with silent, lifting mind I've trod*
*The high untrespassed sanctity of space,*
*Put out my hand and touched the face of God.*

*But the dark pines of your mind dip deeper*
*And you are sinking, sinking, sleeper*
*In an elementary world;*
*There is something down there and you want it told.*
        *"Dark Pines Underwater,"* Gwendolyn MacEwen

EVERYONE KNEW THAT Ricky had changed his name, but Madeleine would have remained comfortably ignorant of his new one had Auriel not said *they*. In that instant it arrived unbidden in Madeleine's mind. Colleen and Ricky's original name. How many Pellegrims could there be in Canada?

The name lay there like a smooth stone collected on holiday. She put it in a drawer of her desk and got back to work, back to her life. She turned on her computer. She put paper in the printer. She sat down and started writing.

*What business are you in?*

*The funny business.*

She phoned Shelly every ten minutes, reading her funny stuff. Then stuff that was not so funny, to which Shelly said, "No, keep it for now. It'll get there, you just don't know how yet." They got together every couple of days so Madeleine could try stuff out. Stuff that didn't require "stuff."

*What are you selling?*

*Stories.*

From time to time she came across the smooth stone. Upon opening her desk drawer in search of a pencil, a paperclip. Sometimes it cropped up in the cutlery drawer among the knives, in the medicine cabinet, under the couch—she had bought a couch. And a bed. Her friends had held a breakup shower for her. Even Christine had given her a gift, a Braun hand mixer. Sometimes, a cigar is just a cigar.

A week after she got home, Madeleine sat cross-legged on her old Persian carpet, eschewing her new club chair, and called long-distance information.

"For what city?"

"Winnipeg."

"For what name?"

"Marjorie Nolan."

"Thank you, here's your number—"

She grabbed a pen and wrote the number on her hand.

She waited until six-thirty central time.

A woman answered, "Hello?"—querulous voice, not Marjorie's.

"May I speak with Marjorie please?"

A rustling as the woman lowered the receiver, her voice a muffled complaint, "It's for you-ou . . . ," followed by a *clunk* of receiver against table or floor.

After a moment, another female voice. "Hello." Crisp. Note of exasperation. Marjorie.

"Hello, Marjorie?" said Madeleine.

"Who's speaking please?"

Madeleine could see her—eyes tightening, ready to defend herself. "This is Madeleine McCarthy. We went to school together in Centralia."

Half a beat, then the woman said, "I'm afraid you have the wrong number." And hung up.

She called every Novotny in Canada. She found Grace's father. He said he didn't know where the hell any of them were any more, but if he ever found out. . . .

She called the Ontario Provincial Police and asked for Missing Persons. "Name of the person?"

"Grace Novotny." She could hear keys being tapped in the background.

Then the female officer at the other end said, "What's the nature of your information?"

*I was right.* "I don't actually have information, I just . . . want to know if there's anything new."

"We can't release that to the public. What's your relation to Grace Novotny?"

Madeleine's answer came so naturally it didn't feel like a lie. "She's my sister."

"Oh. Well I'm sorry, but there's really nothing new since '66."

"Okay. Thanks."

Nineteen sixty-six—Grace would have been fourteen. *Missing.* Did she run away from home and get lost? Like Mike? *Where have all the young girls gone?*

Madeleine left her house, heading for River Street and the Humane Society to visit the desperate dogs. There was no song to soften or explain where some young girls went. Grace had gone to snuff.

Love can work like athletic training, or practice with a musical instrument. Train vigorously for a spell. Then rest—take off the runners, put down the violin. When you return to your sport, your scales, you will have inexplicably improved, due to the intervention of nothing but time.

Madeleine found the scroll and the candle on her carpet in her empty apartment when she returned from her father's funeral. She read the scroll. "*Ma bien aimée,* Enjoy this candle at your leisure. When it has burned down, ask me to be with you and I will give you everything I have. But please don't take too long. I want to have kids. Or you might choose not to light it at all. It will help you to decide because I can't. *À bientôt,* O."

It's broad daylight. Madeleine turns on her computer and lights the candle. When she turns her computer off again, she blows the candle out. And so it goes as, over the course of a month, *Stark Raving Madeleine* begins to take shape.

Madeleine is not unhappy. She has put something aside, she may never take it up again. Is that what it means finally to grow up? To know there are things we have wrestled with and failed to defeat? To make peace with them by allowing them to rest—like a creature in a coma? Is that maturity? Or is it just life? It could hurt many people if she tells what she knows. It could hurt her mother terribly. Whom could it help? Ricky is free and has been for years. No one ever really believed he did it anyway. Why dredge up the past?

One morning in early August, Madeleine rides her bike to the pharmacy and heads for the post office at the back with a special delivery letter for Olivia. O is coming home in two and a half weeks. She reaches into the pocket of her army surplus shorts for money and finds a crumpled "First Notice" from Canada Post. Dated ten days ago. How come she never got a "Final Notice"? She hands it to the elderly Korean lady behind the counter. "Do you still have this?"

The lady pushes her glasses up the bridge of her nose, smiles and nods. She disappears into the back room and after a few moments returns with a package the size and shape of a cereal box. She hands it to Madeleine. "Muffins from Mummy."

Madeleine smiles. "Yeah, would you like one? Let's see if they're still good," and opens it on the spot, fighting her way through enough masking tape to hold together the first atomic bomb. She was right, a cereal box. All-Bran. The joys of aging. She opens the lid, reaches in and pulls out her father's air force hat.

"Ohhh," says the lady.

Faded blue, almost grey. Worn red velvet crown of the cap badge. Tarnished gold braid and vigilant albatross, wings outstretched in flight.

"Very lovely," says the lady behind the counter.

"Thank you."

Madeleine rides back home, goes inside and lights what remains of the red candle. She waits until it has burned all the way down. Then she goes back out to her car.

She tosses the hat into the back seat of the bug, gets in and drives.

> *Two drifters, off to see the world*
> *there's such a lot of world to see*
> *We're after the same rainbow's end*
> *just around the bend*
> *my Huckleberry friend*
> *Moon River, and me*

She drives on because the road pulls her. That's one of the secrets of North America: the roads have a pull of their own, reactive to rubber, to the undersides of car chassis. She feels the tug of the wheel, she doesn't have to steer, the tires follow the bend of the highway, the car knows her destination and so does the road. Let's just drive. We'll find out where we're going when we get there.

*Welcome to Kitchener,* formerly Berlin. All these places named after the real places elsewhere—give them time and they become real in their own right. *London Keep Left. Stratford Next Exit.* She exits. *Welcome to New Hamburg, to Dublin, to Paris....* Outside the car windows, the corn catches the sun; leafy stalks gleam in three greens, arching oaks and maples line the curving highway, the land rolls and burgeons in a way that makes you believe, yes, the earth is a woman, and her favourite food is corn.

From four directions come the X-Men, steel soldiers marching in columns, the distance between them tightening as they close in on their home base just south of here. Cables strung like steel streamers from their outflung arms, thrumming with the drone that sets their martial pace. They are on their way to their underground fortress at Niagara Falls, where house-high turbines fuel the economic heart of the world's biggest democracies and closest relatives, power pronging north and south across the world's longest undefended border. "What nature has joined together, let no man put asunder."

*Welcome to Lucan....* Don't look for that monument now, it's gone, too many tourists left with fragments of the stone. Just sit back and enjoy the beautiful scenery. Think nice thoughts. *Believe on the Lord Jesus Christ and Be Saved ... Kodak ... The Wages of Sin Is Death....*

Deciduous trees like stately homes, painted maples streaked up the side with moss, mile-long driveways, weathered gingerbread framing farmhouse windows. The congenial whiff of cowpies, the rude aroma of pigs and the fierce smell of chickens. Smelled but rarely seen or heard nowadays. Red barns, neat and scrubbed, encroached upon by mysterious long low barracks. That's where the animals have gone, eating and shitting in the windowless dark. Many, but not all. You can still see pale pigs at their troughs, cows in the fields, they blink and flick at flies and live their slow lives. *McDonald's Next Interchange. . . .*

Up ahead, a faded pink ice cream cone tilts toward the roadside, the white shed with its countertop peeling and disused. The cone is still in its party hat, *Where did everyone go?*

The afternoon intensifies. August is the true light of summer. *Trust Texaco.* Dusty gas pumps flash by, glimpse of a screen door emblazoned with a bottle of 7Up, beaded with moisture, poised for pouring. She drives. The sun has sat back to relax on the other side of noon, mellow and magnanimous, with no sense yet that the day is in decline. The best of both worlds.

Smell the sweetness of the grass, look how the hay is almost mauve in the fields; feel how she swells beneath your wheels, the earth in these parts, gentle as the roll of the sea on a blue day. Clouds sweep so gracefully; the high billow of trees that have lived here so long; the narrative pull of the woods; all the crackling lives lived high and low, paths that promise so many stories, and the road itself, always curving just out of sight, the allure of a storyteller and the assurance, "Follow me into the story, it's all right. If it were not, would I be here to tell the tale?"

We're almost there.


Madeleine stands under the beating sun and looks out. The concrete is cracked in places. Uneven with many winters, its grey expanse etched with crooked lines of scraggly green growth. The reclamation of this airfield is underway by the quilted countryside that provided so much safe space for emergency landings. The triangular arms of the runways fan out before her, trembling with heat.

Behind her the hangars loom silent, still white but no longer ship-shape, bordered by grime and weeds that have choked out the hedges. People don't know, unless they trouble to find out, what this place was. Ghost of the Second World War. Relic of the Cold War. Even Kodak pictures fade eventually, and that is what has happened here.

She drove slowly through the PMQs and the base before winding up at the airfield. The pool, empty. The arena, movie theatre, barracks, office buildings—cement steps sprouting grass, black metal railings listing, seeping rust, coming loose like teeth. The sign for the sergeants' mess still hangs next to the dusty green door, the air force crest sunbleached almost to vanishing—why has no one taken it down? There is no longer any such thing as the Royal Canadian Air Force. And just as the services have been unified, so the two Germanys will be, one day soon. The country Madeleine was born in will no longer exist.

RCAF Centralia is Huron Industrial Park now. A government property, leased cheap to any industry willing to relocate and bring jobs to the area. Windows are manufactured here these days, but Madeleine has seen no one and heard not a sound.

The churches are gone. Bulldozed. The officers' mess likewise. In its place a starkly new brown brick building with a sloping roof and smoked windows, Darth Vaderesque. "International School," says the federal government sign planted in the one patch of tended grass. Nothing to do with manufacturing windows. Suitably vague, suitably far away from anyone who might wonder what lies behind the tinted glass, the numbing government designation.

No cars parked anywhere. The tennis court has gone the way of the airfield, its metal link fence flounced and ragged. The street names are still the same: the ten Canadian provinces, the two founding cultures and the famous men who made untold sacrifices to keep us free. The signs themselves remain, rusted now, askew, pointing at sky and ground. Canada Avenue. Alberta Street. Ontario, Saskatchewan, Québec. . . . The Spitfire is gone.

In the old PMQs, the houses are still painted every colour of the rainbow, but not so recently. People must be away for summer holidays, or perhaps not all the houses are occupied. A few people stared at Madeleine's car as she tooled slowly past, but they didn't wave. No swings or teeter-totters in the park any more, but the narrow asphalt paths still wend their way communally among the houses. The open grassy circles are here too, although they are not the vast fields of memory. And that hill she used to run down so recklessly—it's barely an incline.

The confetti bush is gone from in front of her old white house—smaller than she remembered, likewise the purple house across from it. She rolled down St. Lawrence in first gear, past the little green bungalow on her left, to the school. Hardly more than a stone's throw from her old house, yet it was such a big walk then. She stopped in the parking lot near the backstop. Nothing stirred, not even the rope on the flagpole.

How can this place still exist? Barely two hours from Toronto—she could have driven here any time. *Centralia.*

She stopped and got out of the car. Peeked in her old classroom window. New desks. Different art on the walls. A computer. Map of the world, redrawn so many times since her day. She tried the knob of the side door but it was locked. What was in there anyhow? Nothing that hasn't been as close as her own heart for twenty-three years. She went round the front, up the steps, and cupped her hands around her eyes to peer through the glass double doors: framed fighter jets still flanked the portraits of the young Queen and Prince Philip.

This place, Huron Industrial Park, leased to temporary people: for them it's home, perhaps, a community, people raising children, borrowing cups of sugar, keeping in touch after they move on. . . . But for Madeleine it's a ghost town.

She stands on the abandoned airfield. She is not much younger than her parents were when they moved here. She shields her eyes and looks across the baking concrete to the crest of longer grass that marks the ditch where his aircraft went in. For her it was a story, *Dad, tell me the story of the crash.* It belonged to her, the myth of how, inevitably, her parents were brought together in order to bring forth her and her brother. And the unspoken corollary of the myth: if it hadn't been for the crash, Dad might have been killed in the war . . . *two out of three aircrew never came back.* He was not quite eighteen. Mike was nineteen.

She squints up at the control tower, miniature to her adult eyes. She can see the roofs of the PMQs from here. Such a small world. What would she have done in her parents' place? Would she have mustered the conviction "We are a family," no matter where we move? "Here is who you are," no matter whom you happen to live among, "this is your father, the best man and the nicest papa in the world"? Such a big world. "You can grow up to be anything you want to be." Could she have marshalled the optimism, taken the pictures, unpacked the boxes, placed a little family at the centre of that big world? Made herself the anchor of it? Made it make sense?

*Dad, are they going to blow up the earth?*

*Naw.*

A journey of forty years. The Story of Mimi and Jack. *So many nice remember-whens.*

The sun is relentless. The old airfield waits, impassive, a war monument. And perhaps that's why she is moved. These strips of concrete evoke so much about this century. Mass mobilization. Mass memory. Heavy loss.

She recalls seeing a phone booth at the edge of the parade square, near what used to be the PX. She wonders if it still works. She turns and leaves the airfield.

She has forgiven her parents.

A rotary phone in a glass booth. It still takes dimes. The slim phone book is dog-eared, pages torn out, but it may serve. She flips through familiar place names—Lucan, Clinton, Crediton. . . .

She finds him in Exeter. Searches the many pockets of her shorts—crumbs, keys, frizzing tampon, a dime.

She dials, then leans with her palm against the glass while it rings.

"Hello." A woman's voice, tight but pleasant. Career wife.

"Hello, may I speak with Inspector Bradley please."

"Oh my goodness—"

Madeleine assumes she has called another dead man, but the woman continues, "—well, hang on a moment and I'll—may I ask who's calling?"

"Madeleine McCarthy."

"Just a moment, Madeleine," and, calling away from the phone, "Tom," her voice retreating, "Tom? . . . on the phone . . . spector Bradley."

She will tell him everything. About Mr. March. About her father. And Ricky's name will be cleared. The right thing.

"Hello"—manly and businesslike.

"Hello, Inspector Bradley?"

"No such person here, there's just me, Tom Bradley, retired, what can I do you for?"

"This is Madeleine McCarthy speaking." She sees the planes of his face, unsmiling line of his mouth, and feels as though she is lying again.

He pauses, then says, "I know you. . . ." She knows he is probably not thinking of After-Three TV.

"I was a witness at Ricky Froelich's trial."

"Bingo." Silence. The ball is in her court.

"I have new information," she says.

"Well I'm retired, young lady, but I can give you a number—"

"I was a pupil of Mr. March's, he was Claire's—he was our grade four teacher." She hears a sigh. "I think he was responsible."

"What do you mean, 'responsible'?"

"He did it. He murdered her."

"I wish you gals would co-ordinate your efforts."

"What do you mean?"

"You and—another girl, what was her name, Deanne, Diane something—"

"Diane Vogel."

"Right you are, she called me last year, wanting to press charges."

"Against Mr. March?"

"That's right. Is that your story too?"

"It's not a story, it happened."

"Be that as it may—"

"He raped us. Grace and Marjorie included, that's why they lied, he played games involving strangulation—"

"Even if—"

"He did it."

"Yeah okay, look, number one, that was almost twenty-five years ago—"

"So?"

"Number two, he's dead, all right? So much for that. Number three—"

"Thanks for nothing, buddy." She will hire a lawyer. "Goodbye."

"Wait! Wait. Number three: he had an alibi."

And she knows it as he says it. That day in the schoolyard. The afternoon of flying up.

Bradley says, "You know, I'm sick and tired of people digging this up, I did my job—"

She can hear it, fractured melody on the air, struggling out the windows of the gym. Flat trombones, hesitant woodwinds—the school band bleating out a song, reaching them where they lounged on the grass of the outfield, she and Colleen, as Claire rode up on her pink bike. *It's a world of laughter a world of tears . . .*

"Want to come for a picnic?" Her lunchbox in the basket between her handlebars. Two pink streamers. *It's a world of hope and a world of fears . . .*

"Hindsight is twenty-twenty," says Bradley. "Your generation—"

*There's so much that we share that it's time we're aware, it's a small world after all. . . .* Mr. March conducting the band from the piano, pounding out fat chords at odd intervals so it sounded as though the piece were ending every few bars.

"We can look for a nest," said Claire.

"—you like to sit in judgement of every bloody thing we did," says Bradley, pitch rising to a whine—

Claire rode off on her own, and the band was still playing when Madeleine and Colleen left the schoolyard. Mr. March was still in the gym, at band practice, which always went till four-thirty. Madeleine has always known that. *It's a small world after all, it's a small world after all, it's a small world after all . . .*

"—but let me tell you something," says Bradley, "we worked with what we had at the time—"

*. . . it's a small, small world.*

"Thanks, Mr. Bradley."

"Wait now, I'm not—"

She hangs up. Inspector Bradley is retired. He has all the time in the world. She has three hours to make it up to Tobermory, at the tip of the Bruce Peninsula, where the vastness of Lake Superior flows out into Huron. If she wants to arrive before dark. She opens the folding glass door of the booth and feels the sweat immediately begin to dry on her forehead.

For a moment she can't recall where she left her car. But she sees it, beyond the hangars, parked on the simmering tarmac. She has a vision of her tires sticking to the viscous black strands as she tries to leave Centralia. But she runs to it, starts the engine, shifts into gear and the bug leaps forward eagerly, like Noddy's Little Car, *parp parp!*

She doesn't see the white buildings receding on either side of her car as she follows Canada Avenue, she doesn't see the empty guardhouse up ahead. Everything shimmers and melts around her like a mirage, her visual cortex has taken over and will guide her off this old base and toward her destination without her conscious help, because she is seeing something quite different now behind her eyes. It fills the screen in Panavision. Shot from below in rich early sixties pastels, lusher than life, like an illustration from an outdated grade-school reader. Except that this is not a still photo or a drawing. There is a breeze. Caressing the long grass; rippling the leaves in the elm high above, where two or three crows dot the new foliage; lifting the yellow ringlets of the girl to his right. Marjorie. Kissing the curls of the girl to his left. Grace. Playing at the hems of their dresses, their innocent white knees. Mr. March is standing between them in his big grey suit. His glasses glint back the sun, he is holding their hands. All three of them are looking up and to their right, into the sunny blue. Then Mr. March disappears from the picture. And the two little girls are left on their own.

Madeleine passes through the old gates where her father used to touch the brim of his hat to the guard. She passes the cement scar in the ground where the Spitfire once flew on its pedestal. She smells tar and resin and looks up at the telephone pole. Thrusting from a shambles of straw and twigs, a rusting mouth. The old air-raid siren. It's still there, and so are the crows who made it their home so long ago. It hasn't sounded since 1962, the crows have had no need to move. So many years of peace in our time.

She turns north on Highway 4. She will pass through Exeter, Clinton, Goderich . . . the dust will turn to gold behind her car, the lake will wink crystal-blue beyond the dunes, the pines will become more numerous, the landscape rockier and more grand, but she will not see any of it. Instead, she will see what happens after Mr. March vanishes from the picture.

The truth was always there. And it's far sadder than anything she has imagined. But she knows now: it could never have been her, left lying in that tamped down spot.

"WE'RE NOT GOING TO HURT YOU." And they weren't. "We just want to see something."

"Yeah Claire."

They have given her the robin's egg. She has taken it from Marjorie's outstretched palm, its shell perfectly intact. Boys are rough with delicate things, but girls know how to be careful. Marjorie says they know where to find more eggs. "Alive ones," adds Grace

Claire cups her hands around the egg, hollow and weightless, and follows Marjorie and Grace.

The cornfield is on the other side of the ravine, and beyond it is the meadow where, if you are lucky, you might see a deer—if you are very quiet. And bordering the meadow are the woods.

"That's where the nest is," says Marjorie.

They climb the embankment out of Rock Bass. Marjorie leads the way, and Grace lets Claire go ahead.

A buzzy afternoon, warm for April. Trickle of the stream newly liberated from ice. The sound of insects clicketing in the grass. The sound of the sun.

They enter the cornfield and walk single file between freshly turned furrows, careful of last year's cornstalks sticking up like bones from the ground. Behind her, Grace starts turning round and round as she walks. She says, "Get dizzy, then look up at the sky."

Claire tries it. She and Grace laugh with their heads thrown back.

Up ahead, Marjorie turns. "Hurry up, you two, I'm not partial to dilly-dallying." She sees an ear of corn on the ground, still bound in yellowed leaves. She picks it up, light and lean with age, and peels back the papery husk. The kernels are withered, some darkening like bad teeth. She is about to toss it away when Grace grabs it.

"Guess who I am?" says Grace, the cob between her legs, wagging it up and down.

Claire smiles politely but turns away, embarrassed. Marjorie rolls her eyes in disgust and walks on.

Grace swaggers behind Claire—"Squeeze my muscle, little girl"— laughing. She pretends to pee out of it, "Psssss. . . ."

"Don't be so rude, Grace," says Marjorie.

Grace runs ahead of Marjorie, spins around and walks backwards, spraying her with imaginary pee.

"I'm warning you, Grace."

Grace turns forward again, loses interest in the ear of corn and drops it. Marjorie picks it up.

The cornfield gives way to the meadow.

Cows do not even graze here, it's empty but for the long last summer's grass collapsed over new growth, and the few cattails left standing—some broken like spars, others split at their furry tips, spilling seed. The tiny white bell-heads of the lily of the valley release their scent, crushed underfoot, and here and there, brushstrokes of blue like spilled sky, the spreading bluebells. This meadow is lying fallow; in a year or two it may be the cornfield and the cornfield may be the meadow. The ground becomes marshy. They are nearing the woods.

"Are we there yet?" asks Claire.

Grace glances at Marjorie but Marjorie is unconcerned, twirling the cob of corn like a baton.

"Not much farther," says Grace.

Up ahead—standing alone, announcing the woods—is a stately elm.

Claire stops. "I'm not allowed to go in the woods."

"Well I'm afraid you have no choice, that's where the nest is," says Marjorie.

"No," says Claire.

"How come?" asks Grace.

"My mommy said."

"The cornfield is worse than the woods, Claire," says Marjorie.

"Yeah," says Grace.

But Claire shakes her head.

"It's your loss, little girl." Marjorie shrugs. "Oh well, you might as well show us your underpants."

Claire looks at Grace. But Grace is looking at Marjorie.

Claire smiles and raises her dress obligingly, as though to make up for spurning their invitation to enter the woods.

"Oh, they're pretty."

"Yeah, they're really pretty, Claire."

Tiny yellow butterflies. White cotton.

"Take them off."

Claire takes them off. Modestly dropping the skirt of her dress first. A voice in the back of her head says, *Don't take off your underpants when people ask, it's not good for people to ask that.* But there is a lovely breeze and she is out in a field, not among houses or in the schoolyard, where it certainly would be rude to be taking off underpants.

There is another reason why she is taking off her underpants. It's difficult to explain, but she is doing this mainly because she knows how. As if there were already a Claire, an invisible one, perpetually in the act of removing her underpants on demand. So this Claire—the one in the meadow—may as well do so too. And it's not even as though she herself is taking off her underpants, it's as though this is something that is simply going on.

She slips her underpants to her ankles and steps out of them. Grace giggles. Claire laughs. Marjorie picks up the underpants. They are warm.

"Now bend over, little girl," says Marjorie.

Grace giggles, Claire laughs and runs through the grass with no underpants on. Oh it is a lovely feeling. So fresh, like when you first go out without your woollen hat in springtime, the free feeling of your ankles flashing along in running shoes for the first time after a long winter in galoshes.

"Get her," says Marjorie.

Grace runs after Claire, who is delighted to have someone join the aimless race. Let's run and run until we come to an enchanted clearing. There we will meet a fairy princess who will serve us tea in walnut shells, and her attendants will be wearing acorn hats. Grace runs heavily—the more she chases, the more she is weak with laughter, but excited too, and it's the excitement that keeps her going, gradually gaining on Claire, who is politely slowing down. They are about fifteen feet from the elm tree.

Marjorie follows, unhurried, tapping the corncob into her palm the way a teacher does with a pointer.

Claire nears the elm and stops for Grace, and Grace grabs her arm. "Ow," says Claire.

Grace looks back at Marjorie.

Claire scans the ground for her blue egg, which she dropped when Grace grabbed her just now. She spots it in the grass, the shell looks fine, but Grace's grip prevents her from stooping to pick it up. "Excuse me Grace, could you please let go?"

Grace looks at Claire as though noticing her for the first time. There is a look in Grace's eye. Excited and scared, as though at the sight of something just beyond Claire's shoulder. Claire turns to see what's behind her, but behind her are the woods.

Grace hollers, "Hurry up, Marjorie!"—too loud, because Marjorie has almost caught up. *Huwwy up!*

Marjorie is not laughing. She has a grown-up expression on her face. Like when grown-ups are past the end of their tether, they are not even angry any more, but you know that means that you are in even more trouble than if they were. They are just sick to death of you, that's all.

"I'm sick to death of you, little girl," says Marjorie, a worn-out disgusted look on her face.

Claire giggles, because what game are we playing now?

"Bend over and touch your toes," says Marjorie.

"Um," says Claire, "I don't—I want to play—let's pretend—"

"Are you deaf, little girl?"

Grace gives a delighted shriek and holds tighter to Claire's arm, with both hands.

Claire whimpers, "Can I go home now? Want to come to my house and play?"

Grace pushes Claire down.

"I warned you," says Marjorie.

She tosses Claire's underpants onto Claire's face. Grace jumps onto Claire before she can get up. She holds the underpants stretched over Claire's face and hollers, "Smell your bum!" Shrieking with laughter.

Marjorie stands over them, watching. She sees the outline of Claire's nose and open mouth through the taut fabric. It's not enough. "Get off her."

Grace gets up, grinning, her tongue working the chafed corners of her mouth. Claire lies motionless.

Marjorie removes the underpants from her face with the tip of the corncob.

"Get up."

Claire gets up. "I have to go now."

"It's okay, Claire," says Grace.

"Put your hands around Grace's throat," says Marjorie.

Claire obeys.

"Squeeze. Harder."

Grace says, "Mar—!"

"Shut up."

Claire lets go of Grace and waits for the next instruction.

Marjorie tells her, "Pee."

Claire's forehead wrinkles. "I can't," she says, and begins at last to cry.

Marjorie says, "Hold her still."

Grace takes Claire by the elbows, locking them together from behind, and Marjorie puts the cob of corn up Claire's dress, and presses.

"Ow," says Claire, biting her lip. "Don't do that please, Marjorie."

Marjorie presses harder and Claire yelps. The scene resembles agreement, for Claire is not writhing, despite pain, despite fear. It's terrible. The only thing that it isn't is surprising. To any of them.

"Ow-hahoww. . . ." Claire is not screaming, just whimpering. Like a child who knows she is going to be punished.

"Don't hurt her, Marjorie," says Grace, still holding Claire.

Marjorie's arm thrusts upward with a twist, because it can. Claire screams and jolts forward, but Grace prevents her from falling and hurting herself. Marjorie watches. Isn't it strange that someone right in front of you can be screaming about something that you don't feel? Like rain falling two inches away and you stay perfectly dry. "What are you screaming about, little girl?"

Marjorie takes the corncob out from under Claire's dress. There's blood on it. Claire is sobbing.

Grace lets go of her. "It's okay, Claire—hey Claire—Claire, can I see your charm bracelet?"

Marjorie tosses the corncob away, into the grass. A crow drops down to investigate. Claire raises her wrist, hiccuping, and shows Grace her bracelet.

"Oh, that's the prettiest one I've ever seen," says Grace, fingering the charms. "Can I try it on?"

Claire shakes her head, and Grace says, "Okay I won't, Claire, it's yours." Grace lets go of the bracelet.

"Lie down, little girl," says Marjorie.

Claire doesn't move.

"She doesn't want to," says Grace.

Marjorie sighs and says, resigned, "Strangle her, Marjorie."

Grace obeys. She doesn't shriek with laughter at Marjorie's mistake in calling her by the wrong name, because she doesn't notice. She squeezes and squeezes.

Now Claire looks surprised. That's how people look—as though they have just remembered what it was they meant to say. Marjorie watches.

It's all very quiet. Grace isn't grinning, just staring, and it ceases to be funny, ceases to be anything at all. Not anything, just doing this, quiet quiet like under the ocean, the air has slit open. What was there all along, behind the air and woods, and grass and the sky, that painted sheet, is Nothing. You can't stop. You aren't doing anything.

It goes on, it goes on, Grace not doing anything, just not stopping. Marjorie watches.

Falling so fast, all is still, so empty there is no change. It goes on, it goes on, it happens, nothing happens, doing nothing doing nothing doing nothing.

And finally, Claire pees.

Grace lets go and Claire drops to the ground.

It's a sunny day again. They are in a field. Claire McCarroll is there. Insects are there, and from the dirt road beyond the woods, the sound of a car going by. It's Brownies tonight. We are flying up.

"Get up, Claire."

Marjorie will remember that the grass was yellow, but it is newly green. Grace will remember that they were in a cornfield, but there is no corn here. There is the long pale grass. There is the high elm. The corn-syrup sun. All around them is the month of April. It's twenty-five to five.

"Stick your tongue back in."

Claire does not obey.

"Get up."

She will not do as she is told.

"Marjorie . . . ," says Grace, going wavery. "Ohhh," moaning, "ohhh nooo. . . ." *Oh no Marjowieeee. . . .*

"Shut up Grace"—fed up and bored, the teacher marks the failed spelling test.

"Ohhhh. . . ," Grace is turning round slowly, pulling tall grass, bending over, hugging herself, "oh noooo. . . ."

Marjorie relents, as a long-suffering mother might, when her child's misbehaviour has run its course and been replaced by contrition or exhaustion. "It's all right, Grace," she says. "I won't tell."

Grace must make things nice. Pull Claire's dress down. Fold her arms. Bluebells to cover her, Queen Anne's lace, which some people call stinkweed but which is pretty like a doily. Marjorie helps with two long cattails for a cross over her chest, because we may as well do this properly.

"She's sleeping," says Grace, and bends to kiss Claire good night but can't because of the eyes. Claire's face is already changing. Grace finds Claire's underpants in the grass, tiny yellow butterflies on clean white cotton, and places them over her face.

It is time to get out of here.

They walk Claire's bike from Rock Bass back to the dirt road and take turns riding it, but when they reach the intersection with the old Huron County road, Marjorie points out that they don't want anyone to think they have stolen it. They hide it under the willow tree, leaning it against the trunk, where it will be safe from robbers.

Grace pulls one of the pink streamers from the handlebars. "I'll give it back."

That night, Grace called on Marjorie and Marjorie said, "I can't come out, it's too late, I have to do my homework then go to bed."

It was dark. Grace had been out long after Brownies, loitering at the end of Marjorie's driveway with the dented trash cans. Marjorie had seen her from an upstairs window. She rapped on the glass with her knuckles, then opened it and hissed down, "Go home, Grace!" Grace was shivering as though she were cold. Well, the nights were still cool. She wandered slowly away, not in the direction of her own house, not in any particular direction.

Five minutes later she knocked on Marjorie's door again. Marjorie's mother was not pleased. She was sick a lot and it really was a bother. "Marjorie," she called over her shoulder, while Grace waited on the front step. "It's that kid again."

Marjorie came to the door in her housecoat, kiss-curls taped to her cheeks. "What do you want?" she said through the screen door.

And Grace said, "We're best friends, right?" *Best fwiends.*

Marjorie did not invite her in. Grace's lips looked sore and she was gnawing the cuff of her Brownie uniform. Marjorie had just had a bath. She wondered now why she had ever been friends with dirty Grace Novotny.

"I don't know," she said.

"We are so, Marjorie!"

"Keep your voice down."

"We are so," Grace whispered.

"So?"

"So just come out for a minute."

"I can't, I'm ready for bed."

They stood there for a moment, Marjorie behind the screen, Grace on the step below, her eyes starting to wander. Marjorie's mum said from inside the house, "Marjorie, close the door, there's a draft."

"I have to go."

"Claire never came home," said Grace.

Marjorie glanced over her shoulder and tightened the cord of her housecoat. "Are you retarded, Grace?"

Grace looked bewildered. She reached for Marjorie's sleeve but touched the screen. "Marjorie . . . ?" Her voice trembled, tears filled her eyes and she asked, "What happened to her?"

"You killed her, Grace, that's what happened. Now go home." And Marjorie closed the door.

THE SUN IS HALFWAY DOWN the sky when Madeleine puts her car into first and rocks up the stony track toward a log house just coming into view.

The day feels as endless as summer itself, suspended in heat. Trees bask in a cinematic light so rich that every pine needle glints, sharp as resin, against the hot blue. In the upper boughs of a Douglas fir, a spiderweb glitters, prismatic, and a crow sits, as crows like to do, atop the central spire. Birch leaves, responsive to the slightest breeze, blink back the sun with their silver undersides. Birdcalls sound intimate and precise; Madeleine is aware of having entered their home. And appearing with the rise in the road, in the distance between slim scaly trunks, the blue sparkle of Lake Huron. A dog barks. Several dogs.

The house stands on a swell of pink and grey granite—a piece of the Canadian Shield softened by sunset. Is it possible that this ravishing evening light can erode stone, painting it day after day with pastel rays? Veins of mica glitter like strewn diamonds, clefts in the rock cast shadows on patches of moss, grey, green, gold and black, the house itself is burnished ochre at this hour. A wooden ramp zigzags up to the front door.

A dog rounds the house and trots, barking, toward her car: ears erect, sturdy, with a white and grey coat. He escorts her up to a level patch where a shiny Dodge pickup is parked. Nearby is an open shed—firewood neatly stacked floor to ceiling, snowmobile, battered snowplough blade, tools and tire chains, along with several large dog crates and leather harnesses. On the other side of the shed, a vintage Ford Thunderbird rests on blocks, hood propped open like a grand piano, mess of greasy engine guts on the ground. She pulls up and parks.

The dog is part husky, judging by the curl of his tail and the song he is singing now, head thrown back, eyes still on her, one blue, one brown. The rest of the canine chorus is coming from somewhere beyond the shed. She gets out of her car and the dog wags his tail but resumes barking, glancing back toward the house as though waiting for permission to drop the guard-dog schtick.

She can smell a barbecue going. She has arrived unannounced at suppertime. After twenty-three years.

Someone comes out from behind the house. A tall figure. Denim cutoffs. Sneakers and a T-shirt. Lean and brown.

Madeleine shades her eyes with her hand and says, "Hi Colleen."

The dog has stopped barking but he is still at her side, awaiting instructions.

"It's Madeleine."

"I know." Colleen's voice, still smokey and brief but with the added weight of adulthood.

Madeleine says, "Can I come up?"

"What for?"

She hesitates. She is reminded of the day long ago when she met Elizabeth, and Colleen challenged her, *Well say her name, can't you?* Elizabeth. That would explain the ramp up to the veranda. She says, "I've brought you something."

"What?"

*Something that belongs to you.*

Neither has moved. As though each is waiting for the other to jump from the teeter-totter.

*A story.*

Madeleine goes to her car and reaches into the back seat.

*What remains?*

Story. Yours, or one like it, in which, as in a pool, you might recognize yourself.

Memory. Mixed and multifarious, folding itself down, down, for the journey. Story is memory rendered portable. Your memory, or many like yours. Unfold it like a tent. It can shelter a world.

Madeleine holds up her father's air force hat.

Memory breeds memory. The very air is made of memory. Memory falls in the rain. You drink memory. In winter you make snow angels out of memory.

So much remains.

One witness.

*Tell.*

After a moment, Colleen disappears behind her house. Madeleine follows, accompanied by the dog. As she comes level with the house on her left, she sees, off to the right beyond the shed, a compound set half amid the trees. A long low wooden building with several small doors at intervals, like a miniature motel, painted hunter green. Covered runs lead from the doors and open onto a fenced-in acreage of mown grass and trees, canine Shangri-La. Eight or ten adults bound along behind the fence, Labs, yellows, browns and blacks, noses crammed through the mesh, tails wagging.

She rounds the house. The curve of rock obscures the shore, so that the granite's pink is juxtaposed with the open water that stretches to meet the horizon. In between, the blue expanse is dotted with stone islands flat as pancakes, their pine trees permanently wind-tilted and shimmering in the heat like northern palms. A far-off ferry boat inches along, plying the route between the mainland and Manitoulin Island. Beyond where the eye can see lie Michigan and the U.S.

Colleen is tending the barbecue and doesn't look up. Madeleine walks to the crest of the smooth stone, and a dock comes into view below. Water laps at the wooden posts and glitters with the intensity of early evening. She can almost hear the *ting* of light rippling gold and silver, like notes on a xylophone. A battered aluminum outboard rocks against the dock, bleached-out life-jackets mildewing in the bottom where a sawed-off plastic Javex bottle floats, purpose-built for baling. On the shore, a few feet above the waterline, a canoe rests overturned, casting a longboat shadow on the stone.

There is a wheelchair at the end of the dock. A woman is sitting in it, facing the water. It's not Elizabeth. This woman has long gleaming black hair, straight and loose. A head pops out from under the dock—a child. He hauls himself up, water sliding in gleaming sheets from his bare chest. He flops naked onto the dock, a long braid slicked down his back, and stands up. He is a girl.

"Mom, everybody, watch!" she shouts, bounding up the dock, turning to pelt back down again, splashing the silvery wood with ragged black footprints, past the woman in the wheelchair and off the end, cannon-balling into the water. The dog rockets down the slope, onto the dock and in after her. They both emerge, one panting, one laughing. Madeleine looks over at Colleen, who is watching the child from her post at the grill. *Mom.*

Down on the dock, the wheelchair is turning. Madeleine can see from here the sinews in the forearms, tanned and strong like Colleen's, red cotton sleeves rolled up, faded jeans over thin legs. Cowboy boots. The person looks up, a hand raised to shade the eyes. Beautiful smooth face, high cheekbones, cords in the neck rising from the hollow between the collarbones. His hand goes up in greeting.

Madeleine walks tentatively, hat in hand, down the warm stone, feeling through her sandals how welcome it would be to the soles of bare feet.

"Hi, Ricky."

She takes his outstretched hand. He pulls her down to him—there is not as much strength and substance to his arms as was suggested by the slanting light. He hugs her. "How you doing, Madeleine?"

"I'm okay," she says. "How are you?" There is no question that is not inadequate.

"Can't complain." His voice has thinned, but it's clear. Light. How is that possible? "You're beautiful," he says.

She has no reply.

He is beautiful.

His brow is smooth, the only signs of aging the slight hollows under his black eyes. He is both older and younger than he was. What happened to him? She wants to touch his face. She sees him notice the hat in her hand.

He says, "How are your folks?"

She swallows back tears. She was unprepared for kindness. Why can't he be more like Colleen?

"You staying for supper?" He wheels himself up the dock toward the stone, where a ramp traverses the far side. As he rolls past, his black hair swings and the sun catches streaks of silver. He is three years older than her brother would have been.

Feet plunk along the dock behind her; the little girl runs past, droplets flying, followed by the dog, who sideswipes Madeleine with his wet fur, his good wet-dog smell. The girl grabs a crumpled piece of cotton from the rocks, slips it over her head and suddenly she is wearing a dress.

She looks up at Madeleine. "Hi." Ice-blue eyes; the downward tilt at their corners lends them a permanently amused expression. Sharp like Colleen's, but unsuspicious.

"Hi," says Madeleine. She pauses. "I'm Madeleine."

"I'm Vivien."

The girl runs back to Rick, grabs the handles of his chair and hurtles them both forward.

"Mush," he says.

"I'm mushing, I'm mushing!"

Madeleine follows them. They stop up near the house at a picnic table under which sits a cooler. Rick slowly, carefully rolls a cigarette from a pouch of Drum tobacco.

Vivien asks, "Are you the one on TV?"

Madeleine is taken by surprise. "Sometimes, yeah."

The little girl laughs and hurls herself at Rick's lap.

Rick puts the cigarette between his lips and looks up at Madeleine. "Everyone thinks you're funny now but they didn't know-you-when, eh?" He uses both hands to light it with a lighter.

Madeleine puts the hat on the picnic table.

As Rick exhales, the smoke mingles with the freshness of the evening, the charcoal from the grill. Colleen is cooking something in foil. It smells wonderful.

Madeleine says, "That was my dad's hat."

Rick says, "What can I get you to drink?" Vivien announces, "We have beer, Dr Pepper, Mountain Dew and chocolate milk."

"I'll have what you're having."

The child bounds toward the house. The dog flops, still wet and grinning, at Rick's feet. Madeleine sits facing the lake and says, "He's the one who waved at you that day." It feels so small. The words are tiny. Not difficult to say. Not hard at all.

Rick looks away, following the smoke with his eyes as it drifts toward the water. His profile is so pure, cut with the finest instruments, eyes gleaming like jet. He raises the heel of his hand and wipes them. He could have been anything he wanted to be.

A sizzle behind her as Colleen turns the foil package. Madeleine is weeping now too. Because the pines smell so vivid. Because his face is so familiar. Because it's summer and the evening sun is all the clothes you need and school doesn't start for a long time.

"I know what happened . . . ," she says. And down in the schoolyard a boy on a red moter scooter is giving everyone rides. "And I think I know what happened . . . to your dad." But that's too much. What happened to Mr. Froelich and the children he loved . . . is too much.

"I'm sorry," she says, getting up. "I'll put it in a letter."

She is about to leave but the child is there, offering her an iridium-blue tin cup.

"How come you're crying?"

Madeleine takes the cup and replies, "Aw it's okay, it's. . . ."

Rick says, "Her daddy died."

The child puts her arms around Madeleine's waist. When will Colleen turn from the grill and drive a knife into Madeleine's back?

Madeleine says, "It's okay, hey, cheers Vivien."

They clink cups and Madeleine drinks. A dreadful candy clash. "It's great, what is it?"

"My secret recipe," she replies, moustached now in mauve. "Mountain Dew and Dr Pepper and then you put in a bit of real pepper."

"Wow."

The child disappears back into the house.

"Max," says Rick, "get Papa a cool one." The dog gets up, walks to the cooler, opens it with his nose, lifts out a can of Moosehead beer and brings it over. "Good boy," says Rick, popping the tab.

"How did you get him to do that?"

He points his thumb at Colleen. "I'm just the guinea pig, she's the genius. Guide dogs, eh? 'Special skills for special needs.'"

"You train dogs to get beer for blind people?"

Rick laughs, and Madeleine sees the side of Colleen's mouth rise. The same thin scar at the corner. Same rusty thatch of hair.

He has multiple sclerosis—MS. Diagnosed a few years after he got out of prison. He had been working with horses again up until then. "Out west," he says.

Out on the lake a loon flies low across the water, feet skimming to a landing. It releases its effortless liquid cry and is answered within moments from farther down the shore.

"Here!" says Vivien, and thrusts a guitar almost the size of herself into Rick's arms. He takes the pick from behind the strings of an upper fret, places it between his teeth and begins to tune the instrument. He strums—"Not so good at picking any more, eh? But I can still chord some."

"How's your mum?" ventures Madeleine.

"She's great," he replies, "still crazy after all these years."

"She runs a nuthouse," says Colleen.

"A halfway house," says Rick. "For bag ladies. In Toronto."

"That's great."

"Yeah. Look her up if you ever lose your marbles."

Vivien says, "Gran is a Quaker."

"How about your baby brothers?"

"Roger and Carl." Rick shakes his head and smiles. Colleen is chuckling.

"Carl's a biker—" Rick starts laughing. Colleen pokes the coals, laughing now too. "And Roger's a cop." He begins to strum a series of chords.

Madeleine asks quietly, "What about Elizabeth?"

Neither of them answers, and Madeleine is somewhat relieved that they seem not to have heard her. But after a moment he says to his guitar, "She died, pal."

He starts playing a tune. The little girl takes two spoons from the table and starts rattling time with them, a serious expression on her face.

Rick says, "Lizzie got flu."

"She was too sad to get better," explains Vivien. "She's with her dog Rex now."

Madeleine gets up and goes to Colleen. "I'm going to leave now. I'll put it all in a letter for you. I'm going to get in touch with the McCarrolls too."

Colleen finally looks at her. Madeleine is startled, the way she was when she was a child. Wolf eyes.

Colleen reaches into her pocket for her knife. Yellowed bone handle, thumb-faded. Blade curved with age. She slits open the foil and steam escapes. Two big trout.

"Ricky and Viv caught them," she says. She reseals the foil and lifts the package onto a platter. "You're funny, I guess you know that, eh?"

"I know it's weird, me just showing up like this out of the blue—"

"No, I mean . . . you're good at what you do." And now Colleen is smiling. She sets the platter on the table. "Want to see the dogs?"

"Okay."

Rick and Vivien sing softly, "'So hoist up the *John B.* sail. See how the mainsail sets. Call for the captain ashore, let me go home. . . .'"

The two women walk up to the kennels. Soft muzzles at the fence, a Bremen choir of barking. Colleen unlocks the gate and holds out her hand to Madeleine, palm up. There is the scar. Madeleine takes the hand and squeezes it, then lets go and follows her friend along the dog runs, hands out for licks and pats, wet teeth grazing her flesh.

Colleen says, "Tell me now."

Madeleine does. It doesn't take long.

The fish is still warm when they return to the table and join the others.

AN AIR-RAID SIREN is a beam of sound more terrifying than any other.
During the Second World War it was terrifying but now it is more
terrifying, because it was a normal sunny day until the siren went off.
Birds were flying, the fields were buzzing and kids were riding bikes.
The siren screams over wading pools and backyard barbecues, it says,
I was here all along, you knew this could happen. It pauses for breath,
resumes its pitiful rise, mourning its own obscenity, mounting to obliteration. It is everywhere—it makes all places into the same place,
turns everyone into the same person. It says, Run to where there is no
shelter. When the planes come, run, but only because you are alive and
an animal.

And then it stops. The summer sky is empty. Turn on the radio, the
television. Come up from the basement, get up from the ground. It
was a birds' nest. In the siren atop the wooden telephone pole that
stands near the gates to the old air force station at Centralia. Crows.
Who knew the old siren was operational after all these years?

Municipal workers from the nearby town of Exeter climb the pole
to clear away the nest and remove the siren altogether. Bits of tinfoil,
bottle caps, a key glint amid the straw—the shiny things that crows
collect. And a tiny silver charm. A name.

*Claire.*

SOURCES AND ACKNOWLEDGMENTS

Grateful acknowledgment is made to the following. Every effort has been made to contact the copyright holders; in the event of an inadvertent omission or error, please notify the publisher.

Lyrics from "This Land Is Your Land," words and music by Woody Guthrie. TRO © Copyright 1956 (Renewed) 1958 (Renewed), 1970 and 1972. Ludlow Music, Inc., New York, NY. Used by permission.

Lyrics from "Whatever Will Be Will Be" by Raymond B. Evans and Jay Livingston. Used by permission.

Lyrics from "Swinging on a Star" by Johnny Burke and Jimmy Van Heusen. Used by permission.

Lyrics from "Moon River" by Henry Mancini and Johnny Mercer. Used by permission.

Lyrics from "Button Up Your Overcoat." From *Follow Thru*. Words and music by B.G. DeSylva, Lew Brown and Ray Henderson. Copyright © 1928 by Chappell & Co., Stephen Ballentine Music Publishing Co. and Henderson Music Co. Copyright renewed. International copyright secured. All rights reserved.

The epigraph to "Welcome to Centralia" is from *Camelot*. Words by Alan Jay Lerner. Music by Frederick Loewe. Copyright © 1960 by Alan Jay Lerner and Frederick Loewe. Copyright renewed. Chappell & Co. owner of publication and allied rights throughout the world. International copyright secured. All rights reserved.

Jack's thought, "God watches over your first solo, after that you're on your own," comes from Royal Canadian Air Force lore recounted in Ted Barris, *Behind the Glory*. Toronto: Macmillan Canada, 1992.

The epigraph to "Here's to Being Above It All" comes from "Organization Theory: An Overview and an Appraisal," *Journal of the Academy of Management*, Vol. 4, No. 4 (April 1961). Briarcliff Manor, NY: Academy of Management.

The epigraph to "The Mayflower" comes from "How America Feels" (Gallup survey), *Look,* January 5, 1960.

Lyrics from "Unforgettable" by Irving Gordon. Used by permission.

The epigraph to "How Sweet It Is" comes from Heloise, *Heloise's Kitchen Hints.* Englewood Cliffs, NJ: Prentice-Hall Inc., 1963.

The poem that begins "Oh, I have slipped the surly bonds of earth" is "High Flight" written in 1941 by John Gillespie Magee, Jr., an American who served with the Royal Canadian Air Force during the Second World War.

The Dion song quoted is "The Wanderer," composed by Ernest Peter Maresca.

The *Time* magazine quotes that Jack reads are from August 31, 1962, Canada edition, Vol. LXXX, No. 9.

Excerpts from Madeleine's *Girl Next Door* reader come from W. W. Bauer, Gladys G. Jenkins, Elizabeth Montgomery, and Dorothy W. Baruch (eds.), *The Girl Next Door.* Toronto: Gage, 1952.

Wernher von Braun's mother's comment, "Why don't you take a look at Peenemünde? Your grandfather used to go duck hunting up there," is quoted in Michael J. Neufeld, *The Rocket and the Reich: Peenemünde and the Coming of the Ballistic Missile Era.* Cambridge, MA: Harvard University Press, 1995.

The epigraphs to "Oktoberfest" and "Duck and Cover" come from Doris Anderson's editorials in the July 1962 and February 1962 issues of *Chatelaine,* respectively.

The rhyme that begins "There was a turtle and his name was Bert" is from "Duck and Cover," an educational film produced in 1951 by Archer Productions, Inc. and sponsored by the U.S. Federal Civil Defense Administration.

President John F. Kennedy's comments regarding the Cuban Missile Crisis are taken from his television address of October 22, 1962.

The epigraphs to "I Cannot Tell a Lie" and "Flexible Response" come from transcripts quoted in Ernest R. May and Philip D. Zelikow, *The Kennedy Tapes: Inside the White House During the Cuban Missile Crisis.* Cambridge, MA: Belknap Press of Harvard University Press, 1997.

Lyrics from "Where Have All the Flowers Gone?" by Pete Seeger © Copyright 1961 (renewed) by Sanga Music, Inc. All rights reserved. Used by permission.

Norman DePoe's comment regarding the easing of tensions surrounding the Cuban Missile Crisis was made on CBC's *Newsmagazine* on October 28, 1962.

The epigraphs to "Indian Summer" and "Requiem" come from Mary Eleanor Thomas, *Developing Comprehension in Reading.* Toronto: J. M. Dent, 1956.

Lyrics from "Bei Mir Bist du Schon." Original words by Jacob Jacobs. Music by Sholom Secunda. English version by Sammy Cahn & Saul Chaplin. Copyright © 1937; Renewed 1965 Cahn Music Company (ASCAP) and Warner/Chappell (ASCAP). Rights for Cahn Music Company administered by Cherry Lane Music Publishing, Inc. and DreamWorks Songs. International copyright secured. All rights reserved.

Lyrics from "Sloop John B." by Brian Wilson © 1966, renewed New Executive Music. Used by permission.

The epigraph to "Sleeping Dogs" is reprinted with permission of Simon & Schuster Adult Publishing Group from *The Drowned and the Saved* by Primo Levi. Translated by Rayond Rosenthal. English translation Copyright © 1988 by Simon & Schuster, Inc.

The epigraph to "Flying Up" comes from *The Brownie Handbook.* Toronto: Girl Guides of Canada, 1958.

Excerpts from Walt Disney's copyrighted *BAMBI* Story Record are used by permission from Disney Enterprises, Inc.

Froelich's lines "When I saw Dora, it was no longer a mystery how the pyramids were built," "I have a trick. I imagine that I have lived before these experiences," and "I heard once two secretaries from the office, one to say to her friend, 'Hurry up, you miss the legs'" are paraphrased from Jean Michel's descriptions of his own reaction to Dora in Jean Michel, *Dora: The Nazi Concentration Camp Where Modern Space Technology Was Born and 30,000 Prisoners Died*. Austin, TX: Holt, Rinehart and Winston, 1975.

Simon's line "I heard one say he'd trade the whole pack of these former Nazis to the Soviets for a dish of caviar" comes from a remark attributed to an American officer quoted in Linda Hunt, *Secret Agenda: The United States Government, Nazi Scientists and Project Paperclip, 1945 to 1990*. New York: St. Martin's Press, 1991.

The epigraph to Part Four, "What Remains," comes from Primo Levi, "Lead." In *The Periodic Table*. New York: Schocken Books, 1984.

The epigraph to "And That's the Way It Is" comes from T.S. Eliot, "The Waste Land." In *The Waste Land and Other Poems*. London: Faber and Faber, 2002.

Lyrics from "What a Wonderful World" by George David Weiss and Robert Thiele © 1968, renewed. Published by Abilene Music, Range Road Music and Quartet Music. Used by permission. All rights reserved.

The Marianne Faithfull song quoted is "Broken English," composed by Marian Evelyn Faithfull, Joe Mavety, Barry Reynolds, Terence Philip Stannard, and Stephen David York.

René Steenbeke's comment on the part Dora played in launching modern space travel is quoted in "Survivors of Mittelbau-Dora Commemorate Liberation" by Richard Murphy, found in the Jewish Virtual Library at www.us-israel.org.

"You deserve a break today, so get up and get away" used with permission from McDonald's Corporation.

Excerpts from Walt Disney's copyrighted feature film *BAMBI* used by permission from Disney Enterprises, Inc.

The poetry that Madeleine, Mike, and Jocelyn listen to in Le Hibou is from Margaret Atwood, "Procedures from Underground." In

*Procedures from Underground* (Copyright © Margaret Atwood, 1970). Used by permission of the author.

The epigraph to "Hers" comes from Leonard Cohen, "You Have the Lovers." In *Stranger Music*. Toronto: McClelland & Stewart, 1994. © Leonard Cohen 1994. Used by permission.

The epigraph to "The Air Force Cross" comes from Stevie Smith, "Not Waving But Drowning." In *Not Waving But Drowning*. London: Andre Deutsch, 1957.

The epigraph to *"Prête-Moi Ta Plume, Pour Écrire un Mot"* comes from Gwendolyn MacEwen, "Dark Pines Under Water." In *The Shadow-Maker*. Toronto: Macmillan, 1972. Permission for use granted by the author's family.

## Author's Note

The ordeal of Stephen Truscott, his spirit and courage, have been a major inspiration in the writing of this book.

Occasionally throughout the book, there are phrases of colloquial Acadian French, as well as phrases in the Michif language. In neither case are there hard and fast rules of spelling since both reflect an oral tradition. In both cases, the author has consulted native speakers of the relevant generation, and the translations and spellings reflect those speakers' experience.

Thank you for your generous help: Theresa Burke, Louise Dennys, Honora Johannesen, Malcolm J. MacDonald (Royal Canadian Air Force retd.), Alisa Palmer, Clay Ruby and the Ruby-Sachs family, Lillian Szpak, and Maureen White.

Thank you also to the following individuals and organizations for invaluable research information and, in numerous cases, the pleasure of many conversations: Irving Abella, Augustine Abraham, Ginette Abraham, Alice Aresenault and the Bouctouche Museum, Margaret Atwood, Bnai Brith, Professor Stephen Brooke, Professor Chalk, the staff, past and present, of *Chatelaine* magazine, Dr. Trudy Chernin, Charles Clarke, Michael Claydon, Professor Ramsay Cook, Deb Cowan, Olenka Demianchuk, Department of National Defence Directorate of History and Heritage—especially Richard Gimblett, William Rawling, Isabel Campbell and Donna Porter—Mike Englishman, Hugh Halliday, Peter Haydon (Royal Canadian Navy retd.) Geoffrey Hopkinson and the Canadian Broadcasting Corporation archives, Malcolm Johannesen, Sigurd Johannesen (Canadian Forces retd.), Linda Kash, Dan Kaye (RCAF retd.), Douglas Lantry and the USAF Museum, Anne-Marie Lau and The RCAF Museum Canadian Forces Base Trenton, Linda Laughlin, Lindsay Leese, John Hugh MacDonald (Pipe Major, CF), Mary T. MacDonald (RN retd.), Tricia McConnell, Henry Melnick, Montana, National Archives of Canada, Almark Books, Michael J. Neufeld and the National Air and Space Museum, Smithsonian Institution, Ontario Archives, Ontario Institute of Studies in Educations, University of Toronto Archives, Doreen Keizer (Girl Guides of Canada), Danielle Palmer, Jacob Palmer, Gloria Peckam and Dog Guides Canada, Eric Price, the producers of *It Seems Like Yesterday*, Jeanette Richard, Rick Rickards, Bill Randall (RCAF retd.) and the Canadian Warplane Heritage Museum, Alti Rodal, David Rudd and the Canadian Institute for Strategic Studies, Harriet

Sachs, Andrea Schwenke, the Simon Wiesenthal Centre, John Starnes, Gina Stephens, Dave Sylvester, Patrick Szpak, Betty Twena, Tulin Valeri, Cylla von Tiedeman, Lorraine Wells, Joseph White (RCAF retd.) and Zsa Zsa.

Thank you as well to the staff of Knopf Canada and Random House of Canada, especially Nina Ber-Donkor, Deirdre Molina, Scott Richardson and Jen Shepherd. Special thanks also to Susan Broadhurst and an extra special thanks to Gena Gorrell.

I am personally indebted to the spirit and work of Tiff Findley.

ANN-MARIE MACDONALD is a novelist, playwright and actor, and the author of the acclaimed play *Goodnight Desdemona (Good Morning Juliet)*. Her first novel, *Fall on Your Knees,* became a much loved international bestseller when it was published in 1996. Winner of the Commonwealth Prize for Best First Book as well as numerous other literary awards, it also became a selection of Oprah's Book Club. Ann-Marie MacDonald lives in Toronto.

A NOTE ON THE TYPE

*The Way the Crow Flies* has been set in Granjon, a modern recutting of a typeface derived from the classic letterforms of Claude Garamond (1480-1561). It is named in honour of Robert Granjon, a successful French publisher, punch cutter and founder of the sixteenth century and a contemporary of Garamond.